The Northern Clemency

THE
NORTHERN
CLEMENCY

PHILIP
HENSHER

Alfred A. Knopf   New York   2008

THIS IS A BORZOI BOOK
PUBLISHED BY ALFRED A. KNOPF

Copyright © 2008 by Philip Hensher
All rights reserved. Published in the United States by Alfred A.
Knopf, a division of Random House, Inc., New York, and in
Canada by Random House of Canada Limited, Toronto.
www.aaknopf.com

Originally published in Great Britain by Fourth Estate,
an imprint of HarperCollins*Publishers*, London.

Knopf, Borzoi Books, and the colophon are registered
trademarks of Random House, Inc.

ISBN: 978-1-4000-4448-1

Manufactured in the United States of America
First American Edition

For Zaved Mahmood

what he would have ~~done~~ hoped to do for anyone else

—E. M. FORSTER,
Arctic Summer, principal fragment

Contents

Contents

Book One

MARDY

So the garden of number eighty-four is nothing more than a sort of playground for all the kids of the neighbourhood."

"I wouldn't say all," Mrs. Arbuthnot said. "I would have said it was only the Glovers' children."

"All of them?" Mrs. Warner—Karen, now—said. "The girl seems so quiet. It's the elder boy, really."

"I've seen the girl going in there too," Mrs. Arbuthnot said. "It's during the day with her. She's on her own generally. I grant you, it's the older boy who goes in after dark, and he's got people with him. Girls, one at a time. There'll be trouble with both those boys."

"But, Mrs. . . ." Mr. Warner said. He was slow to catch people's names.

"Call me Anthea," Mrs. Arbuthnot said. "Now that we've finally met."

"I mean, Anthea," Mr. Warner said, "why doesn't anyone tell the parents? They surely can't know."

"That I don't understand," Mrs. Arbuthnot said. She was stately, forty-six, divorced, at number ninety-three, almost opposite the empty house. "This isn't the best opportunity, I dare say."

They were at the Glovers'. It was a party; the neighbourhood had been invited. Most had been puzzled by the invitation, knowing the couple and their three children only by sight. Mrs. Arbuthnot and Mrs. Warner had passed the time of day on occasion. They had arrived more or less at the same time; both had the habit, at a party, of moving swiftly to the back wall the better to watch arrivals. They had made common ground, and Mrs. Warner's husband had been introduced. He worked for the local council in a position of some authority.

It was a Friday night in August. The room was filling up, in a slightly bemused way; the neighbours, nervously boastful, were exchanging compliments about each other's gardens; conversations about motor-cars were running their usual course.

"It's a nice thing for her to do," Mrs. Warner said, who always prided herself on thinking the best of others. She had left her son, nineteen, a worry, at home; she thought the party might have been smarter than it was, not knowing the Glovers. Other people's children had come.

"She's a nice woman, I believe," Mrs. Arbuthnot said, who had her own private names for almost everyone in the room, the Warners, the Glovers included. "It's a shame she couldn't have waited a week or two, though."

"Yes?" Mr. Warner said, who believed that if a thing could be done today, it shouldn't be put off until tomorrow.

"There's new people moving into number eighty-four," Mrs. Arbuthnot said. "It might have been nice to introduce them to everyone. They're moving in next week."

"Just opposite Anthea's," Mrs. Warner explained to her husband.

"Perhaps it wasn't ideal," Mr. Warner said. "From the point of view of dates."

"People are busy in August, these days," Mrs. Arbuthnot said. "They go away, don't they?"

"We were thinking about the Algarve," Mrs. Warner said.

"Oh, the Algarve," Mrs. Arbuthnot said, encouraging and patronizing as a magazine.

It was a good party, like other parties. Mrs. Glover was in a long dress: pale blue and high at the neck, it clung to her; on it were printed the names of capital cities. In vain, Mrs. Warner ran her eyes over it, looking for the name of the Algarve, but it was not there.

"Nibble?" Mrs. Glover said, frankly holding out a potato wrapped in foil, spiked with miniature assemblages of cheese and pineapple, wee cold sausages iced with fat. Her hair was swept up and pulled in, in a chignon and ringlets. They had all dressed, but she had made the most effort for her own party.

"I so like your unit," Mrs. Arbuthnot said.

"We got fed up with the old sideboard," Mrs. Glover said. "It was Malcolm's mother's, so he felt he had to take it when she went into a home. She couldn't have all her things, naturally, so we took it, and then one day, I just looked at it and it just seemed so ugly I had to get rid of it. We got the unit from Cole's, actually."

"You got it in Sheffield?" Mrs. Arbuthnot said.

"I know," Mrs. Glover said. "I saw it and I fell in love with it."

"It's very nice," Mrs. Warner said. "I like old things, too."

"I know what you mean," Katherine Glover said. "I love them, really. I just think they have so much more character than new furniture. I'd love to live in an old house."

There was a pause.

"But it's original, isn't it?" Mr. Warner said, helping her out; they seemed to be stuck on the white unit, windowed with brown smoked glass.

"Yes," Katherine Glover said. She gestured around the room. "I think we've got it looking quite nice now. Finally!"

They all laughed.

"We've lived here for ten years!" she said vivaciously, as if hoping for another laugh. "But—"

Karen Warner remarked that it was strange how you didn't get to meet your neighbours properly, these days.

"This was a nice idea," Mr. Warner said, "having a party like this." But he was wondering why, on this warm August night, the party was staying indoors and not moving out on to the patio.

There were five of them, the Glovers, in the room. Malcolm was in a suit, a borderline vivid blue, waisted and flaring about his skinny hips, flaring more modestly about the ankles, his tie a fat cushion at his neck. He carried a bottle from group to group, his smile illuminating as he moved on. "My wife's idea," he was saying to a new couple about the party. "I work in the Huddersfield and Harrogate."

"You work in Harrogate?" the man said. "That's quite a drive every day."

"No," Malcolm said, after a heavy pause. "The Huddersfield and Harrogate."

"The building society?" the woman said. She was a nursery nurse, pregnant herself.

"Yes," Malcolm said, his puzzled voice rising. "Yes, the Huddersfield and Harrogate, our main offices, just off Fargate opposite the Roman Catholic cathedral. It's women like parties, mostly. It was my wife's idea."

"It was a nice idea," the husband said. "We've not met a lot of people in the street."

"We've admired your front garden," the wife said. She sneezed.

"The idea was," Malcolm said, "that by now there'd be new people in number eighty-four. Just over there. They'd have been more than welcome."

"That's a nice thought," the woman said, sneezing again.

"But there must have been a hold-up," Malcolm said. "At any rate, it's still empty."

Elsewhere in the room, people were talking about the empty house, and about the new inhabitants.

"Anthea Arbuthnot's met them," a man was saying.

"Oh, Anthea," a woman replied, and laughed. "What she doesn't know isn't worth knowing."

"We call her the *Rayfield Avenue Clarion*," someone's teenage daughter said, and blushed.

"I was saying," the man said, "Anthea Arbuthnot's met them," as Mrs. Arbuthnot came up, expertly balancing a pastry case filled with mushroom sauce.

"Met who?" Mrs. Arbuthnot said.

"The new people," he said. "Over the road."

"You don't miss much," she said, in a not exactly unfriendly way. "Yes, I met them, quite by chance. The house, it's being sold by Eadon Lockwood and Riddle, which sold me my house too, five years back. It was the same lady, which is quite a coincidence. Her name's Mary, she breeds chocolate Labradors in her spare time, which was a little bond between us, a nice lady. I saw her coming out of the house one day with a couple as I was going down the road with Paddy, my dog, you know, and stopped to say hello. Naturally she introduced me to the people, they'd bought it by then, they were just having another look over. Measuring up for curtains and carpets, I dare say."

The Glover girl, Jane, was at the edge of their circle, listening, her flowery print frock, her lank hair, the empty plate she had been carrying round the guests all drooping listlessly. The adults shifted politely, smiling. She was fourteen or so; just about old enough for this sort of thing. "Are they nice?" she said.

Mrs. Arbuthnot laughed, not at all kindly. Jane Glover just looked at her, waiting for the answer. "Are they nice?" Mrs. Arbuthnot said. "I don't know about that. They're from London. He's very London. She didn't say anything much. They've got two children, nine, and a fourteen-year-old girl, I think she said."

"Were the children nice?" Jane said, and now she was surely being deliberately childish.

"They weren't there," Mrs. Arbuthnot said. "Their name—let me see—it's on the tip of my tongue . . . they're called—Mr. and Mrs. Sellers. That's it."

"London children," a man said, shaking his head.

"I hope they're nice," Jane said, and then just walked away. She knew all about Mrs. Arbuthnot. Under no circumstances would she tell any of these people that she, Jane, was writing a novel. Already she hated the girl, over the road, fourteen.

"He'll break some hearts," someone was saying, in another part of the room. It was Daniel Glover they were talking about. He was sixteen, lounging over the edge of the sofa, his long legs spread. His mouth hung slightly open, and from time to time he brushed away the soft fall of long black hair. Every twenty seconds the pregnant nursery nurse was sneezing, and it was Daniel she was sneezing at. His lush musk odour filled the room, making the air itch; it was the *eau-de-toilette* he'd lifted from Cole's on Tuesday, and he'd practically bathed in the stuff.

Daniel looked at the party. He was thinking about sex, and he counted the women. Then he eliminated the unattractive ones, the ones over thirty-five, his mother and sister—no, he brought his sister back in just for the hell of it. Balanced it out, removed some of the men. Then—what they do, he'd read about it—the men throw their keys into a bowl, the women pick them out, then—

He lost himself in lewd speculation. Or—he started again—you could just have an orgy here. A sex orgy on the carpet. Because that happened all the time, he'd read about it. It just didn't happen here, in this house. But he bet somewhere round here it happened all the time. Probably on this street.

Mrs. Arbuthnot observed with some interest that the elder Glover boy had an erection. She enjoyed the sight: she had divorced six years ago, her long-held ambition to take part in a game of strip poker never having been fulfilled or, indeed, mentioned to anyone, least of all her ex-husband. She envisaged, like Daniel, scenes of satisfaction; for her, they were what Daniel had done, or might be doing, to the girls in the back garden of number eighty-four, watched soberly by its four dark empty windows.

"Hay fever," the nursery nurse said politely, still sneezing, feeling with alarm a little dribble in her knickers.

"They're called Mr. and Mrs. Sellers," someone said. "They paid seventeen thousand for the house. Anthea Arbuthnot told me."

Katherine Glover was relaxing, now that her party was being a success. They were eating the food; she'd made pastry cases with mushroom filling, and prawn, she'd made three different quiches, she'd made Coronation Chicken (a challenge to eat standing), she'd made assemblages of cheese-and-pineapple and cold sausages, she'd made open Danish sandwiches in tiny squares, a magazine idea, and they were eating it all. There were dishes of crisps, too, and Twiglets, but those didn't count in the way of making an effort. They were drinking the wine, Malcolm's choice—she'd had three glasses—and in the background, the music was exactly right, Mozart, Elvira Madigan. It was all being a great success.

The sexes were dividing now: the men were talking about their jobs, their cars, about the election, even; the women about their children's schools, about the cost of living, and about each other.

"Your hand's never out of your pocket," one said, and another observed that her house had doubled in value in five years. One woman, worldly in manner, said that Sheffield would improve when Sainsbury's got round to opening a branch, as she'd heard they were planning to.

"Oh, we know Mrs. Thurston," another said, referring to the head-mistress of one of the local schools.

"She teaches the piano, doesn't she?" the nursery nurse said hope-fully. "On Charrington Road?" She was set right, and the others started recommending piano teachers to each other, boasting about their children's grades, merits and distinctions.

"It's all going to the dogs," a man said. "This'll be a third-world country by 1980," and the others gravely agreed. Malcolm made his rounds again; for the last twenty minutes he had said nothing to any-one, only smiled and offered the bottle, and he was circling too soon. All the glasses were full, and the guests refused with a smile, wondering about their host, who they did not know. Absently, he offered the bot-tle to Daniel, who took the opportunity, his fourth, to refill his glass, still thinking of tits.

"It would have been nice if they could have come," Katherine said again. "Sellers, they're called."

"Your son's getting to be a handsome young man," they said in reply.

"I've got two," Katherine said, laughing.

"Yes," they said, wondering where the other was, the one they wouldn't have meant, since he was, what?, nine years old.

"We invited Mrs. Topsfield, too," she said. "The old lady who lives in the great big house, the old one, at the bottom of the road, the edge of the moor. But only to be polite—she wouldn't be likely to come at her age."

"I've often wondered about her," someone said. "A gorgeous house."

"It's just her in it, apparently," Katherine said.

"I do think they've done their house beautifully," Karen Warner said to her husband; they had been marooned together at one side of the room. It was a handsome room; one wall had been covered with a bold paper in a bamboo print, jungle green with lemony highlights, and the others painted the palest beige. The fat suite, pushed back against the walls, and the carpet were rough oatmeal; instead of a fourth wall, a single picture window gave on to the garden.

"It's quite like our house, the way it's arranged," Warner said.

"Not quite, though," Karen said. The estate, a hundred and twenty houses, all built in one go ten years before, was elegantly varied; there were a dozen or more differently shaped houses, arranged irregularly. There was nothing municipal about the estate; but, of course, she had said this many times before. "Had you heard anything at work about a Sainsbury's opening in Sheffield?" Warner informed his wife that he had not, and that such information would not have come his way in the course of his work at the council. "I do like that unit," she said in a rush, because now she, too, had seen the elder Glover boy, sprawled about his erection.

"I didn't expect to be invited," the nursery nurse was saying, to someone she didn't know, "but I'm glad I came." It had been ten days before; she had been resting in the afternoon, her feet, horribly swollen in this weather even at six months, up on a stool. Through the window she had seen a woman in a sleeveless summer dress stomping up the drive; a familiar figure, some sort of neighbour, with an air of imminent complaint about her walk. What now? she'd thought wearily. But the woman hadn't rung: there was the clatter of something through the letterbox that proved, when her husband got home and picked it up, to be an invitation. "But who are they?" he'd said. "I think we might as well go," she'd said, not answering his question.

But the Glovers had three children, surely: the youngest a boy, wasn't he? Maybe he was in bed.

The youngest was behind the sofa: he had been there most of the evening, slipping behind it quite early on. Timothy had with him his favourite book in the whole world. He had been reading it steadily all evening, letting his eye run over the familiar entries. He had taken it out from the public library eleven months before; he had renewed it once, then stopped bothering. It was now ten months overdue, which caused him great terror whenever he thought of it. In happy moments, he decided that he could conceal the book where no one would find it, and his parents would never uncover the gigantic fine now building up. The fear of punishment was huge in him.

But the terror did not touch the book. It was as good now as ever. The pleasure he found in letting his eye ride over it, touching on category after category, overrode anything else. Whenever he could, he returned to its calm instructions. Even when it was not quite right of him to do so, he sensed, he found a way to be alone with it, as now burrowing behind the sofa at his parents' party. It was so important to him that often in the last months he had found himself telling others—his best friends Simon and Ian, his sister Jane, his mother but for some reason not his brother Daniel, not his father—some facts about his subject. More oddly, he found himself asking them questions about it, as if they could instruct him, feigning ignorance, wanting to find out if they knew what he already did.

The book was about snakes. Timothy gazed at the photographs as if at a family album, committing the names he already knew to a further refreshment of memory.

He had been there for three hours, wedged between the sofa and the large picture window. If the party went outside, they would see him, and probably laugh. From time to time the back of the sofa, the porridgy tweed panels between the wood frames, bulged as someone sat down, swelling towards him, like some inchoate mass searching for him. There was a queer smell of dust down here, and the nasty smell of spilt alcohol. It was his favourite place when there was anyone in the house.

"I don't know where he's got to," Katherine Glover said to a departing guest; it was too warm for anyone to have brought coats, but she made a helpful gesture. "He's a little bit shy."

The guest smiled; her husband made a honking noise, understanding that the woman was talking about her son, not knowing that there was any son apart from the great lout who had been lolling on the sofa, gawping at the ladies.

On the mat was an envelope, which, surely, had not been there earlier; it was addressed to Katherine, and she picked it up. In front of her, the remains of her party; the poor pregnant woman, harassed and tired, waiting for her husband to want to go. But the husband was drunk, his hair rumpled, making a hash of a joke to a group of husbands. Where was Malcolm? Sitting down, his host's bottle in his hand, all refills at an end; and the Mozart had come to an end, too, leaving the patient silence to dismiss the guests.

"You looked so nice," Jane said to her mother, coming up to her in the hall, munching a cheese straw, "in your posh frock and your hair like that."

Katherine felt so terribly tired. "I don't know why I bothered," she said crossly. "They didn't appreciate it at all."

Jane looked at her mother in astonishment. "It was a lovely party," she said. "You should always wear your hair like that."

"What, to work?" Katherine said. "Don't be daft."

"Thank you so much," the drunk man was saying, "for a lovely time, my dear. We've had a lovely, lovely time."

He leant towards her, as if to kiss her, but did not; Katherine had him by the shoulders, a gesture that might have been affectionate, holding him at arm's-length inspection.

"We've had a very good time," the pregnant woman said. But it didn't look it.

"When is your baby due?" Jane said abruptly.

"In November," the woman said, not smiling. She took her husband by the arm, and they went.

"Where's your dad?" Katherine said, but then Daniel was in the hall, up from the sofa for the first time all evening.

"Just going out for a second," he muttered.

"One second—" Katherine said, but he was gone. "Oh, well."

And then Daniel, who had answered all polite inquiries with a brief grunt and a shrug, who had not moved from his perch on the arm of the sofa, like a vast and lurid ornament, proved himself to have been all along the ringmaster of the festivities. Because with his departure the party was decisively over, and the few remaining guests moved towards the front door where Mrs. Glover, her daughter at her side, was standing. In kindness, they bent and said a word to Malcolm, who said something in return, and then, with a chorus of thanks, they were out.

"I do love your unit," Mrs. Warner said over her shoulder, a final kindly thought disappearing into the lush August night. "As I was saying, I do love your . . ."

Goodbye, goodbye . . . and Katherine opened the envelope in her hand. It was an unfamiliar hand, elegant and swooping, in real ink, and the general gist of apology was clear before the signature was deciphered. She read it again, and smiled, her first genuine smile all evening.

"Have they all gone?" she heard Timothy saying, as he got up from behind the sofa, book in hand.

"I think so," his father said, his voice muffled, regretful in the other room. "Where's your brother?"

Daniel was in the street. It was half past nine. The road and the estate, in this summer twilight, had a lush warm glow; in the houses, up and down the avenue, single lights were coming on automatically, guiding the couples home from the party; husbands and wives, arm in arm and in the summer gloaming turned into lovers. The thin trees, planted ten years before, had lost their daylit lack of conviction and formed a delicate orchard, marking the edges of the quiet street. The night was perfumed, and Daniel, perfumed too, sniffed it all up.

Barbara was there, waiting for him. He had told her to wait on the wall outside number eighty-four. It was less suspicious to be casual like that rather than, as she was doing, cowering under the porch at the side of the house. Everyone knew it was empty; anyone could see her from the street. It was asking for trouble. Worse, it showed Barbara didn't trust him, didn't automatically think he was right. He decided to dump her after tonight, or maybe after the weekend.

"I thought you weren't coming," she said, in a burst.

"Well, I've come now," he said, and dived for her mouth. She gave a small squeal, the beginning of a protest; but he knew to let his mouth just stay at the edge of a kiss, not forcing it, and in a second her hard teeth seemed to make way. They stayed like that for a minute; once or twice she made a pretty little noise, almost animal, and each time, not quite knowing whether he was mocking or encouraging her, he made something of the same noise back, but deeper, the sound vibrating through their twinned lips, making them buzz and ache, fulfilling the desire and stirring up more. Finally he pulled away. He looked at her critically; the little squeal, the blonde hair frizzing up in one, the pink roundness of her pinked-up face, lips and tits. Perhaps the boys had it right when they called her Crystal Tipps and laughed at him. Or maybe they were jealous. "I came as soon as I could," he said. "They were having a party."

"You said they were," Barbara said. "I don't know why I couldn't be allowed to come. I'd have behaved."

"It was boring," he said. "There was nothing but neighbours. They didn't know each other, my mum didn't know them. I don't know why she asked them."

"We know all our neighbours," Barbara said with astonishment, "their birthdays, star signs, the lot. The telly programmes they watch, even."

"That's because you live in a terraced house," Daniel said. "You could hear everything through the walls. When they fuck."

"Do you mind?" Barbara said, objecting to the word rather than Daniel's snobbery. But she drew close again, pulling him with her out of the light from the street towards the empty, overgrown garden.

"They were all saying," Daniel murmured, his mouth against hers, running his tongue against her lips as they walked backwards into the lyric night, "they were all saying, who's that gorgeous girl, goes into the neighbours' gardens with Daniel Glover—"

"They were not," Barbara said, her eyes bright, her hand running down Daniel's side.

"They were," Daniel said, his hand, his rippling fingers rising, weighing, cupping, down and under, beneath and within. "And I said—"

"Oh, give over," Barbara said. But Daniel carried on, his hushed, exuberant voice now muted, and as they fell back against the lawn, which had grown into a thick meadow, she gave in to what he knew she felt. There was some indulgent amusement deep within him, and he never completely surrendered to the sensation, was never reduced to begging animal favours or further steps in the exploration of what she would grant him. His gratification, always, lay in seeing her so help-less; his pleasure in the expert and improving knack of bestowing plea-sure. The noises she made were on some level comic, "Nnngg," she went, and an observation post in him kept alert over the expanding border territory between her propriety and her desire. They began when he chose to begin; they ended when he said he had to go, and when he knew that she would say disappointedly, "Do you have to?"

Barbara was in his maths set; he'd heard some of the things she'd been letting out about him. Flattering, really. He didn't talk about her. Another couple of times, and that would be it; he'd seen the way Michael Cox's sister looked at him, though she was eighteen next month. That would be something to talk about.

· · ·

It was not clear to any of the Glovers what the purpose of the party had been. Not even to Katherine, whose idea it had been. He hadn't come, after all. When the last of the guests had gone, the other two children went upstairs, Timothy holding a book. Malcolm sat down and, with his heels, dragged the armchair into a position facing the television. He did not get up to turn it.

Katherine put the letter on the shelf over the radiator, and began to go round the room, picking up glasses and plates. Malcolm had put the empty bottles in the kitchen as he had got through them. There were two open bottles left, one red and one white. The food had mostly been eaten, the tablecloth around the large oval dish of Coronation Chicken stained yellow where spoonfuls had been carelessly dropped. She began to talk as she collected the remains. She was wiping the thought that Nick, after all that effort, hadn't come. He'd said he would.

"They seemed to have a good time," she said. "I thought the food went well. I was worried they wouldn't be able to eat it standing up, but people manage, don't they?"

Malcolm said nothing. She sighed.

"It's a shame the new people over the road haven't moved in yet," she said. "It would have been a good opportunity for them to meet the neighbours. Most people came, I think. There was a nice little letter from the lady in the big house, saying she was sorry she couldn't come. She doesn't like to go home after dark. Silly, really—it's only a hundred yards, I don't know what she thinks would happen to her, and it's not really dark, even now. They get set in their ways, old people."

Malcolm gave no sign of listening.

She couldn't be sure what the reason for the party had been. But for her it had been defined by the people who hadn't come rather than those who had. Not just one person; two of them. All evening she'd felt impatient with her guests who, by stooping to attend, had shown themselves to be not quite worth knowing. She projected her idea of the sort of friends she ought to have on to the new people—the Sellerses—and Mrs. Topsfield, with the exquisite handwriting and supercilious reason for not attending. The Sellerses were going to be smart London people. That was absolutely clear.

"Did you miss your battle re-creation society tonight?" she said to Malcolm, to be kind.

"Yes," he said. "It doesn't matter, once in a while."

"You could have invited some of them to come tonight," she said, although she'd rather not have to meet grown men who dressed up in Civil War uniforms and disported themselves over the moors, pretending to kill each other. It was bad enough being married to one.

"I thought it was just for the neighbours," Malcolm said. "You said you weren't going to invite anyone else."

Upstairs, Jane shut her door. It was too early to go to bed, but it was accepted that she spent time in her room; homework, her mother said hopefully, but, really, Jane sat in her room reading. There were forty books on the two low shelves, and a blank notebook. She had read them all, apart from *The Mayor of Casterbridge*, a Christmas present from a disliked aunt; she had been told that Jane liked reading old books and that, with a life of Shelley, now lost, unread, had been the result. Jane's books were of orphans, of love between equals, of illegitimate babies, treading round the mystery of sex and sometimes ending just before it began.

Her room was plain. Three years before she had been given the chance to choose its décor. Her mother had made the offer as the promise of a special treaty enacted between women, something to be conveyed only afterwards to the men. Jane had appreciated the tone of her mother's confiding voice, but was baffled by the possibilities. It was that she had no real idea what role her bedroom's décor was supposed to play in her mother's half-angry plans for social improvement, and she was under no illusions that if she actually did choose wallpaper, curtains, paint, bedspread, carpet, even, that her choice would be measured against her mother's unshared ideas and probably found disappointing. Would it be best to ask for an old-fashioned style, "with character," as her mother said, a pink teenage girl's bedroom? Or to opt for her own taste, whatever that might be?

In the end she delayed and delayed, and now her bedroom was a blank series of whites and neutrals. She had failed in whatever romance her mother had planned for her; and, with its big picture window, the room showed no sign of turning into a garret. It looked out on to a suburban street. Daniel's room, at the back of the house, had the view of the moor, which meant nothing to him. Over her bed, one concession: a poster, bought in a sale, of a Crucible Theatre production of *Romeo and Juliet*. Daniel had seen it, not her—he'd done the play for O level. Someone had given him the poster, but it was over her bed that two blue-lit figures embraced, one already dead.

She wondered what the new people over the road would be like, and let her thoughts go on their romantic course.

It was the next day, in London. The house had been packed into a van. It was driving northwards, towards Sheffield. On every box was written, in large felt-tip letters, the name SELLERS.

"Nice day for it," the driver said.

"Yeah, you don't want to be moving in the rain," the other man put in.

The driver was on Sandra's right, his mate, the chief remover, on her left. On the far side the boy, ten or fifteen years younger than the others, who had said nothing.

"Why do you say that?" Sandra said. She was pressed up against the man on her left, and the driver's operations meant that his left hand banged continually against her thigh. The lorry's cabin was meant only for the comfort of three. There was a dull, dusty smell in the cabin, of unwashed sweaters and ancient cigarette stubs. The floor was littered with brown-paper sandwich wrappers.

"Well, stands to reason," the chief remover said. "If it's raining, that's no fun."

"And there are always customers who insist on tarpaulins," the driver said.

"Tarpaulins?" Sandra said. "Whatever for?"

"It's their right," the chief remover said. "Say you're moving a lot of pictures, or books, or soft furnishings—"

"The customer, they don't like it if you carry them out into the rain, and sometimes you have to leave them outside for a minute or two, and if it's raining—"

"Hence the tarpaulin," the driver said. Behind them, the full tinny bulk of the removals van thundered like weather. There was a distant rattle, perhaps furniture banging against the walls or a loose exhaust pipe. Below, the roofs of cars hurtled past.

"Because," the chief remover said, "if something gets wet, even for a couple of minutes, if the whole load gets rained on, you get to the other end, see, and it's offloaded and put in place, and a day or two later, there's a call to the office, a letter, maybe, complaining that the whole lot stinks of damp."

"Hence the tarpaulin," the driver said again.

"Course," the chief remover said, "nine times out of ten, it's not the furniture, it's the house, the new house, because a house left empty for a week, it does tend to smell of damp, but they don't take that into consideration. But the tarpaulins, it doubles the work for us, it does."

They were nearing the motorway now, having crossed London. The traffic that had held them steady on the North Circular for an hour was thinning, and the removals van was moving in bigger bursts. The car with Sandra's parents in it, her brother in the back, had long been lost in the shuffle of road lanes, one moving, one holding; a music-hall song her grandmother used to sing was in her head: "My old man said follow the van . . . you can't trust the specials like an old-time copper . . ." No, indeed you couldn't, whatever it meant.

She went back to being interested and vivacious before she had a chance to regret her request to travel up to Sheffield in the van, rather than in the car. "You must see everything in this job," she said vividly.

"Yeah, that's right," the boy surprisingly said, snuffling with laughter.

"Don't mind him," the driver said. "He can't help himself."

"It's a shame, really," the chief remover said.

"A bit like being a window-cleaner, I expect," Sandra said, before the boy could say he'd seen nothing to match her and her jumping into the van like that. She was fourteen; he was probably five years older, but she was determined to despise him. "I mean, you get to see every-thing, everything about people."

"You'd be surprised," the chief remover said.

"That's the worst of it over," the driver said. The road was widening, splitting into lanes, its sides rising up in high concrete barriers, and the London cars were flying, as if for sheer uncaged delight, and the four of them, in their rumbling box, were flying too. "Crossing London, that's always the worst."

"You see some queer stuff," the chief remover said. "People are different, though. There's some people who, you turn up, there's nothing done. They expect you to put the whole house into boxes, wrap up everything, tidy up, do the job from scratch."

"Old people, I suppose," Sandra said.

"Not always," the driver said. "You'd be surprised. It's the old peo-ple, the ones it'd be a task for, that aren't usually a problem."

"It's the younger ones, the hippies, you might call them, expect you to do everything," the chief remove said. "My aunt, you come across some stuff with that lot, things you'd think they'd be ashamed to have in the house, let alone have a stranger come across."

"That's right," the boy said. He seemed almost blissful, perhaps remembering the boxing-up of some incredible iniquity.

"Of course," Sandra said, "you're not to know what's in a lot of boxes, are you? There might be anything."

The three of them were silent: it had not occurred to them to worry about what they had agreed to transport.

"What was the place we said we'd stop?" the chief remover said.

"Leicester Forest East, wasn't it?" the driver said.

Sandra had watched the packing from an upstairs window, and only at the end had she thought of asking if she could travel with the men. She was fourteen; she had noticed recently that you could stand in front of a mirror with a small light behind you, approach it with your eyes cast down, then lift them slowly, and raise your arm across your chest, as if you were shy. You could: you could look shy. Whatever you were wearing, a coat, a loose dress, a T-shirt, or most often the new bra you'd had to ask your mum to buy to replace the one that had replaced the starter bra of only a year before, the shy look and the protective arm had an effect.

The old house had been stripped, and everything the upper floor had held was boxed and piled downstairs; the house had drained downwards, like a bucket with a hole. Sandra had been born in that house. She had never seen these upstairs rooms empty, and they now looked so small. Her clean room's walls were marked and dirty. Only the window looked bigger, stripped of the curtains she had been allowed to choose and hadn't liked for years—the pink, the peacocks, the girly rainbows and clouds. The net curtains were gone too—and if she had anything to do with it, they'd not be going up in her new room.

Her father was downstairs in the hall, telling the foreman a funny story—the confidential anecdotal mutter deciphered by bursts of laughter. Her mother, probably exhausted, was perhaps looking for Francis, who was lazy and clumsy, and had a knack of disappearing when anything needed to be done. She looked out of the window to where the van, its back open, was being steadily loaded with the house's contents, exotic and unfamiliar when scattered across the drive. There were two men, one middle-aged, the top of his bald head white and glistening like lard, the other a boy. She waited in the window patiently, and soon her mother came out with cups of tea. The boy turned to her mother. He was polite, he said, "Thank you, Mrs. Sellers," and when her mother went back inside, he was still facing in the right direction. She did that thing she knew how to do, and it worked; he looked upwards. Her gaze was shy, lowered. It met his modestly, and she gently drew her hand across her chest. Brilliant. She might have slapped him, the way he turned away, but he was the one who blushed. She realized that the driver and Mr. Griffiths from next door, nosing about in his front garden, had also seen her. Mr. Griffiths, who'd always been fond of her, and Mrs. Griffiths too; from the look on his face now, they'd have something to think about if they ever thought of her ever again.

"Have you seen your brother?" her father said, as he thudded up the stairs.

"No," Sandra said. "He's probably down the end of the garden. Can we—" she began. She was about to ask if they could have a tree-house at their new house, but she'd had a better idea. She was fourteen. "Can I go up to Sheffield with the movers in their van?"

Bernie looked startled. "There'll not be room. A bit of an adventure, is it?"

"Something like that."

"I'll see what I can do. Don't ask your mother. She'll have a fit."

So there she was, wedged into the van, clear of London, for the sake of the boy she had glimpsed—a movement of the arms, a flash of blue from the deep-set shadow under the surprising blond eyebrows. But he was saying nothing, and she was settling for enchanting the driver and the chief remover.

"People do this all the time," she said.

"Move house?" the chief remover said. "Enough to keep us busy."

"No, I meant—" But what she had meant was that people leave London by car, drive on to the motorway, set off northwards all the time, perhaps every day. She never had, and her mother, her brother and she had only ever left London when they went on holiday. She had never had any business outside London. "People either move a lot or not at all, don't they?" she said. "I mean," sensing puzzlement, "there's the sort of people who never leave the house they were born in and die there. Dukes. And there's the sort of people who move house every year, every two years. I don't know what would be normal."

"The average number of times a person moves house in his lifetime," the boy said, "is seven, isn't it?" He had a harsh, grating voice, a South London voice not yet settled into its adult state.

"Take no notice of him," the driver said. "He's making it up. He doesn't know."

"But the figure is increasing all the time," he continued.

"He makes up statistics," the chief remover said. "That's what he does. Once we were dealing with a musician, moving house for him—

a sad story, he was divorcing his wife, and we had to go in and pick out the things that were going and the things that were staying. And we were moving his stuff and he said he'd be taking his cellos, because he had two, with him in a taxi, and wouldn't let us touch them, though we handle your fragile things all the time. And all of a sudden this one says, 'There are a hundred and twenty-three parts in a cello,' as if to say, yes, it's best you handle it yourself. He'd only gone and made it up, the hundred and twenty-three parts. There's probably about thirty."

"It sounds about right, moving seven times," Sandra said. "There's a girl in my class who's moved house seven times already. She's only fourteen." Sandra thought she might have told them she was sixteen: she sometimes did that. Even seventeen. "This was two years ago," she added. "So she'd used up all her moves already, if you look at it like that."

"Fancy," the boy said.

"Do you see that sign, young lady?" the driver said. "A hundred and twenty miles to Sheffield."

They were clear of London now; the banked-up sides of the motorway no longer suggested the outskirts of towns, but now, behind stunted trees, there were open fields, expansive with scattered sheep. In the distance, on top of a hill like a figurine on a cake, there was a romantic, solitary house. She wondered what it must be like to look out every morning from your inherited grand house and see, like a river, the distant flowing motorway. It was never empty, this road.

"New home," the chief remover said sweetly. "Sheffield. And The North, it said."

"Have you ever noticed," the driver said, "that wherever you go, anywhere, you see motorway signs that say 'The North'? Or 'The South' when you're in the north? Or 'The West'? But wherever you go, and we go everywhere, you never see a sign which says 'The East'?"

"No, you never do," the boy agreed.

Sandra felt her story hadn't made much of an impression. It was difficult, squashed in like this, to push back her shoulders, but she tried.

"This girl," she went on, "you always wondered whether it was good for her to move so often. I mean, seven times, seven new schools. She never stayed long, so I don't suppose she ever made proper friends with anyone. I tried to be friends with her, because I thought she'd be lonely, but she didn't make much of an effort back. She'd only been in our school for three, four weeks when we found out the sort of girl she was."

"What sort was she?" the boy said.

"At our school, see," Sandra said, "you didn't hang about after school had finished. Because next door there was the boys' school. And maybe some girls knew boys from the boys' school—if they had brothers or something—but this girl, I said to her one day, 'Let's walk home together.' And she said to me, 'No, let's hang around here and see if we can bump into boys because they're out in ten minutes.' We didn't get let out together, the boys' school and girls' school. And she jumps on to the wall, sits there, grins, waiting for me to jump up too. Because she just wanted to meet boys. That's the sort of girl she was."

"Dear oh dear," the driver said. She had hoped for a little more concern: the older men might have had daughters of their own. The levity of the sarcastic apprentice had spread to them.

"So you didn't stay friends with her, then?" The chief remover pushed back his cap and scratched his bald head.

"No," Sandra said. Sod them, she thought. "Five months later, she had to leave the school because she'd met a boy and gone further. In a way I don't need to specify"—the adult phrase rang well in her ears—"and she had to leave the school because she was having a baby. Can you imagine?"

"No," the driver said. He almost sang it, humouring her, and now it was over, the whole invented rigmarole seemed unlikely even to Sandra. "Probably best for you to leave a school where things like that go on."

"That's right," the chief remover said, very soberly, looking directly ahead.

"That's right," the boy said. He plucked at his chin as if in thought. But he was trembling with laughter; the big blue van at their backs rumbled and trembled with suppressed laughter.

The blue pantechnicon, ahead of Bernie, Alice and Francis, formed a hurtling, unrooted landmark.

"I don't know which way he's heading," Bernie said. "Expect he knows a route."

Alice opened her handbag, brown leather against the brighter shine of the Simca's plastic seats. She popped out an extra-strong mint for Bernie and put it to his mouth, like a trainer with a sugar-lump for a horse—he took it—then one for herself. They were on Park Lane. The van was a hundred yards ahead—no, that was a different blue van. Theirs was ahead of it.

"We don't need to follow them all the way," Bernie said, crunching his mint cheerfully. "We could be quicker going down side-streets. They'll be sticking to the A-roads through London."

"I'd be happier, really," Alice said. That was all. Everything she had, everything she had acquired and kept in her life, had gone into that van—the nest of tables they'd saved up for, their first furniture after they had married, the settee and matching chairs that had replaced the green chair and springy tartan two-seater Bernie's aunts had lent them . . .

"That's all right, love," Bernie said. "If you want to keep them in view, we'll keep them in view."

. . . the mock-mahogany dining table and chairs, green-velvet seated, from Waring & Gillow, brass-footed with lions' claws, the double divan bed only a year old—their third since she had first come home with Bernie, him carrying her over the threshold and not stopping there but carrying her upstairs, puffing and panting until he was through the door of their bedroom and dropping her on to his surprise, a new-bought bed, and her not knowing she was pregnant already—and the carpets . . .

"I know it's silly," Alice said, "but I won't feel easy about it unless we follow them."

"Well, we've lost them now," Bernie said. "We'll catch up."

It was true. London had spawned vans ahead of them, blue and black and green, rumbling and bouncing to the street horizon; the Orchard's van was there somewhere, but lost. They ground to a halt in the dense traffic.

"It can't be helped," Alice said bravely. The carpets, all chosen doubtfully, all fitting their space. (She had no faith in the Sheffield estate agent's measurements. The woman bred Labradors, which she'd mentioned more than once when she ought to have been paying attention.) The unit for the sitting room, a new bold speculation, white Formica with smoked brown glass doors, the *Reader's Digest* books, the china ladies, the perpetual flowers under glass; the mahogany-veneer sideboard, a wedding present, once grand and solitary in the sitting room before furniture started to be possible for them; curtains, yellow for the kitchen, purple Paisley in the sitting room, red in their bedroom, the rainbow pattern Sandra had chosen . . .

"Look on the bright side," Bernie said. "If they do get lost, or if they steal it and run away to South America, Orchard's can buy us a whole new houseful of furniture. Insurance."

"They aren't going to lose it, are they?" A voice came from the back seat. It was Francis; even at nine, his knees were pressing hard into his mother. Goodness knew how tall he'd grow.

"No, love," Alice said. Her own worry disappeared in her love for her son. He worried about these things, as she did. Once, on an aeroplane, she had found her own nervousness about flying vanished as she did her duty and comforted him. "They won't lose it, and if they did steal it, they wouldn't get far on the proceeds. Do you think they'd get much for Sandra? She's up there with them, keeping an eye on things."

"I wouldn't give you two hundred quid for Sandra," Bernie said, concentrating on the road. "Maybe if she'd had a wash first. What do you reckon, son?"

"I don't know where you go to buy and sell people," Francis said. "There aren't people shops, are there?"

She hadn't told Francis they were going to move to Sheffield until it was certain. She wasn't sure, herself, how it had happened. Bernie had worked for the Electricity Board for years, the only member of his fast-talking family not to make money in irregular, unpredictable ways. They were at the outer edges of respectability, in most cases only having their churchgoing to take the edge off their quickness. Alice had first met Bernie at church, him and his family in their Sunday best. If it had been a deft illusion, it hadn't been a long-lasting one; you couldn't be surprised with Bernie—he was as open to view as an Ordnance Survey map. His family were proud of him and his proper job, his steadily rising salary, at head office, and Bernie paid back their pride by not renouncing his own quick ways, his broad mother's broad manners.

But in the last couple of years, the job, London, had worn away at him. The series of strikes—every power-cut had driven him to a personal sense of grievance. "Don't say that," Alice had said, the first time the house had gone dark, the television fading slowest, giving out a couple more seconds of ghostly blue light before the four of them were in pitch darkness, Bernie swearing.

"Don't say what?" Bernie said, almost shouting.

"You know what you said," Alice said.

"I can't think of a better word for them," Bernie said, getting up and groping for the fucking candles.

Though the power-cuts, random and savage, affected and infuriated every adult in the country—not the children, who across the nation took to it with delight, like camping, and in later years were to ask their parents when the power-cuts would start again, as if it were a traditional, seasonal thing—they affected Bernie worst. In part, it was the way neighbours, like the Griffithses, or the regular commuters on Bernie's train would inquire pointedly when Bernie and his colleagues were going to get a grip on the situation. Everyone had a story of the power coming on and sparking up an abandoned iron, still plugged in, in the middle of the night, waking up Mrs. Griffiths, as it happened, with a stench of burning, which proved to be her husband's best shirt for the morning. "And a miracle the house didn't burn down," Mr. Griffiths said, suggesting that someone more honourable than Bernie might offer to pay for a new best shirt for the morning out of his own wallet. It drove Bernie mad.

On top of that the winter of 1973 was a hard one, and three or four times the train from the City to Kingston had failed. The first time, Bernie phoned Alice, who went to Morden Underground station to pick him up in their ancient black Austin, the same car they'd had when they first married, a cast-off from Bernie's brother Tony. It had refused to start again in the car park at Morden, and Alice had had to phone Mrs. Griffiths, begging her to give the children something to eat while the garage came out; they didn't get home until after midnight. So the second time it happened, even though by that time Bernie had bought a new car, the Simca, he only called to say he'd be a bit late, got the Tube to Morden and walked from there. The third and fourth time, too; it seemed to be going on all winter, like the winter.

But by then he'd heard of a new job, a promotion, out of London. That would never have seemed like a recommendation before. "Bernard," his widowed mother had said, when they'd gone to tell her in St. Helier, the ranks of crocuses lining up firmly along the path outside. "Bernard. You've never lived anywhere but London. You couldn't stand it for a week." She ignored Alice, apart from a savage glance or two; the whole thing, she could see, was the boy's wife's idea. In a corner, Bernard's shy uncle Henry sipped tea from a next-to-best floral cup, not getting involved; he would have to stay and hear the worst of it afterwards. But if it was unfair of anyone to think it couldn't have been Bernie's idea, you could see why they believed that. His whole manner—the way he blew his nose, the way he ate with his elbows out, as if always demolishing a pie in a crowded pub, his soft London complexion, even—made it impossible to think of him outside London. But it was only Bernie who wanted to move. Alice had been born near the Scottish borders, and had moved to London at the age Francis was moving to Sheffield, nine, at the war's end when no one was moving into capital cities. It was Alice, though, who loved London; she dreaded the North's forgiveness, the way it would look at her when she returned.

But there was no arguing with Bernie and, it was true, the job was a good one. Bernie had been offered the deputy managership of a power plant. It was the best way forward, to take a hands-on, strategic role, Bernie said. He'd left it quite late; but the industry was expanding.

He was like that: he could sell you anything with his enthusiasm. It was for her, however, to sell the move to the children, and she had nothing but her love to draw on there.

Outside the car, the landscape was changing. London had gone on for ever, its red-brick houses and businesses clinging to the edge of the motorway, like small rodents to a balloon suddenly in flight. The soft green of the southern counties, too, had gone, with the cows and sheep, and now harder, more purposeful facts were looming across the landscape. A herd of vast-waisted cooling towers, steaming massively; a terrain untended, brown and barren; one town after another with no name, just a mass of black and brown smoke and soot. It was getting worse; Francis could see that.

He had never thought that his mother would, one night, come into his bedroom and, sitting on the edge of his bed, explain that they might be moving to Sheffield. It was not that he had thought they would go on for ever where they were; it was simply that, at nine, no concept of change had ever entered his head. She had sat there, her face worried, when she'd finished, and he'd wanted to comfort her.

"It won't be so bad," he said in the end. "We'll all be there." He'd wanted to say that they couldn't make her move anywhere—not quite knowing who "they" might be. But he tried to comfort her and, misunderstanding, her face cleared.

"That's right," she said. "I knew you'd be brave about it. And it'll be exciting—a new school, new friends—" She hugged him. It was odd; they'd been trying to console each other. Still, he knew that, in her worry for him, she had expressed some of her own; he'd been right, after all, to think of consoling her.

They'd travelled up to Sheffield two or three weeks later. They'd gone by train, an experience so unusual to Francis, who had only ever gone into London by train, a journey of twenty minutes, that he paid no attention to the view outside. He'd taken fascinated pleasure in the toilets, mysteriously labelled WC, the wooden slatted windows with their frank graffiti, the extraordinary act of sitting around a table, the four of them, and a cloth being laid and lunch being served. You could eat soup on a train, which had bewildered him when he had read of it, in *Emil and the Detectives*. It was all so unlike the rattling compartment train from Kingston to Waterloo when the Lord Mayor's Show was on. Now, in the Simca with its lack of event, he could start to look, with some apprehension, at his surroundings.

The week in Sheffield they'd spent at a hotel. The Electricity had paid for it—"It's all a treat," Bernie had said, once they were settled in the beige rooms, the walls lined with nubbled tweed fabric. "Have whatever you like."

"That's nice of them," Sandra said.

"They're grateful," Bernie said.

"Can I have a glass of wine?" Sandra said.

"I don't see why not," Alice said. It was to be their holiday that summer; they weren't going to have another.

Each day, they took the car the Electricity had provided, and drove out somewhere. Mostly into the countryside. It was different from the countryside in Surrey. There were no hedges, no trees, and the villages were harsh, square and unadorned. Outside, the great expanses of the moors were frightening and ugly; even in bright sun, the black hills with the blaze of purple on their flanks were crude, unfinished. They parked the car and, with a picnic, clambered down into a valley where some terrible catastrophe seemed to have occurred, and about a stream, plummeting and plunging, black rocks were littered, huge and cuboid, just lying there like a set of abandoned giant toys, polystyrene and poised to fall again, without warning. Once they came across a dead sheep, lying there, half in the stream, its mouth open, its fleece filthy and stinking with flies. In Surrey it would have been tidied away. "Don't drink from a stream, ever," Alice said. It would never have occurred to Francis even to consider such a thing.

On these outings Sandra, in the back of the Simca with him, was quiet and sullen. She didn't complain: she followed whatever they were supposed to be doing, from time to time inspecting the sensible shoes she'd been made to bring with open distaste. Francis, as often these days, observed her with covert interest. She was five years older than him. In the room they shared at the hotel, she spent her time writing postcards to her friends, which, when she left them for him to read, proved cryptic or insulting about him in specific terms. Her weariness, never openly stated, only dissipated when they arrived at a market town, and the prospect of shops, on however unambitious a scale, revived her. She bought more postcards; she looked, she said, for presents for her friends, though nothing seemed to fit the bill.

Once they went into the centre of Sheffield, but even for Sandra, Francis could see, this was not a success. It was strange, confusing, and not planned, as London was, to excite. Francis was gripped with the prospect of getting lost; he had no sense of direction or memory for landmarks. They followed Sandra indulgently into one shop after another, and after a couple of hours stopped in municipal gardens by the town hall, an alarming construction like an egg-box.

"We'll have to come back here," Alice said to Bernie. "This is where the education department is. To see about schools."

Francis's dad bought him and Sandra a Coke each, and they sat on a bench in the dry city heat. "This will have been cleared by bombs," Bernie said, "these gardens, in the war. See where the old buildings stop and the new ones start? They'll have been bombed during the war because of the steel, see?" Francis looked around and it was right: a ripped-out space had been created, a kind of shapeless acreage, and into it, dropped in as exactly as false teeth, were new and extravagant buildings, the egg-box, a building with brass globes protruding from its top floor, others whose smoked mirrors for windows made no allowances towards the church like blackened solemnity of the old town hall, a figure poised heroically above the entrance like Eros.

Two boys his own age had sat on a bench directly opposite theirs. It was term-time, Francis knew that, but they had not been taken out of school for a week because their families were moving—a licensed absence that had nevertheless caused him unspoken worry in the course of the week, even while clambering over Burbage Rocks, in case an inspector should materialize from behind a dry-stone wall. These were real truants, their hands dirty, and Francis looked at them in the way he would have studied photographs of Victorian murderers, possessors of a remote experience that would never be his. He sucked at his Coke, and lazily, one of the boys pulled out a packet of cigarettes, offering the other boy one. He felt childish with his fizzy drink and already the object of contempt. Their conversation drifted over with its incomprehensible freight of words—"Waggy nit," one said, and "Scoile," the other said; a long story began, about Castle Market—the Cattle Market, did they mean? Why didn't they say "the"? "Mardy," "gennel"; one punched the other, hard, and the other said, "Geeyour."

Francis tried not to look at them. He feared their retribution, or their mockery; he feared the idea that his father would take it upon himself to say something to them, something inflammatory and adult, and Sheffield would turn upon them.

His parents had planned to spend the next day going round and finding a new house to buy. Although Francis had inspected the pile of agent's particulars in his parents' hotel bedroom with fervour and wonderment at the sums—£16,000—involved, he and Sandra were to entertain themselves for most of the day. His ideas of entertainment were few, and he knew they were not allowed to stay in their room, the cleaners demanding access every morning after breakfast. But his mother had done a little research, and had discovered that a public library was to be found in a Victorian villa at Broomhill, only three hundred yards away. They were to spend the morning there, and find their own way back to the hotel, where they could order lunch themselves as a special treat. Of course, they could not take anything out of the library, not having an address, but if Francis wanted a book to read—there was no suggestion that Sandra was likely to share in this desire—there was a bookshop, only fifty yards further on, where he could buy something. Alice gave him two pound notes, an unheard-of advance on pocket money, and, it seemed, not even an advance: she did it when Sandra and his father could not see, a little squeeze of the hand pressing the money into his fist.

The library filled the morning, but it was short. He sat under the wooden bookshelves that, even in the children's section, bore the intimidating municipal heading "Novels." It took him a moment to recognize some familiar and favourite books there, and it was a surprise to discover that he had been reading "novels" when he thought he had been reading Enid Blyton, or a book about Uncle, the millionaire elephant in a city of skyscrapers, Beaver Hateman at his heels. Chairs were supplied and, greedily taking five books with him, head down and not acknowledging the look of the librarian, whether approving or sour, he went to sit. At first he could hear his sister: she was talking to someone downstairs, in her "mature" voice, as he called it; maturity, much evoked, had become her favourite virtue, and whenever she thought of it her voice dragged and drawled to the point of a groan. "No, we're moving up here in a few months' time. Yes, from London. We thought it best to sample the local amenities. I do hope you don't mind us coming in—my brother's the real reader in the family . . ."

And then the voice somehow faded away. The old library, in Kingston, he'd been going to since he was four, and had read every book in their children's section, except the I-books, which he didn't like, when people told you a story and said I. Here, there were so many new and different books, and what his sister's voice had faded into was a book, a little childish but funny, about a bushranger called Midnite, and "bushranger" was the Australian word for "highwayman," with a cat called Khat, and, look, Queen Victoria, and—

It was quite short, and he had almost finished it by the time his sister, hot and bored, came to fetch him. She had left the library to explore the little parade of shops. "Come on," she said. "Time for lunch." He followed her, the last five pages abandoned; perhaps he could come back later. And perhaps he could keep the two pounds—you could spend it on books in London, too.

"We've found a house," Bernie said, coming into the hotel dining room while they were still eating their lunch. He was glowing with relief and satisfaction. The dining room, hung with velvet wallpaper and dark curtains, had been daytime dingy, and the children had been talking in whispers, not daring to bicker, but there was Francis's dad, as if he hadn't noticed anything. "You'll like it, kids."

"I've found a book," Francis wanted to say to complete everyone's happiness. "I've found lots of books."

"It's nice," Alice said, sitting down in a flop and looking first, with concern, at Francis. She had something to console him with. "You'll like it."

"My name is   "

She began to write. But the paper was resting on the lawn. Her pen tore through the paper on the y of "my," and then she was writing on grass through torn paper. Jane was lying on her stomach in a secret part of the garden. She cocked her head and listened. She kicked her heels up, bouncing them against her bum. There was nobody about.

She took the paper and, rolling over, sat up to write properly. At the end of August, the grass was dry and brown, crackling like a fire. Under her legs, it was itchy with gorse droppings, and she could feel a holly leaf or two. The holly tree in the far corner was constantly shedding leaves. Nowhere in the garden was ever completely free of them. She folded the paper, and wrote: "My name is Fanny."

Jane paused. For as long as she could remember, her name had really been Fanny. Her paper-name, the name of the heroine of her book when it should be written. Now she was fourteen, it was time to write it.

It was a great shame, really, that it was the end of August. She'd let so much of the summer holiday go by without writing anything. Now that she had written four words, she regretted it had taken so long. Until now, it had been a running, contiguous commentary in her head, a third voice putting her smallest actions into a sort of prose—Jane left the house, shutting the door behind her. In the garden there were birds singing. Her mood was black—but now she was writing something.

She had switched on the lawn-sprinkler. The wet earth started to smell dense and delicious in the dry heat. The holly tree dripped with a tropical rhythm, irregular, on to the patio. The lawn-spray flung lazily in this direction with a hiss on each revolution, never quite reaching the little nest. A trickle of sweat, like a darting insect, slipped in a tickle from her armpit down her side; she could smell her own faint metallic odour. She was narrating in her head; she turned and began to write again.

"My name is Fanny. I was born an orphan in the year 1863. My mother . . ."

It was a hundred years before her own birth. Her eyes filled with the sadness that by now Fanny was certainly dead. But she was Fanny, sweating in a sleeveless dress and no knickers in a patch of a Sheffield garden. Presently, as the cool wave of water in air, a jet of perfumed rain, swept over her head, she was lost in the thrill of authorship.

The garden was not squarely established but, like the whole estate, carved out of country and annexed in opportunistic ways. It swelled at the far corner to take in the substantial holly tree. ("A hundred years old," Jane's mother said reverently. She had always wanted to live in an old house, with character.) Elsewhere it wavered about in odd directions, claiming and abjuring patches of land. If the features of the garden seemed deceptively aged, like the trees, that was because the gardens had fenced-in patches of country. A moorland tussock, three feet square, brought in, surrounded by a lawn and a garden wall, like a rockery. The patchy lawn, the spindles of trees on the streets, rooted in squares of earth like tea-bags: those told the age of the development more clearly.

You could nest in the roots of the old holly tree where you were invisible from the house. For Jane's less secret withdrawals, she went to read somewhere she could be discovered. You could sometimes hear a

human noise beyond the garden and, in a series of corrections, understand that it was not, after all, one of the neighbours on either side at
their pleasure, or a walker hugging the shore of the development
before heading off into the wild heather of the country but the child's-
dismay-call made by a sheep, sheltering from the wind beyond the dry-
stone wall.

But there was another better gift from the moor, which no one, Jane
believed, knew about: three thick gorse bushes, brilliant banana-yellow
blossom and always quick to slash at your arms. From the open lawn, it
looked as if they went right up to the wall, but if you got down on your
belly and wriggled through, a little space of secret untended grass
opened up. You could sit there and watch, unnoticed. Her father was
always talking about clearing the gorse bushes but he wouldn't get
round to it. Perhaps he was fond of them too. Here she had pressed
down a space, clearing it of holly leaves and gorse twigs.

Another hiding-place had been the garden of the house opposite,
empty for four months now. All summer it had been the province of
her brother after nightfall; there he prowled and roamed, his girls
coming to him eagerly. In the daytime, it had been hers. After four
months of neglect, it had developed in unexpected, luxuriant ways. At
first it was like a room enclosed, left tidy by the owners to await their
return, and Jane ventured into it with a sense of intrusion. But quickly
it began to grow and dissolve. An inoffensive small plant, a few shoots
above the ground, had exploded, leaping through the trellised fence, a
few more inches and a few more shoots every day. One day, all at once,
a single slap of colour was there: a poppy had burst open, and then,
for weeks, there was a relay of flowers, each lasting a day or two. Of
course, her mother worked in a shop full of flowers, so they were not
strange to Jane; but to watch them work their own stubborn magic,
budding and bursting, fading and moulting on the stem, rather than
dying, yellow and sour, in someone's vase was new to her.

For weeks, the garden expanded along its permitted limits, and only
the plants that Mr. Watson, a gardener as draconian as Jane's father,
had admitted to his garden developed, stretching in their new free-
dom. But then the weeds started: the perfect lawn was scattered with
constellations of daisies and, quite soon, dandelions. There were but-
terflies now and when, once, it rained overnight in torrents, the garden
was filled with snails, come out to drink and feed. Best of all was a marvellous new plant, embracing and winding itself round anything, a
fence, a post, running itself through other plants, with the most beau-

tiful flowers like trumpets, like lilies, like the flowers of heaven. Jane had never had a favourite flower before, and whenever the craze for quizzes had arisen among the girls, she'd always replied, "Roses," when asked, a choice she knew was limp and conventional, as well as probably untrue. But now she really did have a favourite flower.

It was a shock to discover, when she asked her father, discreetly, that it was a garden pest called bindweed. Then he explained the complex and violent steps needed to eradicate it. Jane listened, but it seemed a little sad to her to remove a plant so beautiful, to prefer, as her father did, a border of squat green-tongued plants that would never flower or get anywhere much in life. Jane promised herself, when she grew up, a garden with nothing but bindweed, a dense bower of strangling vines and trumpeting innocent flowers.

Her garden visits were over now. A couple of days ago one of those neighbours had rapped at the window as she had been going in—slipping in, she had thought, unobserved as a mouse in the middle of the day. It had been embarrassing enough to see the neighbour at her mother's party; that hiding-place was now closed to her, and the garden went its way in peace.

She smoothed the paper: she started to write again. Something caught her eye. From here, she could not be seen from the house, if she kept low, but she could see anyone standing near the windows. There was a movement in Daniel's bedroom. Daniel was supposed to have gone swimming in the open-air pool at Hathersage; he couldn't have got there and back so quickly. The figure moved again, and it wasn't Daniel. The day was bright, and in the dimness of the house, Jane could see only the outline of a figure, its shape and gestures. It moved again: a hand travelled towards the face, then paused in mid-air, shifted, went downwards, as if it was going through something on Daniel's "desk."

It was Jane's father. She hadn't realized how absolutely she knew his shape and movements, the way he had of letting his hands start to do one vague thing before abandoning it nervously for something else. "I'll tell you something," she remembered Daniel saying to her once, watching her with an amused horrid gleam, "I bet they don't do it any more." "Do what?" Jane had said. "What do you think?" Daniel said. "And I bet Dad's relieved more than anything."

Lying there, undiscoverable, in the middle of the day, Jane might have preferred a burglar. She allowed herself a minute of speculative romance, but it was no good, it was her father; surprisingly here in the middle of the day, surprisingly in Daniel's bedroom, but that was all.

Twenty minutes later, she heard the front door shut. She hadn't heard it open, she reflected, though it usually made a solid clunk. He'd opened it quietly, she guessed, as if he had sneaked in; he'd thought there was no one in the house so he'd shut it as he normally did. It wasn't much of an adventure, really. She got up, picked up her notebook and went into the house for a drink, brushing down her print dress as she went. She should have gone with Daniel to Hathersage for a swim. She'd said she probably would, that morning over breakfast, just before her dad went off to work.

"We said we'd stop at the next service station," Alice said, noticing a sign.

"Yeah?" Bernie said, not concentrating on what she was saying. "Sorry—"

"I said, we told the removers we'd be stopping at Leicester Forest East," Alice said. "The service station. It's the next one—I think it said seven miles."

Bernie was gritting his teeth: he was stuck between lorries, thundering along at a frustrating ten miles an hour below the speed limit, boxed in by faster lines of traffic solidly flowing to the right. He felt like a box on a conveyor belt. "Not a bad idea," he said. "They won't worry if we don't, though."

"It might be as well," Alice said. "Sandra."

"What about Sandra?" Francis said, his chin resting on the back of his mother's seat, his face almost in her hair.

"Oh, nothing," Alice said.

"Your mum means," Bernie said, "that she might be fed up of riding in the lorry by now. The excitement might have worn off."

"I didn't mean that exactly," Alice said.

"Or on the other hand they might—" Bernie broke off. "We ought to get a radio in the car," he said, after a while. "Aren't you hungry, Frank? I'm hungry. That wasn't much of a lunch."

"It couldn't be helped," Alice said. "Everything was packed away."

"I know, love," Bernie said.

New experiences filled Francis with automatic dread. He had disappeared when the removers had arrived, feeling that demands would be placed on him, but dreading most the presence of rough men in their emptying house. He had never eaten in a motorway service station before; whenever they had travelled, picnics had been packed to be eaten in fields or off the dashboard, according to rain. Now he felt, knowing it to be stupid, that indefinite dangers were presenting themselves, dangers involving crowds of strangers, unfamiliar islands of retail and cooking, the probability of being lost and abandoned. The fear of abandonment was always high in him, and the specific dread, on this occasion, was of the family losing their possessions, now loaded into an untrustworthy, wobbling van.

"Here we are," Bernie said, as the half-mile sign flashed past; he signalled left, and then Francis's favourite thing, the three signs indicating three hundred yards, two hundred, a hundred, with three, then two, then one finger. You could work out how fast you were going: just count the seconds between each sign and multiply by whatever. But, of course, they were slowing down. There was a fragile bridge, glass, metal and plastic, over the breadth of the motorway, and people walking across it as if they did not know they were at any moment to be plunged, shrieking, into the metal river of traffic when the structure collapsed. At this new terror he shut his eyes.

"And there they are," Alice said, with soft relief. The van was reversing into a bay in the lorry park to the left; they drove right, and Bernie found a space. They got out and waited for the men and Sandra; but as they approached, they were a few feet behind her; she was walking with brisk anger. The youngest man had a flushed face, as if he had just been discovered in some peculiarly personal activity; the chief remover's mouth was set.

They waited by the Simca, Alice smiling defensively. "Lovely day for it," she called to them, but they didn't reply. Sandra, scowling, came up and took her father's arm.

"I think it's best," the chief remover said, "that your daughter ride in the car the rest of the way." He had stopped; the other two kept going.

"I thought she'd get fed up of it before long," Alice said hopefully.

"We've got the directions," the chief remover said, ignoring this. "We'll see you up there in a couple of hours, I reckon."

He walked off, following the others. Bernie squeezed his daughter; no one said anything. In a moment, they went inside; Bernie had seen that the men were going upstairs, but there was a nearer café on the ground floor. They went into that and ate fish and chips, all together.

And when the men went out, back to the lorry, they pretended not to notice, and sat there for fifteen minutes longer. Alice even had a piece of cake. Everyone did their best to be cheerful, talking around rather than to Sandra, and by the time they had finished, they could look directly at her. Although she was still a bit red, she no longer seemed about to burst into tears.

Daniel was home by half past four. He'd been at Hathersage all day, pretty well, it had been a hot day, a perfect one. The pool was built on a hillside just outside the Derbyshire village. Surrounded by school-masterly red-brick walls, it was concrete and tile inside; outside were the Derbyshire hills, and the huge sky. If you hurled yourself from the highest diving board, you were horizontal for one moment, poised above the water, framed against the sky and hills. Perfect. He'd got there at ten, in the first bus of the morning, still empty; later buses were full of kids, as he said to himself. Barbara had been supposed to come, and he'd told her to meet him at the bus stop at the bottom of Coldwell Lane at nine, but she hadn't been there when the bus came. He'd got on anyway; not a bad excuse to dump her, especially since she hadn't been on the next bus.

He'd spent an hour thrashing up and down, throwing himself off the diving board in bold, untidy shapes, enjoying more the gesture and the moment of flight than anything else, and grinning when he surfaced after a bellyflop, his stomach red and stinging, joining in with the laughter of the girl lifeguard. By eleven or so another bus had arrived from Sheffield, much more full, and they came in; some he recognized from his school, three girls from his sister's year, finding Daniel splendid in his exercise, brown limbs jumbled, the disconcerting swirl of his turquoise-patterned trunks, flying above the vivid oblong of water which shone with the Derbyshire blue of the sky. He'd met some friends and made some more; he always did. But in the end he went home on his own, hardly saying goodbye, burying his face in a bag of cheese and onion crisps from the machine.

The bus home, the three-thirty, was as empty as the morning bus had been—too early for most people—but with all that day's exercise he ached, sitting at the front of the top deck. Ached, too, slumping up Coldwell Lane when the bus let him off; it was uphill all the way, and just a bit too far; his black sports bag, the one he used for school, banged away in the heat at his bony hips. Half enjoying his exhaustion, groaning as he slouched up the hill, he almost expected Barbara to be sitting on the wall outside their house. Perhaps crying.

There seemed to be nobody in the house. Daniel was terribly hungry; he hadn't had anything to eat since breakfast, apart from the crisps. He went through to the kitchen, dropping his bag in the middle of the hall, and went through the cupboards and the fridge, banging the doors as he went. He poured himself some vividly orange squash; it was always too weak and watery when your mother made it for you, and he liked it about one part to three. In a few minutes, he'd got the stuff for a magic sandwich together, and sat down with a breadknife, contentedly putting it together and eating the constituent parts individually as he went.

"That looks revolting," Jane said, opening the kitchen door. She must have been in the garden.

"You don't have to eat it," Daniel said, putting the sandwich spread on awkwardly with the breadknife. "I'm starving."

"I bet you had some chips in Hathersage," Jane said. She put down her notebook and pen on the table. He noticed that her dress was stained with grass.

"No, I didn't," he said. "What've you been doing? Writing poetry?"

"No," Jane said. "Where's Tim?"

"I don't know," Daniel said. "I only just came in. You know Jason in my year? Him and his brother Matthew were out on the crags a week ago and he said to me, 'I saw your sister. And she was sitting on a rock and gazing at the landscape and guess what she was doing? She was making notes in her little book.' Making notes." He broke into hilarity.

Jane flushed, picked up her notebook and hugged it to her. "I couldn't care less what someone like that says about anything I do," she said. "Whoever he is." She knew who he was: they'd thrown a stone at her.

"Making notes, though," Daniel said, subsiding. "It was dead funny." He leant back in his chair, took a satisfied look at the complex sandwich he'd put together, with ham and sandwich spread, cheese and salad cream, all bursting out from the sides, then took an enormous bite. Much of it fell out, splattering his red shiny shorts and his brown legs.

"That's disgusting," Jane said. "You know what? Dad came home this lunchtime."

There was a noise from upstairs, a little thud and a door opening—Tim coming downstairs. "I thought he'd gone out," Jane said. "I haven't seen him all day."

"Upstairs reading his snake books," Daniel said. "He's made himself a sandwich, though." He nodded at the mess on the work surface. "He'll not have been starving."

"That was me," Jane said. "I was saying, I thought you'd gone out."

"No," Tim said. "I was upstairs in my room. Can I have a sandwich?"

"Make it yourself," Daniel said. "Upstairs with your snake books?"

"Yes," Tim said, and then, in a singing tone, "Do you know—"

"Probably not," Daniel said.

"Do you know what the most venomous snake in the world is?"

"No," Jane said, with a feeling she'd been asked this before.

"Lots of people would say the cobra or the rattlesnake. But it's not. It's the inland Taipan. It can get up to eight feet long. If it bites you you're bound to die. It's brown, it's called Oxy, Oxyripidus something. Oxyripidus—Oxy—I'm almost remembering it—"

"Where's it live?" Daniel said.

"Australia," Tim said.

"Just so long as it doesn't live near me," Daniel said.

"It wouldn't hurt you," Tim said. "It's quite timid, really. It would avoid you and it's probably more scared of you than you would be of it. You wouldn't have to worry about it even if you were in Australia. Most people think snakes would attack you but they wouldn't, really. They only bite if they're in danger. I like snakes. I wish I could have one. Do you think if I asked they'd let me have a snake in my bedroom? I'd keep it in a glass case. I wouldn't let it out and it wouldn't have to be venomous—or not very."

"What do you mean, 'if' you asked?" Daniel said. "You ask them all the time, about once a week, and they always say no. You're not getting the most venomous snake in the world to keep under your bed. Face facts."

"I'd save up," Tim said, reciting his case stolidly on one note, "and I'd pay for it myself. I wouldn't want an inland Taipan—I wouldn't want any venomous snake, really. And I'd buy the mice with my pocket money. They don't need to eat very often, it wouldn't be expensive. I wish I could have a snake. It's not fair."

"I dare say," Jane said. "Go and make yourself a sandwich or something. I'm going to watch the telly."

"There's nothing on," Daniel said. "It's rubbish."

"It's better in the holidays," Tim said. "There's stuff on in the mornings. For children."

"It's still rubbish."

"This boy told me a joke," Tim continued with his dull reciting voice, though the subject had changed.

"What boy?" Daniel said.

"This boy I know," Tim said.

"You haven't seen anyone for five weeks," Daniel said.

"Yes, I have," Tim said, not crossly, but setting things right. "I saw Antony last week. We went to the library."

"Did smelly Antony tell you a joke?" Jane said incredulously. Tim occasionally gave the impression of a rich and varied social life once out of sight of his family, but Antony was its only visible representative. They'd all concluded, with different degrees of worry or amusement, that Antony, a boy as pale and quiet as a whelk, was not the tip of some festive iceberg but probably Tim's best or only friend.

"No, it wasn't Antony's joke," Tim said. "It was another boy, at school."

"You've been saving it up for five weeks?" Daniel said.

"I only just thought of it," Tim said. "There are these three bears, right?"

"I thought this was a joke," Daniel said. "I don't want to hear Goldilocks."

"It isn't Goldilocks," Tim said. "And these three bears, they're in an aeroplane."

"Not very likely," Jane said. "They wouldn't let three bears on an aeroplane. They'd eat all the meals and then they'd eat all the passengers. And they'd open the doors at the other end and there's no one there except a lot of bones and three bears who weren't hungry any more."

"Well, there's mummy bear and daddy bear and baby bear," Tim said, persevering, "and they're in an aeroplane."

"Where were they going?" Daniel said. "I can't remember stories like this if I don't know where they're going."

"It doesn't matter," Tim said. "They never got there, anyway. Listen to the story and you'll find out."

"Is this a joke or a story?" Jane said. "You said it was a joke. Now it's a story."

"I want to know where they were going," Daniel said. "Can they be going to Spain? I'd like a bear who went to Spain. Or can they be coming back? Then they'd have those hats on, those sombreros. A bear in a sombrero, there's a sight you don't see every day."

"They weren't going anywhere," Tim said. "Stop interrupting. I'm telling a joke."

"They've got to have been going somewhere," Jane said, "or they wouldn't have been in an aeroplane in the first place. Go on, tell us your joke."

"All right," Tim said. "So they're in this plane, and suddenly the engines catch fire. I forgot—I should have said there's only two parachutes on the plane."

"There's only two parachutes on the plane?" Daniel said. "For three bears, and a plane full of passengers, and the crew as well? That's not very sensible."

"There's not a plane full of passengers," Tim said, getting red in the face. "There's only three bears."

"But even supposing there are only three bears—I suppose they've eaten all the other passengers, or maybe everyone in the departure lounge saw three bears getting on the plane, and thought, Hmm, do I want to get into a confined space with three hungry bears or, really, do I want to go to Spain that much anyway, and changed their mind and went home—I mean, even supposing that, there's got to be someone flying the plane."

"Or even two," Jane said. "I think you have to have two pilots. When we went to Paris last year there were two pilots in case something went wrong with one of them."

Tim thought for a very long time, breathing noisily. Finally, he said, "Daddy bear was flying the plane. Because he knew how to."

"Oh, that makes perfect sense," Daniel said. "An untrained savage wild beast from the Canadian wilderness who'd learnt how to fly a jet plane. One of the most majestic yet complex machines ever invented by the human race."

"No, it was invented by a moose," Jane said. "Everyone knows that."

"Called Harold," Daniel said.

"And the daddy bear said to the mummy bear, 'There's only two parachutes, one for me and one for you.' So the daddy bear puts one on and the mummy bear puts the other on and they jump out of the plane."

"What—they didn't even try to hold their infant?" Daniel said. "Their poor suffering infant who they loved better than anyone else in the world? They just left the baby bear to die in a plane crash? This isn't a funny story at all. It's deeply moving and tragic."

"No, wait, because they go down, they go down in their parachutes, I mean, and then at the bottom, when they get to the bottom, there's baby bear anyway."

"I've heard this before," Jane said. "It's crap."

"And they say, 'Oh, baby bear oh, kissy kissy, how did you get down safe and everything?' And the baby bear says, 'Me not stupid, me not silly. Me hold on to daddy's willy.' "

There was a lengthy silence. Daniel and Jane exchanged a sorrowing look.

"That's it, that's the joke," Tim said. "It was funny, I mean, it's funny if you don't ask stupid questions all the time."

"What I don't understand," Jane said, "is why they have to be bears. They could be anything. They could be people, or they could be donkeys. It wouldn't make any difference to the joke."

"They couldn't be donkeys, though, could they?" Daniel said pensively. "If you think about it."

"Why couldn't they be donkeys?" Jane said.

"Well, you couldn't hold a cock with your hooves," Daniel said. "If you were a donkey. Have some sense, woman."

"You could try," Jane said.

Tim was crying now, fat tears amassing at his already reddened lids. The other two watched the familiar phenomenon. "It's not fair," he finally said. "No one ever listens to anything I say. I don't want to talk to you any more."

"I wish," Jane said, in her mother's posh or telephone voice, "I wish you two would stop making Timothy cry. It's not kind or clever."

"Do you want to go and watch *Why Don't You?*" Daniel said. "I'm bored of this."

It was at least another hour after Leicester Forest East before the car felt normal again. It felt to Francis like a bubble of discomfort taking its time to rise upwards in him and burst. It was no one's fault; whatever Sandra had done or said, it had been forgiven by the family without inquiry. Bernie's affability towards the men had not crumbled, but his posture had stiffened, a protective, resentful attitude with which there was no argument. But in time the atmosphere cleared; in an hour Francis thought only he was trembling with that strange Francis-dread, the sort of fear that could be stirred in him by what had happened to someone else, or by events that were not about to transpire, that, imagined, could end in some catastrophe, none worse to contemplate than being shouted at. Sandra had been shouted at, in some way, yet she, his mother and father had passed from a stiff front of bravery to a real sense of being in the right. If, indeed, they hadn't forgotten about it.

That Francis-dread came with a smell, a taste in his mouth as of sour clashing metals; it came from inside, and took time to go. He wondered sometimes if he gave off the smell of fear; animals, they said, always knew when you were frightened. Aunt Judith with her dog, making a beeline for him, making him cringe, because the dog could smell the emotion in his mouth. Yes.

But that smell and taste, so strong to him but unnoticeable, he guessed, to the other three in the car, was now being beaten down by a smell of the earth. The landscape had been changing, presenting familiar sights in unfamiliar arrangements—those bald, hopeful trees—as well as the unfamiliar, the monstrous. Hills were rising up, black and softly yielding, the great dunes of a black Sahara; and here, a building, a huge black box on sort of was it *stilts*, there were windows— were they?—but white, opaque, just a grid of white squares. It looked like something you would draw if you couldn't draw, the idea of a big house but just a big black and white square. And out of the side, like a giant lolling arm, an immense conveyor belt. You could see the wheels running, carrying something, some kind of rubble up or down. The most terrible thing: there were no men. It was just a huge machine, a factory—a factory?—like a big black flimsy box, a black hill both flimsy and vast, and that terrible motion of the belt and wheels. Puking out, or forcing down the throat, an endless motion of forced ingestion or rejection, stone and gullet. It would carry on all night, all day. You could see that. The only thing human about it was the retching smell

It was vivid and complicated, and it went by so fast that in a moment Francis was closing his eyes and trying to see it again, a moment after that, wondering if he had seen it at all. But there was that smell. And it seemed there were people, too, who lived in this smell, because there was a town, an estate, of matching red-brick houses. Just below the motorway. But they had somehow left the motorway now. A sign came up: City Centre.

"What city?" Francis said. His voice croaked a little.

"This is Sheffield," Bernie said. "We're almost there. New home. Did you see that factory—the works—some kind of, I don't knew, coking plant? Is that right?"

"How on earth do you expect me to know?" Alice said, smiling.

"You know everything," Bernie said.

"I hate this," Sandra said. "I don't want to come here."

Francis was shocked at her bad manners: she shouldn't say what he was thinking.

After they had returned from Sheffield the first time, when they had found the house, Francis had written to the magazine Sandra liked to read. He liked to read it, too, though it was less use to him. *Jackie*, it was called, with the kindly fashion advice that coloured girls could get away with wearing lovely bright shades, and the page of brisk nice answers from Cathy and Claire to girls who worried about what they should let their boyfriends do to their faces, mouths, breasts, vaginas. (Francis was horrified, not about to need the information.) He wrote, not to decent Cathy and Claire, but to the page before the appeals for foreign pen-pals, the place where readers described their home towns. He was egging himself on, he acknowledged that now, sitting in the back of the Simca with the choking smell of the coking plant in his throat. "When my friends first heard that we were moving to Sheffield . . ." he began, then ran through the events of their week in the Hallam Towers Hotel, blithely equating them with what might be judged the principal attractions of the town. "Don't forget to spend a morning browsing in Broomhill," Francis advised. He had read similar sentiments in his father's *Sunday Express*.

He had not posted what he had written. And now he was glad of it. It seemed as if the Sheffield he had experienced had been created at the tip of a blue biro and had never truly existed. That city of hotels and attentive waiters, of dense Victorian villas dispersed through a verdant forest, breaking out like the frilled edges of amateur maternal pancakes into lavender moorland. It had been replaced by this stinking black city of vast boxes and artificial black hills and unattended vast machinery.

They went on. And poor Francis's selfish focus and fear stopped him seeing the city he was entering, in 1974, its greatness, its sweep, the reason for those black hills and the stink. It was entering on the last phase of its industrial greatness, and Francis, in his little selfish fear, did not see it.

There it was: Sheffield, 1974. Francis saw the artificial black hills, the slag heaps piled up by the side of the motorway. But there were seven red hills in Sheffield too. The city was founded on them. The six rivers, too, the black-running Don, the Sheaf, naming the city, the Porter, the Rivelin, the Meersbrook, the Loxley. Each had its valley, some green and lovely, some lined with grimy warehouses, but all ran together, and they were the reason for the city. The waters, long before, had been harnessed to power forges, small hammering enclaves in dells; the steel masters had built their works, outgrowing the forces of the rivers, and the city had locked its blaze and fire inside those huge blank buildings, rising up on either side of those narrow streets like cliffs. The great noise, mysterious in the streets, continued day and night; those blast furnaces could never be shut down, and men poured in and out at unexpected times. Each man had his fiery function, and as they left their work, their eyes seemed soft, dazzled by the white-hot glare even through their smoked goggles. Francis saw none of it: he did not see the city that had made fire out of water. The rivers were hidden under a mountain of brick; the fires were deep inside those mausoleums. Only occasionally did a black river burst out for a stretch; only occasionally did a warm orange glow against a dark window suggest the fury happening within.

The city had been made by fire out of water. And there was the earth, too, which Francis did see something of. Around the city, in earthworks and diggings, coal was still heaved to the surface. It was everywhere. The city made its money from steel; it was driven by its waters; it was built on coal.

Francis saw almost none of this, as they drove into Sheffield for the first time. He saw a nightmare terror of a landscape; he ascribed evil to it. He had no means of seeing the money and power that these sights produced; he saw black waste, and bursts of fire, and smelt that hard, mineral smell. But he should have looked: in 1974, Sheffield's splendour was coming to an end.

And the motorway, with its raw, uncouth society of fire and mineral gave way now to something like a town. Shops, offices, glass buildings, bridges and, at last, people. "I don't remember *any* of this," Sandra said. It was a shock to hear a voice in the car: they'd been quiet since the Sheffield turn-off.

"No, you wouldn't," Bernie said. "We came up by train, don't you remember?" She subsided again; that wasn't what she'd meant, Francis could tell. She was mostly just complaining.

"I'd feel a lot easier if we could see the van," Alice said.

"It'll be at the house by now," Bernie said. "We'll go up there to make sure, and then we'll go off to the hotel. The men won't want to start unpacking tonight."

"Where are they going to stay?" Francis asked.

"They'll have made arrangements," Alice said.

Daniel, Jane and Tim drew the curtains and switched on the television. They watched *Why Don't You?*—Tim fervently, Daniel making sarcastic remarks about the sort of kids who go on telly. Tim wanted to watch *Blue Peter*, but Daniel got up before it started and turned over to watch *The Tomorrow People*. Then the cartoon—it was *Ludwig*, which was rubbish. "Where's Mum and Dad?" Jane said. They were always home by now—they generally coincided, except on Fridays when Malcolm stayed late and Katherine came home before him on the bus.

The news started. It was boring. There was going to be an election. There'd been one before, Daniel remembered, and that had been boring too, because at school they talked to you about it and tried to get you to say who you'd vote for if you'd got a vote. At school, most of the kids said they were Labour but that was only because their parents were. There was one kid who said he was Liberal but everyone called him a poof, because the Liberals were poofs, everyone knew that. Sometimes Daniel said he was Labour but at others he said he was Conservative and once he told a girl he thought Communism was best. He didn't really care. They were all old and boring.

"I think the Conservatives are going to come first," Tim said, "and the Labour are going to come second and the Liberals are going to come third. That's what I think."

"Why do you think that?" Jane said, but Tim didn't know.

They'd stopped talking. Even when *Nationwide* came on, and there was a story about a dog that drank beer, they didn't say much. It was nearly seven o'clock before they heard the key in the lock. It was their mother. She looked tired and angry; for once her hair was untidy—she'd not really done it since the party the night before.

"Has your father not called?" she said.

"No," Jane said. "Where is he?"

"I don't know," she said. "He didn't come to pick me up. I tried to call the office but they'd all gone home. I came home on the bus."

"These two've been in all day," Daniel said. "He didn't call, did he?"

"No," Tim said. "No one's called."

"I don't understand it," Katherine said.

For some reason, Jane felt she couldn't say she'd seen him at lunchtime. He hadn't wanted to be seen; she didn't feel she should let on.

But Daniel said, "He came home at lunchtime. And then he went out again."

Katherine looked at him. "What did he do that for?"

"How should I know? I didn't see him. I was at the pool all day. Jane saw him."

"Jane," Katherine said, "did he say anything? I don't know where he's got to. If he'd gone to the pub he'd have phoned, surely."

"He never goes to the pub," Daniel said, "except on Fridays."

"But did he say anything about being late?"

"I only saw him," Jane said. "I didn't speak to him. I was in the garden. He didn't see me, I don't think."

Katherine looked at her. It sounded strange, your family avoiding each other, hiding and not speaking. But it made sense to all of them. "I expect he's been held up," she said. "Let's not worry just yet."

"He's never held up," Tim said, his voice emphatic. "He's always home by now."

"He's got a good reason, I'm sure," Katherine said. "Let's not worry. Have you had your dinner?"

The children looked at each other, surprised. The idea of making their own dinner was a new one. No one had ever suggested it.

"All right," Katherine said. "Just let me get changed. There's the food from last night to finish up. That OK?"

"Aren't we going to wait for Dad?" Daniel said.

"He'll be home soon," Katherine said.

They'd forgotten about the party food, which was sitting in the fridge on two big plates under foil, not separated out now, but the remains of half a dozen dishes jammed together. The vol-au-vents were flaking, soft and clothy, the Coronation Chicken a little brown and crusty round the edges; the rice salad, flecked with red peppers, hadn't really been touched the night before, and it didn't look nicer now. Everything seemed sad and unfestive, like tinsel in the full light of day. Jane and Daniel took it out, and she set the table with five places. There was some lettuce and tomatoes too; she made a salad, put out the salad cream.

"I don't like rice," Tim said, following her from the kitchen to the dining room. "I don't like that yellow stuff either. I want beans on toast."

"You be quiet," Jane said. "You're too fussy about your food."

"I can't help it."

Katherine came down, her face washed and recomposed. "Good girl!" she said brightly, when she saw Jane had set the dinner out. They ate; there was nothing to wait for with the food. Daniel ate quickly; he was always hungry, and nothing got in the way of that. Katherine filled a plate for Tim, ignoring his protests; he poked at it, eating a little here and there. Neither he nor Daniel was thinking about their father. Jane put food on her plate—a strange assortment, like the hopeful random selection you make at a party, not necessarily meaning to eat everything but taking a bit of each. She watched her mother nervously; she was looking around her, on edge, not eating. After a few minutes, Tim said, "I don't like rice," again. "I don't like those red things, those peppers, in it."

"Then don't eat it," Katherine said abruptly. "Go hungry." She got up sharply—almost as if she were going to strike him—and went into the hall. They could hear her rifling through the address book by the telephone. Jane and Daniel exchanged a short, scared look. Their parents had suddenly altered. From the hall, the noise of dialling.

"Hello?" Katherine said. "Hello, Margaret? This is Katherine Glover, Malcolm's wife . . . Yes, that's right, at the Dennises . . . Yes, I remember. I know this sounds a little strange, but did Malcolm have anything—Oh, I see . . . Really? That sounds unusual . . . No, I didn't. Well, I'm sure there's some perfectly innocent explanation—he'll be home soon, I expect. Thank you so much—I hope I'm not disturbing you . . ."

And she put the phone down, then came back into the dining room. She didn't sit down and go on with her dinner. She just stood there. "That was your father's secretary," she said, "Margaret. She said he left the office at lunchtime and didn't come back."

"He was here at lunchtime," Jane said, "and then he went out again. I thought he'd gone back to work."

"Yes," Katherine said. "You said."

She went to the window, peered out through the net curtains. She seemed lost in thought. "Look," she said, "the new people are moving in. There's a removal van."

"It came this afternoon," Daniel said, still eating. "They've left it, they've not started unpacking the furniture."

"Did you see them?" Katherine said absently.

"No," Daniel said. "They'll be moving in tomorrow, I suppose."

"I wonder," Tim said, "where my dad's gone."

"You don't think there's anything wrong, do you?" Jane said. She remembered the stories she'd constructed in the garden as she saw the figure in the window. It seemed odd already that she'd imagined burglars.

"No," Katherine said firmly. "There's nothing wrong."

But then she went out again and started making phone calls, to the hospitals first and, finally, the police. One by one the children took their plates to the kitchen; Jane washed up, listening to the repeated query in her mother's politest, most telephone voice. It seemed to her that there was something of blame and guilt in it. She could not understand it.

For years Katherine had been in the habit, in the mornings, of getting into the car with the children and Malcolm. First, Malcolm dropped off Daniel at Flint, the senior school—he insisted on being dropped a good three hundred yards from the gates, and she knew for a fact that most of his friends had exactly the same arrangement with their parents—then Tim, at his primary school, and Jane at the new middle school, less self-consciously getting out at the gate. Finally Malcolm dropped her in Broomhill with its parade of shops and went off to work.

That had been her routine since Tim started school. She did it almost every day, saying, as if it needed justifying, that it was nice to have a regular routine each day, and hers was to buy the groceries before ten each morning, then head back to do the housework. In reality, she hadn't minded the housework when Tim was too small to go to school, just as she didn't really mind it when the children were on their school holidays. It was the days when the four of them set off, leaving her on her own, with no one to talk to and nothing but dull tasks to do, that wore her down. The noise of Radio 2, so mild a burbling complement to breakfast, had to be turned off, or had to be listened to as if it were company; so, by the time Tim was seven, she had taken to getting into the car, going to Broomhill and filling the morning with the day's small shopping—the fishmonger or the pork butcher, the little supermarket, the greengrocer—maybe the bank, and definitely the little tea-shop for a cup of coffee and a piece of cake.

Crosspool was closer to shop in, of course, but it was a 1920s development, a shabby parade with holes in the Tarmac and a hardware shop with Chinese-made plastic flowers in the window, and no tea-shop. Broomhill was stone-built Victorian villas—it was a part of the city that hadn't been bombed in the war. It had a dress shop, a bookshop, and the greengrocer sold courgettes. It was a nicer place, so Katherine put up with the tinny flavour of the brown-coloured filling in the cakes at the tea-shop, the burnt crusty nubbings of Mrs. Milner's rock cakes a guarantee of Broomhill's middle-class, non-shop-bought authenticity. They couldn't have afforded a house there, though.

Malcolm, not really thinking, often said it would be more sensible to go to the supermarket once a week, and was talking about buying a chest freezer to put in the utility room, but she discouraged him. At the words "chest freezer" she saw her life retreating: lifting deep-frozen carcasses from their bed of ice, spending days watching joints defrost, drip by pink drip. In any case, he didn't know that when she said she'd done the shopping by ten, she was dissembling: it was rare that she was home before two—she had so many ways of passing the time. A different woman, she often thought, would have dropped in at the pub for a gin and tonic; the Admiral Codrington was eminently respectable, apparently.

Two years before, Mrs. Milner had said to her, "There's a florist's opening where Townsend's the ironmonger's used to be." She was sitting at Katherine's table: she liked to take the weight off her feet when they weren't too busy and, in any case, the eight or nine women who came in regularly, sometimes inviting each other to share a table, more often calling across if the conversation became more than usually interesting, hardly counted as customers to make a fuss of.

"That's a shame," Miss Johnson, the retired bank clerk, said. "It was useful, Townsend's, for anything small about the house. I'd been hoping there'd be something useful opening up in its place."

"You can always buy a box of screws in Woolworth's, I dare say, Mary," Mrs. Milner said.

"It's not the same," Miss Johnson said. "It was a useful shop to have round the corner, and I don't believe I've bought a bunch of flowers since Mother died, so a florist's no use to me."

"I like a sprig of rosemary with lamb," Mrs. Goldsmith said, intruding into another conversation. "I think it brings out the flavour."

"I don't suppose Townsend's found it easy to keep going, you buying a picture hook once every two years," Mrs. Milner said to Miss Johnson. "Those old family firms with everything in little drawers and the assistant taking fifteen minutes to find anything, they're on the way out, you mark my words. I think it'll be lovely to have a florist nearby. I might even invite them," she went on grandly, "to supply the tea-shop with regular bouquets."

"That'll be an improvement," Miss Johnson said, somewhat nettled, and poking at the limp anemone in a thumb-sized vase on her table. "Goodness, what a day—you'd never think it was June."

"I've never known June such a wash-out," Mrs. Milner said, ignoring Miss Johnson's rudeness. "As for the florist's, they'll all be buying flowers from it once it's there, I think you'll find."

"It's a nice idea," Katherine said. "You never know—it's on the way home from my husband's work. He might take to stopping off there." None of the other ladies knew Malcolm, but politely suppressed ribaldry ensued.

"It's terrible, the parking in Broomhill," Janet Goldsmith said. "I'd remember that, Katherine, before you get your hopes up. Have you seen the new knee-length skirts in Belinda's? Well worth a look."

"Buy yourself flowers and save the heartbreak," Mrs. Milner said, but just then a man, a stranger, came in, bringing a burst of rain with a flapping umbrella, and she got up to fetch him the list of cakes.

Katherine hadn't noticed the shop-fitting work going on at Townsend's old premises, but over the next few weeks she took some interest in its progress. As the work came towards a conclusion, it became obvious that it was going to be a high-class florist's, a cut above the two or three purveyors of scrubby chrysanthemums, tired-out roses and oversized daisies in unnatural colours to be found in the town centre. As soon as the plastering was finished, the decorators put up wallpaper in thin Regency stripes, red and white. Katherine had thought about Regency stripes for her own hall—and she watched with approval when the shop sign, in good solid brass Roman lettering on a dark-blue painted background, went up: REYNOLDS, just that. It wasn't long before the shop opened, and Katherine went in on the first morning. She had plans.

Katherine had had jobs in the past. Before she knew Malcolm, she had worked in a solicitors' office, a family firm in Sheffield that had taken her on when her father put her in the way of one of his old golfing cronies. She'd liked that job. Nice, it had been, hurrying out of the office in Peace Square, down the steps of the Georgian building, sandstone and worn hammocky, at five thirty to meet her young man waiting there with, often, a protective umbrella held high—Katherine had a beehive, high and shiny as precariously roped-on furniture. It was a shock to remember that the young man must have been Malcolm. There hadn't been any other young men. He'd been too shy to come in and wait with the senior partner's secretary even when it was raining, apparently seeing a solicitors' firm, with offices in a Georgian house in Peace Square, as in a social category above that of a Yorkshire building society.

The beehive had lasted after their wedding, but not long after, the changes of fashion and of her own status dismissing it. And the job at the solicitors' went, too, Mr. Collins having opinions about married women in the office that even then he acknowledged as old-fashioned. She didn't mind, never having been brought up to stay where she wasn't wanted, and got another job, actually, in a private boys' school, a day school, a decade old but housed, like the solicitors," in a building meant for more domestic and gracious purposes, a mill-owner's town-house in Broomhill, blackened with soot. A neat line of iron stumps, like orphaned children's teeth, marked the line where the railings had been before the war. There was no prohibition on married women here, and, indeed, they were employed in preference to virgins, though not through any valuing of motherliness—it was not that sort of school, or that sort of time. The masters wore gowns and often carried, actually carried canes through the corridors; rather, it was presumed that the experience of coition had removed from women any illusions about the male nature. Katherine helped out, her tasks too vague and multiple in that scandalous school to remember, let alone define. They went from sticking plasters on knees and sweeping up leaves to "play-ing the pianoforte" in assembly and taking the boys to Forge Dam on a local-history expedition, shivering informatively in the laid-on rain. Everything fell under her title, calculated to distinguish not her but the school in the eyes of prospectives, of Headmaster's Secretary. She was a sort of alternative to the headmaster's wife, who was a hooting mem-sahib with the week's dinners on a list. She'd quite liked that job too; at the end of her day, she could come home and, as never before or since, make Malcolm laugh about it. She had wondered if he wasn't a little too serious, even as she was marrying him; now he was relaxing, and laughing. It was a happy time. It never occurred to her that stories about terrible schools are always funny to anyone.

The jobs ended with Daniel, and then there was Jane. Maybe, as Jane was going to school for the first time, maybe then Katherine was starting to say to herself the sorts of things that women, even in Sheffield, were saying to themselves in the mid-to-late 1960s, with a sense of what very mid-to-late 1960s things they were to be thinking at all. She might well have been thinking that she could, after all, go back to work in some way. But then Timothy came along—how had that happened? She couldn't remember having sex after 1962—but she couldn't remember buying Malcolm's socks either, although she must have done. Maybe it had been a part of her unremarkable domestic routine that had gone on automatically. It was a couple of years after Tim had started school before she dared to think of working, and it was only the florist's opening that put it into her head.

"Ah," the man said, as she came through the door of Reynolds' that morning. The door was open, the flowers still in boxes, the ranks of gerberas like rows of medals, the chrysanthemums like mop-headed boys, the tulips shocked and upright as corn. The empty vases and buckets were arranged on the shelving display, which ramped up against one wall; the other was covered with a sheet of mirrored glass. "Ah—good morning. Good morning," he said again, more cheerfully.

"Are you open?" Katherine said.

"Yes, absolutely," he said. "Just setting everything out. It's our first morning."

"I know," Katherine said. "We've been looking forward to it. Well, you're getting there steadily."

"And you're our first customer," he said. "How hilarious. That calls for something, I feel. I don't know what, exactly. There's no kettle, so I can't offer you a cup of tea, I'm afraid. Perhaps I can give you your choice of flowers gratis, as my first customer. We've got plenty of those."

"No," Katherine said. "Start as you mean to go on."

"That's all right, then," the man said, with a little gesture of relief. "Why don't you sit down? You're not in a hurry, are you? Sit down and talk to me. I'm just putting the flowers out and then you can choose properly. I'm Nick, by the way."

"I'm Katherine," Katherine said. "Is it just you working here?"

"Well, at the moment," Nick said, lifting a row of yellow gerberas from their box in a single fine movement. "I haven't had time to find an assistant, though of course I'll be needing one. I suppose I'll have to advertise and interview and my brother'll want to have a say, and it all seems a bit . . ."

Just then Miss Johnson walked past the front window, her green tartan shopping trolley rattling behind her; she peered into the shop and saw Katherine, sitting on the one chair, apparently at ease with a young man struggling with flowers. Her mouth shut sharply. She walked on. She must have been on the point of greeting the new florist, but now she wouldn't, and Nick would never know he might have been forgiven.

At home, Katherine did not immediately tell anyone that she'd taken a job at the new florist's in Broomhill. She put the jazz-modern yellow and brown plates, twenty years old, in front of Malcolm, Daniel, Jane and Tim; with oven gloves she put one down for herself. On the dining-table was a red tablecloth. She went back to the kitchen, took off the oven gloves and returned. Nothing was really hers. The plates had been a gift from Malcolm's mother—a wedding present. She'd chosen it, Malcolm's mother, as the sort of thing a young couple would like, near on twenty years ago. Now, it looked exactly that: something nobody in particular had ever liked, just some postulated abstract entity of a young couple. The dining-table, another gift or cast-off; a repro of something Edwardian, again Malcolm's mother's—"Your father liked it," she'd said, in a challenging tone, as if Katherine and Malcolm were proposing to get shot of it and not her. Anyway, they'd taken it when Malcolm's father died and his mother had announced that she'd be moving to a cottage in Derbyshire. Snowed in every winter now, too. Katherine put down the five plates, with chilli con carne on them, a new way to make mince interesting mid-week. Malcolm looked at his, perhaps at the patina of violent orange grease surrounding the mound of meat, then started to eat. Really, only the red tablecloth and the melamine-handled cutlery in this room had been her choice. The rest of it represented agreements, and all of it was potential lumber in Katherine's mind. And that summed it up. She felt all she'd brought to this family were innumerable and faintly pathetic minor possessions, effortlessly chosen but easily replaced with something similar, or something quite different. The substantive structures of their existence, like the table they ate around every night, had been foisted on her without anyone ever considering that she might like to choose something herself.

She would start work a week later—no point in hanging about, Nick had said, with evident relief. She'd dropped in once or twice since then to talk over her tasks—it wasn't necessary, Nick said, but she was in Broomhill anyway, as she often was.

"Here, let me," she'd said, on one of her drop-ins, approaching him with opening arms to take a sheaf of sixty yellow roses from him. His lightly bearded face had a suddenly pagan look, a spark of alarm, like an intelligent animal's.

"No, no," he said, controlling the emotion, looking now amused, boss-like. "I can't let you work yet, not until I start paying you."

"Well, I could start properly today," Katherine said. "You wouldn't have to pay me the full day. You obviously need help."

"I can't," Nick said. "I haven't had a chance to talk it through with my brother. It's half his money."

"Where is he?" Katherine said.

"New York," Nick said. "I'll mention it at the weekend."

"Is he coming over, then?" Katherine said, treading cautiously. She was inexperienced in lives and brothers like that, New York brothers; she felt in danger of saying something that showed where she was and where she'd been. What she was.

"No," Nick said. "I'll speak to him on the phone."

"Can you do that?" and "That's an awful expense," came to Katherine, but she managed to say, "Of course," in quite a natural way, and went away quite soon afterwards.

This brother was a new, tantalizing fact, a good one for the tea-shop, but she'd not be in a rush to share it. In repetition, under the unsparing investigation of the Broomhill matrons and virgins, that urbane "of course" would not save her, and she could hardly pass as a woman to whom phone calls to New York brothers were an ordinary matter. Pretence with a Jacqueline Susann flavour made those women's eyes widen, their lips licked even if it were true, a holiday in Morocco with photographs from Boots; she could not associate herself with this bold life without examining her own, and it started with the furniture.

She could not revolt from the second-hand, passed-down nature of her house's furnishings—hadn't she always said she liked old things, family things?—uncomfortably eliding a guilty table her mother-in-law had bought thirty years before with the notion of a "family heirloom." It was rather the sense that her life would pass among superseded objects, things too vast and bulky to throw away without life-changing resolution. She saw herself, elderly, negotiating her own house like a mountaineer with crampons. There was some betrayal of her own existence, too, in the choice of a flower shop. Responsibility; waste; luxury; gardens. That was what it was about. When the time came, she would put on her orange rubber gloves and throw away the stock at the end of the week with a flash of excitement like the anticipation of adultery. Goodness. She would set her face. Nick would fold his arms, study her. She saw the whole scene quite clearly, and she was starting there on Monday. What she had betrayed had, quite suddenly, become not her existence but her husband's.

That oasis of mutable beauty, bought wholesale, was a startling addition to Broomhill's black and, where cleaned, yellowish sandstone. Nick's flowers were the only things sold there both useless and short-lived. Frivolous, unnecessary and lovely.

"Have you seen the new shop? The flower shop?" Miss Johnson said, bumping into Katherine a day or two after it had opened. They were outside the post office; this was Miss Johnson's way of letting Katherine know she had been seen sitting casually with the young man, and had not been seen at all.

"Yes," Katherine said. "Don't you think it looks lovely?"

"Lovely?" Miss Johnson said. "Yes, it does. It does look—" she tried the word out "—lovely. It would be nice to have that *and* an ironmonger's. You see, I'm not in a forgiving mood. I don't know where I'll go for the practical side of things now Townsend's is gone."

"You could go to Marshall's in Crookes," Katherine said, a little impatient at being dragged away from the topic of Nick after so promising a start. "There'll always be ironmongers." She'd been thinking, and couldn't come up with another florist's in the whole of the west of Sheffield, even in the splendid beech-sheltered ramparts of Ranmoor.

"Well, some people might think there's more of a need for ironmongers," Miss Johnson said. "But you're right, Marshall's is perfectly satisfactory."

Katherine wouldn't let on she'd be working at Nick's the next week, and left Miss Johnson to read as best she could the scene she'd witnessed. She was clearly busting to know. She satisfied herself by remarking that the young man seemed nice, and went on. She didn't mind the prospect of acquiring a reputation for slyness when the news got out in the tea-shop.

Malcolm had to be told, of course, and the evening had to be chosen carefully. He was out two and a half nights a week. Tuesday was his battle re-creation society; Thursday the gardening club; Friday he liked to go out with the staff for a drink in the pub and wasn't home before eight. "Liked to" in the sense of "thought it a good thing to do": he didn't have much of a drink, and said they enjoyed it more than he did. Probably enjoyed it more when he'd gone, Katherine always thought. She toyed with the idea of saving it for one of those nights when he'd come in half an hour before bedtime, to limit the discussion. But there probably wouldn't be much of a discussion anyway. On Wednesday she thought hard and recalled what Malcolm's favourite dinner was.

She shopped and bought it to soften him up. She even thought about getting a bottle of wine, but that seemed too blatant.

"Steak!" Malcolm said. "And mushrooms!" He was standing in the kitchen doorway, having changed out of his suit. The room was steamy, loud with the radio and the steak's sizzle. Most food he said nothing much about. But at either end of the scale, he had two responses: after anything new, he'd set down his fork and say, discouragingly, "Makes a change, at least." The other thing, the massively keen one, was what he said now, not even after finishing but before. "Haven't had steak for an age."

"What's so funny?" Daniel said, wandering into the kitchen, looking for something to eat once his dad had gone.

"Your dad," Katherine said, though really it was herself, the neatness of the plan. "Don't start picking, your dinner's nearly ready."

"I'm starving," Daniel said.

"The inexhaustible appetites of the adolescent male," Jane said, coming down the stairs.

"Gi'o'er," Daniel said, lapsing into school talk.

She didn't change the tablecloth, she didn't get out anything but their usual weekday plates. For pudding there was, deliberately, the trifle left from the day before—a delicious one with strawberries in it: she'd been softening them up. The whole thing, apart from Tim saying, at one point, "I don't like steak" ("Why not?" "It's got tubes in it") was a great success. It was almost a pang to remember what she'd done it for; it was quite a glimpse of a perfect family, all sitting up neatly and eating their delicious steak dinner. The kids might as well have said, "May I get down?" at the end.

"Do you know what?" Katherine said, when she and Malcolm were alone. "I've got myself a job."

Malcolm looked at her in assessment; she looked back, firmly; he dropped his gaze to his empty plate. You could see him recalculating the steak, which had been only enjoyment, a treat.

"We're not that short of money," he said.

"I know," she said. "I've worked before. I like having a job. I haven't had one since the children were born."

"What's all this, then, all of a sudden? You've not said anything."

"I know," she said. "I wasn't looking for one. It's just landed in my lap, in a manner of speaking."

"We're not short of money," he said again.

"It's to keep myself busy," she said. "Don't you want to know what it is?"

"All right, then," Malcolm said.

She told him about the shop, which he hadn't noticed although he drove through Broomhill twice a day. That confirmed something she'd instinctively felt. Malcolm, with all his fussing and tweaking at the plants in the garden, the membership of and regular attendance at the garden club, hadn't had his attention drawn by a new florist's. Nick's business and Malcolm's Thursday-night interest, both apparently concerned with the same thing, were in reality sharply separated. He wouldn't have connected the shop with his own interest. They were, mysteriously, different things, and she felt the affront she was offering him.

"Well, I don't see why not," Malcolm said. "If you don't like it, you can always give up. Who's in charge of the shop?"

"He's not in charge," Katherine said. "It's his own business."

"Oh, I thought it must be a chain," Malcolm said. "Interflora. Well, it might not work out for him, either."

And then Katherine told him about Nick.

It had been easy, really. He'd given way limply, and she didn't know why she'd made such a business about it in her head. She'd had an argument practised and rehearsed in her mind, marshalled her points; and they lay there now like gleaming clockwork devices for someone to come and claim them. She was almost disappointed. All those arguments had been, in their different ways, attacks on him. It was only afterwards, sitting in front of the telly, Daniel out somewhere, Tim and Jane upstairs, heads in books, that she started to feel a little annoyed; the things he'd just accepted, the things he hadn't asked about. Shouldn't you ask about the wages, apologetic though they are? She wondered, angrily, about his politeness to her.

At ten, Daniel came in—he'd been at his friend Matthew's, playing that board game they played. At eleven, Malcolm got up, switched the television off, unplugged it, remarking that it was a relief all those power-cuts had stopped at last. He made the same remark twice a week. They went upstairs. As usual, she went to the bathroom first, stripped off her makeup, creamed her face. Malcolm had left his jacket on the back of a chair, and was just putting it away in the fitted wardrobe. She started to undress, unbuttoning her skirt. He went to the bathroom next; she put on her clean nightdress and, as she always did, took off her bra and knickers underneath it, like a shy bather fumbling with a towel. Through the wall, she could hear the fierce sizzle of his piss in the toilet. She got into bed, taking a book and her reading glasses from the bedside table.

He came back, and undressed without saying anything. She looked at him covertly over the top of her book. His hair was getting longer; untidy, though, and he'd be having it cut soon. He pulled his shirt, blue with a white collar, over his head. The first time she'd seen him naked, three months before they'd married, she'd been struck by the hair on his body; the little tufty patch between his nipples, almost circular, not quite amounting to a hairy chest. He turned now, and there was the other patch she'd not known anyone could have, a rough growth at the bottom of his spine, a monkey flourish. He wasn't a hairy man; he'd not have a thick beard if he grew one. She noticed now that the rest of his back, which used to be spotty, was now lightly furred. Odd, the way you went on changing as you got older; that was what ageing meant.

He had an order to things: after the shirt, he took off his trousers, then his socks—his thin white legs! Then he put on his pyjama top, fastening one or two of the buttons, before taking his underpants off. Beneath the hem of the pyjamas, the little purplish tip of his penis, dangling absurdly; she'd had no idea about the penis, apart from Michelangelo's *David*, and it had seemed long and thin, ugly with veins, a little bit sad, always had. It was something she'd read men worried about. Just then the possibility of sex came to her; she'd creamed her face, but she could wipe it off, strip her nightdress from her; her husband could take off his pyjamas again, and then, all that. It hadn't been very much like that, ever; she didn't know why she thought of it like that now. We could get flowers for the house, she thought. All the time; even in the bedroom. Nick, in her head, handed a huge bunch of unsold lilies to her, bearded, solemn, pagan. My life is on the point of change, she said.

And then Malcolm got into bed, and reached for his own book. For fifteen minutes, he read about the English Civil War; for fifteen minutes, before they put the lights out, she read, with less concentration, about an uninvolving girl called Pierrette in a château in Provence.

Although she had started work, Katherine's morning routine remained the same. From the first morning, she took out a more careful outfit, though, one she'd decided on the night before: a neat jacket with a floral scarf, a pussy-bow tied at the neck. When the weather worsened, she would wear a poncho over it; she'd found and bought a purple one in Debenhams, the end of the week before. She'd sneaked it into the wardrobe, and if Malcolm noticed, she'd say, "Oh—this? I don't wear it often, I know." He often didn't notice. It was her money, she reminded herself.

When she arrived, Nick was already in the shop, the flowers in the boxes. It was fifteen minutes before opening time, and when she rapped on the door, smiling, he looked up, first surprised and then, oddly, relieved—had he thought she wouldn't turn up?

"I realized," he said, letting her in, the key fumbling in the thick chamois leather of his glove, "I don't have your telephone number. I forgot to ask." He locked the door behind her.

"I'll write it down for you," Katherine said. "Now. Where have we got to?"

"Well, let's see," he said. "First things first. A cup of coffee. I'm dying for one."

He started to pull off his gloves. He was nervous in some way; after all, it was a new business, the flower shop.

"Let me," Katherine said. "You carry on with what you're doing. Where are the things?"

"I bought a mug for you," he said. "And the milk's in the fridge. I remembered to get it on my way in."

"I tell you what," she said, "let's have a kitty, and I'll be in charge of the coffee and biscuits. I'll need to know about your favourites."

"I can see we're going to get on," Nick said, going back to stripping the stems of the yellow roses. "My favourite biscuits. Well, I like those pink ones, wafers. Or Iced Gems."

"My son likes those," Katherine said. "My younger son."

"They're not a very grown-up sort of biscuit," Nick said. "I'm sorry for that. But I don't think I could face the austerity of Rich Tea."

"My nan liked those," Katherine said. "My grandmother. She used to dip them in her tea. As I suppose you're meant to. So now you know about the biscuit preferences of most of my family."

"I didn't know you had a family," Nick said. "Though of course you've got a family. And what are your preferences in the biscuit line?"

"Me?" Katherine said. "Oh—anything. I just get what the children like, usually."

"The other thing I meant to say—I don't mind if you don't want to work on Saturdays."

"Saturdays?" Katherine said.

"Your family," Nick said. "I'll manage."

"Oh," Katherine said. She hadn't considered that; the arrangements had been vague. She didn't want to reject what, for Nick, was evidently some thought-out kindness, and things could change later. "That's very good of you. You'll manage all right?"

"I'll manage," Nick said again. "Now. Let's have that coffee and no biscuits—I remembered the milk, the biscuits didn't occur to me—and we'll go through the tasks of the week. It's the same every week."

Twice a week, on Tuesday morning—"but I went on Monday this week"—and on Friday morning, before the Saturday rush, Nick went in the little van to the flower market. He'd be back before opening time, and together they'd strip the flowers' foliage, plunge them into the buckets. "I'll just get what tempts me," Nick said. "I suppose in a bit we'll find out what sells and what doesn't." That was the fresh stock, which he was dealing with. Apart from the flowers, there were leaves and other greenery, used in making up bouquets. There was, too, a range of dried flowers and grasses so the shop, even at the end of a busy day, wouldn't look denuded. Some of that, too, could go into a fresh bouquet, like the shining coins of honesty, and some more exotic things: there were crabbed and arthritic fingers of willow twigs, and, against the wall, a fan of peacock feathers. "People come in sometimes, and they just buy honesty and peacock feathers," Nick said. "The trouble is they last for ever, so we won't see them for another year, and we won't get rich on that."

There was, too, a range of vases for sale. "You'd be surprised," Nick said, "—at the number of people—I've already discovered this and I've only been here a week—who come in and buy a bunch of flowers, they're the ones who've got something to apologize for, to their wives usually, I suppose, and then they remember they haven't got a vase. You can charge what you like for those." Katherine looked at the strange collection: some big square greenish glass ones, a Chinese-looking one with dragons, and half a dozen in brownish pottery, a few Victorian ones with blurred transfers of fruit and vegetables.

"Well," Nick said, "I had a flurry of custom on Monday, just after you came in—it must have been you, bringing me luck—and a little bit on Tuesday, but then it died down a bit. I had a good day on Friday, though, and actually, Saturday too. We were closer to running out of stock than I'd expected. Curiosity, I expect—we'll see what it looks like in a month."

"And the vases?" Katherine said, picking at a stuck-on rose on a goblin fantasy of fruit and flowers, bulging like goitres.

"Don't you like them?" Nick said. "I was in York a week or two back, and I saw a florist's, just closing down. I went in and I bought the stock. It must have been there years. He was glad to get rid of it. I thought it was a good omen."

"A good omen?" Katherine said. "Yes, I suppose you could see it like that."

Nick looked at her solemnly, his boyishly blue eyes, his untidy blond hair; she wondered if he knew what he was doing. All at once, he was laughing. "I see what you're getting at," he said. "If they wouldn't buy them in York, they're not going to buy them in Sheffield."

"I didn't mean that, exactly," Katherine said, blushing. She shouldn't kick off by criticizing him.

"But you don't like them," Nick said.

"Well," Katherine said, "not all of them. That one, for instance." She ran her hand over it. It bore a jazz-modern pattern, orange and yellow and brown, the sort of thing Malcolm's mad aunt Susan had had since before the war. "That's fairly horrible."

"You don't think it'll come back into fashion?" Nick said, still laughing.

"And in the meantime we're to have it cluttering up the shop and frightening off the customers?"

"I see what you mean," Nick said. He took off his chamois gloves and, with his slight hands, picked up the vase. "Come on," he said. "We'll christen the good ship Reynolds."

She followed him to the back of the shop. He gave a sturdy kick to the door. It flung open. The brick courtyard was shaggy with weeds, and a cat threw itself up a wall. "Right," Nick said. "Do you want to do it or shall I?"

"Do what?"

"Christen the shop," Nick said. "All right. I name this good shop—" he hurled the vase with one movement against the wall "—Reynolds."

The vase bounced, then rolled along the ground, coming to rest at their feet. They looked at it, soberly.

"It must be melamine," Katherine said. "Or some such."

"I suppose it must," Nick said. "How hilarious." And then they were laughing and laughing; they did not stop until the bell at the front of the shop announced their first customer of the day.

That night, at supper, Katherine told the story; she tried to make it funny.

"I don't understand," Malcolm said. "Why would he try to smash a vase he'd bought?"

"It was so ugly," Katherine said. "I don't know why he bought it in the first place."

"Someone might not have thought so," Malcolm said seriously. "You can't assume that everyone's going to have the same taste as you. He's not going to make a success of it if he goes on smashing his stock like that. I expect he could put it down to accidental damage, though it wouldn't be exactly honest. If I were you—"

Daniel groaned.

Malcolm looked at him in astonishment. "What's up with you?" he said.

"It's funny," Daniel said. "He sounds a right laugh, Mum's boss."

"Yes," Malcolm said. "That's what I'd expect someone of your age to think."

Daniel groaned again.

"That's quite enough, Daniel," Katherine said. She looked down at her plate: the jazz-modern orange and brown pattern they'd always had. She ought to do something about it. And she agreed with Daniel: Nick was a right laugh.

She soon discovered that Nick needed someone like her. The shop was, of course, just a business. It took in perishable stock, relying as well on imperishable steady sellers—Nick ran an illogical but quite profitable line in minor stationery by the till as well as a carousel of cards, and it was surprising the number of people who popped in for a card, some of whom found themselves leaving with some flowers as well. (The cards were much more artistic—Monet!—on the whole than the dismal and ancient range to be had in the newsagent's opposite and, being blank inside, were superior to his faintly common specifications of particular birthdays and particular family recipients.) It was, if you thought of it in an abstract, Malcolmish way, like many other retail businesses.

And yet it was not, because there was the question of the flowers that Nick went to fetch twice a week. Nick, you might easily assume, was a person who had little idea: he projected a kind of uselessness, and a casual Malcolmish auditor might conclude that he had no particular attraction to flowers and no particular aptitude that would make the business a success. But when Nick came in twice a week with his van of flowers, she perceived, without his having to say anything, a kind of magic. That twice-weekly unloading made her feel as if she had carried out some act of betrayal against Malcolm and, in particular, his garden. Malcolm's garden was a matter of mulch and compost, of feeding and pruning, of weeding and trellises, espaliers, reading. Then for two or three weeks the flowers passed the baton of display from one to the next, with perhaps a brief spurt of mass exuberance in late summer; sometimes, despite all the weeding and reading and feeding, it did not happen at all. One January the three camellias had failed to do anything, just stayed there leggily with their glossy dark leaves, like the picture on a jar of face cream; and Malcolm had raised the question at his horticultural society at the church hall in Crosspool. Then, with all the conflicting advice he'd gathered, he'd come back and read some more. "Throw them out," she always wanted to say; and Malcolm had observed that he'd see what happened next year, infuriatingly.

The unloading of Nick's van was a direct affront to that. Thirty perfect roses in each colour, red, white, pink, yellow and, once, exotically green; the masses of carnations, routine and nuptial; the lilies casting their high scent throughout the shop as they slowly opened, the stargazers, the tigers; those were the standards of the shop, and any found not to be perfect was discarded, not nurtured. The glassed-in gardens, heated with oil-stoves, that bred these frail fantasies, she longed to see those. They had to come all year round, the lilies for the Christmas table, the red roses for Valentine's Day, because the dates when people wanted flowers—a wedding, a funeral, what turned out to be the frantic rush of 14 February and the guilty expressions before Mother's Day—did not coincide with the natural lives of the flowers. And along with them came the exotics, things that had caught Nick's eye. Some sold; some, like the almost tawdry beauty of the bird-of-paradise flowers at seventy pence a stem, did not. And Katherine knew that a man who had pinned his future on things that would burst out in colour for a few days and die was not someone who might as well be selling cabbages. That was Malcolm's phrase for anything like that; Malcolm, whose garden, when it flowered, never ventured as far as the numbing scents of the flower shop. It was not precisely disapproving. The bookshop, the art gallery at Hunter's Bar, the new record shop at the end of the moor where Daniel spent his Saturdays, casting out a deafening racket, painted an intimidating black inside, the scarlet legend VIRGIN on the shop face—Malcolm dismissed in them any higher aspirations, any apparently counter-cultural tendencies, with the observation that they were there to make money, they might as well be selling cabbages. But of Nick's shop that was not true.

"I went to university here," Nick said. "My brother too. Actually, I came here because he did. Studied the same thing he did, too. Law."

He was watching her put together a bouquet; she had thought she knew how to do it, but he'd taught her how to do it properly. Start with one, make a spiral round it, alternating the flowers and the foliage, holding the bouquet in the left hand, adding with the right, and there it was: clip with the secateurs, a twist of ribbon and into the cellophane. Easy, after the first five.

"You didn't want to go into the law?" Katherine said.

"Well, I did for a bit," Nick said. "My brother went into a bank in the City, in London, and he's done very well. Legal adviser. In New York for five years, but he likes it there. I think he'll stay. Met an American girl, too."

"I used to work for a solicitors' firm in town," Katherine said. "Before the children were born."

"That's what I did, for a bit," Nick said. "I went to law school in Guildford after Sheffield, and then I got a job in London, big firm. Didn't really suit me, though."

"That was a good job," Katherine said. She couldn't help it. Sometimes she talked with Malcolm's views.

"Oh, I know," Nick said. "Ghastly. I did it for five years, and by the end of it, I was a sort of expert on this one tiny corner of the law. I won't bore you with the details—it was something to do with industrial-property law. It came up all the time, and the answer was always the same, so whenever anyone found themselves in this one sticky situation, they'd be recommended to come to Oldman's, who had an expert in the subject, meaning me, and I'd give them the same answer I'd given someone else the month before. And they'd pay some enormous fee, and I'd go home to my lovely flat in Little Venice— charming, you know, but quite a stink by the end of a hot summer— and have deep existentialist thoughts about the nature of existence. Well, after five years, I was reading Kierkegaard, not quite in the office, but nearly."

A lot of this was obscure to Katherine. "I know what you mean," she said.

"But in the end it was my dear old aunty Joan who came to the rescue. She died and left me a chunk of her money. I suppose she was still thinking of me as a nice little boy with perfect manners and curly blond hair and a velvet suit at tea on Sundays."

"Did you have curly blond hair?" Katherine said. "How sweet." She looked, unable to help herself, at Nick's hair now: tousled but, yes, curly, blond.

"Perhaps not the velvet suit," Nick said. "My father, of course, was furious—he's a lawyer too, great big house in Barnes, wanted us to follow in his footsteps, but I thought, One money-making lawyer's enough. I'm going to sell the flat in Little Venice, take Aunty Joan's money and go—" he pulled a face and threw his hands up in mock horror "—into *trade*. Bugger."

"I could have told you that would happen if you didn't put the coffee down first," Katherine said tranquilly.

"It's gone everywhere. Where's that cloth?"

"By the sink, where it should be. And your brother?"

"Oh, Jimmy? Well, he was tickled by the idea, and I dare say he wanted to annoy the old man, too, so he put some money in. He just wants a finger in the pie. He was always like that, even when we were little boys, wanted to establish the rules of the game himself before we started playing."

"And your mother?" Katherine said.

"She died," Nick said. "Years ago."

"I'm sorry," Katherine said.

"It was years ago," Nick said.

He was not one to accept sympathy, she found out. There were a couple of other incidents when, over the flowers and a cup of coffee in the morning, she tried to offer sympathy, and was rebuffed, first with surprise and then with faint amusement, as if his predicament were more of a shared joke than anything else. She had the impression, for instance, that his relationship with his father was difficult and oppressive, a Marxist nightmare of exploitation and liberation; Katherine had little idea of what Little Venice and Barnes might mean. "He's not as bad as all that," Nick said. "He's quite looking forward to coming up some weekend, actually, to see the shop. My brother said he said, 'Well, at least someone in the family's going to be making some money in an honest way,' as if I was going into the manufacture of—I don't know—steel things, whatever they make in Sheffield."

"How hilarious," Katherine said. It was something Nick said. And the discovery of Nick's response to sympathy there, or over his dead mother or, another instance, over a faintly outlined tale of unsuccessful love, was only one of several things she learnt about him. She was mastering the subject of Nick in pieces, from his favourite biscuit to the envisaged beauty of his future life, and she rehearsed it to herself on the daily bus ride home, on the fifty-one, as if it were her forthcoming specialist subject on *Mastermind*. Rehearsed it, too, in front of her family over dinner each night.

Jane could see that her mother was making a mistake with this. The rhythms of their day had been firmly established: she and Timothy would get on the same bus, the fifty-one, her with her friends and he with his friend, Antony, who lived just down the road. Two stops after, Daniel would get on, his school tie pulled down, a huge fat knot on his chest and just an inch or two of tie poking out, his black sports bag slung round his shoulders—she'd be getting on there next year, when she went to Flint. They ignored each other, Daniel with his noisy friends talking smut or football noisily, evicting the kids who didn't know better than to bag the back seat on the top deck. It was only when they were walking down the muddy track after they'd got off the bus at the top of the road that they coagulated, usually after Daniel had cast a few showy insults their way. But then they'd be home, and there would be Mother, too, having started cooking dinner, the house bright and tidy. They all had keys, even Tim, but they hadn't often used them.

That had changed, and now, when they got home, they opened up the house themselves, and it was grey and preserved from the morning, the breakfast things still in the sink, like an abandoned catastrophe. At first they were bewildered, at a loss, then afternoon television, children's television, rose up like an appalling colour possibility; the telephone, too, which they fought over like rats. And there was, too, the possibility of bickering, always there but never quite bursting out in this way. Bickering: it was mostly tormenting poor Timothy, who nevertheless hardly seemed to suffer, just to accept leadenly the complex feints of Jane and Daniel's mockery. Too often, even Jane thought, after a few weeks of her mother's new job, as Katherine returned, towards six, she must have been greeted with three lined-up children, two faces sweetly composed, hands behind their backs, a third's red and recently washed with a thoroughness surely slightly suspicious.

But if Katherine was suspicious, she did not show it, and her "I wish you two would leave Timothy alone" survived—survived for years, in fact—only in their private exchanges, like a parrot-learnt and comic phrase from a school language that survives fossilized into adulthood when all possibility of expansion into grammatical expression has disappeared. Something decisive had changed when, a few weeks in, their mother came through the door, a little tousled but with a careless glow to her beyond what the weather could bestow, to be greeted with exactly this butter/mouth tableau, and said only, "How hilarious." A phrase Jane knew to be a possible expression but had never heard from her mother before and, reading its origins correctly, found there were more things to blush over than shame at having given your younger brother a Chinese burn while the elder sat on his chest.

But life was quickly full of such embarrassments. She wondered her father was not touched by it. Jane had learnt a lesson in behaviour from Daniel. That year, there had been a new girl at school. There were Indians in Sheffield, you saw them often in town, but they were poor and lost-looking and Ajanta was not like that.

"My father," she said, on her first morning, "is a professor at the university." She said that, just going up to them in the playground at the first break, not waiting to be invited or anything. They'd been about to play a round of Witches and Fairies, but the plan evaporated. Anyway, they all felt a bit too old for that.

"Where are you from?" Anne, always the quickest to nose, said.

"Bombay, originally," Ajanta said, "but we've been in America the last three years."

"Bombay," Anne said. "Where's that when it's at home?"

"It's a city," Ajanta had said, not put off, "in the south of India. Have you heard of India?"

"Have you got brothers and sisters?" Jane found herself asking.

"Yes," Ajanta said. "I've got a sister. She's going to Flint—is that what it's called? And there's my parents and Meena."

"Who's Meena?" Anne said deridingly, trying still to recoup some credit.

"She's my nurse," Ajanta said.

"Your nurse? Are you ill or summat?"

"No," Ajanta said. "You must know the use of the word 'nurse,' to mean nursemaid. We say *ayah*. She's a sort of family servant." Awed, they fell back.

But it hadn't been long—the other side of an alarming birthday party, full of strange puddingy slices, covered with glitter you didn't know whether to eat or not, and everything brought in not by Ajanta's heavy-lidded mother, smoking away on the telephone, but by the tiny Meena who Anne, irretrievably, had mistaken for her—before the subject of Ajanta had taken over Jane's conversation at home. What she said, what they ate, what Mrs. Das had said about the standard of teaching in the West, as she confusingly called Sheffield, the games they had played and what Bombay was like, all a substitute for talking about Ajanta herself. She hadn't been aware of it; it was only when Daniel and, amazingly, Tim had launched into a derisive chorus of "Ajanta says, Ajanta says," that she realized she'd been talking about her for days, weeks. It was something you ought to keep to yourself, whatever the something was you were immuring. She knew that now, at the cost of her besotted friendship—because, of course, you couldn't go on as you had before, even in the playground where Daniel and Tim weren't watching. The observation followed you even there. Ajanta herself hadn't seemed all that bothered, or even to have noticed. But it was something you had to discover. You just didn't talk like that. She'd found that out now.

But her mother, apparently, had never found that out. Here she was, night after night, talking about the flower shop, the day she'd had. It was like an itch in your nose, and you didn't want to watch someone picking his nose over dinner. It was worst on Saturdays and Sundays when she didn't work: she kept at it all day.

"That's looking nice," she said, coming up behind Malcolm, down on the lawn in kneepads. He was tugging at some weeds with a gardening fork, his gardening shirt on. It was a sunny day. Jane was sitting at the table on the patio with a book, the Chalet School; it was getting to an exciting bit, the new girl trapped by a sudden avalanche in a mountain hut with the strict history mistress and nothing but a few dry biscuits to see them through. Her dad had gone out early, and was working round the beds steadily, anti-clockwise, like a battery-powered machine. He'd got to about ten o'clock on the semi-circular dial. She paused, and paid attention.

"Yes," he said. "The hostas, they're doing well this year. Kept the slugs off for once. That trick with the orange peel seemed to do the trick."

"That's a good job," her mother said. "It looked terribly untidy, all those bits of peel scattered all over the place. At least it's serving a useful purpose. That's lovely, too, isn't it?"

"The clematis? Yes, it's had a good year. You never quite know with clematis."

Her mother hummed a little tune. She was on the verge of saying something. She ran her fingers through the climbing plant growing over the fence, the foaming purple; she raised it to her nose, and let it drop. There was no scent. Jane knew that.

"Did we never think of growing lilies?" her mother said.

"What's that?" her father said. Her mother repeated herself.

"No," he said shortly. His voice was harsh with physical effort; his face, turned down, was flushed. "I never did. They come up, and they die off. Not much of a show, unless you've a lot of them, and nine-tenths of the year they're nothing much to look at."

"I love them," her mother said. "Nick does very well with them."

"Who does?"

"Nick," her mother said. "They're very popular—they have a lovely scent for the house. Or there are gorgeous ornamental grasses you can grow now. Or honesty—you know what I mean by honesty? Even tulips. I love a big show of tulips."

"We have tulips," her father said. "Over there. Can always put some more in, if you fancy."

"I'd forgotten about the tulips," her mother said.

"It's not the time of year for them," her father said. "They were doing well six months back. I'm surprised you forgot."

"We've got such a lot of tulips now in Nick's shop," her mother said. "You forget about when things bloom naturally."

"They'll be forced," her father said.

"I suppose that's right," her mother said. She stood, irresolute. Jane's father carried on tugging at the perhaps non-existent weeds, never having turned to look at her; and in a moment she went back into the house. She'd find nobody to talk to about Nick in there, Jane thought. She patted Jane's head absently as she passed.

Jane thought the situation through, and decided the best way to deal with it. Anne was still sort of her best friend. A week or two later, after school, they went round to Anne's house. She lived in Lodge Moor, in a modern house, brick-yellow, surrounded by innumerable stunted shrubs planted by the original builders. The ill-fitting windows rattled all year round with the ferocious wind. They went up to Anne's bed-room: she was allowed to put posters up with sellotape, and her walls were lined with images of big-eyed brown horses, on which Anne was mad, and two or three pop-singers, just as glossy in their brown big-eyed gaze.

"My mum's having an affair," Jane said, once the door was closed.

"An affair?" Anne seemed frightened but impressed.

"It's happening everywhere, these days," Jane said, and sighed. "I only hope it won't lead to divorce. It would break my heart if my parents split up."

"Who would you live with?" Anne said.

"I don't know," Jane said. She hadn't thought things out this far.

"It'd be your dad," Anne said. "Your mum'd be off with her fancy man. It'd be all her fault—you wouldn't let a woman who'd done that walk off with the children too. It'd not be fair."

Jane let the full, lovely tragedy wash over her, its forthcoming bliss. She'd practically be an orphan, her and Daniel and Tim, coping bravely after a family tragedy; how they would look at her, when she moved up to Flint next year! "I don't know," she said, honesty cutting in. "I don't know that it's come to talk of divorce yet."

"What's your dad think?"

"I don't know that he knows," Jane said.

"Well, how d'you know, come to that?" Anne said. "You're making it up." Then Anne got up, apparently bored with the subject. "Look at this," she said. "I got it down town on Saturday."

She opened her white-painted louvred wardrobe doors. That was one of the things about Anne, along with her horses and her snappiness, her incredible wardrobe: there were things in there she'd grown out of, she having no small sister or cousin to pass things on to, all pressing against each other stiflingly. You couldn't help but feel sorry for Anne's clothes, suffocating each other in that breathless wardrobe. "Look," Anne said, and from the bottom of the wardrobe, she fished out a scrap of cloth, white and glistening, its price tag still on it even though it had been tossed to the bottom of the wardrobe, and a pair of strappy white shoes. "I got a halter-top and a pair of slingbacks from Chelsea Girl. The shoes were three ninety nine."

Jane didn't know whether that was a lot or not. "Your mum go with you?"

"Course she did," Anne said. "She paid. I'm going to put them on."

She shucked off her school shirt. Jane looked, with envy, at her starter bra. Anne's mother had bought it for her the first time she'd asked. No one else in their class had managed it, and Jane certainly not. But Anne didn't have an older brother who'd overheard and laughed his head off. She put on the halter-top, twisting and fiddling with the strings behind. She slipped off the heavy brown school shoes, not untying the laces, and pushed on the slingbacks, squashing them on in a hurry, and then, striking a pose, the price tag dangling from her waist over the grey school skirt, she pushed forward her left hip and pouted. She twirled, the strap of her starter bra across her bare back.

"Nice," Jane said.

"Go on, you try them on," Anne said, and so they started to play, the lipstick coming out, the hairbrushes, the materials of femininity. Most of their afternoons turned to this.

"I'm not making it up," Jane said, after a while, their makeup smeared, their outfits half on, half thrown off across the bed.

"Making what up?"

"My mum and her affair. I'm not," Jane said. "She talks about him all the time. She can't stop herself. It's like you and horses."

"Me and horses? What're you talking about?" Anne got up and peered into the mirror, admiring her face, this way and that.

"It's like the way, you know, you love horses, you, you're mad about them, and all the time, it's horses this, horses that."

"I thought you liked horses too," Anne said, drawing back a bit, offended. "I wouldn't talk about them if you weren't just as interested as I am."

"I am interested," Jane said, feeling that the conversation was getting away from her. "But you love horses, you."

"Yes, I do," Anne said. She sank to her haunches, clasping her knees to her chest like great adult breasts. "I'm not saying I don't."

"So you talk about them, don't you?"

"If you say so," Anne said, not quite convinced.

"Well, it's like that with my mum," Jane said. "Every day it's 'Nick says this, Nick did that, Nick likes ketchup with his chips.' "

"Everyone likes ketchup with their chips," Anne said. "That doesn't prove anything, if you ask me."

"Yes," Jane said, gathering the logic of her case. "Yes, that's it, though. If everyone likes ketchup on their chips, why's she bringing up Nick especially? You see what I mean?"

"You're daft, you," Anne said, "I think you're just romancing. Anyway, you don't want your mum and dad to split up, do you?"

"I don't know," Jane said. "It's nothing to do with me."

"Who's this Nick, then?"

"He's her boss. She got a job, working in a flower shop. In Broomhill, it is."

Anne sighed. She was eight months older than Jane: sometimes she took advantage of this difference to make an emphatic point. "I would say," she said heavily, "there's nothing in it. I'm glad my mum doesn't have to go out to work."

"My mum doesn't have to either," Jane said. "She just wants to. I know what. I'm going to go down there one day after school, I want to have a look at him. Do you want to come?"

"What'll that prove one way or the other?"

"Are you going to come?"

"If you insist," Anne said, and then, from downstairs, her mother called something. She rolled her eyes. The call came again. She got up from her squatting position, and impatiently flung open the door. "What do you want?" she shouted rudely.

"There's squash, girls," the polite voice floated up. "And biscuits. I know the sort you like."

"We're busy," Anne yelled. "We're talking about Jane's mum. She's got a lover."

There was a short silence downstairs. Jane could feel herself blushing. "I wish—" she said.

"Oh, I'm sure she's not, not really," Anne's mum called. "There's squash and biscuits. Shall I bring them up?"

But the idea of going down Broomhill the next afternoon had been agreed on. The next day they had geography last thing; Anne had volunteered the pair of them to put away the Plasticine contour map of Yorkshire the class was making, and the labelled cut-away of the strata of rock underneath a coal-mine. The task had been occupying them for weeks—it was supposed to be ready for Christmas Parents' Day and they were all sick of it and Miss Barker's shrill exhortations: "I don't care whether it's done or not, you're only showing yourselves up." For weeks, as if it were tainting them with the nightmarish horror of its incompletion, there had been a rush to the door as the bell rang. But this evening Anne lingered, tugging at Jane's skirt as she, like the rest, got up, slinging her bag over her shoulder. Miss Barker had been about to collar someone at random as usual, but, with a mistaken glitter in her eye, she alighted on Jane and Anne, fingered them as dawdlers for the punishment of putting the stuff away. Anne and Jane, they weren't good girls—they'd already been done for giggling five minutes into one of her lecture-reminiscences, and would have been done worse if Miss Barker had known that Jane had giggled at Anne saying, "It's her wants a lover," meaning Miss Barker. So she couldn't have known that Anne's dawdling was in aid of volunteering for the task, or at any rate—you wouldn't want to show Miss Barker that much willing—allowing herself and Jane to be landed with it. Jane thought she might have been consulted—"There's good girls," Miss Barker said when they were done, which was enough to make you puke—but she saw the point when they'd finished folding the plans, scraping the mess of the afternoon's Plasticine off the tables, put the whole almond-smelling bright geologies back into 4B's geography cupboard, and gone out, fifteen unhurried minutes after the end of school. It was as empty as a weekend glimpse; everyone had gone, swept off in the fifty-one bus. She and Anne shouldered their bags and turned in the other direction, of Broomhill, without having to explain to anyone, and that was a good thing.

All the schools were turning out: the big boys and girls from the George V in their standard black blazers, and the snooty ones, the girls in purple from St. Benet's, where you paid to go, like Sophy next door to Anne, where she claimed you got to learn Russian and, like drippy, bleating Sophy, to produce the horrible sheep-like noise of the oboe, too. They were all heading in the same direction, the opposite one to Jane and Anne. Jane felt like a truant, the two of them in their ordinary clothes.

"Do you think Barker cares?" Anne said.

"Cares about what?" Jane said.

"About Parents' Day," Anne said. "She goes on about it enough."

"I reckon she'll get the sack if it's not ready," Jane said, "if it's not perfect, that geology thing."

"I hope she does," Anne said. "We might get someone who doesn't—"

" 'When I was in Africa,' " Jane quoted, a favourite conversational opening of Miss Barker's, liable to lead to any subject, and they laughed immoderately, clutching their stomachs and saying it three or four times.

"She made me eat cabbage once," Anne said, "when she was sitting in the teacher's place on our table at dinner. I hate cabbage."

"She'll have had to eat worse in Africa," Jane said. "She'll not have sympathy for you, being fussy over a plate of cabbage, when you think what she's had to force down."

"Missionaries from a pot," Anne said. "I dare say."

"Worms and grubs," Jane said. "Toasted over an open fire."

"Only like marshmallow," Anne said.

"Not much like," Jane said.

"But cabbage, it's horrible," Anne said. "She made me eat it, she said it didn't taste of much. I think it tastes right horrible." Jane agreed, and they went on.

" 'When I was in Africa,' " Anne quoted again, but she hadn't thought of how it could go on after that and fell silent. Missionaries, cannibals, and that right funny film in Geography with a black man in a wig like a lawyer's where they'd laughed and Miss Barker'd turned the lights up to talk in low serious tones about (one of) her disappointments.

There was the Hallam Towers on the left, and on the right, the gloomy ericaceous drive that led up to the blind school—there were dozens of blind children up there: you never saw them. And then the library, and then they were in Broomhill. It was a journey you took with your mum and dad, perhaps; it wasn't a schoolday journey. So they were a little bit solemn as they turned the corner into Broomhill proper, with its parade of shops, marking not what they passed but what they were heading towards.

Jane suddenly thought how unwise this idea had been, to turn up without warning her mother. What if—her novelist's imagination creaked into gear and saw, clear as anything, her mother and a young lover, a David Cassidy perhaps, embracing and kissing in a bower of flowers in the shop window. But it could not be helped now. For some unspoken reason, they did not cross the road. Over there, the flower shop's awning, pink and domed, the only one sheltering the Broomhill street, like a flushed, guilty, cross and bad forehead, and, inside, a figure, two figures, moved, gathering, circling, busy.

They stood opposite, watching. Jane clutched her bag. "Let's—" she said feebly, but it was too late. They had been seen. The figures had paused as if surprised, then one came to the broad window, resolving its dark outline into her mother, not bearing the surprised, suspicious expression Jane had envisaged, but a flash of uncustomary delight as the other figure came up behind her. Jane raised her arm to wave, but was arrested by an insight as she took in the worried face beside her mother.

It was Anne's insight, too. "But he's old," she said. "I thought—"

"What did you think?" Jane said, snapping a little. She already felt defensive about this man.

"He doesn't look like anyone's lover," Anne said.

"I never said he was," Jane said irrationally. She didn't need to come closer: she somehow knew what this man was like, better than her mother could, and she could surely see that what animation he possessed was a matter of sparks thrown off by a chill and flinty interior. She was right: Nick had aspects of fire, could briefly blaze, but they were mere sparks, giving little light and no heat, capable only of a short spectacle, of the casual infliction of harsh smarts on anyone standing by, foolishly admiring.

As for Nick: he ran that shop for another ten years. But whenever he looked out of the shop window and saw someone, two people, on the opposite side of the road, inspecting his façade, he always felt that same sudden way. He always felt the same as he did that first afternoon. And then, they were only two schoolgirls.

"It's my daughter," Katherine said. "And her friend. They never said."

"Ask them in," Nick said.

It had been eighteen months or so before when Nick and Jimmy had had the idea. They'd been in Jimmy's new house in Fulham. Jimmy said Chelsea, though it was really Fulham. Miranda, Jimmy's wife, certainly said Chelsea. She was as decisive about that as she was about the fact that Nick, and Jimmy's other not very desirable but probably useful colleagues could be offered drinks at five thirty, but shouldn't expect to stay for dinner. Colleagues! Ha! After all, the nanny'd be bringing little Sonia in her best dress down for dinner: a nice thing—as Miranda said, voice rising—if she grew up mixing with people like Nick.

"You won't have any difficulty finding a taxi on the street," Miranda would say, drifting through and interrupting their conversation. "This is Chelsea, after all. It's not, it's not fucking, what, Streatham or somewhere." Miranda's hair curled out in a single wave backwards about her features. She'd flick it back, give Nick or whatever-his-name-was a level stare, her mascaraed or false eyelashes held painfully apart, go to the bamboo-fronted bar, and, with leisurely disdain, mix herself a Dubonnet and gin, three fat ice cubes and a straw, before returning to the kitchen to shout at Solange, the put-upon au pair, acquired, like so much else in this house, in one of Jimmy's fits of sexual ambitiousness, and now hanging around, disappointing him and annoying Miranda.

The house in Fulham was a step up from the two-bedroom flat in Islington. The money had been flooding in so fast that Jimmy had had a job knowing what to do with it, keeping it in fat bundles (he'd once confided) in a painted oak chest under little Sonia's bed and taking it out periodically to press it into the hands of shop assistants. The results—a pair of gold-tasselled sofas glowering at each other across the drawing room like a pair of retired rival strippers, a whole pack of waist-high china hounds glistening throughout the open-plan living area, vast surfaces of built-in brown smoked mirrors, ankle-high white shagpile and two at least of those horrible leather rhinoceroses you saw in Liberty's. The results all bore something of the bewilderment of the moment of their liberation, as Jimmy brought out a wad of crinkled fivers and counted out several dozen of them in a more than respectable shop. He'd have paid cash for the house if he could; as it was, he was reduced to transferring it from bank to bank to bank first. Nick put the money Jimmy handed over irregularly but lavishly into a bank account and worried about that all the time, though it wasn't an account in his own name.

"I'm fed up of it," Nick had said. "I've done this too often. I'm getting too old for it."

"No reason why you can't go on for ever," Jimmy said. He stretched out in his armchair—a vast leather job, like an intricate wooden puzzle in its manoeuvrability of parts, given to strange hummings and shiftings at Jimmy's fingertip command. He looked as if he might stretch out his arm for, what?, an august cigar. Or just another whisky to go with the one nestling in his fat groin.

"I don't like it," Nick said. "I'll do it one more time, I promised, but that's it. I'm too old for it, you've got to find someone else to help us out."

"The older you get," Miranda said, wandering in—she'd been listening through the serving hatch, "the better you get at it. More believable. No one's looking at you. When you're bald and seventy—"

"Thanks, darling," Jimmy said. "Now go and—" He flicked parodically in the air, readjusting an imaginary blonde hairdo, not taking his eyes off Nick.

"Fuck off," Miranda said, not aggressively, but she went.

"Silly bitch," Jimmy said.

"How hilarious," Nick said.

"Hilarious," Jimmy said. "Unless you're married to it."

"She's all right, Miranda," Nick said.

"I know," Jimmy said, and it was his voice rising now. "I wouldn't. Have her any. Other way. But what are you saying?"

"Nothing, I suppose," Nick said.

They sat there for a moment. Jimmy got up and refilled his glass, a heavy crystal pail. It might have been chosen for its effectiveness when thrown in marital rows. He didn't offer to refill Nick's. In any case he had half an inch or so of gin and tonic left.

"I tell you what," Jimmy said, coming back and flinging his legs over the side of the vast leather contraption.

"What?" Nick said.

"We've got to sort something out," Jimmy said. "This might work out all right." He was talking about the money problem. Nick had meant him to. He'd evidently been on at Miranda about it; Miranda had been on at him. He recognized the rhythm of the complaint. "I reckon a nice quiet little business, you in charge, everything looks hunky-dory. Somewhere outside London."

"Come on," Nick said. "I've always lived in London."

"Not in London," Jimmy said.

"Forget it," Nick said.

"Christ, you're difficult," said Jimmy, who was not Nick's brother. They went right back: Nick's mum had lived in the same street as Jimmy's family when they were children, Nick an occasional holiday visitor—his parents divorced, it was his father who hung on to him mostly, paying for the good school, though his mother got him half the holidays. Jimmy was a permanent resident of the shabby suburb. They'd hated each other, thrown stones, shouted names, then one day they'd met each other down at the shopping-trolley-stuffed Wandle, had tortured frogs together one wide-eyed afternoon with a bicycle pump, and that had been that. "I'm suggesting something might suit you. A nice little shop somewhere, I don't know—Leeds, Manchester, Nottingham, Derby, Exeter, Sheffield, Bristol. Sells stationery. Whatever. Looks nice. You do the books every Friday, no one troubles you, all looks nice and proper, even pay the taxes the end of the year. Why not? Posh boy like you, they'd lap you up."

"Why not London?"

"You don't want to be in London," Jimmy said.

"No," Miranda called through, "you don't."

"Why doesn't he want to be in London?" little Sonia said, coming in in her regulation evening outfit, an inflammable party dress shining like royal icing, red ribbons popping in and out of the hem to match her red patent slingbacks.

"That's enough," Miranda said, following her; she might have meant it for Sonia, but she was looking at Nick. He went.

It seemed to him that nothing had been settled, that it was just an idea of Jimmy's, which had come and would go. Certainly, through all the arrangements for the next trip, he didn't mention it again, or suggest that this might be Nick's last. Nick was more nervous than he'd ever been: the guys out there, they knew him well and obviously thought his demeanour odd. It was almost as if, without him wanting it, his body was conspiring to bring this occupation to an end by crippling his boldness with the appearance of guilt. But he got back all right, and after the last stages had been gone through, the money safely logged and counted, Jimmy had brought the whole thing up again.

It was Miranda's day off, and Jimmy asked Nick to come with him and Sonia ("Don't tell Miranda, and you, don't tell Mummy about him coming with us, darling, and if you're good I'll buy you—what do you want most, darling?") to, of all places, the zoo. It was a dank day, not quite raining but in its London way not quite not raining either; the air was heavy with moisture. Behind bars, the show-stoppers cowered, the lions flat out on their sides, like half-eviscerated carcasses on their way to being rugs. Even the polar bears, presumably used to worse than the gloom of a London November afternoon, had a disgruntled air, casting hungry eyes upwards.

"I like them," Sonia said.

"They'd eat you up in one gulp," Nick said humorously. He was not much good with children, who generally knew this.

"Don't go putting nightmares into her head," Jimmy said. "They wouldn't eat you, darling."

"I know that," Sonia said. "He's just being stupid, this man. I can't listen to things like that, I can't remember them, neither."

"All right," Nick said. "Fair enough."

"I'd like to have one," Sonia said. "I know you can't have one, not in a house, but I'd like one, to have rides on, maybe, and you could put your face in his fur, sometimes I reckon."

"Yeah, that'd be nice," Jimmy said. "You ask your mum. Maybe she'll get you one."

"Don't be so silly," Sonia said. "I want to see the penguins now. They come from the same place as these polo bears."

"No, they don't," Nick said. "They come from the other end of the earth. The polar bears live in the north, penguins live in the south."

"It's a bit cold, isn't it, darling?" Jimmy said to his daughter. "Don't you want to go and see some inside animals?"

"No," Sonia said. Today she was in a heavily embroidered Afghan coat over a puffed and ruched red-and-green dress, more ribbons, but now sort of gypsy ribbons. Nick's nightmare: that Sonia be abducted from his company, and he be obliged to describe her wardrobe to the police. "I think what I want is to see the penguins now, on their slides. I like their slides. I'd like to have a go on one, I reckon. I went inside once and I looked at the inside animals. And I liked the first one, because it was small and furry and you could put it in your sleeve and then it would look out at you and go—" she gestured at her nose with her little fist in its fur mitten, making a small squeaking noise "—but then in the next case there was another small and furry animal and that wasn't quite so nice. And the lady I was with"—adult, drawling boredom—"oh, you know that lady I mean"—normal voice—"that lady I meant, she made me go round every case in the inside part of the zoo, and do you know? Every case, it had in it a different small furry animal, apart from the ones where the animal was supposed to be hiding at the back. And I liked the small furry animals at first but after a while I got really a little bit bored of them all. But she made me go round all of them, and I think really they were all the same animal. They were quite sweet, but they weren't very exciting. I think I want to see the penguins now and the real slide."

"I know what you mean, sweetheart," Jimmy said. He didn't seem to have been listening, but Nick knew what she meant: the world was full of small furry animals with large eyes, and only the first ones you came across would you feel like putting up your sleeve. After that, you'd be wise to their small furry ways, and could step past their cases with a light step. He'd rather go and see the penguins now, too.

"It's all settled," Jimmy said, when they were at the penguins' enclosure, watching their antic waddle.

"Yeah?" Nick said, not following.

"The shop," Jimmy said. "The shop I was on about." The penguins hesitated: over their pool was a double slide, a double helix, and at the top of it they crowded, as if with empty bravado. It had once been white, but the paint was peeling, the concrete coming through in patches, the penguins projecting nerves. At the top, they jostled each other, as if trying to pick on one to shove down first. Nick had seen it before, and knew that as soon as one was sent down, the rest would follow.

"Oh, the shop," Nick said. And then the whole thing was settled.

My God, Nick thought, the first time he saw it. There wasn't much for him to organize: Jimmy was taking charge, dealing with everyone from the end of a phone. The hardware merchant had gone, leaving an interior prickly with shelves and pigeonholes, all painted the same unrenewed cream. The pigeonholes were still labelled "2½'," "60 watt," "mortices," the letters punched out white on those black plastic strips, now, many of them, peeling off and some littering the floor with a detritus of wood-shavings, nails, the screwed-up balls of newspaper used for packing. They would go: a florist's would demand no extraordinary expertise—he'd been on a course, anyway, Jimmy'd thought of that. But the point was that the shop had to be run. It couldn't be like little Sonia, upstairs with last year's Christmas present, an eighteen-inch toy greengrocer's with imperishable plaster-of-paris cauliflowers, pretending to weigh them out and demanding, as Sonia tended to, real money in exchange.

Nick wasn't sure he was up to it. He'd never done such a thing. He'd been a waiter; he'd worked in bars; he'd tried more ambitious jobs, a bit of responsibility, a job in local government, which—you couldn't lose that sort of job, his mum had said—ought to have done him. But it turned out you could lose that sort of job, if you were Nick. And then he'd bumped into Jimmy again, and his life had taken that particular nervous but lucrative direction. It seemed a lot to undertake, running a flower shop.

But without him having to do anything very much, the shop took shape. The workmen came and went, and Nick only opened the door and made them cups of tea as they tore down the shelves and sanded the stained and knobbly floor. "Dost a gnaw—" one workman asked the first day, and broke off, laughing, when he saw that Nick did not understand even that. And he did not know. Nick did not know where—as it turned out he was being asked—the nearest hardware supplier was, this one being thoroughly stripped down and a drill bit needed. After that, whenever a decision was needed, it was to Jimmy they appealed; even the first time a dilemma arose, and they had to have been under Jimmy's instructions in this regard not to appeal to Nick who, they knew, would be the shop's proprietor. They kept a pile of two-pence pieces by the door, on the shelf, like a church's cumulative charity; at least once a day, the foreman took the upmost half-dozen to the phone box to clarify things with Jimmy. Nick made more tea; there was, as yet, no working toilet and they had to nip into the pub at lunchtime or, after two thirty, piss in the yard out the back.

For a few days Nick hovered, an ingratiating smile on his face, then got tired of it, and took himself off. He started to appreciate, with unwelcome clarity, the overt diffidence about him that had made him so useful to Jimmy in the past. Though the diffidence would shortly become useful again, he had only really been aware of it when, as now, it made him risibly ineffective in the eyes of workmen. The area seemed appalling to him. The mincingly genteel tea-shop; the 1950s American-modern laundromat and Co-op; further back, the dismal Victorian philanthropy of the black-pillared Greek-style museum,

with its leaking prehistoric beasts, its dismal paintings of local indus-
tries or, up the hill, that same Victorian philanthropy, the same Greek
pillars in front of a library, and no more alluring. Sometimes, the layers
of change were manifest on a single site: a men's boutique, with a psy-
chedelic shop sign in purple, had kept hanging outside the three balls
of the pawnbroker who must have preceded it. The changes of the district: Nick started to be aware of them as time passed, as the weather
improved and a surprising yellow spurt of, what was it?, crocuses, could
that be it?, emerged from a crack in the pavement outside the shop
and, hardly less cheering, a pod of mushrooms bubbled up beneath the
carpet they'd laid in the lavatory. Became aware of those slower
changes as his business took shape. The scoured-smooth emptiness of
the hardware shop began to be filled. The plasterwork was finished off,
and the Regency striped wallpaper piled up, ready for application;
a display unit, rather like an Olympic podium, but with spaces for
five rather than three winners, was installed and painted a nice dark
maroon; a reproduction desk was brought in at, apparently, Jimmy's
order—he hadn't shared this decision with Nick. Like other decisions
passed up-country by Jimmy—his insistence that the flowers should
bear no prices—it added that crucial sense of class to the enterprise.

All that strange period, Nick behaved and thought much more like a
client than the instigator of a business. Jimmy had booked him into a
hotel while he found somewhere to live, saying he should take his time
about it; but Nick had done nothing in that direction. He returned to
the Hallam Towers every night, dined richly—after five weeks his waistband was uncomfortable with the lobster sauces and no exercise—and
settled down to an early night after his daily phone conversation with
Jimmy. After a few weeks, it looked as if he had set up camp within the
room, the walls lined with bagged laundry, a short shelf of borrowed
thrillers by the bedside.

The workmen knew all about this impermanent existence, returning
to their own wives and children after a day spent not asking for Nick's
instructions about anything. So did the hotel staff, and so did Jimmy.
"Have you got yourself a supplier yet?" Jimmy said one night.

"Supplier?" Nick said, rather thrown by Jimmy's familiar term.

"Flower supplier," Jimmy said. "You been to the market yet?" There
was the sound of Jimmy heavily waiting at the end of the phone.

"I'm planning to go the day after tomorrow," Nick said.

"You should have gone by now," Jimmy said. "Important to strike up
a relationship. I want it up and running by—what did we agree on?"

"Two weeks yesterday," Nick said.

"Two weeks yesterday," Jimmy said. "You think they'll be done by then?"

"I would say so," Nick said. "It looks almost ready now."

"Well," Jimmy said, "this is what you want to do."

The question of the market hadn't gone from Nick's mind, but he'd put it aside as if someone were to deal with it on his behalf. After this conversation with Jimmy, he told the workmen in the shop he wouldn't be around the next day, and asked the receptionist at the hotel for a four thirty a.m. wake-up call. "Hilarious, I know," he said dismally.

The flower market was fifty miles away, in a more urbane, less industrial city that could stretch out its lines of supply in all directions into very different places, some more austere even than Sheffield. Nick had had the whole thing arranged for him, and instructions had been passed down. At a layby on the A1, shortly before six, his hands in fingerless red woollen tradesman's gloves clutched a cup of tea and a bacon sandwich, the hand-drawn map pinned to the bonnet of his little van with an elbow. He knew he would get lost.

But it seemed to work in an all but professional manner, and in only half an hour he was parking outside a grimy Victorian market hall, open to the elements, pillared with flaking green paint over rusting green metal, and everywhere ornamented with idealized brick bouquets, now blackened and snotlike. His *laisser-passer* was accepted, and he went in.

His breath condensed before him. It seemed early, but he could see that the market had, even now, passed the peak of its exchanging, and men and women were pushing wheeled pallets full of ranked blooms towards him on their way out. The market ways were still banked with flowers but great holes had appeared in them as the marauding buyers had carried off the best. Well, he was not here to buy, not today; and that was a useful commercial lesson to have learnt, he told himself. The buyers, the marauders, were men and women, some genteel-looking, the women in capes and ponchos, the men in Harris tweed coats, like Nick, but others rough boys, carrying off the helpless innocent blooms to smaller, more diverse markets, to sell chrysanths beside meat stalls, greengrocers, fishmongers, cheap clothing stalls, provision merchants.

He walked on until he came to what seemed one of the biggest stalls in the market, its depleted fields of carnations and tulips stretching out like blankets. He stood there, irresolute. The man in charge registered him, shook his head in a knowing way and, as his subordinates smirked at this demonstration of who he was, leant forward to spit richly, the abundant phlegm of a smoker's early-morning mouth splattering like puke on the floor.

"Help you?" the man said.

"Yes," Nick said firmly. "I hope so." He explained his situation, or some of it: a new flower shop, a need for a regular relationship with a supplier, and—it did no harm—a frank though not exactly explicit acknowledgement that it was all new to him, he hadn't a clue about what stock to take. Mr. William, he said his name was—Nick was pleased with this: it suggested to him an old-established family in the trade, where the long-retired dad in the nursing-home might be the name on the board referred to as Mr. Gracechurch, the hard-nosed chief remaining Mr. William until his father's death. Nick addressed him as Mr. William in what he hoped was a respectful way at least three times during the conversation. Mr. William was serious, helpful— "You're not thinking of buying today, I take it, sir," he said. In twenty minutes advice had been given about stock—"Though, of course, you'll come to know your customers PDQ"—and an agreement made about the days Nick would turn up—a little earlier, Mr. William suggested, than he had today. It all seemed quite easy. Nick just hoped he hadn't made a mistake in choosing his supplier; in fact, he'd hardly chosen him at all. He took what comfort he could from the greetings Mr. William threw behind his back at passing florists; a popular and— yes?—respected man around here.

"One last thing, though," Mr. William said, as they shook hands. "If we're to do business on a regular like basis, let's not be getting each other's names wrong. My name's Williams, Roy Williams. It's got an *s* on the end."

"How hilarious," Nick said, aghast. "Not hilarious, sorry, I didn't mean—just—sorry," he said, stumbling backwards and, for some reason, bowing. The man wasn't a Gracechurch at all, and though Nick had never heard of the Gracechurch family before half an hour ago, the revelation of Mr. William as the acquirer of the guise of Gracechurch made the original owners seem unattainably grand, the present owner tainted for ever with the suspicion of dishonesty, as if Nick had made a mistake not starting twenty years before, and dealing with those imagined excellencies of the fabled Gracechurches. The embarrassing exchange made him, finally, feel the entire fraudulent nature of the enterprise.

He drove off, face burning, and when, after breakfast, a charity shop presented itself with, in the window, a rigid array of donated vases, there was only one thing he could do. He went in and bought the lot. At least I can, he thought, driving away with the hideous clanking load in the back, at least I can—but reassurance wouldn't come. It would not come, either, when he arrived back in Broomhill and and, in front of all the builders, he had to unload seven unbelievably ugly vases. They had done a good job, the builders, in producing an elegant interior for his shop; they had to see how ugly these vases were. But they said nothing.

It was to this state of concentrated hopelessness that Katherine presented herself. Until then he hadn't thought of taking on an assistant but, of course, shops had them. It was easy for him to understand why he'd taken her on: she had come through the door and, immediately, reassuringly, he had seen someone who was projecting an idea of herself with even less competence than Nick did. She seemed to take him at his word, swallowing brothers in New York. He felt himself growing bigger in her eyes. He didn't despise her for it—in fact, he rather liked the way her presence made him feel about himself. He liked, even, the way she said "Nick" to him, saving herself up, then using his name, enjoying it.

It seemed a good idea. It was a very good idea and, surprisingly, Jimmy agreed. "Why not?" he said. "Don't let her near the books, that's all."

From then on, things improved. Three weeks after the shop's opening, when he looked out of the window and saw two figures opposite, observing his front of a business, he felt only a small shudder of alarm, which subsided immediately as he saw they were two young girls.

Katherine said, "It's my daughter. And her friend."

"Ask them in," Nick said. It was going to be all right.

It was a Sunday morning, a month or two after Katherine had started her new job, when Jane's father put down the *Sunday Express* and said, "We ought to go out somewhere."

Jane had been looking forward to the *Sunday Express*. There was the Foreign News page, a page she always enjoyed, with the story about the man coming back early and disturbing his wife with her lover in an unusual hiding-place—the names and the nation changed from week to week but the story was the same. She'd been looking forward to a boring Sunday, maybe a bike ride down the crags.

"Go out where?" her mother said.

"It's a nice day," Malcolm said. "We could go out somewhere after lunch."

"We never go out somewhere after lunch," Daniel said. He was sitting on the piano stool, one sock off, picking at his feet, absorbed as a grooming monkey. "On a Sunday. Mrs. Kilwhinney, right, she said to us, 'Do you ever go out into Derbyshire with your family, on a Sunday?' and only this one kid, this right spastic, said he did. But no one else."

"I don't quite understand the point you're trying to make," Malcolm said, with the heavy irony he sometimes used in Daniel's direction. "But this afternoon, this family is going to get in the car and go for a drive in Derbyshire. Is that understood? And have a nice time. All right?"

Malcolm got up from the breakfast table and, without exactly storming, walked emphatically out of the room and upstairs; he often retreated to the study and his military books at moments of stress.

"What was that?" Daniel said.

"It's you that's supposed to have tantrums and slam doors," Jane said, neatly swiping the *Sunday Express*. "The problems of adolescence in the young male."

"You read too much," Katherine said mildly. "It's nothing unusual. Your father wants to go for a drive in Derbyshire. I don't know why that's so strange. Lots of people do it."

"It's strange for us," Jane said. "We only do it when Nana comes."

"Well, perhaps it would be a good thing if we started doing it," Katherine said. "There's some of the most beautiful country in England out there, and we look at it once in a blue moon. I don't see that it's 'spastic,' Daniel, and I've asked you once—"

"Okay, okay," Daniel said, and put his sock back on.

"It's disgusting," Katherine said. "But the other day, Nick, at work, he mentioned he'd been to Haddon Hall at the weekend, this would have been last weekend, and he was saying to me how beautiful it was. Well, I was really quite embarrassed to have to admit that even though I've lived forty years in Sheffield, not fifteen miles from Haddon Hall, I've never been there. Of course, Nick, he's interested in beautiful things, he's sensitive to them—a florist, it's to be expected. But don't you think it's terrible that we live here and we never bother to go and enjoy all the beautiful things on our doorstep, and someone who's only lived here for three months, he's making so much more of an effort?"

"We went to Haddon Hall." Tim sounded aggrieved. "Martin Jones was sick in the coach into a bag and Miss Taylor threw it out of the door of the coach without it stopping. I told you we went. You never listen."

"Well, it was only an example," Katherine said. "Of course I remember you going."

"It was boring. I don't think I like beautiful things." Then Tim thought hard for a moment, and said, "Haddon Hall, more glass than wall."

"That's Hardwick Hall," Jane said. "You're mixing up beautiful things."

"No, it was Haddon Hall," Tim said, in a kindly, regretful tone. "Hardwick Hall we didn't go to. I did a project about it, though. I got seven out of ten and I drew pictures. Oh."

"It was Hardwick Hall, wasn't it?" Jane said. "That's got more glass than wall?"

"I don't care which one it was," Tim said. "It might be both of them probably."

"The point is," Katherine said, her voice lowered and slow, she might have been passing on a moral lesson, "don't you think it would be nice if someone, Nick for instance, Mr. Reynolds, said to me on a Monday morning, 'What did you get up to at the weekend?' And I could say—or it could be your teacher, it could be anyone—instead of 'Not much,' or 'Mucked about,' or 'Washed some socks,' I could say, 'We had a lovely day out in Derbyshire. We went to see, I don't know what, and it was really beautiful'? Don't you think that might be nice? I'd really like, once in a while, to say something like that to Nick."

Jane concentrated on the newspaper, as if she weren't listening. She thought of her father's outing, a suggestion out of nowhere; she listened to her mother, lovingly speculating on how she could describe a Sunday afternoon to Nick, the sort of person she could become for his sake. She had never gone on so much about beauty; you could hear the rhythm of her voice changing, as if some contagion had taken hold of it. She doesn't understand anything, she said to herself.

"Well," Daniel said, "you could always say it. It wouldn't have to be true. And then we could have the best of both worlds. We could muck about and you could still say that you'd been somewhere posh and it was beautiful. But you wouldn't actually have to go there."

"That," Katherine said, "is exactly the sort of thing I would expect someone of your age to say."

"How hilarious," Jane said, looking up from the paper and its breathless foreign adulteries, its lovers safely absurd, in faraway cupboards. How hilarious: she meant it to wound. But the outing happened.

After lunch, Malcolm said, "Can you be ready in ten minutes? I want to be off soon."

"Just let me do the washing-up," Katherine said.

"Leave it," Malcolm said. "I want to be off, or it'll be getting dark."

"It'll only take ten minutes," Katherine said. "I'm not leaving the washing-up to fester." And in fifteen minutes they were in the car.

Sheffield fell away from you so quickly, and the gardens joined, broke up, grew and became moorland. There was a garden centre right at the edge, the very last thing of the city, or the first, and Jane had always found something funny about that: it wasn't the sort of thing you could ever say to anyone, or even properly explain, but it was something to do with all that green, rooted life out there, going on without anyone doing anything, and then it got into the garden centre and people sort of then thought it was all right, one of those green things, to pay money for it and put it in their gardens, even though— Jane wished she could explain this thought properly. She just knew there was something funny about the garden centre being at the border of the city, like Passport Control for plants. Ah well. She loved the country, even those walking-distance views and landmarks she had to concentrate to see.

But Jane's pleasure was being ruined by the noises and silences in the car. Her father's concentration on the road had a different quality of silence to it, compared to Tim's dense, bewildered concentration, or the quiet amusement Daniel was extracting from the situation. She wondered what her own pained silence sounded like from outside— perhaps very much like sulking. She looked out for the real boundary, a circular grinding stone turned upright and labelled "Peak District National Park," although no wildness began there. She looked forward to the moment that the car laboured whinnyingly upwards, crested the brow of the hill, and there before them, expected in advance and announced on its appearance, was the Surprise View, a valley opening up idyllically; the only surprise, ever, was if the weather had cleared or condensed on that side of the hill, and they came out of or into low-lying cloud, the view revealing itself or a dense white obscurity descending on the car. The weather today was clear; piles of clouds, seeming less vast than the purple expanse of the moors.

"I thought we'd go to Chatsworth," her dad said, a recognized outing. That was all he said, hardly waiting or seeming to expect any response or excited agreement. But all the way her mother kept up a running commentary, and the texture of it was by now familiar, unvarying. She offered one posh superlative to the landscape after another, comments not exactly hers. And she could not keep off the subject of Nick. They might have been driving through the native country of someone dear to them, a figure of historical renown, and she, speculatively, saying what this meant or might be supposed to mean to Nick; Nick; Nick.

Jane sat there, trying not to listen. No one interrupted. And her father? Well, perhaps he was letting her off the leash in giving her excited voice its indulgence, as if to let her hear herself and shame her out of what, for weeks now, she had been unable to stop saying.

In half an hour, they were through a further gated border, and inside the huge estates of the duke. Just outside was a village, a peculiarly picturesque river running through it and, conspicuously, a pub of some pretensions. Nick had been there; he said the food was exceptional, to match anything one might find in London. Jane thought it was a servile, ugly village, ugly with flowerbeds. Once through the gates the quality of the country changed, not to lawn, exactly, but to well-tended grazing land, prettily organized copses and views. The sheep were whiter, the grazing cows like an illustration on a can of evaporated milk, the river, of a glassy clarity, wending its elegantly serpentine way between trimmed banks. Nick thought it one of the most beautifully landscaped estates in the country, if not the world; he had been knocked out by the beauty of Chatsworth, and liked often to come over here. Perhaps even today.

It was not that she disagreed with it, though the estate had a colossal smooth elegance that was not, Jane thought, exactly right here in the north; it was calculated as precisely as that estate village in orange brick. She thought the whole thing beautiful too, and was pained by how Nick's views, filtered through her mother's mesmerized infatuation, spurred her on to indignant silent disagreement. She wanted, rather, a kind of beauty that required no one to say, "How beautiful," and that, she was convinced, was what Chatsworth had: it spoke to the sort of mind that regarded the epithets of beauty and loveliness with shy scorn. And, most of all, there was the great house, rushing now into view: the encrusted palace, the dense magic of its gardens and beyond, a landing-strip of water with a single fierce jet, forty feet high. Seen from the far side of the house, it flung a firm trunk of water upwards, and at the top the mild wind seemed to carry it away like a willow's foliage.

If Derbyshire had failed, Chatsworth did the trick. Katherine's conversation dribbled to a halt, her gesturing hands froze in mid-air, then fell to her lap. Her head, which had been turning from her husband to her children in the back, now turned to the great house. Malcolm's head and shoulders seemed to relax, his eyes no longer flickering tensely in and out of the rear mirror. They drove into the car park, gravel splashing under the tyres, chickens, exuberant as a flowering bush, scattering. He bought a parking ticket through the window. They all got out; locked the doors.

"You know," her dad said, in his mildest voice, "that village in the park? Edensor, it's called, spelt E-D-E-N, there's an interesting story about that. One of the dukes, a hundred years ago, he wanted to build a model village on the estate for his high-class workers, as you'd call them, the important people, like the chief housekeeper, maybe, the gamekeeper or the head gardener, so he asked an architect to come up with plans for the houses, and the architect, he was nervous and produced a range of ideas, different houses, so that the duke could choose the style he wanted and then they could go with that one. But whether the duke didn't understand—" they were walking now into the main hall of the palace, stout ladies sitting under a fat, gaudy allegory on the ceiling "—or whether he liked them all about the same, he just said, 'I'll have those, all of them,' and so every house in the village, it's in a different style. Two adults and three children, please. Of course, I'm not myself all that interested in the house, it's the garden I like best, but you children, it'll be interesting for you to see the house, you'll enjoy it."

They'd been into the house on school trips and on a family outing—years ago, when Nana Glover was still alive. But they drove through the park regularly, on their twice-yearly trips through Derbyshire, and every time Malcolm pointed out the village, and explained the facts of it. Jane found it comforting, like that longer story about the village of Eyam, the only place, apart from London, where the plague had broken out. She didn't mind being told things more than once: it was a signal that everything was all right in the world. But a moment after they had begun to climb the stairs to the main rooms, her mother started again, her bright eyes glossing over the spectacle of the house and examining the other visitors, waiting for Nick to appear at any moment and, in the meantime, giving her family the sort of comments he might be expected to produce or perhaps already had. She had dropped his name, but there was nothing of her in what she was saying, and she kept it up through those many golden rooms, explaining them, their views, their historical associations, their—now painful word— beauty to her silent family. At last it was done, sculpture gallery, Mary Queen of Scots rooms and all.

"Shall we go and have a look at the gardens?" Katherine said, flushed with pleasure.

Outside on the gravel path, the others said nothing. To the right there were the elaborate gardens, their games and winding path, and the vast single jet; to the left, the car park and the toilets.

"It's getting a bit late," Malcolm said. "It'll be dark before long. Maybe we'll save the gardens for another day. We've had a nice time, though, haven't we?"

It came out more plaintive than you'd have expected, and though Daniel said, "Lovely," and Tim said, "Yes," his voice rising into a question, Jane put herself into it, for her father's sake, and said, "I've really enjoyed it. I wish we did it all the time."

"I thought you were looking forward most to the garden," her mother said.

"Well, I was," Malcolm said. "But we'd better get off. I just want to go to the toilet."

"Can't it wait until we're home?" Katherine said—and whether she now thought it was common to piss on the porcelain of Chatsworth, a thing Nick would never presume to do, or whether she imagined the dukes and their sons, the little lords, drove to Edensor for that purpose, or whether she just didn't want to think about anything so low, nobody could tell.

"I want to go to the toilet," Malcolm said, voice rising in something like anger, and two passing ladies, posh in pearls and dung-coloured sweaters, burst heartlessly into laughter. "Well, I do," Malcolm said childishly, kicking the gravel.

"Go on, then," Katherine said, and with one last look at the posh ladies, retreating up the gravel path towards the formal gardens, he did so, plucking at his anorak.

"You know something," Daniel said, when they were half-way home, "I need to go to the toilet. I wish I'd gone." And Jane's dad—she enjoyed these witty streaks in his character—slowed to the edge of the speed limit, and maintained thirty miles an hour, ignoring Daniel's complaints and the line of drivers behind them.

After that there was no more talk of anyone having a lover. Jane wondered how her mother could be so blind, so deaf: deaf to what she sounded like, blind to the protective shapes her father started to form whenever her conversation took a familiar turn. Anne might have mentioned it once, after that outing to Broomhill, but it was clear to Jane that she hadn't got the force of the situation across, and Anne made her references to the lover in so amused a tone that the discussion couldn't go anywhere; it could only become a joke, like Miss Barker's impact on the continent of Africa. Nor were there any more Sunday outings.

At first Jane felt that she would never get on with her mother's conversation, the way you waited for Nick to enter it at any moment, but time wore down anything. Soon it was the same as Tim's dreaming evocation of snakes, his paragraphs of detail and longing, and they divided the long evenings between them like a pair of madmen supervising the silent sane. That might have been harmless, and there was no chance of it going beyond mad talk, Jane thought. It could never develop into a situation beyond easy horrid embarrassment.

But Jane was wrong, because after some months a suggestion surfaced and her mother had, apparently, decided to give a party, something never done before by the adults. There was no doubting the reason for this party. It was as if Tim had decided to hold a party to which the snake of his dreams would be invited. You could not say that, not to Daniel, not to Anne, not to anyone. Tell a teacher, was the advice in *Jackie* when things got bad for the correspondents of Cathy and Claire. But Jane thought of Miss Barker—and thought that Cathy and Claire didn't know what they were talking about, and she went on thinking that until the night of the party, and the food was laid out to snare Nick, and her mother in a long blue dress, and the doorbell rang for the first time, and it was only Mrs. Arbuthnot from over the road.

Perhaps even then it might have been all right. Tim and her dad were standing in the dining room, looking at but not touching the food. There were vol-au-vents, a dish of bright yellow cold chicken curry, decorative arrangements of cheese on sticks, and a whole Brie, cut open, oozing, but smelling strongly of ammonia. There were loaves of French bread, sliced into rounds and in baskets, and small bowls of pickle and bowls of butter, and on the sideboard, glasses set out in ranks with the bottles of white wine, Malcolm's task, already open. There were bowls of crisps and nuts and, of course, in the middle of the table, and on the piano, and elsewhere in the house, in vases half theirs and half borrowed for the occasion, arrangements of flowers from Nick's shop.

"Are they going to eat all this?" Tim said. "Have they had their dinner?"

"They'll eat it," Malcolm said. "Even if they've had their dinner. And I suppose if they don't, we'll be living off vol-au-vents and Coronation Chicken all week, you'll see."

"How hilarious," Tim said. There was a silence.

"What did you say?" Malcolm said.

"I only said it was hilarious," Tim said, faltering.

"Did you say," Malcolm said, " 'how hilarious'?"

Tim didn't answer; he didn't know what he had said or done wrong. But Malcolm left the room, with two bottles, his face set, and prepared to act like a host to whoever might come through his front door, to pretend they were welcome. Because that was what he had to do, just for tonight.

Mr. Jolly, John Ball and Keith the boy had their routine worked out for an overnight stay and, under Mr. Jolly's direction, they reckoned to clear a good two hundred pounds a year on top of their wages. They worked together as a team. The routine was that you got money from petty cash for a bed-and-breakfast on overnight jobs, but of course you never used it. You slept in the van and kept the money. If they'd been sent out with just anyone, the routine wouldn't have been possible. You'd have to explain each time, and word would get out, and they'd put a stop to it. As long as Mr. Jolly had been with Orchard's Removals, which was getting on for twenty years, they'd kept their teams fixed— maybe not for a day job, within London, but for overnights and more. "It's that sort of consideration," a management wife had once said to John Ball at a works Christmas party, "that sets Orchard's apart, and that's why we never have any trouble with—"

"Strikes?" John Ball had said, and she'd blushed as at an obscenity from an over-familiar acquaintance. Yes, they liked to send you away with your team so, generally, Mr. Jolly, John Ball and Keith could work their routine once or twice a week. Maybe everyone did; you didn't ask.

Mr. Jolly, the chief remover, had a kind of contempt for the management on account of this. Even while robbing it in this small way, he wasn't grateful for the slackness. He'd have put a stop to it. They didn't even ask for receipts, it being believed that the sort of establishments the men would use were not necessarily able to produce that sort of documentation. You just took the three quid each and signed for it. Later, on the way home, you divided it up; John Ball had three quid, Keith the boy thirty bob, and Mr. Jolly took the rest. The firm's accountant was called Perks, something which always made Mrs. Jolly laugh as she took the cash, made a little roll of the notes and put it into the tea caddy on the shelf in their Streatham kitchen for a rainy day, the fifty pee over going straight into her pocket for a couple of glasses of mild for herself later.

"Oi!" Mr. Jolly always said.

"Oi yourself," Mrs. Jolly always replied. He didn't really mind. They'd managed to get to Majorca on the tea-caddy money last year.

But sometimes you wondered whether it wouldn't be better to spend the money in the way it was meant, particularly in the summer. It was still quite warm now, at the beginning of September, even as far north as Sheffield. Mr. Jolly had known worse than Keith—they weren't especially smelly, the three of them. After a hard day's work, you parked, went maybe to a pub for a pint or two and a bite of supper, then back to the van. The van itself was packed with someone's furniture, beds, sofas and cushions, everything you could want for a nice restful night. That's what Keith had said when he'd joined the team, complaining about the real sleeping arrangements. It had never occurred to Mr. Jolly or (John Ball said, amazement in his voice) to John Ball. What an idea! It would be like—Mr. Jolly said—it would be like a doctor treating, er, breaching—a lawyer suing a judge for—er— a thoroughgoing breach of—well, it wasn't to be thought of, and, oddly, hadn't been until Keith said it and then they all started thinking, hard, about those lovely soft beds in the back that they could arrange as they liked . . .

But they had their standards, so they went back to the van and made space for themselves in the cab and in the little loft arrangement over it with its porthole window, just about big enough for two with a blanket rolled up between you. Keith stretched out on the seats, complaining about Mr. Jolly's snoring and about the gear stick in his back all night. It didn't seem so bad when you woke up, nice and warm and toasty often. Then you went off in search of a caff for breakfast and, ideally, a stand-up wash at a sink. When you came back and opened the cab door, phew! It was like something had died in there, and you left the doors open while you did the second half of the job.

"I knew there wouldn't be anywhere," John Ball said.

"Good job you said so, then," Keith said. They were sitting disconsolately on the wall outside the house in Sheffield. It was a quarter to eight in the morning. They'd woken up an hour earlier, and Keith had been sent out on a recce for a caff. They'd looked the night before and seen nothing but, as Mr. Jolly said, they'd been tired, they'd not looked everywhere. It was hopeless. The house was in a new development in the middle of one suburb after another, not the sort of place where anyone would think of opening a nice caff. Keith had come back shrugging. "No joy," he said.

"I knew there wouldn't be anywhere," John Ball said, "as soon as I saw where they were moving from. I knew the sort of place they'd be moving to. No caffs, you see."

"All right," Mr. Jolly said. "You underestimate your uncle Bill. Get out the emergency supplies, John. You'll find a Primus stove stowed under the cabin—"

"That's not safe—"

"I dare say, but there it is, and you'll find some bacon and eggs and a tin of milk too."

"How long's that been there?"

"Not long enough for you to worry about. So there you are—bacon and eggs and a cup of tea. Get going."

Mr. Jolly lit a cigarette and watched, with satisfaction, the preparations for his pavement breakfast. In a moment John Ball came back, Primus in hand. Behind him, Keith balanced bacon and eggs, a packet of tea and a tin of condensed milk. "Where's the frying pan, Bill?" he said.

"Same place," Mr. Jolly said, an awful doubt rising. "Along with the kettle."

"There's no kettle," John Ball said. "And no frying pan."

"We could—" Keith gestured towards the van.

"We could what?" Mr. Jolly said.

"I know where the kitchen box is," Keith said. "We loaded it last. It's at the back of the van."

"No, Keith," Mr. Jolly said, and John Ball shook his head in something like sorrow.

Everything seemed confusing in the Glovers' house. Nobody woke Timothy. He got up on his own, washed his face, dressed himself.

Downstairs people were talking, quietly. When he came into the dining room for breakfast, nothing was being made ready. His mother and sister were sitting at the table, without even a cloth on it, both dressed, his brother standing looking out of the window. His sister had her hand on his mother's. That frightened him a little bit. Then he remembered about his dad.

"I phoned the police," his mother said, as he came in. She seemed to be talking to someone else, not to Timothy. "They said they can't do anything until he's been gone twenty-four hours at least."

"Where is he?" Timothy said.

"We don't know," Daniel said, not turning from the window. Outside, there was a van; there was some activity.

"Daniel," his mother said. Timothy knew, really, that his father had gone and no one knew where. He was just being silly.

"Look at that," Daniel said. "That's amazing."

"What are you looking at?" his mother said. "Oh, the new people. I'm not—"

"No," Daniel said. "Come here."

As if humouring him, his mother got up and went to the window, followed by Jane. They stood for a moment, watching.

"Good heavens," his mother said.

"I know," Daniel said. "That's so strange."

The van was in the early stages of unloading: the men had taken out the first of the furniture, some tea-chests, and left them on the pavement. They must have been waiting for someone with a key. There, on the pavement opposite, was the Glovers' unit. It was exactly the Glovers' unit, and Timothy did what they all probably wanted to do: he ran out into the hall and made sure that the unit, their unit, was still in the sitting room. It was. He came back into the dining room.

"That's extraordinary," Katherine said lightly.

"What is?" Jane said. "What are you all looking at?"

"That," Katherine said. "The unit?"

"What about it?" Jane said.

Daniel stared at her, astonished, but she seemed genuinely baffled. "It's the same as the one we've got," he said.

"Oh," Jane said. "Oh, yes. I suppose it is quite similar."

"It's exactly the same," Katherine said. "I hope they take it in soon. I don't want everyone in the street thinking . . ." She tailed off.

Timothy liked the thought of all your furniture outside, arranged, exactly as it was in the house, on a lawn, or maybe on the pavement. "Can't we move?" he said.

"Don't be ridiculous," Katherine said. "We're hardly going to move just because the new people over the road have the same unit we have. Did you think Cole Brothers had made it just for us?"

"No," Timothy said. "I meant " He didn't know what he meant, and then he remembered he hadn't said hello to Geoffrey that morning. There didn't seem to be any breakfast.

He went upstairs cheerfully. His father hadn't come home, but he expected there was a good reason for that. And maybe later that day the police would come, in a car with the lights flashing on top, and maybe they'd take him for a ride, so that would be OK. He went into his room and shut the door. When you came in, there was a bit of a fishy smell. The books hadn't said. He supposed his mother would find out about Geoffrey soon, though it had been three days now without discovery. Timothy knelt down, and pulled a square, flat glass container from underneath his bed. Geoffrey raised his head and, looking straight at Timothy, flickered his tongue happily. "Sssss," Timothy said, though of course Geoffrey hadn't made a noise and wouldn't. Timothy knew that Geoffrey, flickering his tongue, was sniffing, tasting the air to see what was around, but he liked to think it was a friendly gesture. Geoffrey liked Timothy, Timothy knew that, and Timothy certainly liked Geoffrey. To buy Geoffrey, the glass container and the small objects in it, Timothy had saved all of his pocket money for three years, two months and one week, ever since he had first started being interested in snakes.

But Geoffrey ought to see the world, Timothy thought. He reached into the case, and took Geoffrey out, one hand by his neck, the other holding his tail. He didn't put him round his own neck, of course. He had once seen a picture in the newspaper of a lady doing that, a lady with not many clothes on. The snake had been a yellow python, and gazed out of the picture with an expression of great sadness. That was an awful thing to do to a snake. So Timothy just carried Geoffrey out, very gently, opening the door with his elbow, and into Jane's bedroom, to show him the interesting spectacle of a van being unloaded.

Outside, the men had stopped. They were talking to each other surreptitiously, out of the corners of their mouths. Always in this sort of place, you attracted an audience once you started work. Actually, wherever you were, you got one. It was just that when the house got to a certain size, cost a certain amount, once you got to houses with gardens and trees planted in the street, the audience stayed inside. It didn't gawp on the street, not even the kids. The most they'd do was come out into the garden, pretend to be pruning. It wasn't you they were watching, it was the chance, which might be the only one, to have a really good look at what the newcomers had got in the way of furniture.

"Enjoying it?" John Ball muttered to Keith, as they carried a sofa out, one at each end.

"Oh, yeah," Keith said. "I'm loving it."

"Not you," John Ball said. "I meant them. I hope they're enjoying it. Look at them."

And, indeed, there was quite a lot of discreet attention. At the kitchen window next door, a lady in a housecoat was doing the washing up very slowly. A woman who had walked up the road with a chocolate Labrador ten minutes before was now walking back again on the other side of the road; you could see the dog hadn't expected that, and was looking up at his mistress with a baffled expression. And directly over the road, hardly concealing themselves, a woman and two kids were at the downstairs window, really staring, and upstairs in the same house—

"What's that kid got?" Mr. Jolly said.

"What kid?" John Ball said.

"The kid in the house over the road, the one in the upstairs window. He's holding—it looks like—"

"Christ," Keith said. He was thinking of the girl who'd ridden with them in the van, the way she'd stood in the upstairs window of the house and flashed her little titties at him. He looked back at the kid, and this was, in a way, even more strange. "He's got a snake."

"Do you think they know where they're moving to?" John Ball said.

"Give me Streatham, any day of the week," Mr. Jolly said. "Look at them, all of them staring, and not one of them, it wouldn't occur to one of them to come out and say, for instance, 'Oh, I can see you're hard at work already, I don't suppose you'd like a cup of coffee to start the day with,' or—the least you could expect—an offer to let you fill your kettle at their kitchen tap. Makes you sick."

"We haven't got a kettle," Keith said.

"They don't know that," Mr. Jolly said, shaking his head as he carried on unloading. The pavement was thoroughly blocked with all these possessions; they'd better come soon.

"You've got the coffee-table," Keith said, as Mr. Jolly put it down on the pavement, just next to the sofa.

"So we have," Mr. Jolly said. "Cheeky sod. Right. I'm going over there."

John Ball and Keith put themselves down on the sofa, just as if they'd been hard at it for hours. Mr. Jolly, in a good humour, fetched three chipped old mugs from the cab of the lorry, walked up the driveway of the house opposite. The kid in the window upstairs with the snake—it was definitely a snake, there was no doubting that—he drew back into the bedroom with a look of alarm on his face. Maybe the snake wasn't supposed to come out of its cage; maybe he wasn't allowed to play with the thing before school. He rang the doorbell.

There was a confused noise inside. People talking, their voices raised and muted at the same time. It was a couple of minutes before anyone came to the door. It was a woman; she was dressed—that hadn't been the delay, then—but her hair was unkempt. She held the door half open, looking at Mr. Jolly with her mouth tense. She might have been expecting him, someone like him; she looked as if she was expecting something bad to happen to her, the next time she opened the front door. She said nothing.

"I'm sorry to trouble you, madam," Mr. Jolly. "This is a bit cheeky, like, but . . ." He explained their predicament. She listened to the end; he grew less and less hopeful of success as he went on, she looked so unencouraging.

But then she surprised him by saying, "Yes, of course," and then "It's awful to have to start work without a hot drink in the morning," and "No, I don't know where you'd find somewhere to serve you breakfast, not without going right down into, I don't know, Crosspool," a name that meant nothing to him.

"Thanks very much," he said, handing over the mugs but not inviting himself in.

"Who's that, then?" A girl's voice came from the back of the house. "It's not—"

"No, it's not," the woman said. "It's nobody."

Mr. Jolly overlooked this rudeness, put it down to some kind of distraction as she carried the mugs away, almost at arm's length. She left the front door open and Mr. Jolly standing there.

"It's all with milk and two sugars," he said, calling into the kitchen where she'd gone, having forgotten to ask him any of this.

"Sorry, what did you say?" she said, coming out again, the mugs still in her hand.

"Milk and two sugars," he said. "If it's no trouble."

"It's only instant," she said.

"That'll be perfect," he said, not having expected any other kind.

The conversation was not closed, but he felt foolish standing there. The other two sat on the other side of the road, talking with amusement to each other, watching his suspended embarrassment. Mr. Jolly settled for a performance of head-scratching, whistling, inspecting his watch and looking up and down the road in an exaggerated way. He bent down and ran his second and third finger underneath a flower, a fat yellow familiar one, without picking it.

"Don't do that," a boy said, standing at the open door. It was the boy who'd been watching them from the upstairs window, a snake round his neck. The snake had been disposed of. Made you shiver to think of it. "That's my dad's flowers."

"I was just looking," Mr. Jolly said. He was no good with children, having none; his sister neither, never wanted them, not that they couldn't have had them, him and his wife. "I wasn't going to pick."

"Just because he's not here," the boy said.

"Gone to work, has he?" Mr. Jolly said heartily. "Me too. We're moving your new neighbours in, over the road, there. That'll be nice for you, won't it? Having new . . ." He trailed away. The boy was looking at him, a horrified gaze.

"That's right," he said, raising his voice. "He's gone to work, definitely."

"Good," Mr. Jolly said. "Make a nice early start. I saw you, just then with—you know, your friend—"

"What friend?"

"Your special friend, the yellow one," Mr. Jolly said. "At least he looked yellow from where I was standing. You know—" he made a face "—*sssssss.*"

"I don't know what you're talking about," the boy said. "I wouldn't tell anyone else what you thought you saw only they might think you were mental or something. You wouldn't want that, so don't mention it to anyone, what you saw."

"Here you are," the woman said, bringing out the three mugs, now filled with coffee, on a shamingly clean tray. Amazingly, she'd only gone and put some biscuits on a plate as well. "I do hope my son isn't bothering you."

"Thank you very much," Mr. Jolly said, now rather baffled, and with the door closing firmly, he walked steadily back, balancing the tray carefully.

"That's the ticket," John Ball said comfortably. "Use your charm, did you?"

"They're all bonkers round here," Mr. Jolly said, relieving his feelings a little. "Fit for the hatch, they are."

"Biscuits, too," Keith said. "You should have tried for bacon and eggs."

"That's enough," Mr. Jolly said. "And take your hands off those. This fucking job—"

"That girl, rode with us—" John Ball said.

"Mental," Mr. Jolly said.

"Glad to get shot of her," Keith said.

"Mental," John Ball agreed.

It had been a long night for the Sellerses. They had stayed not in the funded luxury of the Hallam Towers Hotel but in a small family hotel; since the week in the summer, looking for a house, the Electric had ordered a cut-back. Alice had found the Sandown, and apologized for it as soon as they had rolled up there, the night before. She ought to have known. The advertisement, found in a hotel guide, had used an illustration, not a photograph, and a highly fanciful one; you couldn't have assumed that the hotel in reality would have had a horse-drawn carriage with a jolly coachman drawn up outside, but the false impression of window-boxes and carriage lamps at the door surely went further than excusable exaggeration. But there were few hotels in Sheffield, and it was only for one night; the front door already locked at eight, opened up to them by a fat man in cardigan and slippers, masticating sourly on slowly revolving bread and cheese, the slight marshy suck of the orange-and-black carpet underfoot, and the forty-watt lightbulbs casting their yellowish light over a long-term resident peeling the pages of an ancient *Punch* in the lobby.

There was naturally no food to be had, and only a shrug when, their bags deposited, Alice asked after nearby restaurants. Still, they found one and, thank heavens, it had what to the children evidently seemed some quality of fun; an American-style restaurant with flags on the wall and drinks called Fudpucker; they were alone in the restaurant, but it would do to perk up the spirits. Alice wouldn't say anything about what they had left, she wouldn't.

It was a restless night. The hotel had once been three Edwardian semis, now joined together, the gap between the second and third filled with dismal grey prefabricated corridors, and the original rooms split with partitions. There seemed to be few people staying, but, perhaps to save the legs of the chambermaids, all of them were apparently squeezed into the same corner of the hotel. Bernie undressed and, without seeming to pause to think about it, pulled out his red pyjamas from the overnight bag, put them on. It was an agreed signal, undisguised, what he did with them at this point; it was kind of him to know how tired she would be, to remember that there could be better reassurances between them on this hard night than sex.

"Goodnight, love," Bernie said, and as he got into bed, swinging his legs up under the cheese-smelling pink candlewick bedspread, rolling into the same central hollow in the mattress she had fallen into, he gripped her hand and kissed her and groaned and laughed all at the same time. She smelt his warmth; and, as ever, even at the end of the day, the warm smell of his body was a sweet one, like toffee. Always had been.

She was reassured for a moment, could have found the hotel and Sheffield funny as Bernie meant her to, but then, through the wall, there came an ugly noise: a human voice, groaning. It was horribly clear.

"What's that?" Alice said.

"It's from next door," Bernie said, whispering.

"It's not the kids, is it?" Alice said.

"No, they're the other side," Bernie said. "It's—" But then the noise resumed, and some kind of wet slapping noise, too; a single voice giving in to a single pleasure, and Alice clenched her jaw and tried not to think of it, tried not to hear it. It went on, the noise, in a way impossible to laugh about. Bernie coughed, sharply, a cough meant to be heard through the partition. But the noise continued, the animal noise of slap and groan, a middle-aged man—it was impossible not to visualise the scene—doing things to himself in the light of a forty-watt bulb, and not much caring whether anyone heard him through the walls or not.

Presently it stopped and, as best she could, Alice unclenched herself. Bernie was tense, pretending to sleep. It was better than trying to find anything to say. The sound of heavy feet padding around the room next door, clearing up—good God, clearing what up?—was concluded with the sharp click of the light switch and, in a startlingly short stretch of time, with the gross rumble of a fat man snoring. Alice lay there against Bernie's slowly relaxing body, counting up to five hundred, over and over.

In the morning, they dressed and were about to leave the room when she heard the door of their wanking neighbour open and shut.

"Hang on a second," she said to Bernie. "I just want to brush my hair before we go down."

"You've just brushed it," he said.

"I want to brush it again," she said. She picked up the brush, and in front of the tiny wonky mirror she brushed her hair again, thirty times, until it was charged with static and flying outwards, until the man, whoever he was, was downstairs and anonymous. But all the same, when the children had been collected and they were all sitting round the table in the "breakfast room," she could not help letting her eye run round the room. Everyone else there was a man on his own, each at his little table, in various positions of respectability, and the four of them talked in near-whispers. It could have been any of them; she rather wanted to know now, to exclude the innocent others.

"Well," Sandra surprisingly said, when they were decanted into the green Simca, the hotel bill grumpily paid, "I don't think we'll be staying there again."

"Well, of course we won't," Bernie said, turning his head. "We won't ever need to."

"That's not really—" Sandra began.

"I think the Hallam Towers was a better hotel," Francis said. "From the point of view of quality."

"Yes, of course it's a better hotel," Bernie said. "I'm under no illusions there."

"If anyone asked you," Francis said, "Mummy, if anyone asked you to recommend a hotel to stay in in Sheffield—"

"Oh, for heaven's sake," Alice said, her temper now breaking out for the first time, "let's just shut up about it, and never think about the bloody place ever again. I don't know why we've always got to discuss everything."

"Your mother's quite right," Bernie said. "Give it a rest, Francis." He smiled, amused and released from some of the tension of Alice's bravely kept-up face.

"You said 'bloody,' " Sandra said, gleeful and mincing.

"I know," Alice said. "It was a bloody hotel. It's the only word for it."

"Bloody awful," Bernie said. "Bloody awful hotel," he went on. "Arsehole of the world's hotels."

"That hotel," Francis began, "was really the most—"

"That'll do," Alice said. "We all agree."

The thing was that Bernie had taught her to swear, and he liked it, sometimes, when she did. She wasn't much good at it, she knew that. But she'd grown up in a house where you earned a punishment for saying "rotten"; anything much stronger she'd never heard, or heard and never understood. Bernie and his family, they swore; swore at Churchill on the radio ("Pissed old bugger"), at the neighbours ("Stupid old bastard"), at any inconvenience or none, at each other, at inanimate objects and, strangest of all, affectionately. His mother, his aunts, even; and she'd tried to join in, but she couldn't really get it, couldn't do it; she couldn't get the rhythm right somehow, couldn't put the words together right, and it obviously became a subject of fond amusement among the whole clan of them when Bernie's shy fiancée hesitantly described the Northern Line as a bollocks, whatever bollocks might mean.

It was a fine day. As they drove up the long hill towards their new house, a constant steady incline, three miles long, Bernie hummed; she had sworn and made him cheerful again. For some reason, it was nine o'clock by the time they turned into the road. "Here we are," Bernie said. "There's the van. Christ, look!" and, to their surprise, by the removal van, outside one of the houses, on the driveway and spilling out on to the pavement, was most of their furniture. It took a moment to recognize that that was what it was. In the sunshine, it looked so different, arranged in random and undomestic ways, like the sad back lot of a junk shop. The sofa against the dining-table, the dining-chairs against Francis's bedroom bookshelf, one of the pictures, the pretty eighteenth-century princess hugging a cat, with no wall to be hung on, leaning against a unit. Their beds, too, stripped of sheets and mattresses like the beds of the dead, laid open to the public gaze, shamefully. Their possessions; they seemed at once many and sadly inadequate to fill a house. In the old place, they had stood where they stood for so long that you stopped seeing them. But on the lawn, in the driveway, under the sun, laid out as if for purchasers, you saw it all again. Some of it was nice.

"There's the men," Bernie said. "Well, they've made a start, at any rate."

"They might have waited," Alice said.

"Look, Sandra," Francis said. "There's the men."

"I know," Sandra said, angrily. The car stopped: they got out.

"Morning," the foreman said.

From his bedroom window, Timothy watched the family get out. There were four of them. He had taken Geoffrey out of his case again, to let him watch the excitement. The father got out of the little turquoise car, like a bar, and stretched his shoulders back. Timothy imitated him. And there was a mother too, holding her handbag tightly, a sweet nervous expression. The boy was tall, taller than his mother though Timothy thought someone had said that he and the boy were the same age. Timothy hated him already.

But he was really looking at the girl by now. He had no interest in the others. She stood there in a cloud of frizzed hair, and yawned. As she pulled her arms upwards, her wrist in the other hand's grip, her T-shirt popped loose of her waistband, pulled tightly against her chest. Even yawning she was lovely; even from here her beauty was defined. "Venus," Timothy said to himself, and found he was stroking along his snake's back, pointing Geoffrey's head towards the lovely girl. The removers had seen him when he had stood here. But the girl did not seem to see him, to pay any attention to him. He wondered why not. He promised himself something about this sight; he knew it was important; he promised himself he would never forget it. He had heard of people seeing each other, and knowing immediately that was the person they were to marry. He filed it away.

The husbands of the road left for work at seven thirty, at eight, at shortly after eight, to be at work by nine. Some had noted the removals van, blocking half the road; the later departures had observed the furniture being placed right across the pavement, and worried, some on behalf of the furniture, some on behalf of anyone wanting to walk down the pavement, as was their right, not obstructed by household chattels and trinkets. That was quite good, but when the interest of the road quickened with the arrival of the new family around nine o'clock, the curiosity was limited to the non-working wives. Most of them welcomed this; they preferred not to have to share their mood of observation with a man. It usually meant dissembling, pretending not to be all that interested. But if you were on your own, you could take a healthy interest, and not have to explain anything to anyone.

Anthea Arbuthnot, in her flowered housecoat, was paying close attention. She had been finding important things to occupy her around every single one of the windows with a good view ever since the men had started unloading the van. Finally, she had drawn up a chair and a small table by her sitting-room window and made a show of reading the *Morning Telegraph* over a cup of coffee. "They'll not have driven up from London this morning," she said to herself, and started speculating about their arrangements.

In Karen Warner's house, her husband had gone to work an hour before. Her son, nineteen, a disappointment, lay at full length on the sofa. It was one of her rules: he might have nothing to do and nothing to get up for, but he would get up every morning and not lie in bed. In practice, it meant he got up, dressed, stretched out on the sofa and remained horizontal all morning. The telephone rang.

At the other end, Anthea Arbuthnot announced herself; Mrs. Warner agreed that it had been nice at the Glovers', the other night, and nice to have had a chance to meet in a social manner. Karen wondered, rather, why Anthea Arbuthnot was telephoning at the expensive time of day when she was only a hundred yards away. But in a moment she pointed out that the new family had just arrived, that they were standing outside with their furniture spread across the road, and invited Karen to pop round to take her morning coffee with her at, say, eleven. Putting the telephone down, it seemed to Karen that Anthea might have invented some kind of purpose for her telephone call, some occasion to justify the invitation—the loan of the garlic-crusher she'd been so interested by the other night would have done.

"Really, she's no shame," Karen said out loud.

"Pardon?" her son said, after a minute.

But Karen had been talking to herself—he wasn't much company, her worry of a son. "I hope you're planning to get something done today," she said.

"Probably," he said.

Further up the road, the nursery nurse had phoned in sick. Everything about her seemed to be swelling, not just her soft parts, her belly, her breasts, not even her joints, her ankles, her knees, her elbows blowing up like warty old gourds. Everything seemed to be swelling, even her bones, and her face was purple and tight and aching with the effort involved in lying flat on a bed for eight hours. The nursery was growing politely unbelieving—you could hear it in their voices. She knew they'd put the phone down, and start swapping stories about Chinese peasant women giving birth behind bushes in their lunch breaks. The phone rang and she felt it might be something important—she couldn't ignore it.

It was only the woman from down the road, the one they'd met the other night. "I let it ring," Anthea Arbuthnot said, "because I know what it's like. You're at the other end of the house and by the time you get there it stops ringing just as you pick it up and you spend the whole day wondering who it might have been. How are you, my dear?" She apologized, she hadn't noticed the new neighbours moving in; she agreed the other night had been nice; she demurred at the suggestion of coffee later, but there must have been some uncertainty in her voice, because in two more exchanges she had agreed to lug herself down the road. She put the telephone down, and scowled at it.

Taking the key from a willing, smiling Bernie, Alice opened the door to the house. She thought nothing of all these neighbours; she gave no thought to their being surrounded by all those accumulated possessions which in her case were pressed into boxes or arranged haphazardly in the open air. Behind her, the children came in, at first cautiously, craning round corners, and then with increasing confidence of possession, Sandra striding boldly upstairs, already arguing over her shoulder with her brother over bedrooms, something already decided. Outside, Bernie was discussing matters with the men in high good humour: he was good with workmen. Alice thought it would be a relief when the house was straight; she thought, too, that after being left empty for all those weeks, it smelt like a cloakroom, like the smell of dust heating on a long unused toaster, and, a little, of piss. It looked not empty to her but emptied, robbed, and a little pathetic. She walked through the empty rooms; they seemed small, but she reminded herself that empty rooms did seem small. You put furniture in them, and they started to seem larger; you went on putting furniture in them and at a certain point they started to seem small again.

It was the curtains that gave each room its air of abandonment rather than emptiness. All the curtains had been left behind, and still hung limply at each window. It had made sense to Bernie, and to Alice too, at the time: your old curtains aren't going to fit the new windows. And the house was going to be empty for weeks, maybe months. There wasn't much you could do about that, but perhaps if there were curtains up, it might look to anyone passing that it wasn't abandoned. You heard about squatters, these days.

Bernie came in and, shyly, put his arm round her waist where she stood, at the back window.

"Look at that," she said. "Look at the garden."

"I know," he said. "It'll need some work. Nobody's touched it for months."

"Maybe more than that," she said. "Oh God," she said.

"What?" Bernie said. "What's wrong?"

"Just so much to do," she said.

"Not so much," he said. "I tell you what. I'll mow the lawn straight away, it won't look so bad. And then we'll leave it till spring."

That wasn't really what she'd meant, but she said, "You'll need more than a lawnmower. It's too long for that, the grass. You know, I wish—"

"What do you wish?" he said, smiling; it was something they had always come back to, her wishing, his asking to know her wish.

"Oh, I was thinking about the carpets," she said. "What's it going to look like, none of the old carpets fitting properly? I wish we'd persuaded the Watsons—oh, well, never mind. You don't suppose—"

"What?" Bernie said.

"I've just had an awful thought," Alice said. She loosened Bernie's arm, and turned round to look at the light fitting. "I can't believe it."

"They haven't," Bernie said. "They can't have done."

"Maybe they've just taken that lightbulb," Alice said, without any hope.

"Let's go and look," Bernie said.

Room by room, they went through the house, and it turned out to be true. "What are you looking at?" Sandra said, as they came into the room where she and Francis were bickering, and her mother explained. The children stopped their argument, and followed their parents through the house. For whatever reason, perhaps after the negotiations over the curtains and the failed ones over the carpet, the Watsons had apparently, before leaving, gone through the house and carefully removed every single lightbulb. It was incredible. On Francis's face was a look, a usual one with him, of something like fear; he felt these difficulties as catastrophes, personal catastrophes, Alice always thought.

"Well," Bernie said, when they had finished, and had settled, the four of them, on the sofa in the middle of the sitting room, "I'm going to write them a letter. Give them a piece of my mind. How many light-bulbs is it? Fifteen?"

"Problem?" the foreman said, coming in with the smaller of the coffee-tables. Alice explained.

"Happens all the time," the foreman said. "You'd be surprised. Mostly out of meanness."

"My dad works for the Electricity," Francis offered.

"Well, he'll know all about lightbulbs," the foreman said jocosely.

"No," Francis said seriously. "It's mostly other things."

Katherine had made her phone calls now, lying to everyone except the police. To the building society she said that Malcolm was unwell; he couldn't come to the phone, he was sleeping after a restless night. She said this in her best, her bored telephone voice, consciously removing the fact that she had, the night before, called the same woman in a state of panic, telling her about Malcolm's disappearance. She could hear the puzzlement at the other end of the line, and finally his secretary said, "But he seems all right."

Katherine said sharply, "No, he's not well."

"He's asleep at home?" his secretary said. "Are you sure about that?"

"Are you suggesting—" Katherine said.

"It's just that he phoned five minutes ago," the secretary said. "I was sorry to hear about his mother."

"His mother?" Katherine said. "Oh—his mother—"

"Yes, being taken ill like that—what I don't understand—" she went on, but Katherine interrupted her with apologies before putting the receiver down. She sat by the telephone, breaking out into a light sweat of sheer panic, her heart thumping, and in two minutes she dialled the same number and apologized—the confusion with Malcolm's mother, she'd meant to be phoning the children's, Daniel's school, it was Daniel, their son, who was ill. "I must be going round the bend," she said amusedly, "ringing the number next to the school's in the address book and saying Malcolm when I meant Daniel."

"That's all right," the secretary said, obviously thinking there were better things for her to be doing. She phoned the florist's, and this time, to Nick, but with even more of a telephone voice, it was her that was ill. "Eaten something," she said. "Awful bore."

Nick told her not to worry, he'd hold the fort; there was something almost enthusiastic about the way he said it, and then he apologized again for not making it to her party the other night. "I don't know what I was thinking," he said. She had forgotten all about that; almost all about that; but he had reminded her, and that absence, so painful and crucial, returned at once, shamefully battling in her mind against this now more urgent, more dutifully felt absence. To the police, she would have told the exact truth, but now she could only tell them that Malcolm had turned up safe and sound, and in a sense, so he had.

Thank God, with five of them, the washing was constant; thank God that supplied her with something to do. As far as she could see, going through the piles, then, her heart beating, their joint wardrobe, Malcolm had taken no clothes. What that meant, good or bad, she couldn't articulate even in her mind. She took it all downstairs, at least three loads, and deposited it on the utility-room floor. That was where the washing-machine, the boiler, the freezer, all sat together. It was a good thing with the washing machine; an efficient new one, its cycle went into passages of immense fury you couldn't make yourself be heard over when it had been in the kitchen. Even in the utility room, it made the walls of the house shake at its juddering climaxes. She put a load of washing in. That would be something to fill the time, that and the ironing. She could have welcomed the children going off to school, or at least engaging in some kind of holiday activity that would have removed them for a while.

As for her, back in the dining room, she looked out of the window at the activity outside. Then, quite abruptly, she decided to go and offer the new neighbours a cup of coffee. Get to know them. It wouldn't do to give the removal men coffee, and then be remote and stand-offish with the people you were going to live opposite. She stared, hard, at the unit, identical to her own, facing her house for anyone to see. Drawn out by that, she slipped on a pair of shoes and walked out of the house, leaving the front door open. "Won't be a moment," she called.

"There's Katherine Glover," Anthea Arbuthnot observed to Mrs. Warner, both comfortably settled at the window with the best view. "I thought she wouldn't be long."

"Why's that, then?" Mrs. Warner said, enjoying this.

"I wouldn't suppose she'd put up with all that cheap tat lying about in the road," Anthea said. "She's very hot on that sort of thing. Only the other night, she was saying to me that something or other, I forget what, was bringing down the tone of the neighbourhood. One of nature's complainers, I'd say."

"She works, she was telling me," Mrs. Warner said, not believing a word of Anthea's version, quite rightly.

"That's right," Anthea said. "But it's a very superior job, I believe."

"Those children, they're not very superior," Mrs. Warner said.

"Not at all," Anthea said. "Do you know, I think she's just going over there to take a better look. Some people really are appallingly nosy," she went on, but that was a joke, and both she and Karen tittered at themselves and their shameless vigil. "I don't think much of that suite," she went on. "I wouldn't have it in the house myself."

"Hello?" Katherine called, hovering in the front door, calling into the empty house. She didn't like to ring the doorbell when the door stood open.

"Hello," the youngest of the removal men said satirically, coming through with a single chair. "Mind your back."

"Hello?" she called again, and a woman her age, hair untidy, an expression of nervousness, came out into the hallway. At the same time, a pair of children, a boy, a child's face, but too tall, and a girl with an unusual forward stance, dark and unformed, came halfway down the stairs, stood and looked.

"Not there," an impatient man's London voice said from somewhere else, and then "Who's that?" as he, too, came through, his shirt sleeves rolled. The four stood there and looked at Katherine, almost as if puzzled. She gathered herself.

"That's very kind of you," Alice said, once Katherine had explained, had welcomed them to the neighbourhood, had suggested refreshments. Introductions had been made; Bernie had smiled quickly and returned to the sitting room. The children stayed where they were. "We'd like that—" but the children shook their heads, and Bernie had things to do. "Well, I would, anyway." Katherine would have liked to have a look round the house—she'd never really known the Watsons, and the layout of all the houses was slightly different—but in a moment she and Alice were going back together over the road, and Alice was asking what the previous owners were like.

"It's extraordinary," Alice said, "I hope they weren't great friends of yours, but . . ." and she explained about the lightbulbs.

Katherine laughed a little and, no, she hadn't known them well. "Come in," she said, with a big gesture. Alice had stopped halfway down the front garden path and was looking up at the front of their house. "It's wistaria," Katherine said, laughing. "You're shocked to see it doing so well up here, I can see, but it's had a good year, ours," and, seizing Alice's arm in a frank way, brought her into the house. "They surely didn't take all the lightbulbs," she said, and then she was explaining about the Yorkshire character. "You're from London," she said, not asking a question, and then was off on a great paragraph of generalisation. She could hear herself, how faintly mad she sounded, setting out what the people of Sheffield were like, and the people of the whole county too, all three ridings, "though we aren't to say ridings any more, that's all gone," their tightness with money, the way they wouldn't waste a word, their honesty and openness.

"I see," Alice said, evidently wondering a little as they came into Katherine's house. But Katherine went on, unable to help herself, and Alice helped her out with a banality she'd heard or read or seen, that there was a friendliness and openness in the north, which just wasn't there in the south.

"You won't find people keeping themselves to themselves in the same way here," Katherine went on, forgetting that she had said exactly that of the departed miserly Watsons, who were nothing if not Yorkshire, had, indeed, according to Katherine, embodied the manners of the whole county.

"I can see that already, the friendliness," Alice said, smiling awkwardly at this generous neighbour.

"That's kind of you," Katherine said. "But you'll find that we're all like that around here." She thought of saying that there were few people in the area who didn't keep their door on the snib, but fell silent: this new neighbour would quickly discover that it wasn't true, for one thing, and in any case it would have made the road sound a little common. She put the kettle on; she heard herself and her brave party voice, not able to be kind without making a comment on that kindness.

"Normally," she went on, "I'd be at work by now."

"Really?" Alice said. "Where do you work?"

"Well, it's quite a new thing," Katherine said. "I used to work, before the children were born. I mean, when I met my husband I was working at a solicitor's, and then, after we married, I carried on working, though of course there was no real need, not at the solicitor's, I didn't carry on there. I worked at a school, not as a teacher, a sort of administrative job. Do you know Sheffield? No? Well, you must go and have a look at Peace Square. Most of Sheffield was bombed in the war, but that, it's eighteenth century, untouched, really charming. That was where I worked, in the solicitor's. Of course, when the children came along I gave up work, though you know, then, I don't know if it was different in London, but it was quite unusual for a woman to go on working after she was married. You gave up, didn't you, when you married, not when the children came along? It was the done thing."

"Yes," Alice said.

"And, of course, the children—well, there were three of them, there are three of them, I should say, so it's only quite recently that I suddenly thought, I'm bored with sitting at home all day, doing nothing, I'm going to go out there and get a job to keep me occupied. And I did, and it's the best thing," she said emphatically, as if insisting on her point, "I ever did."

"Where do you work?" Alice said.

"In Broomhill—oh, you won't know—a florist's shop, a new one," she went on. "It's only opened a year or two. Nick, the owner, he's from London—he studied up here, and then he stayed, and he's opened this little florist's, and it's doing very well. He was supposed to come to a party here a night or two back, but something came up and he couldn't come. Actually, we were thinking, your house, we thought you'd probably be moved in by then and it would have been a good chance for you to meet everyone in the neighbourhood. That's when we were planning it, and we set the date, thinking, they must be in and settled by then, the Watsons, they'd been gone so long, and then the date was fixed and the invitations sent out and we discovered, my husband and I, we'd missed you by two days. What a shame! You could have met him then."

"Your husband?" Alice said. "I'm sure—"

"No," Katherine said, "Nick, you could have met Nick, except that he couldn't come. And you hadn't moved in. I meant Nick. I don't know why he didn't come. Go away," she said, raising her voice, as Daniel wandered into the kitchen.

"Your son?" Alice said, nervously taking a cup of coffee.

"Yes," Katherine said. "I'm sorry, I should have introduced you. How old are your children?"

"Well, Sandra's fourteen, and Francis, he's eleven," Alice said.

"So they'll be going to—"

"Going to?"

"I meant their schools."

"Oh—I think Sandra's, it's called—"

"The thing is," Katherine said, setting her cup down on the work surface and staring out of the window, "you've really found us at sixes and sevens this morning."

"I'm sorry," Alice said, thinking that the woman needn't have asked her over if it was as inconvenient as all that.

"The fact is that my husband's left me," Katherine said.

All at once there seemed to be an echo in the kitchen, and both Katherine and Alice listened to the noise it made. Katherine had spoken definitely, but she listened, now, to the decisive effect of a statement she had not quite known to be true; she listened to it with something of the same surprise as Jane, sitting on the stairs listening to her mother going on. Alice listened, too; she knew that some sentences needed to be treated, once spoken, with respect, left with a small sad compliment of silence.

"I'm so sorry," Alice said. "Was it very recently?"

"It was last night," Katherine said, almost angrily.

"I'm so sorry," Alice said. "Listen, I'm sure you really don't want a stranger just at the moment—it was kind of you, but I'd better leave—"

"Of course, you've got so much to do," Katherine said.

"No, it's not that," Alice said. "There must be someone who can come and—"

"No," Katherine said. "There isn't anyone, really." It was true. Her party rose up before her again; she found it difficult to call any of them a friend, and impossible to imagine, say, sitting with that pregnant girl and telling her anything. "I don't have any friends."

"I'm sure it just feels like that," Alice said.

"No," Katherine said. "It's true. I've never had any friends, not really. You have friends at school, people you think are friends, but you lose touch with them afterwards. They get married, they go off and live on the other side of the city. And really all you had in common with them was that you were sitting in the same room with them most days, and when that stops, you don't have anything much to talk about any more. And the people you work with, when you work, you leave, you say, 'Oh, we'll stay in touch,' and you mean it, and they mean it, but you don't. Maybe you see them once in a while, just bump into them, and they tell you what they're doing, their children, and you tell them what your children are doing, and then you go on and nothing ever comes of it.

"My God, you're wondering, what have I walked into?"

"No," Alice said. "Don't worry about that, I'm fine. You can talk to me, I'm here."

"There isn't anyone else," Katherine said simply. "I thought about Nick. Nick, he's my boss, he runs the florist's. I thought he was, you know, my friend, but he isn't, not really. I'm just counting them up. There are the neighbours—they're just neighbours, really. There are other people—I used to meet these women for coffee in the morning, but . . . Can you imagine? They say, what—'We're thinking of redecorating our lounge,' and you say, 'That's interesting, my husband's left me.' They wouldn't be able to say anything back. And Nick—I'll tell you something. It's all about Nick, really. I'm sure it is."

"What do you mean?" Alice said. She felt that this woman had really forgotten the situation; she had forgotten that Alice wasn't just a passing acquaintance she'd never see again, but someone who from now on would live opposite her. She, after all, was now exactly one of those neighbours and Katherine didn't seem to understand that.

"I've been silly about him," Katherine said, "I suppose. I like him, a lot. Well, he's honestly not anything like most people in Sheffield. His brother lives in New York."

"I see," Alice said.

"I don't have a brother in New York, I don't know anyone who does," Katherine said. "He's funny, he's really funny, when he talks—that's the only way I can put it. And, you know, I've been kidding myself about him, I see that now. Because he's a bit hopeless, really, and I've helped him out, I've kept him going, or so I thought, and he must have been quite grateful for it, or so I thought. But I had a party, it's the first party I've had for I don't know how long. Malcolm, he just doesn't like the idea.

"It would be a nice idea, you know? I said so to Malcolm. I said, I said wouldn't it be nice if we had a little party for when the new neighbours move in, not just for that but for all the road to meet each other because these days, people, they don't know each other, not because—but—well—I don't know. I don't know why people don't know each other these days. My husband, Malcolm, he works in a building society, but he's got lots of interests, outside interests, and he does know people. You wouldn't think it to meet him, but he's got all these friends through his societies—he's keen on gardening, he's in a society, and of course there's the battle re-creation society, too—"

Katherine, so measured in her speech, had begun to loosen and quicken, her voice now free and bold, her vowels quick and emphatic with the speech of her Sheffield childhood. It was as if for years now she had been answering the telephone under observation. The voice was liberated from constraint and full, of all things, of new love.

"Battle re-creation?" the new neighbour was saying, puzzled.

"Yes," Katherine said. "It's an odd thing. They re-create old battles—they dress up, once a year or so, they act out old battles, just as they were, on the moors. Of course it's usually the Civil War, that's usually it—they can't stretch to different uniforms every time, but once they joined forces with a society from Wales and they did the battle of Waterloo, that must be ten years ago. It takes a lot of work, it's only once a year. Malcolm loves it. He's got friends through that, you see.

"But most people, these days, they don't have the time, and they don't really make friends with their neighbours particularly. I didn't expect Malcolm to agree to the party, but he did. The kids, they weren't around—I can't remember why not—oh, it was—well, we were on our own, and it was a nice moment, not that I'd engineered it or planned it to get a favour out of him. But I asked and he said straight away, 'Yes, let's have a party.' He said it straight out, and he gave me a big smile, and it was something I'd asked, and it was something he could say that would please me. You see, he wanted to please me."

"He sounds a nice man, your husband," Alice said.

"I think he is," Katherine said, almost surprised, it seemed, at the insight she'd been led to.

"And you know him best," Alice said.

"Do you think so?" Katherine said.

"Well," Alice said. "You know, I honestly don't know—I mean, I don't know you, I certainly don't know your husband but—"

She stopped. Katherine withdrew her hand; without her noticing it, she had reached out and rested it on Alice's. "I'm sorry," Katherine said, after a time. Something of her formal voice had returned; she might have been regretting the lack of stargazer lilies, late on a Friday afternoon. "I didn't mean to."

"That's all right," Alice said. "But you do know him best."

"I wonder," Katherine said.

"You must do," Alice said. "Married to him."

"Maybe," Katherine said. "It was just that moment. When he said, 'Yes, let's have a party.' He hadn't wanted to please me like that, not for years. He used to want to, it used to be all the time and you never noticed. You know when it's been dry, all summer, and then one day it rains; and then everywhere there's this smell of grass and earth and flowers, everywhere."

"Yes," Alice said. "Yes, I know that."

"But you never noticed it had gone, that smell," Katherine said. "And after a while, if it goes on raining, you can't smell it any more. It's just the air, it's just ordinary, you take it for granted."

"It was like that."

"Yes, it was like that," Katherine said. "But I'm so stupid. I always ruin everything, always. He said that, and immediately I said the thing I was thinking really. I said, 'Let's have a party,' and he said yes. And then I said we could ask all sorts of people, not just the neighbours, and he said, yes, we could, why not? I don't know who he was thinking of, or who he thought I could be thinking of. But then I said what I couldn't help saying, I said, 'For instance, we could ask someone like Nick.' And he didn't say anything. But I went on, I said, 'After all, he's never been here, he's never come to the house, it would be nice to have him over.' It was an awful thing to say, it really was. I said it anyway. I don't know what he said back. Maybe he said, 'Yes, why not?' but it was awful for him. I don't know what I've been doing to him. I couldn't help it."

By now they were sitting. Alice looked away from the beginnings of Katherine's tears. The kitchen was brilliant with elective cheerfulness, constructed with wallpaper and blinds and spotlights; its morning yellow sunlit and shining with well-kept order and cleanliness. But there was a woman weeping in it, somehow. Alice had walked lightly across the road, and found herself in a place without landmarks. She looked out of the window tactfully; incredibly, her family were there, getting on with the unloading.

"You'll be wanting to get back," Katherine said dully.

Alice turned back to her. Probably better, she told herself firmly, that the woman tell her all this. She was going to have to tell someone, and better her than one of the woman's children. There were things your children should never hear. She'd forgotten the woman's name. That was awful, and now surely irreparable.

"That's all right," Alice said. "It's better that you tell someone."

"Yes," Katherine said. "That's right. It's better I tell someone like you all this rather than the children. Or a neighbour."

"Yes," Alice said, startled. "Of course, I am a neighbour now."

"Yes," Katherine said. "Yes, I suppose you are."

"Listen," Alice said. "Do you mind if I ask you something directly, because—"

"Depends what it is," Katherine said, smiling, wiping her face with a tea towel—the Beauties of Chatsworth, Alice registered irrelevantly. There was something cheeky in her recovering voice; it wasn't true, Alice thought, that you saw what people were really like only in a crisis.

"You don't have to tell me anything at all," she said. "You really don't. But is that really the whole story?"

"The whole story?"

"I meant about Nick," Alice said. "Nick? That's his name?"

"Yes," Katherine said. "About Nick?"

"You and Nick, I mean," Alice said.

"Me and Nick," Katherine said. A formality came into her voice again as she saw what Alice had meant. "No," she said. "I'm not having an affair, if that's what you're suggesting."

"Yes," Alice said. "That was what I was suggesting."

"Well," Katherine said, attempting a light laugh, "I suppose you did ask permission to ask a direct question, and I don't know a more direct question than that. No, as it happens, Nick and I are not having some sort of mad passionate affair. I suppose there isn't an enormous amount of point in my saying that. I wouldn't be very likely to say anything different to you if we . . ." She paused for a second. ". . . we were in fact having an illicit affair. But one doesn't happen to be."

"No," Alice said. "No, I believe you." It was true. She did believe it. Oddly, it was the way the note of deception had crept into the woman's voice that convinced her. The woman, whatever else she was, had no gift for lying, and in most of what Alice had heard from her, the note of helpless truth had been audible. It was only at that point, asked directly if she were, in fact, having an affair, that the voice had started to listen to itself as if to monitor its scrupulous lies. And yet the voice was telling the truth; Alice had no doubt of that. The woman was not having an affair, as she said. But Alice had touched something secret and cherished; she had touched, surely, some characteristic and elaborate pretence. Katherine had lapsed into what, surely, was her usual allusive and interior style where Nick was concerned; she had treasured him up and made a precious mystery out of him before the only audience she had, her husband and children. There was nothing there; Alice could see that. But she'd played it out, and he'd believed what she'd wanted him to believe. The woman sat there in her kitchen, looking firmly ahead, away from Alice. She was smiling tautly, her expression now as she wanted it to be, and that must be bad to live with. An affair would be better; that was something to forgive, to walk away from. To have done nothing wrong, to make a secret of nothing, to coach yourself in the gestures of mystery and deflection, to turn your head away to suppress a manufactured expression of recalled rapture, all that, daily; from that there was no walking away.

"Where's he gone?" Alice said.

"Malcolm?" Katherine said. "I don't know. He's just gone."

"He didn't say anything?" Alice said.

"Nothing," Katherine said. "Not even a letter."

Alice looked at her, seriously wondering. "He's just disappeared?" she said.

"Yes," Katherine said. "Just like that."

"But—" Alice said. "Sorry, but—I mean—are you sure that he's not—well, it could be anything, it could be—"

"No," Katherine said. "He's all right. I know that. He phoned his office this morning. I don't know where from. He'd do that—he'd phone the office so as not to let them down. Me—" She left it at that. "No, he's not hurt or in an accident. If that's what you mean. He's obviously left me. He told the office that his mother's been taken ill and he had to go over there all of a sudden."

"And she hasn't been taken ill?" Alice said.

"Not urgently," Katherine said, and started laughing, an ugly sound. "Not—"

"She's dead, she's been dead for five years. I'm surprised the building society didn't remember that when he said so. It's a stupid thing for him to say to anyone. Honestly, I don't have any doubt what's happened."

"I see," Alice said. She didn't see at all. There must be other solutions to this situation; she just couldn't see what they were.

"It's just the waiting," Katherine said.

"Yes," Alice said. "I can see that. Not knowing."

"When there's some news," Katherine said, "that won't be so bad. Then I'll know where he is, what's happening, even, God forbid, if he's done something stupid, but then we'll know, there'll be things to do. It's the not knowing."

"Yes," Alice said. "Have you talked to the children?"

"No," Katherine said. "Yes. Well, sort of. Not all this. There'll be time enough."

"If I were you," Alice said, "I'd just go and sit with them. You know, be all jolly and cheerful, as if nothing much has happened. They'll be worried, too. I don't know, go and help your little boy, show an interest in the snake, that sort of thing—"

"The snake?" Katherine said. "How on earth did you know about Tim and snakes?"

"Well, I saw him," Alice said. "In the window."

"But how do you know—"

"He was holding it up," Alice said.

"A snake?" Katherine said. "He hasn't got a snake. He never shuts up about them, it's snakes from the moment he wakes up, but I promise you—"

Alice looked back at her, and, incredibly, felt herself starting to blush. "I'm sorry," she said. "I didn't mean to tell you anything you didn't know. But he's definitely got a snake up there. When we were walking up your drive, I looked up and there he was in the window with a snake round his neck. I'd better be going."

Outside on the stairs, Jane had been listening to quite a lot of this. The kitchen door had been taken off, long ago, or perhaps there had never been one, she couldn't remember. There was a sort of open-plan idea going on, and whenever anything was fried in the kitchen, the smell carried right upstairs, the light patina of grease settling on almost everything throughout the house. You could hear anyone talking in there, too. She'd heard everything her mother had to say, but this would bring her out of the kitchen, and Jane got up briskly and walked back to her bedroom. In a second her mother was following her; up the stairs at quite a trot, you could hear. "Timothy," she said, raising her voice, "Timothy!" and into his bedroom. Jane came out on to the landing; so did Daniel. Downstairs, the new neighbour was standing in the hallway; she looked a nice woman, and tried a smile, a confused one, on the pair of them. The moment for her farewell was on the far side of some terrible family scene. She just stood there. Jane would have done the same.

"Is this true?" Katherine said, in the doorway of Tim's room.

"What's this now?" Daniel said.

"Tim's got a snake," Jane said to Daniel.

"Is it true?" Katherine said.

"Is it true what?" Tim said. He had got up from his bed, had backed nervously away to the window. "I haven't done anything."

"You heard what your sister said," Katherine said. "Have you got yourself a snake?"

Tim said nothing for a moment; his fingers, behind him, running fretfully along his little shelf. "I'd love a snake," he said forlornly, but his regular request, so long overlooked or greeted with the same brief riposte had lost conviction. "I really would."

"Do I have to hear from the neighbours that you're hiding a snake in the house?" Katherine said. "Where is it?"

"It smells in here," Daniel said, coming to the door of Tim's room. "It really does."

"I haven't got any kind of snake," Tim said.

"Are you lying to me?" Katherine said. "What's under your bed?"

"Nothing," Tim said, breaking out into a wail, but Katherine was already on her knees, dragging out the glass case with one, then two hands. She pulled it into the middle of the room, and knelt there, staring at the thing. It was like an aquarium of air; littered with small rocks, little toys and, ignoring all of these, curled up, was a snake; thirty inches long, yellow, skinny and ugly. With a gesture of disgust, Katherine got up, pushing the case to one side, and stared at Tim. He started to cry, turning his face away.

"What is that?" Katherine said.

"Let's have a look," Daniel said, coming in and peering at the thing.

"It's—please don't—I didn't mean—"

"That," Katherine said, "is a snake. And where did it come from?"

"I—I—" Tim said, but it was all too much, and his tears overcame him.

"You can't keep it," Katherine said. "There's no argument about that. It's going straight back to wherever you got it from."

"What's he called?" Jane said.

"Geoffrey," Tim said, through his tears. "I only wanted a snake called Geoffrey."

"How do you know it's male?" Daniel said, looking closely. "Look, he's seen me, he likes me—"

"The man in the shop said," Tim said. "And, besides, you can tell the difference between male and female by—"

"That's enough," Katherine said, not letting Tim set out his expertise; it was the way he comforted himself. "It doesn't matter what it is, it's going back to the man in the shop. My God, it's not dangerous, is it? You've not been as stupid as that?"

"No," Tim said. "He wouldn't hurt anyone, he wouldn't. I take him out, I talk to him. You can tell he's not venomous, because the venomous ones, generally—"

"If I want to know about fucking snakes," Katherine said, beyond everything now, "I'll ask for the information and I won't have to think about who to ask, I've heard enough about them now. I could write an essay on the subject with everything we've all had to listen to. All I want to know now is where it came from and then you and I are going to take it back there. And I'm going to give the man in the shop—" and, as she said that, she dropped into an awful, mincing voice of parody, nothing like Tim's voice, but just the voice of loose cruel mockery "—a piece of my mind for selling anything, let alone a snake, to a small boy on his own. My God, what must he have been thinking of?"

Tim's tears, which had been drying up, burst out with great force, and downstairs Alice, still hovering and listening, decided that she would not be missed, and should probably not hear this. She tried to feel pity: not eleven o'clock and all this deposited on top of the situation. But Katherine had sworn at her child, and had spoken to him not even as a sardonic teacher speaks, but as one child to another, a bully in the playground. No one should be heard speaking like that, and Alice let herself out quietly.

"I didn't mean to," Tim said.

"Of course you meant to," Daniel said, apparently enjoying the situation. "You must have saved up for months."

"Years," Tim said. "I thought you'd like—"

"Of course I don't like it," Katherine said. "How do you open this thing?"

Tim, crying, said nothing, and Katherine got down on her knees and fiddled with the case. With a single quick gesture, she reached in and took the snake with both hands, one hand behind its head, the other about its tail, and stood up. The snake buckled and writhed in mid-air, astonished and frightened, its tongue flickering in and out. "Don't take him back there," Tim said, dashing at her and trying to seize her arms. "He doesn't like it there, please don't—"

"All right, then," Katherine said, nearly smiling, "if that's what you want—"

And she walked out of the room decisively and down the stairs, the snake in her hands, her children following her.

. . .

"That was Caroline," Mrs. Arbuthnot said, coming back from the telephone. "You know, nice young thing, she works as a nursery nurse, very pregnant, I mentioned. She says she's just setting off now so she'll be here in five minutes, tops. I'll go and put the kettle on."

"Oh, good," Mrs. Warner said.

"No, I won't, she's coming out again," Mrs. Arbuthnot said, sitting down. Over the road, Alice had opened the front door of the Glovers' house and closed it behind her, very gently. "She's been a time."

"Saw herself out, I see," Karen Warner said. "Too much trouble to take your guests to the door to say goodbye. Manners."

"Terrible," Mrs. Arbuthnot said. "Would you have said that she enjoyed herself, meeting the Glovers?"

"Well," Mrs. Warner said, observing Alice treading, very gently, down the path, as if trying to escape without being noticed, casting a glance upwards at the house. "I expect it was very nice for her, really."

"Yes," Mrs. Arbuthnot said. "Very nice. All the same, I think I might pop over there when they're a little settled. You don't want them to be thinking that we're all like that, do you?"

"Like what?" Mrs. Warner said, rather sharply; she didn't altogether approve of being superior about your neighbours, even if they probably deserved it, particularly two days after you'd drunk their wine and ate their food and admired their furniture.

Mrs. Arbuthnot, who would have said exactly the same thing, hastened to qualify her point. "Not all the same," she said. "People, they aren't all the same, are they?, even if they all live in the same road, and it's nice to meet—well, anyway. It was a nice party she gave."

"Very nice," Mrs. Warner said. "Of course," she went on, offering Anthea a little concession in return, "I'm not sure about letting those children stay up, cluttering up the party. A little out of control."

"The boy," Mrs. Arbuthnot said, enjoying this part of the conversation. "The girl, of course, she's not so bad, but I agree, I wouldn't have them around, any kind of children, particularly when they're at that difficult age. I notice you didn't think of bringing your John along."

"No, I certainly didn't," Mrs. Warner said. "If you ask me, it's nice to have an evening without your great lump hanging around and embarrassing you, and it's not as if he needs a babysitter. They are a worry, though."

"A worry?" Mrs. Arbuthnot said. She remembered Mrs. Warner's John, hopeless. Mrs. Warner explained.

"Well," Mrs. Arbuthnot said finally. "I'm sure it'll all come right in the end. Now—goodness—what—"

Opposite, the front door of the Glovers' had opened again. The removal men at the new people's house, the new family, the husband, the girl and the elongated boy, as well as their mother, were all standing outside in an awkwardly arranged group, and had an excellent view. Through the door of the Glovers' came Katherine. In her hands she was holding a—what was it—something limp but flexible, like—

"That's never a snake she's got there," Mrs. Arbuthnot said. "It is, it's a snake. Goodness me."

"Where's that from?" Mrs. Warner said. "Not the garden, surely."

"I never heard of—" Mrs. Arbuthnot said, but she dried up at what was happening. Behind Katherine and her snake came her younger boy, screaming and crying, tugging at her ineffectually, and the two others standing by. The windows were shut, but the boy was screaming, "You fucking, fucking mother," as Katherine marched down the path.

"Disgraceful," Mrs. Arbuthnot said. "He can't be more than—"

"Eight," Mrs. Warner supplied. "Imagine. Look, here's Caroline—"

But the nursery nurse, just heaving herself down the road, coming into view, stopped dead at Arbuthnot's gate, and, like the new family and the removers and, inside, Anthea and Karen, watched Katherine and the children.

"Don't you ever—" Katherine was screaming at her son, who was screaming back. "And if you ever do anything like that again—this is what happens when you do something as naughty as—"

She ran out of words. She didn't seem to see anyone else around her; the snake, held between her two hands, she raised above her head in a bold, a dancer's gesture, and flung it down on the pavement. "Stop it, stop it!" Tim was screaming, over and over, but she raised her foot and brought the heel of her black shoe down on the snake's head, crushing it in one. It flailed behind her like a whip. The screaming rose, went beyond words, and the little boy's face purpled with terror and violence. His limbs flailed away from him in undecided, unformed gestures, as if some invisible force was plucking at them, and he screamed and screamed. Behind him, his sister turned away and, with a gesture too theatrical to be anything but instinctive, covered her eyes. Over the road, the new people, the Sellerses, stood and stared, and you couldn't blame them.

"My God," Mrs. Arbuthnot said in her house, and Mrs. Warner's mouth moved, and it formed the words without being able to say them. Only Katherine, across the road, seemed composed: she had done what she had meant to do, and now it was all done, all over, and she stood up straight, paying no attention to her screaming son. But had it been enough? There was, surely, a little uncertainty in the way she scanned the houses, at whoever might be watching what she had so publicly done. The doorbell rang.

"My God," Anthea said, hurrying to let Caroline in. "Did you see—" she said, opening the door.

But the nursery nurse, enlisting the doorjamb to support her bulk, was muddily pale, grey to the point of greenness in the face; she had seen it. And it had been all too much for her, the sight of a woman, a mother, flinging down a snake almost in her path and then stamping on it, the snake's head making a vile porridge on the pavement, and then the screaming—Caroline leant forward, as if in a swoon, and Anthea came forward with her arms open to catch her. But she leant forward in a single shy apologetic motion and, for the first time in several months now, vomited over Anthea, vomited copiously over the small glass coffee-table, the hallway rug, the art-deco figurine of a Greek dancer Anthea had always meant to have valued, everywhere.

"My God!" Anthea said—it was all too much and, with a little scream, she ran upstairs, plucking at her puked-over bosom as Caroline, still bubbling over, tried to raise herself up and start apologizing.

"It could have been worse," Mrs. Warner said, coming out gingerly, and trying not to look, guiding the poor girl into the downstairs clock-room, trying to help her without actually touching her. Because if there was one thing she hated—

The van was quite unloaded, and the removers gone, and Bernie had fetched thirty lightbulbs, half bayonets, half screw-ins, a mix of sixty and hundred-watt bulbs, and Alice, Sandra and Francis were sitting in their new sitting room, the furniture somehow arranged. They were surrounded by sealed boxes in the evening light, eating a kind of scratch supper off their knees, just for tonight.

"Sounds like she's not all there," Bernie said.

"No," Alice said. "She'd had a shock."

"I don't blame him," Bernie said.

"Who? Oh, her husband," Alice said. "That's an awful thing to say, love."

"Well, I don't," Bernie said. "I'm worried at the idea of living opposite someone like that."

"She must be mental," Sandra said.

"Imagine what it'd be like being married to her," Bernie went on. "You wouldn't be blamed by anyone, really, for leaving her. Mentally unbalanced."

"We don't know," Alice said. "It might be the shock, your husband ups and goes. That's a terrible thing to happen."

"No, love," Bernie said. "Anyone normal, they just get on with things. They don't—"

"She took the snake," Francis said meditatively, telling the story bit by bit, almost more for himself than for anyone else, "and she threw it down and she jumped on its head until it was dead, and it was the boy's snake, and he was there watching."

"That's about the sum of it," Bernie said. "It's not normal, whatever's happened to you. It's not still lying there, is it? Christ."

"No," Francis said. "The girl, his sister, she came out a while ago with a plastic bag and a broom, cleared it up and threw it away, and she washed the pavement down, too."

"Thank God for that," Bernie said. "Someone in the family's got a bit of sense, apart from him, the dad, had the sense to walk out."

"Poor woman," Alice said. "I wish—" She dried up and took a forkful of Russian salad from her plate of cold food. It was like the supper of a Christmas night, the dinner she'd arranged for them the first night in a new house, and the events of the day similarly cast a sensation of exhausted manic festivity over their plates.

"What do you wish, love?" Bernie said.

"I don't know," Alice said. You couldn't say to your husband and children that you wished you'd kept the information of this woman's situation to yourself. You owed her nothing, you wouldn't keep anything from these three. But she still thought she might not have repeated any of that. "I bet he'll be back," she said, surprising herself.

"Why do you say that?" Bernie said.

"I don't know," she said. "I just think he will be. He doesn't sound like the sort of man who wouldn't come back. He works in a building society."

"She sounds mental," Sandra said. "Killing the little boy's pet like that in front of him. I wouldn't mind a snake as a pet. If she couldn't have it in the house, she could have found a home for it. Oh, well, who cares?"

"You're not to be getting ideas," Bernie said to Sandra, "about snakes."

"No, I don't really want one," she said. "But killing it, that was horrible."

"Yes," Alice said. "It was horrible." But she felt—

She felt what Katherine, across the road, felt.

Katherine was sitting on her own in the dining room. The table was empty and not set; there was no food and Katherine had not prepared any. The children had been into the kitchen and had picked up what they could from the fridge, from the cupboards; children's meals, the sort of thing they arranged for themselves between meals, coming home from school. At least Jane and Daniel had; Tim was still upstairs, gulping and muttering to himself in his room. The last time she'd looked, his face was in his pillow and he refused to take it out at any expressions of regret or apology. Inconsolable. It was just too bad for him; and he liked his food. She didn't worry, not for the moment. What she felt was that the primary drama of the day, the awful thing that had happened to her, was Malcolm's disappearance. But that, now, was inside and had only happened to her. What had taken its place, and remained in its place, was what she had done in the street: stamped on her son's snake at the utmost pitch of despair and rage. Malcolm would come back, there was no doubt about that. That would finish the story in everyone's memory; his disappearance, for whatever reason, would end up being trivial and anecdotal. What would remain was not what had been done to her but what she had done. In the dining room, only the small lamp on the piano was switched on, and the room was dim and gloomy, a pool of light in the blue evening. She sat, her hands on the table, like a suspect in a cell; she breathed in and out steadily, knowing what she had now made of herself. And in time night came, still with no word from Malcolm, whom everyone had now apparently forgotten.

Eventually she got up, switched the lights off, one after another, and went to bed. Over the road, the lights were still on. She looked at her watch and it was only a quarter past ten.

Malcolm came back two days later. She had stopped caring. That morning, she had taken the rubbish out, and over the road, the new people, they'd been coming out at the same time. She had been prepared to pretend that they hadn't seen each other—she just didn't want to think about the things she'd said to Alice. And she'd thought they would probably want to do the same, ignore her politely. Maybe, in a few months, they could pretend to be meeting for the first time, and everything could be, if not forgotten, then at least not mentioned, and they could both pretend they had forgotten. But Alice obviously didn't know the rules of the game. They were getting into their ridiculous little car, some kind of small square boxy green thing, and Alice saw Katherine with her boxes of rubbish, the remains of the party, the empty bottles, the smashed glasses, the chicken carcasses, which had been attracting flies outside the back door waiting for the binmen's day. She hesitated, evidently not knowing what she was supposed to do, and raised a hand. It was a gesture that might have been a greeting, or might have been the beginning of her scratching her head.

Perhaps it might have been possible. Perhaps if Malcolm had never left, she'd now be wandering over, asking how they were settling in, when the children would be starting school, offering advice about plumbers and local carpet-fitters, meeting the children and the husband, inviting them over for a drink with Malcolm and her children some time in the next day or two. But it was hard to see how she could manage that on her own. Alice didn't seem to understand the rules of the situation. All the other neighbours did: the day before, Katherine had been walking slowly down the road, and the door to Mrs. Arbuthnot's had opened, issuing Mrs. Arbuthnot, a scarf on her head and a shopping trolley, setting off for the supermarket. Mrs. Arbuthnot had seen her approaching, and rather than continue and be forced to meet or ignore her, she'd performed a small pantomime of forgetting, slapping her forehead almost and shaking her head, going back inside until Katherine was safely past. Katherine blushed. Of course, she couldn't know anything about Malcolm yet, could only have wondered about him not coming home, the car no longer in the driveway, or maybe she'd seen the business with the snake, heard Tim's wailing. That sort of ignoring would not go on for ever, but only until these things were not the most recent and conspicuous subjects to talk about in a chance encounter. But Alice didn't seem to know that, and raised her hand uncertainly. Her husband, opening the car, saw the gesture, and looked over the road to where Katherine stood. He waited, watching in the interested way of someone who hadn't met her yet. Katherine smiled, but she could not wave because of the bags in her hands. She put them down, turned, and went back into the house.

"I'm sorry I didn't come to your party," Nick said, when she had got to work. "I was terribly looking forward to it. I don't know what happened. It was all a bit chaotic. I went home and called my brother, you know, in New York, and then I sat down with the paper, just for five minutes, before getting dressed and coming up to your party, and all of a sudden I woke up and it was four hours later. I don't know what happened—it must have been getting up so early for the market. And then, of course, it was far too late to come. I felt such a fool. I was so looking forward to it."

"That's all right," Katherine said, stripping the leaves off a box of roses, her sleeves rolled up over her reddened forearms, Marigolds protecting her hands. They were white roses, just flushed with pink at the ends of the petals; lovely, unlasting. She had her back to him, her face down, concentrating on her task, and she let very little into her voice.

"Was it a good party, though?" Nick said.

"Oh, it was just the neighbours mostly," Katherine said. "You'd have been bored."

"Don't say that," Nick said. "I'm sure I would have loved it. Nobody ever asks me to parties. Well, there's nobody I know who would invite me to a party, apart from you. I feel such a fool."

"Don't be hard on yourself," Katherine said, but there must have been something wrong with the way she said it, because Nick came up behind her and put a hand on her arm, as if he was about to turn her round to face him. The touch of him: she actually flinched. She could not endure the sensation.

"Don't be cross with me," he said, taking his hand away. "I can't bear it if you—if anyone, I mean, if anyone's ever cross with me. It's just something I hate. It's so silly, too, to fall out over something like that."

"Oh, no one's going to be cross with you," Katherine said. She meant it to come across contemptuously, but it came out wrongly, as a confession of loneliness. Nick's statement, which ought perhaps to have been that admission of loneliness, had instead been amused, self-reliant, adding to his confidence rather than anything else. Katherine had assured him that nobody could possibly be cross with him, and the words had their face value, a confession of admiration. All at once she was in tears, and gulping, trying to wipe her face with her arm and scratching herself with the rose in her yellow-gloved hand.

"Katherine, don't," Nick said. Without turning she could not tell whether concern or embarrassment would be in his face, but in a moment he took the rose from her, laid it on the pile, the right-hand one, of prepared roses, and he turned her round, her face lowered, not ready to meet his eyes and what might be in them. He so rarely used her name. No one did.

There was still quite some laundry to get through; that had been neglected in the days before the party and now it was keeping her busy. At home, she set the dinner to cook, and went through into the utility room to get on with it in the meantime. The children were in the sitting room, watching the noisy television they all seemed to get something out of. A year or two before they had extended the house. A garage had been built on the strip of land to the side, and what had been the garage, separated from the house, was turned into the dining room and, behind it, an intermediate sort of room, leading from the dining room into the garage.

After dinner, that evening, Katherine went back to the utility room. She had to do something to fill her mind with blankness. You could not hear the telephone from there, but the children would get it, and fetch her. Anyway, there was nobody to ring her, and if it rang, it would only be one of the children's friends. The washing-machine had done one load—shirts and blouses—and was now starting on another, underwear. Normally, she would have transferred the shirts to the tumble-dryer, a newish acquisition, but today she wanted the chores to keep her busy, and she was ironing her way through a damp pile.

The door opened, the one from the dining room. It was Malcolm. She stopped and looked at him. He was wearing the suit he had been wearing that day, but a shirt she had never seen before, and no tie. He's been buying new shirts while he's been away, she thought, with a flush of anger. There were no children behind him; they'd probably taken themselves upstairs, whether to bed or just to be on their own. They'd been avoiding her, but now she didn't care. After all, he'd come to see her first.

"Are you back?" she said harshly.

"Yes," Malcolm said. "Yes, of course I'm back."

"I was worried," she said.

"Yes, I'm sorry," Malcolm said. "But you know why I went like that."

She stared at him, and thumped down the iron. "No," she said. "No, frankly, I don't know why you went like that. I haven't the faintest idea." She had to raise her voice; the washing-machine with its noisy rhythms was going into the racket of its spin cycle.

"You want me to tell you?" Malcolm said. "All right," and he started to speak. He was telling some sort of story, and in his hands, his face, you could see the weight of the conviction behind the story; telling what had led up to this, and what he had been doing the last few days outside the house, where he had been. His face went from pleasure, enjoyment as he thought of something, and rage, pain, irritation and puzzlement. He came into the utility room, and started walking up and down. But she could hardly hear any of it. His voice, always rather soft and low, stood no chance against the furious racket of the washing-machine. She watched, fascinated, and in all honesty not all that inter-ested. It would probably be better, in the long run, not to know. She knew, afterwards, exactly how long Malcolm's explanation had taken, because it was the exact length of the spin cycle. It took four minutes and twelve seconds. The spin cycle came to an end, juddering across the amplifying concrete floor, and made one or two final groans before going into a quieter reverse. It was Daniel and Tim's socks in there, mostly black.

"So that's it, really," Malcolm said finally.

"Yes, I see," Katherine said.

"I don't think there's much point in going over and over it," Malcolm said.

"No," Katherine said. "I'll not be bringing it up, asking for details. We'll just get on with it."

"Exactly," Malcolm said. "That's the best thing, just get on with things, don't go on about them."

"Yes," Katherine said. "The new people moved in over the road."

"Oh, yes?" Malcolm said. "Nice, are they?"

"They seem nice," Katherine said. "Why don't you go and say goodnight to the children?"

"Yes," Malcolm said. "I'll do that. I suppose I could just tell them—"

"No," Katherine said. "Just tell them you're back. That'll do."

"Probably best," Malcolm said. "All right, then."

There seemed to be something more he wanted to say; perhaps he could see in her face that in the last few days something had changed for her as well. But what would he know? For Malcolm, nothing in the situation as he knew it had changed; Tim had not had a snake under his bed, and still did not have a snake under his bed; his wife's conceal-ments remained his wife's concealments; and he was back where he had always been. In a few days' time he would wander across the road, drop in on the Sellerses, ask them over for a drink, and they would come over, none of them mentioning at any point any of the things he had caused or missed, and everything would be quite all right. "Is there any supper left?" Malcolm called from the stairs.

"There's a bit," Katherine called back, but her answer was lost as the doors upstairs started to open, and something like conversation began again, and even the children pretended that there was nothing so very extraordinary, as there indeed was not, in their father coming home in the evening, the only cause for comment a shirt not seen before, the only remarkable detail a man in a suit, and no tie, and no sign of a tie anywhere.

Book Two

NESH

Afterwards he could never accurately reconstruct the rules of the game. The game and its rules had come from nowhere, like myth or tune. It disappeared afterwards, leaving no trace in memory, not even its name, perhaps still being played by generations of children who discovered it, just as Francis had in the autumn of 1974, in a playground and lost it again within the year. But preserved only in that way. What he had in his memory was the sense of a chase, a circle of tremulously linked limbs, some raucous and pungent chant, and, more, the ecstatic terror of wriggling as the quarry turned and buckled under the hand of the pursuer, the ecstasy whichever way the roles had fallen that day; above all, a thick, vivid rise in the chest at the promise or the enactment of violence which, years later, he identified with some shock as an adult sensation, the sensation of erotic desire on the brink of fulfilment. It had been some form of chase, that was all; surely it was the subsequent recognition of its banality that removed its exact excitements from the memory. But a game of chase alone could not have accounted for that speechless thrill, ending with the crack of bone against concrete, a stifled and jubilant cry. There must have been something else.

The school building was new. The school had been recently transferred from an old and blackened building further up the hill to something modern. The old school was a decorated stone edifice, conspicuous with Victorian aspiration and benevolence; with its two entrances, still inscribed BOYS and GIRLS, it looked very much like a school. The new one, oddly, did not. Built in yellow brick, a single storey, the whole shape of the building was difficult to construe as Francis and his mother had crossed the empty playground, that first morning. The building bulged out at either side of a wide external staircase, burst into angry and fanciful geometries of brick and glass, sagging unexpectedly on to rounded banks of grass and, already, well-trodden flowers. He held his mother's hand tightly. An odd pair, given his height; but he held his mother's hand tightly.

Inside the building, they made their way somehow to the headmaster's office. He contributed nothing to this, allowing his mother to make the enquiries, follow the signs, and only when they were sitting on two out of the line of five chairs, the kind lady remaining behind her desk, did he realize that he could not rely on his mother to lead him round his new school from now on. But waiting there, his main concern was for her: in her clothes, the tight smile which was in her mouth but not her eyes, there was something he ought to be able to console. He wanted to tell her that it would be all right, not altogether knowing that himself. But now the headmaster himself was coming down the corridor, buoyant from his assembly; down there, a daunting flood of children, all of whom he would shortly have to come to terms with, all of whom knew exactly where they were going.

The headmaster was affable; the secretary on the way out smiled kindly; a kiss had come from nowhere; and suddenly he was walking by the side of a teacher who, apparently, he had been introduced to, who, apparently, was now his teacher. His mother was gone. It had been her kiss. Once, when he was much smaller, he had in a moment of confusion in a classroom said, "Mummy . . ." before realizing that he was addressing his teacher. He went clammy, as if he had already done it again, as his first act in a new school.

"Quiet, now," the teacher said, coming into a room. It was full of children; they fell silent and looked at him. It was a terrible moment. The teacher had an extraordinary voice. She talked, too, in that strange way, as she went on to explain who he was, where he came from—London, it produced giggles across the classroom—and assigned a boy to show him round; she talked in that way where "castle" sounded like "cattle," a blunt and, to Francis, not very friendly-sounding manner of speech. He was surprised and ashamed on her behalf: he had not thought that a teacher, a person in charge, would speak in the ordinary way everywhere.

The boy he was supposed to sit next to shoved up roughly, and turned his face deliberately away from Francis, placing his hand against it so that Francis could not see anything of him. He was a naughty boy, you could see that straight away; he started hissing and sniggering to two other boys, naughty boys too, across the aisle, who leant forward and examined Francis from a safe, contemptuous distance, their lips curling like crimped pastry. He thought about his friends; they might be sitting at this exact moment, hundreds of miles away, in that sensible classroom, not just-built but old and solid, and there might be—his heart leapt to think of it—an empty chair there now, and perhaps a new person, someone a little like him, being guided to it.

The lesson started, but no one had taken out any books: they were just sitting there. Francis had been dreading that; he thought that he might be the only one without the books, and though everyone would notice no one would help. He had imagined he would go through his whole life in this school without books and, which he had anticipated and accepted, without friends. But there were no books. He placed his pens and pencil, the ruler and rubber on the table; he had brought them with him. He could not understand what sort of lesson this was. The teacher was just talking, and in a moment he listened. It was a while before her words started to make sense. She was talking about the government. He did not know what sort of lesson that could be part of. From time to time she asked a question, and nobody put their hands up so she answered it herself. Some of those questions Francis knew the answers to, but he didn't put his hand up. It was like a party you weren't sure you were meant to be at and he kept quiet, though it was painful for him not to be able to put his hand up to answer a question he could answer. The boy next to him went on talking to the boys over the aisle, and there was a sort of malice in the hiss, which was directed at Francis.

"Michael," the teacher said abruptly. That was the boy's name, which Francis hadn't taken in, and the boy straightened up, lowered his hand from his face, and gave Francis a poisonous look, as if he had betrayed him. There was a smell as if of boiled peas from the boy; it was shocking, he was sitting next to a bad boy who wasn't even clean. "Do you want to tell the class the name of the prime minister?"

"Don't know," Michael said eventually, full of scorn at being asked something so stupid.

"Perhaps our new boy knows," the teacher said, quite gently.

"It's Mr. Wilson," Francis said. He hardly knew how to pretend not to know.

"Very good," the teacher said, enunciating with surprise in her voice, as if talking to an idiot. Francis felt himself getting a little cross. "And how long has he been prime minister?"

"He was prime minister before," Francis said. "But there was a general election this year and he became it again. He's Labour. I thought the Conservatives were going to come first, but they didn't."

"Very good," the teacher said, now really surprised. "Quite a lot of people thought, like—like our new friend from London here"—a wave, a giggle, but why?—"that the Conservatives were going to win. Now, who can explain to me what a general election is?"

The lesson went on, but Francis felt he shouldn't have said anything, should have said, "Don't know, Miss," and swapped what he possessed for something he might have, popularity and the quality of being ordinary. Once the attention of the teacher went elsewhere, the naughty boys on the other side of the aisle said, "Kick him," quite loudly, and Michael, the boy he was sitting next to, gave him a hard angry shove. Francis did not know how to respond, and blushingly rearranged his pens and pencils, his ruler and rubber. In time, the lesson came to an end; it was interrupted—and it had only really been a speech by the teacher, diversifying into reminiscence of a life led partly, it seemed, in Africa—by a bell that, so unexpectedly, was exactly the same as the bells in the school in London. The class got up, their chairs screeching on the floor, and the teacher, too, screeching for them to sit down until they were given permission to go. But half the class were already through the door, and she only wanted to say one more sentence before they were dismissed.

It was playtime. The boy he had been assigned to had disappeared and, anyway, Francis would not follow that boy: he knew well what would happen if he tried to make friends, having said in clear London tones who the prime minister now was. He didn't know what to do or where to go, but he followed them anyway, and was soon in the playground. It was already full, and excited with noise.

All of a sudden, a boy was by his side, addressing him.

"Do you see that girl?" the boy said. Francis recognized him slowly. He must be in his class, he supposed; but there was some familiarity apart from that.

"Yes," he said, though he did not know which girl the boy meant.

"I think she's so beautiful," the boy said. He was a strange boy: his voice was not ecstatic but robotic, as if he was producing an interesting fact. "Venus was the Roman goddess of beauty so I call her Venus."

Francis did not know what to say to this. The boy was looking away from him across the playground. It seemed that he hadn't actually been talking to Francis at all, not specifically. His buck-toothed face was flushed, his hair stuck down against his pink forehead. He called out, "Venus, Venus, my love, my love," and ran away towards the girls. At this they scattered, giving little screams, running off in twos and threes, severally. Francis was alone again; he stared at the concrete in furious amazement. He was alone again.

Francis concentrated very hard on walking round the complete edge of the playground. He pretended that the narrow stone edging to the asphalt square was a tightrope, suspended hundreds of feet above the ground, and he balanced on it carefully, placing one foot in front of another. That was a game you could play on your own and, after a few moments, he forgot almost everything. With arms spread out like wings, he really was walking a tightrope, forgetting whether it was a good game or just something to make yourself look occupied. He was three-quarters of the way round the square when he hit a flight of steps, interrupting its clear progress. On it there was a group of boys and girls mixed up together. He dropped his arms.

"Were you talking to that Timothy?" a boy said, addressing Francis.

"He just came up to me," Francis said. "He said he was in love with a girl called Venus and then he ran off again."

"He calls me that," a girl said. Francis wouldn't have recognized her: she seemed ordinary, not an object of devotion. "I wish he'd stop, it's stupid, I hate him, he's mental."

"Where do you come from?" one of the girls said. "You're in our class."

She rhymed it with "lass," but it wasn't unfriendly, her tone. "I come from London," Francis said.

"She's thick, that Barker," another girl said. "You've got put in the worst class you could be put in. They put people there for punishment, she's that boring."

" 'When I was in Africa,' " a boy said. "She should talk to that Timothy, he's always on about snakes when he's not calling you Venus."

"I'm called Andrea, really," the girl said. "I don't know where he got Venus from. I'm going to tell my mum if he carries on."

"She's always saying that," the boy said. He raised his voice into a dull shriek. " 'When I was in Africa.' "

"Aye," they chorused appreciatively. It was a party trick of this boy's, you could see, the shrieking imitation of, who?, Miss Barker's voice and her usual sentence. " 'When I was in Africa.' What's London like?"

"It's all right," Francis said. "We lived outside London, really."

"I've been to London," a girl said.

"You never," one of the boys said. "You're a right liar, you."

The consensus of the group was that it was obviously a lie, to claim to have been to London. But Francis was surprised: he thought everyone, always, had been to London. It wasn't anything to lie about.

"You don't want to sit with that Michael," a boy said.

"He smells a bit," Francis said.

They all laughed; one of the boys clutched his sides, and pretended to roll about on the ground. "You're a right one," a girl said. "But it's true, he's got a right pong. Miss Barker, she always puts people next to him who can't refuse, it's like a punishment, and you have to sit next to him for an hour. She doesn't mind people who pong. It comes of living in Africa. 'When I was in Africa—' "

"Well, you've only had the miserable torment of sitting next to Smelly Michael for an hour," a sensible-looking boy, in neatly pressed trousers and a short-sleeved grey shirt with a sleeveless home-knitted sweater, said. "You can come and sit next to me, if you like. I've not got anyone sitting next to me because Neil Thwaite's in hospital. He's got something wrong with his blood."

"I heard he's going to die," a girl said.

"No, he's not," the boy said. "I saw him in the hospital, he's bored. But he's in hospital a while, so you can sit next to me."

"She told me to sit next to that smelly boy," Francis said. "At my school in London, you had to sit where you were told and then you stayed there all year. I didn't mind. I was next to Robert who was my friend. But won't I get in trouble if I move?"

"No, no," they shouted.

"Anyway," the boy said, "if she asks, you say, 'I can't sit next to that Michael because I'm allergic to the smell he puts out, it makes me sick and I can't answer questions and my hand wobbles when I write.' That Michael, his family, they live in a maisonette, they're right poor. You can sit where you like, so come and sit next to me."

"He didn't know who the prime minister was," a girl said. "I'm Sally, and that's Paul, and that's the other Paul, and—"

"He was going to be kept back a year because he doesn't know anything," Paul—Francis's new neighbour—said. "But his mum came down and she shouted and they let him go up anyway, but he knows nowt."

"He knows—"

"He knows nowt," the other Paul, the impressionist, the playground raconteur said. "Don't you know what 'nowt' means?"

Soon, that vocabulary, like the shared and tender vocabulary of friendship, was clarified, and Francis was tenderly aware that if he had walked out of that classroom with near-tears of fright and isolation, he had walked back in surrounded by six immediate friends, and his near-tears were from a different source. They were the last back in, and Francis felt that a wave of shy surprise and interest went through the rest of the class, admiring and envying the bold step that that mixed and sophisticated group had taken in befriending the boy from London without waiting to see what the general view was. Francis felt full of pride at the step he had taken here.

The game began every day at half twelve, once they'd finished their doled-out lunch, bolted it down. Sometimes, too, at half ten and quickly at the quarter-past-two playtime as well, till the luxurious expanse of the game they could play at dinnertime to the point of stitches in their sides seemed almost improbable next to the swift trailer of its morning, its afternoon versions. Francis was absorbed here, both anonymous and accepted, whether a blank member of a playtime cadre, or a person with conspicuous friends, but in either case protected.

At break—that was what they called playtime, whether a more serious or just a more Sheffield word—the game began again, returning to the beginning and each time, somehow, getting a little bit further. It was as if with each attempt they had got a little closer to its essential heart, to some prize it concealed, like a team of adventurers taking turns to whittle at some initially unpromising and rude block. Inside there was some prize.

That was it, the allure of the game. Though there was not and could not be any real prize, it seemed far more like a formal, famous game, the sort you played under gracious adult supervision at a celebration, a birthday party, and yet infinitely more violent and exciting. It did not seem like a playground enterprise of shamefaced silliness, of rhymes and stomping that no adult could be allowed to hear, but like a brilliant expansive entertainment with printed rules, played in your best clothes, but with the dazzling promise of unconstrained fury, too. It was a game that should have been put away for best occasions, and was played, irresistibly, every day.

But outside the game and its allotted hours, his social standing was obscure. He felt himself good at the game through something barely commented on by others or previously noticed by him: his height and swiftness. He had grown up into this scale and, in London, the moment to observe any change or the disproportion had never presented itself. But to arrive here in such a state, taller than anyone else in the class and faster too, as the game proved, made him obvious to them and to himself. In the playground, and to his immediately acquired circle, that was something fine, dangerous, admired; outside it, it seemed to make him only conspicuous.

One day, during PE, Miss Barker set them a race in the playground, a relay race between four teams. Each runner was to touch a marked-out point at the middle of each straight border; Miss Barker marked them, and those were the rules. The first runners from each team set off, and ran along the border of the whole playground. It seemed that they had not understood, and when it came to Francis's turn, third in his team, he set off directly, running only between points, carving a small diamond like the points in a game of rounders. He was not stopped, and got home twice as fast as the other teams; the other runners in his team followed his example, and the others, doggedly, to their longer route. He had done the right thing, it turned out, but his height and swiftness, as well as this spirit of enterprise, had marked him out.

A few weeks after arriving, at the beginning of a lesson, as they were sitting down red-faced and busy after morning playtime, Miss Barker came into the classroom. The fourth years had been in the classroom before then, and on the board was an abandoned impatient tangle of x and y, the obscure and useless corners of the alphabet, mixed incredibly with numbers, some normal-sized, some shrunk and sent to the top of a letter like a scratch on the forehead, symbols poetically abstruse and, for the moment, as blank as the hieroglyphs of a kingdom disinterred from the sand; a frail language occasionally glimpsed about the school that it seemed impossible he, or any of them, should ever comprehend or, like French, converse in and, looking at it, he brought a measure of wilful ignorance even of those fragments he could have understood. Miss Barker sighed, sagged. "Francis," she said, her eyes not quite alighting where she spoke, "could you come and clean the blackboard before we start?" She had not quite addressed him by name until then, not since she had introduced him to the class, but Francis was up quickly and taking the board rubber from her somewhat unwilling grasp. "Yes—all right then," she said oddly, with a half-smile to his side that he didn't understand, and let him do the task, slowly and seriously. It was the first task he'd been asked to undertake in front of the whole class, by name; now they couldn't go on calling him "new kid." There was a sort of buzz in the room. When he had finished, he went back to his seat. The two girls behind him were scowling at him, and as he sat down, one of them—yes, her name was Frances, wasn't it?—kicked his chair hard.

"She di'n't mean you," the girl said, not lowering her voice, and Miss Barker, before embarking on another of her unplanned and circuitous "lectures," an improvised and loose chain of her morning's happenstance thoughts, was pleased to say, "Well, Frances . . ." she paused like a skilled comedian awaiting what indeed came, an appreciative laugh . . . "I'm sure you can do it *next* time. If our new friend from London will let you." As if he had no right to his own name, and she'd politely forgotten it out of good taste. The class laughed, and not at the old woman. Francis felt heat in his face.

"He's right tall, that new kid," the girl behind him said derisively to her glued-on friend at the end of the "lecture," meaning him to hear. "It looks ridiculous, being as tall as that. Someone ought to say something to him, that new kid." And then it was time for the game again.

"She's horrible, that old Barker," Anthony said, as they were sitting on the steps, wrapped in coats and scarves, Anthony's coat a broad yellow check, handed down from a brother, with orange mittens hanging from his wrists by sewed-on strips of elastic.

"She's mental," Susan said, a nice girl with an always blocked nose, the snot perpetually at the rim of her nostrils; she had hair like a dog's. "She's boring and mental, too," she said. "The way she goes on, one thing after another, it makes no sense. Are you supposed to be taking notes, or what?"

"And mardy," one of the Pauls said—one of those words, Francis was working out what it meant, the limits of its meaning, and then he'd be using it too.

"I say," Andrew said—he was addicted to this archaic opening style, odd in his Sheffield voice, or in any voice, these days, and had once asked Francis shyly if he had ever heard of a book called *Jennings*, "it was before you came, you know," a tactful way of saying the unmentionably rude, alluding to a time when your friend didn't exist, "but our last teacher in Two CL, she was ill once a whole week and we had Barker, and she just came in and lectured like she does now, and we were meant to do maths and geography, all sorts. Well, she said then that once she were out on the moors driving with a friend, she said, and she sees a little boy by the side of the road and she, they stop and, and they say, 'Can I give you a lift?' and the little boy says, 'No, me mam says don't take lifts off strangers.' And she said, 'Well, isn't that a shame, that you can't offer a child a lift, when he's on his own, out on the moors?' "

"I wouldn't get in a car with that Barker," Francis said boldly, and they all laughed.

"That's it," Andrew said, quite seriously. "I told m'dad, and he reckons that, you know the Moors murders, when they done them kids in, over Manchester, he reckons that after them, they were shut up, there were some more murders, and he reckons they didn't get all the murderers. So m'dad, he says, do you think that old Barker, she's one of the Moors murderers and she never got caught?"

He was so serious in his face, and it made Francis jump when Sally gave him a scoffing push. "Your dad never said that," she said. "Not your dad. You're mental, you."

"No, though," Anthony joined in, quite crossly, "there were this kid, right—"

"Oh, shut up," they all said, and went to play the game.

The girl who sat behind Francis was called Frances, and beside her, her best friend was called Tracy. They had been each other's best friends since the very first day at infants', when they'd been sat next to each other, and they'd always be best friends. They had each other, bossing and sniping, and Tracy thought Frances the loveliest name in the world. She wished she was called—well, not Frances, that wouldn't make sense, but a name that was lovely just like Frances was a lovely name. She thought about it all the time, about not being called Tracy.

"Why did you call me Tracy?" she said to her busy mother in the hall of their Crosspool house. It wasn't the first time she'd asked.

"I just liked the name," her mother said. "Are you putting your coat on, or do I have to do it for you?"

"I wish I was called something else," Tracy said.

"You'll be late for Sunday school," her mother said, "if you don't get a move on." They were out of the house now, the door shutting tight behind them, her mother taking Tracy's hand.

"Why's m'dad not coming to church?" Tracy said.

"He's got to work today," her mother said.

"I wish," Tracy said, but she stopped herself; she was about to say that she wished her dad didn't work in a coal mine. "I wish I was called something else."

"There's nothing wrong with 'Tracy.' It's a nice name," her mother said, not knowing what Tracy had been going to say.

I wish my dad didn't work at the mines, she thought. It took all those explanations. What does your dad do? He works for the Coal Board—not down the mines, he's not a miner, but he works at the mines, he works up at the top, he only goes down the mine sometimes, he doesn't work down the mine. She wished he had another sort of job, a job like, for instance, the job Frances's father had, managing a supermarket. What does your dad do? "Oh, he's a bank manager," she heard herself saying. "I wish I was called Sara," she said out loud

"Sarah?" her mother said. "Why the heck is being called Sarah better than being called Tracy?"

"Not Sarah, Sara," Tracy said. "There's no h, you say Saaara."

"The heavens preserve us," her mother said, "and what's that on your face? My Lord—" and outside the church, she whipped out a handkerchief, spat on it, and rubbed briskly at Tracy's face. "How you manage to get a smut on your face ten seconds after leaving home, I'll never understand."

"Frances doesn't go to church," Tracy said. "She says they don't believe it. They go to the garden centre usually."

"I dare say," Tracy's mother said, not hearing this for the first time, "but in this family, we go to church."

"Is Frances going to go to hell?" Tracy said.

"I've had enough of your cheek for one morning," her mother said, hissing under her breath as they took their places in one of the back pews.

So on Monday morning Roy, Tracy's father, set off for work with a feeling of rank injustice at having had no weekend. On a Sunday, too, he observed. It wouldn't have been so bad, but living right on the other side of Sheffield, it was a good half-hour in the car even on a Sunday morning, and for what? Sometimes he felt like insisting on moving back to where he'd come from, five minutes from the pit. But she was right, really; the schools were better on that side, and with the way he'd moved up from the job his father had done, hacking away in the dark, to a job up top, managing and holding meetings, making decisions in a suit and a tie every morning, it was as well to live somewhere else. These days, particularly. It used to be that the managers lived a street or two from the men, but nowadays those bigger houses, imposing as they were, were lived in by miners just the same or lay empty.

The traffic wasn't too bad, apart from the roadworks on the Wicker, which had been going on for months now, and he was in the car park at quarter to nine, locking the yellow Capri and striding into the office with his hard black lockable briefcase. The car park was full; the men, too, had their cars now, and they'd had to reserve the management's places, each job described with white paint on the asphalt. The charcoal buildings, the meccano towers and conveyor belts had a temporary air, like the great heaps of slag all about; even the sign at the entrance and the gates were cheap and temporary, like the signs on building sites.

He said a quick good morning to Carol and Norma. "You're meeting John Collins at eleven thirty," Norma called after him.

"I'd not forgotten," he said, as he shut the door to his office. Collins was the NUM man, not as bad as some; they were the same age, they'd been at school together, and they got on as well as could be expected after last year's shenanigans. After all, Roy was a miner, had been, and his father; that still counted for something. "I'm down below first, if anyone wants to know," he called, already pulling off the jacket of his suit, hanging it carefully on the coat hanger on the hook behind his chair.

There was nothing particularly wrong; Hoppelton, the mine manager, liked the management to go down the pit at least once a week, whatever was up. Some of them did it at the same time each week; Roy liked to be a bit spontaneous, talk to the men, keep them on their toes. Monday morning was as good as any other time. The girls knew not to come into the office without knocking firmly on the plywood door and waiting for a response. He opened the door of the grey metal locker where the miner's outfit was kept. He neatly untied his tie, undid his tiger's-eye cufflinks—they matched the fat orange-and-brown tie, Tracy's present to him last Christmas though chosen with her mum (they smiled at him from a frame on his desk). He undid his shirt, hung it up, his trousers on the hanger, bouncing them a little to keep them pressed, and then his vest, pants and socks, folding them neatly and placing them neatly, with the rest of his clothes, in a suit-carrier to take over to the pit baths.

It was important to undress completely before starting to put on the miner's kit; it wasn't strictly procedure, but he liked to keep these things separate. Everything was kept separate; there were even underpants handed out from Stores; a bit like being in the Army again, he'd thought the first time he'd collected some. He'd never quite got used to putting on communal pants, owned by the mine, the NCB, the

Government, he supposed in the end. But he wasn't going to buy himself his own special pants. More trouble than it was worth. They were grey and frayed, but as clean as they could be got. The socks, and then the bright orange all-in-one plastic-coated boiler-suit, the hard inflexible plastic boots with the metal toecaps, and with the helmet and gloves, he was ready to go. "I'll be two hours," he said to the girls as he left, walking through the office, his suit carrier in his hand, with a completely different walk from the way he'd walked in, stomping as he went. They nodded; they'd plenty to be getting on with.

"Morning, Mr. Dewmiss," the man said at the pithead.

"Morning," Roy said. The man took two metal tokens, one square, one with its corners shaved off, octagonal, dropped one in a slot and handed the other to Roy. He looked at the number—never been able to help it—four hundred and forty-eight. In his head he divided, and divided again—224, 112, 56, 28, 14, 7. It was just something he did. The more you could divide, the better the morning would be, and halving six times was a very good day. He couldn't have explained that to anyone.

Presently, with a rattle and a roar, the cage came up, a fragile box in a fragile set of supports. The man pulled the concertina doors open, just like a liftman in a shop, and with ten men he stepped in. The doors were pulled to, and with an electric beep, the lift plummeted; you never got used to that. The only light as it made its choking, banging fall, hitting the metal struts as it fell, came from the single weak bulb in the roof, loosely wired up like a casual arrangement. The men had been talking noisily at the top but, as they always did, they shut up at this point. The lift seemed to hit something immense and soft, some elastic substance, slowed agonizingly; you felt it might reach the bottom and bounce back. But it hit bottom, and they opened the doors and set off.

There was a longish walk at first, down passages wide and clean as a hospital's, held up with metal struts. The older miners said they preferred the old wooden ones; said they groaned before they gave way, you had a chance to get out before the roof caved in. There might have been something in that, but then again, it was generally the wooden struts that gave way, not the steel ones. A string of lightbulbs festooned the way and, after ten minutes, he came to a little buggy. All around, the noise and thud of the mine was gathering, concentrating; it was like being inside a huge body, and listening to the remote thunder of the heart. You were inside the earth here, and it might have been the earth's heart that was beating, not just the roar of distant machinery. They set off, Roy and three men, down less established passages, the roof a little lower, and they started talking again. He found he knew two of them; one, Cavan, he was famous, a champion amateur ballroom dancer, and it turned out he and his wife, they'd just won third prize in a contest in Blackpool, two weeks back.

"In the Latin," Cavan said seriously. "My wife, she keeps on at me, have a go at the tango, but I don't know about that."

"No," Roy said. "Stick to what you're good at and you won't go far wrong."

The buggy only went so far; as you went into the mine, the passages were more and more provisional, the roofs lower, the heat greater, the sides just hacked out any old how. They came to the next stage, a roaring conveyor belt, laden with fragments of coal, and left the buggy. Over the belt, a temporary platform stood, like a viewing platform; Roy mounted this, kneeling on the platform, the roof touching his back, and, like a diver, dropped neatly on to the belt as it ran. It had been an advantage to him, being only five foot six; you suffered if you were much taller. On his hands and knees, his head up, he watched the approach, again lit by garlanded lightbulbs, of another platform, now facing this way. Roy half rose and jumped neatly on to the platform, almost like a cat, and, brushing himself down casually, he got out of the way of the man thirty feet behind him. It took a bit of practice, and a new man was always likely to lose his nerve at the crucial moment, be swept away beyond his commuting point.

Now the heat was getting fierce, and the coal dust flying in wet, sooty clouds; the drill was hosed down constantly as it worked, but the stuff still got everywhere. Roy followed one of the men into a narrow crevice, perhaps four feet high, and along towards the huge fury at the centre. The seam was a good one, and yielding beyond expectation; the men liked it, too, he knew, when they hit on a rich fresh seam, liked throwing it out in wheelbarrow loads; when there was nothing fussy about it, when it was more like demolition than dentistry. Not that they'd say anything. He didn't linger, no point, and shortly he was past the seam, and out into what now seemed almost like the open air, a passageway nearly six feet high.

He managed to get round a good part of the works, shouting questions as he went, and was back at the pithead by eleven. On the way back, as always, he was aware of following the great river of coal in the direction it took, following it up to the surface, leaving it as it went on its several purposes; left it as it poured thunderously on to one of those great black mountains, the stocks, and then, subsequently, off to be burnt, to make electricity. He went into the little building by the pit-head. There were no designated showers for management—another idea of Hoppelton's, that it was good for relations in some way too embarrassing to delve into—but the men's showers were empty at this time of day. You weren't likely, having once been a miner, to be shy, though. You couldn't get it all off; you could always tell a miner from the rim of black around his eyes, like make-up, like, ridiculously, one of those pop singers. He peered into the little mirror, and, with fistfuls of cold water, scrubbed at his face. It was almost all off, all but a touch here and there, in the odd crevices of your face. Nothing like a coating of coal dust to make you realize the contours of your face, like a shifting and private geology. If he didn't hurry, he'd be late for the man from the union. He dried and dressed. There was a patch on his back he hadn't reached; his shirt stuck wetly to him there as he hurried across the car park, the cold of the surface air cutting him. Like a knife, he said to himself.

The fragile sense of a protected existence Francis felt from his membership of the game playing group, he couldn't talk about that. The others, the core players, didn't seem to notice it or value it. If they had any kind of status in the playground, they seemed indifferent to it. But the glamour was real, and by the beginning of December, there were twice the number of regular players there had been. With enlargement came a kind of sour irony, an aggression he couldn't encompass, and not all the regular players were, or seemed at all likely to become, his friends. The size of the game was unwieldy now, and often it could only be played in the longer stretch of the dinnertime break. Those shorter breaks in morning or afternoon, they could be entirely absorbed in sour squabbles over the allocation of roles, which they'd never troubled with before.

One day in the playground, Francis saw a new thing, and it stopped him as he was running. Seven, suddenly eight, then nine girls in a ring, not touching, and they were singing a song. Their gestures were grotesque, full and parodic of something, like a mockery, a cartoon, but their faces were shining with a new revealed delight. "I'm Shirley

Temple, the girl with . . ." they were singing in full, hoarse voice, but just then one of the players, a new participant in their game, collided with Francis with deliberate force, sending him to the concrete ground where he lay aching and dizzy.

"That's you, you're spud now," the boy said vindictively, using one of the new terms of the game that had recently crept in, and ran off, spitting jubilantly on his hands while his friends congratulated him raucously on getting the new kid. Francis sat on the ground and watched this new game of Shirley Temple—he didn't care that it was a girl's game. They raised their skirts, explaining in song that she wore her skirts up there. Where had this come from?

"Are you playing?" Andrew said, helping Francis up again without offering him his hand.

"I don't like it," Francis managed to say, when the old group of players was assembled in their usual place on the steps after they'd finished their dinners. It had become a usual thing, and the new, the rougher players would saunter out in time. "I don't like it that there are so many new people playing. I think we ought to go back to how we were."

But he'd said something wrong, apparently, and straight away Susan said, quite rudely, "We were playing it long before *you* came, and if we're talking about new players . . ."

She didn't finish, but Francis was hurt. It was ridiculous, too; Susan didn't like them any better than he did. It hadn't occurred to him, though, that he might seem like a latecomer in any but the most literal sense. It must be absolutely clear to others as it was to him that his natural place, through niceness, was with the kindly, brave band of friends, whenever he had come along, and not with the unkindnesses of the interlopers.

All the same, his loyalty remained with the game at that transitional period, even while, every day, the new game and ritual of the Shirley Temple exchanges drew in more and more participants. A few days in, and there were boy players as well as girl, despite its obviously feminine nature and subject, and not necessarily the sissy ones, either. The boy participants, they made more of a pantomime of girl-behaviour during the game's verses, and exaggerated their boy-swagger to compensate between bouts; they drew their imaginary skirts up to the grey waistband of their trousers and made smacking busses with their lips to each other, before the end of the chant, and they fell in swaggering disorder to the floor, hilarious and shouting, and, almost at once, the song began a new cycle. It looked, frankly, exciting, but Francis's loyalty

remained with the game, their game, feeling like any formerly prosperous man who has over-extended himself carelessly, overestimated
the lasting appeal of the source of his prosperity, and telling himself
unconvincingly that if only the scale of operations could be reduced,
all would be as it was before.

He decided to tackle Andrew on the subject. Andrew was his best
friend. Francis had decided that. The tentative "I say," archaic but
Sheffield and inspiring no mockery in the group or anywhere else, was
probably a superficial link to the culture of London. But Andrew was a
reader, mostly; he knew Jennings, and he knew the Broomhill library,
which had so delighted Francis in the summer and which he was now
filleting week by week. They had both read all the Uncle books, Francis one book ahead, and were now deep in Professor Branestawm. The
dramatis personae provided them with a cryptic bond and a stock of
abstruse insults. The headmaster was Beaver Hateman, and Tracy,
Frances's weak-willed sidekick, was Jellytussle, and a dinner lady Mrs.
Flittersnoop, though she wasn't, Francis thought, quite worthy of it;
anyway, they couldn't be expected, the real people, to see the force of
these labels even if they heard them.

That was a bond, and so was where Andrew lived, at the top of
Coldwell Lane. They got the same bus home, the fifty-one, and got off
at the same stop. Once Francis had gone by slowly extracted invitation
to Andrew's, but it was a bit strange. His father worked at the university, and they lived in a big messy house at the end of an unmade and
unlit road. It was dark and frightening to walk down that road, even
with Andrew who did it every day, and there were shapes to either side
that might be broken walls, or bushes moving of their own accord, or
anything at all. Andrew you could normally get to do what you were
going to do anyway—he had four elder sisters and another, Angela, a
bit younger. But then, for once, walking down the unlit road, he had
been a bit impatient with Francis. "Come on," he said, "it's just here."
The house was alarming; you couldn't put it all in a van and move to
another one. In every room there were books, even lining up sourly in
the toilet, grey-backed and snobbish. It had no television, anywhere,
and was crowded out with burst and broken furniture. The worst and
dingiest of the furniture was in Andrew's narrow room with its one
well-ordered bookshelf; it had just ended up there, like the worn-out
adult phrases he had had to learn, and came out with, surprising people. The five sisters, each with the same long black tangled hair and the
same ugly pink glasses, the ones you got free from the optician, you

couldn't tell them apart, except for their different sizes. Only mooning Angela, scowling hungrily at him: she made Francis nervous in a different way from the others, and so distinguished herself. There wasn't much to play with, it turned out, and you had to get everything yourself—a glass of milk, that was all. Because Andrew's mother, he said, suffered from depression and would be lying down upstairs.

So after that one time they went to Francis's, and sat in his room upstairs. His mother brought them peanut-butter sandwiches, which Andrew had never had before, and sometimes, too, he stayed for tea, chattering through the stare Sandra kept giving him. "It's warm in your house," he said. "You don't need your sweater on when you eat. I expect you've got central heating."

"Yes, we do," Francis's dad said, amused.

"I expect," Andrew went on, still addressing his remarks to Francis, "that's because your dad works for the Electricity Board, doesn't he?"

"Anyone can get central heating," Francis's dad explained. "You don't need to have particular connections or anything."

"We can't, worse luck," Andrew said. "You see, my dad, he works at the university, and he says that wood fires are more natural and self-sufficient, and when they drop the bomb or the coal runs out, you know."

"And what's your poor mother think about that?" Francis's mother asked—the first snow of the winter had already fallen, and she sincerely hoped it wasn't a sign of how things were going to be from now on.

"I don't know what she thinks about that," Andrew said. "To be honest. She's mostly in bed, she's got severe depression. Of course, we can't all of us have baths every day. We've got a rota, on account of the hot water."

"Poor soul," Alice said, aghast, meaning his mother. "I don't think you should be telling everyone about your mother. She might not like it."

"It's an illness just like any other," Andrew said, repeating something and ending the discussion.

They were upstairs in Francis's room after school when Francis raised the subject of the new and violent players of the game. Andrew didn't say anything dismissive, as Susan had done. "I know," he said. "I don't like them either."

"They're Beaver Hateman," Francis said, but he faltered a little bit, not just because there were already other Beaver Hatemans between the two of them, but because in this case, Beaver Hateman no longer did.

"I say, Francis," Andrew said, although there were only the two of them there, "you know—before . . ." He paused, tactfully. It was a kindness in Andrew only to allude lightly, when Francis was in the room, to a time when Francis hadn't been there; it was like, in reverse, a disinclination to refer openly to a future time, after a certain event, by relations about the sentient bed of a moribund, and Francis distinguished even between the kind and friendly on the oversensitive basis of those who, like Susan, say, frankly said "before you came here" and those who, like Andrew, stepped about it with delicate paraphrases.

"You know—before . . ." Andrew said, " . . . there were the same people who weren't at all nice, not one bit, to me or Anthony. They used to throw bits of stuff at me in class—" He stopped. You could see the memory of some specific evolved cruelty, much repeated.

"But they don't do it now," Francis said, jollying him along. "They've stopped it now. They play the game with us. It's all different."

"Yes, they do. I'm not saying it's not," Andrew said. "But they only stopped when we started the game, like something they could see was fun. They're only joining in because we'd got something and they couldn't take it off us, so, you see—oh, I don't know—" But Francis saw: it was the game which, in its splendour, like a performance, had risen up and protected Andrew as it had him, the players like a posse of protectors, and with this infiltration by the envious and the sharp decline in its prestige with the glamorous, unchanging propitiations of the Shirley Temple game, that protection was going altogether.

"I don't want to play it any more," Andrew said bravely. "I'd rather stay in and read."

"You're not allowed to," Francis said, astonished at a terror he had never suspected could be more substantial and historically so much more deeply rooted than his own was, so thoroughly had Andrew kept it to himself. "You've got to go outside unless it's really snowing hard or something."

"I don't care," Andrew said. "I'll hide in the cloakrooms and read."

"It'll make it worse in the end," Francis said, conscious of the adult wisdom of this advice.

"I don't care," Andrew said again. "I don't want to play any more with them. I don't want to have to be friends with those people because they don't like me at all. Timothy Glover, he's really horrible."

"He lives over there," Francis said, looking out through the net curtains of his bedroom, facing the road, and the Glovers' tidy house, thirty feet below on this sloping terrain.

"I know he lives there," Andrew says. "He's always on the bus coming home, isn't he? He's mental, he's horrible, he's a spastic—" and then, with little encouragement, Andrew, the only son among five plain daughters, embarked on a story of hair-raising obscenity and violence, what Timothy Glover was generally supposed to have done the summer before his tenth birthday. Francis had heard it before, somewhat less elaborated, and listened again, believing and not believing it; he did think Timothy Glover was mental and frightening. His whole family frightened him. He wished they didn't have to live here, not exactly here.

"It's teatime," a voice came from downstairs. It was Francis's mother. "Andrew, are you staying?" she went on, her voice coming up the stairs. "Andrew? Francis?"

The two looked at each other; Andrew made a fake-dread face, shaking his head. Francis, with the deliberate sense of being adult again, shrugged his shoulders.

There was a knock at the door, and Francis's mother came in. "Are you staying for tea, Andrew?" she said; there was an affectionate tension in the way she avoided looking at Francis, and Francis remembered what Andrew once, spontaneously, had said, "She's dead nice, your mum." She was pleased that Francis, at least, had made friends so easily, she had said, when the compliment was relayed. And after that, it did seem to Francis as if it had been easy, however fragile the situation. "There's plenty if you want to ring your mother. You're very welcome, though it's nothing special."

"I ought to go home," Andrew said, laying emphasis, however, on the "ought."

"They won't notice you aren't there, with all those sisters of yours," Francis's mother said, but in a nice way. "It must be ever so noisy in your house."

"It's getting into the bathroom that's a problem," Andrew said.

He thought he'd better go home anyway, and got off the edge of the bed.

At the bottom of the stairs there was Francis's sister. She was called Sandra, and she was always around. "It's your little friend again," she said to Francis, as he and Andrew came downstairs, but her scoffing was genuine, done in a miserable, jeering, envious tone. She was wearing a purple loose-knit sweater with a draping roll of a collar, spreading across half her shoulders like a moulded pudding that had lost its shape; a pair of green Birmingham Bags, the square pockets at the side flapping against her thighs, her hair home-frizzed and bushy. She peered at Andrew, angrily, looking at him as if in investigation, closely; it was almost as if she had taken his head in her hands and was investigating the texture of his skin, her own being spotty and ruptured with splashes of dried blood where she'd picked at it. Andrew knew all about that; he'd seen it in his tartan-skirted sisters. "Yeah, OK," she said in the end, and turned away.

"What do you do," Francis said to his mother, when his father and sister were in the other room and Andrew had gone home, "if you don't want to be friends with someone? And they won't leave you alone?"

"I thought you liked Andrew," his mother said, raising her head from the dining-table; she was looking over a pile of cut-out adverts and typed letters; she had a pen and a block of that list-making paper.

"I do," Francis said, surprised. Then he saw the mistake she was making—he couldn't see how she could even think that. He said, "I didn't mean Andrew, he's my best friend. He thinks the same as I do, about these people. He doesn't like them but they won't leave us alone."

"Well, that's flattering, really," his mother said. "Why don't you like them?"

"I don't know," Francis said.

"It's often easier not to like people than to like them," his mother said. "You should think about why you don't like them. There's always something to like about people. If you made a bit more of an effort, if you weren't so picky, you'd end up with lots more friends. I'm not saying you don't have friends, love, but . . ." She put the pen down on the half-finished important list, cast a glance at the door Sandra might be standing behind. He was surprised: he hadn't known that his friendships or Sandra's were of any interest to his mother. All the same, she was wrong: those people, they weren't worth finding good in. "Tell me the whole story," she said.

"It's these other people," he said. "There's a game we play, and it was just us, but now there's too many people playing it, and they're not playing it properly, they don't want to be friends with us. It was much better when it was just a few of us. I don't like it now and Andrew doesn't either."

"Can't you go and play your game in a different part of the playground?" his mother said. "Or tell them to go and play their own game?"

"No, they'd come and join in, and no one wants to tell them to go away," Francis said.

"Well, I understand that," his mother said. "It's not always the easiest thing, to tell someone to go away. What about the teacher? Isn't there a teacher there, on duty in the playground? Couldn't you say to her that you want to play the game on your own, you don't want them to be pushing in the whole time? What about that?"

Francis felt horrified, and it must have showed; he couldn't begin to explain that participation in a game couldn't be considered a matter falling within official or grown-up jurisdiction. The process of adult appeal, which seemed so simple and plausible to his mother, was inconceivable to Francis, and he felt somehow that he had sharply broken some convention even in mentioning the matter to her. "I don't know," he said eventually, then, trying to be helpful, said, "I suppose we could always find a different game to play, me and Andrew and the others," thinking of the alluring Shirley Temple game, which, indeed, that day he had joined for the first time. But as if to confirm that his problems were, after all, laid out to the imperfect observation and understanding of his mother, she now gave an entertained snigger and said, "In any case, I was driving past the playground today and everyone seemed to be playing a big game of Ring-a-rosy. You're a bit old to be playing that, anyway, I should have thought."

It was painful, the apprehension of these several errors; the lumping in of the saucy and raucous vulgarity, so nearly adult in its humour, of the Shirley Temple game with something only known about as if from scholarly research, from classroom discussions, and in any case never played, in any case not called "Ring-a-rosy"; the idea that he was seeking escape from that game, rather than considering it a refuge; all these uncaring errors of his mother's hit him because, really, she did care, she did understand, and was only putting on her adult voice for a moment. "It'll be all right," she said, yielding a little. "You're lucky, anyway—you've only been there a couple of months and you're picking and choosing what friends you have. I wish . . ." She cast another glance at the door. It was true; Francis didn't feel overwhelmed with firm friends, but his sister, it seemed, didn't have any yet. He didn't see why that should be.

It was the next day when it all went wrong. In the morning before lunch old Barker went on about—what?—about the general election, about the Labour Party and why they'd won, about who she'd voted for, about her father, dead in the Stone Age, and something he'd said once, about this woman they'd made leader of the others, the Conservatives, and something about a new broom—it was almost frightening, listening to her mad, insistent, triumphant voice going on, and you knew there was nothing you could say about it, no one you could say it to, that feeling that this was what you were getting when you were supposed to be learning things, this mad old woman going on, very pleased with herself, saying the first thing that came into her mind, and no way of interrupting her, either. He had his head down on the desk and, with the point of a pen, was tracing and retracing a deep gouge made long ago by some other victim. If you didn't do something, anything, you might find yourself listening. It went on for fifty minutes, that voice, uninterrupted, insanely satisfied, and then suddenly stopped.

There was silence in the classroom, and then Andrew nudged him. He raised his head, and everyone was looking at him. "What do you think you're doing, young man?" Miss Barker said. He blushed, hugely; he couldn't explain it wasn't him who had made the mark, but before he could have said anything she was off on a flourish of triumphant unfairness about people from London, yes, London, who don't think we have anything worth respecting in the North, and in a moment, like a jubilant coda to a stupendously enlarged symphonic movement, Miss Barker's understanding of the nation's historical divide into North and South, oppression of labour by the effete, exemplified for the moment by the prevalence of pork butchers, the honourable trades of coal mining and steel manufacturing and one ten-year-old boy.

"Not you, young man," she said dreadfully, as the dinner-bell rang. "You're staying behind." There were, it seemed, many nasty stupid tasks for him to undertake, and for five minutes the supervising simper in her voice had an almost ecstatic quality. So he was late into the dinner hall, and when he arrived, his usual group, Anthony and Andrew and Susan and the others, they'd not been able to save a place for him—you weren't supposed to, but sometimes you could. They looked fairly stricken in apology.

The only place spare was with the people he didn't want to sit with, Timothy Glover and the other new players in the game. He sat down shyly. The others were noisier than his friends, and he didn't feel up to talking in his usual way; they might regard his ordinary London voice with proper hatred. If Miss Barker was licensed to display frank loathing of him because of where he came from and what he might be thought to represent, then the most conspicuous label of that side of his nature, his voice, ought to be kept subdued in front of people without any constraints. They sort of acknowledged him, surprised, jeering in tone even if their remarks were bland items of unspecific ridicule, unarticulated fragments of a general contempt towards any convenient and temporarily current element of school life. In fact, they seemed to be talking—not Timothy Glover, he was just shovelling it down placidly—but the others with their harsh Crookes voices, they seemed to be talking about football, about Wednesday and United. Francis couldn't have joined in, and it was, anyway, a strikingly adult, cynical conversation. Never in his life had Francis heard his father say anything about football. But this, nevertheless, seemed the sort of thing adults talked about. The subject might have been removed from Francis's interests, but it felt directed somewhat at him. The jeering tone of the conversation was pointed his way, surely, and after a few moments, one of them asked him who he supported. "I don't know," Francis said helplessly, and they laughed coarsely, as if it were a funny thing to say. He said only one more thing, when he wanted to have some tomato sauce. Wanting to pass, to erode the improper Southern noise in his voice, he tried to say "tomato" as a Northerner, perhaps, might say it. But he didn't know; the *a* wouldn't go easily into a short *a*, like one in "castle" or "bath" or "pass," and it came out wrong, ridiculous and apologetic. They asked him to repeat himself, unbelieving, and he just blushed and reached for what he had asked for. And afterwards they broke Andrew's leg.

The game began again after lunch, as usual. The others were sitting on the steps outside. Francis would have been sitting with them, and came out, not exactly with the others he'd been eating with. "Get that Jameson," one said, and one slapped Andrew on the back, the agreed signal for the beginning of the game, and Andrew was off and running, the quarry for the chasers. Francis held back, and so did Anthony and Susan and the two Pauls, not really joining in, just running loosely in the right sort of direction. But the others, the new ones, they were playing with some sort of commitment. Andrew yelped, and dodged, jinking through a forming row of Shirley Temple players, and someone's head, not his, was hit, hard, with the side of a hand. Andrew was a fast runner, and dodged well, but there were too many of them; he was nearly safe, had nearly got to the protected territory when two of the chasers, as if by arrangement, ran into him from different directions and pushed him, falling on top, on to the concrete steps, the agreed asylum. They got up, cheering; Andrew moved, and then shrieked, a high animal shriek. He had gone pale; around him, the players gathered, going quiet, and then the playground went quiet, everyone gathered.

"Don't move," a teacher said. "Just stay exactly as you are. Someone go and fetch the nurse," and half a dozen girls sped off, excited at this drama. Francis stood there, awed. Andrew just lay there, making no noise, his face absolutely white; the teacher was kneeling down and talking quietly to him. Quite suddenly, Andrew's eyes rolled back, and his head and neck collapsed limply.

"He's dead, he's dead," a girl shouted.

"No, he's not," the teacher said briskly. "He's just fainted. Everyone, please, just go away, we don't need an audience." They drifted away, but Francis stayed, hovering. The nurse came quickly, brushing them aside—it wasn't just him hovering, but some other people, not even in their year, people who didn't even know Andrew, too—and covered him with a blanket, telling him again not to move. The playground had stopped all its games, and the people in it stood around talking in small excited groups, drifting over to have another look in case Andrew might have died, then walking away again before they could be shouted at.

In a few minutes, an ambulance came, through the school gates and then, amazingly, signalled by another teacher, slowly through the playground itself, scattering people in its stately wake. It wasn't flashing any lights or anything. It stopped by Andrew, and two men got out with a different, professional red blanket. It all took fifteen minutes; putting Andrew in a kind of contraption, tying his leg up, putting him on a stretcher, and loading him into the back of the van like goods, joking all the time and Andrew, forcefully encouraged, responding more faintly. Then the ambulance's doors were shut behind him, and, with the same stately motion, the van drove off. "They'll be taking him to the children's hospital," someone said by Francis's side, and he turned to see that it was someone he'd never seen before who had spoken. There was no one he recognized around. They'd all disappeared, and he was in the middle of strangers again.

The afternoon began with another of Miss Barker's lectures, but after five minutes, a fourth-year came in and interrupted: the headmaster wanted to see the boys concerned. Miss Barker indicated Timothy Glover, and the other boy, the ones who had run into Andrew, and they left, grinning with bravado. Francis felt the empty half of his desk like a badge of grief; he felt ennobled in his loss. "Oh, it's all fun and games until someone breaks a leg," Miss Barker said suddenly; she had been talking about—what? About the seven hills of Sheffield? "I know, I've seen you all, it was bound to end like that. You in particular, I've seen—" and it was like a slow-motion slap, the way she turned again, with some kind of obscure adult delight, to Francis and his London badnesses "—I've seen you, chasing the girls and knocking them over, slamming right into them, making them cry. Well, we've heard of chasing the girls and making them cry before, haven't we, Georgy-Porgy? There's one thing absolutely certain, that sort of carry-on, it's going to stop right now, because we've seen where it ends, and when I see the headmaster, I'm certainly going to tell him," and by now she was almost singing, almost some playground song, never written down, never had to be, I'm GOING, to TELL him, "where I think it's all come from, and I don't think it's the young men who he's talking to now. What do you think? Georgy-Porgy?"

That night, he told his mother and father about Andrew breaking his leg like that; it was a serious story, he told both of them together. He left some of it out; he made it sound like an accident, and he didn't really explain about the game, the way it had been going sour. He didn't go on, either, to say what Miss Barker had said afterwards, the way she'd alighted on something to call him, Georgy-Porgy; it was a name too silly and childish to repeat, and the deliberate humiliation, like the immediate dread of new loneliness with Andrew in hospital, belonged to something that couldn't be easily told, what he felt, not what had happened. She might not call him that tomorrow, Francis explained to himself, she might forget it, he tried to insist to himself.

He finished telling what he had to tell, and took a pear from the fruit bowl on the table. "Poor boy," his mother said. "We'll find out what hospital he's in, and go and visit." Francis snapped off the stalk of the pear. They were bought pears, soft and grainy, not like the hard-fleshed wooden ones that had grown in the back garden of their house in London. He had liked those better.

"I'll give his parents a ring," his father said. "See if there's anything practical we can do."

Francis explained that a phone was one of the things Andrew's family didn't have.

"That's just ridiculous," his mother said.

Francis took a big bite from the pear; he liked the audacious way you could eat a pear, not, like an apple, round the middle then the end bits, but from the very top to the very bottom, leaving nothing but a sort of little plug of twiggy papery brown bits, a sort of belly-button, it kind of looked like.

"When you think of it, in this day and age," Francis's father said. "I can't imagine how the school managed to let them know he'd broken his leg in the first place."

"They'll have phoned the father at work," Francis's mother said. "Well, I suppose we could go round there, see if there's anything . . ."

Francis sat there, not contributing; the flesh of the pear, gritty, almost sandy, its taste like—like—. He tried to think, took another bite, concentrated. "I know where he is," he said in the end. "He's in the children's hospital. I can go and visit, can't I, anyway, I mean, not ask his mum and dad, do I need to?"

"We'll go down tomorrow," Francis's dad said. "I'll take you, as soon as I get home from work."

Andrew wasn't frightened. Was he supposed to be? People kept telling him not to be, and if it wasn't for their feelings, he'd have said, "I'm not." He wasn't excited, either; when the ambulance man had come, he'd said they'd be going in an ambulance, and wouldn't that be exciting? Well, that was stupid, because the ambulance was there, it had come to fetch him, of course they'd be going in an ambulance. It was interesting, really, seeing inside the back of an ambulance, though he'd not been able to have a good look. Maybe when he was well they'd take him home in an ambulance and then he'd look properly—oh, no, that doesn't happen, when you're well again, you don't need an ambulance, so—

His thoughts kept going like that, he didn't know why. The fuss and bother had subsided, and he was in a bed in a ward, the lights turned down, only little pools of light here and there. It didn't hurt; they'd injected him and then it hadn't hurt. There hadn't been time to be frightened of the injection, it had just happened like that.

It was interesting, not exciting or frightening, Andrew decided. It was interesting to know that he'd fainted once or twice. He'd never fainted before, he hadn't known what it would be like. It was like going to sleep but so quickly, and you weren't tired, it was like being swallowed up by something soft and black. And then Caroline arriving, his big sister, with pyjamas and a bag of stuff, they'd got her out of school, and after his dad arrived, having the X-ray taken of his leg, and looking at that, that was definitely interesting. He wondered if they'd give you the photograph if you asked. If you had your appendix out they'd give it to you afterwards in a jar, that's what Paul had said. He'd ask next time he thought of it.

Hospital was interesting, too, with its smell and the ill people all around him and the ugly toys that didn't belong to anyone in particular, but mostly it was comforting and just sort of right. They'd gone home now, Caroline and his dad, and it was nice to be on your own and safe from all sorts of things. He wouldn't have to go back to school for weeks maybe. He could feel a kind of weight on one side of him vaguely—oh, the cast, his leg was in a cast. He closed his eyes, nice and warm, his thoughts nicely dribbling away, falling in stages into a crisp white sleep.

But the next day Francis dragged himself out of sleep; dragged over getting out of bed when his mother called, pulling his bedspread up to his nose, his breath clouding the freezing bedroom air; dragged himself into a dressing-gown, hung silently over his breakfast. His father started to ask something about Andrew, but Francis didn't really know, he said, and then his mother joined in, speculating. Sandra wasn't saying anything; she didn't talk much in the morning, these days, but she was looking at him, preparing to work something out as if she was sharpening a pencil in her head. Time to go, and he went upstairs to dress, dragging until his father called sharply; and then, dropped outside the school gates, he dragged again. He knew what was waiting for him. He felt as if the playground, the pre-school running, all those unfamiliar people were falling away from him as he crossed the space, all spitefully aware of his plight. He put his coat and gloves in the cloakroom, went to the classroom, almost the first, and sat there, getting his stuff out of the bag, arranging it neatly and, in bursts, the rest of the class came in. No one paid him any attention, there trying to fill the half of his desk. But it wasn't Andrew's absence he was thinking about.

In time Miss Barker came in, her fat face smiling, like a preening small bear with whiskers to wipe, the red form register under her left arm. He sat upright, and she let the class quieten down without comment, as if they were on her side; she began to read the register. Francis waited, but Sellers was down the alphabet. "Andrew Jameson," she murmured to herself, "Nooooo—now, let's see . . ." reaching for a different pen to cope with Andrew's absence. Francis waited, his fists clenched, and after twelve names she came to it.

"Francis Sellers," she said, in a voice of glad recognition.

"Yes," Francis said, but his voice croaked and he had to say it again.

"What was that?" she said, looking him frankly in the eye. "Yes," he said, then, "Miss Barker," he added.

"You'll have to sit on your own for a bit," she said gleefully. He waited, and then she said it. "Georgy-Porgy," she said, as if she'd just thought of it, and she got the general laugh she wanted. He knew that was exactly how it was going to be. There was nothing he could do about it.

It was like a river delta, the walk home. When the bell rang, all the kids left, all through the same gate, and half turned left, down the hill, and half turned right, like Daniel, upwards. Then there was a tributary, the stream divided, and some turned off. Not halving again, more like a third or a quarter. It went on like that: at each road junction, the stream divided, and kids went in different directions, tracing their different routes, going to different homes. But they all ended up in the same sea—ah. Daniel smiled. But he liked the idea anyway.

He liked those geographical names; oxbow, crater, fjord lake, plug, and he liked the idea of them; he liked the idea of rivers carving out a huge valley, or a great big dirty grey glacier, thousands of years ago, melting and leaving the land in a particular shape. He hadn't tried to remember any of that; he'd just started listening one day, and he'd remembered it, and got an A, to everyone's surprise. They came to his mind in unexpected ways; yes, it was a bit like a river delta, the way all the kids made their own routes home.

There was a bit at the top of the hill where the road had never been made up properly, a muddy track linking two proper roads. It was unlit, and pitted with potholes. You had to be careful if it had been raining and it was dark; you'd put your leg in halfway up to the knee. Now it was the end of March, and the walk home from school was getting to be a pleasure again. He'd said goodbye to Ben at the top of the road, and was walking down the muddy track. The girl in front of him, he sort of recognized her.

"Hey," he said. She turned round. It was the girl who lived opposite. She'd moved in, what?, six months ago. She was wearing their uniform. He hadn't really known she was at the same school as him.

"Hey yourself," she said, turning back. He speeded up a little.

"What year are you in?" he said.

"Fourth," she said. "What do you want to know for?"

"You live opposite," he said. It amused him as much as anything, someone speaking to him like that straight off. "I see you sometimes."

"Your brother's really weird," she said. Her face was directed downwards, reddened. He knew her now; sometimes she was really spotty, but today not so much. She was all right.

"Yeah, I know he is," he said. "It's not my fault."

"You know what they say?" she said.

"No," he said. "What do they say?"

She shrugged, and whatever the general wisdom was about his little brother, or about pairs of brothers in general, she couldn't produce it for him. "And your mother," she said.

"My mother what?" he said. "Oh, she's weird as well, you mean."

"Not weird," the girl said. "She's frightening."

"Oh, yeah," Daniel said. "I'm terrified of her. I hide under the settee when I see her coming."

"I bet you do," the girl said. They walked on for a moment, the girl not looking at Daniel, just down at the road. "Go on, then," she said. They were walking by the bungalow at the top of the road, the one with the china leaping horse in the front window.

"Go on what?" Daniel said.

"Say whatever you were planning to say," she said.

"Like what?"

"Tell me I'm a stuck-up mardy cow, or I should go back to London, or do me, the way I talk, or whatever it was going to be," the girl said.

"I wasn't," Daniel said, surprised. "I wasn't going to say anything like that."

"You're the first, then," the girl said. With a gentle question or two, he found out her name was Sandra, and she wished she hadn't had to come here. He had seen her, after all; walking home on her own, or sometimes in the corridors, clutching her bags to her, a bit spotty, her face to the floor. There were people like that. You didn't necessarily notice them for any particular purpose. He supposed most people didn't.

After that, the next day, walking home, he kept an eye out for her, and saw her, but earlier. It was on Osborne Avenue, heavily hung with trees, the monumental cliff-like façades of the decaying houses behind falling-down dry-stone walls. He was with Ben and his brother still, and he didn't greet her. She was on her own—he realized how often he'd seen her, hardly registering that thin, resentful, brave stance. She was on the other side. They crossed the road when they'd passed her about a hundred yards; there was no real need to greet her, but he felt the force of her stare at his back, and regretted not being a bit braver, turning round to give her a wave. He knew it would have been the nicest thing that had happened to her today. Once he'd said goodbye to Ben and his brother, at the top of the road, he dawdled on purpose, but she didn't appear; she must have taken a different route home. He felt sorry, and guilty. It wasn't that he fancied her, though.

The next day they did coincide, and a lot earlier. Ben played the trumpet, it was his evening for band practice, and Daniel found himself for once walking home on his own. "Hey," he said to her, hastening to catch up.

"Oh," she said unconvincingly. He knew she'd observed him, been holding herself in against another snub. "Oh, it's you."

"Yes, it's me," he said, really not caring what she said to him, and in five minutes he was producing really quite an irresistible fable for her, all lies. Do you want to know something? he said. Last weekend, him and his brother, the weird one, and his mother, the frightening one, at least according to her, and his dad and his sister, they'd had to go to visit his dad's cousin. He lived in Rotherham, they didn't see much of him, once a year or less than that, really. And his dad's brother, his uncle Ian, he lived on his own because his wife had left him, years ago, on his own apart from his dog. It was new, his dog—at least, he'd got it since the last time they'd gone over there because, to be honest, none of them really liked Uncle Ian, even his mother and he was her brother—

"I thought you said he was your father's brother."

"No, my mother's, he's my mother's brother." And he, Daniel, he'd gone to stroke the dog, just put his hand down in an ordinary friendly sort of way, to pat his head, the dog's head. A sort of mongrel, a funny-looking dog, it made you want to laugh almost just looking at it, and his name's, his name is—

"Are you sure about this story?"

"Yes, I'm sure. I just can't remember what the dog's name was, not that it's of vital importance."

So he, Daniel, just put his hand down to stroke the dog, as anyone might, and the dog, instead of letting him stroke his head, coming up to be stroked, he just pulls back, he whines and he goes and buries himself in a corner. That's strange, Daniel thought, and he asked his uncle Ian about this dog who runs and hides if you go to stroke him, and according to Uncle Ian he's from a home, and the previous owners, or someone, they've only raised their hands to him to hit him. So now he doesn't recognize it if you try to be friendly. He either runs away or, if you're unlucky, he goes to bite you, only he's getting better now. The thing is—

"This was last Sunday, was it?" Sandra said.

"That's it," Daniel said. "I remember because I missed most of the chart countdown, it was half over by the time we got home."

"Because actually," Sandra said, drawing out her London word, "actually, all of last Sunday you were at home, and the car was in the driveway all day, and around four o'clock you changed your shirt, and about five o'clock a girl came round and you and her were snogging in your room without closing the curtains. So that's all a lot of complete rubbish."

Daniel looked at her with appreciation and, all at once, burst into laughter.

"You must think—" Sandra said, laughing too, not unkindly. "Do you know what all that sounded like? It sounded like the sort of rubbish you have to listen to in Assembly, that sort of story, and at the end of it they explain what it's all about. So I'm a little dog, who someone's supposed to have been beating, and you, you're—"

"All right," Daniel said. "But, you know—"

"Yes," Sandra said. "I suppose I do know."

He hadn't fancied her, not at all; anyway, she was two years beneath him, and everything about her until that moment had given off a sense of what he didn't like, the prospect of gratitude. Until the day before yesterday, he'd never bothered to notice her, and until that exact moment he hadn't understood why he was making any effort to speak to her. He didn't need what most people needed, confirmation of what he was best at through the tribute of grateful inferiors, and he wouldn't, unlike Ben and the others, stoop to fingering any girl to be rewarded with panegyrics, ecstatic descriptions of the person he was hoping to become one day. Barbara's speeches on the subject had, as they grew more and more exuberantly tearful, sickened him a bit by the end. He hadn't known why he was taking the trouble with this girl, but she'd laughed at him and it was a little clearer. She wouldn't, after all, be grateful for anything, and if there was still no possibility of sex between them, there was something newer, stranger, the spectacle of someone who gave the impression of being quite a lot like him.

"I hate this place," she said, as they were coming up to their houses, hers facing his.

"Give it a chance," he said, and broke into a run, down their drive. It was a strange thing for her to say. It was a nice clear day; you could feel the sweetness in the air off the moors, and see it, too. Between the houses, a complicated or an ordinary garden, but then, on that side of the road, you could still see the way the trees stopped and then there was just the moor, rolling off into purple and green hills, sunshine, sky. It wasn't to be hated, this place. He didn't mind the houses, the way they were sort of alike but all made slightly different. It was a bit ridiculous, he could see that. They all had the same porch, white-painted and glazed in, which most people left unlocked, and they all had an up-and-over garage—in the morning, you could hear the same creaking and hollow bang up and down the street as people set off—though everyone had painted their door a different colour, making sure they didn't have the same colour as the next house. Some had net curtains up and down, some only upstairs, one or two not at all, and mostly you could see the same thing, in the front bedroom, against the window, the unfinished back of a dressing-table. He supposed it was best to put it there, for the light, when the mothers put their makeup on. His mother, too.

He fumbled in his pocket for his key, putting the moment off. For some reason, talking to the girl over the road, thinking about the estate, he'd managed to lose his family in an idea of a family, an idea of how every family up and down the road was more or less the same, and more or less nothing in particular. He'd felt quite happy about that. It was only at the thought of his mother in particular, and her particular dressing-table, that it came back to him. After all, you did have to go back to your own family, your mum and your dad and your sister and your brother, those particular people. He let himself in. Sandra, over the road, turned and watched the door shut behind him.

Sandra had made a mistake, almost her first day: she'd chosen the wrong girls, chosen them for the wrong reason. She'd chosen the ones brushing their hair. The first day she'd been assigned a place, staring boldly back at the kids, and the fat girl she'd been put next to, she'd answered her questions coldly and shortly. Yes, she came from London. No, it didn't seem that strange. She looked round the class for the people on her sort of level. She thought she identified them.

At the lunch break, the three girls she'd spotted stayed in, clustered at the back, got out their hairbrushes, started to talk. Sandra stuffed her books into her bag, wandered over casually.

"I'm not going again," one said.

"You say that," another said. "You always go, you. You love disco."

"It's always same," the third said. "You get off wi' another lad every Friday, every Monday it's 'I'm not going, I'm not showing my face down there again.' You love that disco, you, it's only because of you—"

She broke off, and they examined Sandra, up and down, still brushing their hair, back from their face.

"Is there a disco?" Sandra said.

"I weren't talking to you," one said.

"I know," Sandra said. "I overheard, though. I love going to discos."

The girls laughed.

"You come from London," one said.

"Yes, I do," Sandra said. This seemed a little less unfriendly; and it hit upon what Sandra thought of as one of her main points.

"There'll be discos there and all," a girl said.

"Right posh ones," the main girl said.

"I suppose some of them are," Sandra said.

But this seemed incredibly funny to the three girls. "I suppose," one said, putting on a voice, a really awful voice. It was nothing like Sandra's. Sandra didn't walk away; she just stayed there, waiting. The classroom smelt of sour milk, of babies; it was the dusty black curtains, like black-out curtains. This was a room for German, and all around it were posters, their corners peeling away from the adhesive like the ears of animals. They showed all sorts of things in sunshine: cathedrals, rivers, a pointy castle made out of white icing like the tower of a beleaguered German virgin, and on each a few words in German. Die, one of them began to advise.

They did German here. They hadn't in London. Sandra expected she'd catch up, learn how to speak it in time. It was on Thursday afternoons, for only an hour.

"What else," one of the girls said, "do you suppose?"

"Oh, I don't know," Sandra said. "I've only just got here. When's the disco?"

"It's on Fridays."

"It's at the youth centre."

They looked at her. There seemed to be nothing more, and not really an invitation. Sandra's prepared account of herself lay there, uselessly. She'd wanted to say some London things; she'd wanted to introduce herself as someone who had been used to going to the West End on a Saturday, to buy a new outfit, once or twice a month; she'd wanted to impress, and had heard herself, in advance, telling the whole class about the time she'd actually seen—who?—in Selfridges once. There were London discos, of course there were. The reality, the trip on the train up to London once a year and, once, tea in Selfridges where they'd seen and marvelled at Thora Hird, would have done to improve upon. She'd have offered it on the slightest invitation.

"Right," she said. "I can't wait." She walked away and out of the classroom. It was better than nothing.

"You've really got everything sorted out," her mother said, at home, passing the door of Sandra's room. It was true. One of the things that drove Sandra mad about the rest of them was the way they left their stuff as it was. They'd unpacked the removal boxes, most of which were standing about uselessly in the room behind the dining room, as if they'd ever find any kind of use for them ever again. It was amazing to her that they'd ever managed to unpack everything they needed to live in this house. It was a perfect outrage, the way this family lived. When she grew up, she would do something about it; meanwhile, she wouldn't live the way this family lived.

Objectively, it was a perfect outrage, too, that only two days after signing on at this glass-fronted boutique of hatred, she was going to be asked to change into stupid clothes and run about for a whole afternoon, less one initial half-hour. There it was on the timetable she'd copied down from her unwilling neighbour. Wednesday afternoon, periods 6–8, Games. Games! Pretentious name. At least when it was called PE, as it had been in London, the stupidity of it had been obvious from the start in a name that was childish rather than ambitious. She'd always hated PE—hated rounders, hated running, hated netball, hated fucking hockey with the clunk-clunk-whack of the bully-off, hated that more than anything. If she'd ever been likely to be any good at it, she'd meticulously trained herself out of it with a slouching derision. Objectively, it was, after all, much more mature not to be keen on games, to run about in a field like a sheep to the directions of a whistle. This attitude, more than one games mistress had remarked in exasperation, spread easily to the other girls until all a class could provide in the way of a hockey team was two keen-as-mustard morons up at the front, and then (they said afterwards, their voices rising) that Sandra

Sellers's cronies imitating her standing round the goal mouth, resting on the blades of their hockey-sticks as if they were shooting-sticks, folding their arms and comparing bosoms, nattering on as if they were in a cocktail bar with a cigarette-holder each. Which was where they'd end up, sure as eggs is eggs.

Well, that was the general view. It amused but slightly disturbed Sandra, since the memory of the games mistress in a fury tended to bring up the reminder of what she didn't now have, a set of cronies. Nevertheless, even the lack of that wouldn't change her attitude to games—she didn't need cronies to shore it up, she'd recruited half a class to her initially solitary stance.

She'd made all that clear to her mother, on that awful day when they'd traipsed round the shops of Sheffield, list in hand, trying on the strictly defined items of uniform. A blazer with a badge, two blue skirts, pale blue blouses (the specifications of the list grew almost hysterical at this point), thick black tights, a tie, and even new black shoes. The shoes were the only thing that could have been carried over from her last, London, school uniform to this one. But whether through absent-mindedness or the misplaced generosity that had been bribing her and Francis for weeks with all sorts of unlikely or undesirable purchases, her mother had decided to buy her new ones. The shoes could have been carried over; everything else from the London uniform was purple, and couldn't be reused. (That was probably the reasoning behind the purple in the first place.) So they trailed joylessly round the department store—Cole Brothers, wasn't it?—radiating respectable necessity rather than any sense of fun. Her mother kept saying, "Well, that's really quite OK," and, objectively, the overall tone of this uniform was less ghastly than the old mad-girls' purple. Finally, they'd crossed everything off List A. They'd half a dozen plastic bags, full of clothes. It could have been the best shopping trip ever. List B was next, and together, by the foot of the second-floor escalators, as people pushed past them, they examined it doubtfully. List B was sportswear. "Excuse me," her mother said, to a passing man in a white shirt and a tie, a green enamel badge at his left nipple, "can you tell me where girls' sportswear is?" Girls' sportswear was, it seemed, over the road in a different building. "Laces *must* be black and 12" in length"; at the turn of the escalators, her mother and she looked at the list and, with a consideration that could only be called mature, concluded that they'd done enough by obeying the crazy force of the instructions in List A. As for List B, sportswear—"PALE BLUE hockey shirt to match school colours," whatever they were, her mother and she were of the same mind, apparently.

"You know," her mother had said, "I don't see what's wrong with the sportswear you've already got. I mean, most of it isn't more than six months old and, let's face it, you've hardly worn it."

"I've worn it from time to time," Sandra said, and her mother laughed.

"That's about the sum of it," she said. "What colour is it? This says everything's got to be pale blue, but what the point of that is when it'll be covered in mud in ten minutes . . ."

"Mine wouldn't be," Sandra said. "I can't remember the colour. I think it might be a sort of navy."

"Not purple," her mother said.

"No, it's definitely not purple," Sandra said.

"Thank heaven for that," her mother said. "No point in looking any more absurd than you would in any case."

"Yes," Sandra said sycophantically, now that she'd got her mother on her side, "you do look an idiot, objectively speaking."

"Well, blue's blue," her mother said. "I can't face sportswear just now. You'll just have to tell them that your stuff's nearly new, that you'll buy the proper colours when it wears out."

"Never, I hope," Sandra said.

"And that your parents aren't made of money. No, don't say that. Shall we go and get a cup of tea? It looked quite nice on the fourth floor."

"Did you like games when you were my age?" Sandra said, when they were settled over tea and two scones, one cheese, one sultana. She put it naïvely, wanting mostly to know

"No, of course I didn't," her mother said. "I hated it. I used to long to be grown-up, because, you know, when I was thirteen, the main point of growing up wasn't boys, or having a house of your own, or a job or any of that. I always thought that the best thing about growing up was that you wouldn't have to go out in the cold and run around in a stupid way once a week. It was Thursday afternoons. I can still remember, I used to dread it. Of course, that was after the war, and there wasn't the equipment to be had. There were only enough hockey-sticks for one match at a time, at my school, so you only got to play that once every four weeks. Not that that was much to be looked forward to. And a bomb had dropped on the tennis courts, which in the winter were supposed to be netball courts, so that was out too. It was three weeks out of four we went cross-country running, as it was called."

"I hate cross-country running," Sandra said. "They've started calling it orienteering."

"What's the difference?" her mother said.

"Well, they're supposed to give you a compass," Sandra said. "But they don't really need to. It was only past the parade and then down the Wandle for a mile, you'd have to be an idiot to get lost."

"Yes, I hated that," her mother said. "It was only running through the woods and being shouted at if you came last, or got a stitch and walked for a bit."

"Are you done there?" a table cleaner said, fat, blonde and permed, hovering over them.

"Not quite," her mother said, pouring out a drop more tea from the bottom of the pot. "I always thought I could never marry a man who had the least interest in sport. But fortunately I met your father, who I don't think has ever run five paces in his life, so the question didn't arise."

It was true; you absolutely couldn't imagine her father taking part in any kind of organized sport. If the television, switched on, should come up with a green field and a cluster of figures, a round object or objects, whether it was football or snooker or bowls, her father would give a prompt yelp and be up and kneeling, stabbing at the channel controls on the mock-teak front of the "box." The only other thing that had exactly that effect was any kind of opera, which didn't come up so often. Sandra tried to shrink him in her mind, gave him a fresh face—the glasses and the quizzical look could stay—as he was in the photos with Grandma Sellers and Uncle Henry, then tried to send the little chap off on a cross-country run. It was no good. He hadn't gone five paces in her mind before he was shinning up a conveniently appearing apple tree, settling among the branches and starting to scrump. That was the sort of thing he could be seen doing.

"I think we'd better go," her mother said crisply, "since they're so keen to have their table back"—this last directed at the permed fat blonde who had returned and was flicking with a dirty tea-towel at imaginary flies. "I tell you what, we've done enough for one day, shall we take a taxi home?"

All in all, it had seemed like quite a daring thing to do, as well as a nice moment of conspiracy between them. Sandra neatly clipped off the price tags from the, to be honest, still horrible components of the school uniform, and removed them from the cheap plastic shop hangers, putting them carefully instead on the aligned wooden hangers, all looking in the same direction in the wardrobe. She had no qualms about facing down any games mistress. After all, her mother's was the more mature attitude. So, it was a bit of a shock when, two days later, her mother went off with Francis to buy his uniform, and they returned not only with the List A stuff, but also with a scrupulously accurate account of the horrible List B demands of sportswear. Maybe he'd already grown out of his old stuff, the weirdo beanpole, but it still looked like a not-very-graceful inconsistency on her mother's part.

It took Sandra a while to see that her mother's first duty, as she saw it, wasn't to the uniform of the two schools, but to the different things that her children needed from her just then. Sandra needed conspiracy and support against an authority that would always be bone-headed and ludicrous, whether in London or Sheffield. Francis, on the other hand, with his shyness and self-consciousness, would be worried, even frightened, by the suggestion that he needn't bother with the petty rules and prescriptions of an authority not yet known in any detail. For him, the reassurance, the sense that his mother was always on his side, would come more convincingly from her serious-minded attempt to kit him out with absolute correctness. All the same, Sandra didn't believe that her mother really gave a toss for the whole paraphernalia of sport. The naughtiness she'd revealed to her was, objectively, much less of an act than whatever serious attitude she'd adopted in the shopping expedition for Francis, and after that they'd not taken a taxi home. Apart from anything else, it was much more mature, not taking games seriously.

That comfort had more or less disappeared by the time it came to Wednesday afternoon. The cloakroom was dank and smelly in a fungal way, the dark varnish on the benches shabbily peeling off like dry skin, lit only by a thick-frosted window high up in the wall, six inches deep, running the length of the changing room. It was almost underground. She was last in, and had difficulty finding a peg, finally pushing aside the over-ambitious claims of one of the sneering girls, and getting pushed in return. It was netball, apparently, and she changed into her old outfit, consciously ignoring the giggles and scandalized murmurs around her. The door was half opened and a rough voice, neither man's nor woman's, called in, "Hurry up, girls, line up quickly." It sounded like Miss Whitaker's voice, the hairy-armed games mistress at Tiffin. Perhaps they all came from the same suppliers, like the uniforms, purple, black, or snot-green. Sandra finished changing into her crumpled games outfit, now becoming a bit tight, and followed the others out into the little lobby. She joined the end of the line, noticing the daunting uniformity of the others, and waited.

In a moment, the games mistress came back in; she was short and broadly built, her chest without a bosom, but stout like a guardsman's in her red tracksuit. The white stripes down the side of her tracksuit trousers curved outwards like jodhpurs, outlining things massive and firm. She came straight up to Sandra. "That's not the correct wear," she said. "And who are you?" Sandra explained that she was new and—

"I can see you're new," the woman said. "Never seen anyone so new-looking in my life. And what in heaven's name are you doing in that unholy get-up?" That, Sandra thought a little unfair; it was what they wore for games lessons at Tiffin, which after all was no more stupid a school than this one, but she told the woman her name and explained about it being a new kit, fairly new, and then, despising herself under the woman's lobster-like glare, suggested that they would get the right-coloured kit before long. All of this was against the fascinated inspection and ugly giggling of the three girls she'd tried to make friends with. They, slightly surprisingly, were straight out of the box as far as their kit was concerned, conforming to the inch with requirements.

"I don't care about any of that," the woman said. "If you're in my class, you turn up in the right kit, or not at all, or rather," she went on, perhaps having seen some opportunistic glint at the prospect of licensed skiving in Sandra's eye, "I'll send you out on the pitch with whatever ends and odds on I can find in the box in my office. Is that clear? I want you in the right kit this time next week or I'll want to know the reason why. Today you get off lightly. Now. What position do you play?"

Sandra had thought all this fury, either fake or, more absurdly, real, both risible and genuinely frightening, but that request she absolutely wouldn't lower herself to give an answer to. In the past, she had been put into positions in netball, could probably even remember the names of some, but out of a sense of her own dignity, she wouldn't give an impression to the class, now finely gripped by this confrontation, that she could honestly be bothered to remember any of that crap. She lowered her eyes disdainfully, shrugged.

"Hello! Hello!" the woman shouted. "We've got a right one here. I asked you a question and I expect an answer."

"I don't know the answer," Sandra said, now losing her temper a little. "You give me a piece of information, and then perhaps I can learn something I didn't know. I thought that was the point of school."

"The point of school is whatever I say it is," the woman said, but that could hardly be true, objectively speaking, and it must have sounded a little limp as a retort even to her, as she then abruptly appointed two captains and ordered them to start picking their teams. Sandra was last to be picked—"That new girl, then"—and it was with a sort of exultation she realized that however long she was at the school, however many games of stupid netball and stupid hockey were organized for her benefit, she'd now always be last to be picked, correct kit or not.

The game of netball was the usual nightmare of legs gone pink and chubby in the chilly wind. The air ached with the predatory chirp of the whistle, and it was usually directed at her. She was holding the ball in the wrong way—how? It was round, wasn't it?—or she'd thrown it to the wrong people, or the right people somehow in the wrong way. There were already people in the class who had apparently concluded they weren't going to like her, and if, outside the netball court, they could best pursue their dislike by ignoring her, here they could apparently make the most of it by paying her every attention. With each new piece of notice paid came, too, an almost gleeful reprimand from the cuboid games mistress, and even the most normally delinquent of the class, the ones who could usually rely on the woman's exasperated fury, could today deflect that fury by making the new girl fail, make her the focus of beadily expressed rage. They threw the ball at her, hard and often. The side of her head pained, her pink thighs, her hands sore with the abrupt slap of the thrown plastic ball, and with nothing to show for it except the games mistress's reprimands and a few sour looks. She wouldn't have wanted sporting triumphs, but she might have settled for the cachet of deliberate, contemptuous crapness. She couldn't fool herself: it had just looked like ineptitude.

"We're going to have to try hard to knock you into shape," the games mistress said to her nauseatingly, when it was all over, beefily falling into step with Sandra as she drooped after the others back towards the school buildings. "And if you're in one of my physics sets, I hope I'm going to see a bit more effort there, too."

"Physics?" Sandra said, confused by the reference—there didn't seem to be much to link physics and physical education.

"Yes, physics," the woman said, insultingly raising and showing her voice. "That's what I mostly teach."

Inside, gripped with the horrible suggestion, Sandra was just about to start changing when another whistle blew, still harsher inside the concrete room. "Everyone *must* take a shower. Is that clear?" the woman called. "And I'm going to sit here and watch to make sure everyone does."

"She's a right old lesbian, that Neve," the girl next to Sandra muttered, surprisingly at Sandra and meant in a kindly way; she hadn't expected anything like generous commiseration, or taking sides against the awful Neve, as she was called. But that surprising and comforting fact couldn't do much at the moment, because Sandra had no towel to dry herself with. She hadn't thought through the implications of that entry on the timetable, sports, periods 6–8.

"You don't have a towel?" Neve said, voice raised, her hands in a what-now position on her hips. The class paused in its undressing, paid attention. "Why ever not?"

"I didn't think—" Sandra said.

"You thought you'd get back into your uniform without showering? How absolutely disgusting."

Sandra wondered what Neve was short for—Neville, perhaps. "The thing is," Sandra said patiently, "it's the end of the day. I can shower when I get home."

"You'll shower now if I say so," Neve said, "and manage as best you can. I expect someone will lend you a towel." That seemed unlikely, and Sandra undressed and walked with the others through the bleak hissing tiled chamber as swiftly as she could.

Around her—she could hardly not see, or hope that she wasn't observed in her turn—was the indignity of twenty girls' bodies, some skinny and boylike, others plain and lumpy with puberty, their square blocky breasts and massive thighs about an exuberant fury of scribbled pubic hair, like a tangled mop-head, and then, here and there, girls who simply looked like women, who had stepped effortlessly from one sort of grace to another, their transformation so recent, making no demands of them, a transformation like that of the heroine of an old book for children stepping across a brook to find herself a queen in one move. Sandra would have classed herself with this last group, despite her spots, and knew quite well that she had not changed much through these processes, that puberty for her was a matter of mild adjustment and not unequal spurt and explosion.

"Here, use this," Neve said roughly, handing her a fairly disgusting greyish towel, the texture of coarse sand. "I found it in a corner of my office. You can use that this week. Don't forget next." Sandra would have liked to drop it contemptuously on the floor, but she was wet; she dabbed at herself, and then dropped it disdainfully in a puddle.

"Well, that seems stupid," her father said that evening.

"She was really cross," Sandra said. "She was yelling at me because I didn't have the right-coloured shirt or something."

"I wouldn't have thought it made an ounce of difference in the long run whether you wore a green shirt or an orange shirt or a sky-blue-pink one to run round a field in," her father said.

"I don't care what I wear," Sandra said, "for playing hockey in. I wouldn't care if I played it in my bra and knickers."

"I bet you *would*," Francis said earnestly. "I bet you a million pounds you would."

She brushed him aside like a moth. It was nice to have someone slightly retarded, even if only in the evening, to practise on.

"It's stupid, and they ought to realize it's stupid," Sandra said. "I've a good mind to go on wearing what I was wearing today."

"Don't do that, love," her mother said, cutting through the principle of the thing in an infuriating way. "We'll buy you the proper wear at the weekend, if this woman insists on you having it. I don't want people shouting at you, even if it's for a nonsensical reason."

"The thing is," her father said, "the world's full of people who make up their own rules and then try and get you to stick to them as though they were important. You know, when I left school, my first job I worked in a bank in the City, a small private bank, and it was starting at the bottom, but it was a good job with prospects. At least, your grandma said so. Your uncle Henry, his friend Eric, he worked near there and he put in a word for me. But you see, in this bank, they had a rule that when you were in your own office, or the office you shared with three other clerks I should say, you could take your jacket off when you were working and even roll your sleeves up—I suppose to keep the ink off your sleeves because in those days you didn't change your shirt every day, you just changed your collar and went on, because your shirts, they all had detachable collars. Gaw, we must all have ponged the place out, but you just—"

"Yes, I bet you did," Alice said, because Bernie's stories, rarely embarked upon, had a habit of running into a sand of memory about cuffs and collars, ration books and next-door's air-raid shelter, the one with a pack of rabbits living in it, the point of the story sinking in his wonderment at the passing of small properties. It came back, wherever he started from, almost always to detachable collars. They all looked forward to the appearance of the collars.

"Yes," Bernie said. "I'll say we did. Well, the rule was that if you were in the office, you could sit without a jacket. But if you left the office for any reason, even if you were just going to the office next door to see George or Joe or whoever it might be, then—" deep breath "—you had to put on your jacket, roll your cuffs down, straighten your tie. It was just a rule, a completely stupid rule, but they made you obey it like it was a rule against, I don't know, stealing money or something."

"It's just like that," Sandra said, "with this woman Neve. She thinks that's the most serious thing in the world, matching shirts with everyone else."

"And what they want," Alice broke in, speaking with an urgency that made them look at her in surprise, "is for you to start believing those rules, not just obeying them, but really believing it matters."

"But the thing was," Bernie went on, "the funny thing was, I worked there for two years and then I thought to myself, Sod this for a game of soldiers. Because I'd done my job as well as anyone could, but I was still doing the same job for the same pay that I was when I went in, and they'd started saying, 'If you carry on we'll have to think about giving you more responsibility,' as if to say to your face, 'You mug.' Coming the old acid but never doing anything about it. And meanwhile, all the time, there were people who'd come in after me, who were the chairman's wife's nephew, or who went to the right school and had the right voice, or who played cricket in the same village team as a member of the board of governors, and they were being promoted, given responsibility, all right, and they weren't much cop, most of them. Some of them went off without a word every Friday lunchtime, going off shooting, they said, for a Friday-to-Monday, as they called it, and it was Friday to Monday, they'd be back Monday lunchtime in their tweeds with some dead wildlife hanging from their wrist. I can hear them now—'Ah, Sellers, have a brace of partridge, my good fellow,' and dropping these dead birds, all their feathers and mud and shit all over them, on my desk."

"I can just see your mother's face," Alice said, "if you turned up with two dead partridges—a brace, that's two, isn't it?—and asked her to start plucking them for your Monday-night tea."

"That's right," Bernie said. "She'd have had a conniption fit at the idea of eating something you'd got from a field, she'd have said, 'We might have had to live like that in the war, but I don't see the necessity for it now.' But you see, they'd got a rule against walking between offices without your jacket on, but they didn't have one against promoting someone because you knew their dad, or because you were having an affair with their mum, or because you were their dad. They weren't bothered about that."

"What your dad means—" Alice said.

"What I mean is," Bernie said excitedly, "is it's stupid, it's a stupid rule you've come across and it's a stupid person that's enforcing it, but it's not going to be the last time you come across one. Sometimes you need to obey the stupid rule, but I tell you, gel, you don't start believing it and you don't start inflicting it on anyone else. You want your own rules, the important ones."

"Don't you have stupid rules at the Electric?" Sandra said.

"Ha," Bernie said. "Of course we do. But I'm in charge of them, more or less."

"All the same," Alice said, "we'll go and get you a proper Flint-coloured games kit at the weekend."

"At the Friday-to-Monday," Francis said dreamily. "It sounds—"

"It sounds ridiculous," Alice said firmly. "Really, it can't be very nice to be shouted at for something so trivial, and I dare say it's not very pleasant for the woman herself to have to shout at people. I shouldn't like it at all."

"No, you wouldn't," Sandra said. "But you ought to see her. She loves it."

"Poor woman," Alice said. "And I expect she's probably a lesbian, too, poor woman."

"Mother!" Sandra said.

"Well, I expect she is, isn't she?" Alice said, over Bernie's chortling.

"She does look a bit like one," Sandra said.

"Well, there you are," Alice said.

All that was quite consoling, but what Sandra couldn't understand was the way the class pretty well lined up against her with the games teacher's attitude. It seemed unlikely, so blown-up and froglike a figure commanding popular support.

Sandra hadn't mentioned the towel question in front of her parents and, especially, brother, partly because it was embarrassing but mostly because she didn't think it was that important. She'd take a towel next week, and it would be a big one, to wrap herself in. She wasn't about to flash her pubes in Neve's lascivious direction again.

But, weirdly enough, it was the towel that had inspired all the interest the next day. When Sandra came into the classroom the next morning, minutes before registration, two of the three girls she'd tried to befriend were at their places, and around them a gaggle of boys in their black blazers, sitting on the tables, some hanging on like perching crows. The look on the girls' faces was of gleeful mock-concern, their voices hushed with pretend worry. But the boys—some of whom, surely, weren't even in Sandra's class—were alive with excitement, hooting mutedly, and when one girl said something, perhaps just "That's her," on Sandra's entrance, they all turned round, almost awestruck, before beginning to laugh in a crude, directed style. Some even stared at Sandra as they laughed. She tried hard to be mature and objective as the suddenly horrible word "towel" floated over.

The classroom door opened, and the third girl of the three came in, in a great rush—she had over her shoulder her own bag, and between her hands another, bigger one, a torn and tattered boy's black bag, holding it out before her like something explosive.

"Give that back right now," the boy coming in behind her was saying, a boy obviously older than this class, perhaps from a year or two above them with a deep, full, cross voice. The girl was playing in a way Sandra objectively recognized. She'd done things like that with an aim of bold flirtation. But the boy wasn't amused and he didn't want to start playing sexy games, Sandra's phrase for it, with this lumpy and short girl. Sandra recognized him at the same time as she recognized the good looks that no uniform could smother. With olive skin, thin-hipped, the rolled-up sleeves of a brilliant white shirt displaying forearms blurred by a dark coat of hair, she recognized his serious loss of patience; it was the boy who lived directly opposite them, the son of the mad lady. He ignored her, or didn't know who she was to recognize her.

"Listen to this, though," the short girl said, handing over his bag.

"I'm not interested," the boy said, but he stayed, drawn into the little group. The boys already there drew back a bit, grew still as if in respect for this story, whatever it was—and it had to have become a story about her body, couldn't possibly have remained only a faithful account of how a new girl with no friends as yet hadn't worn the right-coloured shirt for games and had had to use a communal towel to dry herself. The word "towel" came over again, now pronounced in a mincingly serious way. Oh, God, Sandra thought. The story was now setting off on a journey among the sixth-formers and upwards till the whole city of half a million knew about her as the heroine of a narrative that certainly hadn't happened.

But with this handsome boy as a new and initially thrilling audience, the story seemed to be dying a death. It was as if, standing over them, he had not just a general superiority to them, from age and good looks, but a specific authority over them, as if they were his personal imps. As he looked at it the glee had gone from the story; and there were three very silly little girls, faltering their way through to an under-prepared conclusion. It was suddenly unsatisfactory and not really that funny, even if it was true. The boys were looking not at the formerly excited tellers, or at Sandra, but at the newcomer, holding his retrieved bag. "Don't be so stupid," he said eventually. "That never happened. You're talking a right load of rubbish." He went, not glancing at Sandra, and perhaps he had no idea that the story was about her.

Deflated, the little group sidled to their seats. The short girl, the supposedly fun one who'd stolen a sixth-former's bag and told the story to its unconvincing end, occupied herself, her pink face down like a shy diner's interrogation of a plate, busily rearranging the pens and sharpeners and Snoopy-decorated protractors in her grubby Snoopy pencil case. Sandra eyed her with open, satisfied malice.

"They were saying," her deskmate said, now displaying a wavering and inconsistent support for Sandra in her woes, after ignoring her for three weeks, "they were saying that yesterday in the changing room, you know, after games, they were saying that you'd had your period started in the middle of the floor and you hadn't got your towel, you know, a sanitary towel. But I said that was rubbish, that wasn't how it was, it wasn't that sort of towel at all, I put them right. I've started using tampons," she concluded confidentially, "I find them more discreet."

"Thank you for that," Sandra murmured. The girl seemed to expect more effusive gratitude than that, or perhaps some irrelevant menstrual confidence, but Sandra had seen just how it had been. She'd silently christened this girl Daphne after the four-eyed brainbox in the cartoon. She wasn't the sort of friend Sandra had ever anticipated. She foresaw long Saturday afternoons in the girl's bedroom, talking over David Cassidy's favourite colour (blue), experimenting with diagonal highlighting with blushers, and being jealously allowed after a while to hold pony competition rosettes, awarded for third place.

"That girl who was saying it all," Daphne went on, "you don't want to be seen with her. She's got a reputation. She says she's a virgin but she's not. She let that Michael Williams, I know it for a fact, put *it* in her mouth behind the rec on Coldwell Lane. It was before the summer holidays. She's not a virgin properly speaking."

"Do you think that's entirely true?" Sandra said. She couldn't help herself.

"I know it for a fact," Daphne said, drawing back, dismayed at this wrong response. But of course Sandra, if all things were equal, was more like the sort of girl who put *it* in her mouth than a Daphne with a starter bra who singly deplored that sort of carry-on in others. Anyway, objectively speaking, they would all come in time to be the sort of girl who put *it*, whatever *it* was, in her mouth, sooner or later. Even Daphne. That was a cheering thought. It was history that morning, periods 1 and 2.

"Do let me help you with one of those," a woman said, just behind Alice, a treacly, warm voice.

"Thank you!" Alice said, turning. It was one of the neighbours; a bosomy woman, her front sloping solidly at forty-five floral degrees, less encumbered than she was, but red-faced and pattering up. The woman's name—"One of those disorganized days, I'm afraid."

"Oh, we all have those."

"Normally I do the whole lot at the weekend in the car with Bernie but—"

"Oh, I know," the woman said, taking a bag, just one of five, from Alice and beaming, weighing it in her hand. "Anthea Arbuthnot. You've probably not remembered, it was just the once we met."

"Yes, of course," Alice said. "Thank you so much—it's quite a hill."

"It's quite a nice supermarket, that little one," Anthea said, holding up the bag and scrutinizing the logo. "Crosspool, isn't it?"

"You must tell me the best places to go," Alice said, correctly divining the meaning of this. "To buy groceries. We're all at sixes and sevens still."

"So hard," Anthea said, "to find the shops that suit you in a new place. Of course, when Sainsbury's opens—"

"Oh?" Alice said. "Well, that'll be a familiar name. The thing I find strangest is really—"

"But settling in all right in general, are you?" Anthea said.

"Yes, I think so," Alice said. "The butcher's," she'd been about to say; the way they cut the meat in different directions, dividing beasts in unexpected ways, calling their divisions names all their own, gazing at her as she tried to fit it all back together again, the jigsaw body, and recognize what she knew. She'd felt like a new bride all over again, with that ignorance in the ruddy-faced expertise of the butcher's shop; and meat-knowledge was something she thought she'd acquired.

"I'm sure you'll wonder that you ever thought any of it strange," Anthea said. "I wouldn't live anywhere else now."

"Oh, I'm sure . . ." Alice began, not wanting to offend.

"Apart from anything else," Anthea said, "it's so easy to get out into the country. Just the end of the road, and there you are."

"Yes, I see," Alice said, who had been told this before.

"Let's have a nice cup of coffee," Anthea said, turning in at her drive and, after all, since she was holding one of Alice's shopping bags, Alice couldn't very well refuse. "I'll just pop your perishables in the fridge, then you won't be fretting while we chat. Do go on through.

"Of course," Anthea said, when they were settled, the percolator popping and groaning like colic through the serving hatch, plates of pink iced biscuits, pink wafers, sliced pink and yellow Battenberg before them as her voice grew grander, "one does love London. One always used to."

"Oh—so have you—"

"Well, naturally," Anthea said. "Naturally I've been to London. Many times."

"But you haven't lived there," Alice said—of course people had been to London. "I thought you meant that you'd lived in London for some reason."

"No," Anthea said. "My husband, now, he did live there, for a year and a half, when he was young, a job he briefly had. He often used to talk about it. Hither Green, he lived at. Do you know it?"

"Not so well," Alice said.

"Very sad," Anthea said. "Sometimes when he used to talk about it I wondered whether it was the only really happy time he ever had. But after all, he did come back to Sheffield, and—well, there's no point in wondering about what might have been."

"I'm so sorry," Alice said. "Is it long since he—"

"Oh, he's not dead," Anthea said. "Ran off with someone, awful house on the top of a hill outside Chesterfield with the wind whistling round, two, I believe, small children, well shot of him all things considered."

"I see," Alice said.

"No, I've never lived in London," Anthea said, "but I do make the effort to go down from time to time, for the great occasions of state. They come round sufficiently often, I find. It's quite a regular journey."

Alice laughed politely; she supposed Anthea meant the January sales.

"It was last year, wasn't it, Princess Anne's wedding?" Anthea said, quite serious. "So that was the last time I went down. Well, it's got to be quite a habit now because, of course, the first trip we made along those lines, it was for the old King's funeral in 1952. My mother, she had really desperately wanted to go to Princess Elizabeth's wedding in 1947, but my father thought it was a ridiculous idea, and put his foot down and she didn't go. Do you know, I honestly don't think she ever forgave my father for that, because she didn't ask for a great number of things, but just that once, I remember her so clearly coming out with it. 'Samuel,' she said—it was a Friday night because I remember she always liked to have fish, even though we weren't particularly religious, I suppose it was just a sort of custom, and we were eating fish at the time—'I'd like to take a trip to London to see the wedding of Princess Elizabeth,' she said. But he wouldn't have it. And I know she wanted to go again to London in 1951—now what in heaven's name would that have been for?"

"The Festival of Britain," Alice said. "I went to that. It was wonderful."

"Exactly that," Anthea said, beaming. "But my father stopped us again, only it wasn't that he said anything, it was that he was dying that summer. We couldn't have gone, naturally. But he died that September and the beginning of the next year, when the old King died all of a sudden, she quite perked up and said, 'Anthea, I've decided, we'll dye your old barathea black, and we'll go to the King's funeral. It's what your father would have wanted, to show respect.' Which was to be doubted, in my view, but we did it, we went down and it was thoroughly interesting, I would say. We had really quite a good view—I'd held out hopes for Princess Margaret, but we did have a good view of the Duke and Duchess of Gloucester at one point as they passed, I'll always remember. Not that royalty doesn't come to Sheffield from time to time."

"I remember the King's funeral," Alice said. But that was it: she remembered the fact of it, no more. She hadn't gone near it.

"And the next year—this is really how the habit started—my mother said, and there's a lot of truth in this, she said, 'Well, we've paid respects to the old King, it's only right that we go down to see his daughter crowned Queen.' Which is quite right, if you think about it, and so we went down again. The rain! But you didn't really think of that at the time, you were quite swept away by the whole occasion, didn't you find?"

"I remember the people next door, they bought a television because of it," Alice said. "That was quite a common thing to do, I've heard. And they asked us in to watch it, not just us but it turned out they'd asked about forty neighbours and relations, all squashed in together."

"But you were in London!" Anthea said.

"Yes," Alice said, "but—"

"Well, that I can't understand," Anthea said. "Living in London and not going to look at it in the flesh. But I dare say there was some sort of reason. Well, after that there was a bit of a gap, until Princess Margaret married, we went down again for that and that was nice, there was a little less of a crowd, you could see a lot more. And then when Churchill died, it was just the same time of year the old King died, and that must have reminded my mother of something, and I remember her saying, again, 'We must go and pay our respects, your father would have wanted it, he was always such an admirer of Churchill.' Which I don't suppose he was especially, but my mother had it fixed in her head."

Alice had reached out for a biscuit, but her hand hesitated, as if choosing between a slice of Battenberg and a fondant fancy. It stayed there and, in nervousness, she began to finger, then tear, the paper doily. Anthea Arbuthnot's lounge was soft and beige, the carpet thick and rich, the ankles of the little tables sinking deep into the pile; and now Alice saw that, at the far end of the room, by the side of a polished reproduction glass-fronted bookcase with its load of *Readers' Digest* mock-leather-backed summaries, pink and gold and regal in the face, there was a framed and glazed portrait in pastels of the Queen. Extraordinary. In the picture she was the colour of a mixed bag of Edinburgh Rock misshapes. Alice went on tearing the doily, fixing her look more consciously on Anthea's face. Suddenly it seemed to grow rather close to her own, the little pointed wet teeth bared, a smudge of the vivid red lipstick on the left canine, the flanks of the face warm and powdery and lightly furred.

"Churchill's funeral, I'll always remember that, queuing in the freezing cold for what seemed like hours. Well, it was hours we were waiting. Mother was insisting, but though we'd got there good and early, we'd still to queue, and we'd drunk the Thermos dry long before we got into the hall where he was lying in state. I went with Mother again, though by now I was married. I'd married the summer before, but my husband, he'd put his foot down, he'd said it was a waste of time and money and we'd not see anything much. Mother said, 'Anthea, it's history repeating itself, I don't like the look of this one bit,' and though I wouldn't have it, she lived to see herself proved right. I should have seen how the land was lying from the start. But it was worth it, going to Churchill's funeral and queuing all that time in the bitter cold, I'd say, because we had a great piece of luck: when we got into the hall, there were the four royal princes standing guard at each corner of the coffin. I'll never forget that sight as long as I live. They looked terribly young and slender, all in their uniforms. They'd not announced it in advance, they just wanted to show their respects quietly."

"I never heard that," Alice said. "I'm sorry, I don't really know—which royal princes?"

"Well," Anthea said, "I'm not sure, but we can certainly work it out. It must have been Prince Charles, or would he have been too young? Well, certainly the Duke of Gloucester—the Duke of Edinburgh—no, let me see . . ."

Anthea paused, and thought hard. The direction of her gaze, which had been wandering remotely, seemed to come back within the room. "Do you know," she said. "I don't think the royal princes were there at all. I'm mixing it up with King George V's funeral. That was when they stood guard over the coffin and, of course, I've only read about that, I was only just born. Isn't that a curiosity? It's quite as if I remembered it. But let me show you—"

And she leapt up, briskly going to the far end of the room, opening the bookcase and fetching out a large bound book, one of several.

"I've made it a habit always, after an event like those, to put together a little bit of a scrapbook. Out of the press, and the photographs I like to take, and little oddments, like—see"—she was seating herself cosily next to Anthea on the sofa, opening the book at the beginning—"I know it's absurd, but I even sellotape in the train tickets, and after a while, that's interesting in itself because you forget what old train tickets looked like. This one, it was for Princess Anne's wedding. Of course, the big one, that'll be when Prince Charles gets married if he ever does, but we really had a smashing time at Princess Anne's. This one, it's of my friend Mary, as you see, it's at Sheffield station, just setting off, and here I am, on the train, eating my little sandwich as a mid-morning snack and a coffee out of the Thermos and—"

An hour later, Alice left Anthea's house, as Anthea, glowing ecstatically, waved her off from her porch with a fervour almost patriotic in itself. She had never felt so low as she crossed the road with her five shopping bags.

It was half past four, and Francis was in. He came out of the sitting room as she opened the front door, a book in his hand. "I got trapped," Alice said. "One of the neighbours."

"Oh," Francis said, and went back.

"Is Sandra in?" she said.

"No," Francis called. "I haven't seen her."

She went into the kitchen and started to unpack. A packet of fish; some frozen peas; a tin, a second tin of soup, the same soup; a bottle of orange squash; a bag of potatoes, that was what had been so heavy, and she saw herself as if she were at the task already, peeling them over the sink, which, like all kitchen sinks, was a little too low for her; a bag of sugar and a tin of fruit in syrup; a bottle of green washing-up liquid, a packet of bathroom soap, which they'd needed, and a big bottle of the shampoo they all used; she hadn't been sure about that, it hadn't been on the list, but she'd had a feeling they needed a new one. Alice was orderly, and she set out separately the bathroom things, the cleaning things, as she took them from the bags, first putting the food away. The fish, the peas, she put into the fridge immediately, came back and put the dry food, the tins, into the cupboard. She was lost in her thoughts, and halted there, just for the moment.

"Mummy," Francis said. He had come back into the kitchen, was standing at the door.

"Yes, love?" Alice said, summoning herself and smiling as she turned.

"There's something so interesting," he said. "I found it. I didn't know anything about it."

"What is it?" she said.

"Come and have a look," he said. "In the garden."

"I'll just—" she said, but changed her mind. "What is it?" she said, following him out, leaving the rest of the shopping on the kitchen counter.

"It's a surprise," he said. They went together, Alice following him, through the house, into the dining room and the room at the back, the one they had no particular use for, full of the removers' empty boxes still, and Francis opened the back door, into the garden.

"Was that unlocked?" Alice said—she was sure the doors were locked, always.

"Oh, yes," he said. "I unlocked it. I went into the garden."

"We must do something about the garden," Alice said. They were none of them all that keen on it. They'd inherited the one in London, and Mr. Griffiths, next door, he'd come over from time to time and trimmed shrubs for them, that sort of thing; he rather liked doing it, Bernie always said, and accepted the offer. Bernie could mow the lawn, and he left it at that. They'd inherited this one, too, but, apart from a mow or two when they'd moved in, Bernie cursing at the length the grass had been allowed to reach during the house's uninhabited months, saying it needed a scythe, they'd not done much, and it was a little overgrown. Between the stones of the patio, the beginnings of grass were sprouting up, and even, here and there, tiny delicate plants with the promise of tiny flowers to come.

"Come on," Francis said, his eyes bright, and led her across the lawn. He paused for a moment, and fingered a dark-leaved, waxy plant, leggy and white-flowered, glossy with mysterious health.

"Is that it?" Alice said, amused, but Francis shook his head.

"It's the pond," he said. "Come on. I didn't know there was a pond there, not at all."

"Didn't you?" Alice said. "Well, I'd not thought of it but, yes, they showed it to us when we were looking over the house. I don't suppose we'd given it a lot of thought or I'd have mentioned it."

The garden had been partitioned out, as if into rooms, and it was behind the jutting spur of a bed, planted densely with conifers, curving round secretively, that the pond lay. They rounded the bed, and Francis stood there with her. "But it's not just the pond," he said. "Look."

The pond was dank and dark; it could not be deep, but the water was gloomy, rich with slimy green life, and could have been profound. On the surface, some sort of freckled bright green plant-life, spreading unchecked, and underneath, the lifeless cold depths. The conifers had been planted there so as not to shed on the pond, she supposed, but leaves had blown on to it from elsewhere in the garden, and lay there dead on the surface, slimy and brown.

"Is that all?" Alice said. "I've got dinner to get ready. Oh—"

Something had moved in the pond; a stretch, or so it seemed, of pure muscle, a bank of orange flesh moving in a leisurely, incurious way from the depths to the surface. It was a fish, ten inches long.

"Look," Francis said again, delighted.

"It's a fish," Alice said, amazed. "How on earth—"

"Didn't you know?" Francis said.

"No," Alice said. "No, I'm sure not. They didn't mention that. We just took a look at the pond, said, 'Very nice,' and that was it. I'd almost forgotten about it. They certainly didn't mention anything about fish."

The fish surfaced again, investigating them, investigating it, and then, without any announcement, a second fish, paler and smaller, but that was wrong: the second fish was the first one they'd seen; it was the other that was still bigger, richer in colour. Francis hunkered down on his haunches, and so did Alice; after a moment of joint-cracking, she twisted and knelt on the cold ground, not minding.

"How could they survive?" Alice said. "We haven't been feeding them. I'd have thought they would have starved to death."

"Or frozen," said Francis, because the winter had been a cold one.

"Or frozen," Alice said. And now, as if this was the first interesting thing to have happened to the fish in months, a third one, even, appeared, and for a moment the three fish, fat and sleek, slid over each other, performing some underwater ballet of meaning and touch. "I feel guilty now."

They stayed there for a while, just watching the fish, waiting for each new variation as they moved up and down in the dark pond.

"I suppose we ought to start feeding them," Alice said. "Though they seem to have got on quite well without anyone paying them any attention. I wonder what they've been living on."

"There might have been food left in the pond," Francis said. "Maybe there was enough for a few months."

"We ought to find out," Alice said. "Fancy the people not mentioning it. It would have been terrible to remember the pond one day and come out to find three dead fish floating in it."

"The birds would have eaten them," Francis said. "They wouldn't have left them."

Alice looked at him; he was a strange boy.

"Perhaps the birds would eat them anyway," Francis said, pursuing his line of thought. "Come down, swoosh, carry them off."

"I'd like to see the bird that could carry that one off," Alice said. "That fat one."

"Maybe we ought to bring them inside," Francis said.

"Inside?" Alice said. "Where are you going to keep them? In the bath?"

"No, not that," Francis said seriously. "You could get a tank, they could swim around in that."

"They seem quite happy as they are," Alice said. "If they survived that winter, they must be pretty tough." As they swam up and down into darkness, with each slow circuit of the surface of the pond colliding and slipping over each other, they looked like fat and gorged beasts left when everything else had succumbed.

Francis had had his triumph; he had discovered something, and his gestures were magnanimous as he moved back to let his mother watch. Hardly intending it, she let her fingers dangle on the surface of the pond, stirring the green algae like soup. The fish rose to that, too. Perhaps they were expecting food. They stupidly met Alice's red-painted fingernails, retreated, and in a moment tried again.

"Amazing," she said. "I don't know what they eat."

"Can they be mine?" Francis said.

"Yours?" she said. "To look after, you mean?"

Francis nodded violently, as if to say more might spoil his chances.

"I don't see why not," she said. "That's your father—go and tell him."

He got up and ran into the house. It was the chugging of the Simca's engine she'd recognized, and the clang of the garage door coming down. In a moment Bernie would come out and look at the fat fish, with all the amazement she'd just felt. She could hear, through the open back door, her son explaining the whole thing, excitedly, hardly able to let him get his coat off. In a moment he'd be out and they'd be looking at them together; she could show them to him, and there would be just the same excitement in that as in the way Francis had shown them to her. That ought to be exciting. So why was it that she held this moment for herself, wanted to stay here, just for the moment, with no one else to intrude upon her, and the dank little pond strewn with leaves and bright algae, and the fish, rising, observing, falling, as if that was all they'd ever wanted to do, their whole lives long? Through the hedge she saw Bernie and Francis coming across the lawn, Bernie with his coat and jacket off, in shirtsleeves and his work tie, and realized with a feeling of relief that now she wouldn't have to tell them the story, all at once filled with shame and ugly distortion, of the woman who so loved the royal family, the woman who lived just over the road.

In the house down the unmade road, the witchy house with collapsing gables and rotting window frames, Mary Jameson prepared to go out.

Henry had come into her room that morning, and had spoken to her. He had brought a cup of tea, as he often did, and at first he had spoken in his soft voice, supporting her in her nest of pillows, tempting books, the upper half of his heavily bearded face radiating its usual concern in the greeny light of the curtained room. But what he said was not supportive, not helpful to her at all.

"I'm sorry, Mary," he said. "I know it's difficult, but you have to start going down to the hospital."

She stared at him. She knew it; she knew that all the time, he resented doing anything for her, and didn't take her troubles seriously. No one who loved her could ever ask her to do such a thing. She just couldn't believe it. "I can't," she said, trying to keep her voice steady. "You know I can't."

"I wouldn't say it if the situation was in any way different," Henry said, "but you have to go down there. You know as well as I do what's happened to Andrew."

"I know," she said. "That's why I can't cope with anything any more."

"That's not true," Henry said. "Before Andrew went into hospital, you were finding it impossible to get up and leave the house. This isn't the cause of it."

She plucked at her bedcovers, at her tatty red cardigan she'd taken to wearing as a bed-jacket, picked up the nearest book, sandwiched between two pillows, and raised it between his face and hers. She couldn't believe he was telling her she was lying; or, rather, she always knew that he had secretly thought that.

Henry reached out, and firmly lowered the book. His mouth was set. "I don't underestimate how difficult this is going to be," he said. "But you have to think that Andrew might never leave the hospital again."

"It was just a broken leg," Mary said. "I don't know what they're talking about."

"You know what they're talking about," Henry said. "It isn't just a broken leg. It broke so easily because of—"

"Yes, I understand," Mary interrupted. They wouldn't make her talk about it, not in detail. That, she couldn't bear; it wasn't to be borne that she should be made to talk about it on top of everything else.

Henry let silence fall between them. She looked at the green bedside clock, its unused alarm bells sitting foolishly on its head, a green Humpty-Dumpty with earmuffs. It was half past ten; Henry should long ago have been at work. She didn't know what he was playing at.

"There is such a thing as duty," Henry said. "You can't just refuse to go to the hospital. He needs you."

"He's got everyone else."

"He's a little boy," Henry says. "He's frightened, he doesn't understand—or, rather, he does understand. He keeps saying that it's quite all right, that he knows you can't come to the hospital. I can tell you, it could break your heart."

It was so unlike Henry to use an expression like that. Mary looked up, directly at him. But his face was steady and unweeping. "But he says it's quite all right," she said.

"If you can't—" Henry said. It was almost as if he were about to raise his voice, but he checked himself. "It's quite simply your duty."

But now Henry had gone too far. She knew that they would all start ordering her about sooner or later. She knew all that tiptoeing around and pretending to be sorry with cups of tea and things on toast was just an act, that they all hated her and wanted to get rid of her. Sometimes she'd heard them laughing downstairs as she was crying. "Duty," she said. "How can you talk about my duty? Don't you understand what I'm going through? I can't be made to do things when all this is hanging over me. You don't seem to understand how difficult I'm finding it to cope with anything at all, the slightest thing."

"Of course," Henry said, getting up from the bed, speaking drily. "I had forgotten that, after all, this whole situation—it is, after all, mostly about you. I'm sorry for forgetting that."

She had a horrid morning, one of the worst, but by lunchtime she'd given herself a good talking-to. It would show Henry if, after all, she punished herself as they all wanted her to. So, in small journeys from bedroom to bathroom, back to bed, and then to the wardrobe and back in tiny weeping spurts, she put herself together. She brushed her hair in front of the crowded mirror, and then, step by step, she went downstairs to look for her coat. It wasn't her fault if this would return her to bed for weeks. It was what Henry had bullied her into.

He'd left the number of a taxi company by the telephone, and she called it. Her voice sounded small to her, but the difficult instructions of how to find the house, not used for months, came back to her quite readily. It took her ten minutes to find her coat, beneath the others in the cloakroom, and by the time she'd found it, the car was hooting outside. In a rush, she forced herself to open the door, and pulled it to behind her before she could think about it.

"You're tucked away here," the driver said.

She agreed, getting into the back.

"Children's hospital, is it?"

She agreed again.

"Never mind, love," the driver said, reversing into the empty garage and setting off. "I'm not much of a talker either."

She felt sick all the way, and had to close her eyes when there were too many people. All too soon they were there. She remembered it now—ten years before, Lucy had had her appendix out. That was when she could go out. It was on a main road, an elaborate, flushed palace of red brick, striped with glazing, ornamented with ruffles and cartouches, half château, half public lavatory. The founders of it had built it opposite the university and the park; she supposed they thought that the sick children could look out at the pleasures they'd return to, and think about their future.

"I'll let you out here," the driver said on the main road, just by the entrance. She made herself think of Andrew. It was so unfair, what Henry had said. She was a caring person. She paid the driver.

But, inside, she grew angry again. She forced herself to ask the receptionist—Henry knew how she couldn't deal with strangers—where Andrew was but quickly afterwards she got lost, hardly having listened to the brisk directions. Didn't they know how ill her son was? Couldn't they have spared someone to take her up, the mother of the sick boy? Quickly she was in strange wards; the corridors were lined with terribly sad pictures, done by dying children, all of animals and smiling nurses. And behind a door she glimpsed a horrible menagerie, the drawn animals made plush and stuffed, a whole room of ugly common toys, left there by children who had died and no one had collected them.

"You know where you're going?" A small nurse accosted her.

Mary explained quietly. It was, it seemed, on the next floor up; the nurse took her all the way to the stairs, but left her there. "It's just one flight up," she said again, but laying a hand on her arm.

"He's just there," the sister explained, "in room three, on his own. He's got his little friend with him, the one who comes every day."

No one offered to take her any further, and she walked to the door of the room. There was a square of wire-strengthened glass set into it, and she peered in. There was Andrew, very pale and thin against the propped-up pillows, and next to him in a chair, a boy his own age. He had his back to the door, and was leaning close to Andrew. He was talking, very quietly. Andrew's face was drawn and worried. He closed his eyes, and swallowed; she could see the effort. Then he opened them again, and looked beyond his friend at the door. He saw her face, his eyes opening wide. She went in.

The boy got up, not looking at her. "I've got to go," he said roughly.

"It's my mummy," Andrew said, in relief. "You don't have to come back—" but the boy was gone, making his way roughly past her.

"It's me," Mary said.

"I'm glad it's you," he said, and she sat down and took his hand.

"You've had your friend here," she said.

He closed his eyes. She couldn't understand. It was almost as if he didn't want any of it.

"You know when people start loving you a bit too much?" Daniel said.

Sandra agreed.

"It's ridiculous, they can't help making themselves ridiculous," Daniel said. "It starts out as a bit of fun. Say your friend, he has a party on a Saturday because his mum and dad, it's their twentieth wedding anniversary and they've gone away for the weekend, for a dirty weekend to rekindle the sparks of their dying marriage, and they leave your friend in charge because he's sixteen and he's supposed to be responsible now that everyone thinks he's mature. So he has a party, like a secret party that no one knows about until two or three days before."

They were walking down their road now. There was a brisk wind off the moor, puffing the fat white clouds along; behind them, far above, a screen of unmoving high clouds like a rippling veil. The sky like a diorama, its dramas in clean flat layers. Almost every day now they caught up with each other at some point on the walk home, and fell into conversation. He made her laugh; she, it seemed, could make him laugh too, make him throw his head back and croon with hilarity. She had seen him leave the house in the morning, and his shirt was buttoned up, his tie was pulled up to his neck. He didn't greet her then, he didn't greet her if they passed each other in the corridors at school, but when they met, six hours later, as if by chance on the walk home, the top button of his shirt was undone, or the top two buttons, and his tie, if it was still on, was loosened into a five-inch-wide knot, the tie itself a jutting fat three inches of defiance. He made her laugh with his going on about love.

"And you find yourself in the kitchen, say, or, I know, on the stairs letting people run up and down, and everyone's supposed to be in and out the bedrooms with everyone else, there's someone being sick in the downstairs toilet, because he's only got lager and cider in and everyone's mixing them. Well, you're on the stairs, you know, and without knowing how it happened you're talking to a girl who's in your maths set, you know her but you've never talked to her, really.

"But you're talking, and it's really great, you might be having a deep conversation like about life and the universe, like what's the meaning of life, and you realize that she's really not bad at all. She's called Barbara."

"Daniel," Sandra said, in a mock-adult, reproving voice. "Is this a true story you're telling me? It isn't a story that's happened to you by any chance, is it?"

"It might be," Daniel said, grinning.

"Well, I'll never hear how it turned out," Sandra said, because now they were coming up to his house, with the blue curtains in the upstairs windows, the vase of stargazer lilies and red tulips on the downstairs window-ledge, and to hers, with the red and yellow curtains in the upstairs windows, the handmade model of a tea clipper in the downstairs window.

"Don't you want to hear?"

"Oh, I can't wait to hear how it turns out," Sandra said sarcastically, even though she did.

"OK, then," Daniel said. "Come on, let's go down the bottom crags."

"I've got my bag," Sandra said. Daniel shrugged, and took it from her shoulder—through her school blouse she could feel the manly rasp of the skin on his fingers, and how, indifferently and impersonally, his hand pressed in an investigative way on the strap of her bra. He took his bag with hers, and threw them both behind the neatly trimmed hedge in the Glovers' front garden. They fell into the flowerbed.

"Come on," he said.

"Your dad'll kill you," Sandra said, because she had by now found out quite a lot about the Glovers, their interests, even if the hard neatness of their garden had needed any kind of explanation. "You can't start chucking stuff at his flowers like that."

"No one'll see your bag there," Daniel said, as if that was the point of it.

"There's nothing valuable in it," Sandra said. "I don't care if anyone nicks it or not, they're welcome to my German textbook, my German homework book. It's only stuff like that."

"I hate German," Daniel said.

"I don't know whether I hate it or not," Sandra said, knowing this was the sort of remark Daniel liked. "I never listen to any of it. It might be quite interesting for all I know."

Daniel cracked up and, all of a sudden, they were running together, before Daniel's mother could come out and upbraid them. Not that she would: she probably wasn't home yet. She worked in a florist, came home by six or sometimes an hour or so later. (There was stuff to do after the shop shut, Daniel had explained, now that his mother had been given a bit more responsibility, wasn't just an assistant any more.) They ran down the road, howling madly, and when they reached the bottom, instead of following it round to the right, they turned left, where a track quickly petered out and you were on the moors. This was the bottom crags. The top crags, a wind-blasted path along a low cliff leading you all the way to Lodge Moor Hospital, ran along the edge of the bleak golf course; the bottom crags a rough path between sheep pastures, running quickly into moorland.

At the beginning of the path, glowering over it, was a huge limestone rock, just sitting there, crusty with blots of moss, strangely worn and hollowed. A single crack ran through the whole thing that you could just about wriggle through, a favourite challenge presented to fat kids. You could nestle into one of the hollows and hide there for ever, doing whatever you felt like doing, snogging, smoking, nattering, or something really stupid. Daniel's sister Jane had been spotted there making notes in a notebook, writing a poem possibly. It loomed over the path, and Daniel, followed by Sandra without any complaint or ladylike demur, climbed it in five or six quick grips. It wasn't as hard as it looked, and then, posted on top, you were invisible from the path, conspicuous to the whole world and the miles and miles of purple moor, the miles and miles of double-vistaed sky.

Of course, since the top of the rock was invisible, sometimes you got up there to find that someone had beaten you to it, which meant standing around for a sharpish two minutes saying, "What a fantastic view," in his father's style to nobody in particular before silently cursing and climbing down again. That sort of thing, in Daniel's experience, definitely put the kibosh on things where girls were concerned.

But, of course, today he wasn't there for snogging, he was there with Sandra.

"Go on," she said, when they'd recovered their breath.

"I've got a stitch," Daniel said. "Go on what?"

"We've come down because you wanted to finish your story," she said. "Or," she went on, "so I thought."

"Yes," Daniel said patiently. She'd get bored of it in time. "Yes, I was telling you my story. So I met this girl, I'd known her, who she was, but I'd never talked to her until Pete's party, when his parents went away for the weekend. And as I say she seemed a right laugh, and before you know it, you know, she looks up at you and you look down at her, and it's like two balls rolling towards each other, crash! You can't help it, the way your heads fall together, your face and hers, and then you're snogging without knowing it."

"Is that how it happens?" Sandra said.

Daniel laughed. It was funny how you could talk to Sandra like that. You couldn't talk to girls like that. Most of them believed in love, insisted on all that going on about love. Sandra, he reckoned, was just interested in where love could get her, and that was how he thought about it. He could talk to girls about love all day long, could widen his eyes and slightly open his mouth and run his thumb, very gently, down the front of his chest in a tight T-shirt. But that wasn't talking to a girl about love, not in the way he talked to Sandra. "The thing I sort of didn't think of," Daniel said, in his most worldly way, "was that she was having her period at the time."

"Oh, shut up," Sandra said. "How can you tell?"

"How do you know I didn't find out?" Daniel said.

"Oh, you didn't find out," Sandra said. "You wouldn't have got as far as all that. I can guess what sort of girl she is, holds it out, then says, 'Oh, Daniel, we mustn't.' "

Daniel tried to be offended, but couldn't. "OK, I didn't," he said. "I didn't get that far. But you can tell, they go all spotty, and I remember, she was right spotty at Pete's party—she almost apologized for it."

"So what?" Sandra said. "What's that got to do with anything?"

"I heard," Daniel said, "that girls, women, they're much more horny when they get their period because, it stands to reason, they're fertile then, so Mother Nature, she's going to make them want sex a lot more around then so that they'll have babies."

"That's rubbish," Sandra said, but she wasn't sure.

"The problem is," Daniel said, "that Mother Nature also makes women really spotty and ugly during their period so that even if they want to have sex you don't want to have sex with them because they look like a right warthog, like an oatcake, they can be that spotty. But it's true."

"It's never," Sandra said.

"Finger a filly at full moon," Daniel said, evidently concentrating, "and she'll follow a fellow to Folkestone."

"What's that?"

"I made it up." Daniel stretched out on his back, arching into the odd lumpy contours of the gritty rock. Above him, the clouds scudded across their background of remote white veils, unmoving, high in the sky, and between him and those floating white beasts, a flash of swallow, darting. He liked the clouds, the birds though his respect was with the immovable.

"That's disgusting."

"It's true. And that's what happened to Barbara. She just got a bit keen on me."

"For instance."

"For instance, she phoned me on Sunday, the day after the party."

"Oh, you'd not spent the night together in mad passion, then?" Sandra said, inspecting him scrupulously.

"Gi'o'er," Daniel said, quite as if he was blushing. "She phoned me, and she was all lovey-dovey. And I don't know where I came in her list of people to phone, but when I go into school on Monday, everyone, all the girls, they just look at me and giggle, you know how it is—"

"Yes," Sandra said, though she was thinking of ridicule and hostility rather than sexual triumph, "I know what you mean."

"And then apparently we're going out together, though I don't remember that part of the agreement, and going out together means that you spend every break and every dinnertime together, mostly snogging, and you walk home with her, but she only lives in Crosspool so it's not much of a walk, and then you get home and the phone rings and it's her again, probably been ringing you for the last half an hour just in case you'd managed to fly home in a helicopter or something, and you're on the phone with nothing to say, and most of that saying goodbye to each other."

"Oh, I know," Sandra said.

"And then, before you know it, she's hanging about outside your house, because she's just passing, and then it's the tears and the tantrums and she's offering to hand over the thing you've been asking for. Only now you don't much want it."

Sandra burst out laughing. She poked Daniel, hard, just underneath where his stubby tie ended, on his bony chest. "And so you turn her down flat," she said.

"You sounded quite Sheffield when you said that," Daniel said admiringly.

"I know I dost," Sandra said.

"Not then," Daniel said.

They sat there for a while. You could see for ever from up here, in any direction you wanted. Only when you looked behind you, and there it was just Sheffield. But even in that direction you could still see the moors, the hills, the valleys the houses had been built over.

For a while now Katherine had been staying late at the florist's, one day a week. "Don't bother telephoning," she'd said, when this arrangement was first mentioned. "Nick doesn't answer the phone after the shop's closed. We've got too much to do."

After the two days of Malcolm's disappearance, everything had altered. Nick had moved out of his rented house into a little old cottage on the other side of the ridge, in Ranmoor. He seemed indifferent to the statement of this. His house, a stone-built cottage with four big windows square on, a sloping tile roof, and a door with a red lintel and flowers around it, sat squarely behind a little garden divided by a path, a dry stone wall in front and a blue wooden gate. It was like the houses Katherine's children had so liked to draw; it almost had a round smiling yellow sun above it.

Nick had hardly seemed to cherish or value its prettiness, or what seemed most distinctive about it: that it had been there before Sheffield had spread and surrounded it. Around it, there were quiet leafy roads, and Nick's neighbours lived in what had once been the vast mansions of steel magnates, set back hugely from their big-bellied front walls. A professor lived just there; an old man, a Mappin, one of the last of the family that had given an art gallery to the city, lived over the road and collected books. Nick's house was not grand, but his surroundings were. The place had risen up and surrounded, a hundred years before, what had once been a lonely little house on the raw unclaimed moors. Nick had slipped into this august corner of Ranmoor casually, and hardly seemed to notice.

He had apologized to her, fervently, for not coming to her party, and then, just once, as if he had not been able to prevent himself, had turned her round, had wiped her face, had kissed her. When he took possession of his little house in Rowan Grove, he had offered her a lift home if she wanted to come and look at it. They'd got out of his little van, he'd opened the creaking blue gate, the SOLD notice still over the wall, like a flag stiff in the wind. "This is all going to be wistaria," Nick said, gesturing at the dead-looking vines covering most of the front of the house.

"Going to be?" Katherine said.

"I mean, it is now, only it looks a bit dead," Nick said. "It's not quite right, inside I mean," he went on, opening the door with an unpractised shake and thrust of the Yale key.

"Well, I wouldn't expect it to be that," Katherine said lightly. She'd never seen his furniture—she hadn't been to the rented house, and he had been keeping his furniture in storage, he said—but it made a curious impression in this new house.

It was all bold and new, Nick's collection of possessions. The furniture was expensive, black and metal and bleak, and all with some design behind it. Nothing seemed to harmonize: there was no matching of armchairs and sofas, just a blank standing around of angles and polish. On the table, just above ankle height but long and expensive as a seven-foot glass grave slab, stood a vase. It was rough in texture but as thin as paper; the flowers were placed elsewhere, and this one stood empty and impassive. "It's a Lucie Rie," Nick said, seeing her looking at it, and then he was off, ascribing all his furniture to one name or another, all of it important and all of the names unknown to her.

She was impressed, but all she said was "I don't suppose you bought any of it with a house like this in mind," thinking that the vase was so unlike anything Nick had bought for the shop's use, and wondering about the seriousness that lay behind the shop. He seemed to mount everything for his own amusement in Broomhill, and it was with the same lightness of voice that he would say "Astonishingly, we've made forty pounds clear profit this week" or "How tragic—we're going to have to throw those lilies away," with a giggle and an allusion to the spectre of the workhouse. Everything there was funny; and if he'd never turned her round from the bank of yellow roses, said, "Don't," in that stricken, serious voice and kissed her, she'd never have been prepared for the tone in which he'd said, "It's a Lucie Rie." Nick's ironic detachment, though very extensive, was not all-encompassing, and in his new house, he quickly showed himself when explaining a possession he liked

"No," he said. "I didn't buy any of it for one house in particular. You don't think it looks right?"

"Well," Katherine said, "it's unusual at the moment."

"You're so right," Nick said, seeming relieved by this. "It's the wallpaper, that's all." And, indeed, the wallpaper, as Nick tore at it ineffectually, comically, with his stubby-nailed hands, had been installed by its previous owner with appropriateness in mind. Trellises of spring and summer flowers, in as unnatural and unseasonal profusions as in the florist's shop, ran through the hall and—Nick's word—drawing room against an underimagined yellow ground. It was as if the entangled twiggy growths covering the front of the house had withdrawn, hibernated, and flowered lavishly inside in more extravagant forms. "We don't want any of this," Nick said.

"Leave it," Katherine said, laughing. "Plenty of time to do it properly."

It was all going to be white, plain white, Nick said, though the carpet—he gestured at the plain tufted pale brown, not so different from the through carpeting Katherine had—would do perfectly well. Then the furniture wouldn't look so strange. She could see that but, still, it seemed to her that Nick had acquired an unusually picturesque house that, even if stripped of the rather too bucolic wallpaper, would retain the windows, diamond-leaded like a witch's, the same cosy low-ceilinged proportions and, unless something very radical happened, the same adorable fireplace. It was never going to look very London, Katherine reflected. A thought struck her. "Don't you have any pictures?" she said.

"No," Nick said. "I don't know why. Or books, in case that was your next question."

"Actually," Katherine said, "I was going to suggest we could look at the kitchen."

Nick laughed heartily. "Now that," he said, "I don't think I can face. It's really the worst of it, and I know you're going to say that you really like it. It looks like the sort of kitchen someone would put in a house like this."

It seemed the right moment for a retreat, an apology. "I keep meaning to say," she said, "the other day, when—" she struggled for a point of reference "—when I was so upset—"

"There's really no need," Nick said. "Let's forget about it."

"Yes," Katherine said. "That's best." She turned and smiled, a real smile of relief, sagging with pleasure and, in exact unison, he did exactly the same. They hadn't looked directly at each other for days, had been communicating with each other through glimpses, catching sight of each other through the corner of their eyes, turning away in politeness whenever the other showed signs of looking back, like some game of return and defence. It was immense, their mutual relief, and it made no sense and all the sense in the world when Nick, in pleasure and relief, took a step forward and, quite naturally, hugged her, and, after a relieved and relaxed minute or two, lowered his face to hers and kissed her. She kissed back. It made no sense; it made all the sense in the world.

All at once it was as if the room had changed, not her and not Nick; changed, with the sudden incursion into it of the acts of adultery, and Nick's possessions, into something like a hotel room, planned for this exact purpose, its outer borders now torn and shabby, as if in disgrace. They were turning as they kissed, his mouth and hers the only point of contact between them, their arms flailing about as if seeking an embrace in the dark. She had never noticed until then that she was taller than he was, her neck craning downwards, and as they moved about each other, she sank a little on her knees. He sank too, misunderstanding, and in a second her ankles in their heeled shoes gave, and she collapsed on to the white sheepskin rug. She brought him with her, and then, wildly, he reached round her and pulled the loose cushions from the sofa, throwing them to the floor as he had torn at the wallpaper. "Yes," she said, detaching herself and reaching for the loose seat of the armchair. He threw a glance at the window at the front of the house, small and leaded and half covered with thick unflowering wistaria branches, bare of leaves—"It's all right," Katherine said, breathless, meaning the window, but he could have understood almost anything. She half rose and, fumbling, shakily undid the hook at the top of her zip fastener, tugged at it, her shoulders twisting, pushed down the straps of her dress, undid and pulled off her bra in a disorderly and indecisive sequence, then thrust the dress down to her waist.

She had never presented herself in such a way, and though she did not move, she felt as if she were falling backwards in space. It was only when Nick veiled his spontaneous expression and leant, deliberately, forwards towards her, unbuttoning his own shirt with unshaking deliberate hands, that she started to feel on something like familiar ground. The dizzily unforeseen acts now beginning between the two of them were not familiar, and yet at once she discovered in them a long-trusted pattern, one she knew she could rely on. There, with her dress about her waist, her bra hanging from her elbow, offering herself to a man not her husband, she was discovering what she had, clothed and standing in a hundred different situations, always relied upon: that, in the end, you could force people to be polite to you, and through their politeness, make them act as you chose. No, more than that; dare them not to be polite to you.

And there it was: as the two of them put aside their clothes, undressing and awkwardly tumbling over each other, their limbs meshing into each other's angles, banging against the floor, bone against bone or flesh or the sharp corner of a chair at the height of an eye, even when they were naked and Nick was all at once butting at her in raucous, joyless haste, it was all Katherine, daring Nick not to, and in the middle of it, there rooted the dictates of Nick's politeness. For a few minutes, violently as she clutched at him, fiercely as she pressed against him, she was only matching his fierceness. She saw her own body as if from above, saw it as, in every respect, it was. It seemed inconceivable that she could want this, that she could ever have wanted this.

But then, all at once, the doubt returned, and with it her body tensed. For some minutes she had been lost, transfixed in the thunderous unthinking rhythms of the body, had been taken to a place where there was no thought, there was nothing to say. Only when it all returned did she realize that she had managed to lose it all, that it was, after all, possible. "What is it?" Nick said, pausing at the far end of his stroke, a single line of sweat running down the side of his face, there in front of her own.

"Don't stop," Katherine said, and from then it all disappeared, all thought, all questions, dissolving into a gathering sensation, the air itself seeming to thicken, her body pulling towards some kind of centre, discharging itself in some kind of long thunder, some kind of vast joint-racking yawn, a sneeze, a fit.

He felt all his purpose for her drawn to one point, felt her drawing her body together and hurling it in his direction, and then, as he quickly finished the act for him, going on almost unnoticed through her sighing collapse, fell back and watched her, as it were, pull herself together; the prickled flush across the top of her chest and throat, her pale tight-drawn skin over her bones reddened and raw in spots, her breasts, flat and snub-nosed like deer, rising and falling. He was glad he had not seen until afterwards how much her body bore the marks of her three children, of experience he would never be given access to, and he ran his finger lightly, through her thin layer of cold sweat, down the channel between her wide-separated breasts, and over to mark the diagonal slash, purple and silvery like the trail of a snail against her white skin, faded with freckles, of a long-ago appendectomy. And down, there, horizontal just where the bush of dry, frizzy hair began, untrimmed and lavish, though a little greying, the tight horizontal scar, like a broad smile, of a Caesarean. A child, perhaps more, had been lifted through there—

"It was Tim," she said, understanding that the finger was moving in exploration of the history written on her body, not in playfulness. "He was a breech baby."

But the others had been born normally, and her parts were worn and experienced, he had felt that, shrinking at the time from the observation.

"It's all right," he said, putting his arms awkwardly about her. But the time was past, and she had retreated into what she would allow him or anyone to know. With her hands she made vague, unformed gestures, rather like someone drawing together a *peignoir*, though none was to be had. He understood; he did not linger at this point. He got up, helped her to her feet, and she walked, with wide, almost bowed legs, awkwardly upstairs to the bathroom, gathering up her clothes as she went. He dressed, listening to the shudder and groan of the old hot-water system, the hiss of the shower audible. It was not a large house. Upstairs, the door to the bathroom closed with a click. Nick sat on the sofa, and waited for her to come down, prepared his awkward and kindly farewells.

"It wasn't Tim," she said, coming down. "It was Daniel. I don't know why I said that. You'd think you'd remember." But then she was ashamed, and her voice lowered and shaking, because there was no lover's talking about her body, about what any of her was without a reminder of why she shouldn't and couldn't be here. She had said that it had been Tim who was cut out of her because, in every other way, he had been so difficult, with his wishes and refusals and tears and tantrums and strange obsessions and the worry about what he would become whenever you looked at him. It was not like the removal of an appendix. There was nothing in her flesh that was not written over with the fact of her obligations and her inescapable histories.

She was an hour and a half later home than usual, Nick dropping her at the top of the road in his little purple van with the gold lettering where it was easiest to reverse. She could feel herself shining as she came through her front door, with all the force of the word: "brazen." "Hello?" she called, and from the different parts of the house her children and husband came, not quite approaching her; only the littlest had said, "I didn't know where you'd *gone*," and burst, almost, into tears, and that was only really about his dinner. No one else could reasonably have complained that she might have phoned. Certainly not Malcolm, who was chewing his lip as she explained that from time to time she'd be staying late to sort out some things. He looked at her, not angrily but in the sort of unexplained fear that often seemed to come over him now. She finished her explanation; she might almost have said, "Anyone got any questions?" But without removing her coat, she took Tim off, as sluts do, and drove in her husband's car to the fish-and-chip shop, where she bought supper for all five of them, and hang whatever was in the fridge. She wasn't going to cook it tonight.

The new arrangement, though more irregular than it had been announced, changed the rhythms of the whole household. Daniel took the new irregularity of his mother's hours as some kind of licence, and started appearing from school at odd, late hours. It was only after a few such late appearances—at six, half six, sometimes nearly seven, when the dinner was always on the table—that Katherine brought it up with Malcolm and discovered that, in his opinion, a girl was delaying Daniel. Not that Barbara; she seemed to have disappeared or been dropped. Malcolm seemed relieved about that; Katherine had no view on the subject. No one seemed able to talk to each other in this house any more: they all had their reasons for concealing matters from or snubbing each other.

Across the road, the new family were settling in. Through the Watsons' curtains could be glimpsed a temporary arrangement of furniture; at first, that large front room was filled with armchairs and, crowding over them, the unit filled with objects and a line or two of books. Upstairs, there were more books, a surprising number; it was the boy's bedroom, the boy too tall for his age.

But then, after a week or two, things changed rapidly. Over a weekend, the whole family could be seen pushing the armchairs out of that front room, a dining-table and chairs in. It was a removers' mistake, and then they had their dining room at the front, like most of the rest of the street. (Only Anthea Arbuthnot, who liked to watch, kept it as a sort of second sitting room, one she had had painted yellow, and grandly called "the morning room.") And then, a month or six weeks later, a Cole's van had arrived with sets of ready-made curtains. For the back as well as the front, it was said by the knowledgeable. They'd had them all done at once.

Katherine met the nursery nurse on the street, pushing her tiny darling new baby, Rose, with a face aptly like a tight-gripped rose-bud against the light. "Isn't she good?" Katherine said to the only slightly deflated mother, and, with an air of relief, the nursery nurse agreed.

"For the moment," she said. And then they commented on the expense of having all the curtains done at once but, of course, he worked for the electricity, a responsible job. The baby, Rose, stirred and murmured, and with a sudden red crumpling-open of the face, began to howl. "Oh dear," the nursery nurse said, "time for her feed," and was off.

Katherine hadn't seen the woman opposite since she'd moved in, and wasn't keen to. What was it they said about first impressions—you made your mind up about someone in the first five minutes of meeting them? She thought of how she had been that day, and decided to go on avoiding her. She averted her eyes. In the way of things, she had no exact memory of what she had said to her. The exact memory she had was of what the woman had said in return, her awful sympathy, punctuating Katherine's tale. From that she could understand that she had said what should never be said.

When Katherine was a child, she had longed for a dog. That had been all she ever asked for, for Christmas and birthdays, twice a year. No one could understand where it came from. Neither her mother nor her father had ever had a dog. They were not sociable people, and none of the few people they knew had dogs either. She had argued and argued for a dog, and in the end, her parents had agreed. "But," they said, "it's got to be your responsibility; and we're going to borrow a dog for a week, just to see if you can really look after one."

The dog arrived—where had it come from? She couldn't imagine. It was a white West Highland terrier called Rosie. That was a disappointment; she'd wanted to name it herself, but her mother explained that the dog knew its own name, and wouldn't learn a new one in a week. The first afternoon, she'd played with it inside, calling "Rosie!" over and over, delighting in the way that the dear little dog ran to her every time she said it, never growing bored or suspecting that there was nothing much to run to.

Towards the end of the afternoon, Rosie started to whine, to run to the door, and, after a while, gave a sharp, angry bark. "What's wrong, Rosie?" Katherine had asked, but her mother came out of the kitchen, laughing, and explained that the dog needed a walk. She handed Katherine the lead.

Katherine had imagined a little dog, trotting happily by her side, but Rosie did not do that. She pulled and whined, and stopped dead and had to be pulled forward hard. And, all the time, she stopped to piss. Katherine had never been so embarrassed. It got worse when Rosie stopped dead in the middle of the pavement, squatted and produced an enormous poo. Katherine had felt like crying.

The next morning, she was woken by her mother shouting, and she had to take Rosie out immediately. In the night, the dog had done another poo in the middle of the kitchen. "Rub her face in it," Katherine's father advised, but no one really wanted to do that. The morning walk was even more of a nightmare, and when it was time to turn round and go home, Rosie dug her heels in and had to be pulled whining all the way, her claws skittering on the pavement. At the end of the week, Rosie was handed back—who on earth was her owner?—and there was no more talk about dogs.

But Katherine had told everyone, all her friends, that she was getting a dog. They'd come over that week and made a fuss of Rosie. They all did exactly what Katherine had done, and entertained themselves by calling her from one end of the room to another.

But she'd somehow given them the impression that Rosie was her own dog, her permanent one, and after she was returned, she had to go on answering questions about her, about her tricks, about what she liked to eat, about whether she was going to have puppies. It made Katherine feel sick, pretending that she still had and still enjoyed what she'd once wanted. She had to pretend that no one could come round. It went on for months, and in the end, in a panic, not knowing what on earth else to do, she came to school one day, red-eyed, and told everyone that Rosie had run out in front of a car. "I'll never have another dog," she said, to her impressed audience, some of whom were actually crying on their own behalf. "I just couldn't." It made her a heroine for a number of weeks. Then someone came round, and her mother, unbriefed, told them the whole awful story.

Everything was going wrong in the house. Jane felt that it was exactly the sort of thing she ought to be interested in for the sake of her novel. She'd told everyone she was writing one, and they'd cooed and murmured appreciatively—the grown-ups, that is. The people in her class had chucked spit balls. She ought to be investigating her father, interviewing her mother, observing her brother's behaviour.

Her novel had stuck where it was, in the middle of the nineteenth century. She'd written the first chapter, and by the end of it, Fanny's mother, father, infant brother, her fat nurse proffering sage advice with dropped aitches and (she couldn't help herself as her pen ran dreamily on) even the cruel stepmother with her eye on Fanny's come-by fortune had died in satisfyingly horrible or heartrending ways. Fanny had lost her fortune and two houses (her father's and her stepmother's); and the chapter had concluded with a powerful description of the orphanage on the bleak Lancashire moors burning down. Mrs. Crewkle, the hateful orphanage keeper, had been trapped in the larder, calling bootlessly for Fanny's help. Mrs. Crewkle's too-late repentance and her death surrounded by the larder's hoarded riches, the same ones she'd vindictively denied the starving orphans; Jane was particularly proud of that.

It had stuck there, though. She might be writing about the way they each escaped to their rooms. Her father went to the spare room to tinker with battle plans, or to the garden to thin and weed the plot within an inch of its life, her mother taking charge of the television, or settling in the kitchen—there had never been so many cakes baked in this house, hanging about, forgotten in tins—or in the hall, on the telephone. The three of them were upstairs in their rooms, their different tasks fraudulently described—in Jane's case, and she was pretty sure in Daniel's and Tim's too—as "homework." Or Daniel went out. Nobody stopped him. Everything had gone silent and ugly since that knot of events last year. But no one was talking. They did their talking in other directions and at other people, and how could you write that down? She hadn't managed to get on with it for weeks, perhaps months, but Jane really thought that Fanny, her stepmother, her orphanage and her long-suspended plight on top of a moor where the ruins had now been eerily smouldering for three months might be the thing she could most easily write. It was true, however, that when she sat down, she couldn't see how to get on with it.

It was a surprise, then, when one Saturday morning her mother crisply picked up her car keys from the orangey little wooden table where the telephone and gold-embossed address book sat and said, "I'm going to the supermarket. Coming?" and, without waiting for much of an answer, led Jane out. Over the road, the father of the new family was washing his little turquoise car—an odd thing to do, Jane thought, a Sunday activity rather than a Saturday one. The mother was there too, standing by the bucket. For a moment Jane thought she was helping, ordered out by her husband whose small face, its features squashed together in a rubbery way, gave the impression of a short fuse, though Jane had never seen him lose his temper. But then his wife laughed, and said something; he said something back and she went on laughing, a low and disconcertingly dirty, genuine laugh. "Do it yourself," she said over her shoulder, heading back into the house, but without heat, with affection. She had come outside without a request and without wanting to help. That looked like unfamiliar behaviour to Jane. She was simply talking to her husband; it had an unusual appearance.

Mrs. Sellers turned again, as if she'd forgotten something, saw Jane and her mother before the house, and unhesitatingly raised a hand in greeting. Jane's mother gave a tired little smile and raised her hand, too, but just an upward flick of the wrist. Mr. Sellers followed, an almost satirically enthusiastic wave of his right arm from the shoulder, like a castaway hailing a passing cutter. This Jane's mother ignored. They got into the car and set off.

"They seem a nice family," Katherine said.

"Yes," Jane said. Who, she could imagine Mrs. Sellers saying, did that woman think she was, after that dismissive flick of the wrist. But, of course, Mrs. Sellers was far too nice to say such a thing: it was Jane who was wondering who her mother thought she was. Jane *knew* that something had passed between her mother and Mrs. Sellers, something irretrievable and unforgivable.

"We must invite them over some time," her mother went on, in her light social voice. "It was a shame they weren't here for the party last year. That was what I call a *good* party."

"I don't know that my dad's all that good at having people over," Jane said. "At the moment."

"Rubbish, of course he likes it," Katherine cried. "Oh, watch out, you idiot!" this at a red Mini with a learner driver, edging out six feet into the road, then giving up and staying where he was.

"Isn't this where Nick lives?" Jane said. It was: she knew it was. But her mother overdid it.

"Who?" she said. "Oh, Nick, flower-shop Nick. Yes, I think it must be somewhere around here. I don't really remember. Clever of you to know."

Then Jane was certain, because her mother had said that she'd been to his house, that he'd asked her in, that she'd seen his furniture, that she'd admired his taste but that there were some things that needed to be done, for instance in the bedroom—

No, she hadn't said that. That was Jane filling in. But all that conversation—talking to herself, really—about Nick had passed its long obsessive stage, the casual and constant ostinato to any conversation after which it was not only the overheard name, belonging to someone else in the street or at school that could embarrass Jane, but the coincidence of the mere monosyllable in another word, so that a teacher diverting to the health risks of nicotine, or describing an answer of Jane's to a question about trade in Africa as "slightly cynical" could make her blush. That phase, both of her mother's adoring references and Jane's pained silent registering, went away after the party. Though the references continued, there was for some time an impatience about them and even a dismissive tone. But by the time they stopped, coinciding for no explicable reason with Nick's moving into his new house, they had resumed their fond, almost obsessive tone. The last time Katherine had mentioned Nick to the family, she had been describing the handsome and uncottage-like style in which he had arranged his house. And a matter of months later she was affecting not to know, never to have known, where Nick lived and certainly never to have gone there alone. It was exactly like the way Jane had discussed with Anne the possibility of her mother having an affair, when it had seemed unlikely; when it had seemed altogether possible that she really was having an affair, hadn't she herself stopped talking about it, resisting all enticements to say anything more about what she did or didn't think? "How's your mother's affair going?" Anne's mother had lightly asked once, and while Jane struggled not just for the right answer but for any answer, she'd said, "You're such a romancer, young lady," since she was one of those whom the news of Jane's novel had amused more than impressed. It was just like that, really, her mother's silence.

"Here we are," Katherine said, turning into a neat spot between two Volvos, one blue, one yellow. "Do you know," she said, once they were inside Gateway and pushing a trolley with, for once, not too wobbly a set of wheels. "I haven't seen that Barbara of your brother's for a good long time. What's happened to her?"

"He got rid of her," Jane said, surprised. It had been a good eight months ago. More than once she'd seen that Barbara, poor silly tart, crumpling to her knees almost at the gates of Flint, weeping and half howling in front of her shrugging brother, supported in all this making-a-spectacle-of-herself by two envious votresses, plain and grieving as stone allegories, one at each shoulder.

There was plenty of material there, particularly in what they kept saying to poor silly Barbara, which was obviously not true: "You're better than he is, Barb." Barb was thicker than Daniel, less charming, didn't live in so nice a house, was honestly a bit common and not really so good-looking with her straw-chewing features, the long upper lip calling out for what it would eventually get, a fat moustache. With her silly fat breasts and her silly fat friends, she wasn't better than Daniel in any way.

Daniel had gone his way, and these calumnies clearly worried him about as much as they offered effective consolation to Barbara's red-eyed sorrow.

"Look," Jane said. "Look, that's new—Coca-Cola flavour jam."

"How disgusting," Katherine said. "What an idea."

"I think it sounds nice," Jane said. "Can we get a jar?"

"You'll try it once and never touch it again, and it'll still be in the cupboard in 1980," Katherine said, "and then I'll have to chuck it away, I suppose. No, put it back."

Jane put it back. "He chucked that Barbara," she said. "It was months ago now."

"I thought I'd not seen her around," Katherine said again. "I didn't like her much, though of course I'd not wanted to say anything while they were going steady. Least said soonest mended. He's breaking someone else's heart now, I suppose. You never know anything off Daniel. He's secretive."

"Well, it's that Sandra," Jane said, again surprised, though of course her mother was always at work until six or, one evening a week, seven. "You won't have seen, he always walks home with her now."

"That's nice, walking her home," Katherine said, putting four tins of rice pudding into the trolley. "I hope it's not far out of his way."

The Tannoy announced a good deal for today only in Gateway, ten pence in the pound off beef mince; a voice so weary with tragedy, it might have presided over the fall and decay of a thousand cities, each of them reducing beef mince by ten pence in the pound as its walls fell.

"It's that Sandra," Jane said. "She lives over the road. She's the daughter of those new people, the Sellerses."

Her mother stopped where she was. "Beef. Mince," she said, belatedly reminded by the residue of the voice. "I was planning a shepherd's pie."

"Cottage pie," Jane said. "It's only shepherd's pie if you make it with lamb mince."

"Where do they find these things out?" Katherine said. "I don't think I know the girl—I wouldn't recognize her if I saw her."

"I don't know that they're exactly seeing each other," Jane said. "I mean not going out together or anything, they just walk home together. But they do it every day. Walk home," Jane concluded. She had recently discovered that the word "it" contained a million ruderies from the way the boys would laugh hoarsely with their new, deep, shouty voices at just such a sentence as that. But of course her mother didn't laugh.

"Daniel, he never lets on about anything," Katherine said. "Bleach. He's as bad as his brother, hiding that snake under his bed."

Jane remembered how that snake had ended and said nothing. She thought, out of good taste, her mother might have done the same. They went round the rest of the supermarket in silence, her mother only murmuring the names of products on her neat list. When they were finished and queuing at the check-out, the girl hammering away on her old-fashioned till—Gateway was that sort of shop, a greying one-off with flickering strip lighting greying the tomb-like aisles of frozen food, waist-deep—Katherine said, "Well, we'll have to invite her over some time. Get to meet her." She said it in her light social voice.

Sometimes Jane wondered how her mother saw her own life: a matter of entertaining successive guests and at-homes in tea gowns. "She comes over," Jane said. "Most afternoons."

"Does she now?" Katherine said. "I hope there's nothing I'd have to apologize to her mother for."

"No, I don't think so," Jane said, not liking this role of spy and informant. "They sit in the living room, and drink cups of tea and talk mostly, and then she goes home at half past five, before you get back. I mean, half past five, it's before you get home, not that she goes to avoid you or anything. I don't know why she doesn't come round, the days you're not working. She probably goes in time for tea, has to."

"She seems like a nice girl," Katherine said.

"She is, I think," Jane said. She could see that her mother had shaped reality to suit her. Five minutes before, she'd had no idea of Sandra at all. Now she had a considered impression of her.

"Perhaps she might stay for supper on Tuesday," Katherine said. "I might cook some lamb chops. That would be suitable."

"Why do we eat meat every day?" Jane said. "I really don't like it at all. I think I'm going to become a vegetarian."

"If you become a vegetarian, you can cook your own dinner," Katherine said. "I'm not doing two lots of shopping and cooking two separate meals every night, if that's what you thought."

"You wouldn't have to," Jane said. "Everyone could eat what I was eating. We could all have a vegetarian dinner."

"Very selfish of you," Katherine said. "So no one's allowed to eat what you don't fancy all of a sudden?"

"It's not about fancying or not fancying something to eat," Jane said. "Like not liking—raspberry jelly. It's that I think it's wrong."

"Heavens," Katherine said, infuriated, "how you remind me sometimes of—" she cast around, waving her hands, for an adequately frightful forebear "—of your father's aunt Edith, you really do."

"I can't imagine how," Jane said, since Great-aunt Edith was one of her mother's regular stand-bys. She had begun this conversation, tryingly, in a speculative way, trying out an idea she'd overheard. But now that it had been said it was hardening into a conviction. She saw herself at the front of a glowing army of vegetarians with their vegetarian banners, marching into the future at the head of a clean and grateful flock of liberated lambs.

"Perhaps Friday would be better," Katherine said, half to herself, fumbling in her purse for the £12.37 the girl was asking for. "It's your dad's military re-creation night on Tuesdays."

"What's he doing next?" Jane said.

"It's going to be Cavaliers and Roundheads again, I believe," Katherine said. "I can't remember what battle it's going to be exactly—Naseby, was it? Your dad's going to be Prince Rupert, whoever Prince Rupert was. Not that I pay any attention. I expect we'll all go and watch, but we'll take a picnic and if it's raining, we'll sit in the car."

"It'll have to be a vegetarian picnic," Jane said, feeling that her decision had been lost a little.

"If you make it yourself," Katherine said. "Can you honestly see Daniel living off lettuce?"

"You don't have to live off lettuce," Jane said. "There are lots of delicious meals you could cook that don't have meat in them. You'd hardly miss it after a day or two."

"Macaroni cheese, most of them live off, and end up looking very pasty, too," Katherine said. "Has someone been getting at you? I'd like to have a word with them."

"No one's been getting at me," Jane said, cross at her mother's humouring tone as much as at her suspicion. "I've been thinking about it and I just think it's disgusting, eating dead bodies."

"No one's ever—" Katherine said, guiding the trolley laden with bags out through the supermarket doors.

"And the way they experiment on dogs, too, making them smoke cigarettes—"

"Fortunately," Katherine said, "I don't think the question of eating a dog that's died of smoking too much is going to arise, since we don't live in China. And I don't think having a bacon sandwich is the same as eating a dead body. That's a charming way of putting it. I hope you're not planning to persuade any of your friends to take up vegetarian food along with you."

"I might do," Jane said, now properly sulking, her arms crossed in the front seat of the car. "Why not?"

"Because I don't want Anne's mother on the phone to me complaining that you've talked Anne into something like that," Katherine said. "I know how you two do whatever the other one does. Is it her who's talked you into it? I'd like to have a word with her mother, if that's what's happened."

"I can think for myself, you know," Jane said.

"Macaroni cheese," Katherine said, "night after night. Or are you not allowed to eat cheese either?"

"I'm not a vegan, Mother," Jane said. "I'm going to go on eating cheese. And eggs and milk."

"How cruel," Katherine said. "Snatching the milk from the mouths of tiny calves. I suppose that's a relief. Anyway, you'll have to put off giving up meat until I go for next week's shop, I hadn't taken it into consideration. It was probably too late to save the life of that particular chicken, in any case."

"What chicken?"

"The frozen one I just bought, the one sitting in the boot. I think it was probably dead already."

"It's not *funny*," Jane said.

"Oh, no," Katherine said. "Perish the thought."

"You'd be wanting to go vegetarian yourself if Nick told you to," Jane said, but she only muttered this, and her mother, her hands tightening on the car's wheel, her mouth pursing, her head quarter-turning to give Jane a look as she slouched resentfully, didn't hear or respond to the comment.

Tim left school with the others at the same time every day. They'd stopped asking him, though, where he was going when he left them at the bus-stop and turned in the other direction, walking down towards Broomhill. He had something to do, somebody to see. He'd been doing it three times a week for a while. It was important, and they'd stopped trying to find out what it was. The mystery, solidly maintained, had long since lost its charm.

He walked down towards Broomhill, but stopped before then, catching a bus—he didn't want to walk past his mother's shop. He got out at the university, crossed the road and went into the building. He didn't need to ask anyone where to go: he just went up to the second floor. It was the fourth door on the left. The matron smiled at him as he passed, and he gave her a little wave. She was used to him now. He pushed open the door to the private room peeping through the gap in case anyone else was there. Today there wasn't, and Tim went in. The face on the pillow turned to look at who it was, but the face on the pillow knew already who it was. There was no welcome or pleasure there. Tim didn't mind, and he made himself smile as widely as he could. It was good to cheer people up when they were going through something very very sad.

"Hello, Andrew," Tim said. "It's me again."

"My sister's gone vegetarian," Daniel told Sandra, as they were walking home together one afternoon. It was a warm day; the sun was hotter than it ought to be in May, and underneath the canopy of old trees lining Buckleigh Road, it was moist, fragrant and languid, like the interior of a green canvas tent on a hot day. On the pavement, sticky sap from the trees sucked at the soles of their shoes.

"What's she done that for?" Sandra said. After eight months, she was starting to sound a little Sheffield—"doon that for"—but there was still a hesitancy in her speech, like a competent speaker of a foreign language bringing out a first sentence on holiday after long lack of practice.

"She said she had a vision in the supermarket," Daniel said.

"Which one?" Sandra said.

That made Daniel laugh in a flurry of hilarity, subsiding into a doggy shaking of his head. "Gateway," he said eventually, and that set them both off.

"I must go there," Sandra said. "Or they could put it on their adverts—'Gateway, it's good for having visions in.' "

"It might only be vegetarian visions," Daniel said, "so they'd not put that in an advert. It'd be bad for business unless they could guarantee you'd not have your vegetarian vision until after you'd paid for your meat."

"What's she eating, then?" Sandra said.

"She's just eating the vegetables, with gravy on," Daniel said. "I've told her the gravy's made out of dead animals too, but she won't have it. She says it's—what does she say?—a by-product so that's all right, apparently. She tried to get my mother to cook something special for her, but she won't, and she won't let Jane cook anything for herself because there's not room in the kitchen and she'll leave too much of a mess and she doesn't know how to cook. So she's just eating the vegetables we all have."

"With gravy on," Sandra said.

"The thing is she doesn't even like vegetables," Daniel said. "She won't eat broccoli, and she doesn't like cooked tomatoes, or celery in any shape or form, and potatoes only if they're roasted. She won't eat them mashed."

"Won't she eat chips?"

"Oh, she'll eat chips," Daniel said.

"Well, that's potatoes," Sandra said.

"I suppose it is, when you come to think of it," Daniel said. "I don't know why she's become vegetarian when she doesn't like vegetarian food. It's like going to live in—in Russia if you don't like Russian food."

"What's Russian food like?"

"I don't know," Daniel said. "It's probably horrible, like school dinners. It's probably grey and all mixed in together if you can get it at all. Probably cabbages."

"So why would anyone go and live in Russia?"

"That was just an example—I might have said anywhere," Daniel said. "When you ask her, she just says it's wrong and she won't eat dead bodies."

"That's disgusting," Sandra said.

"That's what she says," Daniel said. "My dad keeps walking round eating cold bits of beef in front of her, saying, 'Yum, lovely dead-body sandwich,' because that's one thing she really does like, cold beef sandwich with brown sauce on it."

"Your dad does that?" Sandra said, because the only time she'd glimpsed Daniel's father was when he'd said hello, in a small, shy voice, as if he thought she might laugh or make fun of his tiny head, and then disappeared as soon as he could. He seemed more like a guest in that house than the man who owned it.

Sandra paid a lot of attention to the way the people opposite, the Glovers, actually looked. Some of them looked normal and others were strange-looking. Daniel was the most normal-looking. People said he was a good-looking boy, and even sexy—she'd become more popular at school, some people in the class suddenly knowing her name without rudely asking a bystander first, once it had got out that she walked home with him most nights. He was that good-looking boy Daniel Glover a year above her, and she was his friend. But actually Daniel, among his family, wasn't particularly good-looking, only normal. His head was the right size, his nose and mouth were the right size for his head, his skin was OK—better than Sandra's, though the Clearasil her mother had bought her without any fuss after a rehearsed request was making some difference. He wasn't thin or fat; he walked as if he was quite happy with the body he was in. His mother was normal-looking, too, though her hands and feet were scrubbed red and huge, like flippers.

Sandra didn't often meet them when she went round to Daniel's. She hardly ever saw his mother close up, since, he said, she came home

later from work than his father, the three days a week she worked, and
once a week quite a lot later. She worked at a florist's in Broomhill.
Their house was always full of lovely flowers, not just the once-in-a-
blue-moon vase of mixed tulips her mother treated herself to, buying
them, she knew, from somewhere other than Daniel's mother's shop.
The rest of the family either didn't notice or, like Sandra, didn't comment. But Sandra knew her mother loved that sight unconditionally, of
bright clashing flowers in a vase, unarranged, lovely. Loved it more
than Daniel's mother did, she knew that. Daniel's family weren't often
there together, and she liked to inspect them covertly from the kitchen
window when they set off in the morning. His droopy sister, her hair
lank and blonde, and never quite washed, hanging down in solid ribbons, her big ears poking through the gaps, peering through ugly
glasses she couldn't have chosen herself. She might have been one of
those Jameson girls, the sisters of Francis's little friend, one of whom
was in Sandra's class, never seeming to notice anything. The sister—
Jane—she was a year below Sandra. She was weird-looking or, rather,
she could have been all right if she didn't always walk in a way that
looked like someone nervously trying out a new and dangerous
machine. But when the five of them walked out in the morning, always
in dribs and drabs, the mother shouting for the last dawdler, which was
usually Daniel, it was the weirdness of the father and the little boy that
took your attention. They really did look objectively weird. She knew
it wasn't very mature to think of people in that way, but you couldn't
help it. When you saw the little boy, you thought that you'd never seen
a kid with so tiny and round a head. It was like a bowling ball sitting on
his shoulders. For some reason he'd had his hair cut in a short back and
sides, probably nits, and his head, with its big nose and the same sticky-
out ears as his sister, was really ridiculous. The three children looked
strange when they stood together, their hair colour all so different,
Daniel's a dark flop over his forehead and falling into his eyes, Jane's a
dirty blonde, but the little boy a real ginger, which must have come
from nowhere. You thought his ball-headedness took the prize, but his
father had exactly the same tiny head. There was a word for the rest of
him, and the word was "weedy." Daniel's mother wasn't much taller
than his dad, maybe only by a fringe and a nose, but with her big hands
and generally bigger scale, the way she held herself and never scurried,
ratlike, as her husband did, she looked much larger, much more normal. Sandra watched them, fascinated. She tried not to think, though,

of her own family's element of freakishness, the way anyone would when they saw them comment on the weird tallness of her own brother. Maybe all families were a bit weird from the outside, until you knew them. But with Daniel's father, you forgot the pinheadedness close up. There was something much weirder: his fingernails. They were scrupulously clean, white as bone, but he had let them grow until they looked like fragile white claws. Not like women's fingernails—they were square at the end and blunt—but they made your skin crawl. She had to stop herself shuddering whenever Daniel's father moved his hands at the thought they might come anywhere near her.

When they were at the top of the road, Daniel was still talking about being vegetarian. She liked these deep conversations with him. She guessed that he'd never known another girl he could talk to like this.

"The thing is," he was saying, "that vegetarians think they're saving the lives of animals, but they're not."

"They're not eating them, though," Sandra said.

"But the ones who are alive, they'll still be killed," Daniel said, "and I'll eat them and you'll eat them."

"That's true," Sandra said.

"You see, if they're not needed for food, they won't exist at all," Daniel said. "No one would call those hens into existence if everyone was vegetarian. Either way they'd be dead or never be born, so they don't win whatever we do. As humans," he finished grandly.

"But do you think we should be allowed," Sandra said, "to destroy the life of a chicken once we've created it?"

"I see what you mean," said Daniel. Sandra, too, had no particular feeling about whether this was a good or a sensible point to make. It might have been total rubbish. She didn't care about the life of chickens, and really she thought it totally stupid of Daniel's sister to alter her own life for the sake of something so totally trivial as the lives of however many thousand chickens.

They stopped for a moment by a house where that woman lived who'd just had a baby; she was outside, staring up at the guttering, or perhaps at the sky. She still looked pregnant, but by her was a pram. The baby couldn't be seen, but it must be getting the sun. The way they'd stopped, it was as if there were now three of them, or four, in a group.

"What's your purpose?" Daniel said, looking at the big blue pram in which a baby lay, absorbed by the sight of the blue sky.

"To be eaten," Sandra said lightly, and the woman heard this, and turned. She looked dazed; she hadn't understood what Sandra said, but her lack of understanding had started long before Sandra said anything.

"Come on," Daniel said, and they started to walk again.

They were nearly home. It was a clear day of fat clouds in the translucent blue, hanging there in a still way. Toys for baby, unreachable. The moon must be up there, and in an hour it would probably pop out of the blue, startling in daylight. She always liked that spectacle. In London, there had always been straight lines drawn in the sky. Every couple of minutes another plane making its way out into the world or back again. Here, there was never anything. The sky was what it must have been before Sandra was born.

"What are you thinking?" Daniel said.

"Nothing," Sandra said. "What are you thinking? Deep thoughts?"

"No," Daniel said. "I was just remembering that my mum asked me if you'd like to come over for tea on Friday."

"Your mum did?" Sandra said.

"I mean, only if you want to. You could watch my sister eating vegetables."

"With gravy. I might go vegetarian myself, keep her company."

Daniel laughed at this idea. She hadn't thought it funny, but to Daniel there seemed no way she could suddenly become a vegetarian. She didn't go into Daniel's house today: she said untruthfully that she'd got a lot of homework to do. It was something to do with leaving space around Friday, to make her appearance then welcome, and not routine. They said goodbye; she shut her own front door behind her and went thoughtfully upstairs. In the pink bathroom, into which someone had thought it a good idea to put an avocado suite, she washed her hands, stained with today's black ink and then her face. She dried her face on the pale blue towel and then, experimentally, she smiled, then bared her teeth in the mirror. Daniel was right, she saw. They were unmistakably the teeth of a meat-eater. She folded the towel, still smiling, but now for herself rather than for the mirror. It was odd. She hadn't expected what had been there for some weeks, and she hadn't really noticed it. It was more like a removal of heavy difficulties than anything positive. She wasn't remotely in love with Daniel, she couldn't be, but in the last few weeks she'd become happy. Her skin was better, too.

"That was Katherine Glover," her mother said, enunciating the name, coming back from the telephone. "I thought she had decided to ignore us."

"What—the woman over the road?" Bernie said. "What's she want, phoning in the middle of dinner? Husband run off again?"

"Well, she wasn't to know when we eat our dinner," Alice said. "She's got a little boy, they probably eat earlier than we do."

"He's in my class at school," Francis said.

"Is he really?" Alice said. "He looks very young. She was asking for you, Sandra—she wanted to know whether you could go over for tea on Friday night. Is she a friend of yours, her daughter?"

"No," Sandra said. "It's Daniel I'm more friends with."

"Ah," Bernie said, in a knowing voice, and they all got on with their lasagne.

The phone call had come out of the blue, but after that, relations were restored to what they might have become sooner. The next morning, the exits of the two families coincided exactly, and rather than wave from the other side of the road, Katherine crossed, all smiles, and had a word with them. She was so pleased Sandra could come to tea—hoped there was nothing she didn't like to eat—promised not to send her home too late. Bernie pointed out it wasn't a school night so it didn't matter within reason, and she turned her gaze on him—she'd hardly met him, they both seemed to realize at once—and agreed to use the phrase, within reason. "We've been so busy," she said, apparently in relation to nothing in the conversation. It was some sort of acknowledgement, apology even, that eight months before she'd sat with Alice and told her everything, and until now there had been nothing between them, perhaps an awkward and half-returned wave.

Katherine, until recently, when they'd seen that Sandra had become much friends with her son, had acquired a name at number eighty-four, and the name was "the mad lady." They got into the car. In the mirror, Bernie watched her make her way back across the road to where her family stood, as if stuck still about their car in the drive. She seemed quite unembarrassable. He thought of launching a sardonic comment, but turned the key and started the car.

When Malcolm heard from Katherine that they were expecting a guest to dinner on Friday night, he misunderstood. For most of their lives together, it had seemed to him that he was admitted only to the public downstairs rooms of Katherine's mind. The more intimate spaces and speculations, the whole upstairs and attics of her thinking were kept from him. So when she told him two days before about this guest, he said wretchedly, "Oh, good," taking the statement at face value. A guest—by which he thought she meant an adult guest—was coming. She made these statements in the tone of one to whom guests for dinner were commonplace and even a bore. She always had. It seemed obvious to him that the only person it could be was Katherine's boss Nick. In a few minutes it became clear that it wasn't a guest in the normal sense but a girlfriend of Daniel's. Why Katherine had implied someone who would need impressing he couldn't understand. He found it hard to forgive her, even for so small a misunderstanding.

On Tuesday night he went to the battle re-creation society. He drove into Hillsborough, down in the valley. The houses here were packed more tightly together, a little shabbier. There was a crowd about, all wearing blue and white scarves, all trudging gnome-like in the same direction, towards the football ground. It was a steady crowd, with none of the urgency and those flurries of violence that would burst out later, after the match. He drove carefully, though, since even before the match there was foolishness in the air, and someone might choose to run out into the road. He made a note to drive back from the society the long way round, to avoid any trouble.

The society met in a school hall over the brow of the next-but-one hill. The school let them meet in it for almost nothing, persuaded by John Ashworth. He taught chemistry there. It was convenient for him, at any rate. There were already twelve cars in the car park when Malcolm drove in, though he was early. That meant twenty already, a good turnout.

Some weeks the society met to plan their biannual re-creation of a battle, which wasn't going to happen until next summer, a good long way off. For those re-creations the core membership of about forty expanded dramatically. Wives and children, colleagues of Richard Thwaite's from the council, John Ashworth's chemistry pupils, all and sundry were pressed into versions of Civil War uniform and given antique-looking guns, or gun-like objects. The quality of the outfits and the power of the delusion varied. Some members of the society were magnificent in hand-crafted uniforms, kept carefully in boxes, and put on appropriate-looking wigs, the illusion only broken, perhaps, by a pair of solicitor-like spectacles peeping out through a cavalier's poodle wig. Others, roped in at the last moment, made do with a cardboard breastplate painted grey, an old trilby spray-painted silver (surprisingly all right from a distance) and a sawn-off broom-handle.

These less plausible warriors were encouraged not to stand together, or at the front, but to melt into the general illusion, their props (of doubtful admissibility) borrowing authenticity from some more scrupulous adjacence. They had as good a day as anyone, and there were some in the society who argued that what they ought to be interested in was battlefield tactics, not the minutiae of breeches and flintlocks, and tactics could as interestingly be re-enacted by three hundred women in flowery skirts if it came to that. Others, more hardline, said that it wouldn't feel right unless everyone was in the right dress for the period, and got into what in the end were surprisingly personal arguments about cuirasses. That was George Burke, who worked for the education authority and who refused to recruit any temporary participants for the re-creations, saying they would get in the way and mess things up. But he always lost the argument when it was pointed out that if you limited participation to people in the pedantically correct uniforms, you'd end up trying to re-create major clashes of civilization with twelve immaculately dressed obsessives. The other point, which no one raised but everyone bore in mind, was that it would also mean everyone submitting their uniform to the approval of George, who was not a generous fellow, in which case you might end up re-creating battles with only one person.

Tonight it was Malcolm's turn to talk. The society alternated planning meetings with evenings on which one of them would talk about an interest of his. It wasn't necessarily the Civil War. People in the society had the widest possible interests—Agincourt, Thermopylae, Bosworth Field, Waterloo, Copenhagen (difficult to do on a moor), El Alamein. If only they could dig up large stretches of the moor, the first day of the Somme might be an enjoyable spectacle. But they'd stuck with the Civil War because the landscape was right, and they'd amassed properties and quite a bit of joint expertise on the subject. But they were all interested in each other's more individual interests, and each gave a sort of talk from time to time. Malcolm's particular interest was in the nineteenth-century little imperial wars. The long-bow membership thought it all very vulgar and coarse, he knew, but, a nuts-and-bolts man, he was going to enlighten them with a lot of interesting stuff about early machine-guns in the Sudan campaigns—the Gatling, the Martini-Henry breech loader, the Gardner and then, what Kitchener relied on, the Maxim gun, "which we have got and they have not." It was a good story. He'd talked before about Fred Burnaby, but in a different context, and they'd enjoyed it.

He'd been in the society for six years now. It'd only been going for a year when he joined. He hadn't known such things existed. He'd been at the city library one lunch time and had come across a biography of Redvers Buller he'd not read—it was in the "recently returned" rack, and normally it was shelved with what he didn't bother with, biography. He knew the military history shelves thoroughly, of course. "What's that you've got there?" Margaret, his newish secretary, said to him as he came back through her room. He showed her the cover, a bristling moustached bruiser in a nineteenth-century uniform, stiff with medals, and with one blazingly mad eye, looking very much as you would expect a Redvers Buller to look.

"Oh, are you interested in army things?" Margaret said. "You ought to meet my husband, he's always on about guns and battles. He's in a society for it."

"What sort of society?" Malcolm said.

"A sort of restaging society," Margaret said. "They restage, re-create, I should say, old battles. They're all going up on Burbage moor next spring and we're going to line up in troops and fight the battle of Naseby all over again, not with people being killed, of course. I'm in it, too, though I don't go to the meetings or anything. I leave that to Richard. I'm going to be a cavalier, because of my hair—" she pulled out her recently permed long hair horizontally, to either side of her face "—and Richard said I can be killed early and then I'll go up and sit on a hill, watch the rest from there."

"That sounds interesting," Malcolm said.

"You could come if you like. They need everyone they can get. I expect you'd be a roundhead, though."

"Oh, why?" Malcolm said, so plaintively that Margaret burst out laughing. It was funny for Malcolm to say that, he could see, but when they'd done it in school and whenever he'd read any kind of book about it since, that hadn't been the side he'd seen himself on. He had been flying through the night on a horse, sleeping soundlessly up oak trees, like anyone else.

"Well," Margaret said, "it's really just your hair. I expect they'd want you to be on the short-haired side, especially since they're a bit overloaded on the other. You've to be grateful for whatever station they see you in."

"Oh, I wouldn't mind one bit," Malcolm said fervently, and Margaret looked with some surprise at her nice but mousy boss. "Do you think I could join the society, really?" he said.

"I'll let Richard know of your interest," Margaret said formally, and returned to a pile of questionable mortgage applications.

At home, he'd mentioned it casually. Katherine was still busy with the little one, who was only three, and barely registered the information. It was a few months later he worked out that somehow she'd thought it was part of his Wednesday-night gardening club. How could she have got that impression? The misapprehension had only become clear when he'd wondered out loud whether Daniel might like to join in at the society's big re-creation in the spring, to boost numbers.

"Some sort of flower show?" Katherine said, and he'd explained about the battle of Naseby, and quickly discovered he had to go back to the beginning and explain what he'd been doing every Tuesday night. He thought then that it wouldn't be difficult to have an affair behind Katherine's back, if she showed so little curiosity in his doings. He had no candidate in mind: it was an instant, disappointing thought, what he could get away with, when there was nothing he wanted to get away from.

He loved the society. He'd always been interested in that sort of thing, but he kept his collection of books about the Afghan wars, the Zulu wars, the wars in the Sudan and the Boer wars upstairs in his study. When they'd moved into the house in 1969, at a preferential mortgage rate, the two things he'd liked about it on seeing it were the south-facing garden, well sheltered (the abundance of rocks in the soil he wouldn't find out about till later) and the decent-sized fifth bedroom. With Tim only a serious toddler, his face usually screwed up in concentration and hardly needing a room of his own yet, Malcolm and Katherine hadn't quite realized their different plans for the house. For her, it was what she wanted, some sort of guarantee of gentility, a spare bedroom, more than you needed so that you could ask people to stay overnight or for the weekend. (Who, though?) Malcolm saw it as a study, even, he said pretentiously to himself, a *library*. In their previous house, his growing collection of books had been kept, forbiddingly, in the hallway or in a dark wood-effect case, vying for space in their bedroom with Tim's small bed. A temporary measure, like Tim sleeping in his parents' room. In the new house, another bookcase joined those two, but upstairs, in the fifth room, and it had become a collection. With the discussions and recommendations from the group, the third bookcase filled up too. Not just with library books and paperbacks. He was doing well at work, and the accidental third child hardly seemed to make any difference to any of their standing arrangements, despite what they'd feared. They weren't the sort of people for expensive foreign holidays; he found himself buying new, expensive hard-backed books on a whim, not always ones about his main interests in life.

Daniel agreed to take part in the first re-creation, though not quite as readily as Malcolm might have liked. Malcolm couldn't have asked Katherine or Jane if they'd like to put a cavalier's breastplate on. Anyway, someone had to look after Tim, but they would all come and watch. At the meeting the week before, all the extras, the schoolchildren, wives, colleagues, relations, crowded into the school hall. There was a festive atmosphere, and the usual members of the society stood at the front, like a gathering of officers before their troops. He felt bold and self-confident, but also self-aware—Daniel was in the front row, chatting happily to someone's daughter. The room smelt of old cheese, and of dust burning on an element, and piled-up black-out curtains left to moulder in corners. Malcolm wasn't expected to say anything, but he felt nervously self-conscious just the same.

Prince Rupert gathers his forty men on the ridge, the other side of Burbage Rocks, beyond the car park; they line up. Their broomhandles, their silver-painted trilbies glitter in the morning sun. The picnickers can see the royal forces, shuffling themselves into line like a pack of cards, shambling about each other on the top of the ridge, a fine defensive position. (Unless the enemy approaches from the back, over the bridge and up the A-road.) Finally, the magnificent army, forty of them, the flower of divine-right chivalry, mostly made up of other men's wives, is inspected by a chemistry teacher. Prince Rupert's thin voice, exhausted by years of yelling at third years about Bunsen burners, drifts across the purple-tufted flank of the moor, across the pleasant noise of the brook, to where the civilians, men, women and helpless children dip their boiled eggs into little heaps of salt in silver foil.

But on the other side, just beyond the brook and the picnicking spot, Thomas Fairfax is drilling his fifty troops. The sympathies of the crowd are already enlisted, and Sir Thomas Fairfax, as he got out of his red Cortina in the car park, silver-sprayed cricket pads and squat silver helmet in hand, was surprised to be booed, at very short range, by two well-briefed chemistry pupils. Now, the parliamentarians, mostly faithful attenders of the society, form themselves into tiny battalions. Over the small rise now comes Cromwell and his thirteen thousand troops, marching in close step; all twenty are grudgingly applauded by the onlookers on their tartan rugs, the faint noise muffled by their holding pork pies, slices of quiche, bags of Quavers and raspberry yoghurts, and soon carried away by the wind. Even from here, you can see their grim-faced determination. They are just by the A-road, the two forces conspicuous on their elevations though separated by the little brook, and the battle is about to begin.

Earl Margaret has the whistle, and is the designated instigator of the hostilities. She scrambles down the heather to a sort of mid-point, raises her whistle, does a little currsy-cum-courtly bow to both sides, and then to the spectators, who are greatly enjoying all this. But before she can blow it, from the road behind comes a furious hooting and a shriek of brakes. A driver in his car has seen the first stages of 14 June 1645 as he descended the rise, and, open-mouthed and inattentive, has wandered on to the wrong side of the road, clipping the wing of a white Mini going in the opposite direction. Everyone, even the soldiers, abandons their position and runs over to see what has happened; Sir Thomas Fairfax remarks to Prince Rupert, as they stand and enjoy the furious altercation between the drivers, that it might not have been a very good idea to mount this event within such close sight of an A-road. "It's all about convenience," Prince Rupert says. "We had this out, we decided it was as well to have it close enough to the car park that we'd not be clambering over miles of moorland before we could start. There was the question of the toilet arrangements, too. It's quite handy here."

Now Earl Margaret does blow the whistle, and the battle begins. Fairfax's men begin to file along the top of the ridge, perhaps overdoing the head-hung exhaustion. After five minutes, Prince Rupert's men—Earl Margaret having rejoined them—mount an attack. Some of the lady royalists break ranks, running down the hill waving their broom-handles and dustbin-lids about their flowing locks like cavemen, uttering very uncourtly yelps and howls, and have to be called back by means of Prince Rupert's rude and blunt-vowelled commands. He wishes he, too, had brought a whistle.

They cross the brook, some treading across delicately on the stepping stones, even queuing politely, others flinging themselves heartily into the stream with warlike shrieks, and when they are all over, mount a charge on Fairfax's cavalry. There are no horses, and, after long discussion, there are no indications of horses, either. "I'm not standing there with a sodding hobby-horse between my legs," was the general view in the society's meetings, and you just have to know that the ten at the back are Fairfax's cavalry. They wheel and retreat, to the spattering applause, like rain on this sunny day, of the onlookers. "Who's that meant to be, then?" the newly arrived driver asks his hosts—it turns out he didn't know there ever was a civil war in England, even, and everything has to be explained from scratch. They all explain from scratch, even the seven-year-old. The royalist cavalry has been routed, and the infantry (six of them) soon follow, stumbling away across the moor. One of Fairfax's men is killed, pinned violently to the moor with a pike, stabbed again and again. This is the first death—they thought they'd just have the one at this stage—and everyone applauds as the first casualty milks his scene, rising up three times before succumbing. He stands up, once thoroughly killed, and bows to everyone, left, right, centre, to general amusement and gratification.

But already the Fairfax forces have summoned aid, and over the hill, just like a Western, the car-driver remarks, come Cromwell and his men. They've been drilled better, and advance in a grim silence, their pikes held out straight. The royalists re-form into battalions, and finally the two armies engage.

The whole thing comes briefly to a halt, with the arrival of the photographer/journalist from the *Star*, who had promised good coverage in the paper but had got the starting time wrong, and then it resumes; they all chase about for ten minutes, and finally return to a position in front of the spectators, where the royalists are ceremoniously killed with bayonets, broom-handles, pikes, most of them for the fourth or fifth time now. The spectators applaud; the dead stand up; they all bow.

Afterwards, the state of his marriage was clear to Malcolm. Other families came along and cheered and joined in; were interested. It had never occurred to him that Katherine might show an interest, and he put her next to the other sorts of wives, the ones who turned up rarely, if at all, the ones who made carping comments, complained about the cold, or ignored their husbands' interest. Ed's wife was like that, by his account, thought the whole thing such a waste of time and money (you could see her, pink candlewick bedspread drawn up to her cold-creamed face, sour eyes watching and nagging), and Ed had been driven to ask Malcolm seriously if he could open a building-society account for his small club and warfare expenditure, all correspondence going to some other designated address. Malcolm couldn't help him,

and things weren't as bad as that in his own household. Amused toler-
ance was about as strong as it got.

On the other hand, there were women like his secretary Margaret,
Richard Thwaite's wife, who'd thrown herself into it heart and soul,
and obviously had the whale of a time, marching up and down the
roped-in irregulars, shouting "Give me a B . . . (B!), give me a U . . .
(U!)," until the picnicking onlookers laid down their hard-boiled eggs
and clapped along with her bugger-chant.

Most of the wives, like Margaret, treated it as a jolly, a day out
in knickerbockers that might as well end in throwing a half-eaten
Bakewell pudding slap in the side of Cromwell's face as he was making
his victory speech. Cromwell hadn't asked for his wife, Margaret, Earl
of Arlington, to throw puddings at him, however merrily.

Malcolm didn't fancy either the open ridicule or the enthusiastic
joining in, which seemed to be the two main alternatives. He would
settle for amused disdain. But he hadn't noticed that amused disdain
was, in fact, what he'd got until the car, in those days a brown Morris,
had stopped in the car park by Burbage rocks and Malcolm could place
Katherine next to the others. He hadn't asked her to show an interest
in his interests, and any curiosity had only shown itself in airy, smiling
allusions. She dusted his books, but never opened one; never commented, either, like Ed's wife, on the stupidity of the *cost* of all of this,
and for that he was more or less grateful. What he mostly wanted was
to be allowed to get on with his interests undisturbed, and he ran
through the various alternatives—an informed interest, a lively unin-
formed one, down to open opposition—before coming to the conclusion that Katherine's attitude wasn't the worst one, though she seemed
capable, if comments afterwards could be read correctly, of mildly
insulting one or two of the more serious members of the society. "As
long as I live," she said, laughing hilariously, "I'll never forget the look
on that Richard Thwaite's face when he realized that his own wife had
thrown the pudding at him. Talk about outraged dignity." What, if
anything, he was grateful for was that she wouldn't be embarrassed by
any of this. It took a lot to embarrass Katherine and, unlike most people, if she found herself doing something, then by definition it was
clearly not an embarrassing thing to be doing.

All the same, it wasn't until the battle of Naseby that it became quite
clear to Malcolm what his marriage was, and what it looked like. It had
taken thirteen years and a Civil War battle to show that.

"Katherine enjoy it, did she?" Ed asked at the next meeting, flushed with success.

"Yes, I think so," Malcolm said, taking off his duffel coat and adding it to the pile at the edge of the stage.

"We'll have to persuade her to take a part next time," Ed said, but this was so evidently unlikely that he faltered while he was saying it. Perhaps he envisaged Katherine in her pale blue summer frock with a pattern of daisies, a white cotton-knit cardigan with mother-of-pearl buttons over her shoulders, her skirt spread over a groundsheet and, by her side, an insulated picnic box in pink plastic to keep everything cold.

"I don't think she'd enjoy taking part half so much," Malcolm said. "She enjoyed it as a spectacle mostly, I would think."

He felt he could live with this; it seemed to him like a stable situation, a sustainable one, and perhaps only in the more concentrated exposure of their two-weeks' holiday each year did it seem as if the long repayments on the initial commitment, as it were, might not reach the agreed term. One fortnight on a barge on the Norfolk Broads, the usual amused allusions, the rather tarter comments made directly to the children on the reading matter their father had seen fit to bring along, turned into something worse. It had rained every day, and the cramped ingenious space, smelling of mould and other people's old dinners, found itself brownly listening to something unfamiliar to Malcolm and Katherine: raised voices and the endless games of Monopoly definitively abandoned long before the end of the evening. It wasn't much of a success, they privately and ruefully agreed later, but the failure had been Norfolk's, the weather, blamed on the idea of managing a barge through the narrow canals. That last one had been Katherine's conclusion. Malcolm felt that he and Daniel had done quite well between them. But he hadn't contradicted her, in the circumstances.

It was only after she'd taken the job in that flower shop that he'd really started to wonder. That was what he said, once, to Margaret and to Richard too, who'd turned up at the office Friday-night drink at the Dog and Duck, the redecorated pub at the end of Division Street, in the nook by the horse-brass-festooned fireplace. "I really start to wonder," he'd said at the tucked-away table, only space for three of them.

"How do you mean, Malcolm?" Richard had said. Katherine had never made much of an effort to get to know them, and he guessed Richard and Margaret only had a broad impression of her.

"Oh, I don't know," he said, almost scared by what he'd said. "I suppose we all have these patches."

"Some of us have nothing but patches," Margaret said cosily, "and very *cross* patches too," punching Richard, but looking oddly at Malcolm, who always seemed to go on so evenly. He couldn't imagine a marriage that worked by making a spectacle of its difficulties, and of small punches in public. After that, he didn't confide in anyone.

After Katherine's party there had been those stupid two days. He always thought of them like that. Even at the time they had been stupid. What the hell are you doing? he said to himself, over and over in that strange clean room, asking questions of the unfamiliar pictures, the unfamiliar wallpaper. All he'd done was move into a hotel for two days, and tell no one about it. It was stupid because it couldn't last longer than a very few days—he couldn't in all conscience stretch beyond that if he was ever to return; a week and it would be easier never to come back and answer the questions about what he'd spent that sum of money on. The day after the party, he'd been left with a feeling of appalling exhaustion, like that after intense physical effort. He'd been tight-pulled for weeks, ever since she'd announced it, or before. He'd had no doubt who this party was meant for, and he waited with his jaw firmly gripped for this man Nick, hardly knowing what he looked like, and it made no difference that he hadn't, in the end, come. Maybe there was an agreement between the two of them.

So Malcolm changed his route home. There was an obvious way to drive from work to home. You went up Division Street, right and past the university, through Broomhill, right up the Manchester Road past Crosspool and left up Coldwell Lane, just before the city came to an end, and then you were almost home. Now he changed his route. After the university, he turned right, before Broomhill, which he wouldn't drive through. He went an extra half-mile through Crookes, every night, humming a little tune that was no tune at all but just one note leading to the next, very calmly. He didn't even express it to himself. It was just a different route home, one he sort of preferred, these days— but he didn't end up driving through Broomhill. He wouldn't have to see the flower shop, open or closed. He wouldn't have to catch any kind of glimpse of Nick. He wouldn't have to drive past the shop, in particular, on those nights when, Katherine said, "Nick" (so Malcolm called him, inverted commas poisonous in his mind) needed her to stay late, just an hour, stay late in the shop to go through the books. He wouldn't have to drive past the darkened closed shop on such a night,

Katherine's explanation that morning as clear in his ears as if on a cassette repeating itself in the car's tape-player, to reach home telling himself that there must have been a change of arrangements, the children watching television and waiting for both him and Katherine. He'd made that mistake once. He wouldn't make it again.

The supper that had so alarmed Malcolm, before he'd discovered who it was really for, occupied Katherine more, perhaps, than it should.

"What does Sandra like to eat?" she asked Daniel in the end.

"You never asked that when Antony came to tea," Tim said immediately. They were walking down the Moor, going to Marks & Spencer. Tim needed a new shirt, having come home from school with the sleeve of a new blue one half ripped off in some act of playground violence. Once, she might have mended it—it had torn neatly at the seam—but now she was damned if she could be bothered to muck about with a needle and thread.

"No," Katherine said heartlessly. "That's quite right. I didn't bother."

"It's not fair," Tim said. "Just because it's Daniel's girlfriend coming you want to butter her up—"

"And pop her in the oven at regulo three," Katherine said, making a witchy face.

"What does that mean?" Tim said.

"You said butter her up," Daniel said. "She's not my girlfriend—" *girl, friend*, almost singing it. "She's just—"

"I thought she was," Katherine said. "I thought you'd got rid of Barbara and taken up with Sandra."

"Everyone in this family's so immature," Daniel said, evidently unable to specify the particular acts that, committed, had made Barbara his girlfriend and, left alone, had put Sandra into a different category. "I don't see why people can't have friends who are girls."

"No," Katherine said. "I don't see that either. But generally people, as you call them, don't. So, you're still going out with Barbara?"

Tim made retching noises, attracting the attention of a startled old traffic warden, her cap and badge perched on top of a superannuated beehive hairdo. Tim's being-sick noises were deep and grunty.

"She seemed a nice girl," Katherine said cheerfully. "I don't suppose it was entirely her fault, having ankles as fat as that."

"It wasn't her *ankles*," Daniel said.

"When she came to supper—'Thank you, Mrs. Glover, ooh, thanks ever so much for passing me the salt, Mr. Glover,' " Tim said, in curdlingly sweet parody "—you wanted to know what she liked too. It's not fair."

"I expect I just assumed that a friend of yours would like everything, and he did," Katherine said. "But it was more likely I just forgot to ask, or that there was no reason you'd know what he especially liked. I'll remember to ask next time you want to ask a little friend to tea. Who do you want to ask to tea?"

"Antony could come again," Tim said.

"You've only got one friend," Daniel said jeeringly. "Slightly Smelly. Just put a nosebag round his neck and let him get on with it. It was horrible to watch."

"That's not true," Tim said, but then they went on to discuss what Sandra might like to eat, going into Marks & Spencer.

"You're both useless," Katherine cried after five minutes, throwing down a pile of shirts, blue, white and military green. "You're both suggesting the sort of thing you'd like to have. I'm going to make a fish pie."

It was an important thing, making a fish pie. Katherine's cooking had retreated to fifteen or so dinners. They didn't rotate with absolute regularity but there was a limit to them. There were the Sunday roasts she'd been taught to do by Malcolm's mother—it was, by immemorial tradition, Daniel's job to make the gravy; he'd been doing it since he was five. There were the dinner-party dishes, such as the beef olives she'd got out of *Good Housekeeping* a year or two back. There were the daily dishes—the shepherd's pie, the lasagnes, the chillis with rice. Katherine was more adventurous a cook than most people with children, and she rather relished the story of Jane coming home crying, a few years before, because she'd reported having trout for dinner and her friend had come back with what was normal, sausage and chips. She hoped, in fact, that had got back to the mother.

Fish pie was one of the things that was halfway between a daily dish and a fiddly special production. She would do it on a weekday, but only if she had the time, and it always landed on the table with a sort of flourish, a sense of a special treat, usually with peas. (Frozen—the children preferred them.) With its layers and the four or five separate things to prepare, it was one of the meals Daniel liked to help with. She wanted Sandra to go back and say, "We had fish pie."

"Bought, I expect," the sardonic father would say, and she'd have to say, "No, Mrs. Glover made it herself—it was great." Those people who said that food was only there to keep you going, that it didn't matter what you ate so long as you didn't actually fall over from malnutrition, hadn't understood anything.

She had only said that to Daniel, "I think I'll make a fish pie," but he understood. On Friday morning, she popped out of Nick's shop and up to the old-fashioned family fishmonger, its bouquets of fanned-out fish with their eyes, shiny as polythene, sprats and perch, a whole half salmon, like the aftermath of some unsuccessful fishy magical trick, its lower body already sliced into tiled fat steaks and laid out on the pallid marble, buried in parsley, half real and wilting, half plastic and spikily vivid, greenly erect, and everything dripping with ice like a forest enchantment. Mr. Gribbins, whose family had run the shop for years—she remembered his father selling her mother herring to fry in oatmeal, when she and this Mr. Gribbins, she supposed, were both children—smiled a ruddy, professional smile as she came in. He was always ready with odd recommendations, the rubbish from the bottom of the net, like pollock, or some Edwardian extravagance like turbot.

"It's only for a fish pie," she said, and ordered some fat translucent cod, some smoked haddock.

"And some prawns, I expect," Mr. Gribbins said. "Me wife always says that fish pie, it's not same wi'out prawns. They're only frozen, what we've got."

"And some prawns, frozen will be fine," Katherine said, then asked him to pop the bag in the fridge and she'd pick it up at five. Mr. Gribbins was a good, popular fishmonger; she expected his fish was better than anything you'd get even in Sainsbury's, which was opening, the city-centre billboard said, that autumn. There'd always be a need for those family businesses.

She left Nick's early, with the groceries she'd picked up in the minimarket over the road and the fish in a heavy, sloshing bag, and caught the bus home. She started work straight away. Four eggs boiled for ten minutes. Onion and carrot fried slowly until they were soft—she hung lovingly over the hissing pan—and some single cream over the top. The potatoes peeled—

"You've done everything," Daniel said, coming into the kitchen. Behind him, Sandra. She was quite a pretty girl, though it was a shame about her skin; she even looked quite nice in that frizzy way of doing their hair that all the girls her age had taken to. Or perhaps it was that you got used to fashions—it didn't look as ugly now as it had only a year ago. She wasn't wearing, either, those terrible clumpy shoes you sometimes saw her in, but quite simple black ones—but, of course, the whole thing, the flattering white shirt and the elegant, demure grey skirt wasn't a meeting-his-mother outfit but simply her school uniform with the tie removed. She hadn't been home. Just as Daniel could, with a plain white shirt and black trousers, Sandra made a dull uniform look like a personal decision. Katherine recognized the bond between them; recognized, too, that the bond was somehow of affinity, and not in any way erotic. They moved towards each other in some other way, neither stiffly self-conscious nor in sinuous enjoyment. He wasn't going out with this girl.

"I've only just started," Katherine said. "Hello, Sandra. Nice to see you."

"Hello, Mrs. Glover," Sandra said demurely. "Can we help?"

"No, you run off," Katherine said. "It won't be long."

"We'd like to help," Daniel said. Though that might be true of him, Katherine was surprised when Sandra competently took an apron and rolled up her sleeves. If the fish pie was Katherine's gesture, it looked as if Sandra had come with some gestures of her own prepared. Daniel went to the kitchen door, swung it shut; on the hook on the back was hanging a red laminated shopping bag and, underneath it, a blue-and-white striped butcher's apron, which he put on.

"Well—I suppose you could carry on peeling those potatoes," Katherine said. "I have to admit that's the one thing I hate doing, so you can say no and do something more interesting, if you like. I don't want to foist stuff on you."

"No," Sandra said, getting to work with the potatoes under a running tap, just as Katherine did them. "I like peeling potatoes, actually."

If the look that passed between Daniel and his mother had had a name, it might have been called what-a-treasure. And then they got to work. Katherine put a few handfuls of spinach on to boil. Daniel competently chopped the fish fillets into domino-sized pieces, and buttered a dish—he always buttered dishes, there was no talking him out of it—and then artistically tessellated the white fish and the yellow across the bottom.

"There's no need to be as fussy as that," Katherine said, watching what he was doing. Sandra came to have a look, and they laughed a little at him. Daniel played up to their mockery, holding the last piece high, parodically examining the space left before putting it down exquisitely and stepping back, like a great artist, to admire the final effect.

"A masterpiece, it is a masterpiece," Sandra said, in a French accent. Daniel scattered the last pieces of fish over the top, then started on the prawns.

"Oh, get a move on," Katherine said, slicing the eggs into quarters and distributing them among the fish. "Mind out," she said to Sandra, taking the boiled spinach in two hands, wringing it out like a cloth over the sink and scattering it over the fish.

"Shall I?" Sandra said, taking the pan with the onion-and-cream mixture and carefully spooning it over everything.

"And that's it," Katherine said. "I just need to mash the potatoes when they're done—I'll do that." She smiled at Sandra, and Sandra gave a big smile back. Somehow, in five minutes assembling a pie for dinner, any awkwardness between them had melted.

"I love fish pie," Daniel said, as they went out, not to his bedroom but into the living room. Sandra turned her head and gave another grateful, almost forgiving smile to Katherine, who returned it.

"What does your dad do, Sandra?" Malcolm said, when they were seated round the table and waiting for Katherine to bring in the dinner. He poured her a glass of water. There was a red and yellow oilcloth cover on the table. It was padded beneath, yielding slightly when pressed.

"He works for the Electric," Sandra said, unthinkingly using Bernie's own abbreviation, or perhaps that, originally, of Bernie's mother.

"The electric what?" Malcolm said, smiling. Though he'd kept his tie and shirt on, he had otherwise changed out of his building-society suit into his weekend clothes, a grey V-necked pullover and flapping grey tweedy trousers, his blue slippers. He didn't always: often he sat all evening in the trousers of his suit, wearing them out fast, as Katherine pointed out. But today he'd made an effort. "Do you mean the Electricity Board?"

"He manages a generating plant, I mean," Sandra said. She picked up the white floral cruet from the boat it sat in, turned over the salt and pepper pots, put them back, seeming to approve as they watched her. "In London he used to work at head office, but he got fed up of living in London, I mean we all did, so he decided to come and work up here instead. I don't really know what he does, exactly."

"How do you make electricity?" Tim said. "I thought it was all like big batteries somewhere."

"They make it in different ways," Katherine said, coming in with the fish pie in her hands, holding it in scarved blue-and-white oven gloves, depositing it with a flourish on the hunting-scene mat in the centre of the table. "And whenever you switch something on it's there."

"That looks nice," Malcolm said, his eyes fixed like a child on what they all remembered now was, in fact, one of his favourite dinners.

"But sometimes they run out," Tim said, going on although his mother had left the room again. "I remember when I was little, sometimes all the lights and everything, they'd go out, even the television maybe, because we'd run out."

"Well, I expect Sandra's dad's making sure we don't run out again," Malcolm said. "I don't know that that's going to happen again. It was because of a strike. It's an important job, your dad's."

"I suppose so," Sandra said. "He doesn't talk much about it."

"He could be a spy," Tim said seriously, his eyes on Sandra. "They don't talk about what they do. They're not allowed to. They'd be arrested or shot perhaps."

"Why don't we always have fish pie?" Daniel said, ignoring Tim, as Katherine came back with the peas and, a concession, a bottle of tomato ketchup. "I like fish pie. Is it too much bother to do when there's not a guest?"

"Honestly, Daniel," Katherine said; Sandra burst into laughter. "You're always showing me up."

But he probably had a point. The big fish pie in the somehow comfortingly chipped and oblong earthenware dish, browned and toffee-like at the edges of the crust where the sauce had bubbled up through the mashed potato, the shared bowl of shiny green peas and everyone eating it all up—it was like a picture of a family in a magazine. Not even the labelled bottle of tomato ketchup on the table could detract from the pastoral sweetness of the scene—that was something Katherine generally disapproved of, but they were allowed it with fish pie and, for some reason, shepherd's pie as well. (Maybe because she liked it, that was a good enough reason.)

The early-summer-evening light came through the window like music. Anyone walking up the street, glancing in, would see a happy family, six of them round a table, their numbers reflecting their abundant easy happiness. And with a guest from over the road, they seemed to be getting on better than usual. They were actually speaking to each other for the first time in months. It was as if family life needed a simple audience, not even to become happy in performance but to take any kind of recognizable shape at all. Without observation, they'd been eating for months now, as it were, from their own little dishes, disparate like strangers in a crowded restaurant asked to share a table and sulking about it. For the sake of a visitor they'd put on a performance of cohesion, but there was nothing false about the cohesion. They all seemed to mean it. And Sandra was a nice girl. Katherine had forgotten Alice's evident niceness, the quality which had invited that instant and embarrassing confidence; all that had disappeared in the shame afterwards. Sandra had some of it, behind her sharp gaze. She was an improvement on Barbara.

"That looks nice, too," Sandra said to Jane, gesturing at her plate, entirely in earnest. It was a cheese omelette with tomato slices placed lumpenly on top—they'd been supposed to go into the omelette, Katherine had forgotten, and she'd put the tomato on one side specially—and the same peas everyone was having. Jane was making it last, but there was no pretending it was as nice as the fish pie, and her new practice looked more stupid than ever.

"Yes, it is nice," Jane said shortly. She guessed what was behind the comment. She guessed that Daniel had told Sandra while they were walking home that, for satirical effect, she ought to turn to Jane with a straight face and say that what she was eating looked nice. Jane was right about this, and about the satiric intent, but she still had to answer the observation and say, "Yes, it is."

"So, why are you a vegetarian?" Sandra said.

"Everyone always asks that," Jane said, not exactly rudely.

"Well, it's interesting," Sandra said. "I want to know—I might become vegetarian myself."

"I can't take the responsibility for sending you back home a vegetarian," Katherine said.

"I don't think there's any real risk of that," Jane said, bending over the remains of her omelette. She was parcelling it out as slowly as she could.

"That's not very polite, Jane," Malcolm said.

"No, seriously," Sandra said. "I was interested. I mean what is it about, the cruelty, or what?"

"Well," Jane said, "I suppose it's mostly about finding it revolting, you know, eating dead bodies."

"Do you mind?" Katherine said. "We are eating."

"That's right," Malcolm said, chortling. "We're eating dead bodies."

"You're as bad as Daniel," Katherine said, but suddenly they were smiling at each other, remembering something between the two of them.

"What?" Daniel said abruptly. "What is it?"

"You don't miss much," Malcolm said, raising a fork with a single prawn on the end of it to near his face, gazing at it, and smiling in a way not all that familiar, smiling over it at Katherine. "I was just thinking—actually, I was just remembering something—"

"I knew it was about prawns," Katherine said, and their eyes met. They giggled. But no one could extract anything further from either of them: they were away, sitting on the promenade front at Scarborough in June 1958, the wind brisk off the North Sea scattering Katherine's young hair about her glowing face, and Malcolm with a wooden prong forking cold pink prawns into her mouth from a newspaper wrap and mostly missing and—no, they wouldn't be sharing that.

"Would you say that a prawn was a dead body exactly?" Daniel said. "I wouldn't bother even about a human body if it was as titchy as that. I don't say I'd eat one, mind."

"It's not the cruelty, then," Sandra said. "You're not bothered about people being cruel to animals for the sake of food."

"I don't know why you say that," Jane said, blushing. She knew she was going to lose this one, and she could only say, in the end, what she thought and felt. "I think the cruelty's the worst part of it."

"That's what I think, too," Sandra said soberly. "I don't like eating eggs because they're from chickens kept in cages. They can't go anywhere. And milk—think how cruel milk is, the cow has a sweet little baby cow, and it's snatched away to make veal, lovely veal, and the poor mother cow just wanting to be left alone with her grief, and she's yanked up to a machine and milked over and over. I call that cruel. No wonder we say 'poor cow.' "

Tim was yelping and applauding, unable to stop staring at Sandra.

"You can choose not to," Jane said bravely. "You can choose only to drink milk from cows who haven't had calves at all."

Everyone laughed, edging Tim's hysteria up a further notch. Jane just said, "Why? What? What did I say?"

"That's worse than being a cod, isn't it? I mean, you've got the whole sea to swim about in, and then you get caught one day and that's it. Your life was quite all right until then."

"Prawns are farmed," Jane said forlornly, but she was losing the argument.

"So, according to you," Tim said, calming down a little, "prawns grow in a sort of farm, with prawn tractors, and in a field, prawns growing in trees?"

"Not like that, but—"

"You have to admit," Malcolm said, "Sandra's got a point. If you were against cruelty, you'd still eat wild things. There are lots crueller things."

"You're all wrong," Jane said, but Sandra, glowing with amusement, hardly even glancing at Daniel, who was her audience, had already started on another topic. They were all enjoying this, Jane thought, all of them; they were keeping up with this spotty girl, and she was enjoying it too.

"I didn't like it up here at first," Sandra was saying. "I didn't want to move. I didn't understand what anyone was saying."

"It's a bit of a shock," Malcolm said.

"Do you know what this means?" Tim shouted; he was getting excited. But it turned out he just wanted to explain what Tin Tin Tin could mean—it isn't in the tin—and, since he'd explained it once already, they all knew that one.

"I wouldn't want to live in London," Malcolm said. "I don't know how anyone stands it. All that commuting—you stand in a big train overground, packed in like sardines, and then in a little train underground, travelling maybe for an hour each way."

"How could you stand it?" Tim said to Sandra. "Did you do that every day?"

"No, I got a bus to school, just like I do here," Sandra said. "It was my dad did that."

"But there's lots more to see," Katherine said. "There's much more happening in London." She didn't want anyone to think they were stupid lumps, going on about the wonders of Sheffield, like Anthea Arbuthnot or someone.

"I don't know that we ever saw any of it," Sandra said. "We've been to more places since we moved up here. My mum and dad, they like to go out on a Sunday, go to the countryside or to a stately home or something. I'd rather stay at home, but they like it."

There was a dangerous memory here, and Malcolm's thoughts must have gone to Nick, and his similar London liking for weekend visits to Chatsworth: he said, "Does your mother work, Sandra?"

"No," she said. "She didn't in London, either. I think she might like to. At any rate she says she gets bored sometimes. But I don't know what she could do. I think she worked as a librarian for a while before I was born. Maybe she could do that again."

"Oh dear," Katherine said lightly. "Tell her to pop over and invite herself in for a cup of coffee if she's ever bored during the day."

"But you're at work during the day," Tim said, who had not taken his eyes off Sandra since she'd arrived, gazing at her with hunger and amazement, spooning gloopy chunks of fish pie, jewelled with bright peas. "You work every day except Tuesdays and Thursdays."

"That's true," Katherine said, taken aback. For one moment, she'd completely forgotten that part of her life with Nick and the shop and his pretty bower of a cottage in Ranmoor. She'd only been a house-wife fulfilled with her family around her at the dining-table. "That's absolutely true, Timothy. Thank you for reminding me. But I'm sure Mrs. Sellers can drop in on a Tuesday or a Thursday."

"She's not miserable or anything," Sandra said brightly. "She doesn't have all that much to do, she says, that's all."

"Oh, I didn't take it the wrong way," Katherine said.

"My brother's in the same class as you, isn't he?" Sandra said to Tim, finally turning directly to the unblinking gaze he'd held, steadily, not looking down even at his plate as his fork rose and fell. Tim blushed, stopped chewing, looked in agony at his mother. He was all right dropping fragments of his own dim, connected thoughts into the conversation. He tended to become unstuck when asked a specific question.

"I don't *like* him very much," he said finally, defensively.

"Oh dear," Malcolm said, chuckling.

"That's all right," Sandra said. "I don't like him much either."

Katherine really rather admired that sort of tact.

You were always coming across odd items of clothing in unexpected places in the Glovers' house. It might be underneath a cushion on the sofa, at the bottom of the stairs and halfway up them, behind a chair, on the work surface in the kitchen, or in a beguiling trail on the land-ing, marking the path Daniel took between front door and bedroom, or bedroom and bathroom. He was always depositing his clothes as he went from place to place, undressing in haste during his progress, so you could always rely on finding an old football sock, a pair of trousers, his blazer, his one school tie or a single shoe left carelessly at some public and shared place. In the same way, after a few months, you could never be sure that Sandra wouldn't be found on her own, relaxed and at ease, anywhere in the Glovers' house. It wasn't that she was treating it like her own house; it was more that Daniel was treating her like one of his ordinary possessions, which no one would question and somebody would sooner or later pick up and return to its proper place. But he invited her in and then deposited her somewhere. She didn't seem to mind; and the rest of the family, even the polite ones, soon stopped asking her whether she wanted anything, a glass of water, something to drink or eat, soon stopped trying to entertain her as they passed. Any time between four and six, you might find Sandra sitting on the washing-machine, in a chair in the living room reading the *Radio Times*, on the stairs where Daniel had left her, or quite regularly lying on his bed, face down, reading a copy of *Jackie* she must have brought out of her bag, quite happy. Katherine was pleased, in a way, that Daniel was getting to know girls as people—it was clear that he was never going to like Sandra for any reason but herself, and Katherine couldn't worry on Alice's behalf about Sandra lying on Daniel's bed.

It was one of those days. Daniel was outside—he'd spotted John Warner mooching up the road, had called to him out of a window and gone out to talk. He was five years older than Daniel, still hanging about at home, doing nothing much; a new friend of Daniel's, and not one anyone thought much of. He'd left Sandra where she was, which was sitting on Daniel's bed, his bedroom door open. She'd been entertaining herself. She'd got down a book of his from school, a Shakespeare play, and had been reading, not the play but the things he'd been writing in the margins. She'd picked up and looked at the model Spitfire he'd made from a kit, its joins hard and rubbery with excess glue—it hadn't been much of a success, that hobby. From the window, you could see the complicated immaculate garden—there was a bed of tulips, supposed to be yellow but they'd all come up purple, to Daniel's father's annoyance. She wrote her name in the dust on the windowsill of Daniel's room, and for a moment thought about opening up his drawers to see what colour his Y-fronts were. But she wasn't that bothered. She sat down on the bed again with *Henry the Fourth Part One*; there was nowhere else to sit in the room apart from on the hard chair at the little desk. She sighed and, kicking off her black slingbacks, not untying them but loosening them with her heel, she put her legs up on the bed. She had a ladder in her tights.

"Hello," she said. Daniel's little brother, Tim, was on the landing. She hadn't heard him coming, but he was outside, pausing as if he wanted to have a good look at her.

"Would you like a cup of tea?" the little boy said awkwardly. It was something he'd heard grown-ups say.

Sandra smiled. "No, I'm all right," she said. "Unless you're making one for yourself."

"No," Tim said seriously. "I don't really like tea. Or coffee. I don't like that even as much as tea."

"Are you still in the same class as my brother?" Sandra said, for something to say.

"I think so," Tim said. "He's not really my friend, though."

"That's a shame," Sandra said. "I expect you're quite different sorts of people, aren't you?"

Tim looked at her; he'd never considered the matter in that light before, it seemed.

"You don't mind being my friend, though?" Sandra said.

"That's stupid," Tim said. But he came into the room.

Sandra looked at him, standing there. He expected something of her; perhaps he had an idea of what she did for his brother. She imagined what he thought, and then, quickly, she undid the top of her blouse, three buttons, opening it to show her bra.

"Do you wear a bra?" he said.

"Yes, of course I do," she said. "All girls do, didn't you know that?"

"I sort of knew that," he said, still looking.

"Do you want to see?" she said, and, almost before he could nod, she reached down between her breasts, undoing the front fastener. "Come and feel what they're like," she said. They were floppy, the nipples pink and oval and big; he came over unwillingly, felt them dumbly. The movements he made with his hands were considered and blunt, like a child making handprints on paper, as if he would only be allowed to touch once. "Not like that," she said, though she felt ashamed, and he pulled his head down, between her breasts. He just put his head there; you could feel the tension in it, knowing that at some level this was fantastic, what he was doing, but not knowing in the slightest what he was supposed to be doing, and she didn't really know either. She just left it there, settling for adoration, and the weird noises of excitement and childish discovery he was making. It was funny rather than anything.

She closed her eyes, not in thrill or physical pleasure, but in relief that, after all, you could make someone do what you wanted them to do. Now, it was only a little boy who didn't really know what he was doing, didn't really know what enjoyment he was supposed to be taking from it. His truffling noises were, Sandra knew, the first imitation of something he could only have seen in films and on the television; they were like the kissy-kissy noises boys made in playgrounds, no more than that. But she was pretending too. And it didn't matter, because you started by making a Timothy do exactly what you wanted him to do; you worked up from there. Five-finger exercises, she thought, detached from all feeling, any practical emotion.

There might have been a noise. The bedroom door was ajar. There was nobody outside on the landing. "That's enough," she said, and pushed his head away. But he pushed it back, and now even started to fumble towards her bottom half. "No, that's enough," she said, pushing more violently and buttoning herself up.

"Will you take your pants off?" Tim said.

"Go away," Sandra said.

"Please," Tim said. "I've never seen one."

"Go away," Sandra said. "Or I'll tell your mother."

He got up, almost tearful, and left. There wasn't much further that the little boy could have gone. He wasn't going to tell anyone.

Whenever Sandra came round for dinner, they took to sitting for a while afterwards, all of them, in the sitting room. It was always nice when Sandra came; she had lovely manners, without being too effortful, and even Tim seemed to like her, always paying attention and listening keenly when she said anything, or even when she didn't. It was always a shame when Sandra said she ought to be getting back. "Come as often as you like," Katherine said warmly. "You're always welcome."

"I'll walk you back," Daniel said, and it was a surprise when they all laughed.

"You never walk Sandra back," Jane said.

"And I think I can manage," Sandra said. "I won't get lost."

"I know," Daniel said. "But I'll walk you back anyway."

Jane made kissing noises, but Katherine told her not to be so stupid.

He didn't know why he'd said, this one time, after she'd been coming so regularly for dinner, that he'd walk her back. He didn't have anything to say to her. And, in fact, he did just take her out of the house, and across the road, leaving her at the gatepost.

"Thank you for a lovely evening," Sandra said demurely, smiled and went to her door. "It's always nice." She didn't try to kiss him; but he knew she wouldn't, and he didn't really want it either. It was odd to feel like this about a girl.

It was a lovely evening, and he stood there for a moment. In the distance, at the top of the road, there was the noise of kids shouting. They'd taken to playing tennis in this quiet street—Wimbledon had finished last week, and set off a minor craze, hitting the ball backwards and forwards, getting off the road when a car came. A little clop, then some shrieks; they didn't often manage to hit it back. It was getting a bit late; they were playing on into the twilight.

The drive to their house was lined with a thick, loose hedge, and as Daniel turned round, a figure stepped out from its shadows. He was startled: he hadn't noticed the woman as he'd left the house, but she must have been standing there. She was chaotically dressed, half-buttoned cardigan over a sweater over a blouse, one collar hanging out, and a loose stained skirt and trodden-down boots; her hair was wild and unbrushed. She called to him, a subdued call, and he went over. He said nothing; raised an eyebrow. She looked terribly frightened.

"Is this your house?" she said eventually.

"Yes," Daniel said. "Why?"

"Is that your little boy?" the woman said.

"My little boy?" Daniel said, not understanding. "I don't have a little boy."

"There's a little boy who lives here," the woman said.

"Yes, there is," Daniel said. "That's my brother, he's called Tim. Why? What's he done?"

"Your brother—" the woman said. Then she looked again at Daniel, looked at him properly. "Oh, I see, you're young, you're not—I thought you must be his father."

This was so strange to Daniel that he said nothing.

The woman said nothing, too. It was as if she had made her point now.

"Do you want to speak to my dad?" Daniel said. "Or is it Tim you want?"

"No," the woman said immediately. "Not him. I've been waiting here, I wanted to say—"

"Why didn't you just ring the doorbell?" Daniel said, puzzled. "We were all in there."

"Oh, I can't do that," the woman said angrily, as if Daniel ought to have known. "It's got to stop."

"It's—"

"He's got to stop, your brother, he can't go on doing this to my son," the woman said.

"I don't know what you're talking about," Daniel said. He had heard people say that; he said it as they said it, reasonably.

"I think you do," the woman said. "I thought he was Andrew's friend, visiting him like that—"

"Stop," Daniel said. "Start from the beginning."

The woman drew a deep, juddering breath. Daniel could not see why this was all so difficult for her.

"My son's going to die," she said. "Maybe very soon. He broke his leg, that was all, and then they found out there was a reason it broke so easily, and by the time they found out, it was too late. He went in with a broken leg, and he's never going to come out."

"I'm so sorry," Daniel said. "But I don't—"

"It's your brother," the woman said. "He's been coming every day, it seems. We didn't know, Andrew didn't say. He's been coming, and he wasn't even his friend, never—he's been coming because he found out that Andrew's going to die, and every day he comes and he asks Andrew what it's like to be dying, and he's made Andrew promise that when he dies he'll come back as—as—as a ghost and—"

"Oh, God," Daniel said. "Are you sure it's Tim?" but that was stupid, because of course it was Tim.

"He's got to stop," the woman said, now crying. "It can't go on, it upsets Andrew so much. He'd kept it to himself and then today I went down, I can't go very often, I can't bear it on top of everything else, and he just came out with it. Day after day. What's it like? Do you think you're going to heaven or hell? Does dying hurt? Are your family upset, are they crying, have you seen any ghosts here in the hospital because so many people have died here, haven't they, and you, you're going to be another one, but when you die—"

She couldn't go on. Daniel tried to put a hand on her shoulder. On the other side of the road, a man walking his Jack Russell before bedtime saw them, then looked away, muttering to the dog as it fussed excitedly around the thin trunk of a little tree. The pair of them must look inexplicable. She shrugged off his hand, angrily.

"I don't want anything from you," she said. "Or your family. I just want it to stop. He hasn't got long, it might be a week or two. I want him to have some peace now."

"It'll stop," Daniel said, not knowing what else to say, and then, having extracted this promise, she turned away abruptly and started to walk down the road. "Don't worry," he called weakly after her. "He won't do it again." She stopped, but more like someone who thought they had been walking in the wrong direction, someone who was about to turn to take the right path. She didn't reply; and in a moment she carried on, her awkward steps taking her to the corner and out of sight. Daniel watched her go. He had no idea who she was.

"—couldn't manage the spear," his father was saying. "There were only adult-sized ones, so he kept falling over it, and in the end—do you remember?—he said 'I hate this stupid spear,' and threw it in the brook, and stomped off in a—"

It was an unaccustomed grouping: his father in an armchair, leaning back and telling a story like a professional raconteur, his mother on the arm, laughing, and on the sofa Tim and Jane, leaning forward and enjoying the story. You couldn't have asked for anything more. Daniel stood in the doorway.

"You were a while," his mother said.

"I bet he had plenty to *talk* about," Jane said maliciously.

He had no idea for a second what she was talking about—it was odd to think that Sandra had made them all cheerful. He looked at Tim, and Tim looked back at him. He looked just as he ever did; small-headed, round-shouldered, slightly bewildered, his face, as ever, not quite getting the point.

"Yes," Daniel said. "We were just chatting."

"I know that sort of chatting," his father said, with a terrible put-on roguishness, and even Daniel had to make himself smile. There might be time before bed to talk to Tim. He knew he couldn't ever say any of it to anyone else, and he watched his brother, rocking backwards and forwards, nursing his own complicated thoughts.

Book Two-and-a-Half

IN LONDON

Much later, that pub in Clapham would be renovated with gold leaf and hand-painted murals; its floorboards would be laid bare and scrubbed; it would take to serving Thai food; it would have to employ a bouncer on a Saturday night, so popular would it become. But in 1983, its walls were covered with wallpaper, its floor was covered with moist carpet, and even on a Saturday night few people went there, and most of those were drinking alone.

Two Australian men sat together.

"I fucking hate her," one said.

"You don't have to show it," the other said.

"She shows it to me."

"You're better than her."

"I don't feel better than her."

"Why do you say that?"

"Like, for starters, it's a Saturday night, what am I doing here?"

"Here's OK."

"There's nothing OK about this dump."

"It's close."

"It's not what I thought I was coming to London for."

"You mean, you want to be somewhere fancy chatting up the girls, yeah?"

"Not now I don't."

"So what's your problem?"

"I didn't think I was coming right round the world to sit in a empty pub on a Saturday night watching old Irish buggers drink until they piss themselves."

Because that had happened two weeks before. It had seemed quite funny.

"Yeah, well."

"It's just that fucking Jane. I don't know what her problem is."

"You just have to look at her as, like, family or something. Just accept you can't choose your housemates in London like you can't choose your sister or something."

"That's hilarious. Chinny tart."

"You're right. She's got a big chin."

"Just think of her as family."

"That's a nice thought."

"No worries."

"Because to tell you the truth, that's really what it feels like, this woman we're stuck with. What's her problem?"

"She went to Oxford."

"She never said that to me."

"She doesn't mention it. She only told me when I asked her straight out."

"That's her problem, you reckon?"

"No, there's no explanation."

"It's just the way she looks at you when you've left a plate on the table without washing it up. Or if she comes in the kitchen and you're there and she's not expecting it. Or—"

"Yeah, I know what you mean."

"I tell you something. This is weird. I was out once, on Clapham High Street, one Saturday morning, just walking along. And I see her coming. And I reckon she sees me, like I see her. But she sort of drops her head, pretending not to see me, so I look away, and I walk on, and when I look back, she's walked straight past, not said anything, pretending not to see me."

"But, mate, you pretended not to see her too."

"That's not the point. I reckon she must hate us both."

"I don't get it."

"And if she was at Oxford, right, what's she doing sharing a house with two Aussies she found through an ad? Why's she got no friends she can live with?"

"She's got friends, they come round."

"Yeah, but why doesn't she live with them?"

"Don't ask me."

"And what's she doing tonight? Staying in, watching the TV."

"You're not saying you want her to come out with us."

"Well, why shouldn't she?"

"She wouldn't want to listen to you having a go at her."

"I wouldn't do it if she wasn't here."

"Yeah, but you'd want to."

"I tell you what. If she was the sort of girl who came out to the pub with a bloke, she wouldn't be the sort of girl you'd want to sit here having a go at. Do you see what I'm saying?"

"Yeah, I see what you're saying."

"I should have found somewhere to live in Earls Court. There's a real party scene there."

"It's expensive, mate."

They went on for a while. The pub got no more full. Outside, by eleven, it might have been a country village. One old man got up to leave, held his chair by both hands, and then, like a learning swimmer at the bar of a pool, pushed off. He managed three steps, then fell, limbs waving, on to the carpet. Some people came to help. They'd done it before. The two Australians watched, one laughing, the other still unamused and cross. The first asked the second to come off it; the second said he didn't know what he was doing in this country. In a moment, time was called, and they went home. It was only a hundred yards.

Music was softly playing from the main bedroom, its door shut. One offered the other a tin of beer, but the offer was refused. The two men went each to their separate bedrooms. After half an hour, one of them, as he had before, put on a cassette of his own and arranged a pornographic magazine open on his bed. He stripped and, standing on a chair, slung a belt over a rafter that ran through his bedroom. He hooked it about his neck, and began to masturbate, leaning quite heavily with his neck on the loop of the belt. In a moment, he slipped, and, kicking out for a foothold, kicked the chair over. Shortly, as he had not done before, he died, making small grunting noises that nobody heard. In twenty minutes, the cassette came to an end, and everything was silent again.

Jane had often been able to recognize moments of significant influence in her life; moments that enlarged her notion of what was possible, permanently. When she was tiny, her family going to stay with someone—who?—and her grandmother being there too, and for some reason she'd had to sleep in a baby's cot with bars you could lower. Tiny as she was, she knew she was too old for this, but her grandmother had presented it as a sort of adventure, and said, "Well, you'll always remember having to sleep in a cot, won't you?" And she had. It was almost her first memory. And at school, once, making pots out of snakes of clay: hers had collapsed and collapsed the more she handled it, until finally it was just a kind of ashtray, hopeless. They'd had to queue to show it to the teacher before firing, and she'd remarked sociably to her neighbour in the queue that hers was terrible, really. The teacher had overheard, and growled at her to go away and improve it, then. A shameful lesson; not to apologize. Or her mother, never knowing that her mother was capable of running out of the house and stamping, in public, on the head of a snake; the idea that had come in a moment that she could go to Oxford. But not Oxford, that wasn't any kind of enlargement, oddly enough.

It was like that the morning she'd noticed she hadn't seen one of her flatmates for a few days, and, before going to work, had knocked on his door, had opened it, found him naked, black-faced, sprawled on the floor with a belt round his neck.

The Australians had been her friend Sarah Willis's idea. She'd met Sarah her first week at Oxford, been drawn to her air of Manchester competency, and Sarah had gone on advising her since. They'd done Old English translations, grapefruit diets, boyfriends from Brasenose and the milk round together, ending up with different jobs in marketing. Sarah's forward, decisive air had got her a job with a company that, it turned out, made almost everything you ever bought and used up— soap, toothpaste, bottled sauces, face masks, savoury spreads to put on toast. Jane had been shocked that such apparently wide and varied consumer experiences all came from the same place under disguised names; the salad cream and the moisturizer might turn out to be exactly the same substance. She hadn't done so well, landing a job with a company everyone knew the name of, a firm that was only ever going to be English, a firm that made exactly what you knew it made, a firm that made, in fact, small metal toys. People smiled when you told them who you worked for. Well, as Sarah said, you could move on a bit later.

Sarah hadn't offered to share a flat with her—or, rather, had explained why it wouldn't be a good idea.

"You see, I'm away so much now. Every week somewhere else, I'd hardly be there. You'd be lonely, really, on your own most of the time."

"I was thinking exactly the same thing."

"And, of course, when I get back, I might want sometimes just to spend time with Dave."

Dave was the Brasenose boyfriend, who, unlike Jane's, had stuck.

"Oh, you don't want to be sharing a flat if you don't have to."

"Well, it's not that so much, but if you move in, and then, in six months, Dave decides he wants to move in—you don't want to be living with a couple, Jane, you're better off like this."

It was probably true; she wouldn't really have wanted to live with Dave's neat little ways in the bathroom, his constant concern for her, as if she was coming down with something, or the cute little messages he left around the flat for Sarah. Anyway, Sarah telephoned one day to announce that she'd actually found a flat for Jane to rent, just round the corner from her in Clapham, a really nice garden square. Three bedrooms—

"But I don't need three bedrooms—"

And £180 a week.

"Get a lodger or two, make it clear that it's your flat in the first place, and turn them out after six months. Of course, if you really like them, they can stay longer, but I wouldn't let them get their feet under the table too much."

It was all very much like Sarah Willis's periodic attempts to find Jane a boyfriend, advertising men she said were really nice but who turned out only to be friends of her own boyfriend; or assuring Jane, without Jane asking for reassurance on the particular point, that yes, she did have a kind of pointed chin but it was really characterful and striking. Sarah finding her a flat looked much like that, making the best of poor material and making you feel worse, honestly, than you had before it started. But by chance it was nice, with a big sunny bedroom overlooking the children's playground in the square. It was an elegant square from the right viewpoint: two and a half sides of it were tall stucco houses in a uniform grand cream. The fourth side must have had a bomb fall on it, and it was now the ugly 1960s back of a fire station.

Her father came down on the train—as he always said, it was all right driving to London, it was getting across London in the car he couldn't face, and what about the parking? Sarah came with her to meet him off the train, and she saw him walking down the platform at St. Pancras with Sarah's Londonized eyes: small and doubtful, his clothes all too beige, his padded anorak and trousers and even his shoes. He greeted Sarah generously enough—she'd been to stay one vacation, and had done her best with him—but, all the way to Clapham, walking from the Tube, letting themselves in and walking round the flat, it was clear there were things he wouldn't say in front of her. He couldn't help admitting that it was a nice flat, convenient for getting to work. They took a walk round, and he admitted it seemed like a pleasant area, though Jane blushed when he asked whether she was sure it was a safe place to live. It was obvious he was counting the black people on the streets. As it turned out when Sarah tactfully excused herself, saying she had to meet Dave, the things Malcolm wouldn't say in front of Sarah were also things he didn't know how to say in front of Jane. When they said goodbye the next day, they agreed that Jane had really fallen on her feet.

"The best idea is Australians," Sarah said, when the question of the lodgers came up again. Jane could manage the rent on her own for a month—she'd saved enough from summer jobs—but not more than that. "They come and go, they're always cheerful, they're not going to want to stay for years on end. And they've always got loads of friends. It'd be good for your social life."

"You can't advertise just for Australians," Jane said. "There's probably a law against it."

"They've got their own publications," Sarah said. She was right; Jane always marvelled at Sarah's knowing everything. Within ten days, she was interviewing a succession of Australians, and within two weeks one had moved in. She thought she'd try just one lodger to start with, and he seemed a nice boy, travelling round Europe and now staying in London for a few months.

The atmosphere in the flat was pleasant. The Australian was tidy, friendly, quiet. He didn't seem to have the busy social life Sarah had surmised of his kind, but when they found themselves in the flat at the same time, he had cheerful stories of his day working—illegally, Jane suspected—as a waiter at a restaurant in Earls Court, the insulting and stupid things the customers had said, the things they'd done to food in return. She quite liked him. The only faint disappointment was discovering what these London terraces were actually like. They looked, from the outside, very elegant, with their tall white stucco fronts, almost like something in Belgravia, but you hadn't been living there long when you worked out that they'd been thrown up very cheaply in the 1820s, with the intention of looking elegant and not much more than that. They were full of odd little gaps between floors and thin walls, through which noise travelled easily; the late-night radio, which sometimes bothered Jane in bed at night, turned out, on investigation, to come from the flat two floors below next door. "I reckon a good hard blow from a sledgehammer would peel off the front of the whole terrace in one go," their neighbour upstairs said cheerily, when they introduced themselves on the stairs. "And if there was ever a fire, get out quick—it'd spread from one end of the terrace to the other through the attics in about ten minutes. There's two hundred years' worth of dry paper and wood lying up there."

Five weeks after he moved in, the Australian said that he'd got a friend who was looking for somewhere to live. Jane had agreed. This new Australian came to see the flat, with a huge rucksack on his back; all his possessions. She knew immediately that she was making a mistake, and this new Australian somehow made the old one seem less nice. Which was odd, because it turned out that they weren't really friends at all: they'd only seen each other once or twice before the second one moved in. He was just someone looking for a room.

Far from improving her social life, the lodgers together created a stale, soiled atmosphere. Jane started heading straight for her room when she got home. The two of them started watching hours of television, switching it on, whatever it was, and going on until they went to bed. Or if she came into the kitchen when they were both there, a silence would fall that she couldn't, with whatever amount of brightness, fill. The flat filled with a sour, masculine smell, of bodies and obscure fluids; the second Australian had a personal neglect that gave the impression of a deliberate personal affront; the streak of black shit in the toilet bowl, the black body hair, embedded in a fatty jelly of what must be spunk in the drain of the shower, the blood-encrusted length of dental floss left on the bathroom shelf; all these she felt deliberately left for her, like the horrible gifts of a cat to its owner.

"My God," she said.

"Jesus," the Australian said. "Don't look. Go and sit in the other room. I'll call an ambulance."

"I can do that," Jane said. She forced herself to turn away, with a physical sensation as if caught in a fierce wind. She had never imagined seeing such a thing. The boy, too, after a gulp or two, shut the door firmly and came after her.

"I haven't seen him since Saturday," he said, sitting down, pale with shock. "I thought he was—"

"No," Jane said.

"I don't know what I thought. He wasn't even a friend of mine."

Jane phoned for an ambulance. Not knowing what else to do, she made a strong cup of tea for them both.

The ambulance arrived; two paramedics, with the useless tools of their trade. They made no astonished or horrified noises, and were more obviously concerned for Jane and the live Australian. In an hour, the police, surprisingly, arrived, and while the body was being removed, asked a few bored questions. "It must be a shock," one said kindly. Once the body had been taken away, covered with a red blanket, strapped down on a stretcher, the police went into the room, emerging with an address book. "Don't disturb anything for the moment," they said. "We'll inform his family. Don't worry, we'll be tactful about it." Jane thought of a London policeman, helmet in hand, making the long sad voyage to Melbourne. A stubby, worried couple in their bungalow, hearing the doorbell, and opening it to find the incredible figure of an old-style foreign bobby in front of their neat square little lawn, edged with shrubs in which poisonous spiders lurked, waiting to pounce, under which deadly snakes coiled and loitered . . . But, of course, it would not be like that. They'd just telephone the details to an Australian policeman to pass on, before forgetting all about the sad and grotesque death, so far from home.

They didn't need to do anything else much, once the body had been taken away. The police took charge of everything, only letting them know, quite thoughtfully, that the man's parents wouldn't be travelling over for the funeral, the cost being too high; he would be cremated and the ashes returned. There was nothing else for it: she and the other Australian would have to go to the funeral to prevent it being an entirely unattended affair.

As it happened, they weren't alone at the funeral. The same thought had obviously occurred to a few people who had crossed the Australian's path in London, and the chapel at the crematorium showed three or four clumps of acquaintances, none showing anything more than a straight face. No one offered to read, and there was no obvious principal mourner that anyone could introduce themselves to; so after standing around outside for a while, they all went their separate ways. "Poor bugger," the other Australian said.

There weren't, in truth, all that many people Jane could have told. She didn't tell Sarah Willis, not wanting to make any kind of story out of it, or her mum and dad—there'd be no end of it if she told them. Certainly no one in the head office of the toy company. Every step of the story was ugly, and she didn't really want anyone to know that any of it had happened to her in any way. It was just too interesting and shocking, she could see that.

"I don't mind," Jane said one evening to the Australian. "If you want to move out."

They'd taken to eating together when they were both in the flat. It wasn't anything very significant, but she had started to feel a little bit sorry for him. Once, going round the supermarket on her way home, she'd deliberately bought a bit too much and, finding he was in, asked him if he wanted some of her dinner. "It looks good," he said and, a day or two later, had done exactly the same thing for her, shyly offering a plate of rice and chicken and vegetables, not all that bad.

"What do you mean?" the Australian said. "Is that some Pommy way of telling me I'm not welcome round here any more?"

"No," Jane said, "not at all. I thought you might be uncomfortable about living here after what happened."

"I don't care," the Australian said. "Well, I do care, but it would be the same anywhere. Poor bugger."

"Good," Jane said.

"This is nice," he said. "Where'd you learn to cook?"

"Anyone can cook," Jane said. It was just a plate of pasta with bacon and peas and cream. "It's not hard."

"You'd be amazed," the Australian said. "When I was at uni, I used to make this pasta bake, and it was a tin of tuna and a tin of corn, and all sorts of vegetables, whatever you could find, and then you poured a cheesy sauce out of a packet over it and put it in the oven."

"That sounds incredible," Jane said. "Did you just invent that?"

"No, it was kind of passed down to me," the Australian said. "The great tradition of student cooking, passed on from mouth to mouth over the years. I even cooked it for other people, would you believe it?"

"I used to be vegetarian," Jane said.

"Oh, yeah," the Australian said.

As if he'd asked why she stopped, she went on, "But one day I just found myself making a bacon sandwich, and I didn't really care."

"Yeah, bacon sandwich, you couldn't give that up and not miss it."

They ate contentedly for a while.

"The thing is," Jane said, "I think I was probably only doing it in the first place to be annoying. It used to drive my mother up the wall."

"Oh, yeah," the Australian said. "I bet your mother went crazy when she heard you'd started eating bacon sandwiches again the second you'd left home and were having to cook for yourself."

"You're right, actually. She put the phone down on me," Jane said. "My dad thought it was funny. I was thinking—"

"You're going to have to think about getting another lodger," the

Australian said, interrupting her. He'd obviously been thinking about it. "There's no point in putting it off."

"God," Jane said.

"Just got to be sensible about it. You can't help but think about it with the room being empty like that. Put someone else in, and it'll be their room before you know it."

"I can't imagine anyone would want to rent a room where, you know . . ."

"You're not thinking of telling them, are you?" the Australian said. "Of course they won't, if anyone tells them. Jesus, sleep in a room where a bloke wanked himself to death three weeks before? No, I don't think so."

The extraordinary normality of the situation kept startling Jane; she placed an advert in the free Australian news-sheet in exactly the same way that she had a few months before, and it cost exactly the same. The girl at the other end of the phone didn't recognize her details, didn't say, "So it didn't work out, then?" or "Yeah, I heard the bloke died with his dick in his fist." There was no reason to think the advert would be any different from any other advert, and Jane had to admit that the flat, even to her, looked pretty much the same as it had when she moved in. No sinister atmosphere had descended on it; in fact, horribly, it was more as if something had been removed from it, and she and the shy Australian had come together into a baffled domesticity.

That Thursday the Australian surprised her by suddenly suggesting going out to a pub. "Why not?" she said, surprising herself in turn. It would never have occurred to her; she went to pubs so seldom that she hardly saw them, like the way betting shops didn't impinge on your awareness. But the Australian, it seemed, knew all the pubs in Clapham, wondering out loud about the Prince of Wales, the Sun, the Feathers, the Alexandra before settling on a pub in a back-street, halfway between the square and the doctor's. Jane had never even noticed it. She wondered if he might be a favourite, a regular at the pub, but they didn't seem to know or remember him. Perhaps that was just London. They drank steadily, sociably; a large television hung precariously in one corner, and a succession of game shows took place. She quite enjoyed the Australian's obscene running commentary on all the contestants and presenters and prizes, and when they'd had three or four drinks, she let him teach her how to play one of the gambling machines in the corner. She'd always thought that the point of these machines was to win money, but this one fizzed and bonged without any suggestion of reward; she called it a "one-armed bandit," he liked that. It was something to do, the game, with an intergalactic space war.

"They have lock-ins here," the Australian said, but in fact the pub closed like any other at eleven, the landlady folding her arms and refusing when he tried to ask for another couple of drinks at five past. "I reckon she thinks you look like a policewoman," he said, returning empty-handed to their table.

"That's a terrible thing to say," Jane said.

"Well, you do a bit," the Australian said.

"No, I don't," Jane said. "I think that's about the rudest thing you could say to a woman."

"Oh, come on," the Australian said. "I'm only joshing. It's the Australian in me. I insult you, and then you insult me back, and then we're best mates, yeah?"

"That sounds insane," Jane said. "You want me to insult you back? You really want me to?"

The Australian was about to say yes, but he caught her eye; there must have been some expression in it, something positively alarming. "Maybe not," he muttered, and they got up and went home.

She'd drunk more than she was used to, but she wasn't expecting the painful hangover the next morning; woken by the noise of the Australian leaving the house at nine, she raised her head before lowering it again, convinced she was about to be sick. It was eleven thirty before she managed to leave the house. By then, the Northern Line had calmed down from its rush-hour insanity; she actually sat down for once.

"Your friend Sarah Willis called," her supervisor, Ian, said when she got in. "Are you sure you're well enough to come in? You look awful."

"I think there's something going round," Jane said.

"Well, stay away from me," Ian said cheerfully, but he was always sniffing and honking away from some cold one of his three small children had picked up at school or playgroup.

"I took the morning off," Jane said, into the telephone. "I told them I was sick, but really it was just a hangover. I felt terrible."

"That's awful," Sarah said. "You don't want to make a habit of that. Listen, I'm really sorry, but you know this evening . . ."

"Er—oh, God, yes, this evening."

She'd quite forgotten, but a few weeks ago, they'd looked at the South Bank brochure and decided to go to a concert tonight together. Last year, they'd so enjoyed *Amadeus* at the National Theatre, and

Sarah Willis had said she'd never thought she'd like Mozart so much, they must go to a concert, a proper concert of his music some time. There it had rested until Jane had booked tickets for tonight.

"It can't be helped. My boss, my big boss, is over from the States and we're all to go out for a brainstorming dinner with him tonight. I'm really sorry, but you'll get the money back on the ticket, won't you?"

There was never anything much like that in Jane's life. The big boss, her ultimate boss, worked upstairs, and though he was much richer than Jane, he went home to Enfield every night at five thirty. Nobody had ever been known to stay late at the toy-maker's.

At six, Jane left the office and walked down Southampton Row. It was a sunny afternoon, and the trees on either side cast a bucolic air over everything, even the hooting traffic, even the four tramps who huddled, as always, in their nests of blankets and rags and possession-filled supermarket trolleys under the pillared porch of the disused old church. She walked over Waterloo Bridge, her soft slim brown leather briefcase, much like a music-case, by her side, and felt she looked somehow different from everyone else hurrying over the bridge at this time. It was a beautiful view, the grand buildings lining up along the green flood as if they were holding back something torrential. As if in planned response, a boat hooted, somewhere down towards the City, its blast echoing between the sides of the canyon, and Big Ben replied with its half-hour chime. She was starting to love this city.

Jane took her seat in the concert hall twenty minutes before the start. She knew that was something her father always did, on their rare visits to the theatre or to a *Messiah* at the City Hall at Easter, and she'd always found it ridiculous. But you couldn't sit in the bar on your own for long, smiling brightly, unless you really were waiting for someone. She put her bag in the thirty-pound empty seat, and realized that Sarah Willis hadn't offered to pay for the wasted ticket. She read the pro-gramme notes, her eyes passing over the superior and baffling explan-ations, and then, with more pleasure, the adverts, the names of the people playing in the orchestra, the Hollywoodish photographs of the conductor and soloist, the message from the London Borough of Lambeth about fire exits. In time, the hall filled, in pairs and parties, and then, all at once, the orchestra, slouching on in their white ties and tails, a crowd of penguins hovering on the brink of the ice, waiting for the first one to take the plunge. It must be odd to wear such things all the time. From the muddle of sound of an orchestra warming up, little fragments of melody, somehow familiar, as they had one last chance to try to get an awkward corner right; and then it all fell silent and, like a crowd all gathering round a single object, they agreed on the same note, hooting and responding like the boat on the river.

A piece by Rossini was listed as coming first, but before that the conductor pointed at the percussion, and a drum-roll. Jane began to struggle to her feet, with a little surprise: she knew that concerts at the City Hall in Sheffield often started with the National Anthem, but she'd always assumed that London wouldn't bother with it, since they could see the Queen's house any time they chose. But she'd made a mistake: no one else was getting up, and she sat down again promptly. It wasn't the National Anthem: it was just the way the first piece began, with a drum-roll. Her face burnt. To her left, a couple nudged each other, smiling. She couldn't listen to the first piece, and applauded at the end with some relief, as though it had been devised only for her discomfiture.

The second piece was Mozart, a piano concerto, and the reason, really, they'd decided to come. But it seemed so hard to Jane to find the pleasure she'd had at *Amadeus*, and though the programme note said that the piece was famous, she couldn't work out whether she'd heard it before or not. The music was shiny, clean and insolent, not really asking anything of her. Only when it came to the second movement did anything start to make sense; she looked at the programme note again, wondering why she recognized this, and it explained that it had been used as the music to a famous Swedish film. That didn't explain the familiarity; Jane was sure she'd never seen the film, which was called *Elvira Madigan*. She must have heard it somewhere, the way music became familiar without you noticing it, and all of a sudden it came to an end. She hadn't been listening. She'd been thinking about something else entirely.

At the end of the piece, when they'd all applauded the pianist, and he'd come back three times, the last time artificially cranking up the applause when it had threatened to die out prematurely, the audience began to shuffle and rise. Behind her, an emphatic voice spoke.

"Of course, it's all very well," the voice was saying, "but I think you'll find that you get much better performances on a Friday night at the Sheffield City Hall from the Hallé Orchestra. Many's the time I've gone back to Rayfield Avenue in Sheffield, quite bowled over by—"

Jane turned in surprise. Behind her there was a man—no, he looked older than he was, his pale hair thinning on top of a pink scalp like mist on a hilltop. He was wearing a slightly crumpled grey suit with an ink stain at one trouser pocket and a blue shirt, but no tie. His knees were pulled up halfway to his chest; he was immensely tall, even sitting down. He grinned at her. "I know you," he said. "You're Jane, aren't you?"

"Yes," she said, wondering. Then she remembered—he was the little boy who used to live over the road in Sheffield. He'd been tall even then. Daniel had been friends with his sister.

"Francis," he said, reminding her. "Francis Sellers."

"I didn't know you were in London," she said.

"I'd heard you were," he said. "Your mother's great friends with my mother."

"I remember you now," Jane said. "And your sister, she's—"

"Sandra? She's just moved to Australia."

"Emigrated?" Jane said idiotically. She didn't know what she had been on the point of saying about his sister; she was probably glad he'd interrupted her.

"Yes," Francis said, looking amused as the people excused themselves around him. It was odd to see him grown-up, with grown-up responses; he was still gangling, but didn't have that conspicuously hovering appearance any more. If anything, he was lounging in his seat.

"That's a coincidence," Jane said, for something to say. But then she realized how foolish her comment really was.

"What is?"

"Oh, nothing," Jane said, not really able to say that she shared a flat with an Australian. "Where are you living now?"

"In Balham," Francis said. "And you?"

"I'm in Clapham," she said. "I don't know why we haven't bumped into each other before."

"Actually, I think I've seen you," Francis said. "I thought it was you, but I wasn't sure. On the Northern Line."

"We ought to meet up," Jane found herself saying.

"Well, we've met up now," Francis said. "Do you want to get a drink?"

He liked music, he explained as they went to the bar. It had come on him in Sheffield. "A lot of adolescents take to music in a big way, I know," he said, and it struck Jane as a strange thing to say; it would have been indecent to use the word "adolescent" five years before, and she almost envied Francis for being able to distance himself from his biological experience in so fast and lordly a way. He hadn't, it seemed, gone to university—he didn't say why, and he'd always seemed like a clever boy. "Do you like Bruckner?" he asked, and she said she didn't know, but pointed out what, of course, he must know, that that was what the orchestra was going to play in the second half. He came often to these things, he said. Jane listened; she didn't quite know how to talk about the way she took this sort of thing, in London.

London was full of opportunities, of interesting things to see and interesting places to visit. For her own sake, Jane was scrupulous about arranging an outing with a friend during the week, perhaps to a concert at the Wigmore Hall or a film, or now and again to the theatre. She'd seen lots of famous actors in all sorts of things, and kept her programmes, some signed, in a folder. There'd never been any choice in Sheffield, just one thing a month at the Crucible and a concert a week at the City Hall, most of which you wouldn't want to go to. At Oxford there'd been a choice, but you had to admit, after a term of going to everything, that hardly any of it was worth going to or listening to. It was really a crime not to go to what London had to offer, and she'd really started enjoying it; she was proud of having seen Antony Sher in *Richard III* and shelling out for tickets near the front. The way he'd hurtled straight at them on his crutches, like a black missile dismantling in flight; Jane had gone home knowing what "starry-eyed" meant, her eyes feeling weighty and luminous on the Northern Line. She'd gone straight to her room and done something she hadn't done for years: written a poem about it. Even Sarah Willis, who wasn't so keen on keeping up with the culture, had to admit that she was glad Jane had asked her to that, though of course the month after she'd yawned her way through a concert—or did you say recital?—of the Amadeus Quartet playing Schubert at the Wigmore Hall.

The outings in the week were interesting and enjoyable, though they sometimes didn't leave much time for talking to your friend. If it was a long evening and they had to get up in the morning, quite often they'd shoot off without having a pizza afterwards, which wasn't really very satisfactory. But there were the weekend outings, too. Jane made a point of visiting a different part of London every weekend. Sometimes she went to a museum or a gallery, either a famous central one—she was doing the National Gallery and the Victoria and Albert and the British Museum conscientiously, two or three rooms at a time—or a local one. She hadn't realized what an enormous walk it was from the tube stop to Kenwood in Hampstead, but of course it was an interesting walk if you hadn't been to that bit of London before. There was the

Horniman Museum, the John Soane, the Wallace collection—oh, she'd been all over.

There were other walks to be had. It was interesting to go for long walks through the parks, through the snooty velvet hills of Hampstead Heath and Richmond Park, the kite-flyers in the one, the deer raising their heads and, all at once, running; Kew Gardens, which rather daunted her with the sense that everything was interesting here if only she knew anything about plants. She'd have to bring her dad here, he'd enjoy it. She went for Sunday walks, too, through particular parts of London, discovering Spitalfields with its blank-faced and picturesque decrepitude, its crumbling brick façades like the long, ruined face of a drunkard. Or the City, so strangely empty on a Saturday. She'd thought it like a horror movie about the end of the world, and then, to confirm her feeling, she'd come across a film crew shooting a film about exactly that, thirty extras horrifically made up like the living dead, sitting around having cups of tea quite naturally. It was all very interesting, and there was never any shortage of things to tell her mum and dad when, once a week, she telephoned them to tell them what she'd been up to.

She was terribly lonely, really.

The ugly, empty feeling of Oxford, the sense that everyone there was conducting a riotous social life in which they all knew each other and had resolved, before even arriving at the place, to exclude Jane and her big ridiculous chin from it, was massively extended into Jane's sense of London. Her friends here were, for the moment, the same friends she'd had in Oxford, obstinately maintained. She felt humbly lucky that she lived near Sarah Willis and her boyfriend Dave, who included her quite often, but somehow she hadn't managed to forge an independent bond with any of their friends. Most of them were Dave's friends from the hockey club and their girlfriends. Sometimes, towards the end of an evening, that sort would start mimicking the way she talked, ask her to say "bath" and "path" and even, stupidly, "cart"; Sarah had kept the way she talked, too, but they never asked her to perform like that. If Jane ever saw any of them in Clapham, she'd say hello, and they'd say hello back, but after a surprised, contemptuous interval as they dragged Dave's girl Sarah's little friend to mind.

The toy-makers weren't much help, either; they hadn't taken on a graduate for some time, and everyone else in the office was married or old. They'd asked her to dance, one after the other, at her first Christmas party, as their wives looked on benevolently, jigging about at more than arm's length, smiling bravely at her before handing her on to another colleague. Anyone would have thought she was the poor ugly girl, and not just marked out by being young and on her own.

The sense of loneliness was a new one on her; she'd felt it first at Oxford, combined with a horrible, stupid, snobbish sense of social inadequacy, and then, renewed, it had taken hold in this bigger city, in London. But she hadn't articulated it to herself until it was forced upon her. This was how loneliness in London ended, she thought, sitting at the Australian's funeral. She wouldn't die like that, exactly, but she could shut the door and go to bed and never get up again; how long, as in the Australian's case, until anyone noticed she was missing? From wondering that, the bigger question of who would miss her at all painfully rose.

There was so much to go and see, so much to visit in London; parks and walks, exhibitions and concerts and films and plays and even, she supposed, operas and ballets. In the couple of days after bumping into Francis, she gave them all detailed thought. She tried to remember everything she could about him, too, but nothing much came to mind except his height, the way he'd always sort of folded himself around himself, his limbs trying to make themselves smaller, his head drooping down between his shoulder-blades. His family hadn't always lived there actually, Jane remembered quite well the summer they'd moved in—but she remembered his sister more than him. He'd sometimes been around when they were a bit older, and when they'd had that gang who used to go down to the lower crags and sit there drinking bottles of illicitly acquired cider, he was sometimes around at the edges of the group. She remembered, too, there was a new year's party once at his parents' house. It was her upper-sixth year; she'd had the letter three days before Christmas from Oxford, and she'd been glowing for ten days. "Jane's just been accepted by Oxford," she remembered her mother saying to everyone at the party, and then, with a shameful grasp of the idiom, "LMH. She goes up in October."

"I'm sure she'll get the grades," Mr. Sellers—Bernie, wasn't it?—had said and meant it kindly.

"Oh, I don't think they trouble about all of that," Jane's mother had hooted embarrassingly, and Jane had stood there like a lemon, as if she were supposed now to start performing or something.

She'd ended up talking to Francis then, and they'd had quite a good conversation. A deep conversation, as they used to call it, about life, the universe and everything. "I don't believe in God," Francis had said, with an air of bravery.

"Well, I don't think I do either," Jane had said, surprised, and before long they were on to the distances between stars and galaxies and how long it would take you if you travelled at the speed of light and how insignificant it made everything seem, and then, seamlessly, on to nuclear war. "You sound like my brother's friend Stig," Jane had said.

"I hope not," Francis had said, with a flash of likeability—Stig was a new friend of Tim's, always around these days, scowling and making sarcastic comments about everything. When people found out she was clever, they often embarked on a conversation that was meant to be deep, and some of the grown-ups at this party had actually started lengthening their vowels as if in deference to Oxford. But Francis laughed at Stig and probably would have laughed at Tim, too. She'd liked him for that, she remembered: she wondered why she hadn't bothered more with him afterwards.

"Weren't you a vegetarian?" Francis said as they were going back for the second half. "That's what I mainly remember about you, that you were a vegetarian."

He was as tall and drawn-out in shape as someone else's shadow, and climbing the steps to the upper half of the stalls, she felt as if the crowd was staring at them; the girl who had stood for the Rossini overture with a man a foot taller than her. What she felt like saying was, what I mostly remember about your family is that once, eight years ago, I was walking past my brother's room, my elder brother Daniel; and I looked in, and there was your sister, with a smeared attempt at lipstick on her spotty stupid face, and bright green eyeshadow on her closed eyes, and she had her school blouse wide open and her bra undone. This was in my family's house, Francis, remember; that was what she wanted to say. And she was in Daniel's bedroom, but it wasn't Daniel who was face down in her stupid tits and making stupid noises. It was my eleven-year-old brother. That's what I mostly remember about your family, Francis.

"No, I stopped all that," Jane said. "Being vegetarian. It was more trouble than it was worth, in the end. Are you on your own here?"

"Yes, I am," Francis said.

"Someone stood you up, too?" she said lightly.

"No, not at all," he said. "I like coming to these things on my own."

"You can sit with me, if you like," Jane said, as they stood at the end of their respective rows. "I've got an empty space next to me."

"If you'd like," Francis said stiffly, and then she wondered whether he might really mean what he said, that he preferred coming to these things on his own. He'd spoken to her, though.

It was a bigger noise that began now, and a sense, despite the brightly lit and optimistic hall, despite the luminous blacks and whites of the orchestra, of plunging into some forest gloom. Something was slowly moving down there, an immense movement, a beast made of a single muscle, like a snake; it took form, and rose, and mounted into a single gesture. She disliked the sensation; before, she had been looking at small exact objects in a glass case, as if she could choose when to move on, but this wouldn't let her do that. It seemed crude, even ugly, but after a while she forgot to think whether she liked it or not. It was just a kind of obliteration, and she had no idea how long it had been going on when it rose into a kind of massive, lowering density, and came to an end. She looked at Francis; he was pale, wide-eyed. She looked at the programme note, but she couldn't understand it; the next part was a set, it said, of "double variations," whatever that meant. All she knew, for the next three-quarters of an hour, was the sense of slow, immense mutation, like layers of geology moving easily, softly and massively under the feet.

"Did you enjoy that?" Francis said, at the end as they were leaving.

"I don't know," Jane said. "I've never heard anything like it, though."

"You haven't heard Bruckner before?"

"No," Jane said. "But it's sort of like how you imagine classical music's going to be if you've never heard any."

"I know what you mean," Francis said, obviously a bit disappointed.

"I don't really know whether I liked it or not," Jane said. "Or whether I was bored or not. I was sort of listening, but it was more like just being in a place, like—"

"It's difficult describing music," Francis said.

"We ought to do something," Jane said, thinking that it probably wouldn't be a concert. She didn't exactly know why. Francis seemed, perhaps, like the sort of person who might quite easily start explaining to her about double variations; men liked to explain about what they did or what they liked to do, all of them. She knew that well enough.

"I'd like that," Francis said outside the Festival Hall, as if saying goodbye, but they'd both forgotten for the moment that they lived in the same direction on the Northern Line, and from Waterloo to Clapham Common they had to find something else to talk about. Jane told him about her Australian lodger; that seemed to do.

The right outing for Francis came to her, and a couple of days after bumping into him, she made an effort and called him. He sounded pleased to hear from her; agreed that the weather was nice enough now to go for a walk; liked a walk; had nothing planned for Sunday; agreed to meet at Putney station and go for a walk along the river. He didn't say anything annoying, like "Do you mind if I bring my girlfriend?" either. She put the phone down; had a thought, looked at the *A–Z*, realized an ambiguity, phoned back and explained that she meant Putney tube station, not the overground station. He laughed, commended her clarity.

On Thursday morning, she was in the bath when the telephone rang. It could only have been half past seven; her alarm clock was set for seven fifteen, and she was just settling in. The bathroom was peach and purple, brown flowers printed on the beige tiles, an old-lady taste, but it was a flimsy insertion, put in when the house was greedily converted into too many flats, twenty years before, and the telephone seemed to ring right next to your ear through the hardboard partition. Jane got out, wrapping herself in her old-lady's bathrobe. There was no point in waiting for the Australian to get up and answer it—he wasn't an early riser—and she hadn't quite got the knack of just leaving a call to be dealt with by the answering-machine.

She couldn't think who would call so early, but the blunt, lazy voice at the other end, announcing itself as Lee—at the hoarse high pitch that could be a man or a woman—said it was calling about the ad in the paper. Jane was surprised: the paper, she understood, only came out today. Whoever it was must have picked it up immediately, and started phoning. "Come round at eight o'clock tomorrow night," Jane said firmly.

"Where is it?" the Australian voice asked, and Jane told it. There was a pause. "Gee, I don't know—that sounds like quite a way. We couldn't meet somewhere more central, could we?" the voice asked.

"Don't you want to see the flat?" Jane said, amused, and wondering why someone would want to live in a flat that seemed too far out to visit even the once.

"Yeah, that's right," the voice said, pulling itself together. Perhaps this was just one in a series of undertakings, and it had had to remind itself, at this early hour, that it was dealing with flat-sharing, not lonely hearts or the exchange and sale of a campervan. They made an appointment.

She had just got into the bath when the telephone rang again, but this time Jane didn't get up, and sure enough another shouty Australian voice could be heard against the clanking background of a railway station spelling out his details, and immediately afterwards a third. She had had no idea this was going to prove so popular— it hadn't been so before. You could have congratulated the dead Australian on his timing. As if to confirm the thought, her hand, reaching behind her head for her shampoo, gripped not her bottle of Timotei but the cheap brand, half-empty and not worth packing with his effects, which the dead Australian had used. The water was getting cold; she shivered. By the time she was dressed and ready to go out, there were eleven messages, which seemed enough; she took their names and numbers to work, and all morning arranged appointments the next night with the ones who could be reached. They all seemed perfectly nice.

"Going out?" the Australian said the next day, wandering into the sitting room where she'd been talking.

"No," Jane said. "I'm going to stay in and watch the telly."

"You've forgotten, then," the Australian said.

"Forgotten what?"

"The new lodgers, they're coming round, yeah? They've been phoning all day to confirm."

"God, yes," Jane said. "Have we got any wine in?"

"Wine? You're going to give them wine?"

"It might be friendly. I wish I'd remembered to ask Sarah to come, too. She always knows about people. I never do."

"I wondered what she was doing here when I came round first," the Australian said. "I thought maybe it was that you didn't want to be left alone with a man, you know, like that woman who disappeared that time."

"Yes," Jane said, not knowing what he was talking about—he had that way of thinking you had access to the precise thoughts his vaguer words delineated. "I never know what to ask them."

"Yeah, I can see that," the Australian said, not unkindly. "They're not going to tell you the truth if you ask them anything directly—like, are you a tidy person, or, do you do drugs or get drunk and smash up my granny's favourite ornaments."

"I don't have any of my granny's favourite ornaments," Jane said.

"But you think they'll say, 'Yes, I'm too tidy really, people complain about how quiet and self-effacing I am—' "

"What does that mean, self-facing?"

"Effacing, quiet," Jane said. "Do you want any dinner?"

"If it's no trouble."

"No trouble," Jane said. "You know, when I was applying for jobs, the first interview I went to, they said, 'Do you have any faults, would you say?' and I'd heard, from my friend Sarah, really, that the thing to say was 'Well, to be honest, I think I'm really too much of a perfectionist—' "

"Everyone says that, it's stupid."

"I know. I said it that once, the first interview I had, and it must have come out a bit wrong, because they all laughed like drains, and I thought, I'm not saying that again. It must have been the tenth time they'd heard it that morning."

"I thought everyone knew that they ask it, you say exactly that, you all ignore it and move on, because if they employ you they're going to find out what your faults are anyway and you aren't going to tell them anything serious, like, 'My main fault in life is that I can't stop myself stealing stuff from my employers.' "

Because half the cutlery in the flat, Jane had recently discovered, had been acquired from the restaurant where the Australian worked. She didn't know why: when she'd moved in, she'd bought a box of cutlery from Habitat, a set of six of everything with red melamine handles, plenty, and the increase in cutlery had in practice just meant an increase in the amount of stuff sitting in the sink, since the Australian never did any washing-up until everything had been used up.

"I'm trying to work out what your fault was that you told them," the Australian said, going into the kitchen and opening the fridge to see what was there.

"Go on, then," Jane said. "I got some mince on my way home. It's on the bottom shelf."

"I'm not mental," the Australian said. "I'm not going to tell you what your faults are, the real ones."

"I don't know that I've really got any."

"Everyone's got faults," the Australian said, when he'd stopped laughing. "But what did you tell them?"

"Oh, I said I thought I was a bit of a chatterbox," Jane said, "because— What's so funny?"

"Nothing," the Australian said. "You're right, I wouldn't have guessed you'd say that."

"Well, I don't see why it's funny," Jane said. "I thought it was quite good, because actually you wouldn't mind working with someone who talks all the time—well, maybe you would if it was all the time. Anyway, it seemed like quite a positive thing, to talk a bit too much, and in any case I said it at the interview for Deacon Barkin and I got the job, and they've been finding out, I suppose, what my real faults are ever since."

"When are they arriving?"

"The first one's at eight," Jane said. "I don't know what we're going to ask them. We ought to have a list of questions, psychological tests, find out what they're like."

"Got to be a bit creative about it, ask them questions they're not expecting," the Australian said. "I don't know what."

"What are you cooking?" Jane said.

"Oh, I don't know," the Australian said, calling through the serving-hatch—it was obviously some sort of amazing mess, to be served up burnt round the edges.

"I know," Jane said. "There used to be this story, about when you went to Oxford to be interviewed, that someone went into the room of the don—the lecturer, I mean—and the man was sitting behind a news-paper and didn't put it down, and the boy sat down and then from behind this newspaper, this voice came, and he just said, 'Entertain me.' "

"That was the question?"

"It's supposed to be," Jane said.

"I wouldn't know what to do."

"The story goes that he set fire to the newspaper."

"Did he get in?"

"I don't know, I can't remember. I don't think it's true. It's just a story they tell you to make you expect anything."

"What did they ask you at your interview?"

"Er, about what I'd done at school, what books I liked, if I was in any clubs, that sort of thing."

The Australian came to the kitchen door. Behind him a mass of steam, the soiled indignant smell of mince frying at too high a temper-ature with a lot of things that had never, in the history of the world, been fried with mince before. His mouth hung open, as he digested this story. All at once, he started to laugh, barking away; you had to join in when someone laughed like that.

"I like that story," he said. "I think we should just ask them that, tell them, 'Entertain us,' and see what they do."

"They might have heard the story and set something on fire."

"No, they won't," the Australian said.

They'd eaten the terrible dinner and, in a great hurry, washed up and returned the kitchen to some state of cleanliness. The sitting room, Jane's bedroom and the bathroom were clean and tidy, but the Australian's room had clothes littered all over the floor, its curtains still drawn, the air thick and fetid. "Honestly," Jane said, and together they picked everything up from the floor and bundled it in a big ball into the wardrobe. They shook out the duvet and laid it over the rumpled and stained bottom sheet; there was nothing much to be done about the pillows, or about the shabby poster, the only thing on the walls, but Jane opened the window to let some air in.

"The other room's fine," Jane said. "I've not been in there."

They'd arranged for the would-be lodgers to arrive every fifteen minutes—otherwise they'd still be seeing people at midnight—but this proved too little time. The first was the earliest telephoner; it turned out to be a short, cross girl, who started on about how long it had taken her to get here, and that she didn't know at all. She had what looked like self-cropped hair, a blocky build; you didn't have to close your eyes to wonder whether she was a boy or a girl still. She poked at everything, stood shaking her head at the view out of the window, asked a lot of questions about the rates and the nearest swimming-pool and the days of rubbish collection, which Jane couldn't answer. "Well, I suppose it'll be OK," she said eventually, sighing, but the Australian explained, on a note of outrage, that they had a few people to see and they'd like a little chat to see if they'd get on, like.

Jane didn't have the nerve, but the Australian sat down next to her on the sofa and said to the girl, Lee, "Well, entertain us."

She stared at them. They both had little notebooks on their laps, thieved by Jane from work, ring-bound at the top, pens at the ready. "How do you mean?"

"Come on, entertain us."

"I can't entertain you?" the girl said, outrage rising with her final inflection. "What do you want me to do?"

"Anything you like," Jane said.

"I don't have any talent?" the girl said. "My sister, she won second prize in a Junior Miss beauty competition? Once when she was eight, when we were on holiday on the Gold Coast? But I never won anything like that?"

"Do you think beauty is a talent?"

"Oh, they've got to show off their talents in the talent round? It's not just about beauty, it's about personality too?"

"What did your sister do?" the Australian said.

"How do you mean?"

"In the Junior Miss beauty competition, what was her talent in the talent round?"

"I can't remember," the girl said.

The doorbell went. The three of them went on staring at each other.

"I don't have a talent like that," Lee said. "I'm not a performing donkey?"

"What's a performing donkey do, when it performs?" the Australian said, when she had gone with instructions to let the next one up.

"Heaven knows," Jane said. "She was horrible."

The next one was someone the Australian actually knew, who announced himself as Clive. He was immensely fat and breathless, red in the face, mopping himself and his damp hair with fat hands. He took a moment to remember the Australian, but it turned out they'd been at school together when they were nine. Jane was more amazed at this than either of them seemed to be; they took a cursory walk round the flat, then sat down and started reminiscing heavily.

"And that Mrs. Blewitt, she was a bitch," Clive said.

"Oh, yeah, a prize bitch," the Australian said. "Do you remember that day Carol Walmer pissed herself in class because she kept putting her hand up to be excused and Mrs. Blewitt wouldn't let her go, kept telling her to put her hand down and wait until break?"

"I thought she pooed herself."

"Yeah, that's right, she pooed herself. What happened to her?"

"Carol Walmer? Oh, she's got herself a good job on a television station, news reporter, and a rich husband and a house in Manly. She doesn't look like the sort of girl who'd poo herself these days, and I don't reckon she'd thank you for reminding her of the incident. You're always seeing her standing on a beach with a microphone talking about the jellyfish."

The two of them laughed merrily at the thought.

"Do you want to see anyone else?" Jane said miserably, when the fat man left, waving goodbye all the way down the stairs.

"How do you mean?"

"It's a stroke of luck, having an old friend of yours from school turning up like that."

"Clive Franklin? He's not an old friend of mine, I fucking hate him, fucking gutbucket. We don't want him living with us. If I never saw him again in my life it'd be too soon."

"Entertain you?" the third applicant said; he had a nervous appearance, his thin brown hair parted dead down the centre of his head, falling away lankly to either side. If his face was sallow, the skin underneath his hair was dead white, forming a diagnostic line from his forehead to the crown of his head. He spoke in a whine, too loud for the small room.

"You don't sound Australian," Jane said.

"*I'm* not Australian," the man said, as if acknowledging that there were queues of Australians waiting outside. "Nobody ever thought I was before."

"No," the Australian said. "It was just—well, we thought everyone who came for the flat would be Australian."

"Are you only prepared to let to Australians?" the man said. "Because if you are, I can inform you that it's illegal to discriminate on racial grounds. I'm a law student. I know about these things."

"It was only that, you know, the magazine we put the ad in," the Australian said, "it's mostly meant for Australians in this country. I didn't know anyone else read it. We'll let you know."

"Ah," the man said. "I think we've established that your firm intention was to discriminate on racial grounds in the letting of the room in this flat. So if you now let to an Australian then I have very strong grounds for suing you. I don't believe you have any choice but to let the room to me."

"Ah, piss off," the Australian said.

"No, I'm Australian all right," the fourth one said. She was a girl, round-faced, her hair in a black bob, wearing a short skirt and leggings and Doc Martens. "I guess if you advertise there that's what you get mostly. My dad was born in Greece. He's a dentist."

"Oh, yeah, a Greek dentist from Melbourne," the Australian said, bafflingly, but they both laughed; it must make sense somewhere. Jane's Australian stereotypes were limited to people standing on their head on the other side of the world, calling each other "mate" with corks in their hats and eating turkey on the beach on Christmas Day, but there must be more stereotypes to enjoy.

"I'm a walking cliché," the girl said. "I'm Sophia, you don't want to know my last name."

"Why? What is it?" Jane said.

"It's Papadopolous, you'd never manage it," the girl said.

"Papadopolous, that's not too hard," Jane said.

"I'm amazed," the girl said. "So, what can I tell you? Shall I entertain you or something, make you like me?"

Jane and the Australian man exchanged a glance; he shrugged, smiled.

"I can't believe it," she said. "You really are—you're saying to people, 'Go on, tell us a funny story,' aren't you?"

Jane told the story about the Oxford don and the burning newspaper; it went down quite well.

"Well, I can juggle," the girl said, "or I can play the guitar, though I only know three songs. I busked in Munich in the summer and every fifteen minutes 'Streets Of London' came round. I was outside a pizza restaurant and after two days the owner came out and paid me forty bucks, no—what?—marks just to go away because he couldn't stand it any more. I haven't got my guitar with me, though."

"It doesn't sound that entertaining," the Australian said.

"So what happened to the bloke who used to have the room?" the girl said.

It was a bad thing to say; she couldn't know.

"He just went," the Australian said.

"Bummer," the girl said. "I bet he left you with a phone bill and half a month's rent, too. So, do I pass the test? I like you guys." She bounced up and down on the sofa. It wasn't her fault, not really.

"Listen, we've got a couple more people to see," the Australian said. "Can we call you tomorrow?"

"OK," the girl said, puzzled. She hadn't expected that: she'd always been liked where she wanted to be liked, and she was likeable without doing the popular thing. It wasn't her fault, not at all.

"I hate that fucking song," the Australian said, at the end of the evening. They'd been too ambitious, and the interviews had stretched out, the last of the Australians coming in and saying they'd have to be quick, it wasn't long till the last tube. They'd had a glass of wine with each of them, and they'd grown laconic and precise towards the end, framing their questions in their mouths before trying to bring them out. Not much towards the end had made a lot of sense, and the marks on the notebooks had grown big and bold and unreadable. On the last page, Jane had written in firm, sloping letters, Her Name Was Lola. The whole idea of living with someone who didn't know what they knew, about the way the previous occupant had quit his tenancy, had grown more and more horrible. She wondered why she hadn't seen that one coming.

"I hate, just hate, that fucking song," the Australian said, stumbling off. " 'Streets of London.' "

"I didn't know," Jane said, "what you meant."

"I hate it," the Australian said, and went into his room, shutting the door behind him. The decision seemed to have been made.

On Sunday, she met Francis at Putney station. It was a beautiful day, and he was waiting at the entrance with a newspaper under his arm. The sun was shining through his thinning hair as she came through the barrier, a glowing halo about his pink head. It was eleven, but not many people were about; they'd both had breakfast, and went down Putney High Street towards the river. She'd brought an *A–Z*, not quite sure of London still, but he seemed to know where he was going.

"I can't remember what you do," Jane said. "I'm sure your mother's told my mother, but I don't know if she ever told me."

"It's very boring," Francis said. "I went to Leeds University, but I didn't like it, and I left after two terms, so I had to get a job. I work for the Civil Service, in the Department of Energy, but it's not very exciting, I mostly do filing and book rooms for meetings, and photocopying."

"That's, what, mining and power stations and that sort of thing?"

"That sort of thing. It's very boring. It's not what I want to end up doing."

Jane told him what she did.

"That sounds fun," he said.

"It's not that exciting," Jane said. "It's not as if we're allowed to play with the toys all day long."

"I think I had a train set made by them," Francis said.

"Everyone did," Jane said. "I hope you enjoyed it."

"Not really," Francis said. "I wasn't really a train-set sort of small boy. It took a long time to set up, and then I didn't know what to do with it. It just went round and round. In the end I was making up stories about the people who might be sitting in the train carriage. It didn't really have anything to do with toy trains as such."

They stopped and watched a rowing team go by, their movements as smooth and satisfied in the glossy river as an expert chef stirring the last stages of a complex soup.

"Do you live on your own?" Jane said.

"No," he said. "I'm renting a room in a house with a couple of others. They're all right—I didn't know them before. I just found the room in an advert in the paper. I wouldn't have them as my best friends otherwise. You can't ask anyone back ever, the house is always such a tip. I'm the only one who ever does any tidying up."

"Everyone always says that," Jane said. "No one ever says, 'I'm the one everyone has to tidy up after.' "

"Maybe," Francis said. "But actually it's true. I do do the tidying up in the house. I'd really like to live with someone a bit nicer. What about you?"

"I'm sharing with an Australian," Jane said. "But it's the same, I just found him through an advert. There used to be another one but—"

"What happened to the other one?"

Jane paused. "Look at that," she said. "Is that a heron?"

They looked. It was, fastidiously picking its feet through the dense mud, peering down at the water like a treasure-hunter. "I thought the river was supposed to be filthy," Jane said. "I thought nothing was supposed to be able to live in it."

"It's getting cleaner, supposedly," Francis said. "I read in the *Evening Standard* that someone caught a salmon at Battersea or was it a trout? I can't remember. We're quite a long way up the river here, too."

"Look at it," Jane said, and in a moment another heron emerged, walking precisely about the first one but somehow ignoring it, as if waiting for a proper introduction. All at once, the first heron plunged its beak into the water, and emerged; in its beak something glittered, writhed with a spasm of muscle. "Do you know, I think it's got a fish—" and the heron lifted its neck, straightening itself, the white streak down its front against the dark sleek river like an exclamation mark, and exultantly swallowed. It seemed to pout, and then from its beak shot a long pure jet of water, exactly like an ornamental fountain. In its throat, the fish went on bucking and wriggling, like an Adam's apple going down. The heron seemed to blink, hugely, and froze, starting to look for another fish; the second heron, bored, stalked away.

"I've never seen that," Jane said. "I've never seen a heron eat a fish before."

"Did you see—"

"The way it sort of spat out the river water—"

"And you could actually see the fish—"

"Sort of going down its neck, still alive, the way it was wriggling—"

"I've never seen that, either. You were saying about the other Australian," Francis said. "The one who left."

"Actually," Jane said, "it's not a nice story. He killed himself about six weeks ago."

"Christ," Francis said. "Where?"

"In his room," Jane said. "I found him." It hadn't, oddly enough, occurred to her until she said this that she might be the object of concern in this situation; the ugly scene, which kept presenting itself as a vivid image, wasn't, by conventional judgement, her problem at all. She was there by chance, an onlooker, and yet it had been mainly horrible for her.

"Jesus," Francis said. "Did you have any idea that he might be, you know . . ."

"What do you mean?"

"You know—depressed . . ."

"Oh," Jane said, seeing that she was going to have to explain the whole thing. "No, he wasn't depressed, we couldn't have known. Are you sure you want to know this? It's not very nice, I said it wasn't a nice story. He didn't mean to kill himself, he was just—ah—sorry, he was masturbating, and for some reason he was hanging himself from a belt at the same time."

"That's shocking," Francis said.

"You would have thought," Jane said, "that anyone could have seen in advance that that really isn't a very sensible thing to do, tie a belt round your neck."

"What a way to go," Francis said.

A little later, Jane said, "You know, you're not very much like I remember you."

"In what way?"

"I don't know," Jane said. "I remember you as being sort of shy."

"Yes, I was shy," Francis said; he seemed amused.

"But you don't seem shy now," she said.

"No," he said. "I'm not."

They walked a little further—Francis told her to mind out, and helped her over a deep hole in the rubble-strewn path. To the right, there were two bicycles on the grass, as if they had fallen drunkenly and stayed there, on the slope down to the river; their riders were at the water's edge, two teenage boys with their trousers rolled up and their knees to their chests, mirroring each other's posture, looking out to the river as if it were going to take them somewhere, as if it were some road. It was a strange place for anyone to pause: from the landward side, a strong odour of rotting tomato soup came, the smell of a brewery at a particular point in its cycle. It was a smell Jane knew—there was a brewery at the west end of the town centre in Sheffield, and some days, if the wind was in the right direction, the smell would drift up the Moor.

"I know about the shyness," Francis said. "It was the weirdest thing. I was going to Leeds in October, to university, and at the beginning of the summer holidays I decided to sort myself out. Because they'd always been six weeks, but then it would be an extra four, ten weeks. It was something my mother said. I'd always eaten with my knife and my fork the wrong way round, my fork in my right hand—because you do more with your fork, it just seemed more sensible. You could always tell when I'd set the table, everything the wrong way round. My mum said one day, after I'd got the letter from Leeds, she said at dinner, 'You're going to have to start eating properly. You can't go to dinner and eat with your fork in your right hand, people will think you're an idiot. It's starting from now.' So I put the knife and fork the other way round—it was really difficult at first—and persevered until I'd got the hang of it.

"And then I started thinking about anything else that maybe I could do something about. Everyone else in my year who was going to Leeds was doing a different subject, so I probably wouldn't be seeing much of them. I thought, It doesn't matter what I've been like, I can start being a different sort of person and no one would ever know. Well, I didn't think exactly that at the start. It was more like, well, I ought to start wearing proper shoes with laces, and not just slip-ons, because I never liked doing up laces. I know it sounds stupid. And I made myself try different food and tried to get used to red wine, and I even had a go at whisky, though I still don't like that. Just little things, making me seem a bit more grown-up because if you're as tall as I am and you eat like a child, people do think you're an idiot, there's no way round it.

"The really big thing was the shyness, though. I'd always been shy. I never liked meeting new people. I was scared of making a phone call. I couldn't ever go first into a room, even into a classroom. And then one day I thought, I'm going to stop being shy. It suddenly seemed really stupid to be shy. It wasn't hurting anyone else, it was only a problem for you, getting in the way of what you'd really like to do. I'll give you an example. You know Bigg and Cleaver, the bookshop?"

"Yes, I know," Jane said. "Off Division Street. I used to go to the café next door."

"Diamond—no, I can't remember what it's called."

"Ruby Tuesday," Jane said. "It's a Beatles song they've named it after."

"That's it," Francis said. "Well, they've got second-hand records in the back room. You can get good things there, and you know I like music. I signed on over the summer before I went to university, and after a few weeks a cheque came for a hundred and twenty pounds, and I thought, I'll spend it on records. So I went to Bigg and Cleaver, but there's a big notice over the door saying, 'Please leave your bags at the front,' and I had a bag. I can't explain it, but I was that shy, I couldn't go up and say, 'Can I leave my bag?' or whatever it is you'd say."

"You wouldn't have to say anything," Jane said, incredulous. "You'd just put it down."

"But," Francis said, "but—well, I thought, you'd have to say something, so they knew it was you who'd left it, or they might challenge you when you came to collect it, or they might think you were weird for not saying anything to them or—"

"I've never heard anything like it," Jane said. "You really used to worry about all of that?"

"Yes, of course I did," Francis said. "I thought everyone did."

"So what did you do?" Jane said. "With the bag."

"I didn't do anything," Francis said. "I didn't go in the back room and I didn't spend my hundred and twenty pounds. When I got home and thought about it I almost felt like crying."

"I don't wonder," Jane said. She felt herself growing more Sheffield in her speech. "That's ridiculous."

"I know," Francis said. "So I just decided, like that, without telling anyone, I was going to stop being shy."

"What did you do?"

"Oh, all sorts," Francis said. "I went up to strangers, I started conversations on buses, I went on my own to pubs, I began arguments. All sorts."

"I wouldn't do any of that," Jane said.

"It worked a bit too well," Francis said, "because, of course, when I wasn't shy any more, it was like I'd woken up and I was in Leeds, and I wondered why it was that I was in Leeds. I wasn't the same person as I was when I'd applied there. I could have had a go at Oxford, I reckon. You went to Oxford, didn't you?"

"Yes, I did," Jane said. "You're probably right, you don't need to be that intelligent to get into Oxford. There were some people there who wouldn't have been at the top of an A-level class at Flint. You'd have been all right."

"Well, thanks," Francis said. "In any case, it was too late, I was at Leeds, and I kept thinking, the only reason I applied here was because I was shy and I thought it would be quite like Sheffield, and it wouldn't be far from Sheffield, and if I thought I could get in there then it would probably be full of people like me. Of course I didn't say any of that. Do you know what I said at the time?"

"You know, actually, I do. Because someone told me what you were going round saying. You were saying you wouldn't want to go to Oxford or Cambridge or back down south, even though you'd come from there in the first place, because there weren't any hills and you wouldn't like a town without any hills. I thought it was the most stupid thing I'd ever heard, because I'd just finished at Oxford, or maybe I was in my last year, and I thought, There's lots of things to object to about it, but one of them isn't that there aren't any hills."

"That's horrible," Francis said, "having people remember stupid things you said. Anyway, it all went wrong. I carried on with my programme for not being shy, and it got a bit out of hand, and I didn't like it at all because it was a bit like meeting yourself when you were younger, living in a decision that a stupid version of yourself had made. I was living in this hall of residence, basically a huge tower with the walls made out of grey breeze blocks and I didn't like one single person, I don't think, so after two terms I left. I'd have failed the first-year exams anyway."

"What were you studying?"

"I can't remember."

"Oh, come on."

Francis had finished his story. It seemed like a sad story, but he'd told it before, and now he'd told it evenly. A bell sounded behind them; it was the two cyclists who had been resting by the river. Francis and Jane moved to one side and let them pass, clattering as they went. "Did you see—" one called over his shoulder to the other, not caring, "—did you see that giant?" and they were a hundred yards down the path. Jane looked at the ground; Francis wasn't so enormously tall, she'd seen taller, though not much. It was really just the way he held himself.

"I love that building," Francis said bravely—it was the Harrods

Depository, or so a huge sign said, flushed red and lavishly curlicued, smothered in brick fruit and flowers. "It's just a warehouse, I don't know why they'd make it so fanciful."

"I've never seen it," Jane said. "I suppose Harrods would naturally want to have the best of everything, even their warehouse, it would have to be—"

"The thing is," Francis said, breaking out in a sort of frustration, "the thing is I was wrong, I'm sure I was wrong, deciding not to be shy. I really think that now. Because if you're not shy you go out into the world, but if you are shy then you stay at home, and it's really better to stay at home. You're going to be happy if you stay at home. I wish I hadn't come to London, really. I hate where I live, I hate the people I live with, I hate my job. I don't feel I belong here."

"But you were born here," Jane said. "Weren't you?"

"It doesn't feel like it," Francis said.

She left it.

"I'm really glad I met you," Francis said. "It just made me feel like Sheffield again."

She couldn't answer; she had felt something like that, too, but at the same time not what Francis had felt. What she rested on was the conviction that you had to value what you had. You might want something, and most times you ought to realize that what you wanted was what you already had. You couldn't move on restlessly, trying to annex new possessions in the hope, like Sarah Willis with her expanding address book, that what you wanted might be out there somewhere; but on the other hand you couldn't stay exactly where you were. You had to leave your family. She felt, looking at the Harrods warehouse, filled with the stuff of acquired lives and the stuff of possible rooms, that hanging in the air between them was an expectation that she, now, would invite Francis to come and live with her in her flat. She saw herself coming home from work, getting out a bag of potatoes and a leg of lamb, starting to chop and peel to the smug noise of Bruckner making the walls shake; she saw herself in twenty years' time with three gawky children, never having found the right moment to say to Francis that, in fact, in reality, she had never cared all that much for Bruckner, it had never been any kind of bond between them. So she said nothing.

"I've enjoyed this," she said, when they were getting on to the train at Hammersmith together. It was a long journey, but she'd get off at Sloane Square and take the bus to Clapham, leaving him. She might as well say the polite thing, the Sarah Willis thing, now. "We must do it again soon."

"Or a concert," Francis said, almost angrily; she felt confirmed.

"Where've you been?" the Australian said, as she let herself in.

"Hey, Scott," Jane said, with real pleasure. She hadn't known how much she was looking forward to him being in.

"You've been out hours," he said.

"Oh, I've been on this enormous walk," she said. "I met someone I used to know, years ago, and he wanted to go for a Sunday-afternoon walk down the river. I'm knackered."

"I've done nothing," the Australian said. "I was trying to find something to watch on the telly, but it's all crap. Have you seen this crap?"

She looked; it was three old actors, mugging embarrassingly on a hill in Yorkshire. "You're right, it's crap," she said. "Let's go out."

"You've just come in," he said. "Your friend Sarah called. She said you could go there for dinner if you liked. And some people about the room, but I just told them to piss off."

"I'd rather just go to the pub," she said.

"What, with me?"

"Unless you've got any objections," Jane said. The whole question of the third lodger seemed to have been abandoned; and perhaps that was right. They would manage the rent between them, surely.

"You're on," Scott said. "Put your coat back on."

Book Three

GI'O'ER

The great mass of Torcombe, seen from the London–Bristol railway line, which ran a mile or two away along the foot of the valley, was blurred in its outlines as if by charcoal scribbles. Its many blackened pinnacles, towers, minarets and chimneys extruded upwards, as innumerable gargoyles and waterspouts extended horizontally from an architectural body already complex with cubes and domes, its shape symmetrical in no direction. All along the battlements stood shroud-like shapes in blackened stone, statues of some sort. Originally they had been regularly positioned, but now gaps had appeared in the ranks like spaces in an old boxer's teeth. The sheep in the meadows stood and gazed at the hideous prodigy, all year round. For decades, people had been saying that it would come to be seen as beautiful as well as remarkable—"After all," they tended to say, "the Brighton Pavilion . . . ," the point of comparison trailing away in their voice. But the moment never quite came, and its appreciation stuck at a few specialists in the field, and occasionally someone wrote an article about its Indian features. (It was built by a jobbing architect in retirement from a career in Calcutta, and the gardens, in a moister climate, retraced the plans of the gardens at the Taj Mahal, in raised brick beds with a single central fountain.) Sometimes the BBC had come to see if it would do for a house in a Sunday-afternoon serial, but the novel had never been written that could contain Torcombe, and they always went away again.

It had all the fractal elaborations of a wart. The valley it looked over, too, had its disappointed aspects. The railway line was older than the house, and as long as the house had been there, hundreds of passengers every day had used it as a bold, ugly landmark on their journey. The river at the bottom of the valley was a slow, shallow, muddy affair with no fishing of any account, meandering cursively through the sodden meadows like a handwriting exercise. In this heat, the river flowed even more slowly, a smog rising off the morning meadows like the air of a pub saloon bar. Almost as soon as the house and estate had been put together, the mercantile fortune that had funded it had turned out to be inadequate, and within a decade or two the slow process of dis-robing had begun. The estate had once stretched right down to the river, but that had gone in the 1920s, and a sour line of electricity pylons strode through the valley. The land had gone in pieces, until there was just a couple of acres of garden, the drive and the house. And then that had been sold, too, and these days the letters from the pro-ducers of BBC serials got a rude rebuff, or no response at all.

Nick saw none of the embarrassments of the estate as he turned off the main road to Salworthy on to Torcombe's drive. He saw only his own colossal embarrassment. It had never seemed worthwhile, in Sheffield, acquiring another car when Reynolds's van did perfectly well. You could get your shopping in it, or drop in on Rose, his new girlfriend, in her cottage in the Rivelin valley, or go out to the pictures or the theatre or even a pub in Derbyshire in it. It was perfectly ser-viceable, even a little bit jaunty to go about with your business adver-tised on the side. He hadn't thought of this aspect when Jimmy had said, a couple of years ago, "Got myself a big new place in the country," or, a fortnight ago, "Well, if there's something you want to discuss, you'll have to come down to my place in the country for the weekend. Nice idea. Show you over." If he'd envisaged it, he'd probably thought of a prosperous farmer's house, but not this. It was the sort of place you glimpsed in passing and wondered who the hell managed to keep up a pile like that, these days.

Steeling himself, and certain that the van, his shabby suitcase and the two changes of clothes inside it wouldn't do, Nick drove up the overgrown drive and round the circle of dry, unkempt grass in front of the massively windowed façade. He'd misjudged, badly. The worst of it was the last horrible thought: that the van's gold Roman lettering on deep purple, to match the shop front, always had the effect, in Sheffield, of *class*.

It was extraordinarily hot. He'd set off in a T-shirt and shorts, quite cheerful in the early-morning sunlight, but by Derby and after break-fast, he'd had to peel off the T-shirt. His back and thighs had been clinging to the plastic seat, despite the wide-open windows; his hands, gripping the steering-wheel, were almost wrinkled with sweat. His hair, drenched with sweat, dried in the breeze. Outside this huge and alarming house, he put on his T-shirt again, at any rate. He was rather hoping it had occurred to him to put his summer jacket into the bag as well as a pair of summer trousers.

He got out, hanging his head, and slammed the van door. What the hell did you do when you came to a place like this, anyway? Did you ring the doorbell, or just walk in? He was getting his shameful bag out when the vast door opened, and there—oh, Christ—was what could only be a butler. Nick steeled himself to explain, before the bugger could send him round to the tradesman's entrance, that he'd been invited, that, yes, he sold flowers in a shop, but he was—Christ, these days, how did you say, "I am a gentleman"? The bloke came over, not at all butler-like in his demeanour, but slouching and shuffling his shoes through the gravel. Maybe he was just one of Jimmy's, but then he said, ludicrously, "Welcome to Torcombe. The master's expecting you." He was suppressing some kind of accent in a kind of gurgling yodel. He took Nick's bag, hardly hesitating, and led the way in his crisp uniform, Nick following in his shamefaced 10CC rock-concert T-shirt, bright red shorts and sandals. The butler still looked cooler, in this heat, than Nick did.

Miranda was long gone—divorced and, by all accounts, making a success of her own business on the pay-off. She had a keep-fit studio, a gym they were calling them now, in Covent Garden "and good luck to her," Jimmy always said, as if they really were, as he went on to claim, "on the best of terms." Gone too, the next wife—Susie, or stupidly-spelt Soozie, it had been, one of the girls Jimmy had always picked up from time to time but on that occasion, light-hearted and released from Miranda's minatory supervision, had unaccountably gone and married. Eighteen months of trying to meet Soozie's showbusiness demands, culminating in a disastrous week when she'd played a cat in a musical before being rudely sacked, and that had been that. The one who came forward now to meet Nick in the cigar-box entrance hall, glauconsly lit by stained-glass windows and fragrant with mould, was the latest trading-up; gentry, Jimmy'd said or, more exactly, "Posh tea-head. She's over the needle, all that, now. Name of Laura."

"You must be Nick," Laura said, bonily attractive, her voice low and grand, leaning forward as if she might put out her hand to be shaken. She was wearing a simple white dress, hung with two straps over her buttered-toast-coloured bosom. It looked as if it had cost nothing, had come from Marks & Spencer, but something about the way it swung as she came forward, some suggestion of asymmetry in the cut suggested immense expenditure of a sort not visible to people such as Nick. She smelt deliciously of jasmine-scented soap, and no perfume.

"And you must be Laura," Nick said, smiling, wondering what on earth he must smell like. "What an amazing house. I had no idea."

"No?" Laura said, her smile now chilling a little. Nick understood. There was to be no reference to the acquisition of Torcombe, anything to suggest that it hadn't been in Jimmy's family for generations. "You're just in time for tea—"

Tea?

"—and I think he's in the library. Thank you. Take Mr. Reynolds's luggage up to his room."

Library?

It was, of course, to be expected that Jimmy would obstinately hunker down in some baronial spot, waiting for a supplicant like Nick to be ushered into the presence. In fact, given what Nick had come here to say, he wasn't sure that he wasn't as frightened as Jimmy wanted him to be. But the idea of Jimmy in a library was a new one; Nick could remember when he had said "front room," and he wondered what slips from Jimmy and well-mannered corrections from Laura had edged him into the state where he had tea—real tea, not tea-head tea, presumably—in the library in the afternoon, and perhaps even describing it in that exact way.

Laura led him from the hallway, not into the library but into a sort of long gallery, gloomy and heavy with mahogany, but here and there, recognizably, a piece of furniture from the old Fulham house. Hardly any of the day's fierce sunlight filtered through to illuminate these rooms; their atmosphere was as of undergrowth in which familiar objects nested. Here was a white sofa placed where no one, surely, could want to sit on it. Further along, surely, a white polar-bear rug, bought, if he remembered, at little Sonia's insistence. It had overwhelmed even the generous spaces of the Fulham sitting room, but here it looked sadly isolated, as if it expected to greet a yawning mate at the far end of the gallery. The rest of the furniture, the paintings, the shabby carpets, you couldn't imagine Jimmy choosing them, or even owning them.

"Shouldn't I go and change first?" Nick said, gesturing at his *déshabille* with an apologetic hand.

"Oh, nonsense," Laura said, hardly looking at what he was wearing. "It's only Jimmy." He understood her to mean "It's only you." "The other thing is," she went on, "you can send a guest off to his room and then you never see him again."

"Are your guest rooms as irresistible as that?" Nick said heartily.

"It's not as much a rabbit-warren as it seems at first," Laura said, ignoring his comment, turning into another room with the height of a cinema and in much the same grottily gilded style, also not the library. "We only really live in about a dozen or fifteen rooms. Heaven alone knows what goes on in the rest."

A *dozen?*

"And here he is," Laura said, pushing open a pair of double doors into the library. "I told you he'd be in time for tea, darling."

Against Nick's expectations, the library really was a library; one whole wall lined with sets of bound books, up to the ceiling. The case was ecclesiastical, Gothic, with pendentives and ogives and, with a shock, Nick recognized that the whole construction was a huge scale model of St. Pancras railway station. No, not quite that, but almost. The shelves went up to the twelve-foot ceiling, encrusted with more doomy Gothic plasterwork, but the single ladder had at least four rungs missing, and the top shelves must be more for show than use. Nick wondered what could be up there: mice nesting in antique pornography, probably. In any case, a few of the bottom shelves had been cleared out for what books Jimmy owned, and among the ranks of bound sermons, fat paperbacks screaming LUDLUM, coffee-table volumes of illustrated popular anthropology and *Learning to Paint With Nancy Kominski* were closer to hand. The windows here were floor-to-ceiling, giving on to a long vista of terrace, sad, intricate, twiggy garden with blackened statuary and leaf-filled dry fountain bowls, a grizzled pepper-and-salt meadow where sheep piled up in the shade of the Cedars of Lebanon. Beyond, the railway line, the glistening meander of the river, the glistening lines of the pylons, and a flash of mirrored windows as the London–Bristol traversed the valley. Inside, the room was dense with the flight of dust-motes, the long torn red velvet curtains, their cream lining poking through, in a collapse over the windows like a two-day-old pudding.

"And you were right," Jimmy said, rising from the heavily padded green leather sofa. He greeted Nick with a wave that just failed to become a handshake, and a showy kiss for his new wife, who patted him reassuringly on the back, detached herself and left them alone.

"You'd have told her to shut up and piss off once," Nick said, "if she'd said that to you."

"Who? Laura?" Jimmy said. "Never."

"Not Laura," Nick said. "I didn't mean Laura, I meant, I don't know, Miranda."

"Why'd you say Laura, then?" Jimmy said, but mildly, curiously.

"What I meant was if, in the past, Miranda had said to you even 'I told you he'd be here for tea,' like, 'I told you I was right and you were wrong,' you'd have said, straight away, 'Piss off and shut up.' It must be the country life."

"Christ, it's hot," Jimmy said. "One of the hottest. Went out this morning, thought about walking down to the lake, see how the trout are coming on. Twenty feet out of the door, couldn't stand it, too fucking hot. Ten thirty in the morning, mind. Not hot travelling down?"

"Very hot," Nick said. A silence fell.

"She's a fantastic woman," Jimmy said miserably. "I bought it for her, you know."

"The—?"

"The house, you berk," Jimmy said. "Or hadn't you noticed?"

"Oh, I noticed all right," Nick said. "Going it a bit, aren't you?"

"You're telling me," Jimmy said.

The last move of Jimmy's was only a mile or so westward, but in its own way a colossal one. There'd been a rationale behind Fulham; Jimmy, he let you know, could have afforded something flasher but you'd be running a risk, making yourself conspicuous. Nick wasn't convinced, and the Fulham house was flash enough. Sure enough, in time there was a new house overlooking a Chelsea square with nannies in uniform and old generals in scarlet frock-coats, most of the first and second floor interrupting the splendid stucco with a vast studio window. Some painter had lived there when painters could afford Chelsea. Soozie had wanted to keep it as a studio, Nick remembered, with a barre and a mirror and a white grand piano, but Jimmy'd refused. There he'd stopped, and Torcombe was a new addition rather than a replacement for the Chelsea house.

"You must be doing all right," Nick said.

"I'm doing all right," Jimmy said. He reached over to the table by his side, where there was a plate of sandwiches and a cake, but instead of tea, a glass of whisky. "Some of it was mine, and some of it was Laura's. You know her husband died? Just died, when I met her. Another tea-head. Usual story. She'd cleaned herself up, found out she'd got more money than she expected, met me."

"Did you know her before?"

"Knew the husband a bit. Everyone knew the husband. Lord, wasn't he? Viscount or something. She's all right, Laura. Educated. Knows about all this stuff—" a wave of the hand at the Victorian age "—and I reckon it makes her laugh, cleaning up and then marrying into the business when it don't interest her no more, the goods. Makes me laugh, too. Never thought I'd marry a customer, despised them. She's all right."

"She seems great."

"I tell you what," Jimmy said. "It's just us this weekend, but there's a fan of yours coming down. Might be here already, don't know. Remember Sonia? Thrilled to bits when she heard you were here too. Remembers you."

"Little Sonia," Nick said. "I haven't seen her since she was eight. I didn't know I made such an impression on her."

"She's nearly twenty now," Jimmy said. "Bought her a house, too, in the—get this—in the East End, Spitalfields. My old mum'd never in a million years contemplate living in Spitalfields. Sonia, she's studying art, I bought her this mouldy old house falling down round her ears and she loves it. You never know about kids. I think it's mostly floorboards and plaster falling off the walls still. Didn't cost much, or I'd have had a job stretching to this monstrosity. Did I tell you about it?"

"No, not at all," Nick said.

"Do you want the guided tour?" Jimmy said. "Laura'll give you that—she knows all about it, where Mata Hari slept and the pisspot King Edward used in 1906 and which Chinese emperor made what vase and all that. So we get married and I thought Laura, she loves the country, so I'll surprise her. I'll buy a house in the country. Now I was thinking rectory, five bedrooms, couple of acres, rose garden, that'll do me. But I went out and looked and rectories, that's exactly what you can't find any more, they're all done up and twice what they should be costing. And then, suddenly, I was driving round this neck of the woods with a local estate agent and he mentions that the family here are thinking of selling up after I don't know how many generations. And no one in their right minds wants a place this size, so it's going for a song.

"You should have seen them. There was just an old brother and sister left, and one housemaid who I think had been their nanny, she must have been eighty, and they lived in three rooms, just a bedroom each and a little room they sat in and watched an old black-and-white telly. Poor as church mice. All the money had gone, and they'd sold all the land they could sell. But I looked around, and, you can see, it's not in first-class nick, but there's nothing much wrong with it—it doesn't leak much. So I took it off their hands and they're living in a nice little cottage in the village with central heating for the first time in their lives, and four hundred thousand pounds in the bank. Happy as Larry. They left most of the furniture, too—they hadn't seen it for thirty years. It'd been under dust sheets. I don't say I like it much, but it fills the house, and you can't fill a house this size straight off. Do you know how much it costs just to put curtains up in one room?"

"No idea," Nick said.

"No, I don't know either," Jimmy said. "But it couldn't be done. Couldn't stretch to it."

Nick looked around him. They lived in a dozen rooms, the wife had said, which didn't seem a lot until you totted up the rooms in your own house—five, not counting kitchens or bathrooms, and that seemed plenty to Nick. There were more rooms out there for Jimmy and Laura to colonize as time went on, too—billiard rooms, morning rooms, smoking rooms, menageries, the long-gone paraphernalia of wealthy lives. How had even this been stretched to? Nick knew to a penny how much of Jimmy's finances went through the Broomhill flower shop; it was a good deal, but it wouldn't have begun to fund this on its own. He had always assumed that, despite the close bond between him and Jimmy, there were others in exactly his position, channelling Jimmy's heroin money through launderettes, newsagents, sweet shops, stationers, all serving an apparently decent purpose in provincial cities. He had no idea who those other people were or might be. But there had to be a lot of them.

Over the few years the decency and usefulness of his own flower shop had been creeping up on him. Next door to Reynold's, there was a madam shop, run by a handsome haughty Jewess, selling "robes" to the middle-aged ladies of the area. The mannequins were old-fashioned, based on the sort of Parisian models that the New Look had hung off in the 1940s, and on them Mrs. Grunbaum hung well-made suits and dresses, expensive and heavy with buckles to show where the money was spent, and a few years out of fashion. Nothing too alarming.

For a time Nick had assumed that Belinda's, as Mrs. Grunbaum's shop was called, was the sort of madam shop gifted by an elderly businessman to his mistress. Mrs. Grunbaum's title was certainly a courtesy one; she had laughed hoarsely when it came out that Nick thought there had ever been a Mr. Grunbaum. But Belinda's was, in fact, all Mrs. Grunbaum's work—there had been no wealthy lover to give Mrs. Grunbaum the money and indulgently help her choose the pink-and-white toile-de-Jouy style of the showroom, patiently listen to her agonizing over stocks, or assist her in a commanding, humorous way when she burst into tears over the books. That was the way it would have been in London; there were Jewish madam shops all over London exactly like Belinda's, and every one run by someone's mistress as a surprisingly successful hobby. In Sheffield, Mrs. Grunbaum had taken the money her mother had been saving up for years—"God knows for what, Nicholas"—had sold the house in Ranmoor and bought a shop with a flat over it in Broomhill. "I'd always longed to be in the fashion industry, Nicholas, but my people, they'd always looked down on people of our sort doing that sort of business." She did well, Mrs. Grunbaum; she knew what sold, and what wouldn't.

Nick, it seemed, had always longed to be in the floristry business. It was just that, unlike Mrs. Grunbaum, it hadn't been a long-nursed and exact desire. He hadn't known he'd wanted it until he had it. His assumption about the funding of Mrs. Grunbaum's shop had been, as well as an inference from previous experience of similar shops, a projection of his own situation. It seemed quite normal, the idea that Mrs. Grunbaum would be set up in business by an admirer for reasons of convenience since that, more or less, had happened to him. He hadn't, he supposed, thought of the fishmonger, the newsagent, the little greengrocer's in this light, or as anything other than old family businesses, but it came as a shock, the idea that he might be the only shop in the parade funded by a large donation of capital by a backer who expected no particular financial return, who thought of his business, inevitably, as a sort of light-hearted hobby.

This sense of the shop had been sustained by Katherine, whose employment was not, in any sense, a serious one. She was, at first, just company and they shut the shop if they felt like it, and were able to deal with customers in an unctuous or a dismissive way for no other reason than their own amusement. But after that ugly mistake, the after-hours encounter in his own house, the single occasion that they circled round without comment for months, their light-hearted relationship altered somewhat and so, he eventually realized, did his attitude towards the shop. They carried on working there together, and he concentrated as never before on the shop's success. Before, he had simply bought more or less what he felt like buying, never troubling about discounts or analysing what sold and what didn't. It hardly mattered if you ended your Saturdays throwing away twenty pounds' worth of browning tiger lilies. But he could see where the new awkwardness between him and Katherine would end, and he began taking an interest in the shop itself, having nothing much else to think about. The

wastage of stock fell right off; the shop became more heavily fre-
quented, as if the people of Sheffield had been given their first opportunity to buy flowers and had discovered a need they had never known
they had. Perhaps for Katherine the enterprise became less fun, more
like work. She couldn't say that, though, without admitting what the
whole enterprise had been about for her in the first place.

"Those narcissi went well," she remarked out of the blue one May
evening. "They were pretty. You could get some more next week."

"They were nice," Nick said. "I thought people would go for
them—they're cheap, but they're quite unusual. People who don't like
to buy daffodils because they're a bit—"

"A bit newsagent," Katherine said.

"Exactly," Nick said, and indeed Price's opposite had three bright
orange buckets of custardy daffodils and tragic dyed carnations
plonked down on the pavement next to the ruffle-like display of papers
outside. He held up a last narcissus; looked at its curious, inquisitive
face, pulled a face of his own.

"I thought that'd be no good for us when he first did it," Katherine
said. "I mean, he never thought of selling flowers until you opened.
But I suppose people look at his"—she gestured over the road at the
orange buckets, each with its star-shaped lurid green tag in cardboard,
with its felt-tip price—"and think, Ooh, flowers—I know, I'll buy some
nice ones, and cross the road."

"Maybe," Nick said. "I might try jonquils next." That was the sort of
conversation they tended to have, about the business. The narcissi
were lovely, it was true: there was a bridal virginity about their
blanched virtue, costing almost nothing, which, properly presented,
could lure customers in. But it wasn't disguising anything to talk about
them in terms of turnover. He couldn't deny it: one of the things he
liked best about this new line was that it had sold incredibly well.
"How's your son getting on?" he said, returning from the backyard
with the empty mock-lead container the narcissi had been in. "He
moved out, didn't he?"

"Daniel?" Katherine said. "He's fine, I think. He's got a room, a big
bedsit, really, at the top of a house in Crookes. I haven't been there
since he moved in, but I think he's coping all right. He was always a
tidy boy. Still comes home with his washing."

"Oh, I was like that," Nick said, but for some reason Katherine
blushed.

"I don't know about this new job, though," she said. "I'd have preferred him to go to university, and his A levels were good enough, but he said he didn't know what he wanted to study so there didn't seem much point."

"He's in an estate agent's, isn't he?"

"Eadon Lockwood and Riddle," Katherine said promptly. "He likes it. He sold his first house all on his own last week. It suits him much better than the last job. I knew it wouldn't suit him, working in a building society like his dad. He likes to be out and about a bit, and with this, he gets a company car soon, of course, which you certainly don't with the Midland Bank. No sign of any steady girlfriend, too busy breaking hearts. I dread the mother of some poor girl turning up on my doorstep. He keeps telling us about houses he's seen, as if we were ever likely to move."

"No, you're all right where you are," Nick said. They carried on for a time in silence, Katherine stripping away the leaves on some long-stemmed red roses—one of those things that never sold at 40p a stem, but you had to have them, like a gesture of high class. Nick, behind the desk, watched her. A customer came in, not a regular but passing trade, discussed her requirements at some length, went away with a big load of stargazers and two blocks of oasis. A lengthy debate could lead to that or a fistful of carnations.

"I've been thinking," Katherine said eventually, having turned off her smile. She seemed to be concentrating on her task. "How long have I been working here?"

"As long as we've been open," Nick said. "Five years, is it? Six? I remember you came in on my first day. We didn't know anything, then, did we?"

He knew what she was going to say, and in a way didn't mind the prospect of it. But for the moment he'd try to fend it off with a cosy reminiscence.

"You hadn't a clue," Katherine said. "Do you remember trying to smash that vase in the backyard?"

It was still there, on the shelf: no one would ever buy it, and it was a sort of mascot for the whole enterprise.

"The thing is," Katherine said. "I've been thinking about what I really want to do."

He listened, kindly, as she explained that she'd enjoyed it, but she might as well stop; she might, she thought, even do an Open University degree now that the kids were grown-up. "Of course," she said, "I'd stay until you found someone to replace me."

But that hadn't taken long, and in only three or four weeks he and Katherine were sitting in a pub, the mysteriously *soignée* school-leaver left in charge on a Thursday lunchtime, having a farewell drink. It was busy, for a Thursday lunchtime, and embarrassingly they had to settle for a fragile little table in a nook, hidden from the rest of the half-lit mahogany interior, just like adulterers. The time, unexpectedly, flew by—Katherine was thinking of taking a little holiday, a City Break perhaps to Munich, which she'd heard was nice, just her and Malcolm, leaving fifteen-year-old Tim to fend for himself, and they looked over her brochures together. It was surprising when the landlord rang the bell for time at half past two. They'd managed to have a conversation for once without awkward corners, and would still see each other, of course . . . Privately, Nick doubted it.

That had been two years ago, and his relationship with Amanda, the school-leaver, had gone in a quite different direction. He'd even found himself ticking her off when, very occasionally, she turned up late. There was no question of her being anything but an employee, with her boyfriends and her silly concerns, and with her being—how had that happened?—young enough to be Nick's daughter. The shop, too, seemed to change with Katherine's departure, less like a game or a toy, with its Regency stripes and its absurd, comic vases that nobody would ever buy. Some vases people did start buying came into the stock: massive, greenish glass vases from Czechoslovakia, oblongs, hourglasses, rosebowls, simple and modern, and for the first time when Nick did the books he paid attention to what the real figures would have been, and realized that beneath the shop's apparently spectacular profits lay a small but true one; enough, certainly, to live on. It seemed to be growing, too, and for two years he'd been summoning up the energy to do what he was doing now: spending a weekend with Jimmy in the country and telling him at the end that he was very grateful for everything, and would like to pay him back his original investment, and run the shop as a straightforward business from now on. That was what he was here to do. He saw no reason why Jimmy would be difficult about it. It seemed perfectly reasonable to him that, having run a shop for Jimmy's benefit for ten years, and having gone on who knows how many dodgy and frightening journeys to Morocco, and Iran before that, Jimmy would be happy to hand over the shop as a kind of retirement reward. Jimmy was doing well: perhaps he'd even give it to him without asking Nick to pay back the capital. No, he wouldn't do that—Nick couldn't see him standing in the hot, creaking hallway, handing over the deeds with tears in his eyes—and in a moment a more plausible scenario arrived, in which Jimmy and the thuggish "butler," by the side of the lake, a good hearing distance from the house, kicked Nick to the ground and beat him into gratitude.

Well, it still had to be done, but probably as late in the weekend as possible.

Jimmy yawned, theatrically, in the library. "Tea" was over, in the form of four fat whiskies for Jimmy, and, eventually, to coincide with the last, one for Nick—"There's no ice, though I could get some, I suppose." A smiling maid had come in at half past five to clear Jimmy's glass and the tray; she had looked broad-faced and foolish, like a milkmaid with a touch of mongolism. The air in the library was stale and heavy as tweed. The yawn might have been connected to some bell-pulley system; in a moment or two Laura came in noiselessly, suddenly appearing by the side of Nick's chair.

"Nick'll be wanting to see the grounds," Jimmy said. "You're not deep in anything, are you, darling?"

"Nothing I'd like better," Laura said. "You'd like to see the grounds, would you?"

"I'd be fascinated," Nick said.

"Where's Sonia?" Jimmy said. "She's here, is she? Thought she was looking forward to meeting her old friend again."

"I'm amazed she remembers me," Nick said weakly. "I can only have met her—"

"She's up in her room on the phone," Laura said, ignoring Nick.

"Never off it," Jimmy said. "Well, off you go. We'll have dinner at eight."

"Do you dress for dinner?" Nick said ironically, and in any case he had nothing to dress in, probably not even a jacket.

"What—for the pub?" Jimmy said. "No, fuck off. Tell Sonia if you see her that she can come out with us too this evening."

They went. Laura ruffled Jimmy's hair as she crossed the room, getting a grunt in return. She pushed one of the tall windowed doors, shards of paint falling as the door opened, and stepped out on to the terrace. Nick followed her. "We're getting there, I believe," she said. In the puff sleeve of her dress was a handkerchief and a pair of sunglasses; there was nowhere else to keep anything, and she pulled out the sunglasses and put them on. "At least, there always seems to be some little man or other tinkering away at something or other. I expect it's a bit like the Forth Bridge—once we get to some kind of presentable state the little men'll just start doing it all over again."

"It's amazing," Nick said, meaning it, and following Laura down the terrace. The sun was obese and orange, entangled with the upper branches of the hill-cresting grove on the horizon, and the terrace faced it. A little man had been at work, perhaps today, and though half of the terrace was thick with grass, growing through the interstices of the paving-stones and even through the cracks, the other half had been recently stripped and scrubbed, the bald stones clean. The workman or -men had gone; they had worked up to where a crudely carved statue, a shrouded and weatherworn figure, lay in three broken pieces on the paving-stones, themselves broken and sagging like a mattress.

"Fucking nora," Laura surprisingly said. "I thought we were supposed to be doing something about those wretched statues. Jimmy! Jimmy!"

Jimmy, in time, appeared at the open double doors of the library. "What is it? Oh, fuck," he said. "They're supposed to be fixing those things. How can they still be falling off? You could understand if there was a gale or something."

"When did that fall off?" Laura said. "You've been in the library all afternoon. You'd have heard it, surely to God."

"I nodded off for a bit," Jimmy said. "But it might have been this morning, when we were down in the village. I've not been out here all day. Christ knows how my fucking statues keep just falling off. It doesn't make no sense. That's four gone in a year and a half. You think I'm going to shell out to replace them?"

"No, darling," Laura said. "I don't think anything whatsoever. In any case, they're going to keep on falling."

He came up and, scowling, bent over to inspect the four-foot figure, its head separated like a carved-up fruit from its shawled torso, its torso from its swathed stumpy legs, joined together. "I can't understand it," Laura said. "It's awfully bad-quality stone, though. You see how it breaks when it falls—it must be, I don't know, shale or sandstone or something."

"I know it breaks when it falls, darling," Jimmy said. "I don't know why it should fall in the first place when there's not a puff of wind."

"You know," Laura said. "It's so hot, and it's been like it for days. It might be that, you know, being made out of low-grade stone, it dries out and then, I don't know, it cracks and falls over, bang. Something like that."

Jimmy scratched his head, hunkered down, poked ineffectually at the statue. The stone was something grainy, blackened at its old surfaces but orange as old butter where it had cracked open. At the bottom was carved a single word: DEMOSTHENES. Nick wondered why, since it could hardly be read from the ground and, if the figure had ever been supposed to be identifiable by anyone, the stone's carved features had long since worn away to a snowman-like anonymous bluntness. From the base, three rusty iron spikes protruded where it had once been attached.

"I don't know about that," Jimmy said reasonably. "I don't see where it's supposed to have cracked in the heat. It looks as if it fell over in one piece to me, just like the other one last month."

"Come on, I'll show you the rest," Laura said.

"Don't go too close to the house," Jimmy said, walking back, waggling his arms as he went, flexing his fingers like a pianist against the sticky heat. "Or the philosophers'll get you."

"What philosophers?" Nick said, when they were safely down the steps into the formal Italian garden, out of the range of any more projectile statues.

"They're all philosophers, supposedly," Laura said. "You saw the statues, caryatids, whatever, round the top of the house. The one that just fell over. There's supposed to be twenty-four, they're all supposed to be the world's most famous philosophers or something. Most of them have togas on—well, I think they all do, even the ones who weren't Greek, probably because, you know, it's easier to carve a toga than whatever it would have been that Kant"—"Carnt," she said, and Nick had to struggle for a moment to recover a strange pronunciation of a barely familiar name—"would have worn, I don't know whether Kant"—"Carnt,"—"is actually up there, we've not made a proper list of them. Well, we know one of them now, the one who fell down. Did you see who it was?"

"Domestos," Nick said. "Or something."

"That doesn't sound right," Laura said. "The man who built the house, he had an interest in those old Greeks, supposedly, and when he wanted to put up twenty-four statues around the house, he decided to make it philosophers, though of course even by thinking up ones called Domestos he'd have run out of names. Strange thing to choose, philosophers, on a country house. The sort of thing you see on a school or a library or something in Oxford but here you'd have thought he'd choose, I don't know, something a bit more countrified."

"Fox-hunters," Nick said.

"Not exactly that," Laura said, looking sidelong at him. "Do you know? I believe Sonia pushes the statues off whenever she feels bored."

"Surely not," Nick said.

"Well, it's always when she's here that it happens," Laura said. "Not that you could tell that to Jimmy. Tell me, how long have you known him?"

The Indian garden was intricate, tawdry and spikily barren, like an ugly Victorian mourning brooch. It had recently been heavily over-grown, you could see, and had been cut back to its raw brick raised beds, the dried-up shrubs trimmed back to the recently moistened black earth. Here and there a new shoot was spurting out; at the centre of the knotty brick garden, a marble fountain copied from the court-yard in some Cairo palace, dry and stained with tears of soot. Nick started to tell her the whole story, but her attention was taken by some-thing beyond the fountain, emerging from the hedges that bordered the whole formal garden. It was a slim graceful figure in cream; its clothes were a little middle-aged, a pair of elegant slacks and a plain man's shirt, and the way the hair was piled up on top of the head, too, was middle-aged. But the shy walk, sidling through the narrow gap in the hedge, approaching them as if their meeting would be a matter of the sheerest coincidence, was that of a girl.

"You don't remember me," the girl said, coming up to Nick and Laura, who stood with her arms folded, waiting obscurely for some apology. "But I remember you. You came with us to the zoo when I was awfully little—you showed me the penguins. I must have been a terri-ble pain. I'm Sonia."

"I remember you very well," Nick said, after a moment. Standing in the heat of the afternoon, it dazed him. He would never have seen the child in this tall and inspecting girl, the child's spoilt demands and insistence turned in a matter of a decade into a cool, assessing gaze that would get its own way. In that decade he had sat in a flower shop in Sheffield, and learnt to think of that as the limits of his own possibili-ties; the same period had transformed Sonia, and she looked at him with the eyes of one proposing to buy a mechanical vehicle. "I took you to the zoo," he said, and both Sonia and Laura laughed at his dazedly confirming what she had happened to say.

But he saw her that moment as if down a long event-lined vista of years, as if with this meeting, not the first but a meeting so transformed for him as to give it a sense of primacy, he had embarked on something he would always preserve and keep in a safe padded box, to take out and play with in special treasured conversations. Around them the caged beasts seemed to press against their bars and pause as they watched, and at so many points in the future he seemed to see himself saying, "I think I fell in love at once." Sonia stood by him, with her bundled-up hair the shining colour of cold tea, the translucence of her skin and the luminous ox-like darknesses of her eyes, and was transformed from the small girl he recalled, if at all, as a scowling blonde juvenile with curls, her demands reshaping her remembered features into what a spoilt child should look like. Her features, once bunched together and resentfully squashed in a round scowling face, like a tight-pressed Brussels sprout, had spread and smoothed as she had grown, and no tension was in her calm milky face.

It had never happened before with such an unladen freight of stupidity falling on him all at once; love had come to him differently, whether for Caroline Stacey, the tennis-playing girl down the road he had followed and lurked after when he was fifteen, or in other crushes, growing shorter and more comic with age, the girl who cut his hair and pressed her bosom to his head with, in the summer months, a dizzying wash of metallic flesh odours, who (he discovered only when he turned up one month) had married three Saturdays back and moved to Peterborough, or the tiny Indian girl, Gita, who had lived above him for six months, tormenting him with her tight black T-shirts and her heartbreakingly tiny mini-skirts, tormenting him too with her love of terrible pop records and her noisy illicit boyfriend, who stayed over Friday and Saturday nights, Marc Bolan's breathy moans and squeals or Gita's for some weeks giving him real anguish through the floorboards before she moved and, unexpectedly, the anguish and even the memory of her face and walk, once so vivid, evaporated in just a day or two. The girlfriends, too, though they came to mind more slowly and with less sense of a lesson to be learnt, shy clinging Susan French who had cried so, or Margaret Bollom, who had taken charge of everything, from his virginity but not hers with quiet efficiency, or Rose who he'd been seeing for the last three years in exactly that Gita-like way of staying over at weekends at her cottage in the Rivelin valley. She might have proved to do quite well for him until this very second. It had never happened before to him in such a way, such an infliction of a moment as it now happened, dazed in a hot Devon garden of ugly elaboration. It seemed an unwanted gift, when he wanted nothing to tie him further to Jimmy, least of all a daughter, and he tried to translate that vista of years into an effective barrier, the line of years between him, nearly forty and hopeless, and Sonia at only eighteen. It couldn't be done.

"I don't mind," he said, realizing with astonishment that he had been following the conversation and Sonia had asked him whether he would object if she, rather than Laura, carried on showing him round. "If you don't mind," he went on idiotically.

"No," Sonia said. "I don't mind one bit."

So it was that he found himself walking with careful steps, as an amputee trying out his new-given legs which would never wear out, as a funambulist who can see the narrow woven path in the air and knows that he can, surely, walk the rope he feels beneath his rolling soles, through the garden behind this beautiful girl. She was talking about the garden—

"I can't see how it's ever going to come right," she was saying. "They've ripped everything up, but no one seems to know what to do next. I don't think anyone's even thought about planting anything, it's just what was there before, hacked down a bit."

"It's strange," Nick said. The geography of the garden was clear to him; he felt the need to explain what he had seen. "In these houses, it all relaxes into wildness, doesn't it?"

"If you say so."

"As you get further from the house, I mean. You get the terrace, with the pots and the bay trees, and then there's the garden with beds, where—you know—where I met you—"

"That's really ugly," Sonia said, picking her way through an untrimmed gap in the hedge, the one she'd come through, into a lawned expanse.

"Then there's this," Nick said. "It's probably got a name."

And here the trees stood about in small groups, irregular and picturesque, as if by nature; but Nick saw the same principle of flower-arranging, that you grouped in odd numbers, and these threes and fives, the carefully varying sizes of the trees planted together had the air of cunning natural disposition. The rough lawn ran down to a ha-ha, and beyond it a water-meadow, the river, the railway-line.

"My dad just calls it the parkland," Sonia said. "I don't know what it's called properly. I suppose it's just a bit of countryside that somebody put a wall round and decided it was theirs once. You'd have to let it go a little bit wild after a bit. You couldn't keep it up otherwise."

"I suppose so," Nick said. "Don't you like it?"

"Me?" Sonia said. "What? The whole caboodle? The whole malarkey? The entire kerfuffle?"

"The whole caboodle," Nick said, smiling. "I don't think you really mean kerfuffle."

"Oh, I suppose I like it," Sonia said. "Kerfuffle Towers. I don't know why my dad decided to buy it. He keeps saying he bought it for Laura's sake, that she liked this sort of thing, or even that he bought it for me, which is rubbish. I quite like bits of it, but I just wish it wasn't so incredibly ugly, every bit of it."

Nick laughed.

"I wasn't expecting something quite like this, it's true," he said.

"Well, you couldn't reasonably," Sonia said. "Unless you were prone to nightmares, you couldn't imagine anything that looked like that. The thing is, I don't believe my dad really wanted to live in the country. He's much happier in London."

He paused, and let himself look at Sonia as she walked ahead, her loose-jointed walk across an English lawn. Her talk of ugliness seemed remote and exotic, like the appearance of a word looked at so long that it has lost its meaning.

"I remember you," Sonia said slowly. "But I can't remember how you fit in. You live in Yorkshire, don't you?"

"Yes," Nick said. "I've got a shop in Sheffield." He didn't know what Sonia might know about her father's business. "Jimmy, your dad, he helped me when I was setting up. We've been chums for years. He's got a sort of stake in the shop."

"Look at that," Sonia said. It was a flight of swallows, circling above their heads. "They always do that around this time of day, I don't know why."

"Actually," Nick said, "I've come down about the shop—I want to ask your dad if I can buy him out."

"Have you asked him?" Sonia said. She seemed bored. "It sounds like a big deal."

"No," Nick said. "I don't know what he'll say. He might think it's his shop as well, I suppose."

"Leave it with me," Sonia said. "I'll raise the subject."

"Really?" Nick said.

"I don't see why not," Sonia said. "Come on, I'll show you something interesting."

She turned and, with Nick briskly in tow, went back up the hill towards the house. A tattered path started, then a sequence of Roman vases, one every ten yards or so. They came to the house at the far end from the library, and walked through what must once have been the stableyard, the doors shabby and hanging ajar. Sonia pushed one open, and they found themselves in the servants' quarters, flagstoned and scrubbed; there seemed to be no one about.

"These are the back stairs," Sonia said, trotting up. "I could show you the whole house, but this is the interesting bit. No one comes up here apart from me, as far as I know."

They went on up, past a big door covered with baize, and on to the second floor; a grim workhouse-like corridor of narrow doors opened up—"The servants' bedrooms, if we had any," Sonia said—and on upwards. Beyond, there was space for storage, cluttered up with detritus, a broken sofa with its springs out, boxes, an antique pram. "We go through here," Sonia said, weaving through the rubbish. It was hot and stifling, smelling like the underneath of an old horse blanket. Nick trod on something; he bent and picked it up. It was a lead soldier, painted red like a Grenadier, the relic of some long grown-up, long-dead child's nursery pleasures. He showed it to Sonia. "Oh, you'll find everything here if you look hard enough," she said. "They didn't take much away when they went. It's like the Victoria and Albert Museum." She took the little figure from his hand, seeing that he didn't know what to do with it—it came so close, the touch of her hand, and he almost closed his about it—and, with a casual gesture, flung it over the detritus.

"Come on," Sonia said, and she was halfway up a fixed ladder; there was a trapdoor at the top. "No one knows you can do this, get up on the roof. I suppose you could crawl out through one of the top-floor windows, but this is the easiest way. I'm the only one who's discovered it."

She pushed with her shoulders, letting out a little grunting shriek, and the trapdoor gave way. There was an immediate breath of air in the stuffy room. She pushed herself out, hands on either side of the opening, lifting herself through the narrow square, her hips, her knees, then finally her ankles disappearing. Her foot caught on the edge as she went, and her sandal fell into the room. "Bugger," she called, and her head appeared in a lovely frame in the ceiling, framed against the perfect blue of the afternoon sky. "You couldn't be a sweetheart and fetch it up, could you?"

"Of course," Nick said, and picked it up from where it fell, between two piles of green-bound books. He looked up cautiously; her head had disappeared again. He took the golden leather of her sandal, worn just a little at the sides—but he would not have had it new, not for the world—and with an urge that could not be resisted he brought it to his face, and snuffled deeply in its complicated smell. It was disgusting, what he was doing, he knew that, and the smell was not truly hers, not Sonia's, but just the smell of worn leather and anyone's feet. And yet it was hers, and for a quick surreptitious moment he breathed it in and found it wonderful. What must you look like, he said to himself, and, shoe carefully in one hand, he climbed the ladder steadily, assembling his features.

"You need shoes, you see," Sonia said, standing on one leg like a flamingo, gesturing downwards at the verdigris'd copper roofing. "It's agony to stand on in this heat."

He had seen one of the statues down below, on the ground, but wasn't prepared for the slight comedy of them up here. With his toga'd back to them, each looked out idiotically at the landscape. The roof was ribbed like corduroy, sloping gently into runnels; and about them the countryside.

"This is really the best of it," Sonia said. "And the best of it is that you don't have to look at this hideous house. So everything is beautiful."

"Yes, it is," Nick said. "It is."

"These fucking things, though," Sonia said, walking casually up to the edge of the battlements. Nick had a terrible flash of fear; he had to stop himself leaping forward to throw his arms round her in rescue. She pushed at one of the statues. "You see, they're quite loose." It rocked a little on its base. Sonia turned and smiled.

"Don't," Nick said, but smiling too.

"Why ever not?" Sonia said.

"Well," Nick said, "you've already pushed one off today."

Sonia laughed. "Perhaps you're right," she said. "But it's fun. I'd rather like to. My dad thinks they're falling off of their own accord. But it's well worth it."

"Until it falls on someone's head and kills them, of course," Nick said.

"That might be worth it, too," Sonia said. "Depending on who it was."

All the rest of that day and evening, Nick could not concentrate on anything. In his bath before they went out, his mind went round in circles and, changed into a shirt and long trousers, he waited in the hall with Laura only for Sonia to come down, trying not to watch the staircase like a spaniel. "I hope you saw the house properly," Laura said admonishingly—she had changed and wore now what could only be described as a little black dress, unremarkable but clearly expensive, her legs bare and brown and glistening. "Sonia always starts with enthusiasm, but then her attention tends to wander and nothing ever gets finished."

"Oh, Sonia and I are old friends," Nick said calmly; it made no sense as a response, but seemed to satisfy Laura, as if he had agreed with her. And then, after Jimmy's appearance, when Sonia came downstairs, a sight filed away for the future, that was all the evening seemed to need.

In the pub, a very ordinary place where they did their best to find dinners out of the usual chillis and chicken pies and ploughman's, no-one seemed to know or acknowledge Jimmy. Nick couldn't tell whether it was through deliberate intent, a wish to put the rich interloper in his place, or because they didn't know who he was. He joined in with Jimmy's reminiscences, hardly paying attention to what he said, he had gone through it so many times before. Only occasionally did he remember that he was supposed to raise the subject of the shop, and fell silent.

In the end, it was Jimmy who brought it up, the next morning. The same fat-faced maid had brought his breakfast in bed—a shambolic affair on a stained tray and someone had made a heart-rending attempt to fold a napkin in an elaborate way to the side. It seemed as if, in the meantime, Sonia had mentioned Nick's shop. When Nick came downstairs, Jimmy was pacing about in the hall. He made a gesture towards the door, a not exactly unfriendly gesture, and soon they were taking the same route out into the parkland that Nick had taken the day before.

"I don't blame you," Jimmy said, when he'd allowed Nick to stumble through his proposal. "I don't see why not."

"Really?" Nick said.

"Course not," Jimmy said. "It's not the end of the world from my point of view. It's not the first time someone's decided to cut the apron strings, you know."

Nick wondered again about the extent of Jimmy's concerns; it was something he would never know, he supposed.

"Tell you the truth," Jimmy said, "I'd be pleased to see you making a go of things. You like it, then, the old flower business?"

"I do," Nick said. "I couldn't tell you why."

"Your timing might be quite good," Jimmy said.

"What do you mean?" Nick said.

Jimmy took out a cigar and, from the inside pocket of his linen jacket, a cutter. He made a swift incision in the end, then, replacing the cigar-cutter in his pocket, fetching out a box of matches, he lit it, puffing in a leisurely way until it caught. It seemed early to Nick, but he stood patiently.

"I'm not that easy about the future," Jimmy said. "One of the boys, in Birmingham as it happens, he's got the impression that people are sniffing around, asking some strange questions. Things aren't as easy as they were."

"I see," Nick said. "I haven't had anything like that. I'd have told you."

"Course you would," Jimmy said. "I start to think I'd get out myself if there was anything to get out to. You, you're all right. You've got a nice little flower shop, doing all right—it's doing all right, isn't it?—and no one's ever going to ask where the money came from in the first place, or why the takings used to be so good. No reason at all."

"I hope so," Nick said.

"You know," Jimmy said, "I've sometimes been round houses like this one, in the country, great big jobs, as a tourist, like. And they tell you who made what and who this painting's by and who that woman's supposed to be and what the ninth duke did until you're wondering how much longer it's going to go on. And at the end of it, I always wanted to ask the same question, but it's a question you're never allowed to ask—they'd stare at you if you did."

"What's that, then, Jimmy?"

"I always want to ask, 'Where did the money come from to build this in the first place? I mean, they must have made a pile. Was it coal, or were they importing stuff, or was it land, or what was it?' They never tell you that. Course, you know where the money comes from to run it now. It comes from you buying a ticket and a guidebook. But how did they make the money to build the place in the first instance? They never tell you that."

"No, they don't," Nick said.

"I like to think of that," Jimmy said. "I like to think of people on the train, down there, looking up and saying, 'I wonder who lives there, and I wonder how he got the money to buy a place like that.' "

"They wouldn't like to know," Nick said.

Jimmy stood and puffed contemplatively. "I tell you what," he said. "Have it."

"Have it?"

"It's yours," Jimmy said. "The shop. Forget about it, the capital. I don't want it back."

"I couldn't do that," Nick said.

"You're going to have to," Jimmy said. "Look, if you're getting out, you don't want anything to connect you with me, do you? Like, you know, regular monthly payments of a thousand pounds for I don't know how long. That's a risk you don't want to be taking. No, I tell you how it's going to be. In a couple of hours, we're going to go back inside, and we'll have lunch together, you and me and Laura and Sonia, and we'll have a nice time, talking about old times. And afterwards you get in your little van, and you drive home nice and safely, but that's it. It's best you don't keep in touch, and I won't get in touch with you. There's nothing to connect you with me—I tell you, you try to sort out all those bank accounts, because I'm fucked if I can—and from now on, you're running a nice little flower shop and that's it."

"Come on, Jimmy," Nick said. "We don't have to go that far."

"Trust me on this one," Jimmy said. "Not even Christmas cards. So, say goodbye nicely to Laura and Sonia when you go. And be thankful I'm writing off the, whatever, eighty grand was it, and not asking my Glasgow friend who opened the door to you to come out here and break your legs. Some people might."

Nick thought; his thoughts were all on Sonia. "Is he from Glasgow?" he said eventually.

Jimmy turned round and stared at him. "You stupid, fucking, cunt," he said. But something behind him caught his attention, and his arms fell; his lit cigar dropped on to the dried-out grass.

"Careful," Nick said. "That'll catch—"

"Sonia!" Jimmy was yelling. "What the fucking—"

And, of course, on top of the house, there was Sonia, purposefully rocking another of the statues to and fro. It was incredibly dangerous, her position; she might easily go over with it. It seemed to stick, but she gave it a fierce pull, and it came back towards her; a firm grip, a big push forward, and the statue perched forward, hanging for a second at the utmost limit of its safety before something snapped and the weatherworn philosopher toppled. There was a crack like a rifle shot; Sonia raised both arms above her head like a champion. She had seen them, it was clear; she was doing it for Nick. But she couldn't know it was his farewell present.

Lunch was brief, and Sonia sat opposite Nick, eating silently, half smiling while Jimmy and Laura took turns at berating her. Nick said little; from time to time Sonia gave him an ironic smile, acknowledging that he hadn't split on her and she wouldn't give him away. By two, the three of them were standing outside, saying their goodbyes. Behind them, in the doorway, the dark Glasgow butler stood; watching him go, but not saying goodbye.

"Come again soon," Laura said brightly.

"Yeah, that's right," Jimmy said, with a raised eyebrow.

Sonia said nothing.

"Thanks for everything," Nick said. It didn't mean anything, and no one took it to mean anything. In a moment, he got into his little van, the purple one, with "Reynolds" written on the side in classy letters, and set off, waving as he went. He concentrated on the road for two or three miles. A pub car park presented itself. He pulled in, unable to help himself any more, and then, in the heat of the afternoon, his van slewed across the marked parking spaces, as Sunday pub diners came out and looked curiously at him, he sat in the driving seat and wept without restraint. He had nothing of hers; he had been with her for only twenty-four hours; she would never remember him, never know what she had driven him to.

The windows had been replaced, the walls removed, and the floors stripped and re-covered, the rooms gutted and opened up, the furniture carried off, and everything new and reflective and transparent. It had been going on most of the spring and summer. The Huddersfield and Harrogate had been unchanged in outward appearance for decades, as long as Malcolm had worked there, which was twenty-five years. Longer than a marriage. It had squatted in one of the stone terraced houses in the stone-flagged pedestrian street that ran alongside the Roman Catholic cathedral, august and dour. For decades, the Huddersfield and Harrogate had held itself back, its front as little like a shop as possible, announcing itself with bottom-of-the-range signwriters' lettering and the logo of an umbrella that anyone might have thought up. The ugliness might have been deliberate: they weren't about to splash anyone's money about on pot-plants.

As long as Malcolm could remember, any changes in the building had been mere tinkering. Every few years, someone would remark that the upstairs offices were looking a bit dingy; some debate would discover who it was, exactly, among the senior staff was responsible for the building's upkeep; and, to everyone's astonishment, it would prove to be almost fifteen years since those rooms had been painted. The walls would be refreshed, the curtains and the carpet from time to time replaced, not preceded by any discussion about possible changes, just replaced much as they were. The walls stayed off-white; on the floor hard-wearing carpet tiles, and the hunting prints and eighteenth-century views of Derbyshire on the walls stayed the same as they had always been. Occasionally—often after people had discovered who it was, exactly, in charge of this sort of thing—the managers succeeded in getting rid of their old chairs, and replacing them with a new, swivel-type job, getting another from lower in the same range for their secretaries. But that had always been about the extent of it. The building society's customers appreciated the lack of splash in the branch and the offices. If the question had ever arisen, Malcolm, or anyone, would have said that the customers liked knowing where their money wasn't going.

It was odd how all that changed, quite suddenly. Somewhere in the previous three years, everyone who had agreed on one thing without ever bringing it up suddenly seemed to agree on another, also without bringing it up. It might have been allotted a date in a memo—say, 15 June 1982. The building society was all at once awash with money, awash with other people's debt, and a memo might have gone round, instructing that on 15 June 1982 the staff would look at their immediate surroundings and agree that a general overhaul was long overdue. An architect was called in—it was astonishing that there was such a creature in Sheffield. But here was a real one, talking to everyone and telling them to call him Harry.

By the end of the summer, the warren of rooms was gone. Most of it had been temporary partitions, anyway. There was nothing—Malcolm found this weirdly, ironically inappropriate—load-bearing. The offices were opened up, and the top brass, the only ones to have their own secluded space, sat in plate-glass boxes. Everything was planned to match, from top to bottom; the desks all pale ash, black leather chairs, and a range of splashy abstracts. "I like them," Margaret said defiantly. "I think they're up-to-date." But actually everyone else liked them, too, and Margaret's up-to-dateness went unnoticed. The old windows in practical white plastic, installed only twelve years before, were ripped out and replaced with hand-made sash windows, quite in the style of the original building. They were solid, though, with a steel core and reinforced glass. There were blinds instead of curtains. On the floor, throughout the building a single pale beige carpet ran. "It'll look terrible in two years," someone said, but the designer assured them that it was practical, stain-resistant, and it looked, you had to admit, amazingly expensive. And, for the first time, smoking in the building was forbidden. Downstairs, the girls sat behind gleaming steel windows, secure in their new Huddersfield and Harrogate smart blazers, with smart yellow-and-blue scarves round their necks and little name badges. There were ties in the same colour for the men at the counter too, though naturally they were allowed to wear suits of their own choosing, so long as they were dark blue. There was some discussion, even, about the senior management, the third- and fourth-floor people wearing the new yellow-and-blue tie, to identify them. But word got up to the fifth floor, where Mr. Regan OBE liked to wear his regimental tie, and no more was heard of that. All in all, it was a great success.

Not everyone had his own office any more. Malcolm, though, had been promoted only months before to the level, it proved, of a glass box. He'd have been open-plan without that promotion, any event. His office was open to view on all sides, with a glass door set into the glass wall, which tended to confuse new visitors trying to find their way out. On the way in, Margaret tended to lead the way. She still sat outside his office, connected to him by a new telephone system, one with twenty lines on it. He and Margaret were only six feet apart, though divided by a wall of sheer plate glass, and had to pick up the phone to speak to each other. It would have been unimaginable to summon her by waving. Though they'd always been chums, and whenever he'd wanted to suggest a cup of tea, or she to him, they'd fallen into making a capital T with their forefingers, these days he came out of his office before doing it. He just couldn't communicate with her through the glass wall. Even when they spoke on the telephone, they automatically swivelled their chairs to face away from each other, as if to preserve the other's privacy, the telephone right to pull faces unobserved.

This afternoon, she was typing with demure concentration, eyes down; she'd recently been inspired to have a hair-rethink, as she put it, and it was now looser and a little bigger than it had been, as well as a new rich colour, artificially streaked with red and deep brown and flashes of gold. The shape of a chrysanthemum, it was still a slight novelty to him. Malcolm brought his attention back inside the room.

"Yes," he said to the couple, not having paid complete attention. "Go on."

If the interiors of the building society had been taken up a few notches, been polished, the shabby and serviceable replaced by the impractical and expensive, the customers, Malcolm sometimes thought, had gone in the opposite direction. The couple sitting opposite him now might, in the past, have come in, but they would never have ventured beyond the ground floor. For them, the building society would have meant a little green book, with handwritten entries of deposits, perhaps for a son, perhaps five pounds a month or even less. They would never have come upstairs. That was for the bold, the swaggering, people who looked at Malcolm and told him what they expected him to do. These people were different. They had put on their best clothes; a Burton's suit, which the man's occupation would not require, and a tie. The man fiddled at the fat knot, checking something. His wife had a black shining handbag like the Queen's, chubby and square and capacious; it had been gone over with boot polish, leaving its mark on the tight gold clasp, gripped like a mouth.

They were a Sheffield pair, fat-faced and middle-aged, though both—Malcolm looked down at their forms—barely forty. They had the local build, neither with much in the way of a neck; their square heads sat firmly on their shoulders, and their complexions were pale and moist. They had dressed up for an interview with Malcolm, as they must have done once, years before, for a vicar, and he came to the end of the catechism he would always associate with these years with the same sense of an almost spiritual gravity. It was a matter of such importance, and his voice was full of seriousness. He kept from it the excitement, the love almost, which rose in him on these occasions. Such people had always been the bread and butter of the society's business, but now they were becoming more than that. They were realizing their power, and they were coming upstairs for half an hour with Malcolm, in increasing radiant numbers. Behind his serious face, the desk with the neat arrangement of the necessary papers, his heart, in its peculiar way, shone.

"You think we can afford this?" the wife said, after a long pause.

"Certainly," Malcolm said. "Of course, it's my duty to stress that you must keep up repayments or risk the repossession of your house—"

"We've never missed a rent payment," the husband said abruptly. "Never. Or been late, even."

"I'm sure of that," Malcolm said. "That was just the requirement of what I have to say to you, as it were. But it's certainly in your interests to move from renting your property from the council to being its owners."

"They couldn't take it back, could they?" the wife said. "Take it away from us again?"

"Don't be daft," her husband said. "They couldn't."

"No," Malcolm said, allowing her a kind smile. "They couldn't in any circumstance take it back. *They* couldn't. And you would find that your monthly payments would be an investment, rather than a monthly sum of money you'd never see again. Though your property could conceivably decline in value, it is much more likely to appreciate."

"Appreciate?" the wife said.

"Go up, he means," the husband said, and he wasn't impatient, it was a look of unlikely love he gave her, real love between the two of them. All at once, Malcolm saw them, twenty years younger, perhaps at a youth-club dance, taking each other in their arms for the first time, starting to talk to each other and finding out everything they had in common, and that same look they would both come to know so well passing between them.

"It's just our house," the wife said. "We've lived there for so long, we feel it's ours. We'd never want to sell it. But when we heard that they'd passed this law, that you could buy your own house, Geoff said—"

"I said, let's go for it," the husband said. "Maybe that sounds daft."

"No," Malcolm said. "No, it doesn't sound daft at all."

They had confessed something private, and as Malcolm went through the remaining details, now smiling freely, they visibly relaxed. It was so small a sum of money in the end, and for it they would have something of their own, a little plot, a house they loved. It didn't take long, and in ten minutes Malcolm was getting up to show them out. They fussed with their belongings—the wife held her handbag proudly but incompetently, something she wasn't used to—and the three of them performed a small, embarrassed ballet of after-you at the glass door.

"Goodbye, Mr. Glover," the husband said, shaking his hand, "and thank you." He let go and, turning, took his wife's beloved hand, and together they walked down the stairs. Malcolm watched them go with pleasure.

"New customers?" Margaret said.

"Buying their own house," Malcolm said. "Council-house sale. Those are the ones I like best, almost."

"I'd like to know where people are supposed to live when they've sold off all the council houses," Margaret said. "Poor people, who couldn't get a mortgage, I mean. Selfish, I call it. The waiting lists, they're going up and up, since they passed that law."

"Yes, I suppose it is selfish," Malcolm said weakly, not quite knowing how to say what he thought, that if you couldn't be selfish about your own house, you couldn't be selfish in any respect. It made him happy to help people like that even fill out one of those impossible forms. In the end, he said all he could say, which was "It's good business for us, though."

"I suppose so," Margaret said. "It'll all end in tears, mark my words."

She returned to her typing, and Malcolm, after a moment's thought, went back into his office.

It wasn't a busy day, and he left on the dot of five thirty. Something was going on in the Roman Catholic cathedral, and through the open doors a dark, glowing interior could be glimpsed, and what you sometimes smelt, a whiff of perfumed smoke. He'd never been in. Outside, there was a small group of women, shaking their tin cans. Not a charity, but what you expected more and more in Sheffield in the last few weeks, a collection labelled "Dig Deep for the Miners." At the feet of the women, a pile of tinned food—a sad collection of donations, like an urban harvest festival, tins of beans and sardines and ugly soups, and at the front a solitary tin of chick-peas. That amused Malcolm; he could well envisage the Broomhill intellectual who had donated something as dreary as that. Probably a vegetarian, too. Malcolm didn't know many miners, about as many as he knew vegetarians, but he could imagine how that would go down as a donation when it finally arrived. They were supposed to be miners' wives, drifting in from the mining villages around Sheffield, and some probably were.

Less connected to the industry, Malcolm guessed, was a group awkwardly aligned to the headscarved wives; they were young men and one girl, shabbily but decisively dressed, not quite mixing with the miners' wives but next to them, like competing stalls at a village fête. Malcolm recognized the one at the front. It was Tim's friend Stig, wasn't it, with an awkward armful of their nutty newspaper? The *Spartacist*, produced by half a dozen people, half of it written by Tim. Malcolm heard all of it every day, but driven by an obscure impulse, he jingled in his pocket for a fifty-pence piece, went straight up to Stig.

"Hello, Stig," he said.

The man looked appalled at being addressed by anyone in a suit and tie, carrying a briefcase; or perhaps he didn't recognize Malcolm. His name, Malcolm believed, was really Simon. His dad was the vicar up Lodge Moor.

"It's Tim's dad," Malcolm said. "I'll have one of those, please."

Stig said nothing, but handed over the newspaper with a sneer, and took Malcolm's fifty pence. "No change," he said.

"That's all right," Malcolm said, folding and tucking the newspaper under his arm as if it were *The Times*. "Give it to a worthy cause."

"Oh, we will," Stig said contemptuously, and as Malcolm walked away, he broke into a chant, soon followed by his three or four grubby followers. They'd been alternating two chants all day. In his office, Malcolm couldn't hear the words, but you could tell what each one was just from its rhythm. "Maggie Maggie Maggie!" Stig shouted after Malcolm as he cheerfully went off. "Out out out!" his followers joined in. Malcolm wasn't sure that he didn't prefer that one, on a purely musical basis. The other, which they could keep up for hours, was "Coal not dole! Coal not dole!" That really got on your nerves, as Margaret was always saying. "I say 'Mine not whine,'" she regularly remarked, oddly not objecting so much to the youths chanting, apparently, for her removal just outside the office. Malcolm wondered when they knocked off for the night. They tended to show up about ten thirty in the morning.

"Who the fuck was that?" Trudy said, sidling up to Stig. "Maggie Maggie Maggie."

"Out out out," Stig shouted. "Tory scum with a briefcase. Don't ask me."

"Seemed to know you," Trudy said. She had a scowl, a pair of Doc Martens, black 501s, and granny glasses. "Maggie!"

"Out!"

"Maggie!"

"Out!" Stig said. "He's Tim's dad. You know T."

"Little T," Trudy said, curdlingly. "That's his daddy, then, is it? And he lives at home, diddums, getting his clothes washed by mummy."

"That's not fair," Stig said. "Might as well take advantage while he can. The alternative being pouring money into some fat landlord's pocket."

"There are other ways," Trudy said mysteriously. "There are squats, or there's the people's housing. Maggie Maggie Maggie!"

"Out out out," Stig said dubiously. He, too, still lived at home, with his dad the vicar. Trudy, as she kept reminding them, lived in the people's housing, or Park Hill Flats on the fourth floor, a nice view, plastered inside with posters of nuclear explosions and unlikely geopolitical figures kissing each other, a flat she also referred to as a Women's Space, not admitting any men on Mondays to Thursdays inclusive. "I don't know," Stig went on, "but there's enough pressure on ordinary working-class families as it is. There's not enough of the people's housing to go round without them as don't need it claiming it."

"What's that supposed to mean?" Trudy said.

"Maggie!" Stig said. "I just meant him, he's got housing as it is, no point adding to the obligations of a local authority trying to establish socialist principles in a fascist larger environment. They've not the resources to offer to freeloaders. It's right he's taking the larger view."

"It's not everyone as can take the larger view, which anyway is supporting fascism, if you think about it," Trudy said. "If you bring down the local authority, which in any case is implicated in the larger fascist system, then the whole thing will follow, you shouldn't make things easy for any of them. Blunkett."

"Fascist," Stig said. "Anyway, that's his dad, works for a building society."

"Fascist," Trudy said. "Should have spat in his face."

"We're off home now," one of the mining wives said, a woman with carefully prepared hair and a thin, raw face. They'd been dividing up the food donations, which weren't that many, into solid woven-plastic bags. "We'll not be back while Thursday. Mary and that lot from Pontefract'll be down tomorrow."

"We feel your pain," Trudy said exuberantly, and, as she always did, tried to embrace the chief mining wife. They sort of submitted to it, but you could see what they thought about Trudy, who, with her views on the systems that made deodorant, both vaginal and armpit, and shampoo seem necessary, wasn't all that nice to be embraced by or even come very near to.

· · ·

Malcolm had parked the car in Cole's car park as usual, and he whistled a little tune as he turned into Fargate. It was a tricky tune he was attempting—what was it?—an old one, a hit from *Oklahoma!* was it, with its little notes so close together, quite close but not quite the same. With a new black leather briefcase in one hand, a copy of the *Spartacist* neatly folded under the other, and whistling "People Will Say We're In Love," Malcolm found that the previous few years had developed his sense of irony about his own existence to an unexpected degree. There was hardly anything in the briefcase—for years, he'd suffered a kind of briefcase envy at all the young executives who, at the mid-point of the 1960s, had abruptly materialized with almost the sharp suits of the five-years-before Mods, a sharp oblong black briefcase in their firm grip. What did they carry in them? Malcolm hardly ever had anything to take from or to work unless he felt like taking sandwiches, and for some time he'd loaded up his case with unnecessary work, which would stay in the locked case until morning, when he'd take it back again. But then he concluded that many of those sharp-suited men had, like him, nothing in their briefcases from the way they swung them. They were just a signifier of a sort of existence, and Malcolm went on bearing his existence to work, empty, and back again. They would have been scandalized, the girls at the Huddersfield and Harrogate, if a man of his station had gone through the doors in the morning with no bag in his hand. Anyway, today there was a library book in it, a life of Wavell.

At the head of Fargate was another small group of ratty, raw-faced women, in the bright Crimplene fashions of ten years before, their floral skirts at or above their knees, like the women outside his office touting for donations to the miners, their husbands. Competition. He wondered whether there were arguments over the best sites to collect, whether they joined forces, whether what they collected went into a general pool at the end of the day, the neediest getting the tinned meat pie, the less needy a tin of chick-peas or nothing. Or whether each donation was kept by whoever received it. Probably sold it at knockdown prices. Odd how your interests changed over time. Ten years ago, he wouldn't have bothered with any of the viceroys, or India at all. These days, the whole thing struck him as extraordinarily fascinating. He looked forward to a good hour or two after dinner, undisturbed, with the life of Wavell. Dig deep for the miners. Stupid, when you came to think of it, and not serious either, going on a coal strike in

May. They'd starve to death long before demand rose sharply in November. Stupid. They didn't deserve anyone's chick-peas.

All the way home, his thoughts ran on pleasantly. He followed his usual route, hardly paying it any attention. As he approached the university swimming-pool, a police van turned out, full of policemen, then a second and a third. Curious. Then he realized it was probably their afternoon off. Extras, called in from neighbouring authorities to deal with all those flying pickets, terrorizing the students with their dive-bombing and Australian crawl—was that still what it was called these days? It was a shame, when you came to think of it, that Tim didn't go there or that they didn't go to the cockroach-looking old Glossop Road Baths where, three times a week, Tim did. He must be getting to be quite a good swimmer.

In fact, Tim was coming up the road now, his black hair plastered down and a plastic bag in his hand, with a heavy rolled towel at the bottom of it. It was one of his swimming days. If you didn't know him, you'd think he was quite respectable. There was nothing he wore that owed anything to any kind of fashion, as far as Malcolm could see, unless those horrible old granddad shirts without a collar and those sleeveless Fair Isle knitted jerseys had come back into fashion. Tim found them in junk shops, second-hand clothes shops, like the suits he liked to wear. You saw other kids dressed like that. But you couldn't, it seemed, get the shoes quite right from a junk shop—anyway, Tim's shoes were always a bit strange. Today they were the sort of platform shoes they'd been wearing ten years before. Perhaps the other kids gave up, and bought their shoes new to go with their junk-shop clothes.

Over the road, Katherine and Alice were standing in Alice's kitchen, watching Malcolm get out of their new red car, a hatchback.

"That's a nice big car you've got there," Alice said.

"I know," Katherine said. "I don't know what Malcolm was thinking of. I suppose once you've had three children hanging round the house and all wanting lifts at the same time, you go on thinking in those terms even when two of them are gone."

"Useful if you ever wanted anything moving," Alice said, and they giggled a little.

"Ah, well," Katherine said, and they took a regretful sip from their glasses of white wine. "I suppose I'd better be getting back."

"No hurry," Alice said, reaching for the bottle.

"No, they can wait," Katherine said. "I know what we'll be getting all evening, anyway, from Chairman Mao over there. No point in hurrying the inevitable."

Since Katherine had given up her job, she'd taken to dropping in at Alice's around four thirty or five. It was at Alice's suggestion, and they both enjoyed the regularity of it. Of course, at first they'd had a cup of tea and a cake, but one day Alice had said, when Katherine was getting up to go, "Do you fancy a glass of wine?" And Katherine, of course, had said, "Oh, I didn't know it was as late as that," and Alice had assured her that it was a real offer, not one to get rid of her. Since then, they'd dropped the tea, taking turns to bring a little bottle of wine. It was nothing too awful, a bottle lasted them two days, and they'd carried on with the cake, but there was no nonsense about cups of tea. "Oh, Mother," Alice's boy Francis would say, before he'd left home, if he happened to come in, but not seriously, and it was generally only when Bernie came back that Katherine put her glass down and, regretfully, went.

"I saw that Nick the other day," Alice said. "In the post office in Ranmoor. He was struggling with the mysteries of recorded delivery."

"Did you say hello?"

"Oh, he wouldn't know me from Adam," Alice said. "Do you not miss working there?"

Katherine considered, taking a ladylike sip. She could have been remembering anything.

"I don't think so," she said. Then, eventually—it was not a logical answer, Alice had not asked it but she was answering the question that was hanging in the air—she said, "It was only that once. And that was ages ago. It seems ridiculous for it to have become something to make all this fuss over."

Between the two of them, they had gradually, over the years, slipped back to the point they had started from, attained by degrees their initial level of intimacy. It had come about by degrees, by little allusions on Katherine's part when she felt ready, and by an ordinary decent pretence on Alice's part that she didn't know any of it. These were necessary steps, and by this mutual process of respect and pretence they'd got to the point of being able to talk frankly and openly about the situation when no one else was about. It was almost the most interesting thing that had ever happened to Katherine—the most interesting thing she'd ever done. In return, Alice had been able to tell her all of the most interesting things that had ever happened to her. They were not, by comparison, all that interesting or tellable, but she talked expansively to Katherine as best anyone could who had, after all, met her husband when she was eighteen, who had married him at twenty-two, who had never been to bed or been tempted to go to bed with anyone else. Alice's story was less forceful than Katherine's, which tended to circle round one episode, one event, one afternoon, even, but it had aspects that she couldn't tell to anyone else.

"It wasn't exactly just that one time, though," Alice said reprovingly.

"Oh, but it was—"

"I mean, that's not what's worrying you," Alice said. "You might only have done it, taken that step, once, done what you're not supposed ever to have done, but in your head it went on a lot before that and a lot after."

"I suppose there's something in that," Katherine said.

"It was the thinking about it in advance, and the extracting yourself from it afterwards, that's what did the damage."

"I suppose so," Katherine said humbly. "Though the afterwards part, that was when the whole situation became a lot easier. It was doing it when I didn't want to any more."

"They'll be wondering where you are," Alice said, nodding at over the road. "Have a bit more."

"I will," Katherine said.

"But afterwards . . ."

"Well, afterwards," Katherine said practically, "naturally, I couldn't feel the same about him, I didn't even like him that much. I couldn't see what it was all about, and then I noticed that in the six months before I'd actually called in sick three times. Of course, I'd not been sick, I'd just found I had other things to do those days. Before—you know, I couldn't have imagined being sick on a day when I might see Nick, spend a day with him putting stupid flowers in vases. I'd have dragged myself in even if I'd had bubonic plague. And then all at once I was looking at him one day, and I thought how completely stupid and—you know, somehow *unmanly* he looked, stripping the foliage off lilies. I never compared him to Malcolm, I never let myself go down that route, but then I thought, you know, what Malcolm does, it's just a bit better, a bit more dignified. And then Malcolm got this promotion, and he gets bonuses now, and he said at the time—in a way this was funny—he said, 'You don't seem all that keen about going to work any more. You used to look forward to it and talk about it more.' And I said, 'Yes, I suppose that's true.' I thought about it for a minute. I'd rather not be doing anything."

"Even though there's less to do around the house, I suppose," Alice said.

"That's true," Katherine said. "Though Daniel, even with his little flat in Crookes, he still comes home with his washing, to save time. Jane's always been a bit more self-reliant, I imagine she's coping quite well in London   at least she never says anything that makes you think otherwise. We were going to go down next month, Jane's got a sort of sofabed in the sitting room she says we can sleep on, a kind of Japanese thing called a futon, though Malcolm says he doesn't much fancy that and what about a hotel—"

"London prices," Alice said. "Stick to your Japanese affair, save yourself a hundred pounds."

"That's what I said," Katherine said comfortably.

"What did Nick say in the end?" Alice said.

"I think he was secretly a bit relieved," Katherine said. "That sounds terrible, but I think he was. Anyway, he's got a school-leaver. It all seems to have worked out very well. Here's Bernie, I'll have to be off."

"All right, Katherine?" Bernie said, coming into the kitchen. "Don't dash off on my account, it's nice to have company."

"No, I saw my boys coming in twenty minutes ago," Katherine said. "I'll have to go and make the peace."

"Make the peace?" Bernie said. "Hello love," he said, kissing Alice.

"They'll be hammer and tongs by now," Katherine said. "You don't know how lucky you are."

"Oh, we all have our little crosses to bear," Bernie said, smiling because, after all, they didn't really. "Is that a letter from Sandra I saw?"

"Alexandra," Alice said. "Yes, I left it until you got home. The post didn't come till ten."

"Shocking," Bernie said, and together they said goodbye to Katherine, before together going into the sitting room, opening the envelope with the Australian stamps, and Bernie, as they'd got used to, reading it out loud to Alice.

Tim had got to the city library, as was his habit, within half an hour of its opening. Sometimes when the porter opened the yellowish varnished double doors at nine thirty he was already waiting on the chalky white steps with his two old plastic supermarket bags, one filled with pads and paper, foil-wrapped sandwiches, biros and books, the other with a towel and swimming trunks, soap and shampoo for later. The porter had a pitted beetroot for a face, and, neckless, chomped on his ill-fitting dentures as he let in Tim and the other two or three impatients. He never acknowledged these early regulars as his jaw rose horribly into the middle of his face like a horrible motor. Tim did not acknowledge him, either: his blue uniform with its insistent badges, shiny as if it had been through a rainstorm, put him on the far side of some line of demarcation.

There were three doors leading out of the echoing marble lobby; in front, the general library, for anyone who thought reading was for entertainment, cheap sops to keep them quiet, and to the right, the business library, full of telephone directories. Tim despised them both. Two at a time, he went up the august marble stairs to the first floor, where the reference library was. If you carried on up, or took the strangely two-doored lift, which made the exact same clank at the exact same spot in its ascent, you got to the art gallery with its op-art café, furnished with tables and chairs all red and plastic and circular. Tim despised that, too, with its sense of money and fatuous donation. But he liked the reference library, liked the sudden squeak of the floor under your shoes as you came through the double doors, liked the newspaper smell of it, and the light through the high, many-paned windows. He didn't go into the main library. That was where his dad went.

There was a new security check at the entrance, a sort of arch detecting some small slip of metal in each book. Until six months ago, you could still get a small book out in the inside pocket of your parka, hidden in the orange quilted lining, as Tim's bookshelves at home demonstrated. Quite big books, too, though he couldn't now remember taking the illustrated survey of European reptiles, and it had been so long since he'd looked at it, he'd often thought of smuggling it back in. But he didn't know if the detecting device worked in both directions, or just when you were leaving.

The girl at the entrance was settling herself for the morning. It was the blonde one, the Alice-in-Wonderland one with the hairband and the high-necked dresses with flowers on them. Tim knew all her dresses. She raised her head a little when he came in, but not enough to look at him. Some of the other librarians did look at him, the older ones, boldly, and making comments to each other, but she never did.

He made his way to his place. Marx had had his desk in the British Library where he wrote all of *Das Kapital*, a copy of which Tim now had in his plastic bag, the book bag. Tim had his own table, D3. It was in the politics niche. The compressed thoughts of ideal lives rose lavishly around him. Politics was not a school subject, and though in other niches, schoolgirls attempting revision nested with their notes in their round, vacant handwriting, whispering and giggling, the only people Tim ever shared a table with were serious idealists, their lives' works in frayed plastic bags too. It was good to have left school. There was nobody here to mark what he did, and his own approval was unalloyed by dissent. Sometimes he thought of showing one of the old men over the table the sheer body of his notes, preparing for something, he didn't know what, just knowledge in the urgent spiky handwriting, half pressing through the thin paper. He knew his own handwriting so well and approved of it so much. He could effortlessly construct their ideal responses.

Taking his seat, he placed his bags on the table before getting out his block of blank lined paper, and his copy of the first volume of *Das Kapital*. It wasn't the mock-shouty edition Penguin published, but the fat blank one, the size of your hand, that a small English publisher kept going by the Soviets published. The cover was thick and flocculent, like beige blotting paper, and the title printed in plain red ink. He put the bags underneath the table. He'd spent a good deal of time making it look read, before bringing it out in public. But now he really had worn it down with reading, little vertical lines next to important points, stabs of exclamation marks next to really important points, all like streaks of blue rain at the edges of each page.

On the other side of the table, Mad Mary was putting down her books and bags. She was a regular. Recently, he'd even started having his sandwich with her, though she had nothing to talk about except her neighbours' unreasonable complaints about her six cats. "I ask you," she always ended up, "is it really too much to ask for, to be left in peace?" She had an exploded air: her hair, the contents of her pockets, her stuffing almost escaping from the gaps in her surface, held together inadequately with safety-pins and amateurish tacking. She must have been nearly fifty, and spoke sometimes of her mother with unspecifying regret. Where she lived, he didn't know; or what she was working on. She liked to build up piles of books about anarchism, truffling through them, snuffling with amusement for, surely, Tim's benefit. She wouldn't speak to him until she was settled, and he watched her, muttering, "Let's see—ah—I think . . ." gather twelve books, one by one, laying them carefully on the table. Tim regretted, as ever, not foiling her in some small way, perhaps by claiming that biography of—who?—Ba-ku-nin, he read upside-down, before she got here.

"Good morning, Tim," she whispered noisily over the table when, at last, she was settled. "Awful developments *chez* Brewster. I'll tell you later what the swines said to me last night."

"Oh dear," Tim said, and got his head down, with his blue biro chewed to bits at one end, not encouraging her.

The library filled steadily in the course of the morning. By twelve thirty, he was hungry, and faintly radiant with the sense of absorbed wisdom. How right Marx was! How he saw through everything! If only people could be given the opportunity to read what he said, everything surrounding them would crumble into dust, and something never yet seen on the face of the earth would come into being to solve everything. He rummaged in his bag for the foil-wrapped sandwiches and the little Thermos of tea. It was a nice day, and he'd have it sitting on the wall outside the theatre. Better, he genuinely couldn't remember what the sandwiches were this morning. A nice surprise. Mad Mary was too fast for him and, pretending to be finished with her work at exactly the same time as him, entirely by chance, stood up with her own lunch bag in her fist.

"I thought one might go to the Peace Gardens today," she said, in her grand, throaty gurgle. "I don't suppose you'd care to join me?"

"Why not," Tim said wretchedly, only hoping that the Sparts weren't outside, selling the paper, to witness his horrible friend again.

"The most frightful thing happened," Mad Mary said, sweeping out of the library. It was an oddity of hers that, while working, she was hot on shushing anyone who made a noise, even an accidental dropping of something, but as soon as she stopped, she would scamper through the library talking at normal volume without noticing that she, sometimes, was being hushed in her turn. "Those awful neighbours of mine. They said that Arthur had done his business in their garden. They came round and accused me, face to face. Well, of course, they don't know Arthur from any of the others, they think all cats are the same, and they didn't say Arthur, naturally, but I knew it was Arthur they were accusing."

With a series of encouraging hmms, Tim got Mad Mary through the doors and down the library steps. The Sparts weren't there, thank goodness; probably down Fargate supporting the comrades' struggle in the mines. Mad Mary's story wended on. It seemed to be heading towards actual violence but, as most of her stories did, ended up demonstrating her absolutely admirable grasp of the issues involved. Still, she was an anarchist.

They ate their lunch on a bench in the Peace Gardens, people staring at them as they passed, a teenage boy with his mad granny, listening to her stories of cats. Afterwards he gave her the slip, walked three times round the City Hall before returning to the reference library. The Alice-in-Wonderland girl was out, having her lunch. Tim thought of going straight to the swimming-pool, but his mother's warning about cramp and death if you swam after eating intervened. He went back to his desk.

After lunch it was never the same and, to be honest, he footled with Marx for an hour or two, his head bent over the rumpled book with its stains and deliberate coffee-mug rings, not taking much in, just enjoying the thought of himself reading Marx and how he must look to everyone else. The girl at the desk. His eyes went repeatedly over phrases; he came back in his head to Mad Mary and her seven cats. He was not sure what he thought, what he ought to think, about animals and their rights. Trudy thought one thing; Stig thought another. They'd argued about it, whether it was at the root of everything, or whether it was a distraction, even if it was a symptom of something else. Stig and Trudy had gone on, quite late into the night once or twice, in Trudy's flat on the fourth floor with its twinkling view of Sheffield and the remote hoot of the last trains into the station at the bottom of the valley. Tim wasn't sure what he thought. But there was something to be thought about ownership, and private property, and Mad Mary's seven cats were definitely that, in a sort of illusory way.

He always started to get a little sleepy around three.

Tim packed his things, trying as ever to look as if he was just popping out with both his bags and would be back soon. A "goodbye" with Mad Mary often turned into a hissed revival of her last anecdote, now that she'd had time to brood further over it. But today she just waved vaguely.

The swimming-bath at Glossop Road was usually quiet between three thirty and five. The school parties had gone, and the few after-work swimmers not yet arrived. It was an old bath, with still some slipper baths in the basement—he had no idea whether anyone still used them, now that everyone had bathrooms at home. He thought of the 1930s, a grand pity coming over him as he undid his shirt in one of the many little lobbies and odd square corners of the changing rooms. He'd never much enjoyed coming here from school—he was always a bit shy, and hadn't liked the noise or the violence or the smell of mould everywhere, ascending the joints in the tiles like trained creepers. He liked it now, though: the stern square ford of the disinfected trough at the exit, the ugly bluish light from over the swimming-pool, always with one humming on and off, throbbing like a migraine, and the weird ranks of seating in the gallery for some swimming gala that would never happen.

The bored hunched lifeguard, in flip-flops and faded red trunks, a whistle hanging between his knees, didn't look up from his book as Tim tripped out, shivering a little: it was always cold in here, and sharp with the unregulated stink of chlorine. The first few days of the month, after they'd tipped a new load in, it really made your eyes sting; then again, by the end of the month, you hesitated about getting in sometimes, it was so ammoniac and cloudy with other people's clandestine piss. There was an old love, ploughing up and down like a shabby tugboat, and a couple of kids, mucking about. At the shallow end, a regular stood, the water just at his huge thighs; he was one of the length-murderers, churning up the whole pool with twenty lengths of bloodthirsty butterfly. Just now, he was having a pause, or about to begin, or just about to finish, his insect-goggles and skull cap taking away any personality. Tim hated him.

Tim lowered himself into the water—he wasn't a diver, he'd leave that kind of showing-off to Daniel and the insect-faced professionals— and, after a moment, stretched his arms out behind him to the rail, hunched up his legs against the wall, and kicked off. It was a steady breast-stroke he did; he knew it was a rubbish one, with his head achingly up and his ladylike circular sweeps, all out of time with each other. Before he was halfway up the pool, just at the point where the painted blue letters thrillingly indicated six foot, his own height, there was a heavy crash behind him and, as it were, a vast swallow as the butterfly-merchant launched himself. In five more strokes, he'd overtaken Tim; ten yards from the far end, he performed an immense gymnastic twist, sending half the pool up Tim's nose. Tim carried on manfully, doing three lengths at a time before pausing, but after eighteen, he'd had enough and got out. The lifeguard had never looked up from his book the whole time, and had read five more pages.

"So, what did you get up to today?" Malcolm said, letting Tim into the house after him.

"Nothing much," Tim said, dropping his bags on the floor of the hall.

"Well, you went swimming," Malcolm said patiently, gesturing towards the bag with the towel in it.

"Yes, I went swimming," Tim said.

"Did you go to the library?" Malcolm said. "I see you've got your books."

"Yes," Tim said in a silly voice. "Yes, I did go to the library."

"Did you remember to sign on?" Malcolm said. "It's a Wednesday, isn't it?"

"No," Tim said. "Strangely enough, I didn't remember to sign on. Because amazingly enough it isn't today that I sign on. It's next Wednesday. You only have to sign on every other Wednesday."

"Oh," Malcolm said. "I thought it was this week, for some reason."

"You probably weren't listening," Tim said, making as if to go upstairs.

"That must be it," Malcolm said calmly. "I saw some friends of yours today."

Tim paused, halfway up the stairs. His face, when he turned, was instantly full of loathing. "Oh, yes?" he said, snarling. "What friends of mine would that be, then? Were they my Russian friends, you know, the ones in the Kremlin? Or the Chinese ones, like Chairman Mao?"

"He's dead, isn't he?"

"Or was it some other sorts of friends, like Fidel Castro, you're talking about today?"

In some ways, Tim had a point, Malcolm conceded; that was, in fact, usually who he was referring to when he mentioned Tim's "friends," far away old men, ruining their countries. "Actually," Malcolm said, "I meant real friends of yours. I saw what's-his-name—Stig, isn't it? He was standing on the street selling his newspaper and collecting money."

"Yes," Tim said, though he hadn't known that Stig had been out today. "He's doing his bit. For the miners."

"So I gathered," Malcolm said. "He tried to ignore me, but I bought a copy of his paper."

"Very funny," Tim said. "I hope you choke on it."

"I enjoy it," Malcolm said. "I think they have the best television pages."

This was a joke: the *Spartacist* contained nothing but three or four shrieking calls to order, denunciations of anything to hand, and a few contemptuous paragraphs here and there giving an individual take on major news stories of the day. Trudy's lurid twenty-word account of the marriage of Prince Charles and Lady Diana was still enjoyed by all, three years on. Most of the articles tended to finish at the end of a line, though not often at the end of a sentence, let alone a paragraph, but their conclusions were usually fairly clear.

"And how's the job hunting going?" Malcolm said.

"There are no jobs," Tim said. "There's no point in looking."

"You've got A levels," Malcolm said. "You could find a job if you tried. And what are you going to say at the dole office when they ask you?"

"I'll tell them the truth," Tim said.

"You'll make something up, you mean," Malcolm said. "There's no point in refusing to look for work because the revolution's nearly here, you know. Anyway, when the revolution comes, they won't put up with idle sods like you refusing to work, they'll send you down the coal mines."

Tim turned and took a step or two down.

"I expect you're going to say that you'll happily work down the coal mines when they're run by the People for the People, aren't you?" Malcolm said. He was getting to the point in this argument beyond happy enjoyment, and was starting to fume.

"And you?" Tim said. "What did you do today? Make lots of money, did you?"

"Personally, you mean?" Malcolm said. "The usual amount, the amount that pays for your food and keep, I suppose. No, I'll tell you what I did today—I made a couple very happy. Listen to this, son, you might learn something. This couple, they've been living in their council house for years. It's their own house, in their own minds, but they've only ever rented it from the council. And today I helped them take out a mortgage so they could buy it, and then it'll be theirs properly, and they can pass it on to their children. I don't suppose you'd like to live in a council house, but they loved their house. You know something? It's really quite satisfying when you help people to fulfil their dreams like that."

"Christ, you fucking fascist," Tim said. "Does it never cross your mind, the struggles ordinary working-class people face, and then participating in flogging off public assets for a cheap profit, bribing people like that to keep fucking Thatcher in power?"

"Well, oddly enough, that's exactly what Margaret was saying on the subject. Not Thatcher, my Margaret, my secretary. No, it didn't occur to me."

"Well, it's all just false fucking consciousness," Tim said. "And they'll wake up one day."

"They've woken up," Malcolm said. "That's what you and your friends don't realize. They haven't a clue. Call a coal strike in May? What a pack of idiots. They haven't a clue."

"Fascist," Tim said, stomping upstairs, and slamming his bedroom door.

Malcolm hummed a little tune to keep himself calm. False consciousness all right. He pretended to everyone, even to Katherine, that these nightly confrontations amused him as much as anything. It was really the only way he could explain why he didn't let Tim sulk in his room, silently, but goaded him into name-calling. It wasn't as if he even cared that much. But he didn't, honestly, find them that funny. When it had all started, the summer after Tim's O levels, he'd at first been easily infuriated by beliefs only acquired to hang adolescent tantrums on. Then they'd carried on, and he had managed to find a little amusement in the predictable course of Tim's assertions. But always, as the argument went on—and it was always the same argument, night after night, starting from a raw expression of total personal contempt—he found himself full of rage. He tried his best to keep the whole thing as a joke.

"Tim's come in?" Katherine said, coming through the front door.

"He's upstairs," Malcolm said. "I'd leave it a while, if I were you."

"I wish he'd learn to put his own swimming stuff in the washing-machine," Katherine said, picking the wet towel out of the abandoned bag. "And he gets so annoyed if it doesn't get done overnight. You haven't had a row already, have you? You've only been in twenty minutes, the pair of you. I saw you come in—I've been over at Alice's."

"Only a little one," Malcolm said. "Hello, love," and he kissed her quickly, negotiating the wet fat sausage in her right hand. Besieged, they were finding consolations in each other these days; maintained the rituals of love and the fronts of amusement for each other's benefit.

"You're as bad as he is," Katherine said, disentangling herself. "I honestly believe you start them deliberately."

"He talks such a load of codswallop," Malcolm said.

"He'll grow out of it," Katherine said. "Eventually."

"That's the trouble," Malcolm said. "I just wish he'd find a job."

"And move out," Katherine said heartlessly. It had taken time for them to come to that acknowledged point, but once they'd reached it, said openly to each other that they wished Tim would move out, they enjoyed repeating it. To most other people, they managed to go on saying that they were happy for him to go on living at home, it was quite nice still to have one child with them now that the others were gone, Daniel in a flat in Crookes and doing well at his job in the estate agent's, Jane, after three years' university thoroughly independent, sharing a flat in London. But they didn't say that to each other, or to people who knew, like Alice and Bernie. To them, they said quite openly that they looked forward to the day when Tim moved out, and both of them thought of Kenneth Warner, up the road, his thirty-year-old son still at home, and drifting from job to job, and nothing Kenneth could do about it. And at least Kenneth Warner's son was only a gormless lump; he didn't go on about the petty bourgeoisie all day long at the top of his voice.

"I'm going to watch the news," Malcolm said.

"It's all the coal strike," Katherine said. "I'm sick of it."

"All the same," Malcolm said, going into the sitting room and picking up the remote control from the white unit. They really ought to get rid of it—they couldn't remember why they'd liked it, with its white plastic surfaces, and now one of the smoked-glass doors was gone, smashed after Tim had gone too far and hurled a mug straight past his dad's head late one night. They'd been on the point of throwing it out when Alice and Bernie's identical one had appeared on the pavement for the dustmen to take away. (They wouldn't, either, so it stayed there for five whole days.) So, of course, they'd had to hang on to it for a while longer. It would just look stupid, otherwise.

Katherine was right: it was all about the coal strike. There was a shot of the prime minister, then a shot of the miners' man, while the reporter talked over the top about the day's particular failure. The pair of them looked far too pleased with themselves; Malcolm wondered, too, and not for the first time, which of them got through more Elnett to keep their hair in place. He had voted for her, twice now—or, rather, for Osborne, a son of the steel-makers, a man he'd never seen round here and didn't believe he'd think much of if he ever did. The news shifted to film of men on strike outside a Pontefract mine. They were in T-shirts; the weather was nice. It might have been the same film they'd used yesterday. It would have looked better if they'd been able to stand outside the mines in donkey jackets round a hissing brazier, rubbing their hands to keep out the winter chill. As it was, anyone could see that no one was urgently in need of coal at the moment, and now, when Scargill came on to say that the mines that the Government wanted to close down, they'd do better to supply pensioners with fuel for nothing, he looked an idiot.

"Taking an interest," Tim said. He'd come downstairs quietly, in his socks; his white big toe was poking out of one like a potato out of a bag.

"It's all a bit ugly," Malcolm conceded.

"You won't find the truth out by watching the news on television. It's all staged."

"How do you mean?"

"I mean, as everyone knows, the television companies, they're going down to the picket lines and paying people at the back of the crowd to throw bricks at the police. It makes a better picture."

"That can't be true," Malcolm said. "That's crazy."

"Of course it's crazy," Tim said, sitting down in the brown armchair, the survivor from the last three-piece suite, his hands chopping at the air in explanation. "But the media's stirring up trouble, and the Government's paying people to infiltrate and start up violence so that the police can charge the legitimate strikers and beat them up. It's true. Not that you'll find any of that on the television news or in your *Daily Telegraph*."

"Is that a fact?" Malcolm said.

"The fact is—" Tim began, picking at his socks, but then his mother came in.

"I don't know what you'd like for your dinner," she said. "There's some pork chops, or I could get some cod out of the freezer. Did I tell you, Tim, I was talking to Alice and she said she's just had a letter today from Sandra in Australia? Go over and find out what she's up to some time."

"Sandra?" Tim said. "Over the road? Why should she have anything special to say to me?" He was fiddling with his sock, pulling it out to cover his big toe, twisting it round to make a little knot. "She never had anything to say to me while she was living there. I don't know why she should suddenly be interested in me now." There was a sharp tone, almost of anger, in his voice.

"I always thought you were great friends," Katherine said. "No, I remember, it was Daniel who was great friends with her—" She looked away, suppressing something that promised to have been a smile; she might have been remembering those hungry wet-eyed gazes, unmodified by shame or experience of the response such things got, that Tim used to direct at Sandra over their dining-table. "I don't know why I thought it was you. Of course it was Daniel, we all thought they were going out together, and then, of course, they weren't, they were just friends."

"You never knew where you stood with Daniel, did you?" Malcolm said.

"Still don't," Katherine said. "Don't start off reminiscing at your age, Malcolm, nothing so likely to turn you into an old man. I ought to give Daniel a ring, tell him, he'd be interested at what Sandra's up to. She calls herself Alex now, Alice said."

"Confusing," Malcolm said. "Alex and Alice."

"Well, they're twelve thousand miles apart," Katherine said. "Anyway, he'll be up before long, I haven't washed any clothes from him for a week and he'll want his best jeans for the weekend. Now, I still haven't had an answer to my question about dinner."

"Look at that," Tim said, rising from his seat and pointing, wraith-like, at the television. It had wended its way through the day's other news, picturing disasters in other parts of the world. The violence might have visited parts of the world in strictly alphabetical order, and today it was Iran and Iraq and India, with a shot of a badger-haired woman who might as well have been Mrs. Thatcher in a sari. Now it had returned, in its last minutes of summary, to the miners, and to shots of a dense, dusty crowd throwing bricks. "Do you think there's any point in getting a job when none of this—" he waved his arm around at the sitting room, its one wallpapered side, its three cream walls, and the three-piece suite and coffee-table with three books in a neat pile on it, the vase filled with lilies scenting the room "—is going to last? Why buy into a system that's on its last legs?"

"I thought you said all that was staged by the television," Katherine said.

"It is," Tim said. "But they're still angry, the people of this country."

"Just not angry enough to throw bricks," Katherine said. "I see, I think. Did I ever get an answer about what you want for dinner?"

"The fact of the matter is," Tim began, but Katherine had given up, and gone back to the kitchen to start cooking whatever she felt like.

"The pork'd be nice," Malcolm called. "Or whatever you feel like, really." And in a moment *Nationwide* started, which he couldn't stick, and he had an excuse to get up and leave Tim addressing an empty room, Frank Bough and a dog that liked to drink beer.

. . .

Halfway through dinner, the telephone rang. Tim left off what he was saying, and went to get it. It was usually for him around this time, and usually it was Stig. He'd been supporting the miners all day with Trudy, and had something to pass on: CND were holding a big meeting in ten days' time. There was going to be some kind of rally in London, and this was a planning meeting.

"They'll be handing out puppet-making duties," Stig said. "And painting their stupid banners. Trudy wants to go along and smash it up. Are you on for it?"

"Yeah," Tim said. "It's just a stupid distraction."

"That's right," Stig said. Their feelings didn't go further than this; they listened with awed respect to Trudy's view that a nuclear war would smash capitalism once and for all.

"Are you coming down tomorrow?" Stig said in the end. "It was good today, we achieved a lot."

"Yeah, I will," Tim said.

"There's another thing," Stig said. "But I won't tell you over the phone. There's a meeting of minds taking place later this week we ought to be at." A meeting of minds was their term for a confrontation, one the listening police and MI5 wouldn't understand. At the moment it meant a flashpoint of the miners' strike.

"Where is it?" Tim said naïvely.

"I can tell you tomorrow," Stig said. "We're still trying to arrange—" stressing these last words, as if he knew quite well how stupid the euphemism was "—a venue."

Stig had been at the forefront of resistance since the fifth form at school. Tim had sort of known him, skulking at the back of the class and answering questions in a bored, parodic way when directly appealed to; he couldn't be disciplined, since he usually knew the answers, but the teachers didn't like his tone of voice, or the look on his face, or that he wouldn't make an effort, and sometimes hilariously said so. Tim's proper admiration began on the day of the dinner-ticket protest. Dinner tickets were obtained from machines or, if you were on free dinners, handed out by the school secretary; they were identical, and you weren't supposed to know who paid and who didn't, but everyone knew anyway. It was a rule that once you had your little sludge-green ticket—it was supposed to change colour day by day, yellow Tuesday, blue Wednesdays, but in reality it was always sludge-green— you had to write your name on the back in case you lost it. Their form teacher, Mr. Kay, always liked to tell them something important on the mornings they didn't have Assembly and were stuck with him for half an hour before lessons began. One morning, in the stuffy form room in the geography block, lined with maps where an engorged yellow America, a shrunken grey Africa were supposed to demonstrate the world's riches in graphic terms, Kay started on the importance of this rule. Stig—then still Simon—put his hand up. "But why do we have to do it?" he said.

"So that if you lose it no one else can use it."

"But the dinner ladies don't know who we are."

"They can certainly check if you report your ticket lost."

"But isn't it our right to lose it?"

"What?"

"Why is it a rule?"

"I've just explained that."

The girls at the front were sighing now as they brushed their hair, examining themselves in their own little mirrors, exchanging humorous what-now glances with Mr. Kay.

"Why shouldn't we be free to write our names on the back or not, so that it's our own decision?"

"Well, it would just be foolish."

"Isn't it our right to be foolish?"

"It's just a school rule."

"But why is it a school rule?"

It went on for twenty-five minutes, until the bell rang. By the end of it, Mr. Kay was having a very bad morning, and Tim was full of envious admiration. Since then, Stig had been not only his best friend but the object of constant emulation. Tim adopted his style of dress, with zigzag Fair Isle tank tops over granddad shirts and a pair of round wire glasses like John Lennon; he observed, with speechless envy, Stig's sardonic habit of addressing his parents, to their resigned faces, as "Vicar" and "Fat Marge," something he could only translate into a sneer when talking to his own parents. Of course he'd go along with Stig and smash up a CND meeting.

He put the phone down and wandered back into the dining room, but he'd finished his plate of pork chops, peas and potatoes; he'd not been concentrating, and had finished it before noticing.

"I'll be upstairs," he said, turning round.

"Don't you want any sweet?" his mother said.

"No, thanks," Tim said. "I'll be upstairs."

"It wasn't anything special," she said. "Just what was left of the crème caramel yesterday." Tim took the stairs two at a time, glad no one was overhearing the words "crème caramel."

He could have moved into one of the bigger bedrooms, Daniel's or Jane's old ones now they'd moved out, but he'd stuck with his own. It didn't really matter. In the same way, it hadn't been decorated for ten years, since he was a little boy, and the walls were still a pale blue, the colour of Blu-tack. They'd offered to redecorate a year ago, but when he'd said he'd like the room painted black, they'd refused and he'd said he wouldn't want anything else, so nothing was done. He didn't really see the room any more—perhaps only when Stig or someone came round. It had a little desk and a low bookcase; in the bookcase were fifty favourite books, the three Shakespeare plays he'd done for O level and A level, some Marx, this week's library books and, behind them, tucked away, a packet of Benson & Hedges, only three smoked. He'd bought it a month ago; he'd decided he ought to smoke, he could see himself cadging a light from a miner on a picket line. He didn't want his mother to find out, though.

Underneath the bed, two drawers, and in one of the drawers, a shoe-box, his Sandra box; in it, some photographs of Sandra that Daniel had taken, an essay of hers Daniel had borrowed once and then, as he thought, lost, some of her writing, a spoon she'd once used, a postcard she'd sent to Daniel with her address in Australia on it, which he'd got to first when the postman had delivered it. There was no reason he'd find out why he'd not received it, or probably ever know that she'd sent one in the first place. Tim thought about Sandra, still, all the time; he was sure Daniel never did. On the walls, the poster of the woman tennis-player scratching her bum had gone, and there was a big poster of Che, another one, a streamlined spiky Soviet one in red and white and black, of Lenin; he'd got them from the radical bookshop, not understanding much beyond his own blushing embarrassment when the woman had smirked when he'd bought a life of Che at the same time. He could have gone on with what he'd been reading today, *Capital*, but he wandered over to the window and looked out on to the street. He'd taken down the net curtains last year.

It was quiet outside; the man opposite, five houses up, trimming his hedge, and there, running across the road, some small animal—a squirrel. It would be a squirrel here, Tim thought. Squirrels were a sort of middle-class right-wing animal. A car approached, its diesel engine ticking, labouring up the little slope; he watched it go, turn the corner, fade away. God, this was dull. But then another, and as it turned into the road, he saw with alarm that it had the white and blue of a police car. Don't be stupid, he told himself, don't panic straight off, but the two policemen inside were looking out of the window, counting the house numbers, and slowed to a halt directly outside their house. They got out, and cast a brief, severe glance upwards at where Tim stood, framed in his window. He quailed. But then he remembered. He had always known what he was getting into. He knew a hell of a lot. He had always known that the police would take an interest, and it seemed that now the time had come. He concentrated on his telephone conversation with Stig. If he had said anything, he reminded himself in the words of Trudy's instructions, it was all completely deniable. He had said nothing, and Stig had too much sense to give anything away. He watched the two big blue corruptible policemen, one a woman, walking up the drive as if they had some heavy task, weighing down their arms and legs, and prepared to be called downstairs.

Daniel had just got home from work, had just climbed the stairs, when he heard the phone ring on the ground floor. He knew it would be for him—it always was—but he carried on taking off his suit jacket and tie. The old sod on the ground floor always surrendered to temptation and got it in the end. He'd had quite a good day: all morning, he'd gone round properties in Nether Edge with a youngish married couple. The wife was pregnant—with twins, she'd confided—and they needed a house with more space than they'd got at the moment. He'd gone around with Jennifer in her Eadon Lockwood and Riddle car—he was just tagging along to watch and learn—and hadn't said much. The wife would have been quite sexy before she'd got pregnant, and even now had a kind of bloom to her that was quite appealing. He'd done his special smile, levering her into the back of the car, and she'd blushed hormonally, as she was meant to. At first, he'd thought the whole thing a waste of time: they'd gone round eight different houses, and with every one, there'd been something wrong and apparently unacceptable, as far as the husband was concerned. You'd have thought he couldn't believe anyone could ever live in dumps like these, and it was a disgrace that Eadon Lockwood and Riddle were prepared to try to sell places so horrible. But Jennifer had just nodded as the wife echoed the husband's strictures—yes, she didn't know what they were thinking of either with that décor in the bedrooms, no, speaking personally, she wouldn't be very keen on taking on a house at that price where there was so much work to be done, he was quite right, it didn't look as if anyone had touched it for thirty years—and in the end, Daniel was surprised when the husband had asked for five minutes alone with his wife, in the garden of the last house, and had come back afterwards and said they'd be making an offer for the fifth one. "I never thought anything different," Jennifer said, when they were back in the office. "I could tell they were serious. Some people just like to look at a dozen houses in one shot and then take the pick of what they've seen. You get to recognize the type."

When the time came, Daniel thought he'd be that type as well. For the moment, he was living in this big bedsit at the top of a house in Crookes. It was cheap, and because of that his salary was building up in his bank account—that was all you could say for it. He thought there was something wrong, even professionally questionable, about an estate agent living in rented accommodation. The house belonged to a family dentist—the Glovers' dentist, in fact—who'd bought it and converted it into three flats at least twenty years ago, and never touched it since. Daniel had seen the card in the waiting room, before he'd gone in to have his teeth declared fine, just like last year. The interior paint in the house was the same colour as the front door, a gloomy racing green, a shade obviously going cheap at the time, and the communal parts of the whole house were wallpapered in aggressive florals. At each turn of the stair, there was a forlorn spider-plant in a wicker basket, its children broken off and dead on the dark green window-sill, or a chipped porcelain figurine, a souvenir dish from some English seaside resort, objects that had been downgraded twice, first from the dentist's elegant home and subsequently even from the waiting room of his surgery. In the hall, letters piled up in the names of tenants from years ago, some with angry instructions to open immediately on the envelope. Somewhere, in anonymous office blocks, machines toiled and spat over the affairs of these lost tenants; one day, perhaps, someone would turn up and demand to see them in person.

It wasn't a bad place to live, though the furniture was a bit grandma-ish, and there wasn't a lot you could do in the way of cooking, nothing but a Baby Belling on a shelf, its enamel chipped and the rust beginning underneath, and a cramped fridge with its freezer compartment too frozen up to post even a bag of peas in it. He shared a bathroom, too, with the woman immediately underneath, the sod on the ground floor having his own. But the woman underneath was a devoted sherry drinker, and never got up until long after Daniel did, so it wasn't much of a problem. When it all got too much, Daniel went home with a bag of washing and ate his mum's cooking. But he did all right, and the bedsit was decent enough, considering that he hadn't looked at any other flats.

The only really annoying thing was the phone, which was always for him, and on the ground floor. It was a payphone, and right next to the old sod's door; when the money dropped into the box, you could hear him tutting away inside his flat. You could swear he listened to your conversations; probably the most excitement he got all day. Now he could hear the door of the old sod's flat opening tetchily, and the phone being picked up; a complaining voice, the words not clear, then a throaty yell: "Phone!" Never his name. Daniel came out, and trotted neatly down the stairs. He liked this moment, not knowing which girl was calling him up. The old sod was standing there, holding the receiver in his fist like a weapon, slippers and green-grey zip-up cardigan on, glaring at him.

"It's for you," he said. "If you would answer the telephone some-times, it would be much appreciated, since I'm not an answering-service, last time I looked."

"I'm sorry," Daniel said. He went to take the telephone.

"One other thing," the old sod said, holding it back. "I've asked this before, but it's not right to come in at all hours of the day and night, banging about and waking folk up. I don't know what unearthly hour it was last night. Bringing girls in, too, a different one every time."

"I don't think that's your business," Daniel said, painfully aware that the girl waiting on the phone would be hearing this, since the old sod hadn't covered the mouthpiece. "Even if it were true, which it isn't."

"I'll be speaking to Mr. Bullock," the old sod said. "I'm sure he wouldn't be happy to learn about his tenant treating his flats like a bor-dello. And your way of life isn't my concern, but the fact that I get woken up, night after night, by your antics, that's something I'm not prepared to put up with. I'm not going to mention it again."

"Oh, good," Daniel said. "If you don't mind—"

"I'm telling you," the old sod said, but gave way; he handed over the telephone, and went back into his flat, banging the door.

"Sorry about that," Daniel said into the receiver before anything else. "Who's this?"

But it wasn't a girl: it was his father.

"Can you come home?" he said directly. He sounded remote, his voice high and strained. "There's something happened."

"What is it?" Daniel said.

"I don't want to say over the phone," his father said. "No one's hurt, it's not that, but—"

"I'll come over as soon as I can," Daniel said.

Some nonsense. He put the phone down, and almost immediately it rang again. Daniel picked it up, and this time it was a girl.

"It's me," the voice said, maddeningly. The old sod opened the door to his flat and glared at Daniel. "It's for me," Daniel mouthed, and the old sod raised his eyebrows and slammed his door. He'd got the phone, hadn't he? What more did he want?

"Pardon?" the voice said.

"I was just saying something to my neighbour," Daniel said. "Hi . . ." He trailed languidly away.

"What are you doing?" the voice said.

"Oh, nothing," Daniel said, trying to guess.

"You don't fancy a drink?" the girl said.

"Tonight, I can't," he said. He had no idea.

"It's just I haven't seen you for, what, two weeks, is it, when we went to Benjie's?" Ah, it was Kelly. "And I'd not heard from you, though I expect you've been busy."

"It's been terrible at work," Daniel said, peeling back a stretch of floral wallpaper contemplatively. "But not tonight, I can't. I've just this second said that I'll go up and see my mum and dad."

"I see," Kelly said. She was a dark girl, who had swimmer's shoulders, her hair in a sharp bob, her lips an atrocious pillar-box red and a beauty-spot painted arrogantly above her mouth, but in her eyes you could see what she was really like, and what she was really like was nineteen years old. "I don't want to get in your way."

"It's not that," Daniel said. "Don't be daft. I'd love to do something with you, you know that. But not tonight. I've nothing on Sunday."

"Sunday," Kelly said, as if being offered an insulting and inadequate substitute for what she'd rightfully demanded. Perhaps she was right: there was a whole weekend, a whole Friday and Saturday night, she was being excused from. "Well, I suppose I could—"

"Course you could," Daniel said. "I'll give you a ring, shall I?"

"Let's arrange it now," Kelly said with assumed briskness, all difficulties gone. They arranged it, and he went back upstairs. The old sod was right: he wasn't an ideal person to have living in your house. There'd been, for instance, three different girls since he'd last seen Kelly, two weeks ago, and it was fair enough, they did tend to stumble through the front door at two o'clock in the morning, knickers round their ankles, clawing at Daniel's shirt, smearing their mouths, their much-repaired lipstick, all over his face. That, you couldn't deny; and they did, most of them, phone him up afterwards.

He undressed, and, with a towel round his waist, popped downstairs for a quick bath. The woman never cleaned the tub, and a single long grey hair lay like a calligraphic squiggle on one flank. Trying not to think too much about it, he sluiced it quickly, and ran a bath, the pipes clanking in objection as if, somewhere in the house, they were being hit with spanners. He prepared himself as if he was going out for a date; he stood up in the bathtub and, with his floral soap, worked up a lather, covered himself all over with a half-inch-thick coat of suds. There was a little mirror over the sink, now clouded over with steam; in it, the cloudy reflection of his brown face. It was a tiny bathroom; he leant over and with a sudsy forefinger drew a smily face, outline, two dots for eyes, a vertical line for a nose, a little O of moueing astonishment for the mouth, and he leant back, bare and soapy, and bent his knees a little until the vague reflection of his face coincided with the drawn outline. But underneath the surprised mouth, his own reflected real one was smiling broadly, and he leant forward again, and with his palm wiped the steam from the mirror, and there was his face; dark, listening, with kindness in the eyes and a gleam of a smile, even here in this shabby hired bathroom. He greeted his own face like his best friend.

It was getting a little cold; he plunged back into the bath, splashing noisily, once, twice, three times. He pulled the plug out, and lay there as the water fell to the drains, running his fingers with pleasure through the dense black hair on his chest. He liked that feeling; he liked the clean smell of his own body, like an expensive scent, as he towelled it dry. A girl had once told him that he should live his entire life dressed in nothing but a white bath towel, about his hips. He tried to remember, bouncing up the stairs, soap in hand, who that had been, exactly.

Soon he would have a car of his own, paid for by the company, but for the moment he got around in a tatty old yellow Cortina. He'd bought it because it was wide and low, and had, if you chose, a faint echo of those big glamorous American cars. Walking out of the house in a clean white shirt and tightly pressed black trousers, he felt he deserved something more. It was one of those things, like living in a rented bedsit, that would have to be seen to when his life became what it was becoming. He drove with one hand on the wheel, the other stretched out across the back of the front passenger seat; he might have been setting off on a long Pacific journey. He had forgotten to bring a bag of washing; it would wait until the next time. As the car whinnied up the hill, he entertained himself between thoughts of girls by focussing on random houses as they came into view, and pricing them. Location; condition; size; adaptability; the office mantra went through his head, and he produced confident figures as if out loud, to a vendor. At the top of the hill the houses drew back behind massive walls, park-like estates, and here and there even a new set of gates at the bottom of their drive. Behind these mansions, the more modest estate of his parents; he slowed, signalled right, turned with a sense of almost American scale to the sweep of the Cortina's manoeuvre.

His father must have been waiting and watching for him—the car, it was true, made an unmistakable and incredible noise as it laboured up the last bit of hill. Daniel had hardly rung the bell before his father had opened the door. He didn't say anything, just made a gesture towards the sitting room. His mother wasn't there; Tim was on the stairs, just nodded and went up to his room.

"What's up?" Daniel said, but his father said nothing, just closed the door behind him. "Where's Mum?"

"She's fine," Malcolm said. "I don't know what's happening. It was an hour ago, an hour and a half. The doorbell went, and there were two policemen. They've taken your mother down to the station."

"The police?" Daniel said. "What is it?"

"I don't know," Malcolm said.

"It's probably nothing," Daniel said. "It's probably some driving thing or, I don't know, your television licence."

"I don't think so," Malcolm said.

"You didn't go down with her?" Daniel said.

"No, but I'm just going to," Malcolm said. "I wanted you to come along, though, if you don't mind."

"I don't mind," Daniel said, "but I'm sure it's nothing. There's nothing Mum could have done."

There was a pause. Malcolm got up and went to the window. Turning, he looked suddenly quite old and drawn. He had always, in the past, changed out of his suit altogether when he got home, hadn't he? But that was a work shirt, and work trousers, though he'd taken off his tie and shoes. He hadn't wanted to ask Tim to go with him to the police station. Daniel could understand that.

"I know that, really," Malcolm said. "I'm worrying about nothing probably. I wish I knew what it was about, though. You don't mind?"

"No, I don't mind," Daniel said.

As Katherine stepped out of her house, the policemen walking, discreetly, ahead and behind her, not flanking her, the neighbours appallingly watching, she felt an inevitability about the whole thing. In whatever house she had ever lived—on the other side of every front door, the solid green door of her childhood, the door with a stained-glass inset of her teenage years, and then the three front doors of her married life, the flimsy one of the terraced house, the solid Victorian one with its two windows, and finally this modern white-painted one, behind which they'd lived for how many years—she'd always felt there would one day arrive some chariot of judgement to bear her away in exactly this fashion. Perhaps some people always lived in fear of the police knocking on the door. Katherine hadn't. The judgement she had waited for and expected was a more general thing than that. It hadn't been, either, a fear of being found out in whatever she might have been doing, but really the expectation of a judgement that in the end might be a positive one, confirming that there was nothing wrong with her life. She felt she needed that from outside, and without it, she would always feel as she did: slightly ill at ease. She didn't know what form such a judgement might come in; in the event it came, as it often did in the real world, with two mineral-faced policemen.

The room she sat in had only a ribbon of reinforced window running round the top of the wall. It was not an interview room, but a sort of waiting room, rather like the rooms in hospitals where doctors tell next-of-kin of a death. She had been led in here by the policemen who had brought her in, and told someone would be along shortly. She felt almost calm. In a few minutes, a policewoman came in with a sheaf of papers, and said as if reading from a script that Katherine understood she was attending voluntarily, that she had not been charged with any crime, and then asked if she wanted to have a solicitor present at her interview. "I can arrange the duty solicitor," she said. "It won't take long."

"I think that would be a good idea," Katherine said, then asked what this was all about. She had never thought it was some traffic offence, as Malcolm had found time to say while she was leaving the house. She knew it was not. Her thoughts had gone first to Tim—who knew what he was doing in his spare time? But he had not presented an object of interest to the police, and immediately her thoughts went, more securely, to Nick. It was an unspecific insight, but it was clear to her that if her life had contained any squalor-harbouring fissure that might ultimately interest the authorities, it related somehow to Nick. She wondered how she had never seen that before.

Around her, outside the room, the life of the police station continued, a rattle of talk, of machines typing, and a man shouting unintelligibly, somewhere remotely. Katherine wondered how long Malcolm would be, though of course he would have to wait outside, she supposed. Time passed: no one came to offer her a cup of tea. It must have been nearly an hour before the door opened, and a young Asian woman came in, introducing herself as the duty solicitor. It was true: as you got older, police officers looked younger, and so did solicitors. She had expected one of the partners from Collins Rathbone and Ostler, the firm she'd worked at before her marriage, someone like that with a solid old suit and a grave manner, not a tiny woman with glossy big hair and a cheap big-shouldered suit with gold buttons, a chain-store imitation of something expensive. But she was the duty solicitor, and she began to talk. At once, Katherine was unnerved by having heard and instantly forgotten her name.

Speaking from a script again, she explained Katherine's rights in the interview room, and then—this was troubling—stressed that Katherine was not under arrest. She might well have said "yet." She had said that many times before, wearily, in her voice, throaty, with only a trace of a Sheffield accent. "I understand all that," Katherine said. The solicitor nodded, and went on with her standard explanation. She shuffled her papers, then started on the specific reason for Katherine being here: and it was, as Katherine had somehow thought, about Nick.

The solicitor finished, and asked Katherine if she had any questions at this stage. Katherine had, but she shook her head. "Right," the solicitor said, and left the room. This time it wasn't a long wait: in five minutes, a uniformed sergeant came in and led her down a corridor, confused noisy offices behind open glass doors to either side. At some point, the solicitor joined her, and they went into a different room. It, too, was bare, only four chairs about a table, and again that narrow strip of window round the top of the walls. Katherine and the solicitor sat on one side; the sergeant stood by the open door. Promptly, two men came in, in ties and rolled-up shirtsleeves, carrying papers and recording machinery. They set them down; the door was shut; they began to talk.

"When did you start working at Reynolds?"

"Was the job advertised?"

"Did you know Mr. Reynolds before you started work there?"

"Do you expect us to believe that?"

"Why would he employ a stranger?"

"We will, of course, be checking all this, you understand."

"What previous jobs have you had?"

"Do you know this man?" A photograph across the table.

"What were your duties at the flower shop?"

"Would you describe the shop as a success?"

"Did it seem to be making money, from the sale of flowers, I mean?"

"What was Mr. Reynolds's typical outlay on flowers in the course of a typical week, a month?"

"Explain your duties at the flower shop to us again."

"You must have had a loose sense of how much money the shop made from the sale of flowers in the course of a typical day."

"When you say that you had nothing to do with the shop's accounts, do you mean that it was not your responsibility, or do you seriously expect us to believe that you never even saw them?"

"How long did you work there?"

"Why did you leave?"

"Again, I want to ask you, why did you stop working there, and I would very much appreciate a full and truthful answer."

"Could you describe the shop? I mean, its storage arrangements."

"You haven't mentioned the cellar. Did you ever go down there?"

"What was stored in the cellar?"

"Did you ever see anything unusual being stored in the cellar?"

"What deliveries were made to the shop while you were there?"

"What do you know about Mr. Reynolds's financial backing? I mean, where did the money come from to open a shop in the first place, because we know perfectly well it wasn't from any kind of bank?"

"We haven't heard about any brother in New York. Can you tell us some more about him?"

"Have you ever met this supposed New York brother?"

"Have you ever spoken to him?"

"Could you tell us his name, or his address?"

"Would it surprise you very much to learn that Mr. Reynolds has no brother, in New York or anywhere else?"

"I am going to ask you again, do you recognize this man—" A photograph pushed across the table.

"What do you know about the girl who replaced you in the shop?"

"How would you describe your relationship, in general, with Mr. Reynolds?"

The interview went on for an unquantifiable time, the dull, unexcitable voices of the urban policemen treading wearily over the ground, going back, pressing at some point that interested them, producing papers, photographs, asking for years ago details with solid persistence. From time to time, the duty solicitor cut in, not sharply but judiciously marking some boundary. The interviewers accepted the point each time, and moved on. Katherine went on answering the questions, even when, as the solicitor kept saying, the point had been raised and answered. Under examination, how unmotivated ordinary life seemed; her actions deriving from nothing very concrete, and certainly not from the decision and the rational assessment of advantage the policemen seemed to believe must be there. Her ignorance, neither wilful nor feigned, but no more than a not-knowing, could not satisfy them, and she could not explain how much of her connection with Nick and his business, now revealed by the tenor of these questions as empty and criminally fraudulent, had come from the way his hair, years before, had fallen over his childishly puzzled brow. Nothing more than that; and it was not evidence.

Katherine answered all the questions calmly, and said what she knew. Only when it came to that last question, of how she would describe her relationship with Nick, did she consciously keep anything back. It was not their business; it had no conceivable relevance to their investigations. She went on answering, and in time a foolish and ugly scenario became clear from the outline of their questions.

A man had come to Sheffield, and had opened a shop. But it was not selling flowers at all. Despite appearances customers had come in, had selected blooms, had watched them being wrapped, had handed over money, which had been conscientiously placed in the till and scrupulously registered afterwards—the shop had not been selling flowers. It was doing something completely different. Nick had been taking money from somewhere else, in regular amounts—dirty money, soiled by its origins—and slipping it in underneath the respectable money involved in the sale of narcissi. He was a useful tool for someone; she had looked like—what? She had looked to him like a useful tool, too, her foolishness and clear, shameful devotion a positive benefit. She would gaze, cow-eyed, at his lovely face, but in the end never want to say, "Nick, I don't understand where this two hundred pounds has come from. We haven't sold a blade of grass since yesterday."

All the same—and this was a thought that she rather kept from her mind than hugged to it—he had, in the end, made love to her. Screwed her—done sex to her—fucked her. If she thought of that one occasion at all, she would uglify it as much as she could. He hadn't needed to do that. He must have wanted it.

It seemed incredible to her now that she hadn't wondered where the money had come from to buy the charming Ranmoor cottage with its London furniture. She had never thought that it had come from the flower shop. If she had considered the matter at all, she would have thought that Nick had a deep reservoir of his own money. Quite natural that such a person could run a shop, making no money, for years, and not take the matter remotely seriously. The question for Katherine now was not what she had believed at the time, but what the police could reasonably presume she had believed, as the time went on, the questions dully circling, setting out what Katherine could now see was the substantial truth of the situation. She wondered where Nick was at this moment; perhaps in this police station, locked up. She almost felt like asking.

There was nowhere to wait in the police station; nowhere but where everyone waited, out in front of the public desk. The walls were shiny with washable yellow-white paint, and hung with firmly advising posters about drink and drive, about drugs, about guns, about all manner of things. There was a leisurely traffic through the reception area, some drunk and noisy, more drunk and rebuked, their heads down. One defiant prostitute, her frizzy, hennaed, half-greying hair plastered down with sweat, her white leggings obscenely hoisted into the cleft of her cunt, greeted the desk sergeant by name and was greeted, sardonically, by name in return; she looked round, grinning, and found Daniel to stare at. Malcolm had never seen such people; Daniel said, when appealed to, that it was more like you had seen them, glimpsed them out of the corner of your eye when walking through town. You wouldn't want to look directly at people like that. They sat on the orange plastic chairs, bolted in rows against the walls in case someone decided to throw them at the policemen, and read the posters, over and over, passing desultory and general observations, like a conversation struck up between strangers on a bus. At one point, around half past nine, on the other side of the desk, the station filled with hundreds of policemen, appearing from nowhere, dishevelled and dusty, their tunics open and their helmets in their hands, shouting with the hoarse voices of men occupied all day in the open air. They didn't have Yorkshire accents; they had been called in from elsewhere, and had been policing a miners' picket line all day. "Where can we get something to eat round here?" one called out.

"In the canteen," the desk sergeant said, in his normal voice, breaking off from a discussion with a worried old man.

"They're in no hurry," Malcolm said, attempting cheerfulness, but Daniel wouldn't answer that. If they started wondering about how long they were going to keep her, they would start thinking about what his mother might have done, and it obviously wasn't a parking ticket.

"I should phone Tim," Malcolm said a little later.

"I'll phone him if you like," Daniel said. "Have you got any two-ps?"

"There's not a lot of point," Malcolm said. "And he won't be worrying. Do you think we should phone Jane?"

"When we know if there's anything to tell her," Daniel said. "It's probably nothing."

"Yes," Malcolm said desolately.

But the time went on, and they went on reading the posters; so many useful telephone numbers.

It was late when the Austin Allegro drew into the driveway. Across the way, a light in the front room of a house snapped off sharply, so as not to reveal the woman standing up and peering out. Katherine—you could see how the story would run—had been carried off in a Black Maria, and they wanted to see if she was coming back tonight. There had been no question about one thing. Daniel had come home with them, riding in the back as if he were a child again. No one had mentioned dropping him off in Crookes and he hadn't thought of it until they were halfway up the Manchester Road. Anyway, the car was still in Rayfield Avenue.

Certainly, it had always been his job to jump out smartly to open the garage door, one of his household tasks, like gravy-making. But tonight it was his mother who made a point of getting out. She had thought, evidently, during the long, silent exchanges of their drive home, of the neighbours' watchfulness. She fumbled with the key at the lock, lit by the headlight beam, and with a wrench lifted it up over her head. She stood aside to let Malcolm drive in, and Daniel caught an unguarded glimpse of her face, as a stranger might see it. The faces of his parents were surely just as they had always been, ever since he had been able to identify them, they had grown no older, but now he saw Katherine's face as the worn generic face of a middle-aged woman, its lines full of some unknowable care, and only the eyes were definitely those of his mother. She had found time to change not only her shoes but all her clothes. She was wearing the little jacket and, underneath it, exactly that sort of piecrust pussy-bow-collared blouse Mrs. Thatcher so liked to wear on the television, exactly the same shade of baby shit as the Austin Allegro, now a bit wilting at the end of this long guilt-strewn evening.

His father leant over to lock the passenger door before getting out and locking his own. Katherine was standing there, her arms upraised on the garage door, her back to the street. She seemed tall; but she had her high-heeled shoes on. Malcolm looked at her, a volunteering expression in his eyes.

"I think," Katherine said, swallowing as she spoke, "I might go for a walk before bedtime. I feel—" she lowered her voice as if she could be overheard "—all wound up, if you know—"

Daniel looked at his watch. He had no idea what time it was, and it was well after eleven. But as if he'd made a rational objection with the gesture, Malcolm seized Daniel's forearm and held it. She pulled the garage door down, and swiftly walked away. Above, the snake-hiss of a curtain opening, a slash of light in the upper floor. Tim was watching her go. Katherine clicked away down the street; her increasing speed made it seem as if the clicking was growing louder the further away from them she got.

In a moment, the two of them went inside. Unseen by anyone, Tim drew his curtain again, and in ten minutes the light in his bedroom went out.

Katherine started walking at an ordinary pace, hardly knowing where she should go—she walked so seldom, unless it was to the postbox at the corner of the road. But she reached the corner and did not turn right, following the greasy line of yellow lights, but left, off the road, on to the crags. Here, at the very edge of the city, was the big old house behind its double gateposts. An old woman lived there, a posh old woman whose family had owned it for years, perhaps for ever, perhaps had built it. Katherine had invited her to a party once; she'd accepted, then written a kind, regretful note of apology, as if she'd remembered she'd ignored the estate growing up round her big square

sandstone house on the edge of the moor, and couldn't start acknowledging it now. Katherine went past, on to the stony irregular path,
walking more quickly as she went, and to her surprise the windows on
the moor side of the house were lit up, curtainless, empty of people
observed or observing, like a lighthouse to a broad dark sea.

She went on, almost trotting, into the darkness of the path, her
ankles bending impossibly from step to step. The light cast by the big
house faded after a couple of hundred yards. On the right, a steep rise
of hillside grazing where sheep sometimes wandered, their flanks
striped with a slash of blue or green. To the right, a sharp fall of rocks,
almost a fifteen-foot cliff. She could see neither, only down below the
glowing sequence of street-lights masking the road. It was the Manchester road, just losing its name and turning into the pass over the
Pennines. Katherine went fast, her breath catching. She never walked
down here, hadn't since the children were old enough not to want her
company when they explored or escaped. She hadn't missed those
maternal outings, and she knew they'd all come here on their own.
Daniel with girls, Jane to dream, Tim to bury himself in a crevice and
hide, she guessed. She couldn't be sure of the path—her feet wouldn't
carry her unthinkingly over the rubble-strewn way, but she hurried on.
It hardly mattered, what would become of her, and her thoughts ran,
not on Nick or even on her husband and children, still less on that specific chain of circumstance, but on all that, transformed and melting
into a black cloud of dread. It was bigger and more horrible than the
mere idea of public prosecution, even prison; bigger even than the
notion of being found out and having to account, as she had tried so
haplessly to do in that thin-windowed interview room, for a broad
stretch of her own behaviour. It was just a weight, a blanket of dread
spreading out to the dark horizon and covering half the starless sky,
like the embroidered ownerless moors, with great strata sleeping deep
beneath it.

Her right foot went through something, a gap between two rocks.
She pulled, but her heel was caught fast. She tugged again, letting out
a little cry, and all at once she felt the narrow heel snap. Even here, the
immediate thought was of cost. They were new shoes; that was why
she'd put them on. She bent down, gasping, and felt. It had snapped off
cleanly, leaving her only the sole to walk on, and though she rummaged around in the loose detached fragments of the wild earth, she
could not find the heel. For a moment Katherine paused, scrabbling
for breath—she had been almost running—and without stopping to

debate her immediate thought, walked directly to the right, where the precipice must be. That was the best thing to do.

But she fell, not a bone-breaking ten yards, but directly forward, on to grass and heather. All at once the exact image of the lower crags in daylight came to her. Sideways in her vision, in the garden of the big house, a new light appeared. It was like a torchlight in the garden, moving about with pendulum regularity, a little hand-held light, a fleck like a glow-worm. It could have moved, pointed in her direction and shown her fallen, not tragically, but absurdly flat on her face in a damp, cold field. There was only a drop at the very beginning of the path. After that, the fields rose up to meet it. She lay, awkwardly twisted, bruised but no more than uncomfortable, and looked at her ridiculous position. After all, it seemed as if she hadn't wanted to fling herself off a cliff at all. She hadn't wanted to die, but rather, for once in her life, to fall over like a risible idiot, unwatched. Had she ever, since she was a girl, fallen in such a way? With this fall, her shoe broken, lying helpless like an overturned beetle, Katherine felt that the worst had now happened to her, happened in a fall, a second. Nick, the police, authority could peer at her, and do their worst. But she didn't know what grey position in this new configuration of inspectors was occupied by Malcolm. She lay there until the damp and prickle of the undergrowth took the place of all other thoughts and sensations.

The shoes were unbearable, and she carried them one in each hand, all the way home. By the time she let herself quietly in, her tights were worn through at the heel and under the balls of her feet. Her feet felt as if she had been a day walking over cheese graters. She paused at the kitchen and switched its light on. In the dark house, the strip-lighting had the same metallic sour quality of a glass of water drunk on waking at four in the morning. Noiselessly, she dropped the new shoes, one broken, one whole, into the kitchen bin on top of a heap of potato peelings. It seemed so long since her last domestic task, and Tim had left the washing up from dinner time just where it had been left, in the sink.

A voice from upstairs, frail and sleepy, calling in the dark: "Is that you, Katherine?"

"Yes," she said, not raising her voice. "I just felt like some air."

The door to their bedroom opened, rustling against the thick pile of the fitted carpet. Presently, a thin figure, slightly hunched, pulling the skirts of his dressing-gown to him, coagulated at the top of the stairs looking down like a dark spook on the landing.

"You've been a time," Malcolm said, in his normal, quiet voice.

"I wanted some air," Katherine said. "Can I bring you anything up?" She hitched up her skirt, and in a broad gesture, hooked her thumbs under the waist of her tights, pulling them off with their ruined heels. They crackled over her legs; she'd shaved them last a week ago. She screwed them up into a ball and threw them at the kitchen bin.

"What happened to your shoes?" Malcolm said, but mildly, as if reminding her of something she might for very good reason have forgotten or mislaid. "And what—"

But that was evidently to hold her too much to account, and he stopped, leaving Katherine to survey her torn skirt, with a thick gash of mud and crushed grass down her left hip, where she'd fallen and slid.

"I don't know," Katherine said, but it sounded stupid. "I thought I'd walk down the path—you know, what the kids call the lower crags—"

"In the pitch dark?" Malcolm said.

"Well, I broke the heel of my shoe," Katherine said reasonably. "In the dark. And I fell over, as you see. So you're right, it wasn't a good idea."

By now they were in their bedroom. Katherine handed over the unrequested second glass of water she'd brought up, as she did every night, one on each side of the bed, on his bedside table, on hers. Malcolm in his old pyjamas with the drawstring waist and his woollen tartan dressing-gown; it was the same evidently comforting one, much washed and faded in its now soft fog of colours, running into each other, that she'd bought for him a Christmas soon after they'd married. He looked so like an aggrieved big-eyed child, one ill with some harsh wasting disease rendering him old before his time. He spoke, too, with the sort of grievance a child might have.

"Now, Katherine, what's all this about—"

Or more accurately, a child trying his best to be terribly adult. It infuriated her, instantly.

"Is that how you speak to customers at the building society? The bad ones?"

"I don't know what you're talking about."

"The ones who've fallen behind with their payments?"

"Katherine, there's really not a lot of point—"

"Do you think there's a single woman in the world would put up with being spoken to like that? *Malcolm?*"

"I don't mean to put your back up," Malcolm said, blinking in his most owl-like way. "I know you've had a shock, an unpleasant experience—"

Katherine almost delighted in that, though her face remained perfectly solemn. He hadn't expected her to throw up so solid a wall to block the customary allusions and retreats of their customary way of speaking to each other, the ways in which he always tried to head off her capacity for the blunt statement of a situation by the shy exhibition of a patch of tender skin. Nothing was to be gained by not speaking plainly, she felt, about their situation if not her particular one, and she saw her way forward quite clearly.

"I'm worrying about you," Malcolm said in the end. "And about how you—I don't know—about how this has all come about. It must be—" he said, hanging on in case she should ask where, exactly, he thought the blame lay "—it must be some stupid mistake, a silly misunderstanding."

"That would be the *easiest* thing," Katherine said. She remained standing, taking off her clasp earrings. It was a surprise that they were both still there. The familiar physical release, at the end of a long day, was like an exhalation.

"Katherine," Malcolm said. "I don't understand why you're talking to me like this. Anyone would think it was my fault you seem to be in trouble with the police."

"That's really not fair," Katherine said, lowering her voice. "And not accurate. I'm not 'in trouble with the police.' I've done nothing wrong."

"It's Nick, I know," Malcolm said. "But what did he get you involved in, that's what I'd like to know."

"I see," Katherine said. "So you and Daniel, you've been puzzling it all out between you—"

"No," Malcolm said quizzically. "It's more, really, that you came out and said, 'It's Nick.' "

Had she?

"I didn't know what I was saying."

"Do you now?"

Katherine sat down—not next to Malcolm, on his side of the bed, but in the armchair they'd always had in the bedroom, Lord knew why. Perhaps no one had ever sat in it before, with its hard red chintz and its narrow hipless seat. But Katherine sat in it now. She was quite calm, not hysterical, as Malcolm seemed to think—he was treating her gently, as a woman who couldn't remember what he'd said, one who had no grasp of the situation. Clarity was best and, actually, clarity was what she had to spare. She had walked out into the unlit country to clear her head, and her head was now quite clear.

"What's that noise?" she said.

Malcolm cocked his head; in a moment the same rasping sound came again. Of course, she knew it, she didn't know why it had seemed so unfamiliar. "It's Daniel snoring," he said. "He must have left his bedroom door open."

"I'd got used to not hearing it at night," she said. "I'd practically forgotten what a noise he makes. Why did he come home with us?"

"He left his car," Malcolm said. "I suppose he thought he might as well stay overnight, drive in tomorrow."

"He'll have to be up early in the morning," Katherine said. "Is there still an alarm clock in there anywhere?"

"Oh, I'll wake him up," Malcolm said. "I'll even give him a lift to work, don't worry."

"I thought you said he'd got his car."

"Yes," Malcolm said. "That's right, he's got his car. I don't know what I was saying. Of course he's got his car."

"The best thing," Katherine said. "The best thing all round is if we get divorced."

The curtains were drawn, the room small and full of stuff; on the floor, a pile of books had been kicked over and tangled with his abandoned shoes. There was a chaos in the room that never used to be there; they'd always been good, the pair of them, about putting things away, dirty clothes in the bedroom laundry basket or folding them neatly on the back of the armchair. Somehow, the room wasn't like that now; it was full of detritus. There'd been an effort recently: she'd put a little vase of chrysanthemums on the bedside table, on his side, a week ago. They were starting to brown and wilt; a few curled-up petals, like monkey fingers, lay on top of his book. Malcolm got up and, with his bare foot, poked aside his shirt from where he'd dropped and left it, a gesture of disgust. He went to the window, pulled the curtain aside a little, looked out. There was nothing out there; he looked at the silence.

"You're not straight in your mind," he said after a while.

"Stop saying that," she said, gripping the arms of the chair. "I'm perfectly straight in my mind. The best thing all round is if we decide to get divorced."

"I don't understand what you're saying," Malcolm said, coming back. He raised his hands; he might have been about to hold her face in them.

"I'm saying," Katherine said, "it's best all round if we get divorced. I'll move out in the morning. I won't need much stuff, it'll go in a suitcase, and I'll find a hotel first, and then a bedsit, maybe like the one Daniel lives in, and—and—"

Her plans ran out. She shook her head, as if to shake some notions loose into speech.

"Just go to sleep," he said, sitting down on the bed and pulling the cover over his knees. "It'll all seem different in the morning." But he didn't get into bed; he stayed there in a halfway position, waiting for the rest of the conversation.

"No, it won't," she said savagely. "Whatever it seems like, it'll all be the same in the morning. Don't speak about it, don't look at it, don't think about it—it's always there, whatever you do. I don't know how you can—"

Her speech was failing her now, perhaps in exhaustion, like a garaged car on a frosty morning.

"You want to speak about it?" he said levelly. "Katherine, I'm telling you, you've had a shock. Don't say anything you won't want said in the morning, because you don't really mean it. Whatever it is."

"But you've said it now," Katherine said, and then, parodically, "whatever it is. You've said yourself there's something I won't want said in the morning. You might as well come out with it now."

"I don't know what you're talking about. I don't want to know."

"Yes, you do."

Outside, remotely in the night, perhaps as far down as the Manchester Road but carrying across the outdoor open silence of the suburban night, there was a piercing remote noise, the yowl of a siren. Katherine, convulsively, got up out of the chair and went to the window, a bone cracking in her bare ankles as she went. She pulled the curtains tighter shut, held them with her fists.

"They wouldn't put the sirens on for you," Malcolm said. "Anyway, they're done with you tonight, they said."

"I don't know how you can—" Katherine said. "You've no idea, what it was like in there."

"I can imagine," Malcolm said. "And you're right, I know. I just don't want to know."

"You don't know anything," Katherine said. It was the worst thing she could have said to her husband, worse than any confession, a frank statement of unretractable contempt.

"I didn't think I did," Malcolm said, holding the bedclothes tight to him. "Till a couple of weeks ago."

"A couple of weeks ago?" Katherine said.

"Yes," Malcolm said. "He told me then."

"He?"

"Listen," Malcolm said, getting up with a convulsive gesture, "just let me tell you, and then, you know, everything's been said, like you want. I was out in the garden, I was pruning the abutilons, I remember because it said in the *Telegraph* gardening column that it was this weekend you ought to be pruning shrubs back, and I thought, That's funny, shows I'm on top of things because that was one of the things I'd definitely decided to do that weekend, trim back the abutilons—"

"Oh, for heaven's sake, Malcolm," Katherine said. "Shut up about the shrubbery. I can't bear it. It's nothing to do with the abutilons."

"Katherine," Malcolm said, not raising his voice. "Just sit down and let me tell the story in my own way. And if abutilons come into it, then they come into it. There's not everything in my head that's all about you. Some of it's abutilons, and some of it's stuff which I go out into the garden and do to get you out of my head, and the kids, and everything that sometimes makes me want to think about something else entirely for an hour or two. Right? It was still quite cold out there—I had my gloves on—so it was strange when Tim came out. He watched me for a while. I ignored him. Actually, I probably went out so I didn't have to talk to him, I just couldn't face it. And then he said, 'I don't know how you keep it up,' or something he'd been thinking about saying, something horrible. I pretended I thought he was being interested, so I started saying that with a garden you had to keep it up, just a little attention now and again, going round doing a bit of weeding, a bit of pruning, a bit of planting, and the plants'd look after themselves, or it seemed like it. You had to keep it up.

"I probably gave him a bit of a speech about gardens, and he just listened for a while, and then he smiled and said, 'I wasn't talking about shrubbery,' exactly that, exactly the thing you've just said. I don't know where you get 'shrubbery' from but I know where he got it from, it's just what you say when I'm out in the garden. Teaching your children contempt for their father, that's a nice thing for you to do. Wait a second, I'm not done. 'That's a shame,' I say to Tim. 'It might do you good to take a bit of interest in something.' And I thought he was going to start on the urban proletariat again, that, you know, there were more important things than hobbies, as he calls them, there's the revolution, blah blah. It doesn't take a lot to set him off, you know as well as I do. But he didn't, he just said, 'I wasn't talking about gardening. I was talking about your wife.' 'Your mother,' I said. 'I don't know,' he said, 'how you can take an interest in something and pretend nothing wrong when your wife's behaving like she behaves.' "

"Oh, my God," Katherine said. "What on earth—"

"No, there's more," Malcolm said. His voice was steady, and now he was almost in Katherine's face. "I just looked at him, and I sort of knew what he was going to say, and I think I said to him what I just said to you, that there's things that are best if no one says them even if everyone knows them, that if you don't say them—no, I didn't say this, but this is what I think—that if you don't say something it can't become important, but if you say it everyone's ever after got to walk round it like a pile of rocks in the living room, and it might just go away. I thought it had gone away. I thought it really had. I thought I'd ignored it and you'd stopped it, whatever it was, and we were getting on all right again. We've been fine, the last three or four years, better than ever, there's no reason—"

"It's Nick, isn't it?" Katherine said.

"There's no harm in saying it," Malcolm said. She hadn't surprised him. He'd known one of them, soon, was going to say exactly that, and he swept on. "Or no more harm now, I suppose. That's what he said. He said it wasn't recent information, it was something he'd seen years ago. He said he'd been going down through Broomhill, what, six, seven years ago, he'd only be a little boy, and he looked in through the window of the flower shop to see if you were there. And, I suppose, to get a lift home—I don't know what he was doing in Broomhill, coming back from town in the school holidays or something. But he looked in through the window and, he said, 'You know what I saw? I saw your wife with her arms round that man she used to work for, and they were kissing.' "

"That's not true," Katherine said.

"Oh, come off it," Malcolm said.

"No, I'm completely serious, it's not true, it can't be true," she said. She was incredulous that something like the truth should be represented by something so false. Tim had never seen anything of the sort, and it was ridiculous to pretend that he had. Never in her life had she embraced and certainly she had never kissed Nick in the flower shop, in the window of the shop where anyone passing, anyone in Broomhill, could have seen them. He had just made it up. "I've never kissed Nick in the flower shop, I've never put my arms round him. He can't have seen that because it didn't happen there."

Malcolm looked at her gravely. "I wish you hadn't said that," he said. "There's been a point, I think you know the point, where we could just ignore it and the whole thing would come to an end, though I wouldn't know when it came to an end, and then you'd stop thinking about it and so would I. And it would fade away in time without anyone ever talking about it. But you just said, 'It didn't happen there.' "

She had heard herself saying, "It didn't happen there," but the time was too late to hold back confessions. Malcolm, too, was going to do it all for her. It was unfair of him to say that it was her fault it was coming out now.

"I thought it was all over," Malcolm said.

"It is, it was, a long time back, it was hardly ever anything, it never started, it was a mistake, it's—"

"I don't know why you want a divorce," Malcolm said. "If it's all so very much over and finished. I don't know why you wouldn't first want to forget all about it, or if that's not possible because your husband's found out, why you wouldn't first ask him if he can forgive you, because that seems like the sensible thing to do in the circumstances."

That dropped like a stone. It was true: she didn't want a divorce now. It seemed extraordinary that she had wanted a divorce only so that she wouldn't have to talk, as a married woman, about the short affair she had had with Nick. The one occasion. It seemed a high price to pay so that she wouldn't have to listen to anything he said in response, but she had said it, and had said it with a conviction that things were clear in her head. Now that, it seemed, they were about to have that conversation, her wishes had changed; her wishes, which had always been for convenience above all.

"You see, the thing is," Malcolm said—and it was exactly the voice in which, surely, he started raising objections to someone applying for credit when holes in their application had become apparent, "I thought we'd been through all that. I thought it was all over and nothing had come of it, and, really, I still think I was right. When you said first, 'I want to go and get a job,' I thought, Well, we don't need the extra money, though extra money is always nice, but I'm not going to be selfish, I'm going to think about you. And maybe that was right. I know it can't have been much of a life for you, being at home all day, looking after the kids, shopping, cleaning, tidying, cooking dinner, it would wear anyone down. And I know you used to like going to work—you used to go on about it, but I know you enjoyed working in the school, having a position of responsibility. You're an educated woman, you're not stupid. It's not like Alice over the road who's never worked and never missed it.

"So I thought, Well, maybe that's a good idea, though to be honest I didn't really like the idea of the flower shop, and just you and Nick working there. I don't know why. And then you started coming home and—well, I tell you what. When you used to work in that school, you'd come home and there'd be stories about what the headmaster'd said or what the headmaster's wife'd done, or about that woman you used to work with, what she'd lost or what some boy had said to you, some funny story or an interesting story or something like that. I could see that when you stopped work, you missed that, because you weren't that good at telling funny stories about what the kids had said or done today, mostly because, well, they're my kids and I love them, even Tim, but they aren't that interesting when they're so small. I never thought that and I know you didn't. So I sent you out to work—"

"You didn't send me out anywhere," Katherine said. Her anger at the way Malcolm was putting things had been growing. "I went out and got a job and told you about it afterwards. And you didn't let me go, either."

"Well, however you want to put it," Malcolm said.

"Yes," Katherine said. "However I want to put it. I won't let you put things for me. That's how it was. I'm not yours to let go or keep in, I did what I wanted to do."

"But you didn't ask me," Malcolm said. "You didn't even ask me."

"I know what you'd have said," Katherine said. "You never ask me about—Listen, do you think I've never wanted to move house, move to a nicer house, a bigger one? You know I've always wanted a big old house and we could afford one—we could move to Ranmoor if we wanted to. But we never could, because this is where your garden is, and it's where you want to live, and it doesn't matter."

She caught a terrible glimpse of herself in the long mirror inside the wardrobe door, hanging open; her hair anyhow, mad and even drunk-seeming; there was a yellow streak of earth on her face, and her clothes—her beige blouse with its frills and furbelows torn to the elbow, her skirt thick with mud. Barelegged, barefoot, she seemed like a desperately refugee presence in her own bedroom.

"Katherine," Malcolm said, "I don't know what you're talking about. We were talking about you working at the flower shop, and whether you want a divorce, and now we're talking about whether we should move to Ranmoor or not. I can't keep up with you."

"All right," Katherine said. "Tell me everything about when I was working at the flower shop. You know all about it, don't you?"

"Yes, I do," Malcolm said. "I'll tell you something, I know what it's like when your wife comes home every day and she talks about her boss, how marvellous he is, how fantastic, how she goes weak inside whenever he speaks to her—"

"That's not fair, it's not—"

"—and the whole time listening to this, night after night, and knowing that your wife's having an affair with someone and she can't stop herself talking about her boyfriend, her fancy man, her lover, whatever you called it to yourself in your mind—"

"That's not true, I never, ever—"

"Oh, come on," Malcolm said. "You must think I'm stupid. Going on like that? And in front of the children? If you didn't, then don't tell me you didn't want to, and tried your hardest to make it happen. Tell me it never happened, not once, nothing, not even a little kiss and a cuddle in the back after closing time, and then we'll forget about it."

She said nothing. She had been about to say, with perfect truth, "I never had an affair with Nick," but the way he had put it, she could not answer and not tell a lie. She had not thought his standard of the unacceptable would be set so low when it came to voicing the situation. There was a heavy click from the bedside table; the digital alarm clock's black and white numbers had flicked over. It was two o'clock. Suddenly she felt appallingly tired; she felt as though this conversation could now be put off until tomorrow, until never.

"You see?" Malcolm said. "You see? You can't. And the thing is that I'd stopped thinking about it, I'd stopped torturing myself over it, thinking about how humiliating the whole thing was and what it was going to be like when, eventually, you actually said to me, 'I want a divorce.' It wasn't going to be in these circumstances. It's almost like I'd forgiven you. I don't know what happened, and I'm not going to ask, and I don't want to know, but you just stopped going on about it, and then you said, I know, 'I don't want to work there any more.' I thought the whole thing was over."

"What did you say to Tim?" Katherine said, after a long silence. She could not look at him. She could feel him staring heavily at her. It seemed so unfair that it was up to her to make the situation right again, and what she had proposed should be rejected so sharply. There was no question of their getting divorced, she could see that.

"What do you think? What would anyone say? I told him it was a load of rubbish, that you'd never do anything like that, and I told him to shut up and never tell anyone what he said he'd seen."

"He hadn't seen anything," Katherine said. "He was making it up, the whole thing. He had to have been. Believe you me, he had to have been."

"I believe you," Malcolm said.

"I don't know what we've done," Katherine said, "to bring up a child like that. I hate him."

"Like what?" Malcolm said. You could say that his eyes were blazing, but eyes could not blaze. It was perhaps only a small physiological change, a rush of liquid from the tear ducts, made them shine brilliantly, angrily. "A liar, you mean?"

She left that.

"I've been quite successful in dealing with the whole thing," Malcolm said. "Even after that, I never thought I'd have to talk to you about it. I thought it was all ancient history. But now what's going to happen? Do you have any idea what's going to happen?"

"I don't know," Katherine said. "Malcolm, I'm exhausted, I can't talk any more, I can't—"

"All right, I'll tell you what's going to happen, and then you can go to bed," Malcolm said. "First off, we're not getting divorced. Second, I'm going to stand by you all through this, whatever it is, because I still don't understand and you still haven't told me, because whatever Nick's done, I don't believe you knew anything about it and I don't believe you knew you were doing anything wrong, whatever it is. But he's a stupid man, a weak man. He'd never have done anything if you'd not made him do it, I mean the two of you, not whatever it is the police are after him for, and I just want you to accept that. And the last thing is, whatever it was between the two of you, I don't want anyone else to know about it, ever, and I don't want the children saying anything like that. I can stand it, knowing that my wife once went to bed with someone else, so long as nobody else ever knows, and he's a bad person, but I don't believe he's the sort of person who would go round boasting about it, whatever it was that happened. Tell me it doesn't make any sense, but I can cope with being in that position so long as I'm the only one who knows I'm in that position. Let me keep a bit of dignity here."

"Malcolm, everything you think is completely wrong," Katherine said. "Or nearly everything."

"No, it's not," Malcolm said. "I know it's not. It's not like I set a private detective on you, but I know all the same. Don't ask me why. Now I'm going to bed."

He got into bed and turned his face to the wall, away from her side. All her life, Katherine had had a bedtime routine, and now she did it, muddy and torn, bruised and untended as she was. She took off her mud-encrusted skirt, her shredded slip, her torn and earth-painted blouse. In her bra and knickers, she sat down at the dressing-table. She took a puff of cotton wool from a transparent plastic tube, and opened a pot of cold cream. It seemed appalling to her that these familiar things had lain there, unused, since her life had changed so much, and it was only twelve, eighteen hours. There was no makeup to remove: her routine of creamy foundation, blusher, blue eyeshadow, lipstick, everything had gone, as if wiped clean by the moors and the crags. Only her mascara remained, though smeared and spread across her face. She must have cried at some point, and the smutty coal of its deposits had run; tearproof it was called, but its manufacturers had not thought of the sort of weeping that had, it seemed, come across Katherine at some point in the evening, whether in the police station, on the moors, in her own bedroom. Across her face, a splat of earth; in the last few months, Katherine had stopped using the scarlet blusher she'd always used, had followed a piece of unwilling extracted advice from Alice, the genuine blush spreading underneath Alice's applied one, and changed to bronze. It was the same colour; but this was the same earth that had got everywhere. She cleaned herself with the cold cream, the same calm, circular movements she'd always used, and even found herself, as she always did, faintly humming. Malcolm lay with his face to the wall, his knees drawn up underneath him and a pillow hugged to his stomach, not pretending to sleep but in the position of unconsciousness. Her nightie was on the back of the dressing-table mirror, and she dropped it over her head, unhooking her bra underneath it, dropping it to the floor, but she kept her knickers on. She switched off the light, and got into bed, her back to Malcolm's, in the same spooned position. "Goodnight," she said, but he didn't reply. "I said, goodnight," she said, more tetchily, and he grunted. She had no idea why she had thought, at the end of all that, they might have sex.

They lay there together, facing different walls, and listened to the faint, throaty roaring of Daniel's sleep. It was like the whole house breathing, in and out.

The next morning, she lay in bed, unmoving, until Malcolm got up, dressed and left. She listened to him and Daniel moving about downstairs, chatting, the metal twang of the toaster popping up twice, the tiny rumble and click of the kettle coming to its climax. They seemed to be talking quite naturally—you couldn't hear the words, but the noise of their voices was unconstrained. At one point Daniel laughed. They left together, and from outside Katherine heard, first, Daniel's crappy car, then the Austin Allegro starting up and driving off. She hadn't said anything to either of them, and Malcolm hadn't said anything to her, taking her stillness for sleep. And, God knows, she was tired.

Eventually she washed, dressed and came downstairs. Tim was in the kitchen with a plastic Gateway bag and a pile of books, making himself a sandwich in a ham-fisted way, poking at it disgustedly. He was dressed, but barefoot, and didn't turn round when Katherine came in.

"I hope we didn't wake you up when we came in," she said politely.

He said nothing for a moment, but put down his knife, staring out of the window. "I heard you," he said eventually.

"I'm sorry," Katherine said. "It was a bit of a—"

"I heard what you and my dad were saying," he said. He turned round; his face was congealed with rage.

"It's not—" Katherine began to say, but all at once he hit her; swinging ineptly with his right arm stiff, his hand open. She flinched, but he caught her, not hard, on the cheekbone, making her give out a small cry, more like a breath.

"I know what I think," he said, his voice choking with what could only be emotion, and turned back to stuffing his things into his plastic bag. She went into the sitting room, slamming the door. She had never smacked the children; she'd thought it would teach them habits of violence. And when he left in a few minutes, she went to examine herself in the cloakroom mirror. If he had hurt her, she could not distinguish that bruise from the other bruises and scratches of the night before, or tell that one sting apart from all the others.

. . .

There was a house in Rayfield Avenue that excited comment. Most people who drove or walked through the estate either lived there, or were visiting someone there, or were perhaps thinking of moving there and were having a look at the houses on a Sunday afternoon. It wasn't a short-cut to anywhere, so anyone who drove or walked up the road tended to look carefully at the houses. It was a well-kept estate; the gardens were at worst bleakly tidy, and at best, like the Glovers', elaborate witnesses to a keen hobby. Quite a few had had their pristine irregularity added to with extensions and conversions, extra bedrooms and side conservatories making the asymmetrical houses still more saleable. The fronts were painted every three to five years, the window frames and front doors in bright white and the garage doors, to demonstrate individuality, in a variety of vivid shades; Mrs. Arbuthnot had just had hers done again in imperial purple after a few years of lime green, but something had gone wrong, and the paint was bubbling all over like bubonic plague. "I could kill that painter and decorator," she kept saying, "and he says it'll all be all right in a month or so, having pocketed my money in the meantime."

It was a tidy, respectable place, but one house excited comment. It was the Warners'. There, in the front, the lawn grew unchecked over the pathway, and the asphalt in the driveway had cracked as weeds forced their way through. The doors and windows hadn't been attended to in years, and the paint peeled off in long strips, showing the already rotting wood underneath. In the porch, addressed and unaddressed mail formed chaotic drifts; outside, half a dozen unwashed milk bottles, half full of rain and antique mould had been sitting for weeks—the milkman wouldn't collect them, and neither Warner nor his son was likely to take them back inside to wash them. It was generally thought that sooner or later someone—"Probably me," at least half a dozen civic-minded people, busybodies really, from different addresses tended to think—would take pity, go up the drive, pick up the milk bottles and wash them themselves. It couldn't be hygienic, leaving them mouldering and festering away like that, week on week.

Pity was what most people felt about the Warners' house. In any other circumstances, someone would have had a word with the owner, pointed out that the shabbiness of the house might affect the value of the houses to either side, and that the weeds flourishing in the garden, both front and back, were no respecters of fences. Of course, nobody said any of this since Karen Warner had died of a sad, fast liver business, even though it was three years and more before. It wasn't to be expected that Kenneth Warner would cope—not because he was bereaved but because he was a man; the allowance for incompetence spread happily even into masculine areas of ability, such as house and garden. Offers of help had been made, but were not renewed when, in practice, Kenneth Warner had taken advantage, pointing out to Caroline that he didn't care for lamb stew twice in one week, and it was eating heavy food like that that had made her put on so much weight, which wasn't polite or grateful in the slightest degree, and in fact it had been moussaka, not "lamb stew," and her with a ten-, an eight- and a five-year-old to think about too, probably the cause of her putting on weight in the first place.

Complaint against Kenneth was, all the same, muted and tentatively voiced; it was a sad situation he'd found himself in. Resentment tended to come out more vivaciously when the subject turned to John Warner, nearly thirty and never left home, never had a job for more than six months, a constant worry to his poor mother even on her deathbed, and showing no signs of doing anything with his life other than lie on the sofa and hang around in pubs and nightclubs.

"Two men living together," Anthea Arbuthnot often said. But in fact the house, inside, was neat to the point of bleakness, though worn and frayed about the edges. They neither of them cooked very much—you could get quite good lasagne from Marks & Spencer these days—and it had really only been Karen who had taken an interest in things like ornaments and cushions and vases. The vases went unfilled, and were dusty as the ornaments on their shelves. Kenneth hardly saw them any more: the pretty floral bowl, a stylish 1920s figurine of a dancer, skirts in her hands and her hands raised up, something Karen had always thought might be worth something. They all sat on a shelf and were just "the ornaments." The pictures were always cocked at a quizzical angle, and each wore a disapproving, elderly single eyebrow of dust. The carriage clock on the mantelpiece was stuck at quarter past three—the battery had run out more than a year ago, and nobody had got round to replacing it. There was always at least one lightbulb gone somewhere in the house—at the moment the one on the landing—and elsewhere areas of peculiar dusty dimness, because both Kenneth and John tended to put up with intermittent darkness for three or four weeks before replacing the bulb, and then usually with the wrong or a randomly selected wattage. There had been cushions in the living room, and when Karen was alive they were always neatly posed in the corners of the settee, one at a rakish angle on each armchair. For a while they had a habit of migrating together, ending up in a squashed pile of four at one end only of the settee, and then one day Kenneth picked one up and saw how stained and smelly it was, its tassels now intermittent and even chewed, as if by a dog. John slept with his head on them in the afternoons, with the television on. So he threw them out and hadn't replaced them. Cushions were things women liked, really.

They were coping all right. Kenneth had mastered ironing and washing—it wasn't hard, after all—and presented a decent face in the office and even at weekends. They were clean, but not much more than that. Kenneth saw now what women brought to a house; he wouldn't have minded it; he didn't know how to do it. In a moment towards the end, when Karen had taken to saying the sorts of things she'd never in her life come near to saying, she'd said, "Make sure John sticks to things, makes something out of himself," and then, horribly, unforgettably, "I think you'd be best off if you got married again afterwards." He couldn't say anything to that; he didn't even want to. It wasn't to do with cherishing anyone's memory. It was more to do with a sense of decency.

When he came in, John was standing in the kitchen holding what looked like a big yogurt pot in one hand and a fork in the other. It was steaming, and John was blowing at it. He was wearing a pair of tight drainpipes, the button undone, his stomach bulging through a gap in his shirt buttons.

"I don't know how you can eat that stuff," Kenneth said, putting his briefcase down.

"It's all right," John said. "It's convenient, at any rate."

"You ought to eat some vegetables," he said.

"There's vegetables in this. It's mushroom flavour."

Kenneth grunted. John got on with puffing at forkfuls of noodles.

"I went for a walk," John said, between mouthfuls, "and then I came back and read the paper and a bit of a book, then I watched a film this afternoon."

"Pardon?" Kenneth said.

"You were going to ask me what I'd done today," John said.

"Doesn't seem like very much," Kenneth said. "And I don't even believe you went out for a walk. What was the film?"

"*Bringing Up Baby*," John said. "I've seen it before, though, more than once."

"Yes, I know that," Kenneth said, kicking off his shoes without untying the shoelaces. Next time he might well buy a pair of slip-ons. They were quite smart, the slip-ons they made these days. He went into the sitting room. On the television screen, there was the cast list of an old movie—*Bringing Up Baby*, presumably—paused on the video. A thick white blazon cut across the screen, hiccuping up and down.

"I've told you before, don't do that," Kenneth said. "How long's that been there?"

"What?" John said, through a mouthful, wandering through, his holed socks dragging baggily loose. "I wanted to see who was playing the friend, I couldn't place her and they go past so fast you can never see."

"It's bad for the tape to leave it like that," Kenneth said. "It'll break next time you play it and probably ruin the machine. That's an expensive machine, you know. And," he said, remembering what he always forgot, to try to look at things from John's point of view, however stupid it might seem, "then you won't be able to watch *Bringing Up Baby* until the next time the BBC broadcast it, will you?"

"They show it all the time," John said. "It's not my favourite Cary Grant."

Kenneth went over, stopped the tape and ejected it, not listening to John wondering out loud about which of Cary Grant's movies he liked best, and switched the television back to the BBC, to the news. It was all about the miners.

"The rent arrears," he said, "it's terrible, I was talking to someone from Housing in the canteen today. They don't know what to do, the miners, they can't pay their rent, but you can't just . . ."

He paused and watched the scenes of violence. A policeman, his helmet knocked half off, had blood streaming down his face.

"Stupid buggers," John said.

"Are you in tonight?" Kenneth said.

"No, I'm off out," John said. "Daniel's coming round about eight, we're going off down town. Don't wait up."

"I wasn't planning to."

Many things in John's life were a mystery to Kenneth, but the biggest was probably his nights out with Daniel Glover. They'd never been particular friends till a couple of years back—there was three years between them—but now they regularly went down town together, drinking in pubs before going to a nightclub, even. Kenneth wouldn't have exactly trusted Daniel Glover, but he had to see that most people would think he was a lot more respectable than his own son. He had a decent job, was polite and friendly enough. He was what used to be called "clean-cut." Really, what Kenneth didn't trust about Daniel was only the strangeness of his being friends with John. John shouldn't have been able to afford to go out on nights like that. "I pay my way," John had said, when asked directly. Kenneth didn't believe it, and couldn't work it out. It wasn't as if they were queers; that would have made more sense.

Daniel drove down the road so that he wouldn't drive past his parents' house, making them wonder why he hadn't dropped in on them if he was in the neighbourhood. He stopped outside John Warner's house and hooted twice, not turning the engine off. He was twenty minutes late; John was never ready on time. Daniel could never face sitting around making a sort of conversation with John's dad, who hadn't yet realized that Daniel wasn't fifteen any more. It was always freezing cold in their house, too. I don't mind the blue suit, Daniel said, but please, just tonight, when I've got other things on my mind to worry about, please not the chocolate-brown tie with the naked lady on it. He himself was in a showy new suit, black but with silver thread shot through it, and a new white shirt with a butterfly collar and no tie. The day after all that business with his mother at the police station, he'd checked his bank balance and, amazed that there was as much as that still there at the end of the month, he'd gone shopping, and had his hair cut too, though it was a fortnight before it would really need it. He hooted again, and this time John came out, calling something to his father. With a kind of delight, Daniel saw that he was wearing not just the blue suit but the chocolate-coloured tie with the naked lady on it. He'd have to say something.

"What've you got on?" he said, leaning over to open the passenger door—the handle outside didn't work.

"What d'you mean? It's my suit, you've seen it before," John said.

"Not that, your tie," Daniel said.

"You've seen that before, too," John said. "And you said you liked it. What's wrong with it? It's that whole nineteen-forties thing, like Betty Grable."

"Has anyone—I mean, has a girl ever come up to you and said, 'I really like that whole nineteen-forties Betty Grable thing you've got going on with your tie'?"

"I wouldn't necessarily expect them to," John said. "You've got a lot to learn about women."

Daniel knew how it would go from here: the next time they went out, John would be wearing the same tie, without comment. But after that he would throw it away. John looked up to Daniel, while maintaining the belief that it was up to him to explain the facts of the world. He'd actually said that: "You've got a lot to learn about women." It was a strange friendship they'd started up, more of a convenience. Daniel had been out with a girl in the Frog and Parrot, and had seen John on the other side of the bar, recognized him. The pub was a new one, but got up to look old, sawdusty, picturesque; the floorboards were bare, the pillars about the bar, through which the customers ordered, were painted casually green, with amateurish bleeding edges. It was supposed to look like an old rough pub, and different from the real rough pubs, with dartboards and dank sucking carpets; the barmaids were sexy, not in a big dyed blonde way, not buxom, but sexy as girls were ordinarily sexy, and they scowled at you. John had been on his own, and Daniel had raised his glass in greeting to him, half wondering as he did so whether he really knew the face; but after a moment, John had responded with the same gesture. Like Daniel, he had been drinking bitter, the murky small-scale productions with weird names the Frog and Parrot specialized in; the girl Daniel was with, not having been there before, had allowed herself to be talked into a half before saying, "There's bits in this," and going on to gin-and-orange. And later, unexpectedly, John had been at Casanova's, propping up the bar or circling the banquettes, striking up brief conversations, but never quite making it on to the dance floor. "It's good here," he shouted into Daniel's ear, when they'd crossed each other's paths for the fourth time. "Is that your girlfriend?"

Of course, the friendship might have rested there, such as it was. But a day or two later, Daniel had been up at his parents' for Sunday lunch. He liked to take the opportunity of borrowing his dad's hosepipe and bucket to wash his car, and John walked past with a letter to post, stopped, chatted, and somehow they'd arranged to meet next Friday in the Frog and Parrot for the same sort of night out. Who had John written a letter to? It was hard to imagine.

"We've only had the police round," Daniel said, when they were sitting in a corner at the Frog and Parrot.

"What was that?" John said. Daniel repeated himself.

"What, at Eadon Lockwood and Riddle?"

"No, at home," Daniel said. "It's my mum, she had to go down the police station the other night."

"What's she supposed to have done?"

"It's not her," Daniel said. "Well, I don't know exactly, but I think, what it is, she used to work in this flower shop and it turns out the fellow who owned it, he was up to all sorts."

"Oh, aye," John said.

"My mum's in a right state," Daniel said. "And my dad."

"Is she going to prison, then?" John said.

"Don't be daft," Daniel said. "She's done nothing wrong, she just didn't know."

"How could she not know, then?" John said. "What's he been up to, this flower-shop fellow?"

"Could be anything," Daniel said.

John took a long drink of his bitter, narrowed his eyes. He might have been thinking. "My dad's out of sorts with me, an' all," he said. "He had a right go at me today."

"What now?"

John explained about the freeze-framing of the video, his failure to remember the name of the actor, and most of the plot of *Bringing Up Baby*. After five minutes of it, Daniel went to get two more pints; he came back, and John carried on, just where he'd left off. "It's not true, either," he wound up eventually. "I've never heard of a video just snapping because it's been paused. I don't know what he's on about."

"I wouldn't have thought so," Daniel said comfortably. That was the thing about John Warner. Look at it how you liked, Daniel's life was more eventful and more interesting than his. But you could say anything you liked to John, and he'd ask three questions, then tell you about something that once happened to him; something much more boring, but something either very similar, not very similar, or not really the same thing at all. Daniel didn't mind. From time to time he went as far as making up something sensational—a woman client's lewd suggestion to him when he was showing her the bedrooms of a house for sale, for instance. Nothing like that had ever happened to him, but John seemed to think that sort of thing would be completely ordinary, and just started talking again about the last girl he'd gone to bed with, months ago now. Daniel had friends enough, but most of them were going to do what John had just done; if you told them your mother had been arrested, they'd probably go, "What for?" and then in a minute start going on about the argument they'd had with their dad about the video-recorder, or something. He let the subject drop.

Casanova's was at the other end of town, down towards where the cheap markets were. Round the Frog and Parrot it was all bookshops

and cafés, and those stupid shops selling joss sticks and Indian cushions. Casanova's was on the other side of the dual carriageway and
from the outside just a bleak concrete outcrop of the market complex,
its name incongruously written in swirling purple copperplate. "All
right, lads?" the bouncer said, not really giving away whether he recognized them or not; they were quite early, and there was no queue.
Daniel was embarrassed about these early appearances, and didn't
think they led to success. When girls arrived, they naturally looked
about to see what was already there, and you were the sad furniture.
John wouldn't have been that successful in any circumstances, but he
didn't help himself with this obstinate idea of turning up early and
watching the girls as they came in.

The purple nooks and mirrored niches of Casanova's were all familiar to Daniel now; what must be basically a big square space had been
made intricate with partitions and semi-circular seating, little intimate
caves of velvet and plush, lowered ceilings at unexpected points, raised
platforms and short flights of stairs, so that you could hide yourself,
place yourself on display, make entrances and disappearances; pools of
luxurious downcast lighting melted into gloom and fug. In some of
those corners you could imagine going a long way with a girl. There
were two bars, one with a mirrored surface where the expense-
accounts stood with the people they'd come with. The other was a
mock-marble island between the two dance floors, where the dancers
repaired with the new partners they'd acquired mid-record, or where
you might buy a girl a drink.

Daniel bought John and himself a vodka and tonic each. The ultra-
violet light made the drinks shine like radioactive mercury as they went
across to a discreet booth where they wouldn't be clocked by new
arrivals; lit up the constellation of scurf across the shoulders of John's
suit.

"Don't you possess a clothes brush?" Daniel said, flicking his hand
over John's jacket. "Or haven't you heard of Head and Shoulders?
That's terrible."

"It's only the lights," John said. "I've not got that bad dandruff, it
only looks like it in here." But he took off the jacket and, holding his
collar in his fist, gave it a good shake before inspecting it and putting it
on again.

"You want to have it dry-cleaned once in a while, too," Daniel
said.

"I'm not made of money," John said. "You sound like my dad."

They settled back in the gloom. It was a good spot; you could see them arriving, but they wouldn't be able to see you unless they came right in. Three were already on the dance floor—old favourites, determined to have a good time and ignoring the rules of precedence, the rule that admitted the confident to open the dancing. They'd accepted they'd be going home on their own, and were settling for the pleasures of the dance. Around the floor, here and there, some little groups; a few schoolgirls, probably on their first time here, hunched together and with over-elaborate makeup to advance their real ages. Some were sexy and would do all right; one was spoon-faced and too tall, and in a dress she'd been persuaded into, probably some other girl's. Her left arm was behind her back, awkwardly grasping the back of her right elbow; she laughed too much, too brightly. She wouldn't be back much. And the others, the real crowd, were starting to come in now. John and Daniel watched them.

There were all sorts of girls. There were the old favourites, the Kellys and the Julies, the ones who'd give you a jolly and not think anything much of it. There were the Tinas and Gayes, who would dance with you and have a drink with you, even buy you a drink, and at the end of the night would say, "You must be joking," and "You're terrible, Daniel," or "Well, you get full marks for trying, anyway," but with good humour, because you didn't ask a girl if a fuck was out of the question if you thought it wasn't. If he'd been them, he'd have said much the same thing. Then there were the hopefuls, who came here looking for someone rich. Chapeltown or Intake, ugly dirty places, had somehow produced something Chapeltown or Intake had thought like Miss World, and they turned up in their ra-ra skirts, rearranging their bosoms in Daniel's direction. Daniel wasn't rich, but to girls like that, he looked clean, and in Casanova's, he looked like a star on a video. There were the old eyesores, too. Daniel had been through the regulars in Casanova's like a barium meal, and there were a few Tricias and Wendys, girls who'd been in his life for two, three months and had left angrily. There were quite a few stares to confront in Casanova's these days. The peculiar thing was that the accusing stare was never a single one; these Tricias and Wendys, they always had a new boyfriend who'd been primed with the history, or more usually the same fat best friend. It was always the fat best friends who said, "Get lost," when Daniel made a point of saying, "All right, Tricia?" to these embittered old conquests; always the fat best friends who wouldn't in practice mind if Daniel ever had a go in their direction; always the fat best friends who

John had most success with. The situation never became difficult, because it looked as though, with John, once was enough.

"Quiet, isn't it?" Daniel said, leaning over and shouting.

"I wouldn't say quiet exactly," John said. He always said this, pretending not to know what Daniel meant by "quiet," since the music was at top volume, hopeful in the still-empty club. He got out his cigarette case and lit up. The cigarette case was an affectation to hide the cheapness of the cigarettes he smoked, though he only offered a girl a cigarette where he thought he saw real prospects.

"It's early yet," Daniel said. "I said, it's—early—yet."

"They're not going out," John said, in his sagest style. "It's the miner's strike."

"What's that got to do with it?" Daniel said.

"It's the first thing to go," John said, with narrow bravado, "when things are tight, a night out."

"What—you think they're miners?" Daniel said, nodding over his vodka at the loose groups around the bar; his attention was taken by a girl in pixie boots and no skirt, her long loose RELAX T-shirt coming to the top of her thighs.

"No," John said. "It's more that there's not really—"

A girl slid quickly into the booth where they sat; it was Helen. She was someone who'd been around for years, a good sort. She'd history with Daniel; they'd got off the first time they'd met, here, and then one New Year—last New Year—the girl Daniel had come with had slapped his face and walked off, and Helen'd split up with the lad she'd been seeing right after Christmas, so they'd done each other a one-off favour. No charity on either side. She was all right, no phoning or weeping or unspoken plans for their future together. She'd turned down John when he'd had a go at her.

"You've not moved since the last time I saw you," Helen said. "Do you live here or something?"

"You can talk," John said, in a way not exactly friendly.

"They ought to put a sign up," Helen said, "and a letterbox, you'd never have to go home. I saw you, last Tuesday it would have been."

"I never saw you," Daniel said.

"You were driving past the hospital in that terrible old car of yours," Helen said. "You can hear you coming a mile off, it's like a bad case of whooping cough. I was coming out, I'd just finished my shift."

"Did you kill anyone this week?" Daniel said. Helen was a nurse at the Hallamshire Hospital.

"Mopped up a lot of shit, I'll tell you that for nothing," Helen said. "With some people it's the blood, with me it's the shit. Had an old fellow start wanking when I was trying to give him a bed bath."

"It's a sort of compliment," Daniel said.

"You can't blame him," John said.

"Sod off," Helen said.

"So do you have to carry on when that happens?" John said.

"Oh, for Jesus' sake," Helen said, carrying on talking only to Daniel. "No, I get called away urgently and send in Kevin to finish him off. Is your friend going to offer to buy me a drink any time soon?"

The financial arrangements for these evenings were firmly established, without either John or Daniel ever discussing them. The basis was that John had no money. He bought the occasional round in the Frog and Parrot, to show willing, but when they got to Casanova's, it was easiest for Daniel to say, "Two," at the door. The drinks inside were twice the price they were in a pub, and Daniel bought them all night without question. John earned his keep in ways Daniel couldn't explain, and he paid for his pleasures with the humiliation of his position. He was the serf on the floor at a medieval banquet, waiting with cupped hands for whatever might spill from the laden salvers.

"Well?" Helen said.

Daniel was pretty sure that Helen knew John had no money, and it was outrageous of her to insist, to make John buy a drink for a girl he couldn't benefit from. "It must be my round," he said.

"No, it's mine," John said, flushing at Daniel's well-intended lie. "I was just going."

"I'm all right," Daniel said, letting John pass.

"Whisky and Coke," Helen called after him, watching him go with a sardonic smile. "He's a nice lad," she said. "Deep down."

Daniel shook his head, laughing.

"What's up, then?" Helen said. "I heard you're seeing that Kelly."

"What, do you know her?"

"Course I know her," Helen said. "Her mum's a physiotherapist at the hospital, she was telling me all about you, what a nice boy Kelly's found herself. It was a shock when I worked out she was talking about you."

"I don't know about seeing," Daniel said, with the hot sense of parts of his life drawing together. He could almost feel the tight black shoes, the carnation being placed in his unwilling buttonhole.

"That's not what she thinks," Helen said. "I'd make a run for it, it sounds like she's choosing the cushions and drawing up lists of children's names."

"Oh, for Christ's sake," Daniel said. "I quite like her, I'm not complaining."

"Well, good luck to you," Helen said, drawing back in her seat. "How's your week been?"

"Oh, Christ," Daniel said. "No, it's been great. Fantastic. This thing, though, my mother—"

"Bad as that?" Helen said, interrupting him, probably not hearing what he was starting to say; he was quite glad of it, didn't know why he'd even begun to bring it out. "I didn't mean to offend."

"?"

"About Kelly."

"Oh, that's fine. Forget it," Daniel said. "Just got things on my mind."

"I really didn't mean it about the car, though," Helen said. "I quite like your car. I said, I quite like your car."

"Now, that you're allowed to be rude about."

"I like the fact that you can hear you coming a mile off, make yourself scarce if need be."

"It's not long for this world, I reckon. I'd get something better, only it won't be long until the company car. Seems stupid not to struggle on a bit longer."

"That I look forward to," Helen said. "Is it going to have the name on the side? Your company's name, I mean, not yours."

"I'm not selling wet fish," Daniel said. "It's all very discreet, very tasteful. We're doing well, they've said I'll get the promotion before long."

"What is it you do again?" Helen said.

"It's Eadon Lockwood and Riddle," Daniel said, disappointed. "The estate agents."

"I like the car you've got, though," Helen said. "It's one of the nice things about you."

"Oh, there's more than one?"

"It's one of the things that shows you're not a twat," Helen said. "I thought you were a twat at first, when I first met you. Most people think you're a twat, you know, Daniel. But there's things like your car, and the fact you can't really dance, and sometimes you'll say something, I don't know—well, you're not a twat."

"That's one of the nicest things anyone's ever said to me," Daniel said. "Am I a twat, though?"

"I've just told you you're not," Helen said. "I'll tell you who is, though."

John shuffled back with two drinks; there was some element of defiance in the fact that he'd bought himself another one, even though the first one, still on the table, was only half finished. If he were a girl, Daniel thought, you could discreetly slip him a tenner; but to do so with John would be to acknowledge too much about the unspoken conventions between them. He placed the drink in front of Helen. She looked at it, lifted it up, drank.

"Thanks, love," she said. "I wanted a whisky and Coke, but that'll do just as well."

Daniel said nothing, recognizing in the vodka and tonic a familiar low-level gesture of hostility John often resorted to; it had once, in similar circumstances, been a pint of lager he'd thumped down, something harder to overlook.

"Takes for ever to get served here," John said. "I was standing there with ten pounds in my hand, and he's seen me, and he serves them who were there before me, fair enough, but then this girl comes up after me and flutters her eyelids at him and he serves her, and I say something, right, just to make the point, and he says nothing, just serves two more people, they've come after me too, before he finally agrees to serve me."

"We were just discussing whether Daniel was a twat or not," Helen said. "I don't know what you think."

"Fuck off," John said. In other circumstances, he might have taken a different opportunity, directed his hostility towards Daniel. "Dan's my mate, he's not a twat."

"He just looks like one, a bit," Helen said. "And acts like one."

"Don't mind me," Daniel said, amused.

"But there again," Helen said, "he's not one, because he drives that car. It's true, Daniel, you spend too much time in front of a mirror, and you worry more about split ends than a girl does, and you obviously think too much about whether you're going to undo just one button on your shirt, or two, and that's the shirt of a twat if ever I saw one, and you've got the sort of job most people would be embarrassed about admitting they did, but you're a nice lad apart from all that."

"There's the girls," Daniel said. "You've not mentioned the girls."

"Kelly and that? I wouldn't give you the satisfaction. You're not half as much a twat over them as you think you are. Or you want to be. Do you fancy a dance?"

"Go on, then," Daniel said, not minding at all, and he and Helen stood up, taking their drinks. John stood up, too, but changed his mind about coming with them, and stopped, half crouching over the table; he seemed to be making the sort of courtly gesture he didn't know how to make. Daniel followed Helen across to the half-filled dance-floor; they placed their drinks on a shelf running round one of the boundary pillars; she put her handbag on the floor, and they started to dance. For a moment Daniel was self-conscious as he started to move, following the instructions he had once been given about dancing in a disco, to move nothing except the vertical foot between navel and upper thigh, but in a moment Helen gave him a broad, saucy grin, lowered her handbag to the floor and started dancing in an almost professional way, her little clenched fists moving from one shoulder to another, her hair tossing. He could smell the fragrant steely scent of her chemical hair-spray; he guessed she could probably smell the fresh clean breeze of his lemony cologne, of Cacharel. In a few minutes, after three or four records, one after the other, the dance-floor was almost full, and he was enjoying himself. At the edge, a crowd was forming, watching the show; at the front, his eyes wandering from girl to girl, nursing his anxious drink, was John. The sight of a good-looking couple doing the moves had, after all, been the signal of approval the nightclub had been waiting for, and all of them—the Kellys and the Julies and the Tricias and the Wendys and the Gayes, and the men who came with them, all of them with their different motives and ideas about what a good Friday night out might be like—they all followed Daniel and Helen onto the dance-floor. That was exactly what they'd been waiting for.

When the car horn sounded in the early-morning street outside, it echoed in the silence like the hooter of a tugboat, melancholy and raw. It was so silent in the early mornings, only a single bird singing in wan hope of a mate in the holly tree in the back garden. Tim had been awake and half dressed for twenty minutes; he'd had a bath the night before, so as not to wake anyone in the morning with the hissing and clanking from the boiler.

In his brown cord trousers and bare-chested, carrying his favourite T-shirt, he went downstairs. He'd made himself a big mug of tea, and cut off a hunk of granary bread, savagely, an almost pyramidal slash, then slathered it with butter. If it hadn't been more trouble than it was worth, and likely to raise the house, he'd have fried some bacon and made a bacon butty with the HP sauce he'd made his mother buy. It was the sort of breakfast a man on a picket line deserved. But he ate the breakfast he had made for himself in the kitchen of the house with its view of a neat front garden, with its Italian tiles on the walls and its specially air-pocketed flooring, warm and yielding under bare feet in the winter.

He'd almost finished his tea when the car's horn sounded outside. He looked outside; it was Fat Marge's orange Marina, which had become Stig's vehicle. It was going to be warm today; he quickly put his T-shirt on, rinsed the mug under the tap and put it upside-down in the rack. He went outside, and immediately Trudy stuck her head out of the open window and hissed, "You can't wear that."

"Why not?" Tim said. "It's what we're here for." The T-shirt had a slogan on it: DIG DEEP FOR THE MINERS. It had been printed by some-body unprofessional, on the sort of T-shirt material that didn't last more than a dozen washes; even now, only a few months into the min-ers' strike, it was grey as a prison flannel, its capitals, printed in trans-fers, cracking like dry earth. He'd told his mum to wash it inside out, but he suspected she deliberately didn't, or didn't pay any attention to what he asked her to do.

"That's exactly why," Trudy said. "It's because it's what we're here for that you can't wear it. Haven't you heard? The enforcement's stop-ping cars and turning them back if they're obvious radicals."

"Back from where?" Tim said. He wasn't in the mood for this, and especially for Trudy's invariable habit of calling the police "the enforcement." There was some justification for this, and he'd tried to use the term, but they'd looked strangely at him, as though it was Trudy's copyrighted word. Trudy and, surprisingly, Stig, at the wheel of the car, were dressed with almost excessive respectability; Stig, satir-ically, in an old tweed jacket, certainly one of his dad's, over a plain white T-shirt, Trudy in a beige top with laces tying up its slashed neck.

"Back from where they're going to," Trudy said. "They won't let you anywhere near the picketing sites if they think you're going to be trouble. And that spells trouble."

"Have you had your breakfast?" Stig said, speaking for the first time. "We're in a bit of a rush."

"Fat Marge got up specially early," Trudy said, "and made us a spe-cial breakfast. She thinks we're going hiking on the moors. Thanks, Timmy," Trudy said satirically, as Tim went back to the house to change his T-shirt. He stomped slightly, aware of them watching him go. He bounded up the stairs, not caring whether he woke anyone now, and went quickly into his bedroom. He pulled out another T-shirt. None had no slogan on it, whether home-made, printed on home-tie-dyed cotton from stalls at radical fairs, or occasional semi-professional jobs from the radical bookshops. Everything was promoting or protesting, making some statement; it was either that or they did what Daniel's clothes did: announced the multi-national exploiter, which profited from the making of these things, in external labels or even printed on the front, like slogans, announcing the triumph of sweatshop and profit. But the top one was ambiguous in its protest: the slogan was ETCH COPPER FOR ZAMBIA, a cause exotic even to most of Tim's immediate circle, and written, as it happened, in ingratiating and suitable copperplate.

They were in a hurry to get to the picket, Tim knew. He stood up and looked out of the window at them, waiting outside. Trudy had got out of Fat Marge's car and was leaning against it. It was early—nothing short of class warfare would get Trudy out of bed at this hour—and she was yawning. She took her left wrist in her right hand, and, like a triumphant boxer, raised both above her head as she voluptuously yawned. Her T-shirt broke loose of its moorings in her waistband, and rode upwards, exposing a pale and rounded patch of her belly. It was as if Tim had slipped sideways on some unseen patch of black ice underfoot, and found himself, a second later, shaking and unbalanced, but still standing, at the same place, a thousand years before. Trudy standing like that, just there, yawning like that, brought back a memory to him; the first time he had ever seen Sandra. She had got out of her car and stretched and yawned, on just such a morning as this.

She must have been much younger than Trudy was now. But just as the trees outside the window, though now presumably much bigger, seemed exactly the same as they had been ten years before, so Trudy seemed exactly as Sandra had been. There was nothing to connect them; Trudy possessed only a fragment of that beauty which Sandra had so fully inhabited. He had looked at Sandra for ten years, every day until she had got on a plane and left for Australia, and with every look there was a precious fragment of that wash of desire he had felt in his uncomprehending childish way the very first time. He never saw her now. But this memory, brought back all at once, was something that often occurred to him. He had looked at her carefully; had made as solid a set of memories of her speech and words as if he had stolen keepsakes of her and locked them in a box. He had stolen a letter of hers to Daniel, before he had seen it. But that was all the physical avatar of hers he had, safe between the pages of a long history of the Cuban revolution. Now, mere thoughts of her were solid and regular in his mind. He thought they always would be.

She had gone from his life. Perhaps all he could do was to try to find those women, like Trudy, in whom his desire could mine a fragment of that pure quality now embodied on the other side of the world, in one woman he hadn't seen for years.

"You took your time," Trudy said, as he got into the car.

"Are we all right, then?" Tim said to Stig.

"You'll get away with that," Stig said, meaning the T-shirt. "You know something? Trudy was just saying. Your house, it looks completely mad."

"My dad's idea."

Whenever it was the right season, and, as everyone always said, the climbers about the house shot all at once into bloom like a moment, prolonged into weeks, of applause, and the house itself, no more interesting or remarkable or special than any other house in this road, turned for a long moment into what might have been a house of blossom and nothing else.

As Stig started the car, Mr. Sellers opposite was coming out in his suit, keys in hand. Something in the way he shut the door made it clear that his wife, Sandra's mother, was still asleep. Of course, there was nobody else in the house to wake up: Sandra was in Australia (a sudden shot of her in bikini, laughing as she ran out of the surf) and that Francis had left home, was in London, wasn't he?

"He's up early," Stig said, setting off.

"Works for the Electricity Board," Tim said. "My mum's friends with his wife. She says he's always having to leave the house before seven."

"I don't wonder," Trudy said. "They ought to be supporting the action, and they'll be working against it. We should go and let down his tyres."

"What's it got to do with him?"

"Who do you think's buying the blackleg coal, if we don't stop it leaving the pits?"

"Oh, yeah," Tim said. He was vague about the destination of the coal: he always thought of it as going into people's fireplaces, but of course nobody did that any more.

They quickly left the western suburbs, the blackened stately villas of Broomhill with their remains of railings like cut-off blackened teeth. Nobody was about; the morning was high and blue and slightly steaming, the dew smoking above the municipal gardens. It was going to be hot. They drove through town, round the Hole in the Road, hardly being stopped by lights at all, and only now was traffic beginning to build up. Tim saw a single, boarded-up shop, and turned to make sure. There'd been shops like this on the outskirts, in the poor places, as Tim could never stop himself thinking of them. He'd seen shops in frazzled arcades which had discovered they served no need, and where no one else could see a need either, and had been boarded up. But that happened in the poor places. It hadn't happened in Broomhill, where Nick's flower shop had already been turned into a bookshop, with forty copies of *Frost in May* fanned out in the window round a left-over vase of Nick's with a sprig of blossom in it. It hadn't happened, before, in the middle of town. That had been a trendy clothes shop, selling jeans mostly; he'd bought a pair of cords there once himself. He hadn't noticed it was closed, and now it was boarded up. Perhaps Sheffield itself counted as a poor place now.

There was an increasingly sour smell in the car. You might have thought Trudy would have taken the opportunity to have a bath before she set off in a small car on a warm morning. "We're not picking you up," he said in surprise, turning round to her; they were driving past Hyde Park Flats in its immense sour concrete ribbon on the hillside above the station. It hadn't occurred to him that it was odd, Trudy being in the car from Lodge Moor, nor had he really understood what had been meant when she'd said that Fat Marge had made them both breakfast. He hadn't been paying attention.

"I stayed at Stig's last night," Trudy said. "We thought it would be easier." She had a sort of triumph in her voice; he hadn't known she saw him as some kind of rival for Stig's attention, though Tim knew he thought of her in that way.

"It's quicker," Stig said. "Trudy wanted to borrow a book, so she came up last night and stayed."

"You don't have to explain," Trudy said, her voice rising. "Not to little Timmy. Oh, and by the way, Timmy. We didn't screw or anything."

"I never thought you had," Tim said. "I don't make those sorts of assumptions. Where are we meeting the others?"

"At the service station car park, just on the M18," Stig said. "Throw them off the track a bit."

"Where are we going?"

"Orgreave," Trudy said. "No harm in telling you now."

And now the roads were widening out, leaving Sheffield behind. The carriageway ran like a mournful mountain pass behind high peaks of slag, lowering and black. Down in the valleys, the palaces of the steel-makers, vast and cubic and full of fire; up here, the unworking coal-sorters, huge and yet frail, their sides dustily clamped with metal stairs, like drawings executed in dust. Tim wondered what they looked like, in their car with bricks in the boot. To the other drivers, they could be normal. Just then, like a physical thrill, a police van drove past; not just a police car, but a whole van, its windows lined with chain-link and filled with shadowy dark figures. As it overtook them—Stig was driving at an ostentatiously moderate speed—Tim felt sure that they would wave them over. But in the back window, two heads, leaning forward, helmet-less, in intimate conference. The three of them in the Marina must look like what they were not, students off to Manchester for the day.

"Pigs," Trudy said, with obstinate routine.

"They must be stupid," Stig said. "If they knew their job, they'd be putting roadblocks up for miles around."

"You can't stop democratic protest," Trudy said. "It's not just us supporting the miners, it's the ordinary people of Sheffield. You'll see."

And this seemed to be the case because, in ten minutes' time, they slowed at the signs for the service station turn off, the three fat white stripes on blue, two, one—signs that had always fascinated Tim when he was young. They turned off, and drove into the car park. There seemed to be nobody there, or just families getting in and out of cars, but Stig seemed to know where to go. He parked at the far end of the car park, overlooking the motorway, and almost at once the doors of cars near them opened, disgorging half a dozen people like them.

Stig and Trudy knew them, and there was quite a lot of pumped-fist hand-shaking going on. "I'm Tim," Tim said loudly, because you didn't wait for people to say who you were, and the others introduced themselves, too—Johnny, Vikram, Billy, Kate, and half a dozen others. He'd come across two or three before, met them while selling the *Spartacist*, and knew the faces of most of the others.

There wasn't much time, and Vikram, who seemed to be the leader, explained quickly. "We can't stand around here," he said. "They'll spot us and take us in if they see us grouping. We're all here now, I reckon. We're going to drive off at five-minute intervals—you first, then us, then you, OK—and this is what you do. You stop outside Orgreave—

there's a little car park by the community centre, you'll see the pay-and-display sign on the toilet wall. Drop people off there and make a move pretty sharpish. Don't wait for us. It's about fifteen minutes' walk from there, it should be OK. The men make their way to the site of the action as discreetly as you can. The women and me, we'll take up viewing positions wherever we can. If you're just sitting on a wall, not doing anything, they can't tell you to move on."

Everyone laughed at the policeman-like turn of phrase. Tim thought, on the whole, they could move you on, but out of curiosity just said, "Why are you staying with the women and not coming with us?"

"Come on, Timmy," Trudy said.

"Do you think I look like a miner?" Vikram said. "Have you ever seen a black miner in South Yorkshire? They'd spot me as soon as look at me."

"When do we meet up again?" one of the boys—Johnny, perhaps—said.

"This is an engagement," Vikram said impressively. "It doesn't run to a timetable. We'll see how it goes. You might have to get out on your own."

That was it. Perhaps the others had discussed more specific and military tactics, or perhaps they were expected to use their own initiative. Trudy took over the wheel, and they set off again, accelerating away down the ramp. It was a beautiful morning—you couldn't help thinking that. The landscape was torn away in slag heaps and pylons and this fat grey slash of a motorway, but there were trees, too, and green hills as if it were the English countryside. Torn and scarred, it still swelled and dipped like Gloucestershire. Once, people might have come here to admire the scenery; the earth had been beautiful before it had proved useful. If they had their way, Tim thought with deliberation, it would only be beautiful all over again, and useless, and filled with the ragged foraging unemployed. But you couldn't help responding to the lovely morning. There had been some early mist on the ground, and the sun was lifting it off by the minute, like a transparent child's blanket. You could see the layers of air; still misty down in the dips, and thinning into a blue lucid heat, solid and tangible like crystal fifty metres up. The air seemed like a reflection, as in a still lake, of the dense layers of geology below, the mist like a white negative of the seams of coal beneath the thin surface of turf, under what might even have been lawn. It was a beautiful day for it. He could have got out and danced on the roof of the moving car.

"I'm going to drop you and make off straight away," Trudy said. "I'll find somewhere to leave it inconspicuously. I'll make my way back somehow, but I'll be watching from a distance, like Vikram said."

"It's not my car," Stig said. "Leave it in the car park, it makes no odds."

"Don't be stupid," Trudy said.

"It might be quite funny if the police turn up and ask Fat Marge what exactly she was doing in Orgreave yesterday. She'd have a fit," Stig said.

"What does she think you're doing with it?"

"God knows," Stig said. "I just took the car. I didn't ask her."

"And, Trudy," Tim said, drawing out her name cruelly—Troooody, "you're just going to sit on a hillock overlooking the event with some egg sandwiches and some salt in a wrap of foil, are you? Doesn't seem very brave to me."

"You heard what Vikram said," Trudy said. "There's not going to be many women out there on the line. I'd stick out like a sore thumb. Don't worry, Timmy, I'll be doing useful things. I'll be seeing Orgreave women. I know plenty of women activists here. Don't worry about me."

Tim thought of the women who stood in Fargate, shaking tin cans and shrinking from what was now very pungent in the car, Trudy's animal odour, when she embraced them. Most were probably a bit too houseproud to be real friends with Trudy; she flourished her friendship with working-class women as something extra to ideology, something she would have done anyway. He didn't have the knack of that. He saw their houses, with yellow leather sofas and fat yellow leather armchairs; he saw the dado-effect stripes of wallpaper running at waist height round the sitting room; he saw their doorbells ringing, and them rushing with their (practical, he made himself think) floral housecoats on to answer the door. He saw their back kitchens, with nothing in them but donated tins from Fargate and a little caddy of tea. They would answer the door, and there would be Trudy, foul-smelling with her self-cut hair and granny glasses, in her collarless striped shirt, her arms wide to embrace them. He could well imagine how welcome she'd be.

"Sounds like you're actually a bit frightened," Tim said. "Not to want to come."

"Trudy's not frightened," Stig said as Trudy, simultaneously, in a querulous whine, said, "How do you mean, frightened?"

"You know, frightened," Tim said. "Frightened. Frit. You know, couldn't take it, couldn't stand it—I don't blame you, it's going to be pretty tough."

"It's going to be *pretty tough*, is it, Timmy?" Trudy said. "Oooh, I never realized."

"Gi'o'er, you two," Stig said.

"I think Timmy's been giving himself nightmares about it," Trudy said, but in the jeer, there might have been some kind of admiration, too. "Here we are. We turn off here."

When the news came, Alice was in Katherine's kitchen with her bag on her arm, sipping a cup of coffee. She wasn't supposed to be stopping long. Alice knew about the whole business. Katherine had to tell somebody outside her immediate family about the court case, about Nick being in trouble. Everyone inside her immediate family was scornfully disapproving and enjoying it (Tim); bewildered and hurt and withdrawn (Malcolm); just not understanding and constantly asking for tactless details. That was Daniel. Or they were in London and not to be bothered. That was Jane. Somebody else had to be told so that she could look at it and see it for what it was. It was like when you bought a picture in a sale, or a dress on a whim. Your family had too much history of responses to your whims to be of much use. You had to call in a friend, an outsider, to look at the fact of it and then, without them even saying anything, you had a view of the fact of it through their eyes, from the way they stood and looked at you, or at it, even.

Perversely, it was Alice she had told rather than anyone else. She was the obvious choice, because Alice was the only one who knew the whole story about Nick. She knew more than Malcolm, who would now never listen to it, or believe it. Perhaps she knew more even than Katherine, who had only steeled herself to tell the story that once quite plainly and honestly. On every other occasion, reflecting on it, she found herself providing embellishments, romantic touches, exaggerations of humiliations and inventions regarding disgusted rejections. When she had told Alice the full plain account of the affair, such as it was, and then, more recently, when she decided that of course Alice was the person to tell about being in trouble with the police, the whole evening down the station, which Rayfield Avenue must be absolutely dying to find out about, given the appearance of the police car outside their house and her being taken away, as it were, virtually in handcuffs, Alice had behaved well. She had only said, "But did he say . . ." and

"I'm sure what he really meant" each time quite plausibly. She had been a good listener. She had enquired, carefully, and with the appearance of objectivity, and had in the end cleared Katherine of culpable wrongdoing with a consideration that might almost have been professional. It would have been nice to be sure that the court, when it came to it, was going to do the same thing.

The cherry tree was in blossom in the front garden; she gazed out at it through the yellow and white kitchen blinds, and thought of nothing but her problems.

But it was perverse, her choice of Alice as someone to tell the whole story to, and exactly because of what might have recommended her in the first place, that she would never tell anyone. Katherine knew that perfectly well. She would never tell even Bernie. And what was needed now was someone who would tell the story completely and authoritatively. Since the appearance of the panda car outside Katherine's house, Anthea Arbuthnot had never "popped round," had never so much "just happened," had never existed half so much "on the off-chance" in her entire life. Her being had never had so much excited casualness about it as it did these days. She was forever appearing for no very good reason, with a gift of half a dozen scones too many she'd just happened to make, or a recipe she'd cut out from the *Morning Telegraph* on the off-chance Katherine might find it useful, or bearing a pot of home-made jam. Tim had answered the door. "Thanks, I'll donate it to the miners' collections," he said, taking it firmly off her, but it hadn't put her off.

Anthea was round here because she'd seen the police car, and couldn't produce an explanation for it even she could believe. Her own inventions were, almost certainly, not remotely credible even to herself. It wasn't her fault if Katherine couldn't produce an explanation for it either, but that didn't seem to cross her mind. It would have been much easier all round if Katherine had taken Anthea into her confidence as well as or instead of Alice and just told her what was going on. It would have saved a lot of trouble. Sooner or later, she'd have to start telling people—she had no illusions that the case would come to court, and it would certainly be made public then. If they already knew, through Anthea, it would save a lot of trouble. Katherine envisaged Anthea, hastening up Rayfield Avenue in a muck sweat, brushing the streetside blossom from her glistening face where it fell, popping up one red Tarmac drive after another, ringing the bell and, as the door opened, producing a small token gift from behind her back, an excuse to come in and gossip. It would be very much like that. It probably had been very much like that, since by now they probably all knew her constructed and invented version. Already the haggard and worn figure of poor Caroline had made a habit of crossing the road to offer inept expressions of sympathy over the knee-high grey brick wall when she'd seen Katherine in the front garden. They'd been inept expressions of sympathy about greenfly on the roses, as it happened, but Katherine identified the general intention and where it had come from.

She'd only told Alice, whose practical expression of sympathy was to induce her to join her keep-fit class. It was run by a lady in Crosspool, a nice girl called Tracy Bowness, who said she'd been at school with Francis and—a polite little afterthought, turning from Alice's glowing face to her own—with Tim, too, she thought. She rented the church hall by the term—she had some connection with the church—and got them all going for 50p a lesson, or "session," as they said. She was very good, with an array of legwarmers and a large range of different-coloured all-in-one leotards as the weeks went on. She hadn't left home, and kept house for her dad, who was a mine-manager—you weren't supposed to know that, but they all did. Her mother had gone off with a teacher from Flint, years before, run off to Exeter with him. You weren't supposed to know any of that, but they did, and it added a degree of sympathy to the enjoyment of the class. Poor Tracy, with nothing but her legwarmers to keep her warm, with her Kept-Fit figure and spoony unkissable features. They all knew she had nothing but a grumpy old mine-manager of a dad in a little house in Crosspool to go home to.

Alice was in Katherine's kitchen, the cherry blossom thick in clouds just at the window, when the news came. She was drinking a cup of coffee. Tim had gone out somewhere very early. They'd been woken by the front door slamming, before seven o'clock. "Heaven knows where," Katherine said, though Malcolm—who was for some reason still in at ten o'clock on a weekday—said he could guess. That was mysterious to Alice, as Malcolm greeted her amicably enough and went off upstairs. The telephone rang, above their heads and in the hallway. They'd installed a Trimphone extension in Malcolm's study, directly above the kitchen, and they heard the sound of his voice saying their number rather than the actual words, "double one double six?" in a tune with a rising inflection. There was another comment, a silence, then another rumbling, unintelligible and short sentence, before he called, "Katherine—it's important," and came out of the little study.

She went to the phone in the hall and picked it up, listening, white-faced. Malcolm hung up the phone upstairs, and came down. Alice, following Katherine, made a quick tactful gesture of leaving in Malcolm's direction, but Katherine saw this. She reached out to grip her wrists. Malcolm, more weakly, shook his hands and pointed at the ground, to say, "No, stay here." Whether Malcolm knew that Alice had been told the facts of the case or not, he wanted her here.

There was nothing to be gathered from Katherine's short, neutral sentences, hunched over the phone with the wings of her hair hiding the secret of the Trimphone handset. Malcolm led Alice into the kitchen.

"It's the solicitor," he said calmly. "She's phoning to give us an update on the case."

Alice noted that "us." "Good news, I hope," she said, words that even she knew would probably sound even more fatuous. And then they started talking, in the agreed social manner of those days, about the miners' strike and the weather. Started talking about them in connection, too, as if they had anything to do with each other, as if the miners, on top of everything else, had managed to arrange lovely weather for their strike. Alice and Malcolm did it on this occasion with graceful, pointed practice, as if the whole of their social intercourse over the last few decades had prepared them to carry out exactly this difficult conversation, even with a more difficult one happening in the hallway on the Trimphone. But, all the same, they broke off as soon as she put the phone down and straightened up.

Katherine came into the kitchen with elaborate casualness. She was sometimes so much like a small girl, Alice considered. Not like her own daughter Jane, whose body had always had that gawky frankness that never mounted much of a defence or dissimulation of her own thoughts. When fed-up, Jane drooped; when happy, she perked up; when bored (Alice had noted last Christmas when they went over there for drinks), she still sighed and moaned and rolled her eyes. Katherine was more like Alice's daughter Sandra, who had made a point of complicated poses at odds with her situation or feeling, being upright and staring when she was frightened, looking angry when she was in love and, like Katherine now, draping herself around in casual unconsidered shapes when there was something clearly important to be conveyed. Of course, Alice didn't know whether Sandra still did this; she hadn't seen her in eighteen months.

"That was the solicitor," Katherine said. "Tricia. She was phoning about the case. She was just giving us an update."

"Is there any news?" Malcolm said, after a pause.

"I thought you'd spoken to her," Katherine said, going to look out of the kitchen window. She turned the kitchen taps on, and started to wash her hands. "Well," she said, raising her voice, "they've decided not to bring charges."

"They're not going to—" Alice said, as Malcolm, simultaneously, said, "Against Nick, you mean?"

"I don't know about Nick," Katherine said. "She didn't say anything. Of course, she's not his solicitor. No, she, they, they're not going to press charges against me. They know I didn't do anything wrong."

At that point, Alice realized that that was how it was always going to be from now on. The moment of frank openness—a short moment, no more, in their lives—like an eye opening and shutting again in sleep, had gone away. Because the news had come when there was an audience, in front of whom pretence had to be kept up: from now on it had never been the case that Katherine had done anything wrong, that she had ever been in danger of being prosecuted and taken to court. Alice could feel the buttress-like projections of the last few weeks dissolving like pissed-on bubble-bath. That was how it was to be.

"Are they going to prosecute Nick?" Malcolm said, with a visible effort.

"Well, yes, they are," Katherine said. She was going now into that style which was almost the first thing Alice had found in her, when they first met; the tiny recoil when an unwelcome and inconvenient question was asked, the tiny beginnings of a party-like smile as if at a personal comment in bad taste from the friend of a guest, brought and welcomed under sufferance. "They must be. Tricia said that they'll want me as a witness when it comes to court."

All this behaviour was mounted for the benefit of an audience. It wasn't clear, though, who the confidant was, and who the audience before whom appearances had to be kept up. Katherine ought to be pretending that things were as she had expected in front of the neighbour, in front of Alice. In fact, it felt much more as if she was protecting Malcolm from the full knowledge of the scenario. There was now no hope that she would ever be honest with either of them, or anyone, about what she had once so clearly feared. She had been let off; and from now on, Alice knew, should she ever again mention the fact of Katherine's affair with, her feelings for Nick, she would be greeted with that faint party-like smile and twitch of surprise, and a change of subject. None of it had ever happened.

"They couldn't find anything to pin on her," Bernie observed, later that night, as they were getting ready for bed. He took off his string vest, dropping it in the bedside laundry basket, and then his old watch with an unhooking gesture. He laid it carefully on the bedside table next to the alarm clock. He sneezed, and shivered in his pyjama bottoms, string-tied at the waist. He rubbed his sides.

"I don't think there's anything there *to* pin on her," Alice said, sitting up in bed, looking over her book—she'd been reading *The Far Pavilions* for four weeks now, persevering with it; handling seemed to have increased its bulk by half as much again. "She didn't know anything about any of it."

"She must have wondered," Bernie said, and sneezed again.

"I worry that you're not eating properly," Alice said. "That's the fourth night running you've come in late and just picked at cold."

"It's nothing, just a summer sniffle," Bernie said. "It can't be helped, working late at the moment. I don't like it any more than you do, you know. It's not like you to start nagging."

"I'm not nagging," Alice said, astonished that Bernie could even think such a thing. It must be his tiredness. "I'm just worried about you, working all the hours God sends. We didn't move up here so that you could start knocking yourself out like this. You're working yourself to a frazzle."

"Won't go on for ever," Bernie said. "They can't last six months."

"Who can't?"

"The miners, love," Bernie said, laughing despite his exhaustion. He never got over how vague Alice could be about what he did at work for the Electric. There was a day, when they'd been married five years, when he actually asked her what she thought they made electricity out of. He'd never do anything so cruel again—it was agonizing, how painful she found the explication of her own ignorance. "I'll tell you something—if I were Scargill, if I wanted to make things difficult, I wouldn't have called a strike in spring. Look at the weather—demand for coal's never been so low."

"That's what Malcolm was saying," Alice said, cautiously and nervously. "At least they're having nice weather for their strike."

Bernie wondered again, but left it. "So she's in the clear?" he said.

"In the clear? Katherine. Yes, I suppose she is," Alice said, obscurely.

"They couldn't pin anything on her, as I say," Bernie said.

"Yes," Alice said. "Yes, that must be right."

"So—"

"What do you mean, so?"

"What's on your mind, then? You don't seem relieved that she's out of trouble."

Alice paused, setting down her book on her lap. That was true. There was some kind of fret tinging her thoughts when she contemplated Katherine's escape. And there had been something in the constantly maintained dissatisfaction and bewilderment in Katherine's face that made her think that Katherine, too, couldn't understand why she wasn't more relieved. Alice felt that Katherine, much as she loved her, had got away with something that she'd actually done. She hadn't cooked the books, she wouldn't know how—Alice often found it difficult to ascribe skills to women she knew that she herself didn't possess and couldn't have mastered. But she'd done something wrong, she knew that, and she wasn't being held to account for it. Where the court was that would judge Katherine, and find her definitively guilty or not guilty, that Alice didn't know, and understood that Katherine didn't know either. Those decisions had been promised, and now she was back where she had always been, with the ongoing sensation, not the single redemptive statement of guilt.

"She's still got to be a witness," Alice said.

"She won't like that," Bernie said. "Either sticking up for Nick or owning up to what he's done. She'd decided she didn't want anything more to do with him, yeah?"

"It's not a pleasant situation," Alice said.

"It's her own fault," Bernie said. "I don't know how Malcolm puts up with it, to tell you the truth."

"I don't think he does," Alice said. "What time do you have to be up in the morning?"

"Six thirty, love," Bernie said. "I'm sorry about all this. It's not going to go on for ever. You should find yourself a nice posh boyfriend with a flower shop, keep yourself busy while your husband's fannying about and worrying himself to a frazzle over the levels of coal stocks."

"That's not funny," Alice said, getting out of bed in her summer nightie, frilly and halfway down her thighs. "I'm just going to put my face on," she said, sitting down at the dressing-table and pulling the jar of cold cream as she always did.

"Not just yet," Bernie said, as he always did.

"Well, all right, then," Alice said, wondering whether there was anyone else in the world who still went to bed together, meaning, well, went to bed, every night, as the two of them did after thirty years of marriage. She didn't much care whether anyone else did or not. Good old Bernie.

"I saw him once," Bernie said, nuzzling into her neck and taking the hem of her nightie, scrunching it up on either side in his fists, in the way he had. He had lost his pyjama bottoms. She felt the sharp hair on his back and shoulders against the soft skin under her chin as he buried his face in the gap, which, yes, it seemed her neck and shoulder naturally made for it, yes, it did. "I saw him once, her Nick. I went into the shop, and I bought a bunch of flowers. Kept him running around. I was playing the Century bigshot, didn't know what I wanted, might be orchids, might be roses, might be lilies. Couldn't believe his luck. Running around with his 'Yes, sir, no, sir, a very wise decision, sir.' Posh little sod, isn't he? Not much sense in his face, though. I wouldn't lend him twenty quid and hope to see it again."

"You never brought me flowers home," Alice said.

"I'll tell you why. That's because I gave them flowers to me girlfriend," Bernie said.

"Get off," Alice said. She didn't even have to think about it.

"No, straight up," Bernie said, but he couldn't keep it going, and started laughing in the middle of what he was doing, perhaps envisaging the girlfriend he could never have had. "To be honest, what I did, I asked him to make up this bunch of flowers, told him I was just taking a leisurely stroll around the block to collect, I can't remember what I told him, say it was my dry-cleaning I had to collect. And would he make it up before I got back. Forty-pound bunch of flowers it would have been, like a bleeding wreath. And then I strolled round the block all right, but I strolled round the block to the car and I drove home."

"Bernie," mock-pushing him away, "that's terrible."

"Getting my own back, or not my own back, revenge on Malcolm's behalf. Husbands sticking together. Little sod."

"I still think that's a terrible thing to do. He'd not done you any harm."

"Course, she'd stopped working there by then, or it was her day off or something, she wasn't there or she'd have recognized me. She'd have known I wasn't serious. Forty-pound bunch of flowers."

"He'd have told her about it—Bernie, hang on, just a second, let me—I said, he'd have told her about it when she came in the next day," Alice said. "Described you. She'd have known who it was."

Because for Alice, there was only one person in the world who could ever have looked like Bernie.

"I'm not surprised you keep out of her way now," Alice said.

"Oh, I don't care," Bernie said. "He probably sold the whole bunch to the next mug who came in, anyway." And, pretty soon, Alice didn't much care either. There were things that were always worrying Katherine, making herself fret and nag on the other side of the road. There always had been and there always would be. In Bernie's arms, though he had to get up in seven hours' time, Alice thought there had never been much reason to join in, and that was the end of it.

The heat of the morning was turning even Orgreave into an idyllic setting, it seemed. Tim and Stig had been dropped by Trudy, who had hurtled away, hardly even slowing to let them out, and they had taken an indirect route through the little town, not wanting to be seen by any of the groups of policemen gathering at the street corners. They were trying to look as much like sons of the miners living in Orgreave as possible, and dived down one cul-de-sac after another, jumping over back walls and into back ginnels, kicking over dustbins. They only had the faintest idea of where they were going; the coke works was at the far end of the town, they knew, that was all. "Oi!" a woman shouted from her back door, and they jumped over another wall and ran.

They came to the back end of a cul-de-sac, and paused; there was no one around, but you could feel something brewing nearby in the tension in the air. It was just heat; it was just the pressure of history in the air; it was just the mutter of voices somewhere within a few hundred yards. One of those. Stig straightened in an unsuspicious way, gesturing with his thumb, and in a second, joyously, Tim and Stig were suddenly among what must have been a late group of miners, slipping down against all attempts by the oppressive forces of the police, and there they were in a crowd of T-shirted and bare-chested miners at the gates of the coke works. There they were.

On the grassy slopes about the gates to the works were hundreds of idling miners, like seals on a beach, or perhaps like pleasure-makers in a municipal park. It was already hot, and most of them were lazing in the sun; booted and trousered, but in T-shirts, like Tim and Stig, or bare-chested, as if they were sunning and tanning themselves. Tim and Stig walked a little way up the slope, sat down in an empty stretch, reclining back on their elbows. Stig set down his rucksack with the radical leaflets inside; they'd distribute them later. "Who the fuck are they?" Tim heard someone say, and was about to turn his head to stare.

Stig murmured, "Don't look round," and he was right; some of these people had a weird proprietorial attitude towards their legitimate protest; some even objected to the presence of people like Tim and Stig, directing the ideological aspect of the martial festivities. It didn't seem to occur to these people that they might be doing the ruling class's bidding, policing the substance of the protest on their behalf. It didn't seem to occur to these people that this struggle was not just a battle over pay and conditions, another in the long line of particular protests. This was a battle over the substance of the country, the nature of the land and who owned it, and it was not just for the miners, the card-carriers, to fight, but for the people of the land, all of them, the concerned ones. So if an unenlightened miner said, "Who the fuck are they?" you didn't turn round. You didn't turn round and say, "I'm fighting for you, but I'm fighting for everyone, too." In any case, at the moment, everyone was sitting enjoying the sunshine on the grassy slope, so it would have sounded a bit daft.

Everyone, that is, apart from the policemen. The town had been full of policemen, standing around on street corners like old women nattering; they'd been there to stop people like Stig and Tim, but Stig and Tim had got through. Down here by the coke works, there were lines of them by the gate. They hadn't been allowed to take off their shirts and jackets; they were red-faced with the heat already at nine thirty in the morning. They looked good humoured, and were even swapping caustic comments with the groups of miners down there, some kind of tense banter, you could see. Behind them, the police vans; spilling out of them, like a mound of winged insect carcasses, the riot shields, the helmets, that might be needed later.

Tim started to look around him, now that they were settled and somehow absorbed in the group, a little less the object of curiosity. There were small islands of miners here and there, some reclining like them or sitting, others squatting or standing, their characteristic bow legs apart, their hands up to their eyes, shading them. They were gossiping, swapping stories, in high good humour. Some of the men were going from group to group, bearing information, instructions. He couldn't imagine what this could be, until one passed them, and, looking at them with only a touch of scepticism, said, "The scabs' coach, it's set off now." At the top of the hill, there was a phone box, and men were crowding round it. That, clearly, was the nerve centre of the operation, the place where information spread from, a field telephone in a red box with broken glass windows. Tim looked back, towards his nearer neighbours, and the lad in the group next to him, reclining just like them, gave him a frank grin and, with a disclosing gesture, lifted up the edge of his screwed-up T-shirt on the ground. It was covering half a brick. Tim grinned back, self-consciously. He wished he'd thought of that. Give them something to do with the riot shields.

"There he is," Stig said, in a voice that said he'd been expecting this all along. Tim looked and he was right: it was Arthur there, visiting the men, striding from group to group with a little entourage. He was dressed more like your dad on a weekend, and his hair, complicated in arrangement but perfectly held, glistened in the sun like a badge of distinction.

"Who's that with him?" Tim said.

"You're kidding," Stig said.

"No," Tim said. "How the hell did he manage that?"

Because at the back of the little entourage, there was Vikram, of all people. He didn't seem to be with any of the others from their gang, and it was pretty clear from the way Scargill's temporary friends and associates were looking at him that they didn't know who he was, and didn't think he should be around. He must have found himself in the midst of the Scargill entourage, and taken the opportunity to tag along, but if he had any sense he'd peel off soon. Tim restrained the urge to wave; anyway, Vikram was looking directly towards them without making any gesture of recognition.

Time passed; it was quite pleasant sitting there. You almost wished you'd brought something to eat, a picnic. The policemen went on chatting; the miners wandered from group to group, and it looked, as the half-hour succeeded the hour, much more like social exchanges than the dissemination of strategy or tactics. It occurred to Tim that this might, in the end, turn out to be nothing much, that their information was wrong. They'd sit in the sun for a few hours, and drive home with burnt red face and arms. He'd put some factor sixteen on before he left home, slightly embarrassed about it; but he did burn, and it was painful when it happened. If they were there for more than three or four hours, he'd burn anyway.

"I reckon they've lost their nerve," Tim said in confidential tones to Stig.

"How do you mean?"

"I don't reckon they're coming at all," Tim said. "I reckon they're avoiding the confrontation, sending the scabs off somewhere else."

"I don't know about that," Stig said. "There's got to be a confrontation sooner or later, unless they're admitting defeat already. They're not about to do that just yet."

And as if in confirmation, the police—it might have been at a signal—seemed to break off their edgily cosy exchanges with the miners and, with not so much as a polite nod of farewell, drained away in one blue movement towards the gates and their heavy-sided vans. It was like the draining of a mass of water, the retreat of a sea before a tidal wave, and the miners, as if in shock and offence at the social affront, began to stand. First the miners at the front, the ones the police had been talking to, and then the whole crowd stood, rippling up the hill towards the back in a single wavelike movement. They all stood there, on the hill, a mass of disparate men in their uncertain groups, and for the first time, Tim noticed a huddle of Yorkshire Television people, journalists with notebooks, photographers at the main road, all standing together in fear or safety. What are they frightened of? he thought, but then remembered it hadn't started yet. It was just starting.

The police had withdrawn to arm themselves, and when the first of the insect battalions turned about, their surfaces reduced to blank geometries that blazed under the Yorkshire sun, the miners made a noise: an angry, offended noise, a murmur that turned into a grumble and a roar and a shout within a couple of seconds. It was this noise that seemed to coagulate the mass of men into order, turn them from a rabble on a hill standing around into a crowd, a rank, a battalion.

The police stand there, facing them in silence, and the men roar, and go on roaring; their weapons, if they have thought to acquire them, now in their hands: half-bricks, stones, bottles, even a park railing like a javelin. They brandish them openly, and the police raise their hard plastic shields, each with a slash of sun reflected on it like a blazon.

And the roar proves an incantation because it summons the police, calls them into their places, their orders of battle; it calls up something else, too, the thing the miners have been waiting for. The roar falls, just for a moment, and there in the gap is the noise of an old diesel-fuelled charabanc, put-putting away, just over the hill, accompanied by some remote and more human noises—off-stage shouting, something being thrown—and the roar on the hillside rises again, as everyone compresses, forms themselves into a mass, and their noise seems to call up an apparition, a noonday ghost, a terrible vision. Now, like the chariots of the dead, like tumbrils of pure evil, the scabs' vans come into sight. They are a morbid green, splashed, too, with paint, not thrown, but an attempt to obliterate the windows, so that the scabs cannot be seen. There is no point in it: people know. From here, the outline is blurred; the coaches are almost entirely encased in wire cages.

They need to be. The hurling of rocks and bricks starts immediately, and even from Tim's position the yelling, the thudding of bricks against the coaches is deafening; inside it must be terrifying. He catches himself, thinks again, yells louder. "Scabs! Scabs! Scabs!" The police are moving forward, in their regimented way, pushing back the miners who are rushing forward to the vans; but the pressure is too much, the police are being pushed back themselves into the path of the coaches, which slow. There is a redoubling of rage, fallen rocks and bricks being picked up and hurled again, and now the miners are at the sides of the vans, and starting to push and rock. In the hail of stones and rocks, Tim is pushed and pushes, the stink of—incredibly—the mineral stink of deodorant from a miner's armpit in his nose, and all the time yelling in his ear. He is a few inches taller than most, and there are only three or four miners between him and the van's side. All at once he sees, through perhaps a scratched-away patch of paint, a face—no, really just an eye, and one with clear terror deep in it. Good, Tim thinks, serve the—serve the—"Scabs!" he yells.

Something hard descends, there, to his right, and the sound of bone being struck very heavily. Stig has disappeared, somewhere in the mob. The van has stopped, and a thunderous banging on the sides and doors; it is beginning to rock, pushed by the men on the other side. They will turn it over, and open it up, and then, Tim thinks, they'll kill them, they'll kill the scabs—there is a rise in the thrill in his throat at that. He turns, yelling, feeling himself at the head of this violence, this uprising, leading it, but everyone is yelling, everyone is calling out instructions. Everyone is calling, "Kill the scabs," and they will; but there, next to him, a man, he has been struck with something, and there is blood running down from his bald head, through his eyes and features, making him unrecognizable. He could be anyone.

He looks again, and there, from behind—how?—pressing behind him, there are the police. What had descended a moment ago descends again, hard, and hits the bleeding man; it is a police truncheon. All at once, a gap opens up, away from the police and their hard shields, their truncheons, and, half stumbling, Tim steps sideways, running and tripping over himself as he goes. He is heading up the hill towards a bunch of stone-throwers; now they are throwing not just at the vans but into the united front of the police squadrons, unified and tight as a Roman battalion behind their contemptuously transparent shields. There are some direct hits; you can hear the thunder of the bricks on shields and, as Tim stumbles directly up the hill into the path of the throwers, he ducks and finds his hand, as he falls on to the earth, closing on a rock—no, a heavy lump of coal. He has no time to pause for the irony of this, if there is any irony, if it isn't just what the coke works deals in, what the earth here gives up; he turns and he throws it as hard as he can, into the police lines, the lump of coal describing a perfect parabola, curving just over the edge of the shield, hitting a hot and frightened policeman on his shoulder, inflicting some grave injury. Or so he thinks: his rock just disappears in a hail of stones, and could have gone anywhere. All at once a policeman is hurtling up the hill towards him, having seen him throw a rock, the copper's truncheon out, and Tim is legging it.

The violence ebbs away, in flourishes and bursts, and after a time, the men are sitting again on the grass, now torn and scattered with rocks and bricks; quite a lot of them are now nursing bleeding heads and bandaging themselves with handkerchiefs, whatever comes to hand. Tim is looking for Stig: he has the pamphlets to hand out. At these moments—Lenin said something along these lines—class consciousness falls away in the liberations of violence and the revolutionary spirit prevails. Lenin said that. Or he said something like that. So Tim looks for Stig with his rucksack of information, but he can't find him. He is just wondering how, really, he is going to get home, since he doesn't know where anyone is or where the car is and he doesn't think there's going to be much in the way of public transport running to Orgreave today, when a fine thing happens. The great man himself has been present all through today's events, leonine, magnificent. Tim has seen him from a distance, stirring up the troops, inspiring them. And then, all at once, at the end of the day, Tim stumbles into a group of miners, and one turns round and it is Arthur. He looks directly into Tim's face, and Tim looks into his—bruised and broken, heroic and bleeding. He seems to be expecting Tim to say something, inspecting him knowingly.

"The people, united—" Tim says. He can't think of anything to say, and it sounds, all of a sudden, completely stupid. But the great man has more of a sense of history than Tim does. He has more of a sense of the moment than his lieutenants, who are eyeing Tim with a sense of ludicrous wonderment.

"The people, united," Arthur says, seizing his hands, "will never be defeated."

Timothy, stirred, turns away to look for Trudy and Stig or Vikram, anyone who might have a bit of space in the back of their car to give him a ride to Rayfield Avenue or Sheffield town centre at a pinch, with a sense that here he has been at the cutting edge of history, and has the innocent blood spilt on his turn-ups to prove it. Scabs.

It had been hers, the idea of an outing. Daniel thought it marked a particular step in going-out-together when she started suggesting "an outing" of a Saturday. It would be the first time they'd met during the day. Daniel drew on his experience of women, and concluded that it might even mean dropping in on her parents—girls, Daniel knew, liked to show him off. Helen was more sensible than that, and it wasn't completely clear that they were, in fact, going out together. But it might mean dropping in on her parents, and he bore that in mind when he got dressed that Saturday morning.

Daniel also thought that the yellow Cortina might not do. Helen, when she arrived, came immediately to the same conclusion. "Are we going out in that?" she said, poking at the gap where the back bumper was held on with duct tape.

"It looks a lot worse than it really is," Daniel said.

"If it looked any worse," Helen said illogically, "it'd be lying in the road in pieces. It couldn't look much worse, Daniel."

"The fact is," Daniel said, and went on to tell her, as they stood in the street outside his flat on a Saturday morning, looking at the sad failure of his yellow Cortina, that two days earlier, he'd been driving into the car park on top of Gateway, where the turns in the ramps were sharper than you expected, and someone had been coming down who obviously didn't think there was anyone coming up in the other direction, and they'd had a glancing but catastrophic collision. The chap had given a cheery wave, which Daniel assumed meant "Carry on up to the next level as best you can, park, and I'll be up in a second to swap insurance details." But in fact it meant "I'm off as fast as I can, pal, before you can take my number."

"You are an idiot, Daniel," Helen said. "It looks terrible. Doesn't it?" she went on, appealing to a passer-by.

"I've seen worse," the passer-by said, a brown man in a hat and a pipe, a festively bounding King Charles spaniel at his dour crimplene ankles. "But not many."

She'd be asking the views of the old sod on the ground floor of Daniel's house next, who was peering out from between his net curtains with undisguised enjoyment of the scene. He hadn't thought it worth the bother of putting his teeth in. "I thought you liked my car," Daniel said to Helen, ignoring the old sod's horrible expression. "You said it was the one thing about me that made you think I wasn't a gormless twat."

The passer-by gave a sage nod, and walked on, as if something he'd thought had just been confirmed. "I must have been drunk," Helen said. "Or it can't have been daylight. Or it must have been held together by something other than parcel tape. One of the three. Do you think it'll get us there?"

"Oh, aye," Daniel said, dropping a bit further into Sheffield, as Helen so often made him do. "Get you all the way to Rotherham, that. And back again, probably. Where are we going, anyway?"

"We're going on a little outing," Helen said. "I thought we'd go to Tinstone."

"That's on the other side of Rotherham," Daniel said.

"Well done," Helen said. "I thought you never went further in that direction than the Hole in the Road."

"I've been to Rotherham," Daniel said, always fearful that Helen thought him a bit of a snob.

"We'll take our chances with the car," Helen said.

"Tinstone, that's a terrible rough sort of place to be going for an outing, though," Daniel said. "That's a mining town. Why are we going there?"

"Have you ever been there?"

"No," Daniel said. "Just to Rotherham. I've never had any reason to go to Tinstone."

"Well, you've a reason to now," Helen said, in her most practical voice, her bed-bath voice to an unwilling patient. "I thought you might like to go there to see where I grew up, as a matter of fact. And, by the way, my father's a miner, before you start saying anything else about terrible rough towns like Tinstone."

Daniel subsided, fairly amicably, and got into the car. He leant over and opened the door on Helen's side, and she got in, putting her bag on her lap. "It'll start in a moment," he said, after it had failed to do so twice, with the straining sound of an unsatisfied but deeply resounding cough. "It's just that it's been parked on the hill. There's nothing wrong with the engine, as far as I know."

"Is that a new shirt you've got on?"

"Fairly new," Daniel said, pleased that she'd noticed. The engine caught at last, and Daniel lifted off the handbrake with relief.

He hoped the car would make it there and back—it wasn't just the duct-tape, he was a bit worried about the little whinnying noises the engine had started to make. He didn't know how far Tinstone was or, really, where it was. "You're going to have to guide me there," he said to Helen, who was already chattering about that week's most amusing sick cases.

"You just head down to the Wicker," Helen said. "Now, that's a terrible rough part of town. I once had a disgusting curry down there, and someone hit me on the head with a poppadom."

"That'll have been me, last week, in the Kashmir," Daniel said. "Did you get the bits out of your hair?"

"Not while Thursday," Helen said. "The whole ward was at it, picking bits out. It were the mango chutney that were the bugger." And by the time they got down to the Wicker, she was explaining the connection of every tenth building to herself, or her friends, or her family, starting with her aunty Muriel's pork stall in the Castle Market.

"That was the first job I had, after leaving school," she said. "There, in there, in British Steel. It was an office job. I hated it. I were just sixteen, and my dad asked a friend of his in the Latin if he could suggest anything for me, and he worked at British Steel, so there you go."

"How do you mean, in the Latin?" Daniel said, thinking of the *amo amas amat* they did up the road at King George V, going on as if they were still a grammar school. They didn't do it at Flint.

"In the Latin. My dad, he's a ballroom dancer," Helen said, "in his spare time. He loves it. Him and me mum, they've won all sorts of cups. They specialize in the Latin—they won at Blackpool two years ago in the tango, that's what he likes best. They used to be just tango, but now they're Argentinian tango."

"What's the difference?"

"Oh, it'd take too long to explain to you. He's always saying that one day they're going to go to Argentina to learn about it properly—he's that mad about it, he was on their side in the Falklands war, said they should have the Falklands if they wanted them. Course, my mum wouldn't go, even without the Falklands. She says mostly it's the food she couldn't deal with. Crete were bad enough."

"You must be a bit of a disappointment to him," Daniel said, looking at the vast brick cliffs of the foundry, blackened brick rising above a sad and depleted car park, its signages soiled and half readable, even the main hoarding-sized announcement at the gate. He hardly ever came down here, and he'd never really looked at any of the huge ugly buildings on either side of the route. It was difficult to imagine Helen, so neat and clean in her movements, working in so savage and untended a place.

"How do you mean, a disappointment?" Helen said.

"You not taking it up and all," Daniel said.

"Oh, he doesn't mind," Helen said. "I learnt it for seven years, until I were sixteen. I even got to dyeing my hair black and greasing it down, because you can't do the Latin with blonde hair that's fluffy like mine. And I did a few competitions, a nice boy I danced with called David Horniman—he lives with his boyfriend in Middlewood."

"You drove him to it, then," Daniel said. He meant madness, since Middlewood was where the mental hospital was, but too late he saw the insulting ambiguity of his comment.

She batted it aside. "He works in the steelworks, the boyfriend, on the factory floor. I'd say that was quite unusual, he's called Michael. Insists on that, he does, not being called Mike or Micky or Mick, pretends not to hear you, then, 'No, my name's actually Michael.' That's what he says, just like that. He worked in this one coming up, Osborne's, as a matter of fact. It's just closed down. They're all closing down, aren't they? I don't know what happened to that Michael. I wouldn't have thought he'd find it easy to get another job.

"Well, I went in for a competition or two, but we weren't even placed, and it weren't David's fault, because he's very good, it were me. I could get round floor, I could do it piece by piece, but it never looked quite right. It's because of the shape I am, and in the end Dad had to give up hoping and David found himself another partner."

"Not Michael who worked at Osborne's?"

"Oh, no, they wouldn't stand for that, they'd be up in arms. I had a job teaching the little ones at the dance school in Rotherham the summer I left school, just a summer job. I were quite good at that. They could always see what I was trying to do because I couldn't ever quite manage it. But then I went off and worked at British Steel—it's not much of a job, teaching the little ones the rudiments of the waltz—and then when I got fed up with that, I went to train as a nurse at the Hallamshire and took to going down Casanova's on a Friday night and here I am. How did I get on to that? Oh, you asked about Dad and the Latin."

"My dad's in a battle society."

"What's that, then?"

"They re-create famous old battles—they get dressed up, and go out on the moors, once a year, every year."

"How do you mean?"

Daniel explained.

"I'd like to see the photographs of that," Helen said. "It sounds daft. Did you ever do it?"

"I've been a roundhead and a cavalier," Daniel said. "When I was younger, I mean."

"I'd pay good money to see that," Helen said. "Look, there, that's Linda's, that house standing on its own."

"Oh, I know about Linda's," Daniel said. "At school, everyone always said it was a brothel because there's a red light outside."

"It's not a brothel," Helen said. "It's where the gay boys go. Everyone knows that."

"Well, at Flint we didn't know that. We thought it was a brothel. There was one lad who said he'd been there and dozens of beautiful women were lying around with nothing on. I knew he was lying. You've not got a relative who works there, have you?"

"The very idea," Helen said. "But here, at Cooper's, my uncle, my mum's brother, he's foreman there, or he was. He managed to get early retirement. He says he's lucky, they'll not be there in twelve months' time. All this, along here, it's the Golden Mile. Every steelworks, every factory, everything, it's all closing down. There'll be nothing here in five years' time, nothing except buildings. They won't bother knocking them down, but there'll be no one to work in them, no one's going to take them over."

"Sad when you think about it," Daniel said.

"Oh, aye," Helen said. "When you think about it."

He'd hardly ever been out this side of Sheffield. It was as if the landscaped half—the groomed and gardened, the sunlit park side out towards the moors where he'd always lived and gone to school—had been ripped up from its bedding, and its rough dirty roots held up for examination. On this side of the city, there were stretches of waste-ground between the foundries, half-standing walls and raw fields of rubble and soot-painted leggy weeds. Only every so often a single building, left whole, such as Linda's the brothel, like a single tooth in a foul old mouth. This side of the city had been destroyed by German bombs, decades ago. Where money could be made again, those foundries had been built or rebuilt; the steel foundries, the cutlers', the great names, they went back a hundred or more years. He knew that: the school "houses" at Flint, the ones you were put into when you arrived at school and had to struggle to remember what you were in when it got to sports day, there had been four, each a different colour, each of them had been named after a different famous steel-maker. He'd been, what? Firth. It had been green.

"The cutlers, they'll be all right," Helen said. "People are always going to want 'Sheffield Plate' on their knives and forks. The foundries, though, they can't go on. It's not economical, they reckon."

"Once, at school, they said to us, there are places in America where they just decided to call the town Sheffield so that they could make knives and put 'Sheffield Steel' on them."

"I never heard that," Helen said.

"I can remember her saying it—what was her name, that teacher? She said it was a dirty cheap trick people would play. I'm glad I don't have to do that kind of work. Steel, not teaching."

"You sound like my dad when he's talking about mining," Helen said. "And he actually does it. Says nobody ought to have to do something as bad as that."

"Is he on strike at the moment?"

Helen looked at him, a proper old-fashioned look. "You're not going to meet him, you know."

"Where did that come from?"

"I'm just saying, you're not going to meet him. Least, not this afternoon you're not."

"I wouldn't mind."

"I dare say not. But, yes, he's on strike, and he's not very happy about it."

"I still don't understand why we can't go and say hello."

"Because then they'd have to invite you to stay for tea, and we'd probably end up staying because they're not going to take no for an answer."

"I'm not going to look down my nose at them, if that's what you're thinking."

Helen shook her head. "I don't care whether you look down your nose at them or not. I'm not having them laying every blessed thing they have in the kitchen on the table for the sake of company. They're managing, and I'm helping out, my brother's helping out a bit more, but I don't think it's easy at the moment. All right? It's not all about you, you know."

"I'm sorry," Daniel said. That morning, he'd gone through his fridge; there was cheese in it, milk, which had gone off because he'd forgotten about it; a pack of mushrooms he'd bought thinking he'd do something with them and never had, gone grey and wrinkled under the cellophane; an old onion at the back and a pound of mince he'd never got round to. He'd thrown it all out, just as when he made too much for himself he threw the rest out, not thinking about it. Last week, he'd opened the boot of the car for the first time in weeks, and found a bag of shopping there; stuff for salad, dripping brown water by now, and a whole ready-made chilli from Marks, and a bottle of wine. When he was a kid, they'd had to go sometimes to his nana Glover's for Sunday lunch, or she'd come for Christmas lunch, and when he'd try to get out of eating the sprouts or the horrible parsnips leaking water on to the plates, or the potatoes that were never quite mashed properly, his nana Glover, a whiskery old woman with the sweet smell of wee and parsnips, she'd always say the same thing: "Eat it all up, there's starving children in Biafra," or "in Bangladesh," or just "in Africa." But Bangladesh and Africa and Biafra were a long way away—where the heck was Biafra, anyway?—and Tinstone was only the other side of Rotherham. No one could be starving in Tinstone. It was a load of bollocks.

"Is your dad on strike, though?" Daniel said.

"He's supposed to be," Helen said. "He's just staying at home, though, and not working. He's not going down the picket line or anything. He doesn't approve of it."

"Why's he on strike, then?"

"You don't know what it's like," Helen said. "You can't carry on working in those towns if everyone else is on strike. Your life wouldn't be worth living."

"But what would happen if everyone felt like that?"

"Everyone does," Helen said. "Sometimes I can't believe you were born in this town—you don't seem to understand anything about anything. I suppose you just left school and thought about what you wanted to do, and started doing it, and if you got fed up of persuading people to buy houses, you'd go and do something else. Is that about the size of it?"

"That sounds normal," Daniel said.

"I don't think it's much like that for most people in Tinstone," Helen said. "Here's Rotherham."

The blasted abandoned streets had given way to a few houses, an estate, and then a stately old municipal school, rising behind preserved railings and gateways at the top of a rise of lawn. Suddenly, people, too: groups of boys, sitting on walls, a mother hunched over a pram loaded with baby and shopping bags, and everything so poor. If Daniel didn't think about it, he could imagine himself in this big car as a rich man, cruising smoothly through charred settlements he would never walk through; if it were not for the insistent whine and grumble of the motor, and Helen sitting by his side, to whom he could never say any of that.

"I tell you what," Helen said, "we will go and see my mum and dad. If you want to."

"Course I want to," Daniel said. He'd thought she always wanted to, yet this struck him as a genuine change of mind, one somehow in his favour. "What's changed your mind?"

"I'll ask you a question," Helen said. "Do you ever use the expression 'That's how the other half live?' "

"I don't think I've ever used it, but I've heard it."

"And what do you mean by it? Or what do you think people mean by it? If you hear them use it."

"What's all this?"

"Just answer the question."

"Well, it means—what people are like, people who aren't like you, don't live like you. I mean, you know, people who don't—all right, if I used it, I'd mean people who didn't have any money. 'Let's go to Castle Market and see how the other half live.' I suppose you could say that, though I wouldn't—it doesn't seem very kind."

"Well, there you are. You see, Daniel, when most people say 'the other half'—normal people, I mean—they don't mean poor people. They mean very rich people."

"I thought you were explaining why we weren't going to see your dad and now we are."

"It just occurred to me," Helen said, turning sideways and thoughtfully inspecting Daniel's face, "that if we go there now, they'll have finished whatever they've had for lunch, and we can get away before the

question of tea arises. There's that, and there's the thought that if anyone sees me in Tinstone they'll hear, and wonder why I didn't drop in
on them."

"That's a good point. What are you looking at?"

"I'm just looking at you. Don't you ever get spots? You've got skin
like a girl."

"I've had a spot."

"I bet you cleanse."

"Fuck off."

They were through Rotherham, with its discount shops, its women-
folk with trolleys, its jammed mess of blue and white buses, and soon
turned off the A-road to Tinstone. Only one of the front windows in
Daniel's car opened, the passenger window, and through it came a
dense choking smell, as of tons of burning stone and metals. But you
could see even here there was countryside, too; the slag heaps intervened in front of some hills, which swelled and were green. It was
really a lovely day; those distant hills with their fields glowed, and
through what must once have been a valley a line of glittering pylons
was frozen in some vast rural dance. The little town was a mass of identical houses, all built at the same time, and at the far side, a winding
mechanism rose up, the head of the mine where they worked.

"Are they all on a picket line, then?" Daniel said, as they turned off
again.

"Probably," Helen said. "My dad won't be, though. He says he's
done enough, withdrawing his labour. He's been down there thirty
years. Left again here."

"I don't know why you like me," Daniel said, quite suddenly.

"And it's probably quite good for you not to know very well why
someone likes you. That's what I think."

The street where Helen's parents lived was very much like the other
streets they'd passed through. The houses were in pairs, identical
except for the various colours of the front doors. The gardens were
neat, and well-kept, but not much more for the most part. Only once or
twice did something more ambitious appear: a complicated garden of
roses, doing as well as could be expected, witness to a serious hobby,
and once, an absurd plaster porch in the style of a Greek temple, shining brilliantly against the yellow-grey brick of the semi-detached house.
The cars in the drives were small and clean; there was nothing like
Daniel's terrible Cortina. It wasn't like the towns of the poor he had
always imagined, nothing like a place where people worried about food.

Helen's parents lived at number forty-two, and their front door was a cheerful blue, the front garden neatly kept with a sort of standard border of marigolds and lobelias. It wasn't the house of a tango champion, and when the woman opened the door, too quickly after Helen's brisk ring, she didn't look much like a tango champion either. There was only a suggestion of neatness about her figure and an upright stance to imply any of that.

"You could have phoned," she said to Helen, with a degree of reproachful but delighted welcome, inspecting not Helen but Daniel. "And who's this, then?"

It had been one of Philip Cavan's worse days. They'd grown more frequent since the men from the NUM had decided to leave him alone. When they'd first gone out on strike, announced it without a ballot, Philip had been one of those who'd grumbled. "It won't get anyone anywhere," he said. "We'll be out on strike for four months and then they'll close down the pits just as they would have done." There was a lot of talk of "solidarity," though, and talk like Philip's wasn't popular, however many might have agreed with it. "Solidarity with who? That's what I'd like to know," he said.

"Solidarity with the lads, Phil," Thiselton, the new NUM man had said—he was twenty years younger than Cavan, and a firebrand.

Philip had liked John Collins well enough, Thiselton's predecessor as the union man, but this one talked too much about the working man's struggle and the fascist Tory government for his liking. Philip would never have admitted it to anyone, not even to Shirley, but the year before, the only reason he'd not voted for Mrs. T was the nonsense in the Falklands. Apart from that, she was doing the country a lot of good, he reckoned. Thiselton was Scargill's man, and Philip couldn't stand Arthur. "It's all very well him calling us all out on strike without the courtesy of a ballot," he'd observed to Thiselton, "but it's not him going to lose his job at the end of it, is it, now?"

All these observations were made during a series of visits by the union men to Philip's house in the early days of the strike. At first they'd tried to get him to come and do his stint at the picket line. "I reckon giving up my wages at Arthur's command is solidarity enough," Philip said, and they'd stopped trying to persuade him. They settled, in the end, for a promise that he wouldn't go back to work against the clear majority wishes of the mine-workers. "What majority wishes?" Philip asked. "Show me the ballot results." The man from the NUM explained that there was no ballot, because the requirement to hold a

ballot was one imposed on working people by the fascist Tory government in a clear attempt to frustrate the democratically expressed
wishes of the working classes. "Oh, aye," Philip said laconically, then
kindly observed that he supposed the lads had mostly come out, and
that was a majority, any road.

Having extracted this minimal promise, the NUM left him and
Shirley alone to fill their days as best they could. They could practise
the tango in the community hall, cluttered up now with banners and
collection tins and boxes of donated cans of food, waiting for the boot-
faced NUM wives to hand out to supposedly deserving cases. The food
got collected in Sheffield town centre, half by the boot-faced contin-
gent and half by a lot of silly students being supported through university by Mummy and Daddy and all the tax Philip Cavan had paid over
the years. Shirley'd made it clear, when the NUM wives had come
round at the start to gather names, that she wouldn't demean herself by
accepting hand-outs, hadn't in her life eaten dinner out of tin cans and
didn't propose to start eating tinned food now, donated or not. She'd
kept them on the doorstep with their little clipboards, rudely hadn't
asked them in, had made it plain that solidarity wouldn't now require
her to ask women into her house she'd never have asked in before.
Philip was proud of her, even if the bit about not eating tinned food
wasn't strictly true, and as they practised the tango, she took care, at
least once each session, to kick over a pile of tinned beans with one of
her famous, neatly timed turns.

But there was not much to practise for, and even those competitions
on the horizon, they wondered whether they could justify the expense
of travel and accommodation. Not that they'd say so to each other.
The practising only took up a couple of hours a day; in the evenings
there were books to read; there was the trip, once a week, to Rotherham to the library to change their books—they both liked biography,
Shirley at the moment reading a life of Disraeli, Philip on the third
volume of a life of Tchaikovsky. The house had never been so clean,
the garden so well weeded. People left them alone. Everyone knew
what Phil's position was. He wasn't a blackleg, but he wasn't part of the
strike either, and anyone with any sense would have worked out that he
wasn't far off retirement, and wouldn't much care if the pit closed
down. It was all right for him: he'd take the redundancy money and
he'd have his pension soon enough.

But they were left alone, and it was clear how much Philip had enjoyed his audience in the first days of the strike, how much he'd enjoyed explaining to them why he wasn't going to join in, why they were wasting their time, what he thought of Arthur Scargill, all in all. He hadn't said to them that he thought Mrs. T was doing a good job for the country, Falklands nonsense notwithstanding, but if they'd persevered, it would have come in time to that. What he missed, now, was an audience. He'd allowed himself to assume that the professional duty of the NUM men, coming round to lecture him, would go on indefinitely, allowing him to ask them awkward questions and lecture them more extensively as long as the strike lasted. Perhaps he'd thought that once Thiselton had run out of things to say, he'd bring in the regional heads of the NUM to talk to Philip, and so on upwards until Philip found himself, with great joy, talking down Scargill himself in his own front room. What he hadn't imagined was that Thiselton would just give up, go away and leave Philip in peace, with no one to lecture on the iniquities of the strike, the foolishness of the whole enterprise and its inevitable disaster, no one but Shirley. Shirley couldn't give up. She had to put up with it.

She was dusting in the front room when, through the curtains, she saw Helen coming up the path with a young man she didn't know. Her first reaction was relief, fast followed by wonderment at what the young man seemed to have on. She dashed to the front door, taking off the housecoat she wore for cleaning and hanging it quickly in the cupboard under the stairs. She wanted to have a better look.

"You could have phoned," she said, looking him up and down. "And who's this?"

The young man was wearing the sort of clothes—well, she wouldn't want to say what first came to mind. But the second thing that came to mind was the sort of pantomime they'd taken the children to at Christmas. His shoes were black and shiny, and witchily pointed—you'd fall over your feet in shoes like that. His trousers were jeans, but black and tight enough to cut off his circulation. The young lads in Tinstone liked to get dressed up, and that was only to be expected. But they wouldn't wear a shirt like that, though it was brilliantly white and obviously brand new; the sleeves billowed like a girl's blouse, and the collar was just daft, a butterfly collar of the sort old rich people used to wear with dinner jackets and bow-ties. He wasn't wearing a bow-tie, though, but had two buttons undone; a dark flurry of hair, trimmed short like pencil strokes, showed at the top of his chest. He was a handsome young man, with shining white teeth, long eyelashes about his dark blue eyes, and a little flush of pink in his dark face as he smiled, but his clothes couldn't have been more ridiculous.

"This is Daniel," Helen said. "I'm sorry about his car, lowering the tone of the neighbourhood, but it couldn't be helped."

"We don't care anything about things like that round here," Shirley said, ushering them in. She turned and had a look; it was a long yellow car, badly bashed in, but she wasn't in much of a position to say anything, and this might be the sort of young man, like a student or something, for whom a car like that might be amusing. They used to drive old London taxis, young men like that, years ago, she remembered. "I think your dad's in the garden."

Once they were in the front room, the young man produced a cellophane-wrapped cake, a shop cake, from behind his back. "We thought we'd contribute something in case you were going to make us a cup of tea," he said cheekily.

"That's nice of you," she said, but she recognized it as one of the cakes you could get from Rita's shop in Tinstone. She didn't think much of shop-bought cakes, and the sort that Rita sold, she wouldn't ever have offered those to a guest. If they were going to bring a cake, they could have got one in Sheffield or even in Rotherham.

"Daniel wanted to see where I grew up," Helen said.

"Well, there's not much to see," Philip said, coming in from the garden. Helen introduced Daniel to him. "There's where you went to school, and the playing-fields out the back, but I wouldn't go anywhere near the mine this afternoon. They've been having trouble down there."

"Is it the police?" Daniel asked.

"No," Philip said. "It's a lot of idiotic hot-heads with nothing better to do than sit there day after day. It's worse elsewhere, I hear—they're throwing rocks and Molotov cocktails at each other down at Orgreave coking plant. But it's bad enough here."

"There's people down there never worked at Tinstone," Shirley said. "People never been down a mine, come to that, don't care anything for it, just want to make trouble."

Daniel blushed for some reason. "Are those your cups?" he said, getting up and looking at the mock-mahogany display cabinet, crowded with trophies, large and small; they were almost an extra source of light in the little room, they shone so sharply. "I've heard about your winning prizes for dancing."

"Ballroom dancing," Philip corrected mildly. "In the Latin."

"I'll put the kettle on," Shirley said.

"I was telling him on the way over," Helen said, putting her bag on the floor and sitting down, "about the Latin competitions you've won. I was saying—"

But Daniel's attention had been caught by the way Helen sat down, in a single graceful movement, and by the way her knees, popping out from her above-knee skirt like bashful bald angels, held together and slid with somehow the same grace to the side of the armchair, her lovely unclad calves making an ideal chevron to the floor. It was beautifully done, something only a finishing school or perhaps a dancing school in Rotherham could have taught; or, perhaps, something to be acquired by natural elegance. It could have been Princess Diana sitting there, and he himself sat down with a feeling of comparative lumpiness. You wouldn't have thought this little parlour, with its ugly highlights of the elaborate cups in a glass-fronted cabinet, could have produced such natural discreet elegance.

"My dad just asked you a question," Helen said.

"I'm sorry, Philip," Daniel said. "I was away admiring all your trophies."

"Oh, aye," Helen's dad said, with what might have been amusement; Daniel must have been staring at Helen's legs clearly enough. "I just wondered where you met our Helen."

"Oh," Daniel said. "I think we first met at Casanova's, in Sheffield, the nightclub. We've got friends in common," he added, in a rush, in case they should think their daughter was the sort of girl who picked up strangers.

"There's a lot of skill in disco dancing," Shirley said gnomically, calling through from the kitchen; it wasn't far to call. "There's competitions for it."

"Of course, we're too old for that," Philip said. "High kicks and that. I've not seen our Helen do it. Is she good at it?"

"It's not like that, Dad," Helen said sharply, and Daniel could see the difference between "disco dancing," as Philip and Shirley had perhaps seen it executed on stage in a Blackpool ballroom, men in all-in-one rhinestone-encrusted Lycra doing their damnedest to kick their own eyebrows, and the sort of "dancing" that happened on the under-lit dance-floor at Casanova's, which was basically estate agents in suits, like him, shifting from one foot to another, and making odd clay-modelling gestures with their hands.

"Oh, I dare say," Philip said. "Do you like dancing, Daniel?"

"I've never really learnt," Daniel said, seeing this as the easiest reply. "I enjoy it, and I'm sure I'd enjoy it more if I knew what to do properly."

"He's an embarrassment on the dance-floor, this one," Helen said.

"Try and be a bit more polite, love," Shirley said, coming through with, obviously, the best china, the milk in a little pink floral jug and the shop-bought cake in neat slices on top of a pile of matching floral plates. "You want him to come again, don't you?"

"He'll think you weren't brought up to know how to behave," Philip added, with that married-couple thing, not exactly finishing each other's sentences, but chiming in with matching responses. "Would you like to learn?"

"Learn to dance?" Daniel said.

"I can show you the first rudiments of the tango," Philip said, and was, incredibly, up on his feet in a second, his arm outstretched. Daniel couldn't believe he was serious, and was half expecting the two women to burst out laughing—apart from anything else, there was no space to dance in this little room, with its bulging fat tasselled three-piece suite decorated with a brown forestry pattern around the low coffee-table. But Helen and Shirley were looking at Philip with shy indulgence; they knew what a generous thing he was offering to a non-dancer like Daniel.

Daniel's hesitation was clear, and Helen said, "Go on, he's just going to show you the first position." So Daniel did, and with his elbows stiff, allowed himself to be held by Philip, a good eight inches shorter than him.

"That's no good," Philip said. "I can see you've not learnt to dance. It looks like a stiff dance, but you can't hold yourself as stiffly as that," and he took one of Daniel's arms, then the other, shaking it until it seemed to move in a single wave from wrist to shoulder. "There," Philip said, "and try not to hold your head like that, and your feet like—no, not quite, more like—" he kicked Daniel's right foot, then nudged it, then the left "—no, don't move your right foot, that was just right, and then, soon as I touch your left, you move it, let's try again."

It took half an hour before Daniel was remotely in the correct starting position for a tango; Helen and Shirley had drunk the teapot dry, and when Daniel finally collapsed, amazed and exhausted, into the armchair, Shirley had to go out to boil some more water for the pot. Philip looked at him, his eyes shining with laughter.

"It's not as easy as it looks, is it?" he said.

"It's not as easy as it looks," Daniel said to Helen, later in the car, as they were driving back towards Sheffield.

"It's easier if you start learning when you're younger," Helen said. "You've got used to putting your body in all sorts of strange positions, so standing naturally, it doesn't seem natural at all to you. You could still learn, though."

"Really?" Daniel said. "It's not one of those things you have to start when you're six?"

"Well, if you wanted to be really good, you'd have to start young," Helen said. "I don't say you couldn't learn to do it so that it would look all right."

"I'd like that," Daniel said. "Do you think I could learn?"

"I don't see why not," Helen said. "I don't know what your mother was thinking of, not sending you to dancing lessons. Everyone ought to learn how to dance."

"I'll find a dancing school in Sheffield," Daniel said. "Do you know one?"

"You want to ask my mum and dad to teach you," Helen said. "You won't find anyone in Sheffield knows as much about the tango as them. It'd be good for him. It wouldn't always be him holding you, you know. You'd mostly get to dance with my mum."

"Oh, that makes all the difference," Daniel said. "Wouldn't I get to dance with you?"

"You can dance with me at Christmas," Helen said. "When you've reached the required standard. I've not the patience of my mum and dad."

"Would they really teach me?"

"I don't see why not," Helen said. "It'd give them something to do. They might even start thinking about taking on other pupils. They're not going to be competing much longer, and my dad's going to retire from the mines as soon as he reasonably can. They ought to have something to do other than sit around moaning about Scargill and the NUM. The heavens bless us, what's that terrible noise?"

That terrible noise, just there on the Golden Mile where everything else was decrepit and broken and closed, was the bang and slap and howl of a broken fan-belt. It was the one thing Daniel hadn't thought about in his worries for the Cortina's ability to get them there and back. The car limped to the side of the road.

"What are we going to do now?" Daniel said. "Shall I call the AA?"

"If I were you, Daniel," Helen said, laughing hilariously, "I'd leave this wreck where it's landed up, and forget about it. I think it's a bit beyond the care of the AA."

"You can get in trouble for just abandoning a car," Daniel said. "And how are we supposed to get home?"

"Well, let's see," Helen said. "There's a bus stop over there'll take us into town, and from there you can get the fifty-one all the way home. It's what normal people do, Daniel. And I tell you what, tomorrow, if you like, you can go out and buy a brand new car. I bet you've got enough money. How does that sound?"

"Gi'o'er," Daniel said. "Are you cross, love?"

He'd never called her love before, but she didn't seem to mind. "No, I think it's right funny," she said. "Are we going to get that bus, then?"

There was nothing else to be done. Daniel emptied the car of anything he wanted to keep, and locked it one last time. It was quite sad, standing at the bus-stop looking at the rusted, reproachful expression of its front grille.

"Do you want to do something later this week?" he said eventually.

"Oh, I'm coming home with you," Helen said, with astonishment. "What did you think, Daniel?"

It seemed both as if the day would never come, and as if every day it slouched a little closer, lumpily approaching from across the moors as the seasons came and went. Whatever tasks occupied a day, at some point the thought of the court case would elbow its way in, and it was always a painful one; her heart would kick off, the sensation of ants running up and down her arms. Katherine could be in town, or doing the housework, or cooking, or out for the day in the car, or in anyone's company. If she managed to go on talking—and nobody raised the subject, even Malcolm through kindness or renunciation, an unspoken decision that it had nothing to do with him—then it would keep at bay. She could go on about the weather. She could agree with Anthea or Kenneth Warner or any of the neighbours that the state of the road was shocking for something only thirty years old, that the council certainly neglected this side of town out of envy. She could talk about the coal strike. She could discuss anything trivial and meaningless, expounding on the children's careers. Daniel had taken to coming for Sunday lunch almost every week, and often these days bringing his friend Helen too. They were good at talking about their lives, what they'd been up to, and Katherine was grateful that for days afterwards she could keep conversation going with any number of people with the news of what Helen's father thought of the coal strike, or the interesting and surprising fact that Daniel had started taking informal dancing lessons from him—he'd been a champion ballroom dancer until very recently. All these topics of conversation, carefully cultivated and mentally practised, and brought out with care for each listener—she tried to remember not to bring them up more than once, though of course it happened—successfully kept the ugly hot thought from her head. The thought that before long she was going to have to go to court, and be questioned in public as a witness against Nick. If she made an effort, she could take an interest in whatever they had been up to, as well, and that would have the same sort of effect, too. But if silence fell, as it sometimes did even when she was sitting with Anthea and Caroline in Anthea's lounge in the morning, she could guarantee that the immediate horrible thought of her approaching day in court would come to mind, draining her features and tensing her wrists. "Are you all right?" Anthea said once. "You look quite pale."

Nick's trial had a horrible Christmas-like aspect, the way it trod closer and closer with gleeful and unwarning annunciations. Nobody was opening Advent-calendar windows, or reminding the world in shop windows that there were only twenty-seven days to go until Nick's trial. But as time went on she was contacted by the authorities; had to be interviewed again by the police; had to be informed of the practical questions of being a witness in a criminal trial. These she kept to herself, only telling an unresponding Malcolm afterwards. They were horrible not in themselves but as reminders of the unexperienced unpleasantness that was still to come. The worst of it was that she could not believe Nick was going through a tenth of this dread. Wherever he was—was he in prison, was he out on some kind of licence?— she knew that his temperament would accept whatever was coming for him with acquiescence, and would, if it came to that, take prison with the same spirit. Sometimes she was encouraged to believe that the fatalist in him would let him plead guilty and make a fair end of it. But that wouldn't happen. He was one of those who would be surprised, in any circumstances, to learn that anyone could think him guilty, and he certainly didn't believe himself to be anything but innocent. In any case, she knew she would never see him again.

Cole Brothers had moved in Katherine's lifetime. Where it had been had once been a favourite meeting-place. When she and Malcolm had first known each other, they, like most of Sheffield, had been accustomed to meet at that point, and still she thought of that turn at the end of Fargate, now occupied by Chelsea Girl and the Midland Bank, as Cole's Corner. Now it was in a glassy sixties block opposite the City Hall and the war memorial, facing the new prancing statue that looked a bit like an emaciated Princess Anne on a thin rearing donkey. The women's clothes were on the first floor, and Katherine quite often bought hers there—she'd given up on Belinda's in Broomhill and, in fact, on Broomhill altogether since she'd stopped working at Nick's. Today she was buying a suit. The case was on Thursday.

"What is it for?" the shop assistant said—the first one she'd approached had said it was just about her tea break, and passed her on to an older colleague with a violet rinse in her hair, only needing rhinestone horn-rims to make the resemblance to Mary Whitehouse complete. "Is it a wedding?"

She hadn't waited for an answer, and Katherine was glad. "Yes, that's about the size of it," she said.

"Is it your daughter who's getting married?" the woman said, sizing up the suit Katherine was trying. "Perhaps she ought to come and advise you, too."

"No," Katherine said. "It's an ex-colleague of mine. We never thought it would happen to him, but it finally has. He's in his late thirties."

"Well, I do call that nice," the assistant said. "There's no need to be too sombre, though, even so. That's a nice suit for a professional woman, a very smart work suit, but I think a navy that dark might make you look a bit too sombre in the photographs. You could almost wear that to a funeral, now, couldn't you?"

"All right," Katherine said, shrugging off the jacket.

"My ladies always think they can jazz up a dark outfit with a brightly coloured shirt or blouse, but it's never quite right," the woman said. "Now, it's definitely a suit you're wanting, is it? What about a smart dress with a little bolero jacket on top? We've got something—"

"No, I don't think so," Katherine said. "I think definitely a suit."

"You've got the figure for a little dress," the assistant said, "and you could just shrug off the jacket when it comes to the wedding breakfast. No? All right, let's see, now. There's this—"

"That's too bright," Katherine said. "I couldn't wear that shade of red, not to this sort of occasion."

"You should try it on," the assistant said. "I'm sure there are lots of lovely bright colours you could get away with that you haven't considered. For instance, you should consider more warm greens, gold and rust. You shouldn't be wearing that scarf, it's salmon pink, that's more a sort of pink-and-blonde lady's colour, like teal or periwinkle."

"I'm not sure what periwinkle is," Katherine said.

"Well, it doesn't matter, because you won't be wearing it. Now, just for the sake of it, let's put you in this long dress. I know it's not what you're looking for."

"No, it certainly isn't," Katherine said, because it was a gold taffeta strapless ballgown, ballooning out. She would never wear such a thing, though the idea of turning up to give evidence in it—again that familiar glitch, like a needle skipping over a scratch on a record—was an impressive one.

"I know," the assistant said. "It's just to give you an idea of the way that colours you've probably never considered could do the world for you. Just slip it on, and you'll see straight away."

Katherine meekly obeyed. She came out of the dressing room with her eyes cast down, feeling ridiculous, but the shop assistant clapped her hands; a pair of shoppers who had been sorting through the ra-ra skirts in the middle distance paused in what might have been impressed amazement.

"You see," the assistant said, leading her to a mirror. "Just take a look at that, see if it isn't a fantastic colour for you."

Katherine didn't know what to expect, but certainly not the full transformation; in this aisle-wide dress, the cloth rustling, its skeleton creaking, she seemed not the apologetic worm she had expected, but an ageing beauty who hadn't had time to do her hair properly. In this extraordinary colour, she just glowed.

"Welcome to the 1980s," the assistant said.

"It's just the dress, though," Katherine said. "I couldn't ever wear something like that, I don't have the occasions."

"No, it's not just the dress, it's the colour," the assistant said. "Now, let's have a look for suits, but something in your colours, warm green, golds and rust."

"Not too gold," Katherine said, making a gesture at the luminescent dress, which, splendid though it was, was still a little like the Christmas turkey wrapped in gold foil.

"Perhaps a nice warm green tweed," the assistant said. "I know what you're thinking, but it'll be a nice modern sort of take on tweed, a tweed suit with—a classic with a twist. I might have just the thing. And you'll be wanting a hat."

"I'll leave the hat for another day," Katherine said. "I want to think about that a little bit first, see what people are wearing, these days."

So, surprisingly, as Katherine entered the Sheffield court building with Malcolm three days later, Daniel following behind soberly dressed—they'd both managed to take the day off work with a made-up excuse—she was wearing something she'd never thought of wearing, a tweed suit in a warm green she'd been persuaded into. Her shoulders moved experimentally within the wide board-like expanse of the jacket's cut. She'd thought of livening it up with a blouse to match her usual American Tan tights, but in the end she'd taken the advice, and wore a white silk shirt with a sort of pussy-bow collar and something she'd not worn for years, a pair of black tights. She'd not announced them as new when she'd come home with them; Malcolm must have understood when she came back with the big Cole Brothers bag why she'd bought a new outfit, but he'd not said anything, and this morning, when she'd come down in all this for the first time, he'd only told her something reassuring about repeating exactly what she'd said to the police, and that would be fine.

It had been explained to Katherine that she wouldn't be allowed to listen to the evidence of other witnesses, just as they couldn't meet her or listen to her evidence. But she could, if she liked, listen to Nick defending himself later in the day. She wasn't sure if she wanted to, or what she would gain from that. She didn't mention it to Malcolm. So she was separated from Malcolm and Nick, and settled in a kind of private space, with nothing to read or look at apart from a neutral pair of old prints, pictures of Sheffield before the war. A cup of coffee was brought, and another. She waited, emptying her mind as much as she could. She remembered what she had been told, that a good witness listened to the questions, and answered only the question that had been put; a witness did not get angry, or try to explain the whole situation, or the witness would be stopped. It all seemed impossible, and had never been further away.

But soon an officer of the court stepped in and asked her to follow him. The corridors were plain, not the wood panelling she had expected, and when he opened the door and led her into the court-room, that was a surprise, too. It was a smaller room than she had thought, and full of people; it seemed strangely smoky, its dust rising up in the light from the high windows. Nobody looked at her. She allowed herself to be led to the witness stand, and took the vow on the Bible. Then, before the barrister started to ask questions, she managed to glance around, and there, suddenly, were a few people she knew; in the public gallery, Malcolm and Daniel and, unexpectedly, Helen too; and her eyes fell on Nick, looking exactly as he always had, his gaze anywhere but on her. He only looked bored, that was all.

One of the barristers rose; he was fat, broad-faced, and his wide mouth seemed almost to cut his face in two, like a toad's. His gown swelled out before him; he rested his two hands on either side of his pile of papers, crouching there like malignant amphibians about to leap. The questions started, and they were much the same as the questions the police had asked her the first time, and the more recent occasion when they had gone through the whole business again.

"When did you begin work at Mr. Reynolds's shop?"

"Did you know Mr. Reynolds before starting work there?"

"What drew you to apply for a job there?"

"What experience did you have working in a shop before then?"

"Why did you want to take a job at all?"

"How would you describe your family finances?"

"How many days a week did you work there?"

"How would you describe Mr. Reynolds's methods of running the business?"

"Did you see the accounts of the shop at any point?"

"Did anything ever strike you as peculiar about the amounts of money coming into the shop?"

"What banking arrangements did Mr. Reynolds have?"

"Is that the only bank account you are aware of?"

"Did Mr. Reynolds ever ask you to pay any money into the bank?"

"Did you ever question Mr. Reynolds about the accounts?"

"Did you ever see the bank statements pertaining to the shop?"

"Did you ever go to Mr. Reynolds's house in Sheffield?"

She paused then.

"Just answer the question, please, Mrs. Glover," the judge said gently.

"Yes," Katherine said. "I went once to Mr. Reynolds's house in Ranmoor, just after he had bought it."

She could almost feel the stiffening from the public gallery, a willingness not to hear what was about to be said.

"How would you describe Mr. Reynolds's house?"

"It was a very nice house."

"Would it surprise you to learn that it cost seventy-eight thousand pounds to buy?"

"No, I would guess that that was about what a house like that in Ranmoor would cost. I live quite nearby. It's a very good neighbourhood."

"How did Mr. Reynolds find the money to buy a house like that?"

"I have no idea."

"Did he never mention how he was buying the house?"

"No, I don't believe he did."

"Would it surprise you to know that Mr. Reynolds bought the house outright, without needing to take out a mortgage?"

"If I had known that, I would have thought that he had bought it with his own money."

"Did it not strike you as strange—"

There was an objection here, for some reason, the defence barrister popping up like a black jack-in-the-box, and the judge asked the barrister to move on with his questions. Katherine felt released from something; she would not have to answer at least one question, though it was a question she hardly cared about or worried over, and with the release she found herself trembling.

"How would you describe your relationship with Mr. Reynolds?"

"We had a good working relationship," Katherine said carefully. "I liked him."

"How close was that?"

"Well, I invited him to come to a party my husband and I were holding once," Katherine said. "We were good enough friends for that."

"So you socialized together."

"I wouldn't say that," Katherine said. "He didn't come to my party, and I only went once to his house."

"Did he take you into his confidence on any subjects?"

"I don't know what you mean," she said, seeing that there were too many ways to answer this question.

"Did you believe, from anything Mr. Reynolds said, that there was anything improper about the way he was running his business?"

Another objection, again sustained. The courtroom—she was able to look around her properly, now—was modern, but wood-panelled, the panelling brought from some older and more august building. For the first time, she saw to one side of the room a box of people in two short lines, inspecting her with frowning disapproval, boredom, concentration. It was the jury. She wouldn't turn to the other side and look at Nick again.

"What were Mr. Reynolds's suppliers?"

"I can't remember their names," Katherine said.

"Was he supplied, for instance, with flowers, by Gracechurch's?"

"Yes, that's right," Katherine said. "Those were his suppliers."

"What other suppliers did he have?"

"Later, he found a different supplier, I think—yes, they were called Bradstone. He got fed up with the others, he said they never had much of a range."

"So he dropped Gracechurch's?"

"Yes."

"When would that be?"

"I think it was in the very early spring one year."

"Would it have been in 1977?"

"Yes, it could have been. In fact, yes, it definitely was, because I remember Nick saying that he was worried Gracechurch's might let us down in some way when it came to the Silver Jubilee if there was a high demand for flowers, so we ought to change a few months in advance."

"Did Mr. Reynolds ever, to your knowledge, use more than one supplier at the same time?"

"No, definitely not."

"How much of a mark-up did Mr. Reynolds generally make?"

"Could you explain, please?"

"Mrs. Glover, there's no need to dissimulate."

"I'm sorry?"

"You must be aware of what the shop's mark-up was. What did Mr. Reynolds pay for flowers from the wholesalers, and what did he charge for them?"

"I'm sorry," Katherine said. "We always used a different word. I think if he paid five pounds, he would try to charge enough so he'd make between eight and ten pounds if he sold all of them. Lilies, that would have been. I think that's about right."

"So between sixty and a hundred per cent mark-up, is that right?"

"I don't know," Katherine said. "I really don't know."

"That would follow from what you've just said."

"Yes, but," Katherine said, hoping to help Nick in some way here, "I don't think he ever really made a hundred per cent profit at the end of the week. There were all sorts of other things he had to pay for, like the van, and rent, and then, of course, there were lots of flowers which had to be thrown away at the end of the week because they hadn't sold—"

"Mrs. Glover, the court is quite familiar with these concepts of business," the judge said. "Could we move on?"

"If your lordship pleases," the barrister said. "Now, Mrs. Glover, I wonder if you could take a look at Exhibit G." It was passed up to her by one of the clerks, sitting in the well of the courtroom. "As you see, these are three pages from the accounts for September 1976. These are sample pages, m'lud. And with it, the business's bank statement for the same month. You will see that recorded sales and the amount paid in on successive Friday afternoons by, I presume, you, amount to £1,223, £1,076, and £1,150. Is that correct?"

"I don't remember ever seeing any of this," Katherine said. "I don't remember those weeks in particular."

"Does that seem like the sort of amount that you were being asked to pay into the bank around that time?"

"It sounds about right," Katherine said. "But I didn't really pay very much attention."

"Now, please look at Exhibit H." Again, three sheets of paper in a folder, passed up in an unfamiliar hand. "These are the relevant pages from the order book of Mr. Reynolds's supplier at the time, which you have testified was his only supplier, is that correct?"

"Yes, that's right, as far as I know."

"You will see that for the corresponding weeks, Mr. Reynolds paid £220, £240 and £215 to the supplier for flowers. You have testified that Mr. Reynolds's usual mark-up was somewhere between sixty and a hundred per cent, a usual commercial rate. These rates suggest, however, something more like five hundred per cent or a little more. Can you offer any explanation?"

"We sold vases too, sometimes," Katherine said hopelessly. "And stationery, as well."

"Did you ever sell as much as six or seven hundred pounds' worth of those goods in a week?"

"I can't remember."

"Try to remember, Mrs. Glover."

"I don't think we could ever have done," Katherine eventually said.

"Did nothing about any of this strike you as being remotely strange at the time?"

"No, it didn't."

"What other business associates did Mr. Reynolds have, apart from the suppliers?"

"I don't know of any."

"Come, now, Mrs. Glover. You must have been aware of the sources of this extra income in the shop. Who brought the extra money to Mr. Reynolds?"

"I never saw anyone."

"We know they came very regularly, these sums of money."

"I don't know that."

"We also know that they were most likely brought in person."

"I don't know that, either."

"Were there never any regular visitors to Mr. Reynolds's shop whom you became familiar with?"

Katherine paused, looking to the public gallery as if for assistance. She could see her family, Daniel leaning forward in concern; behind him, there was a girl in a beautiful cream jacket and perfect hair. She stood out; and though she was not looking at Katherine, or at anything in particular, there was something about her forced stillness that had a significance. Katherine had no idea what that significance might be. "I only knew the regular customers," she said. "There was nobody apart from that, as far as I know."

"Let us move on," the barrister said.

By the time Katherine was dismissed, she was exhausted. Under her warm green tweed suit, her blouse was wringing wet. She looked up, helplessly, at the public gallery. There was not only Daniel and Helen and Malcolm, but, unexpectedly, Alice Sellers, too. Alice was the only one looking directly at her, and on her face was an expression of relief. Katherine was surprised; and then she realized that, horrible as it had been, they had come near to the horrible story of her real relation with Nick but had failed to discover it. The whole thing was over. There seemed no hope for Nick, but there was no reason now to think that anyone would ever discover any of it. She could, if she liked, go home.

The court broke for lunch, and in a moment, Malcolm and the others were there outside the courtroom.

"Thank God that's over," Malcolm said. "It makes me so angry, your being dragged into all of that."

"It was horrible," Katherine admitted. She couldn't say anything else.

"You can listen to the evidence, now, can't you?" Helen said. "Now that you've done what you had to do."

"I suppose I can, love," Katherine said, surprised. She had thought of going home now; but of course they would want to stay to hear what

Nick had to say. His evidence would be that afternoon, the lawyers had told her.

There was a canteen and, depositing Katherine at a table with Alice, they bought a range of dried-up sandwiches, children's fizzy drinks and bags of crisps—a lunch for a school outing. Katherine ate it all, gratefully, shrinking into herself, not saying anything much. She kept her head down to the table. There was no risk of seeing Nick. He would be shuttled in vans between the dock and prison each day; he would be taken down to the cells between the morning and the afternoon sessions. She had no real doubt that, at the end of this, he would be sent to prison and never appear in their lives again. She was safe from him now. But she still kept her head down to the table. She felt that the barristers, with their wigs and their robes off, but still with their white bands, the instructing solicitors in their neat suits, all had listened to what she had had to say and had interpreted it lewdly, had heard the obscene innuendo in the barrister's questions. If she raised her head, they would stare at her.

There was no conversation to be had, or made, surely: but steadily she found herself being drawn out of her inturned concern, and found herself listening to a conversation, which seemed all but natural, about Helen's parents, and particularly her father. Katherine knew that he was a miner, and she knew that he must be on strike, but hadn't enquired any further. It was out of a combination of good taste and self-absorption.

"Why doesn't he go back to work if he feels like that?" Malcolm asked. He seemed genuinely puzzled.

"It's not as simple as that," Helen said. "He could, of course he could, but they live in a small place. Everyone knows everyone in Tinstone, and there's a bit of—I don't know how to explain it."

"They call them scabs," Malcolm said. "I know that much."

"And not only calling names," Helen said. "It's not a playground thing. They'd paint it on your house, and throw bricks through your window. The police, they can bus you in every morning but they can't mount a guard outside your house night and day. And it would go on after the strike was over. They never forget that sort of thing in a place like Tinstone. There was a lad I were at school with, some of the other kids weren't allowed to associate wi' im because he were the son of a scab. That'd be during 1972, his dad were a scab, but people in Tinstone, they went on crossing the road when they saw any of them coming for years after. They probably still would, but they upped sticks and moved to Nottingham."

"How terrible," Katherine said. "It's like bullying in the playground."

"Well, my dad," Helen said, "he doesn't feel that strongly about keeping the mine going, anything like that. But he hates Scargill and he hates the union men." It was apparent that, even here at the table in the noisy canteen, she had lowered her voice.

"I'm sure a lot of miners feel like that, really," Malcolm said.

"You'd never find out, though," Helen said. "What time does it start up again?"

They looked at the big digital clock on the wall; surprisingly, the hour had passed.

"I wonder how the judge stays awake in the afternoon," Helen said sociably, as they got up. "I'm sure I wouldn't be able to. It's like wading through treacle between three and four for me." Then she seemed to realize that Katherine, at least, could not fall asleep during these hearings and, squeezing her arm, said, so as to be heard only by her, "I bet you're glad to have that over."

"Yes, I am," Katherine said.

"It can't have been pleasant," Helen said. "You came through it all right, though. Here we are."

Here was the public gallery. From here, the courtroom looked larger, and was filling up with people she had hardly observed before. Giving evidence had been like an intimate exchange between three or four of them, the larger crowd and the officials a blur, like intricate wallpaper. Katherine settled herself, making a single ineffectual gesture at her hair, and all at once, just behind her, there was a conspicuous arrival: the girl she had noticed, the girl in cream with the perfect hair. She made no kind of signal in Katherine's direction, which was unnatural: she had spent an hour that morning staring most intently at her, and there might have been some kind of observation, the sort of covert investigation that most of the other inhabitants of the public gallery were carrying out. Instead, Katherine found herself taking stock of this girl; her long thin bony legs out of the mini-skirt, the perfect clarity of her skin, and the jacket—there was something unfamiliar and yet intended about the odd cut of it, like no jacket Katherine had ever seen close up before. She felt herself dressed in what a chain store could manufacture.

There was a call from below; the court, the judge, the accused assembled themselves in their intricate order, fulfilling their roles. The public gallery grew quiet; the accused was Nick. At length, the agonizingly non-directed conversation was over, and she went back with

Daniel, Helen and Malcolm into the public box. There was no harm, apparently, in her listening to Nick's evidence on his own behalf now that she had given hers. She had avoided looking at him, and only now, in the witness box, did she see how quite unchanged he was. She hadn't seen him so unaltered during the whole period of her working there, when he would, every few months, undertake a change in his hair, sweeping it from one side for a few weeks before another, having it trimmed right down; acquiring a whole set of pullovers in a previously unenvisaged shade, taking to turning up every day in a green tweed suit or in a sequence of dreadful T-shirts and shorts, as if he were playing with what might be his identity. His face, too, was the first to display the slightest change in his weight, sometimes puffing out after Christmas or narrowing after two weeks' holiday in the sun. Now it was as it had been at bottom. He was always in a state of flux, but now, oddly, he was as he always had been, in a grey hound's tooth jacket and a sombre blue-and-purple striped tie; that had always seemed to her to be, as it were, his default position. He took a vow; his evidence began.

"Yes, that's correct."

"Yes."

"I had a succession of not very interesting or important jobs. Offices, temporary jobs, serving in shops, that sort of thing."

"No, I didn't have any kind of education for anything better. I thought I was lucky, to be honest."

"No, I've never had any such connections. I've never even seen anyone smoking a joint, to tell you the truth."

"Yes, that's correct."

"I went there on holiday."

"Yes, I know—I liked Morocco a good deal, I'd made friends there. What—don't you ever go back on holiday to places you've had a good time in?"

"Mr. Reynolds," the judge said.

"I'm sorry, Your Honour," Nick said, before the judge could say anything more, but the judge explained anyway that this was a serious matter, and that it was not for him to ask questions of counsel.

"Mr. Reynolds," the lawyer said, "when did you have the idea to start a flower shop?"

"It must have been around 1972."

"What made you decide this?"

"I had an aunt who died, and left me some money," Nick said bravely.

"We will return to this aunt, but what I was really asking was, why should you have opened a flower shop? Did you have any great interest in flowers?"

"Yes, I always liked them."

"And yet we have heard from Mr. Williams, your supplier at the time, that when you began buying from him, he was struck by your almost complete ignorance, not just of business but of flowers. We have his word for it that: he wondered who had told you to get into the business. How would you respond to that?"

"I don't know how I gave that impression," Nick said. "I always loved flowers, it was always my dream to sell them."

The wrangling went on a little.

"Let us return to the question of your aunt. In what way was she a relation of yours?"

"The relationship was complicated—she was really a sort of cousin, I think. I never met her."

"Could you tell us, however, what her name was?"

There was just the faintest flutter around Nick's eyelids as he came out with the name; a lowering and a hovering of the gaze; whatever this name was, it wasn't one that had ever belonged to any human being. Katherine could not bring herself to look at the jury. The lawyer went on remorselessly, exploring the biography of the aunt/cousin who had left all her money to Nick, despite never having known him, with something close to sarcasm.

"And, Mr. Reynolds, could you perhaps explain to us why, exactly, it might be that an elderly maiden aunt living in Cheltenham might channel her financial business through a banking organization in Belize?"

The court, horribly, burst into laughter and was reprimanded. The girl behind Katherine did not laugh; you could feel her knees being drawn together, her face becoming prim with disapproval.

"I put it to you . . ." the lawyer said, grasping his advantage, and went on to outline a tale of a Mr. Big, funding Nick's little flower shop in Broomhill, laundering money through it, all of it connected to Nick's suddenly sinister repeated trips to Morocco. To Katherine, who had sat for long hours in Nick's little shop making up bouquets, trimming bits of stalk and thorn off roses, talking nonsense for hours on end, it seemed hardly less unlikely than Nick's tale of a maiden aunt. Deep down, she still believed roughly what Nick had told her about the basis of the flower shop, long ago. That seemed the most probable thing.

"That, Mr. Reynolds, is the plain truth, is it not?" the lawyer said.

The lawyer for that side came to an end, and the lawyer for Nick's side took charge.

"My learned friend has set out a scenario under which your flower shop was funded, and a secret purpose it was designed to serve. Is there any truth in this scenario?"

"It isn't true, and it couldn't possibly be," Nick said. "If it was, everyone else would have known about it."

"Who do you mean by everyone else?" the lawycr said.

"For a start," Nick said, "my assistant would have known all about it. She would have had to."

Katherine felt herself becoming the subject of interest again; in her armpits a prickle of shame began.

"Are you referring to—" a quick glance downwards "—Mrs. Katherine Glover?"

"Yes," Nick said. "We were very close, she would have noticed if anything was amiss."

"You had a close professional relationship, you are saying."

"More than that," Nick said. "We had an affair."

There was no intake of breath, no cross-court murmur in the way there always was in American films of courtroom scenes; there was no kind of movement in the well of the court or the public gallery. Was it Katherine's imagination that the observation of everyone around her stayed absolutely fixed on where they had been, that they would not, did not shift back to look at her?

"I must object," the lawyer for the other side said, rising. "I really don't see what possible relevance this has."

"Does this form part of your client's defence? Mr. Reynolds is entitled to defend himself," the judge said, dismissing the objection.

"Could you explain the nature of your relationship with Mrs. Glover?" the lawyer said, and they proceeded, together, on to the cooked-up story. It was absolutely horrible; it was almost entirely invented; from a single episode had spun out a passionate, two-year affair, brought to an end through Mr. Reynolds's feelings of honour.

"Yes, I loved her—I adored her. I would never have kept anything from her."

"And yet she knew absolutely nothing of any such scenario as the one my learned friend has presented to you."

"She would have known. She knew exactly what I knew. She was probably much more in love with me than I was with her. She would have taken the opportunity to find out everything she could about me—you know how people are when they're deeply in love, almost obsessive. She had exactly the same degree of access to the books and to the financial arrangements of the shop that I did. She was telling you the truth, she didn't know anything wrong. Anyway, I absolutely trusted her."

"Why was that?"

"Because she had a lot more to lose than I did."

The other lawyer objected, and this time the judge decided that they had heard quite enough of all of that. Katherine could hardly move, could hardly breathe. There was no question of it: Nick's testimony was so full of holes, so patently absurd, such a complete mess of lies that he was going to go down for this. For a moment she thought of tying her innocence to that string of lies, of assuring everyone that he was making up a ridiculous story, making it up to save his pasty skin. It might have done, and much of what he'd said did sound like a pathetic lie, all that about loving her, adoring her. It was simply that one unnecessary addition: the suggestion that she had loved him much more than he had loved her. Everyone who had known her at the time would have recognized the truth of that. She really had, and it was horrible to hear it put out in this way, in a courtroom, in front of everyone. At the front of the public gallery, the men from the *Star* and the *Morning Telegraph* lazily scribbled her adultery in the loops of their shorthand. She'd once have been able to read it; she'd had the training.

She hardly listened to the rest of Nick's evidence, and only when he had quite finished did she really bring herself back into the room, focus on him as he was being dismissed. He looked up, into the public gallery, and she tried her best to look outraged. But his gaze wasn't seeking her. He hadn't even been thinking of her. He was looking, with amazement and pain, beyond her, trying to fix the gaze of the tall-boned girl in a cream suit. She was ignoring him, making her own exit, pulling her lovely toffee-coloured bag to her side, rising and excusing herself in a drawling-posh-Cockney tone, pushing past. Katherine didn't know who she was; but she'd come to see something, and Nick knew who she was, and it pained him. Only then, as she turned quite away from the court, did he happen to notice Katherine; and his eyes dropped from her, quite abruptly. He knew he was going to prison. There was no point in anything that he had said about her. Alice, sitting next to Katherine, took her hand and squeezed it tight, between both of hers. Katherine was grateful for that.

Every Thursday evening now, after work, when the men outside the pit had settled down to a small handful, loitering about something that wasn't there, it being too warm for braziers, Daniel came to the little community centre in Tinstone and danced. Helen sat on a box of donated tins; Philip sometimes sat, only to leap up, as if there was something hot underneath him, and brush Shirley aside to demonstrate something, taking Daniel clinically in his arms without any meaning. "You should have started all this before you were ten," he'd say, but demonstrate anyway, and sometimes Daniel got it right, sometimes he was allowed to dance a little with who he wanted to dance with, Helen. The battered old tape-machine with its one unvarying tape sat on a ziggurat of tinned charity, wheezing through the same seven Argentinian tangos every week, and Daniel adored it. Mostly he danced with Shirley, who was neat and precise in all her movements. He could not see how; when she moved, she moved so swiftly like a dart to its board, but she gave him the sense in his arms of slowness, of stillness, even. "You might be getting it," Philip started to concede; they did it every week, and Helen came along, pretending to mock and laugh, but her eyes shining. She remembered what it was to dance in such a way.

And that Thursday, Alice sat down in the quiet of her house and, while she waited for Bernie to come home, made a start on replying to Sandra's last letter. It had come yesterday; Bernie had made a point, tired though he was, of sitting up and reading it with Alice. When the weekend came, he'd write his own reply to it, but Alice made a start now. She read it again; she looked at the photographs of Sandra's new flat, of an evening out with some new friends, lined up around the heel of a table and smiling, of Sandra on a beach rug raising a glass of wine to her new friend Basil, who must have been the one taking the photograph. Basil was Chinese, but had come to Australia as a baby. There was a photograph of a kangaroo, too, not in a zoo but sitting on a lawn-like expanse of country, under a tree that might be a eucalyptus. If you looked, Sandra said in her letter, you could see the kangaroo's baby, his little nose poking out from the lumpily filled pocket. Alice looked, not for the first time, and saw the little nose. "I'm glad . . ." she began. "I had no idea . . ." she went on. "Your new flat looks . . ." she continued. "I'll think about whether it might be possible to come . . ." she wrote. "We'd love to meet Basil . . ." she responded. Everything she wrote was a reply to something Sandra had said. "I hope . . . I hope . . . I hope . . ." her letter went, disconsolately. There was nothing much of her own to say. She couldn't think Sandra would be interested in the Glovers' goings-on, and about Francis there was little enough that she knew, what might be happening to him. Bernie was doing something important, but she could leave all that to him. She'd got into the habit of turning out the lights in the house when she wasn't in each room, though Bernie had never said anything. She sat in the warm pool of light cast by the green-shaded Tiffany lamp over the green-topped leather desk in the spare room. With her father's old fountain pen, on the heavy embossed Italian writing paper Francis had given her last Christmas, both saved for special occasions such as a letter to Sandra, she went on writing, perseveringly.

At the end, when they came through the door, the others melted away somehow. She had the sense, when she was sitting at the right end of the sofa as if washed up by the tide, her hand resting like a claw on the shell-embedded box that had always sat there on the green-leather-topped table, that the others had tactfully disappeared in some way. But that wasn't true: only Daniel and Helen had made a mumbled excuse and headed off. Tim had taken one look at them, coming in, and levered himself off the sofa in the living room, taken himself off to the armchair in front of the small television in the dining room. The television and the armchair had replaced, a couple of years ago, the old upright piano in shades of marmalade and Double Gloucester, an old square marmalade cat showing its silent teeth, that had been Malcolm's mother's. Nobody had ever played on it once the children's lessons came, at their own wailed request, to an end. The replacement television was used pretty constantly by Tim, if no one else; he didn't like anyone to think he watched television in any kind of frivolous spirit, and having to peer at the fifteen-inch screen gave him some kind of puritanical licence to watch even quiz shows. She did think, however, he might have asked how it had gone first. She thought, too, Malcolm might have done something different from lowering his head and going upstairs, following Tim. He was probably going to spend the evening in the study, leaving her to her own devices. It occurred to her that she had no idea what they were going to eat for supper. It hadn't come to mind in the morning, as if she were accused and might not be returning to her house that evening.

But she, at any rate, had not been on trial, and whatever it was that the jury would return with in their hands in the days to follow, it would not constitute any kind of judgement on her life. What she had had to do was now finished, and it could never have had any public consequences. But Nick had said what he had said, and it was not just everyone but Malcolm who had heard it, and knew that everyone else had heard and believed it. Underneath the new jacket, the warm green tweed, her new blouse was soaked and limp; her hair, which had been teased into a difficult and precarious height that morning, was collapsing about her head in slides like the shale of a Derbyshire mountain. She took her jacket off, slinging it carelessly over one arm of the sofa. She didn't feel that, at the end of this, she could turn the television on and sink into the unfeeling events of any normal day. There was Malcolm in the doorway. He was carrying a pile of fat-leaved leatherbound books, chin-high; she recognized the photograph albums that lined up along the bottom of the bookcase in the study.

"I was thinking," Malcolm said gently, "we've got too many photo albums. We stuck everything, almost, in them. I thought we ought to have some quality control."

"How do you mean?"

"I thought we might go through them, separate out the best ones, put all the best ones in the same album. People like to see photos when they come round, but no one's going to go through fifteen albums."

"Are there as many as that?"

"I counted," Malcolm said. "There's five don't match—I couldn't get the same ones we used to buy."

"That's a nice idea," Katherine said. She wasn't in the mood to refuse anything Malcolm suggested tonight. Perhaps this was the moment to renew her offer to leave him, to move out, but she hoped he wouldn't bring it up, now that he had so concrete a reason for doing so.

Malcolm placed himself down beside her, quite solidly, and opened a volume. "No," he said. "That's not the first," and indeed it wasn't, since there were three children on the first page, all quite young and all with that funny page-boy haircut children used to get in the early 1970s. Once, Daniel in a shoe shop had been offered girls' slingbacks; he was so pretty and his hair so long and shiny. Jane had never let him forget it. In the background, a white railing and a blue sea; it must have been Scarborough, or perhaps Whitby. But Malcolm set it aside and, humming, opened another volume and then another. "They've got out of order," he said. But that one was the first, and they settled down to it.

First, there was an overlit quartet, the two of them and Malcolm's friend Eric and his girlfriend—what was her name?—her hair gone greenish in the odd colour printing of the time. There was a solid white frame about them all. They were outside a pub, standing by Eric's Hillman Imp. Who had taken the photograph? It was before they'd married, and probably in the depths of winter, judging by the girlfriend's whited-out face and the white fur collar on Katherine's winter coat. She remembered that coat; Malcolm had promised to buy her a new whole-fur coat when they were married. It was an elegant thing, cream and A-line. What had happened to it? And then there were more of Malcolm and Katherine, some on the same sorts of outings into the country. It surprised her how, in so many of the photographs, whoever was with them, Malcolm was caught looking directly at her, as if impressed and surprised by something she had said. The look of love, she supposed.

And at some point in this album, they'd married, but all the photographs from the wedding were in a different album, a white and silver-embossed one. Malcolm hadn't brought it down, and in any case that was the album that had had most wear over the years. Jane had had a positive mania for poring over it at one stage, it must have been at her ballerina-phase. She'd needed to be reassured about who everyone was in the bigger crowd photographs, and Katherine had got thoroughly reacquainted with it. So here they passed imperceptibly from what must be pre-wedding outings for nothing in particular to the ones after the honeymoon. The best of the honeymoon photographs—there weren't many, it had rained with a warm Atlantic persistence for two weeks in the Scilly Isles, so much for the Gulf Stream and the palm trees—were in loose bundles in the other album. She couldn't quite tell at what point she and Malcolm went from anticipation to settled couple, the Kodak happiness was so uninterrupted. She selected ("That's in your cousin's garden, isn't it?") and Malcolm pulled out a photograph from under the clinging transparent skin.

There was their old house; there she was, in the beehive, which, to be honest, had always looked a little silly. It was as hard to coax her thin hair into one of those high piles as it was now to persuade it into the big waves people seemed to like. Her hair had always been thin, even before she'd had the children. But she had to admit, in this photograph, in an overall spattered with cheerful blue paint, her hair coming loose from its loaf, flushed and smiling, it didn't look as stupid as all that. The gaze of the camera was almost tangible, its pleasure. He must have taken that photograph at the end of a long day. She was kneeling, and you couldn't tell but they must have been doing up the second bedroom in their first little house because Daniel was on the way. There was probably a reason scientists would tell you about nowadays that would stop you painting a spare bedroom if you were pregnant. For the sake of the photograph, she was glad no one had thought that at the time. She slid it out and passed it to Malcolm; without thinking, following it with the photograph on the next page, of Malcolm, similarly smiling and tired-looking in the finished room, in front of the little cream crib stencilled with cartoon woodland animals. It had served them well, that crib, through all three children. She could remember the shock of coming in, one day, and peering over the by then very shabby and well-known bars and seeing, instead of what she had expected, the calm expectation or funny screwed-up understandable rage that Daniel and Jane had displayed, the unnerving face of Tim as a baby, like no baby she had ever seen, lying there on his back observing and calculating with what looked unmistakably like adult resentment.

The album came to an end just as reels of film did, with some miscellaneous and unidentifiable shots of bluebells in a wood, moorland, a stretch of marsh and estuary she had no recollection of. They all looked oddly period, just as if bluebells and moorland and estuaries everywhere had changed markedly since the early 1960s; of course it was the colour in the photographs that dated them. They moved on to the next volume, and all at once it was Daniel; he was a funny Chinese-looking baby with his dark colouring and screwed-up eyes, and on the verge of screaming in photographs. He couldn't possibly have been so green in the face as these pictures made him look, though.

As in the image she craned her neck to peer, amazed, into Daniel's face, and Malcolm in those heavy horn-rims peered over with the goofy smile he seemed, from these albums, to have developed around then; it was hilarious to see how incredibly cross and grumpy and uncooperative the baby looked, and went on looking in subsequent photographs, as they held him up, one at a time, for each other to view. Daniel had been an easy baby, really, never rejecting even unfamiliar food and sleeping easily, taking to the potty early, never being shy with strangers and hardly a tantrum to be seen; he'd been an easy teenager, too, come to think of it, and the troubles Katherine had foreseen hadn't, after all, come to pass. He was a good lad. There were only two or three photographs with all three of them, Katherine, Malcolm and the baby Daniel; mostly the photographs were taken by one or the other of them. (It worried her, Katherine, who had taken the ones of the three of them; she wished Malcolm had noted that rather than what had seemed the obvious thing to write on the back, that it was of her, him and Daniel; they could see that for themselves.) Malcolm had known how to set the shutter speed and all that, and they'd all come out well, whoever had been taking the pictures.

She carried on, Malcolm turning the pages with her, and craning over at them as he had in the photographs with Daniel as a baby. She carefully extracted photographs, she passed them to him, he placed them on the arm of the sofa beside him.

And then it seemed as if it had been sensible for Malcolm to note who it had been on the back of the photograph, because there was another baby, Jane. Katherine and Malcolm looked exactly the same, but there was a little brother, too, in a grey pullover with a red train appliquéd on the front—his grandmother's offering—and here in a white shirt and a turquoise bow-tie, the sort of thing little boys were forced into for parties then, and didn't his scowl show it . . . There was a different house now in the background. With a shock, Katherine saw that they were sitting, her and Daniel and baby Jane, just where they were sitting now, at that exact place. A different sofa, a different pattern on the walls behind them—they could only just have moved in, it was the builder's idea of decoration still—but the same house and the same place. The outings began again; aunts appeared, a cousin of Malcolm's, and his friend from the battle society with their children. Here they were on the moors with a picnic—she must have taken this one, with Malcolm in a Civil War uniform holding the baby in a soft pink woollen blanket, silk-margined, and Daniel gazing up at his father in excited surprise. He looked—of all things—dashing in his get-up, Malcolm did. She had to admit it; she'd complained, but she had sometimes secretly quite enjoyed those afternoons. Last year she'd even told Malcolm that she'd started enjoying them, though it was the battle of Naseby again, and she'd seen that one, frankly, a few times before.

She started recognizing, to her surprise, outfits of her own, things still hanging in the wardrobe upstairs. That white cardigan—she hadn't worn it for years but it was certainly still up there. It was Jane's fifth birthday party, and an artistic shot, her eyes pitched between the candles, and made to glow. Behind her, there was Katherine, big with what must have been Tim. You didn't know what Jane was thinking; she'd been made to look like an angelic Victorian tot, open with wonder at the four candles and the pink ballerina in royal icing on top. Katherine extracted and passed a photograph; they started on the next album. "Look at Tim," Malcolm said, gurgling with amusement, and, absorbed, she had to laugh too: it must have been the least prepossessing photograph of a newborn child ever taken, his eyes already big and open and calculating. He'd been terribly thin, and his aged ugly face, like a gnome's or a changeling's, was one not even a mother, as it proved, could love. (How they'd recoiled, all those initial visitors!) She'd had difficulty with Tim, and difficulty telling Jane and Daniel that they had to love their new little brother. He hadn't slept, hadn't liked food, had pushed her away almost constantly. She'd wanted, sometimes, to push him away, to be honest. There weren't so many photographs of Tim, at least not in so much of a starring role: he tended to creep in at the edges of family gatherings, at Christmas and the children's birthdays and on holiday, and only two or three of him in particular. There was one of him being christened. She hadn't quite got round to it with the elder two, but with Tim, for some reason, she'd got it into her head, as Malcolm had expressed it, that he ought to be "done." Perhaps she thought that someone ought to love him, and it might as well be God.

Daniel with a football; Jane in a ballerina's dress—poor Jane, second-row fairy at Miss Brackenbury's dance-school summer show, before she decisively lost interest, or lost sight of her once great goal, to stand on a stage in pink on *pointes*. Katherine felt for her: she could remember wanting exactly the same thing. And then suddenly a flush, a whole run of photographs of Paris. They'd never been, and it had seemed like an adventure; taking children had proved, indeed, an adventure, and suddenly, where the albums had been patchy and isolated, glimpses only of the stream of their lives, here was the whole thing, photographs taken in succession, fifteen a day, all of them minus the photographer (Malcolm wouldn't have trusted a passer-by in a foreign country, just as he wouldn't trust a running dog abroad), underneath the Eiffel Tower, on a famous bridge of some sort, the Arc de Triomphe, Notre Dame. She passed the photographs; the album was ended.

"There's plenty more," Malcolm said, and he was smiling. "Do you want to carry on?"

"We're not doing very well," Katherine said, indicating the substantial pile of photographs she'd taken out of the albums, quite two-thirds of them all. She hadn't realized how much of their recorded lives was, in fact, worth saving. "There's too many there for one album already. We might as well put them all back."

And then, all at once, she was crying, the stripped album open on her lap in front of her, and not knowing how not to. Malcolm squeezed her shoulder, and smiled too, in a way that suggested he, too, might at any moment start crying, and got up, placing the albums carefully on the coffee-table in front of her.

"Do you remember," he said in the end, "years and years ago—"

Katherine nodded.

"Years and years ago," he said, "I just took off that once. I just went off for two days and I didn't say where I was going, I just went and came back."

Katherine nodded.

"I never said where I'd gone, did I?" Malcolm said. "I don't think I ever told you why I'd gone, either."

Katherine tried to say no; she couldn't.

"The thing is," he said, "it's not important why I went, or where I went. I just went to a hotel for two days, then I came back. That's all I did, it was nothing much. You know what the important question is, though?"

"You're being deep," Katherine said, or tried to say; she couldn't.

"Yes, well," Malcolm said, "the important thing—I think the important thing is why I came back. Anyway. I'm just going to get the rest, love," he said. "The rest of the photographs," and he went to the door.

"I don't deserve you," Katherine said, hardly managing to get the words out, shaking her head.

"Love you," Malcolm said, and went upstairs. He was there a while, allowing her to finish, to dry her tears on the handkerchief she kept, as she always had, in the wrist of her blouse, and when he came back, it was with the rest of the albums. "We might as well," he said judiciously, and his eyes were, surely, a little red around the rims themselves, "finish going through these tonight. I'm enjoying this."

Beyond and below the crags, heading down into the bottom of the valley that divided Rayfield Avenue, Ranmoor and Lodge Moor on one flank from Hillsborough and the moors on the other, there ran the Rivelin through a thick line of trees. The beechwoods stretched like a thick dark wash along the floor of the valley, like sediment that had washed to the lowest point, flourishing along the meandering line of the river as far up the flanks as the twin A-roads on either side, heading in the direction of Manchester. It was a place of mysterious lights and shadows, which under rain hissed and drummed; the river formed pools and deep, sibilant cascades. It was always dark down there. Even when the sun shone, the trees met overhead and cast heavy green shades over the paths, carved by custom rather than arrangement. In the winter, the limes and beeches bare, it was a favourite place for rooks to congregate, their sawing calls echoing down the narrow, extended forest. It seemed like a very old place, and was; probably the remains of a much larger forest that had extended right up the sides of the valley, where now were fields of sheep and stripped moorland, and even crawling masses of houses.

It began at the western edge of Sheffield. The lengths of suburb started to contain some things that suggested an older, more rural past: an old forge, preserved now as a museum, which school trips favoured, and, among the suburban houses, a stableyard and field tilted at thirty degrees, now a riding school. There was even a little working farm, with hens and geese and twelve pigs tucked somehow into its yard; there must once have been more land to that, and the farmhouse itself was blackened, rough and eighteenth-century. But the land, if it had existed, had long ago been sold off to build bungalows and semi-detached houses on, each with a sunburst motif on its gates and a garage added at some later date. It must have taken some doing to live in the houses directly backing on to the pigsties.

The houses gave way to a last garden centre, or nursery, according to taste, as the Rivelin woods and the Rivelin valley began their sinuous path. After this point, the river ran behind the backs of houses, unfollowably, and was even directed into narrow pipes. At the edge of the houses, it was full of rubbish, old bicycle wheels, plastic supermarket bags, a trolley from Gateway, which must have been pushed uphill a good two miles before being dumped here. But if you followed the river upstream, the detritus in the water, the flotsam and jetsam, soon thinned and then disappeared; you came across a municipal pond, a little reservoir constructed out of the Rivelin's stream like a lido. Children often came here with their shrimping nets in search of frogspawn and sticklebacks, taking the sticky trove home in funerary jam-jars. And then you could go further upstream, tracing the river that fed this pond, and all sorts of fish under the rippling green shade. Most kids—Daniel was explaining, as he and Helen walked up the side of the stream together—most kids round here, they came to the pond, and stopped there. But if you went on—

The pond, with its concrete edges and warning notices, was ruled by the gods of municipal holiday. But further upstream, leading up from the runnel that fed the pond itself through a concrete pipe, in most seasons under water, beyond this pond the events of the river became more surprising and suggestive. There weren't often many people around. Often you came across the remains of a dam constructed out of rocks and mud by boys, once effective but after a few days scattered and ineffective; the naughtiest boys—

"You weren't one of them, were you, by any chance?"

"I was not," Daniel said.

—the very naughtiest boys used to beg or steal a sheet of plastic from building sites and underpin their dams with it. It was the only thing that ever successfully stopped the river, constructed a proper pool; rocks and mud never had the same effect. From such a pool, you could after a couple of hours scoop the gulping tench with your bare hands, more or less. But grown-ups, if they ever came across one of these more ruthlessly efficient dams, would usually step in and pull out the plastic sheet with an impressive roar and cascade as the built-up pool gave up its swelling bulk, its gasping and ungrateful fish.

The concrete paths stopped above the municipal pond, and the only paths were worn down by people following the river out of curiosity and the occasional gang of naughty boys. Most kids went to Forge Dam, with its ice-cream vans and its shallow reach. You could only drown in that if you set your mind to it, like those government adverts starring man-high talking squirrels about the murderous potential of six inches of water. Some kids, like Daniel, had gone to the stretch of Rivelin that went between the pond and the old post office two miles into woodland, which only survived on the sale of drinks to cyclists and quarters of sweets to the dam-making boys. He loved the summer here; loved the hover of the dragonflies over the soupy surface of the river's pools in summer; loved those clouds of gnats like a hot fog about your head, clustering under the stickiest trees; loved the underwater hover, like a mirroring of the dragonfly hover above, of the stickle-backs, and the occasional glimpse of a bigger fish, or the thought of a bigger fish as the surface of the water gulped like a hiccup, and it must have been a carp, perhaps, taking an insect. Nobody came to fish here, apart from the naughty boys with their home-made means, which most fish easily evaded. You were supposed to have a licence, according to the notice at the western edge of the Rivelin ponds. But Daniel had never seen anyone fishing seriously here. He liked it—he'd always liked it—because not many people came here. It wasn't really anything special, but it felt very old, and it was always quiet, so—

"You mean you could take girls here," Helen said.

"I worry about you," Daniel said. "I worry about what a cynic you're becoming."

"Well, it's not cynical if it's true," Helen said. "And I bet you did bring girls here."

Daniel thought. "I don't think I did much," he said. "If it was for a kiss and a cuddle—"

"A *kiss* and a *cuddle*?"

"—if it was for a kiss and a cuddle, I used to take girls more to the crags. It wasn't so much of a walk from home."

"It's lovely here, though," Helen said. "We've nothing like this in Tinstone. Just the moor tops—if you took a girl up there, you'd not have much luck asking her to take her jersey off."

"Look," Daniel said, "no one else knows about this . . ."

And he took Helen's hand and dived off into the woods to their left. There was no path at all. They could have been going anywhere. They thrashed and plunged through undisturbed plant growth; Helen put her hand on a tree-trunk, and it came away reluctantly, smeared with sap. "This had better be worth it," she said. The noise of the river behind them, the plunge of the fall over rocks and, above their heads, the song of birds as their huge crashing alarmed them; but when they stopped everything seemed quite still. There was a whoosh ahead, perhaps a couple of hundred yards, the unexpected noise of a car. The woodland was dense and untouched, so close to the Manchester road. "It's wet, Daniel," Helen said, but he just held out his hand to help her along. The ferns and grass were moist, and her tights were wet round her ankles as if she'd plunged into the river. But they carried on.

Suddenly the woodland came to an end, and they were at a clearing. There was a building in the middle of the wood. She couldn't understand why you didn't see it until you were absolutely on top of it, but it was quite hidden. It was an old, two-storey building, its windows made blank with wood panels that were themselves old and shabby. Its door—wide enough to have been a double door once—was covered with another panel, but hanging half off, and its roof bald and patchy, the joists displayed like the bones of a dead animal under its fur. It didn't look like a house; there was a kind of shed to one side, or the remains of one, its roof completely off and open to the elements. The walls of the shed were eroded like the ruins of a medieval castle, as if it had been stripped for masonry or dry-stone walls. The main building, however, was still pretty well whole. There were the remains of two external staircases, leading up to door-sized windows on the upper floor, one at each end, like wrecked fire-escapes.

"I don't think many people know about this," Daniel said. "I found it. I used to come here. Not with girls, I just used to come here. Come on."

They went to the building across the grass-strewn clearing. Under the grass, there were some sort of cobblestones, though they'd been grown over for years, perhaps decades. Daniel slipped through the broken door; Helen followed him.

"It's some sort of old forge, I found out," he said. "It went on working till before the war, but no one's done anything with it since."

"What's a forge doing out here?"

"It's perfect for steel-making," Daniel said. "Or it would have been once. There's the forest for firewood—if you look round the back, there's still a pile of timber rotting, it's been there fifty years. There's the river—I reckon there used to be a pond came right up from the river, but it's dried up and overgrown now. I don't know how that happens. There's the road, too. They'd have wanted to build something near a road, for the transport."

"What—you think they built this because of the Manchester road?"

"It's old, the Manchester road. It'd have been there long before this was built. It's only a hundred yards in that direction. Didn't you hear the car go past?"

"That's amazing," Helen said. "Someone must own it."

"I don't know who," Daniel said.

"People own everything," Helen said.

Inside, there was nothing much to be seen. If there had ever been forges or machinery, it had long been stripped out and taken to be melted down or reused. Though, from the outside, it looked as if it had two storeys, and the wrecked staircases showed that it must have done, there were only the broken-down remnants of a ceiling, mostly joists and rafters, hardly any floorboards, and what might have been a staircase had been efficiently removed, leaving not much more than markings on the wall where the horizontal beams had gone. The sun slashed through the grand ruined space; great diagonal girders of light struck haphazardly, just as they did through the forest. Whether it was from their entrance, or perhaps its normal state, the airborne dust of forest-eaten ruin was as heavy as a thin brown fog.

Helen walked round the circumference of the building, running her fingers over the lovely texture of the worn brick. "There's mushrooms growing here," she said.

"I bet you could eat them," Daniel said.

"I'll watch you eat them," Helen said, "and die soon of the adventure."

"There's nothing growing inside, though," Daniel said. "Have you seen that? The ferns, they're only growing just inside the door."

"Why's that, then?"

"There's a cellar underneath, a big one," Daniel said. "You get to it through that archway, over there."

"I'd be careful," Helen said. "The floor's going to collapse if you don't watch out."

"It won't collapse," Daniel said. "It's stone and brick, this floor, it's made to last for ever. It's only the first floor that was wood. Do you want to see the cellar?"

"You must be joking," Helen said. "It'll be dark and full of rats, I've no doubt."

From his pocket, Daniel produced a little torch, smiling. "There's no rats," he said. "Or, at least, none I've ever seen. There might be a frog or two, they like it down there, but they're not going to hurt you."

"Were you planning this?" Helen said. "I'm not one of your girls, you know, you can ask to lie down on your mackintosh in a wet cellar in a derelict building."

"I told you," Daniel said. "I never brought any girls here."

The archway, which looked like a cobwebby niche in the wall, no more, showed itself to be the top of a flight of stone steps. He brushed aside the curtain of wet cobwebs, their makers long gone, and with his torch shining a path down the steps, took her arm.

"I'm not going down there," Helen said, but she let herself go down with Daniel, step by step, until with a kind of damp crunch under her shoes they reached the bottom. He turned her gently, as if she were the blindfolded birthday girl being taken into her own party—for a second she almost felt that as he swung his torch round, there would be all her friends, and her family, waving balloons and calling, "Surprise!" But there was a huge space there, pillared with brick, twelve feet high.

There must be some other opening; the torch lit up a dense gloom rather than complete blackness.

"If I were a serial killer," Helen said, "this is where I'd come to leave the bodies."

"That's a charming thought," Daniel said. "If I were a serial killer, this is where I'd live, under the staircase, lying in wait for the next pair of my victims."

"—!" Helen shrieked, as just then Daniel, with a sharp fingernail, had reached round her back and pinched her bare arm, just where a serial killer might seize her. "That's not very funny."

"Well," Daniel said, shining his torch around the whole space quickly, "don't you think it's fantastic?"

"I wonder who owns it?" Helen said.

"That's what I'm going to find out," Daniel said.

"What for?" Helen said. "You know, sometimes I get the impression there's something you're not telling me."

"That might be an accurate impression," Daniel said. "I'm going to tell you now."

She looked at him; he brought the torch back to his stomach, and shone it upwards, giving his face heavy shadows, a horror-film expression. She couldn't help thinking, though, what a charmer he was, even with the special effects.

"We're going to buy it," he said.

"You must be joking," Helen said.

"I'm not joking," Daniel said. "We're going to buy it. If we can find someone who can actually sell it, we're going to buy it. It must belong to someone, and if we can find out who that is, I'm going to make them sell it to us."

"And who in the name of Beelzebub do you think 'us' is, Daniel?"

"That's the thing," Daniel said. "By 'us,' I mean you and me, and your dad Philip and your mum Shirley."

"Very funny," Helen said. "I suppose we're all going to live down here like the frogs."

"No," Daniel said. "We're not going to live here."

"To be honest, Daniel," Helen said, "I don't mind you bringing me down here to see where you used to hide yourself away, but I don't appreciate you making a joke out of my mum and dad. I thought you might have noticed that about me by now."

"I'm not joking," Daniel said. "I've never been more serious."

"Well, I'll tell you something," Helen said, "you might have started going out of your mind, but I can tell you my mum and dad haven't. There's no reason on earth could persuade them to get involved with any kind of scheme, being polite for the moment and assuming this isn't some kind of stupid joke."

"You're too late," Daniel said. "They're quite keen on the idea."

"You what?" Helen said.

"I said, they're quite keen on the idea," Daniel said. He switched off his torch; the gloom surrounded them. "Do you see?" he said. "There's a sort of trapdoor over there. I bet it's where they used to deliver the timber, they must have used this for storage. The raw materials."

"I don't doubt it," Helen said. They stood there in the dark, and in a moment Daniel came towards her, took her folded arms, one in each hand, and tried to kiss her. She wouldn't kiss back, and in a moment he stopped it.

"I tell you what," he said. "We'll walk through as far as the Manchester road—we're not far from the post office, they'll do us a cup of tea—and I'll tell you all about it."

Book Four

THE GIANT RAT OF SUMATRA

Well, have a look at this," Damon from the direct marketing said. "We just had the boys in Design—" blood-curdling chuckle "—'run up' a little example of the sort of thing we might be talking about. ETA in the press, eight weeks."

Nine of them were standing around in the central sort of discussion-space thingy in the office. It was lucky there were four pillars holding the roof up, or nobody would have had anything to lean against, and they'd all, like Jane, stand there formlessly. Would it really be so much, she asked silently and not for the first time, for a table and chairs around it and a door you could shut? But this was called hot-desking, which meant you didn't have one. Russell's idea from some American nonsense weekend in Berkshire. Two of the younger lads had dragged over low leather armchairs from the sort of reception-area thing, and were sitting in them with embarrassment, looking upwards. Jane didn't care, though she would have liked a desk and a room of her own where you could put a vase of flowers and a photograph or two. Instead, there was just a sort of plinth-arrangement thingy with a computer on it every now and again; that was supposed to be for everyone or anyone's use when inspiration struck. What you were supposed to do when inspiration hadn't struck? . . . In practice everyone had their own little computer on a pedestal and their own armchair nearby, where paperwork piled up on the floor alongside. You couldn't be neat without a desk with drawers, and Jane looked forward to Russell's experiment soon being modified, then abandoned altogether.

As the most experienced person there—they didn't do "senior" in Barney Spacek Boughton—Jane took the piece of A4 laminated card from Damon from the direct marketing. She inspected it. It was an advertisement for a weekend in a holiday camp, the same old chain of holiday camps that the poor kids at Flint used to go to and claim was great fun. Things had moved on. This weekend was reserved for queer-boys. There was a lot of talk about how much money they'd all got, the queer-boys, not having children and not talking to their elderly parents or anything else that looked like responsibilities. Russell had an expression for it; the "pink pound." "We'll be doing more and more of that sort of business," he said to her. "It's where the money is." When the question of doing the marketing for this weekend had come up, he'd gone for it with a degree of enthusiasm that had, frankly, surprised the clients, lowering the fee as they were taking their coats off, looking round fruitlessly for somewhere to hang them (and would a cupboard really be too much to ask?).

As it happened, it turned out that nobody really knew whether the queer-boys, despite having more money than anyone else, thanks to not having any kids and not talking to their elderly parents, were all that likely to part with it in exchange for a weekend in the lowest of low seasons, in dead February in a holiday camp in north Wales facing Liverpool across the Mersey. Jane had always seen these places quite clearly: a swathe of yellow-painted plaster peeling off the surface of grey concrete, and a middle-aged clown trudging round the corner with his soiled yellow-plush props dangling from his hand in the rain. That didn't seem very gay, in any sense at all.

She looked at the mock-up, reading from the bottom right upwards. "Is that what the costing came out as?" she said. "It seems quite a lot for the—a lot to ask."

"We queried it," Damon said. "Actually, the boys in Design queried it. They wondered whether the price was right. But the client said they'd run it past their focus group and it seemed to stand up. Fifty-eight per cent of the ITA taking part, I think—where is it?—fifty-eight per cent said that they *would* be prepared to pay up to, ah—"

"You see, Jane," one of the boys in the armchairs piped up, "the intended target audience have a high disposable income. The Pink Pound. The thing is, they don't have—"

"Yes, I know," Jane said. She and Scott didn't have any children, or any obligations to elderly relations, but no one was trying to lure them and their supposed riches to holiday camps in north Wales in February. It seemed like a lot of crap. "I know all that. Could I just ask a question? You said it was the boys in Design who queried the figure. Now, I don't really know about these things, but I would have thought that Design is the place where, if anywhere, you were going to find, well . . ."

She shrugged, looked at Damon.

"I don't follow," Damon said.

"Well, are none of the boys in Design, themselves, are any of them themselves . . ."

Damon stared at her. "Are you asking whether they're gay?"

"Yes," Jane said. "They often are."

"I honestly haven't asked them," Damon said, affronted. "I don't think it would be an appropriate thing to start an inquisition into."

"I see," Jane said.

"The thing you have to remember," the boy in the armchair said—a helpful type, "is that this is a sort of experimental exercise. The client's never done anything like this before, and he wants to cover his costs and quite a bit more. After all, there might be a consequential effect on his core business."

"That was really quite a serious concern," Damon said.

"The families don't want to sleep in beds where the queer-boys have been a week or two before," Jane said, "so the queer-boys have to pay for getting the AIDS off the sheets too—is that it?"

"Well," Damon said, "I wouldn't put it quite like that myself, but—"

"Let's have a look at this, then," Jane said. More and more, she found herself thinking, quite happily, some awful word whenever someone passed her in the street, or sold her something in Boots, or even spoke to her on the telephone. Nig-nog, Jew-boy, Paki, queer-boy—it ran through her head like the nursery rhyme from hell as she walked the streets or waited for a tube train to arrive, counting them like cherry stones, and more and more often she found herself discovering excuses to say them out loud. If Scott died before her, she'd be a mad old woman within days, yelling obscenities in public, there was no doubt about that. "Well, it looks—"

"What we've done," Damon said happily, "is really more tweaking than anything else. It's really quite similar to the mail-out the client always uses. We took out the family going down the water slide and put in—well, you see, and the sort of glitterball there, there's usually a clown with two kiddies instead of that. But the rest of it, it's just the adjectives."

"Pardon me?"

"We've just tweaked the adjectives in the copy. So, where it talks about the rooms—"

"Fabulous double rooms."

"That's it. Normally that says, 'great double rooms.' We ran it through the focus groups and they responded very positively to that. 'Great' is a terrific family word, families with two-point-four kids like that a lot, but the target market didn't really go for it, it was too family. They like 'fabulous' a lot. A full twelve PCP more said—"

"What?"

"A full twelve percentage points more said that they were extremely likely or fairly likely to book this holiday when the change was made, and the not-at-all-likelies fell from twenty-seven per cent to thirteen. Which is amazing."

"Or fabulous," Jane said. PCP, for heaven's sake.

"Yes, it's a fabulous result," Damon said, risking a drag-act squeal and throwing his hands in the air. Everyone duly laughed.

"I'm going to call this meeting to a close now," Jane said, "so that we can all look at this and think it over and brainstorm it and come back to you—what? Day after tomorrow? OK, thanks, everybody."

"Right," Damon said, disconcerted. But they did everything differently at Barney Spacek Boughton, everyone knew that, no meeting lasting more than half an hour. They'd won awards. He picked his coat up from the back of a chair where he'd left it, and his team let themselves be shown out.

Jane came back in five minutes, wearing her coat. They were all still milling around, passing the proposed advert between themselves. "I'm going out for lunch," she said, her hands in her pockets, grumpily.

"OK," the juniors said. They knew these moods of hers, always after a presentation. Some people thought she was taking herself off to think about strategy, others thought that she quite often considered the whole thing a load of crap, though it was daring of them to float the possibility that anyone might think their business a load of crap. When she ended meetings abruptly with most questions undecided, or took herself off "for lunch" at a quarter to twelve, like now, it was, some people thought, to stop herself saying something unforgivable, unretractable. There'd almost been trouble a year or two back at a management training weekend she couldn't have walked out of: three-quarters of an hour of direct questions to the facilitator about the exact meaning of the terms he was using, one after another, and, they said, that glare. She had some licence in the office. She was the only married person who worked there, for one thing. And she always came back from these two-hour absences, whatever she did in them, talking sense. The load-of-crap school was in the minority.

"Do you want company?" Robert said mildly, calling over from behind a pot-plant.

"Yeah, why not?" Jane said. The others watched them go.

"Tell me something," Jane said, as the two of them got out of the lift into the lobby, shared with twenty other companies on different floors. "This is a load of crap, isn't it?"

"Total crap," Robert said comfortably. They had known each other, worked with each other, for ten years on and off, in different companies here and there. She'd come over to Barney Spacek Boughton when it was just starting up and Russell was looking for someone with a portfolio of tame clients. He'd brought the subject up, of all places, at their wedding, and she'd found herself discussing the salary and BSB's client list in her wedding dress. She'd come back from the honeymoon safari to find an invitation from them to come over and talk a bit further, and she'd been there for four years now.

"Jesus," Jane said. "When he started on about 'great' and 'fabulous,' I really thought—"

"Oh, we all know what you thought," Robert said.

"Was it as obvious as that?" Jane said, as they went into the car park.

"Well, pretty obvious," Robert said. "Obvious to me, anyway. It was like you'd already put your coat and hat on. Where are we going?"

"To be honest, I was just going to drive around, let off steam a bit," Jane said. "I suppose lunch was going to come into it at some point."

They set off in Jane's new red saloon—she'd argued for a BMW but Russell said they couldn't stretch to it and they couldn't justify it just yet.

"How's Scott?" Robert said. "And the new house?"

"Oh, it's fine," Jane said. "He's fine. So much to do. New curtains, new carpets, the furniture looks all wrong, there's no bookshelves, new kitchen, new bathroom. Improvement on the Scott front, though, now he's not the entremetier any more—he gets in before two, these days, and he does something other than sleep on his days off."

"Remind me."

"What? Oh, entremetier—it means the vegetable cook," Jane said. "Sorry, you pick up all this jargon. They made a new job for him, he's canapier these days."

"Is that a word?"

"Well, they didn't know what to call it, but they invented canapier, he's in charge of canapés and nothing else. People like those best—that and the petit fours. They don't care much about anything in between. So he's always thinking up new little canapés for them. What they like is miniature food, tiny versions of proper dinners. Not that the rest of it isn't fairly miniature anyway. He made a shepherd's pie the size of your thumbnail, they liked that, and, you know, cold soup in a thimble, that sort of thing. He keeps trying to get something Australian in there—he had a go at kangaroo carpaccio with a dab of truffle oil, but it kept coming back to the kitchen untouched. They'll eat anything when it's that small, but they didn't like the smell or something. Tripe in a garlic and champagne gravy, that wasn't a success either."

"I can't say I'm all that surprised."

"The good thing, as I say, is that he does get to come home a bit earlier—he's really done by eight o'clock."

"Does he cook for you?"

"Scott? Are you joking? Poor sod, I wouldn't ask that of him."

The traffic was quite heavy, for some reason, and then, without warning, it ground to a halt in both directions.

"What's going on?" Jane said.

"I should have said," Robert said. "This is my way in, there's road-works."

"Now you say," Jane said. They sat there for a minute or two, the traffic stationary.

"Where are we going?"

"I thought," Jane said, "what about that pub in Farringdon, does proper food? You know?"

"Yeah, go on," Robert said. "At least you don't get everything with a coulis or a sabayon in a pub."

"It's a bit sabayon, strangely enough," Jane said, "but not that much. Gastro-pub, they call it."

"Sounds like what you experience in the loo afterwards."

"It's all right, it's nice. I'm going to ask this policewoman what's going on with the traffic."

"She looks off-duty," Robert said. She did. Coming up the hill away from the roadworks, however far away they were, the policewoman was carrying her policewoman's cap in her hand, and on top of her uniform was a black wet-look PVC raincoat, tightly belted. "That's not uniform, surely?"

Jane wound down the window and called across the road to the policewoman. She looked around her, then sauntered over, weaving between the unmoving cars facing the other direction. In her tightly belted raincoat, she had an exaggerated figure, heavy on top and bulky below; she was mid-thirties, somewhere between voluptuous youth and the heaviness of middle age. "Did you want me, love?" she said. Her voice was Northern; she was wearing a surprising amount of makeup.

"I just wondered whether you could tell us how bad the traffic is ahead," Jane said.

"Jammed solid, love," the policewoman said. "Where are you heading?"

"Clerkenwell," Jane said.

"That's a coincidence," the policewoman said. "That's exactly where I'm heading. Well, you'd be as well to do as I'm doing and get the tube. You won't get there any time soon the way you're going."

Afterwards, they said to themselves that they'd never seen a policewoman wearing a shiny PVC mackintosh, or taking the underground to get to where they had to go, and probably should have wondered about that. But Jane's attention was taken by something else; she was looking the policewoman up and down with a puzzled expression.

"Well, you'll know me again," the policewoman said, but not in a hostile way.

"You're not from Sheffield, are you?" Jane said.

"Is it as bad as that?" she said. "Most people say Manchester down here, but they coon't tell difference between Leeds and Liverpool 'less you told them direct, like. He's not from Sheffield." She pointed.

"No," Robert agreed. "I'm from Maidenhead."

"You're not Barbara, are you?" Jane said.

The policewoman leant forward, lowering her head to the window in an interested way, as if a suspect had just let drop a valuable admission. "Who are you, then?" Barbara said.

"You used to know my brother," Jane said. She couldn't really say that she'd recognized Barbara, not from her face, which had coarsened and grown wide and, anyway, was forced into a general approximation of what women should look like by too much makeup. She'd recognized her in a sort of dim flash of familiarity, from her shape, pulled in and falling out, almost comic, like a drawing of a woman by a twelve-year-old naughty boy; she'd seen that shape waiting outside in the dusk, years before. "My brother Daniel. Daniel Glover."

"Oh, aye," Barbara said, leaning back and standing up straight as if she had now won her point. "I remember Daniel."

That seemed to be all there was to be said on the subject.

"You couldn't give me a lift, could you?" Barbara said. "I can't be late. I'll direct you, I know a better way than this."

"All right," Jane said, and leant round to unlock the rear door. Nobody ever sat in the back of her car, and she had to pull her seat forward a little bit to give Barbara leg room.

"Right, do a U-ey," Barbara said. "And next left, no, next but one. I don't remember you, love."

"I was only little," Jane said. "You probably wouldn't. You never came in, that's what I remember about you."

"Wasn't allowed to," Barbara said. "Your brother!"

Jane doubted this, but she said nothing. The car was already full of a chemical, heavy floral smell, more like a room disinfectant than any kind of perfume. "I'd never have thought," she said, "that you'd end up like this, doing that."

"Like what?" Barbara said. "Oh, right," she said, looking down, almost as if in surprise. She laughed. "Oh, I see. That's surprising, is it?"

"Well, it is a bit," Jane said. "I must have had the wrong idea of you. Of course," she said, turning to Robert, who was wearing a questioning expression, "I didn't really know Barbara. All I knew was she went out for a bit with Daniel, my brother. He was a bit of a ladies' man, to be honest, even then."

"He's a bit of a twat, I know that much," Barbara said.

"No, he's not," Jane said evenly. "He just got through quite a lot of girls. They were throwing themselves at him. Still do. He's spoken for now, though. Girl called Helen."

"Good-looking boy, your brother?"

"Throwing themselves away on him," Barbara said. "What's he up to, now, then?"

"He's got his own business," Jane said. "He used to work for an estate agent's, then he gave it up. He's converted an old steel mill, not in town, in the country, really. It's half a dance school and there's a restaurant upstairs. It's doing all right."

"He's never teaching dancing," Barbara said.

"No, it's his girlfriend's parents look after all that," Jane said. "He was a miner, Helen's father, he put his redundancy package in, Daniel found the rest. It's doing all right."

"Strange combination of things," Robert said. "Restaurant and dance school."

"I can't imagine Daniel doing anything like that," Barbara said. "Still less making a success of it."

"People change so much, don't they," Jane said. "It's doing all right. It's a lovely setting, it's getting to be quite fashionable as a place to go of an evening. Some people go for a dance lesson, some for dinner. Daniel says quite a lot of them do the one then stay on for the other.

It'd been derelict for years, the building—the council owned it, but they weren't going to do anything much with it. They got quite a good grant just for restoring it."

There was a little silence in the car. "I didn't really know Barbara at all," Jane went on. "You know, if you'd said to me twenty years ago, what Barbara was likely to end up doing for a living, I'd never have guessed."

"Why's that, then?" Barbara said.

"Well, it just goes to show what a wrong idea you can have about someone," Jane said. "To be honest, I thought, because you dressed like you did, and because you didn't live in such a nice house as we did, and because Daniel would never let you come in and meet us, and because—" meeting offensiveness with the sort of frankness that always won "—because you were having it off with my brother, I just assumed you couldn't be very good at school."

"Oh, aye?" Barbara said. "And what's changed your opinion, then?"

"Well, you know, to get in the police, you need O levels, don't you? And A levels even? I never thought one of Daniel's girlfriends would be the type to—"

"Get through them, did he?" Robert said.

"Quite a few," Jane said. "A month or two and then that was generally it. They used to come and go. You'd not meet three or four in a row, just hear about them. He's settled down now—Helen's got him on a leash all right—but he used to just throw them away. I never thought you'd do well at school, Barbara, it never occurred to me."

"So what makes you think I did well at school?"

"As I say, you'll have had to have got O levels, A levels. They're strict about that, aren't they?"

"What—before they'll let you get your kit off in an Irish pub at lunchtime?" Barbara said. "Left again here."

"You—"

"You thought I was in the police?" Barbara said. "I tell you what, it's not me but you that must be a bit thick if you think real policewomen go round dressed like this and looking like this, lot of lesbians. Someone said I could be a model. No, love, you've got the wrong end of the stick. I'm a strippergram. I'm a sexy policewoman today—it's an Irish lad's twenty-first, his granddad's laid me on as a treat for him. Other times I can be a sexy traffic warden, or—I tell you what, this is funny—I can be Jane. It's a double act with a Tarzan. He's gay, the Tarzan, you'd never know, though, big fella. Hundred quid a time, hundred and fifty for the double act. Your name's Jane, in't it? Or a sexy secretary, dressed up like you, in a suit. I'll tell you love, no one's going to pay you to take your clothes off. The next corner's fine."

Jane braked abruptly. "You can walk from here," she said, not turning round. "Nice to meet you. I'll remember to tell Daniel I bumped into you and that you're showing your hairy bucket to drunken Irishmen in pubs for a hundred pounds a time. He'll be so interested, if he can remember who you were."

"I'll sithee, love," Barbara said. "And give my best to, Helen, was it? Poor cow, whoever she is. Bet she's working her fingers to the bone. And tell him from me, that sounds like a stupid business he's got himself. Bet he's happy spending other people's money, though. Sithee." She got out quite gracefully, and walked away. As she walked ahead of them, she made one exaggerated movement of her hips, an old-fashioned, insulting bump-and-grind gesture.

"You know the extraordinary thing about getting older?" Robert said. "Police officers, they all start to look like really raddled old strippers."

"Don't they just," Jane said.

"Could I ask you?" Robert said. "Hairy bucket? Where on earth did that come from?"

"Honestly," Jane said. "Do you know, I almost want to go and watch her act. Did she say what pub it was?"

"No, thank God," Robert said. "I want my lunch now. I hope she's not performing in the Eagle."

"Not very likely," Jane said. "I can't wait to tell Daniel. Do you think she had a python concealed about her person?"

"I like the idea of a stripper-policewoman," Robert said. "Not much worse than a dancer-restaurateur, though, if you think about it."

"Honestly, it's doing well, Daniel's business," Jane said. "I wouldn't have thought it, but there you go."

"But that woman," Robert said. "Of course, it's disappointing she wasn't really a policewoman. Imagine. I was stripping in a northerly direction, when I observed—"

By the time they got to the Eagle, they were laughing raucously about the whole story. The pub had recently been reduced to floorboards and exposed brick; an elaborate kitchen was behind the bar, and on blackboards was listed the sort of food that pubs didn't sell. Jane had scallops wrapped in prosciutto; Robert had a porcini risotto; she had Pellegrino; he in a nod to their being in a pub had a pint of bitter from an Ipswich brewery, not finishing it. The subject kept them going all through lunch, and by the end they could start talking seriously about the holiday-camp project. Jane heard herself talking sense, incisively; she was good, really, at what she did, which was handling a lot of nonsense.

Rosalie was loitering a bit as she came up to the entrance to the building. She was sure she'd seen Muriel getting off the same tube train; there had been something characteristically complaining in the set of her shoulders. She knew what that meant for her: ten minutes of Muriel making herself feel better by commiserating about Harold, Rosalie's son. Muriel always knew what Harold had been up to, or what somebody had told Muriel Harold had been seen getting up to. Rosalie didn't need it, so she hung back.

If she was arriving after Muriel, she was late. Without thinking about it, she pushed back the cuff of her coat, forgetting that her watch had gone the way of the carriage clock on the mantelpiece, her mother's set of four silver candlesticks, and, three times, most of the contents of her purse, left around thoughtlessly. It was the candlesticks she'd minded, though she'd not noticed their disappearance for weeks, probably. The watch wouldn't have fetched much, surely. Well, she hoped he'd got some enjoyment out of it in the end. Brendan, the supervisor, would be sure to point it out if she was late. But Brendan always made a point of finding fault with something; it might as well be lateness tonight as anything else.

Sanjay was on tonight; she liked him best of the security guards. He was actually a student, working one night a week for a little cash. Some of the other women were saucy to him, but Rosalie approved of someone bettering themselves and calling her Mrs. Simpkins.

"You like your book, Sanjay," Rosalie said.

"Mr. Macinnes isn't in yet," Sanjay said, making as if to conceal it, though it was nothing but a school book, nothing to hide or be ashamed of. Mr. Macinnes was Brendan. He never quite looked you in the eye; his unexpectedly pale ones just fixed themselves on your neck.

"It my lucky day, Sanjay," Rosalie said. "I'm thinking I'm late and Brendan kill me."

"It's not seven yet," Sanjay said. "I keep telling you, Mrs. Simpkins, you got to buy a watch."

"When Brendan start paying me a hundred pounds an hour," Rosalie said, passing through the security barrier and calling behind her as she went, "then I buy me a watch. Or it matters so much to him, he buys me a watch himself, with diamonds on it, OK, Sanjay?"

There were worse places to clean than offices, Rosalie thought. The worst was a hotel; the mess some people made, you wouldn't believe, and they were so particular about folding the toilet paper in an arrow, having it hanging flat against the wall, dozens of little thing like that, you were always in some kind of trouble with the housekeeper. She wouldn't do that again, but she still worked for people in their houses, too, like most of the girls. A lot of the girls said they preferred that to office work. Rosalie didn't know. They could be nice, and you got to know them—you got to know a lot about them, more than you wanted, sometimes. But there was the looking-grateful when they gave you something extra at Christmas, and when you were a coloured lady they were always thinking that surely there'd been a ten-pound note on the bedside table before Rosalie came or where had my husband's best cufflinks disappeared to, that type of kerfuffle. Offices were really best; if it was untidy you left it alone, you hoovered and you wiped down the surfaces and emptied the bins, and you cleaned the toilets and the kitchenette. But people in offices generally left those in the sort of state they wouldn't mind their bosses seeing. It wasn't too bad.

She went up to get the cleaning stuff out of the general cupboard, and down again to the fourth floor. She couldn't understand the fourth floor. It wasn't like an office at all. There were just little podiums here and there, and sofas. There was even a snooker table and a darts board hanging on the wall; there was a room enclosed with glass for no other purpose than smoking in and, of all things, a cupboard hanging on the wall full of alcoholic drinks. Rosalie was fifty-three, and in all those fifty-three years she had never in her life stepped inside a public house; but it was with confidence that she thought and frequently remarked that the fourth floor more resembled the inside of a drinkers' den than a respectable place of business. It wasn't Rosalie's place to wonder what sort of business was conducted by Barney Spacek Boughton, the name written like careless two-foot-high handwriting in moulded plastic on the wall where you got out of the lift. She read it as "Spack"; she couldn't really imagine. There were no desks anywhere. Sometimes there were piles of papers left by the side of the sofa, as if they'd tried to hide them; Rosalie did her best, but she always thought of that one time years ago when Saul had still been alive and they'd had company, the minister and his wife. Harold, he'd have been no more than three, he'd disappeared out of shyness, and they'd thought nothing of it, until there'd been this terrible smell; the minister's wife had been raising a best teacup to her mouth and she'd stopped and lowered it without saying anything. And it had been Harold, hiding behind the sofa, he'd dropped his trousers and pants and done his business on the carpet, the Lord knew why. It had been a terrible thrashing Saul had given Harold when the minister and wife had gone. That was what those shameful little piles of papers always made Rosalie think of, secreted behind the sofas.

There was a sharp spatter, a shrill military drum-trill, as if against a virgin's bedroom window a lover had thrown a fistful of gravel. It was starting to rain in the spangled City dark beyond those ten-foot walls of glass, to rain with abrupt, flung severity. There'd been no sign of it when Rosalie had set off from home in Tottenham this morning, or she'd have taken her brolly, or when she'd left her last job of the day, Mrs. Franklin's house in Clapham—Mrs. Franklin was all right, she wouldn't mind if she'd borrowed an umbrella from the cloakroom in the circumstances. For an awful moment Rosalie suddenly wondered whether she still had an umbrella. But that was ridiculous: you couldn't sell an old umbrella for anything, you couldn't buy any amount of heroin with the money someone would give you in exchange for your own mother's old umbrella, surely you couldn't. You couldn't: Harold couldn't; nobody could. It must be somewhere.

Rosalie did everything in order. She washed up the mugs in the kitchen, and the glasses with their ugly smell of smoke and earth, the smell of whisky. (Whisky smelt of burn and destruction, beer smelt of not washing, wine smelt of sick, vodka smelt of money, of sour old coins, gin smelt of room freshener, and the rest, they smelt mostly the way desserts smelt when you'd already had too much to eat and you'd dread another helping being forced on you; all that specific knowledge Rosalie had and would never find a use for or take any pleasure in.) In the men's toilets, she cleaned the sinks, she cleaned the two toilets, she mopped the floor; she did the same in the women's, which could be worse. She emptied the full ashtrays in the smoking room, the full wastepaper bins; she wiped the surfaces everywhere. When she'd done everything else, she ran the vacuum-cleaner round; a fat circular red thing on wheels with a face on and something like an old-style hat, like one that old Charlie Chaplin used to wear. Some clever person had thought all that a good idea once, rather than, for instance, quite a stupid one. They paid her two pounds seventy an hour here.

Even so, Rosalie felt quite light-hearted, she didn't know why. She hadn't had to talk to anyone. She hadn't been got at by Muriel or shouted at by Brendan. If it was raining as hard as this in Tottenham, then Harold would have stayed at home; he wouldn't be out causing trouble. She ran the vacuum-cleaner round briskly and, without really paying attention, she ran it hard into a pile of papers she hadn't noticed, just by the side of one of the sofas. They went everywhere. Rosalie switched the grinning red round thing off, and went to pick the papers up. She couldn't help looking at them, what someone had written on them. It was written by a woman, a child could see that—men, when they wrote, they didn't do those little fat loops and all—but Rosalie read the single sentence at the top of the page and didn't think very much of it. No decent person would have written such a thing; she almost felt like putting it out with the rubbish from the bins. Not that she knew in every detail what "buttock-featured TLA-mongering vadge-brain" could mean. She put it back in its pile; she squared them; she continued in her job, and in a moment the doors to the office opened and Brendan came in. She could have said something sarcastic about him turning up at last, but she didn't. And, of course, he went without saying hello into the office kitchen, and came out again. "I hope that's next on your list," he said, "because you've obviously not done it properly." She gave him a thumbs-up and a sort of smile. There was no point in anything else.

Jane went home with the good feeling of having got somewhere, and knowing exactly what to do tomorrow morning, and it would be easy enough. Nothing much lay in wait for her. Scott wasn't back yet. She let herself into the hallway of the new house in Clapham. It still gave her pleasure, a month after moving in. There were still movers' boxes in the outer hallway, emptied but not disposed of—they used to use old tea-chests, but nowadays, apparently, movers had their own name and details printed on the side of special cardboard boxes. There were more boxes, not unpacked yet, in the conservatory, but the house was getting pretty straight now. Her mother had said, "Live in it for three months without changing anything, then you'll see what needs to be done." But Jane thought she could see by now what needed to be done, with the curtains too short and the kitchen, which had seemed all right but now seemed really quite awful.

There were messages blinking red on the answer-phone, three of them—she ran through them. Scott saying he'd be home by eight, Sarah Willis confirming, for the second time, that they were going out for a drink next Wednesday, and someone sighing and putting the phone down. Poor old Sarah Willis, as she'd become again since her divorce; clinging a bit too much, talking a bit too much about the good old days in Sheffield—no, Oxford, Jane corrected herself, she'd met Sarah in Oxford. Just went to show. It was odd how things changed between people: these days, it was her inviting Sarah round out of kindness, though, God knows, Scott complained enough about asking people for dinner on his night off without, on top of that, being asked to be especially nice to Sarah because she was having a rough time; a rough time that was made obvious to everyone since she arrived drunk and carried on drinking steadily, asking everyone round the table to tell her their names three separate times. Well, never again.

According to her mother, Daniel had got himself a mobile phone. "It really is amazing," she'd said. "He can justify it against tax, or something. Daniel was showing it to us—you know they used to be about the size of a brick? Well, they've really shrunk them down, they're not even as big as the remote control for the television. Your dad said, 'You'll be spending all your time hunting for that,' but Daniel said, no, he just keeps it in his pocket all the time. It's as small as that, you can keep it in your pocket." She'd had his number written down somewhere, but it must have disappeared for the moment. Jane knew perfectly well what mobile phones looked like, these days, but she let her mother run on. Sooner or later, she'd have to get one, she supposed, and as Russell kept saying; and then there'd be a complete end to escaping for three hours where no one could reach you. Daniel had always liked gadgets; she remembered, years ago, his digital watch—it wasn't the flickering electronic winking, which came in later, but just a dial with numbers on it that rotated slowly behind a window, just an ordinary watch, really, but Daniel used to go round showing it to complete strangers. He must be terrible with his mobile phone. But in any case she didn't have his number.

She left a message at their house—"You'll never guess," she said, "who I saw today. You've got to phone me, you just won't believe it." They lived in Walkley; Daniel said it was up and coming, and they'd bought a bigger house than they could afford anywhere else. He also said, laughing, that once you got a bank manager who believed you, you might as well take advantage of it, and of course he still knew all the dodges when it came to buying houses, hadn't forgotten how property thought into the future. Jane herself, she'd never have wanted a friend who lived in Walkley when she was at school. She found it difficult to imagine.

But then, afterwards, she started to consider who else there was she could tell, if there was anyone at all. She almost started to phone Sarah Willis before remembering that, of course, she'd got to know Sarah Willis at Oxford, and she'd never have heard of Barbara. Weird how the past sank into a single conflated pile. Tim wasn't likely to remember Barbara, and in any case there was no point in telling him anything of that sort; he'd always been keen on Sandra Sellers, who'd come afterwards, always gazed and admired and gawped at her in a way that made you think she must be the first girl he'd noticed in any solid way. But thinking of Sandra Sellers, she suddenly remembered her brother—Francis, wasn't it?—and that he lived in London. She hadn't seen him for a while; they'd met at a concert by chance, and had gone for a walk afterwards.

These days, they only had one address book between the pair of them. Scott's old one with all his Australian addresses was somewhere in the bottom of a tea-chest, and, in any case, it was completely full on every page. It made Jane feel quite inadequate, until she saw that it wasn't that Scott had so many more friends, just a habit of noting down the addresses of acquaintances, and then their new addresses, and then their temporary addresses, and their Australian addresses for an emergency in case any of them wanked themselves to death and it turned out once more to be Scott and Jane's responsibility to inform their parents, not that either of them put it like that. They all moved so often between shared houses and bedsits, Scott's Australian acquaintances from his own house-sharing Europe-touring days, that he was forever crossing out and writing in. But he was older now, and hadn't seen most of those people for years, or only briefly, at their wedding. He just made sure that Jane had his parents' address and his sister's in Amsterdam where she'd been learning to play the flute for seven years now, had them written down in her address book, and then that did for the pair of them. They didn't go out much in any case, and the green padded address book, its spine fraying and its gold-lettered function worn thin, sat undisturbed underneath the *Yellow Pages* and the phone book and, for some reason, an old copy of the *Guardian*—oh, it was the one with a review of Scott's restaurant in it. They mostly knew the numbers of people they called.

London had divided, and the small part on which Jane had had her haphazard landing had claimed, unnoticed, her allegiance. It seemed unlikely that Jane, and Scott too, could ever have lived anywhere but Clapham, that something in them denoted South London. She loved the common and its featurelessness, even the little duck pond and the curious, hunched pub on their side, like an old rural pub that had once been a London outing and was now just a London pub. She loved the good butcher and the terrible one, the Edwardian adverts for long-useless businesses—piano rolls, stabling for horses and hire—painted indelibly on the sides of houses. She loved the occasional noble square, and the weird passages where council housing had been thrown up in the gaps left by wartime bombing. She liked it all.

She found the address book, and there, amid a thicket of crossings-out, was an address and phone number for Francis Sellers. They'd gone for a walk a couple of years ago—no, Christ, it had definitely been just after the Australian killed himself, so just before she and Scott had started going out. That was ten years ago. Christ. He'd have definitely moved by now, but she dialled the number anyway.

"What?" the voice at the end of the phone said. It was the voice of a heavy mouth-breather. Jane was prepared to apologize and hang up, but then it said, "Oh, yeah. I'll just go and have a look."

At the other end, the phone was clunked on to some surface, or dropped on to the floor. There was a heavy thudding upstairs, and then, after a minute or two, the same noise in reverse.

"There's a note on his door," the voice said. "It says he's gone away for a while, says he's gone home, says his mother's seriously ill or something. Hang on, I thought he was supposed to be going to Rome, though. Says if anyone calls to tell them but I don't think no one's called. Except you."

"When did he go away?" Jane said.

"How should I know?" the voice said.

"OK," Jane said. "Do you live there?"

"Course I do."

"Well, when did you last see him?"

"I don't know," the voice said. "All right?"

Jane was about to leave it, but the other person, whether man or woman, had already hung up. In any case, she didn't think, on reflection, Francis Sellers had ever known Barbara or even Daniel that well.

There was the nice rattling sound of Scott's key in the lock. She looked at her watch—it was later than she'd thought. She got up from where she'd been squatting—with all this unpacking still to do, it was a bit like the office round here—and went to kiss him.

"Hey, stop running everywhere," Scott said.

"I'm not running," Jane said. "I just got up to give my husband a kiss."

"Well, don't do it," Scott said. "I bet you haven't had a rest at all."

"I feel fine," Jane said. "Think of all those Chinese women who go on working in the fields until the last moment."

"Yeah, well, I'd like to see their miscarriage rate," Scott said. "You'll never guess what happened."

"Don't do that," Jane said, as Scott ran his hand over her stomach, still flat.

"Don't do what? I'm not allowed to touch you all of a sudden?"

"No, it's just—" Jane said, not quite able to say that it was sort of hers now in a way it hadn't been before and, more than that, she knew how, when you were visibly pregnant, people you hardly recognized had a way of laying their hands on your belly for luck. She might even have done it herself. "So what happened, then?"

"Your friend Sarah Willis called me," Scott said. "They hauled me out of the kitchen."

"Christ, what was it?" Jane said, going over and laying herself down carefully on the sofa. He'd always impressed on her that you didn't call him at work.

"Well, it seemed she'd been calling you and leaving messages," Scott said, "and you were unavailable at work and you weren't answering the messages she'd left here."

"She's left one message," Jane said. "Yesterday. No, the day before."

"And she thought there might be something terribly wrong. Which there isn't. So she called me to see if you're still having a drink next week. Tell her she's not to do that."

"I'll give her hell," Jane said.

"Good," Scott said. "I hope you're not having a drink with her, though, I mean, a drink."

"Oh, don't worry," Jane said. "I'll stick to tomato juice. I think we can probably tell people now, anyway."

"She'll only want to be the godmother," Scott said. "Silly bitch."

"That's not going to happen," Jane said, laughing. "I suppose we ought to think about it, though."

The kitchen was a naff flash one, with metal work surfaces and glass-fronted cupboards; when the previous owners had heard that Scott was a chef, as they were going over the house for the first time, they'd visibly relaxed, as though the sale was now in the bag. But the kitchen didn't get a great deal of use. These nights, now Scott came home from cooking and then cooked dinner for them, they ate the same few simple things. It might have been easier to reheat something ready-made from the supermarket, but they were full of additives, Scott said. So it was plain things, full of iron; he'd fry a plain steak with mushrooms, and steam a big pan full of spinach, a huge pot of greenery reducing quickly to a kind of slimy undergrowth. It didn't taste too bad at all. And for dessert, a succession of mineral supplements and vitamins. Scott was taking it all very seriously. But she liked the way he faced her across the table, and watched her eat every mouthful, making sure all that goodness went in, making sure, as parents did, she chewed every mouthful thirty-six times before swallowing.

There were four whole weeks' holiday in the working year. Twenty days—it meant four weeks. And there were bank holidays, too, nine of them—New Year, May Day, Good Friday, Easter Monday, Spring, August, and about three days off at Christmas. Francis knew them all, particularly that horrible long stretch at Easter, when it seemed as if one Sunday was succeeding another. The four weeks' holiday you had to take for the sake of the other staff in the office, who actually wanted it. Oddly enough, you had to call in sick at least once or twice a year, too, because everyone thought that was normal and pretty well your right, so you had to do it whether you were sick or not.

Usually Francis took his holiday in as large chunks as he could bear, whenever it was convenient to everyone else—always in school term-time, which couldn't affect him. He never did anything much. Often, he went up to see his parents in Sheffield. One of these days, he thought, he was going to go to Australia to see Sandra. He hadn't seen her for five years. There was no reason why not: his salary piled up in his bank account, depleted only by his CD habit. But it didn't happen. He was quite happy as he was.

For some reason, he'd suddenly thought that, after all, there might be something to be said for going abroad. He was getting too set in his ways. He thought, and decided that he really would quite like to go to Rome. He booked his holiday from work, bought a ticket, three months in advance, and reserved a hotel by letter. He went to the post office, filled in the forms, and in some weeks his passport arrived; he'd never needed one before. And then he remembered the cat.

Francis had lived in the same house since he'd moved to London. It was quite pleasant, but it wasn't his. He'd moved into one bedroom in a shared house, and in time the original people had moved out. At first he'd had the smallest room; when the others moved out, he moved into their rooms, until he was living in the best room in the house and paying a little more for it. There were five bedrooms in the house, and at first five lodgers. In time, he asked the landlord whether he could have an extra room, and the landlord agreed. He'd lived there now for ten years, and now he had three rooms. There were two lodgers downstairs; he had a whole floor. He didn't really know them—anyway, they were so much younger than him they didn't have much in common. They'd move out soon, he expected.

Francis was so settled in his three rooms on the top floor that it seemed a natural step to acquire a cat. He'd got the idea from one of his friends in the queue for a Proms concert in the summer. The Proms were his social season. He'd been going for years, and knew almost all the old hands, the regulars. They all had their favourite places on the rail at the front of the arena, and they looked out for each other. If anyone tried to let someone in at the front of the queue, or muscle into a reserved space, the dedicated Prommers had their ways of making sure they didn't succeed, and didn't ever come back. "I'm surprised you don't get a cat," Stephanie said. She was twenty stone, her long, half-washed grey hair in a wet-looking cascade down her back, which, even now, she sometimes liked to flick in girlish ways, and loved oratorio best. "It's so nice when you come back to your flat and there's Dame Kiri there, so excited, she can't wait to jump up into your lap."

"I didn't see you at the Rattle, Francis," someone else said, perhaps surprised at a mental picture.

"I thought I'd prom in the gallery," Francis said. "I think you get the best sound in Mahler Two up there."

Stephanie worked for the Civil Service, too, in the Department of Health, where she had her own little things, her own coffee-machine and pictures and special chair for her back problems, they all knew all about it. Francis could see the pathos of a woman like Stephanie coming home and being greeted by a cat; she kept the animal's birthday, and bought it Christmas presents too. But, of course, a cat needn't be like that. A cat of Francis's wouldn't be like that at all. It might be quite nice to have an animal dozing away in the corner of a room. You couldn't have a dog in London, but a cat was perfectly possible, and a degree of company more than the lodgers downstairs. And, of course, the cat wouldn't be called Dame Kiri.

It was called Samson.

"I wouldn't have thought of you as a cat person, Francis," Mr. Knowles, his line manager, said in the lift. He was hearty and fat and, though dad-like, actually the same age as Francis; his stomach bulged against his striped shirts, turning straight lines into arabesques. He looked up cheerfully at Francis. "I'd have thought—"

"Do I seem more like a dog person?" Francis said, surprised.

"Oh, no," Mr. Knowles said. "Definitely not."

"Definitely not," a woman in the lift agreed. Francis wasn't sure he even knew her.

"I would have thought . . ." Mr. Knowles said. "More—a fish, maybe."

Francis didn't know what to say to that. The woman started sniggering. But luckily it seemed to Mr. Knowles as if he'd said something rude, which Francis might complain about.

"So what are you going to call your cat?" Mr. Knowles said.

"He's called Samson," Francis said.

"That's a curious name for a cat," Mr. Knowles said. "Big fellow, is he?"

"Well, it's more that—" Francis began, but then the lift arrived at the fifteenth floor, and Mr. Knowles led the way out as if the conversation was over.

Francis had brought the cat home in its cage-fronted box; had set out its basket, its litter box, and then had opened the front. The cat, still unnamed, had peered at them with its black face from the dark like a panther in a plastic cave. After a moment, it ventured out, padding heavily. It went all round the room, under chairs and into crevices between furniture. For some reason, watching it walk with its soundless, weighty tread, Francis remembered something horrible he had once heard: that if you died alone in a house with a cat in it, it would sooner or later start eating your body. The cat came to the CDs, piled up high in towers; he seemed to see something interesting in the gap between two balancing piles. He turned away and, with his rump, knocked against one of the towers. It teetered, wavered, and fell with a crash, sending the cat rocketing to the other side of the room and up the sofa. "It's all right, you silly animal," Francis said. "You don't know your own strength." So, of course, the cat was Samson. He'd have explained to Mr. Knowles if he hadn't been in so much of a hurry.

"I couldn't take the responsibility," one of the lodgers said, when Francis asked her about looking after Samson for a week.

"I'm not going to be here," the other one said, barefaced, staring at Francis as if challenging him. "Where are you going?"

"I thought I might go to Rome," Francis said apologetically, as if he hadn't quite decided yet. He thought about everyone he knew, which of them could look after Samson for a week. It wouldn't be much of a burden; he didn't do anything much for Samson himself, beyond feeding him and emptying his litter tray, and Samson never went outside. All the same, it seemed a lot to ask people. In the end, before he found himself tracking down Stephanie in the Department of Health, he phoned his mother.

"Yes, of course," his mother said. "I don't mind. It won't be any trouble for a week."

She sounded tired, accepting.

"What shall I do?" Francis said. "Shall I bring him up on—what—the Friday?"

"Why don't I come down for a change?" his mother said. "I could make a trip of it—come to London, stay overnight with you, take the cat back the next day."

"There's not really the set-up here," Francis said. "I don't see why you should be put out. I'll come up."

"It wouldn't put me out," his mother said. "It's not like you, popping off to Rome. What's got into you?"

"I don't know," Francis said. "I suddenly thought I wanted to go somewhere for a change."

"Say hello to the Pope for me," she said.

After Bernie had retired, the days seemed to lengthen for Alice. The question of his retirement had come up earlier than she had expected, when he was still in his early fifties, and she'd known what it meant: it meant being held accountable, in the friendliest way possible, for how she spent her days. There wasn't much to it. The house didn't take much keeping, now the children were gone. She liked to have ten minutes on the exercise bike in the mornings—she'd always kept herself trim. There were a few small hobbies she'd taken up, too; not elaborate pastimes like Malcolm Glover devoted himself to, but taking a particular care and interest in stuff that most people did carelessly and inattentively. She'd always been a reliable cook, and even the plain stuff she'd cooked night after night for the children had been interesting to her; now she became an inquisitive one. Although she took care not to become overelaborate or showy, and, anyway, as everyone said, you shouldn't eat food that was too rich any more, she discovered and mastered new dishes, repeating and refining them over a few months until they were really delicious, then moving on to something else.

The little brick-bordered patch outside the back door she cleared of the few dismal perennials, and turned into a little herb garden—lemon balm, mint, rosemary, thyme. She picked them over, trimming them neatly, weeding the bed, finding a use for each. After rain in summer, the waft of perfume was a delight to her. She experimented with remedies to exclude the neighbourhood cats from the garden, pouring five jars of chilli powder round the boundary in a cordon. It didn't work, and she moved on, with a sense of keeping herself busy, to the next idea. She made a hobby of her face, trying out moisturizers, toners, eyebrow-pluckers, cleansers, foundations, shifting the tones of her makeup in small ways that no one but she was ever likely to observe. Occasionally she even had a face-pack; she liked the fun of the peel-off ones. She read; not buying books particularly, but going weekly to the library. She'd always liked reading, but now her reading became serious: if she liked a novel by an author, she carried on reading all his novels and perhaps even his biography. She saw a notice in the library for a reading group, one afternoon a week, took the plunge and went along. She enjoyed that; she started drinking up something that had always horrified and frightened her, direct argument. She found out about things; there was so much to discover. They kept her going, all these small, ordinary hobbies.

When Bernie was still working, her unassuming activities could be compressed into ten or twenty seconds of explanation at the end of the day: "Oh, I read a book, I had coffee with Anthea Arbuthnot, I did a bit of weeding in the herb bed," and that seemed good enough. It would be different, however, when he was always there to observe her pottering. She loved him, and she would never conceal anything from him. But she couldn't help thinking it would be odd when he was there every day to watch her putting on a face-pack in the middle of the day, for no particular reason. She supposed she was asking herself, in reality, how it was that Bernie was going to fill his days.

Bernie decided that the sensible thing to do was to stay on until after privatization, then leave gracefully. It was a good idea, greeted with relief all round. Bernie had proved himself during the difficult stretch in the summer and autumn of 1984, when the electricity had kept running. Probably, Walter Marshall had said, in the handwritten letter he'd sent at the time—not just to Bernie, but he had sent one to Bernie—not one of the general public had noticed that the electricity in his house was still there, or had worried about its disruption for one moment, "and that, if I may say so, as the Prime Minister has said in person to me, can only be a tribute to . . ." Bernie would get one last promotion, it was agreed—a promotion in post, a kindness more for the sake of the pension than anything else—and walk his privatized successors through the process. The Electricity was going to come to an end, guided by Bernie, then he would hand over and go. He was splitting in two, it seemed: there were going to be two generating companies where there had been one. Politicians' decisions. There was some talk, even, of asking Walter Marshall himself to Bernie's leaving party; he was, indeed, asked, and a charming letter of regret came back, that he was, unfortunately, long scheduled to be in America on that day. But he would have come.

The day approached, and a difficulty arose. The difficulty was over Bernie's retirement present. Davina, Bernie's secretary, was "o.i.c. Bernie's present," as she, incomprehensibly, described herself on the telephone; she was a foghorn of a woman, much imitated by Bernie and rather feared by Alice. She was Yorkshire gentry, five-ten and Harrogate, well-shod and well-brought-up, as she was the first to tell you, the twice-married daughter of a Harrogate solicitor called (of course) David, married the second time to a second cousin of her own called (of course) David. For fifteen years, Alice had never telephoned Bernie at his office if it could be helped. To do so always involved talking to Davina first. "We're racking our brains down here," Davina said, over the telephone, "and we would really like to mark Bernie's departure with something special, something he'd use, or something he'd very much enjoy in his retirement. You know how fond we are of Bernie." It was astonishing how, even before his departure, everyone had become "fond" of Bernie. It made him sound like a dribbling nonagenarian in his wing-chair already.

His family had been interested in all sorts of things. Alice had never quite got over the conviction that his mother, with her perm the colour of pewter and the up-and-down assessing gaze, had been the black-market queen of St. Helier during the war, keeping the grassed-over

Anderson shelter at the bottom of their garden stuffed with nylons. In the years before she died, in the late seventies, she'd taken to continental tours in what she went on calling charabancs, to the Italian lakes, to the châteaux of the Loire, to the Austrian Alps, to Switzerland in summer. She'd return with sixty slides, a china figurine labelled Innsbruck or a hand-turned wooden spoon at the top of her luggage and, concealed elsewhere, something to get past Customs. She couldn't read about an allowance without flouting it, setting off with a hundred pounds in cash over the legal limit stuffed in her knickers, returning with four hundred cigarettes more than you were allowed. Lily, no doubt about it, was interested in all sorts of things. And there were those uncles and cousins; some a bit shady, like Lily, or Bernie's brother Tony, who had been lucky to escape prison that once. Even Bernie's shy uncle Henry, who seemed much more out of place in that family than Bernie did, he'd got his interests: until he was fifty, he'd gone cycling somewhere in England with the same man, every year for twenty-five years, a man who, like Uncle Henry, had never married and who Uncle Henry every now and again talked about setting up a house with to save money. Bernie had been incredulous, then hilarious when Alice had pointed out what to her was perfectly obvious, that Henry's friend Eric was his boyfriend. "But they only spend the two weeks together in the summer," he'd said. "It'd kill Mum if she ever thought—" Even Uncle Henry had fiddled with bits of radio in the garden shed, and he took endless photographs of Eric in front of anonymous backdrops. "Here's Eric again," he'd mutter, handing another one over, "in front of Boots in Hereford. We cycled forty miles that day."

But it was hard to think of Bernie's interests in the usual sense, and impossible to think how they might be boiled down into a present that Bernie would find either beautiful or useful. It was difficult enough at Christmas and birthdays, but various conventions had evolved there, and Bernie accepted his tie, this year's book, his whatever-it-was-the-house-needed with good grace. A retirement present was more difficult. Alice herself suggested a clock, a canteen of cutlery, garden furniture. In the end, Davina thought up something really quite original, a gold-plated vent, or valve, or tap, or something—something industrial and very ordinary, something Bernie would have seen every day of his working life, turned into a useless gewgaw and put in a glass case. "He'll love it," she announced briskly. "Some people suggested a scale model of a generating plant, but I put the kibosh on that. I couldn't imagine anything more hideous, plonked in the middle of your sitting room or, if you've got any sense, straight into the attic. But this is rather unusual, a conversation piece—" she finished off, barking with mirth "—as one used to say." It made Alice wonder how Bernie, so hard to buy a gift for, was going to fill his days.

The day came. Bernie retired on his fifty-sixth birthday, and there was a big party. She'd been to parties like this before at the Electric, and they'd often been dismal affairs; sometimes there'd been only one or two other wives attending apart from her, almost everyone else coming out of duty. But Bernie was popular, he'd always been popular, as well as being quite a high-up; they hired a venue and paid for everything. Everyone's wives came, and they asked a few of their own friends too. The Glovers came, and Daniel and his girlfriend, Helen, and Helen's parents, too, Philip and Shirley; and people from the reading group, even, with their husbands, and other friends; people they'd met because they'd had children at school together, Jillian Kirkpatrick, who had tried to teach Francis the piano, and people they'd only met at parties, friends of friends who had become proper firm friends themselves. It was astonishing how embedded they were in this place.

"You know Walter Marshall was supposed to come," Davina said, plonking herself down with worrying heaviness on one of the hotel's thin-legged gilded chairs. "No, honestly, David, go away, we've got girl things to talk about. Go and pick up a bird or something."

"Lord Marshall," Alice said—she wondered how the topic of Lord Marshall qualified as a "girl thing." She watched poor old David, a bear-like figure, plod off with a glass of wine in each hand. Big bones ran in their family, evidently.

"Oh, we all call him Walter," Davina said. "He's awfully nice."

"I know, I've met him," Alice said. "I don't suppose he would really have come."

"Don't you believe it," Davina said, finishing off the wine in her lipstick-rimmed glass. "He's got the highest regard for Bernie. Terribly fond."

"I'll be glad to have him on my own for a while," Alice said. "Bernie, not Lord Marshall, I mean." She looked sideways at Davina: a big woman in a little black dress, she had held her knees together but, as if that was effort enough, her legs sprawled off in quite different directions and her elbows kept wandering away in search of something to rest on. The dado rail, as her right elbow kept discovering with a jerk and a slip, wouldn't do.

A waiter approached the two of them with a salver of food.

"I love these little things," Davina said, taking a sushi roll, then a second and, with the waiter's smiling forbearance, a third. "It was a brilliant suggestion of yours. It's perfect for a party."

"I thought it would be a little bit unusual," Alice said. "When I saw the Hallam Towers had started doing Japanese food, I thought it would make a bit of a change."

"Brilliant stuff," Davina said. "Hasn't he got good-looking, your son?"

It was kind of Davina, but Alice looked with surprise. "Oh, no," she said. "That's Daniel, he's our neighbour's son." She raised her glass to Daniel. "Excuse me," Alice said, getting up.

"I've come to save you," Daniel said, smiling. "Is she drunk?"

"What have you done with Helen?" Alice said. She felt terribly tired; it was a mistake to wear new shoes to a party, a mistake she'd known she was making even when she was buying them.

"She's off somewhere lecturing some bigwig about privatization," Daniel said. "I left her to it. They didn't seem to be minding too much."

"She's a nice girl," Alice said.

"Sandra couldn't make it, then," Daniel said.

"We never expected her to," Alice said. "It's a long way to come just for a party. She said she's hoping to come over some time next year, but she's very settled now. Do you ever hear from her?"

"I had a Christmas card from someone calling herself Alex the year before last," Daniel said. "I couldn't think who it was."

"Oh, yes, she's changed again," Alice said. "I never got used to Alexandra, either. It never occurred to me that Sandra was short for Alexandra—anyway, she's Sandra on her birth certificate."

"You ought to go out there, now that Bernie's retired," Daniel said. "She's not married, is she?"

"No, nothing like that," Alice said. Then she saw she hadn't answered the question. "It'd be nice to go out there. It's just such a long flight, and Bernie—"

She left that where it stood.

"He's like me," Daniel said kindly. "He likes his home comforts."

"I hear the dance school's going well," Alice said. "Helen's dad was telling me he's never enjoyed himself so much in his life. And the restaurant, too—Anthea was saying—"

"What was I saying?" Anthea said, turning as she heard her name.

Alice hadn't seen her there, talking to Bernie's brother Tony and his new wife, though she was conspicuous enough in her black-and-white vertically striped dress, for the slimming effect. Tony and his new wife saw their chance and slipped off. "I heard you, just now, saying, 'Anthea was saying.' I'm sure it was something very reprehensible."

"I was telling Daniel what a nice time you had at his new restaurant, down in the Rivelin valley."

Anthea Arbuthnot looked Daniel up and down, never having quite lost her ambition to play a round of strip poker with him. He looked her up and down in return, observing with fascination that on the huge bosom of her horrible dress she was wearing a brooch that, amazingly, contained a kind of pastel portrait of the Queen's profile. It looked as though a second-class stamp had fallen there, and stuck.

"We had a lovely time," she said. "It's the most gorgeous setting and, though it's a converted factory, if you think of it that way, they've converted it very nicely, I must say. We had a girls' night out. I went with Caroline and my cousin Ruth, who normally lives in Wales, she retired with her husband to Tenby, and Katherine too, and we had a high old time. It was Katherine's suggestion—she wanted to support Daniel's restaurant, but we needn't have bothered, it was nearly full. I had the fish pie, and Ruth and Caroline splashed out and had a steak, both of them, and Katherine—what did your mother have, can you remember, Daniel?"

Daniel burst out laughing. "You know, Anthea," he said, obviously having decided that he was now old enough not to have to call her "Mrs. Arbuthnot" any more, "it's a strange thing, but I find it quite difficult to remember what every one of my customers ordered from weeks and weeks ago. Even if they are my mother."

"That's no way to talk to valued customers," Anthea said, laughing herself. "But in any case, I remember now, she had the fish and chips. Some people might think it was a little bit odd, having fish and chips on the menu, but everyone likes it, and it was lovely and fresh, I must say. It was a Thursday we went, or I'd never have advised the fish— never, ever eat fish in a restaurant on a Monday, that's my advice, even Daniel's restaurant. He's got a hard head, this one—there was no discount for the owner's mother, even. And we had two bottles of wine and it came to forty pounds with a starter each but no pudding, which I call good value, these days. You ought to go, Alice. We're going to go back and we're going to be taking dancing lessons too. You had a lovely write-up in the *Morning Telegraph*, Daniel, did you see?"

"We've got it framed," Daniel said. "I think they're going to make a speech, Alice."

She excused herself and went over to stand by Bernie. He'd always liked parties—as she came up, he was surrounded by a circle of people, all laughing at something he'd just said—and he took her hand with a quick smile and a raise of the eyebrows, to make sure she, too, was having a good time. In fact, she was looking at Francis. It wasn't hard to spot him, though he was in the middle of the crowd. His head was six inches at least above anyone else's, and she couldn't see how Davina had mistaken anyone else for him. Had he been talking to anyone? She couldn't see. Whenever she'd spotted him, he had been wearing the same slightly baffled expression, moving through the room as if looking for someone in particular. He always looked like that. It was nice of him to come up for his father's party, even on his own, not having anyone else for them to invite. Alice turned back to Bernie. "Do you know what it is they're giving you?" she whispered.

"I'm not supposed to," he said, "but I've got a good idea."

Franks was on the stage now, bringing his wrists together in the action of an orchestral conductor, and by stages the noise in the room subsided. He began to speak; Alice was pleased to see that, though he'd obviously thought what to say, he'd not found it necessary to bring notes to refer to. There were some office jokes about Bernie's manners. "We may feel sorry about Bernie leaving us," he said, "but Davina's swear box, which Bernie's sole efforts have kept so full over the years, is completely bereft. No one else could possibly have kept it so busy." There was a ripple of laughter, even from the people who didn't know what Bernie was like at work; and "busy" didn't seem the right word, anyway. He was a good speaker, though; if all the stories he told about Bernie were familiar to Alice, and to most people there, he told them as well as Bernie did. And Bernie, on this telling, sounded like the man who had kept the whole thing on the road. That couldn't be true, and Franks's speech was just threatening to get too serious, too heartfelt, too much a history of the electricity industry and its tribulations over the last thirty years when he cut short the beginnings of his audience's murmurings and went into the last straight. She was proud of him; there was no reason not to be; and she was almost surprised when suddenly her own name came up. What had she done? She'd supported him—"And we who only worked with him can guess at the patience that must have taken over the years." That was what was to be said about her life; and Franks, in a last gracious sentence or two, handed the gilded valve to Bernie and, with a pat on the back that only looked slightly like a push, handed Bernie over to Alice for good.

It was a successful party; everyone admired and commented on the Japanese food, and she said hello to more people in one evening, probably, than she had ever done in her life. She kept glimpsing the most unlikely people in conversation with each other, and seeming to get on. Only once was there any kind of awkwardness: passing one group, towards the end, she heard a woman's voice saying, "Not that you give a toss."

She looked: it was Daniel Glover's girlfriend, Helen. She was talking to Mr. Franks and his wife.

"That's a bit harsh," Simon Franks was saying.

"All I know is, my dad and everyone he worked with, they crippled themselves, out on strike for a year, and if anyone, anyone at all, had come out in support of the miners—"

"It was our job, young lady," Simon said, in his most insufferable way, "to keep the lights on in this country. I'm happy to say that our workers understood that, from beginning to end of the crisis."

"All I'm saying is—" Helen said, but Alice slipped away. It was horrible, the sight of anyone making a spectacle of themselves.

The gilded valve, without either of them discussing it, went on the wall in the spare bedroom where nobody went, and for the first couple of weeks Bernie kept himself busy. A surprising number of people wrote to say how much they'd enjoyed the party and, once he'd worked out how to use his new computer—that took a few days, it having been Davina's responsibility at the Electric—Bernie enjoyed writing back to them. Even with his near-total incapacity to type, though, that task was eventually done. And then what?

"Where are you off to?" Bernie said, coming out of the sitting room, the newspaper hanging from his hand. He had heard her opening the cloakroom door and, twisting round in his armchair, had seen her putting on her coat. It was six weeks or so after he had retired.

"Oh, just out," Alice said. She waited where she was. She rather wanted to make Bernie go through everything, just once, so that she could tell him to stop it.

Bernie ruminated. It was perfectly clear to Alice what was going through his mind; he was telling himself not to ask if he could come too, like a small boy. Bernie could understand that much.

"If you're going to town—" he said eventually.

"No, Bernie, I'm not going to town," Alice said. She wasn't going anywhere so very special or secret; she wasn't going to carry on accounting for every one of her movements, and she waited again.

"OK," Bernie said. He still wanted to come, with his newspaper dangling pathetically from his hand. "When will you be back?"

"Bernie, love," Alice said, and she took the opportunity. Leading him back into the sitting room, placing him back in his chair and sitting herself down, still in her coat, she explained perfectly kindly that, all in all, the only way you could possibly live from this point onwards was with some degree of independence. "I won't ask you where you're going all the time, and you shouldn't ask me where I'm going," she said.

"It's not much to ask," Bernie said.

"No, it's not," Alice said, "but if nothing else, it's nice to have something to tell each other in the evenings, and if we go everywhere together, do everything together, explain everything in advance, we won't have that. All right?"

Bernie didn't see, not really, but she left him there. It seemed harsh, even cruel, but Alice could see that if she didn't do exactly this, she would very soon find herself responsible for finding things to fill Bernie's life, as well as her own. She saw herself bringing him jigsaw puzzles to do, like an invalid. Not for the first time, Alice reflected that the conditions women existed under were apt to strike men like the cruel imposition of suffering, and she remembered how very bad Bernie had always been at coping with any kind of illness.

Bernie made an effort, and improved a little. He remembered not to ask her where she was going all the time, and contrived a few activities of his own. He started talking about things he might conceivably do in the future, as if reminding himself that, after all, he did have a future. "One of these days," he'd begin, and though they were mostly unimaginable—Bernie writing a book, or doing a degree at the Open University—Alice thought that showed willingness. Some of the real activities they did together were his idea: they had a regular afternoon at the cinema, and often drove out to see some historic sight, some country house. Alice quite enjoyed the films, and even the country outings. She let him in, too, on a couple of her own activities, and together they experimented with steadily more stringent ways to keep the neighbourhood cats off their lawn. He cancelled the delivery of the paper, and instead made a point of walking to the newsagent's every day. At first, he was gone only thirty or forty minutes or so; and then, to Alice's curiosity, he started being gone two hours, even until lunchtime. He would come back with a cryptic smile and, they'd made an agreement, she wouldn't enquire. In time, she discovered, not from Bernie, that he'd taken to dropping in on one of four or five acquaintances, housewives living on the way to the shops, and nattering over a cup of coffee. It took a weight off Alice's mind.

"Nothing much," she heard Bernie saying once, on the telephone to Francis. They spoke every week, and it broke her heart to hear Bernie say, with every attempt at cheerfulness, that they'd done nothing much in the last seven days. Bernie was filling his time as best he could, being cheerful about it, and it seemed to be her who was forced by his retirement to wonder what, if anything, her life had ever consisted of. Nothing much. Bernie went uncomplainingly through the motions of what, after all, had been her daily existence, and for him, painfully obviously, the emptiness of it was nearly unendurable. Perhaps it ought to have been so for her. What he took pleasure in—she had never seen this so clearly, and at first she could hardly credit it—was her own constant company, and he hurried to share small things with her, saved stories and cartoons from the newspaper to show her. If he was developing an Arbuthnot-like avidness about the most local and minute events, it was only for her sake. It was exhausting to see how much he lit up when she came through the front door.

For Alice, her worry about Bernie—and she had never worried about Bernie—added itself to her long-standing worry about poor Francis, and even to her worry about whatever might be happening to Sandra, Alexandra, Alex in Australia. Francis, who had seemed such a clever child, had a life that no one could have wanted, and there was something about it she could not understand: he had never had a girl-friend, and though she had tried to train herself into thinking he must be gay, that seemed false too. There simply seemed some kind of blankness there, some kind of puzzled lack where everyone else had, surely, something. She worried steadily about them all, individually, and in time the individual worries coalesced, united, turned on her and made her ask what, in fact, she had done to the three of them. She felt herself growing old, exhausted, and she could not help what occupied her mind.

It was something, at least, when Francis told her he'd got himself a cat, and when, a few months later, he announced he was going on holiday to Rome, it was an encouragement to her. She remembered, long ago, when the two of them were children, when they'd first moved up from London, how much she had worried about whether either of them would settle in, make friends, and how much comfort she had drawn from even very small signs, even the mention of a name by one of them. Of course, she had been worrying then about nothing. Children settled in and made friends easily enough. On the other hand, in feeling relieved over Francis at thirty getting himself a cat, or taking a holiday, she was admitting there was something to worry about. She wished she knew what it was.

It was, however, mostly selfishness that made her offer to come down to pick up the cat. Alice hadn't been to London in years. She hadn't any way of making the offer, however, other than in terms of being helpful, and Francis refused it as soon as she came out with it. It might have been nice. If only Francis had said he'd think about it for a day before deciding that he'd come up, she'd have had a day of thinking where she might go, what she might do; as it was, not only the trip but the smaller pleasure of anticipation was taken away from her. He certainly meant well, though.

In the same spirit of sparing them any trouble, he turned up on a Friday morning without announcing himself, catching a taxi from the station. Alice had heard the guttural metallic rattle of a taxi in the road, and gone to the kitchen window to see. "Francis is here," she called. She watched him untangle himself from the back seat, setting down an overnight bag, a plastic bag from a supermarket and a black cat-box on the pavement, patting his pockets and finally paying the driver. He'd always had difficulty finding clothes his size, and he was wearing all grey and beige. If his habit of carrying his stuff round in old plastic bags was the habit of a schoolboy, his clothes were the clothes of someone thirty years older. His padded beige anorak on its own could make you weep. She went to let him in.

"You could have phoned," she said, as he bent down to kiss her.

"There was no need," he said. "I can perfectly well get a taxi. You all right, Dad?"

He shook Bernie's hand; there was some kind of agreement between them that they wouldn't kiss, and they had settled on this when they met and when they said goodbye.

"I don't know when you're going to learn to drive," Bernie said.

"There's not a lot of point keeping a car in London," Francis said. "And it's no trouble, getting a train up here. It must be a lot faster than driving, and you can read on the way, too."

"There's something in that," Bernie said. "Well, come in. Is this him, then?"

They shut the door, and Francis bent down to open the cage. There was a glint inside as the cat looked at them, withdrawn into the far corner of the box.

"He'll come out in his own time," Francis said. "Here's his litter tray and some fresh litter for it." He handed over the plastic bag. "There's some food there as well. You can put it in the kitchen, he's quite clean. Have you got any butter?"

"Any butter? What for?"

"It's an old trick," Francis said. "To make him feel at home. A friend of mine, she knows all about cats, she said you've got to do this straight away. You smear some butter on their front paws as soon as they get to a new place, a place they'll be staying, and once they've licked the butter off, they feel much more at home."

"Do we want him to feel at home?" Alice said. "I've never had a cat to look after before."

"They've got to feel at home, apparently," Francis said. "If they don't, they get confused, they start wandering off, trying to find somewhere they know and then they never come back."

"I don't think he's in the mood to wander anywhere," Bernie said, peering in. "I don't think he has any intention of coming out."

"It's got to be butter, has it?" Alice said, going into the kitchen. "We mostly eat spread nowadays."

"I don't think it makes any difference," Francis said. "How can you eat that stuff?"

"You get used to it," Bernie said. "I didn't much like it at first. The doctor told your mother to get her blood pressure down, so we've switched to all sorts of things. Oily fish, twice a week."

"Nothing serious?" Francis said.

"Oh, no," Alice said. "It just comes with old age. Everyone we know's had to give up butter and cream, they talk about nothing else."

"You're not old," Francis said, taking the box of yellow spread and the teaspoon from his mother. Perhaps he meant to banter, but in that case it came out wrong; he looked and sounded quite anxiously concerned. He had always been the sort of small boy you couldn't tease or banter with; he'd always taken everything with a fearful literalness. And Alice remembered that when you knew and lived with someone for years, they went on looking exactly the same to you, never seeming to change. Bernie was just as he had ever been; and she probably seemed just the same to him and to Francis. "I hope this works."

Choosing his own moment, the cat came to the brink of the cage, its nose and whiskers venturing outside. It took one step, another, not appearing to look about it or register Francis's presumably familiar presence. "What a pretty boy," Alice said encouragingly, but in fact there was something slightly skewed about the animal's handsomeness, its face coming to a point and not quite symmetrical, one eye a little higher than the other. Its ears, too, pricked up and rotating now like radar receivers, were absurdly large for its angular little head, as if, like an adolescent boy, some spurt of growth had inflated only one of its features, and was waiting for the rest to catch up. "What a lovely glossy coat he's got," she said, more honestly.

"Let's give it a go," Francis said, kneeling with the tub, and taking a teaspoonful of spread. He took the cat's front right paw, and, with a finger, smeared it over the pink pads. The cat pulled the paw back, and tried to lick it; but Francis took the other, and, after a short tussle in which both of them were trying to do quite incompatible things, Samson gave up and let the same thing happen to his left front paw.

"He's not going to walk butter into the carpets, is he?" Bernie said. "Hell of a mess to get out."

"No, look, he's licking himself clean," Francis said. "And after that, he's supposed to settle down."

It appeared to be working. Samson finished with his paws, and then gave himself a thorough wash from top to bottom. The three watched; Samson ignored them.

"We ought to leave him in peace," Alice said. "It doesn't seem very polite to watch."

"He's all right," Francis said. "He doesn't care. Look, he can reach everything with his tongue apart from bits of his face."

"That's a useful talent," Bernie said.

"I suppose so," Francis said, and there was that lack again; it was a little like talking to someone who couldn't understand jokes. The three of them seemed mesmerized by the cat, and when he'd finished his bath, and set off to find out about the house, they followed him into first the kitchen, then the sitting room, watching him prowl the margins. They only let him go off on his own when he went out again to map the rest of the house.

"He can't get out, can he?" Francis said.

"I don't think so," Alice said. "I don't want to be rude, love, but how long are you here for? I'm only thinking about meals."

"I've got to go back this afternoon," Francis said. "I'm sorry."

"Oh," Alice said; she'd got a leg of lamb in for the evening meal. She couldn't understand the overnight bag.

"I got a really cheap flight to Rome," Francis said, "but it leaves at four thirty in the morning, tonight. It would have been twice the price otherwise. I've got to get back and get packed."

"That's a shame," Bernie said heartily. "We haven't seen you since Christmas."

"Can you stay a bit longer when you get back?" Alice said. "I mean, when you come to pick up Samson?"

"That'd be nice," Francis said. "I don't see why not."

"Never mind the cat," Bernie said. "I reckon it's you we want to put butter—we want to put butter on your paws, make you feel at home again. It's always your home."

But his voice dropped as if he had been trapped into saying something serious. Disconcertingly, Francis put out his long pink tongue and pretended to start licking the palm of his hand. "I know," he said sadly, and Alice couldn't help looking about her at the house: the new Turkish rug, the old wood and glass coffee-table, the glass-domed preserved flowers on the shelf and the other knick-knacks, the new pair of sofas, which had replaced the three-piece suite, and Bernie's ancient comfortable high chair he swore he couldn't do without, and the ten-year-old television that couldn't help being at the focal point of the room, the Liberty brown-and-purple curtains that had been there ever since they'd moved in. Like Francis, she knew; it seemed to be her home, too.

He stayed, at least, for lunch—she wished she'd known, it was a bit of a scant affair of shop-bought stuffed pasta and shop-bought sauce with a salad thrown together on the side. She'd got used, too, to cooking for herself and Bernie, and had somehow forgotten that Francis was six foot eight, and ate about twice as much as anyone else you could think of. Bernie insisted on driving Francis to the station, and she'd only just started doing the washing-up when he returned.

"That cat's watching you," Bernie said, coming through the front door.

"I haven't seen it since it arrived," Alice said. "Where is it?"

"Here on the stairs," Bernie said. "He's watching you do the washing-up."

It was true: it was watching her from a distance and through the kitchen door, but very intently. It was on a step, too, which was not much below her own eye level.

"Daft thing," Bernie said. "Do you know something? Francis didn't say goodbye to the cat."

"There's not a lot of point in saying goodbye to a cat," Alice said.

"You'd have thought, though," Bernie said. "I'm going to let it out into the garden. It seems settled enough."

He went through the dining room, making little kissing noises as he went, and into the utility room. Alice stopped her washing-up, and turned to see what the cat was doing. As soon as she looked directly at it, it looked away, as if embarrassed, and started washing itself energetically. From the utility room, Bernie's encouraging smacking and bussing could be heard and, after a cursory wash, for display purposes, the cat lowered itself with unnecessary care from one step to another, slinking into the dining room. Alice followed at a few feet; it walked into the utility room, dropping itself after a short hesitation off the single deep step, and inspected Bernie, standing by the open door to the back garden. The cat looked Bernie up and down, and thoughtfully sauntered to the door. It paused; something seemed to stiffen in its frame; it gave a tiny sneeze and, quickly, another, then turned and ran back into the house.

"Ah," Bernie said. "I forgot. The garden's about half an inch thick in chilli powder."

That hadn't occurred to Alice, either. "At least we've found—" she said. She was about to say that finally they'd discovered one cat the deterrent worked on, but it was as if something, at just that moment, had hit her from behind on the head. She staggered.

"What is it?" Bernie said.

"Ah—" Alice said. A brilliant horrible light was exploding in her eyes, and behind them, some shock of pain. "Bernie—"

He was turning to her, and, starting, almost to run—and Bernie never ran—and she was holding out her arms in order not to be anything but caught when she—

It was a long journey back. Francis hadn't thought to check the train times to London—he'd vaguely thought they ran every hour, and they did, apart from the occasional longer gap. As it happened, his dad dropped him off at the station—"Don't wait," he said. "I'll be fine, I'll see you in a week"—just after a train had gone, and another not due until a quarter to six. He filled the time as best he could with a copy of *Gramophone* magazine, which, he realized after a few dimly familiar pages, he'd read already, and a cup of coffee in the station café.

It was a busy train, and he had to share a table with three noisy women who were heading down to London to take in a show, whose festivities were beginning here; they had two bottles of wine with them, which they invited Francis to share, laughing at him quite unkindly when he refused, and when, after Leicester, that ran out, they raucously asked him to pop along to the buffet to get them some more. "Don't fret," one said, pretending to be outraged, "it's not like we won't give you the money." He was appalled at the thought that any-one around them might think he was with them, and appalled at their broad and wrong ideas of the pleasures of London. It was *Phantom* they were going to see; Francis had never seen a London musical in his life.

The tube train fell into that lull between the rush-hour and chucking-out time; most people who were going out would already have gone out, and it was quiet. Opposite were two Middle Eastern students, talking in their gurgling labial language, smelling of cloves in a way that made Francis feel slightly sick. He remembered he had no food in the house; he'd been using things up before his Rome trip, and had come to the end of everything a day early. He'd have to stop at the corner shop to buy something, or—that would be easier—pick up a chicken kebab from Mo's takeaway at the end of the road. The best the corner shop could do was ready-stuffed pasta, and he'd had that for lunch.

The house was dark—the housemates downstairs were always out on a Friday night. As Francis was fumbling with his keys, he could hear the phone ringing. He didn't bother hurrying, it would certainly be for one of the housemates, and as he let himself in, the greasy bundle warm in his hands, it stopped before he could turn the light on. He went upstairs, put the kebab on a plate, poured himself a glass of water, and put the little television in the corner on, quite indifferent to what-ever the programme or the channel was. He'd wait to pack his bags until after he'd finished eating—he couldn't really say "after dinner." It wouldn't take long. He could have read his guidebook about Rome, but he had a feeling that over the next week, he'd be filling in a few hours alone in his hotel room by reading it in detail, and there was no reason to start on that early. The phone started ringing again; Francis ignored it.

He finished his plate of food, and went to wash it and his hands. Then he started to pack. He suddenly thought that he didn't know what the weather was like in Rome at the moment. He had thrown out all the newspapers when he'd got home from work the day before—they carried information about the weather in foreign cities. In the end, he packed a series of short-sleeved shirts and lightweight trousers—all his trousers were grey or beige, and drip-dry, so they would do for relative heat. He put in a pair of thin sweaters—even if it was still warm over there, he'd heard it could be cold in the evening. Then, spending more time thinking about this than about any other, he went over to his bookshelves and pulled out one, then a second fat Russian novel. Most of the books on the shelves were old ones, favourites from his childhood, *Uncle* and *Professor Branestawm* and *Midnite*. But others were fat books he'd read, had always meant to read, had been saying to himself so long he had read them that he believed they had actually been read. He packed *The Idiot;* he packed *Dead Souls*. Finally, with a quick look round the room, he went to the bottom drawer of his desk, on top of which an Amstrad computer sat stolidly, its start-up disk hanging from the slot like a tongue. Francis took out the half-finished bulk of his own book, eight inches thick, an A4 notebook with black binding and three green Pentel pens. He'd always used those Pentel pens; he liked the flow of the ink-soaked ball under pressure.

The book was the third novel Francis had written. He had sent the first out; he had sent the second out; he rather thought he would finish this one and put it back into his drawer.

The telephone started ringing again. Francis looked at his watch; it was past eleven o'clock. If he was going to get even two hours' sleep, he would have to go to bed soon. They'd been phoning every half an hour since he got in. It was completely unreasonable. They'd probably go on phoning and preventing him sleeping, too; or, if they stopped phoning, he would probably be lying awake wondering whether it had been someone phoning for him with an important message. By the time he had thought half of this, he was down the stairs, sure he was going to reach it just as they rang off.

"Hello?" Francis said. There was some ambient noise at the other end of the phone, and the clunk of a payphone. "Hello?"

"Francis," the voice said. "Thank God."

It sounded quite unlike his father—a broken and absent voice—and in a second it went on. Francis could not understand what it was saying. He had been so clear in his mind that it would be one of the lodgers' idiot friends, calling repeatedly from some pub on Balham High Street that he couldn't for half a minute quite understand what it was that his father was saying, or understand that it was his father talking.

Still, he must have understood something, since he found that he had, after all, said, "I'll come up as soon as I can." It was his own voice, sounding still in the quiet and dim-lit hallway of the house that seemed to break the spell, and, as if in reverse, he heard what his father had been saying.

"Your mother's had a brain haemorrhage—she's in a coma—she's in the hospital, in the Northern General. The doctors say it's too early to—"

And some terrible gulping breaths. He had been phoning all evening—with a sort of grisly relic of paternal concern Bernie had started asking whether Francis had had a reasonable trip back, thinking perhaps it had taken him until now to get home, and worrying about the state of public transport in London rather than his more immediate concerns. Perhaps he had gone on ringing without any expectation that the telephone would be answered, and had not been prepared to have to tell anyone yet what he would soon have to tell to so many people—Francis thought of the masses of people at his retirement party, six months before. In any case, he had started, and in a few moments had found himself gulping.

"I've looked at the trains," he said, pulling himself together. You could hear the noise in the background, some sort of lazy yowling call between nurses ending their shifts. "The last train to Sheffield tonight's gone, the first one in the morning's at quarter to six. You don't need to get that, you can come later in the morning. You will come?" he added in a rush, remembering perhaps that Francis had been going to Rome, remembering perhaps what Francis, with a shudder, thought, that he'd not left the address or phone number of his hotel there with them, that he might not have known any of this for a week, and what might happen in a week.

"Yes," Francis said. "I'll come."

He went upstairs and sat in his room. A stretch of time elapsed; Francis found that he could not sit, but kept having to rise and walk from one room to another, pacing. Outside, in the street, it grew quiet. Francis picked up a book, set it down. All at once he thought of Sandra; he worked out the time difference, and saw that it was lunchtime there—whether Friday lunchtime or Saturday lunchtime, he couldn't work out. His brain would just not go in that particular direction. He switched on his Amstrad computer; it hummed, and in a moment he pushed the programming disk in. At this point, he usually went to make a cup of coffee, coming back to find the computer ready to go, but now he just sat there and listened to it run through its cacophonic recitation. He could almost sing along with it. The list of options came up, sour green on black—if you worked too long on the computer, you could look away and see your work printed, purple against a white wall. He replaced the disk with another, and opened up the file with all his addresses on it. He printed out the document, noisily—he had never quite worked out how to print anything but a whole document—took the sheet with Sandra's address and telephone number on it, and went downstairs. He couldn't remember ever having phoned her in Australia of his own accord.

The quality of the air down the line changed noticeably when he was finished dialling, and then an unfamiliar ringing tone. It rang six times, and then there was Sandra's voice. It was unmistakably hers, but with a distinct Australian swing to it. He started to say, "Hello? Hello, Sandra?" but it was only a machine.

"Alex," it began. He started to put the phone down, but stopped; he left a short message, saying what had happened, and that he was going up to Sheffield. He put the phone down, a cream plastic comma, slotting neatly into its place, and went upstairs again.

At two the housemates came in, shushing but thumping about noisily.

At three, they came out of the kitchen and went to bed, murmuring their goodnights to each other.

At half past three, Francis realized that anything would be better than walking up and down in this confined space. He wrote a short but clear note to his housemates, explaining what had happened, and taped it to his door. He thought again, and wrote exactly the same note, and left it on the telephone table as he left the house with his already packed bag. He imagined them waking for a moment, puzzled, wondering why the bloke upstairs was going out at such a strange time, and then turning over and going back to sleep; he imagined them waking late the next morning, saying, "What a night," and then seeing the note on the table. He imagined them regretting their sarcasm towards him, their lack of sympathy. As he hailed a rare and lucky taxi, it struck him that for the first time he could remember, he was in the middle of a serious drama. He wanted it to be taken away from him.

It was always incredible to Francis that the whole of his journey afterwards disappeared, as if that itself was the trauma, from his mind. He knew that he must somehow have spent at least an hour and a half at an empty and shuttered King's Cross station waiting for the trains to begin again; he must have travelled in a slow train to Doncaster, and changed there for Sheffield; he knew that from Sheffield station he must have taken a taxi to the Northern General hospital, travelling up quite unfamiliar hills to a campus of sickness, at some remote and unknown quarter of the city. All that specifically remained in his memory of that horrible journey, going through the end of a dark night into a grey and wet dawn, was the general sense of not knowing what was at the end of it; and, from time to time, turning his face to the rain-washed windows because, he found, he was crying as if in anticipation, as if in practice. There was nothing else afterwards, except the memory of coming into the hall of the Northern General, the sense of nurses falling away to right and left, and finally coming into a room with his mother and, bending over her, his father. There looked to be nothing much worse with his mother than, perhaps, a touch of flu; she was flushed around the eyes and mouth, and her hair was damp; nothing, that is, other than what was suggested by the array of tubes and the battery of bleeping machinery. Thank God bleeping. It was his father in whom something seemed to have broken; it was something that had been keeping him upright for years.

"The doctor thinks she's stable," his father said. "The doctors are going to come round in a while." There seemed nothing more for him to say, and, on either side of the white hospital bed, in a room on their own, they pulled up a chair each, and took, each of them, one of Alice's hands.

When it became apparent that Tim was going to get one of the refurbished offices on the fourth floor, Hester Carver obviously made a decision that she might as well dress it up as her personal favour. Anyone could see that, in fact, there was nothing she could have done about it, even though she was the faculty secretary and, for all purposes, the person with the power around here. Her personal campaign against Tim, based on nothing more than personal antipathy and carried on without a break for the three years since he'd finished his PhD and been taken on as a junior lecturer, had taken quite a few forms. He'd been refused almost every item of furniture he could think of to request. The office computer he'd been assigned had been an old one, overladen with five years of files that his predecessor had built up before taking a fatal overdose and leaving a vacancy. Everyone, it seemed, had been given an updated model before him, and then the budget had run out. There was talk of the faculty going on to the Internet, but not in Tim's direction. He lived in a windowless breeze-block hell-hole in the basement with his name handwritten on a slip on the door.

The basement, however, was being handed over to Film Studies, which seemed quite happy to be subterranean. It was probably something to do with them all having had a misspent youth watching old movies with the curtains drawn in the afternoons, and Hollywood blockbusters made intellectually respectable by being viewed at suburban Gaumont matinées rather than in the evening, with popcorn. In whatever other ways Hester wanted to neglect Tim, she was in the end defeated in this. He was to be moved, he was informed, to one of the refurbished offices on the fourth floor, with quite a decent view of the station and Hyde Park Flats behind. She chose to take advantage of this by putting it to Tim not as a defeat but as the result of a certain amount of strings-pulling for which he ought to be grateful.

"I wish I had an office as nice as that one," she said, in her own cosy space, accreted with a bonsai tree, photographs of the grandchildren, a lingam-sized vacuum flask with a tartan transfer and a rolling screen-saver of kittens in a bowl of pasta. One of her many cardigans, this one in apricot, was over the back of the chair. "I'm sorry you've had to wait for it, but I'm sure you'll appreciate it all the more now you're settled in it. There were quite a few people after that office, you know."

"I'm very grateful," Tim said, not believing her and giving her something not to believe in return.

"Have you been up to have a look at it?" she said. "It's not quite finished yet—the men'll be wanting to paint it next. You can choose your colour, you know. Any colour you like."

"Isn't it all going to be white?"

"Oh, no," Hester said. "In any case, if you mean like this, this is actually magnolia, not white. White with a hint of cream. Whatever colour you like." And she hoicked out a paint chart from her top drawer. Some of the samples were already annotated with what looked like room numbers.

"Can I have anything at all?"

"Anything you like," Hester said, turning back to her typing. It was a letter from the professor to a first-year student who'd missed four Cultural Criticism seminars in a row without explanation. Not that they'd fail the ignorant little sod, she allowed herself to think.

"I think I'd like this nice dark brown," Tim said.

Hester looked over the top of her glasses—a habit, she hadn't her bifocals on. "I don't know about that," she said. "They dry darker, you know, Tim. That'd be quite dark and depressing to work in."

"Are you sure?" Tim said. "I thought paint dried lighter."

"No," Hester said. "It dries darker."

There was an embarrassed pause between them, which Hester quite enjoyed.

"What about this one?"

"What's that? Prawn Sunrise, is it called?" Hester said.

"That can't be right," Tim said. "No, it's—well, you're right, it is called Prawn Sunrise."

"That'd give you a headache, that shade of yellow," Hester said. "It might be all right for a kitchen. You want something fairly neutral, really. No, I wouldn't have that green either. People are driven mad by green, you know."

"I thought it was restful," Tim said, looking as if he were starting to resent this utter waste of time. "Or meant to be, anyway. Backstage at theatres, the green rooms, where the actors rest, aren't they green? Well, they're not green, but they used to be. Aren't they green because it's supposed to be a restful colour?"

"That's quite a vivid green," Hester said, enjoying this thoroughly. Actually, if she'd predicted, she'd have thought a grumpy idiot like Dr. Tim Glover, presented with his run of a paint chart, would unerringly go for having his office painted black, like a seventeen-year-old boy who liked heavy-metal music. And in the end she got her own way, as she usually did. Tim's office was to be painted a very suitable pale brown, quite a lot like Demerara sugar or maybe wet sand, but called Peanut Butter. It was quite nice if you didn't think about the name they'd given it.

"You see," Trudy said, when he told her the whole saga, "everything's been bought up and sold off. Even colours." They found a lot to chew over in Hester's campaign against Tim and her whole Tory demeanour, unbelievable in someone who worked in what was supposed to be a radical department teaching the social sciences.

"How do you mean?"

"It's all part of the system," Trudy said. Her face under the energy-saving forty-watt bulb in the kitchen—you could only tell when onions were browning or just burning by the smell—was full of the shadowed troughs and valleys of a much older person. Her frizzed-out hair was full of grey already. She was only thirty-four. He was becoming embarrassed by these grand claims of hers, but he said nothing, knowing she enjoyed insisting on what embarrassed him. "Everything's owned, even colours. You can't just call a colour what it's called. The name of a colour's owned by some paint company. Brown, the colour brown or its name, it's probably owned by Dulux."

"That can't be right."

"So they've got to think up ludicrous names for colours. All the ordinary ones were sold off and bought up years ago. Things can't be just blue or green any more, because blue and green are owned by, whoever, Rupert Murdoch. They've got to be Italian Ladder or Blush or Clouded Rose or something stupid. The ordinary person, he has to ask permission from a company before he can call his own door blue. Mind you, it's all about the illusion of choice. The multiplication of options . . ."

It took Trudy a good fifteen minutes to explain why it was stupid to have your room painted a colour called Peanut Butter and why in any case you didn't have any real choice in the matter. It wasn't that Tim disagreed with her. But when he moved in, he found the room quite restful, even if it was the colour of a capitalist plot. Finally, he'd got something that looked like proper furniture, and not things that might have been rescued from the departmental rubbish heap. "I wish I had an office chair as nice as that one," Hester said, rotating in the comfy old swiveller she wouldn't give up if you paid her. The view was surprisingly pleasant—you could see that old flat of Trudy's from here. He'd never wanted to hang around the office in the basement, only arriving when absolutely necessary and leaving when his tasks were done. But this office started to seem—well, not nicer than home, it would be an insult or an admission of failure to say that, but definitely an alternative place to sit and think. For the first time, he organized his books in alphabetical order, rather than in random piles, acquired and started using a filing cabinet, started sticking up pictures of Bose on the walls, that poster of Thatcher and Reagan in a *Gone With the Wind* embrace. The new orderly airiness up here had an effect on his work. Where before his intellectual explorations had been limited to what was required, like his office hours, now he wondered about all sorts of things. It was as if he needed tasks to undertake to justify hanging about, often, until seven or seven thirty in the evening.

Some of these were ideas for articles, true—some spilling over with unrestrained vitality from the mainstream of Tim's work. He had gone to university in the first place two years late, and from the beginning had been more purposeful, better read and more focused than any other undergraduate. Cleverer, too; the choice to come here was only down to the fact that it was local, and he wanted, by then, to be near Trudy, who wasn't moving. He'd always been brighter than the mass of the intake, he had no illusions about that, and they'd been delighted to take him on as a PhD student and, when the time came, to appoint him to a job. It was proof of the excellence of the institution that it could appoint from its own ranks of postgraduate students; *le patron mange ici.* But he'd been dopily devoted to the narrow line of his own research, down there in the basement, like a duckling head-down pursuing a laid-out line of corn, a duckling narrowly denouncing far-off Erving Goffman and following wherever the despised master chose to go. Up here, with a view of Park Hill Flats and the railway station, he found his mind expanding, and in the first three months he wrote an article on something quite off his usual track. Gestures of refusal enacted between the public bourgeoisie and the vendors of radical media in an English urban setting. (He and Trudy, they still sold the *Spartacist* outside Sheffield public library on a Saturday, and in his fifteen-page analysis, tabulated according to gender and perceived social class, my God, he got his own back on the deradicalized lumpen bourgeoisie.) More than one of his colleagues, bombarded with offprints, called it "witty," and he started to think of more, fresher work to undertake.

Up there, too, he started to think of other things he'd like to write and, all at once, found himself writing cogent and furious letters to the *Guardian, The Times Higher Education Supplement, New Left Review* on all manner of subjects. Most of them were no more left than the *Daily Telegraph,* he had no illusion about that, but the letters page (he found himself explaining) was the point at which radical voices sometimes made themselves heard, almost despite the media's best intentions. "The voice of the people," Trudy said piously, and Tim agreed. It wasn't an expression he could have used himself in good conscience, these days, and doubted that Trudy, in the sixth year of her own PhD, was allowed to get away with it in an academic context any more. But he let it go for old times' sake. Some of his letters were published, though—of course—they were cut down and their point and cogency removed. Even so, colleagues noticed; he was developing a reputation for controversy.

There were other letters, too. On a rare visit to his parents, he saw, shamelessly pinned to the kitchen noticeboard, an invitation from a public utility. He looked, amazed, and saw his own name written in by hand, along with Daniel's, Jane's and his parents'. "What the hell's this?" he said to his mother.

"It's just an invitation," she said. "You can see for yourself. It's for Bernie's retirement. It's nice of them to think of you at all. I'm sure Trudy could come as well if she wanted to—I'm not sure that they've ever—"

"Trudy wouldn't want to go to something like that," Tim said. It was incredible to him how dense his mother could be. "Do you seriously think I could possibly want to go to a party hosted by a company like that? Don't you think Sellers is totally implicated by that job he's done?"

"Well, I hadn't honestly given that aspect of it a lot of thought," his mother said. "Whatever you're talking about. Why don't you tell your father all about it? I'm sure he'd like to hear."

"Hear about what?" his father said. "You're not leaving me alone with Tim's principles, again, are you, Katherine?"

His mother was laughing heartily as she left the kitchen—it was always like this since Tim had left home, an atmosphere of teasing that Tim couldn't remember ever having been there before.

"Well, I'm sure we'll all miss your merry banter and Trudy's sense of fun," his father said. That was supposed to be a joke. No wonder Trudy said it made her feel physically sick to visit his parents.

It was incredible to him that the Sellerses, Sandra's parents though they were, could possibly have so little sense of him that they could think he might come to their stupid party, and the very next opportunity, at the end of the working day, he sat down and wrote a finely argued letter over five pages of the departmental writing paper explaining why, whatever he thought personally of Bernie Sellers, he couldn't in all conscience go to such a party. A condensed but savage account of the CEGB's role during 1984 formed the main bulk of the letter, with an astonished and wounded paragraph on the Tory programme of denationalization to wind up. It was seven thirty before he was done. It wasn't until two weeks after the party that he had any kind of reply, and then it was only three unoffended and inappropriately lighthearted lines, which he read once before throwing away and, unlike his original letter, didn't bother showing to Trudy.

It wasn't just him who felt more at home in the new office. Students, he noticed, were coming to see him of their own initiative. And an odd thing started to happen: they were mostly girls. Women, eighteen-year-old women. At first he could hardly credit it, and for several weeks pushed the suspicion to the back of his mind as an unregenerate thought from some reactionary and uncorrected fragment of his personality. But it seemed to him at last undeniable that, for the first time, the physical irresistibility of his brother Daniel, now lost as he had gained a couple of stones, had passed on to him, and the women, some ten years younger than him, had started to pay him visits. They came to talk, nominally, about their work, but their eyes widened, their mouths fell open like ruminating beasts of the field, they allowed their hands to brush lightly against his as he went over their poor essays, lying on the desk. There were half a dozen favourites; or, rather, he was the favourite of half a dozen. He was inoculated against their charms. He never considered whose the imaged face was that protected him.

He hardly knew how to talk about this with Trudy, and, as it was not her face he thought of, decided not to; it was too easy to imagine what she would say on the fantasies of men about strong and independent women under their supposed academic control, and then straight off into some page of Foucault or other. The oddest part of the phenomenon was its cyclical nature. It didn't happen steadily: it came and went. Even the most devoted of his followers, if accosted in a corridor at the wrong point of the cycle, would look at him with slight puzzlement from clear complexions, not quite understanding what it could be he wanted to talk to them about. (He had no doubt: the students here might not be the brightest.) But in a couple of weeks the same students were booking appointments with him, the next day if at all possible, and soon sitting there, in as few feet distance from him as could be decently contrived, a galaxy of acne crossing their features, breathing at him with their mouths open, as if they wanted him to lie back and let them lick him.

It baffled him. Tim had never been particularly expert with women, or known a lot about them, until Trudy had happened along; she was only the third woman he had ever slept with, and the first two had, to be honest, hardly registered for long. What started to strike him was the peculiar odour that accompanied his visitors, the weight of their breath in the room; it was an odour at once eggy and metallic, a smell that it seemed to him he had always known, or known how to respond to, almost a primeval smell. It wasn't a body odour or, exactly, bad breath, but it certainly came from them.

Perhaps he was a little slow. When the explanation came to him, he was walking down the main concrete stairs of the polytechnic building, cased in glass; one of his half-dozen girls had been coming up the same staircase. "Hello, Mandy," he said cheerfully; only ten days ago she had been in his office, glowing with tears and acne and emotion over nothing more than her essay on farewell gestures in public places.

"Hello, yourself," she said, remote and surprised.

It had happened before, that shift of relationship. It was as if she couldn't remember quite why she had been so warm towards him, or even that she had. If she had been surrounded by friends, unwilling to be seen to suck up to a lecturer, he could have understood it, but she was on her own. He observed that her skin had much improved since he'd seen her; there was none of that eggy odour but, rather, a clean waft of recently washed flesh. All at once, an amazing explanation came to him: could it be that they came, these girls, midway in their need, at the centre of the menstrual cycle? Could essay-checking be taking the place of mating in their primeval skulls? He checked. It took an entire day with this year's diary, but it seemed indisputable: his six most regular attenders, his most loyal fans, they had made appointments at intervals of four weeks, regular as clockwork.

The revelation left Tim entirely aghast. He hated any kind of personal revelation to the point where he shrank from his own insight. Though he could undertake the kind of Goffman-like investigations into the behaviour of strangers, that was different. There was nothing biological about that, but acquired, willed behaviour. And in any case he didn't know the people who refused to buy copies of the *Spartacist* in, if they only knew it, one of five distinct ways. To see students at the mercy of their biological imperatives in so elevated a practice as writing and discussing essays with their academic tutor horrified him, and after some thought he wasn't surprised that he'd pushed away the explanation in his own mind. But, worse than that, there didn't seem to be anyone he could discuss it with. Trudy was out of the question: he knew her likely response so well, he could have recorded himself talking about the power of women being rooted in their menstrual gift, and the intellectual structures imposed on them by male institutions being (and so on). There was no way he could have raised it with any of the girls themselves. Women. They would have been horrified—he was worldly enough to understand that. And it didn't seem altogether a matter for the faculty's welfare officers. He expected they would wonder out loud what, exactly, they could do about it, and if it were really a faculty matter at all. It seemed incredible, but Tim went back and forwards through the Spartacists and his colleagues and the remoter correct regions of his acquaintance, and there seemed only one person that he could raise the subject with without fear of consequences. For the first time in months, he phoned Daniel.

"Why ever not?" Daniel said, when Tim suggested lunch, a little heartily. "Do you want to come out here?"

"I've only got my bicycle," Tim said.

"It's not far," Daniel said. "You could cycle that, easily. But all right. What about in town?"

Daniel took a day off, once a week, leaving either his partner Helen in charge of things or the boy straight out of catering college, who, Daniel said, could manage perfectly well on his own so long as he knew exactly what he was supposed to do. Daniel suggested Tuesday, which was the day when Tim's teaching finished at twelve anyway. Tim suggested they meet at Ruby Tuesday's.

"Are you home tomorrow afternoon?" Trudy said, over the vegetable curry and rice that evening—it had been her turn to cook, and she'd put sultanas in it again. Tim could never decide whether she liked sultanas in her vegetable curry, if it was a memory of those dried Vesta curries, heavy with mincemeat, or whether it was meant to demonstrate that she couldn't cook and it was an insult to assume that women could cook and that that was where their interests lay. Once she'd put glacé cherries in; that was pretty definitely a protest.

"No," Tim said. "Not till three or four."

"I wanted to go up the nursery to fetch some potting compost," Trudy said, "but I can't manage it on my own."

"I've got a meeting," Tim said, which was more or less accurate. If at all possible, he avoided telling Trudy when he was seeing any of his family, or even mentioning them. It wasn't often, their meetings or phone calls, but he embarked on them stealthily—once, when Trudy had asked about a London number on the phone bill that turned out to be Jane's, it had led to a whole evening's disquisition. If he ever had to phone her in particular, he saved it for the office. Trudy had something specific against all of them, and the mention of their names was generally enough to spark off a detailed recapitulation of the specific account. She'd followed his mother's court case in gleeful detail; and then there was what his father did for a living; what his brother did, and also what his brother had done for a living, somehow in cahoots with his father's activities; there was what his sister did and who his sister was married to. Worst of all were Daniel's Helen and her parents, who perhaps ought to have been OK but were somehow included in the sweeping arraignment as class traitors. It wasn't that Tim didn't agree—it was all right for Trudy with her unfaultable connections and the brutally cut-off culpable ones, like her rich cousin James sending his kids to public school. But most people had family that couldn't be looked at as ideal, and most people, like Tim, thought you probably shouldn't cut them off entirely. Even Daniel, who Tim had more time for now that he was a bit overweight.

Ruby Tuesday was a café, but a vegetarian one, and quite OK. It had been there for more than twenty years; Tim had started going in for long-spun-out cups of tea when he was in the sixth form at Flint. It was on that radical stretch behind Division Street that started with Bigg and Cleaver, the jazz-playing second-hand bookshop, next to an old bookbinder's and a radical print shop. Inside, it was painted a dark racing green with its Edwardian cornices picked out in vivid red. The tables were scrubbed old kitchen-tables from junk shops and skips; the plates, glasses and chairs didn't match, and the salads, quiches, home-made cakes and the till rested on a similarly reclaimed bank counter. It was run by a kind of collective, most of whom were pretty rude to you, and did very well. There were handwritten menus on the tables, but if you sat there you tended to get neglected, and the customers never seemed able to decide whether you waited to get served and paid at the table, or did both at the counter. Neither tactic was reliably effective.

Daniel was late, and when he came through the door Tim was sitting there with a cloudy apple juice. Tim hadn't seen him since Christmas, and he'd trimmed his hair right back; it was as short as Trudy's skull-crop, but somehow more expensive-looking. There was a new goatee beard, as well; whenever Tim had allowed his beard to grow, he'd wondered about the unfairness with which Daniel had been able to grow one densely and quickly. His shirt hung carelessly over the waistband of his black jeans.

"I knew it would do well," Daniel said, once they were sitting down. He was talking about his business. "I just knew it. We're turning people away on a Friday and Saturday night."

"Good for you," Tim said.

"You ought to come," Daniel said. "Bring Trudy. We do a vegetarian option. It's roast Mediterranean vegetables and couscous this week."

"Remind me," Tim said. "What's your restaurant called?"

Daniel looked a little abashed. "Get High on Your Own Supply," he said. "You must know that, though."

"Why's it called that?" Tim said; he did know, perfectly well.

"I know," Daniel said. "But we're stuck with it now. It seemed like a good idea. It was that we were told there was no chance of getting a licence in time for the restaurant opening, and not for at least eight months after that, if then. So we thought we'd make a feature of it, you know, the restaurant where you have to bring your own booze, and you only get charged, what, fifty pence corkage, for us to open it."

"You charge fifty pence to open a bottle of wine?"

"It's not fifty pence a bottle," Daniel said. "It's a flat charge. I think it's some kind of legal requirement. Anyway, we called it that, and then, as it turned out, the licence got fast-tracked in some way, or we'd been given rubbish advice in the first place, because it came through a week before we opened. But by then we'd put out adverts and everything, had the menus printed with Get High on Your Own Supply on the top. Phil said—Phil's Helen's dad—Phil said that people would think it was the sort of place like in Amsterdam where you go and smoke cannabis, but people seem to get the hang of it being called that."

"I don't know when you learnt to cook," Tim said.

"I don't do the cooking," Daniel said. "I'm just the—I don't know, the host or something. I wander round and I make sure everyone's having a good time, that sort of thing. I do all the boring stuff, too, the ordering and the invoicing. Helen does the menu—she's got a real knack for it. She knows what people like and what's going to sell. I put a word in from time to time but I don't get it as right as she does. She said people would go for the calves' liver, and I thought it wouldn't work, people wouldn't go out to have liver, but she was right. It's one of our best sellers."

"I don't think I could eat any sort of veal," Tim said.

"No, I wouldn't expect you to," Daniel said. He was in very good humour, and not allowing himself to be snubbed. "As I say, we've got a vegetarian option. It's quite popular."

The food arrived.

"This is terrible," Daniel said cheerfully, banging the back of his fork against a potato in the salad. "It's practically raw, it's like a water chestnut. It's not hard to cook potatoes and serve them with mayonnaise on top."

"I like it here," Tim said, but Daniel was off again.

"Helen's got a new idea," he said. "We're going to have a seventies' night in the restaurant once a month. I'm going to dress up in flares and a loud shirt and she'll put an Afro wig on."

"Where are you going to get flares from?"

"Oh, there'll be some in my dad's wardrobe," Daniel said. "But we're going to do seventies food, too—there'll be prawn cocktail and chicken Maryland and melba toast. Helen thinks we ought to put glasses of fruit juice on the menu as a starter, just as a joke, I wouldn't expect anyone to order it. People really like that stuff still."

"But, Daniel," Tim said in his most superior way, "there are certainly restaurants in Sheffield which still serve all that. I bet the restaurant at the Hallam Towers still does prawn cocktail."

"Not ironically, though," Daniel said. "It'll be a blast. Anyway, they don't, I know they don't."

"You don't eat at the Hallam Towers, do you?"

"Not regularly," Daniel said, "but when we were starting up the restaurant, we thought we'd go and eat in every restaurant in town, and everywhere that was any good in the countryside near here. So we went to the Hallam Towers. We just had dinner, we went on a night we knew'd be quiet, and we'd order things off the menu that you knew people wouldn't order much. And then you'd start up a conversation with the waiter about what was popular, what went well, what did most people like to eat. They'd always tell you. It's interesting. But, no, they don't do all that stuff any more."

"I'm amazed," Tim said sardonically, but he was surprised; "prawn cocktail" along with "dinner-dance" were shorthand pieces of abuse between him and Trudy for the pleasures of the *petit bourgeoisie*. He wondered what they actually ate nowadays when they wanted to go out for a bit of a splash.

"And we went there again, it must have been six months ago, and it certainly wasn't prawn cocktail. It was Bernie, you know, Mr. Sellers, lives across from Mum and Dad, he was retiring and they gave him a big party there. It was Japanese, the food, sushi, it was really good. I thought it was going to be warm white wine and a master of ceremonies inviting us to tuck into the vol-au-vents, but it was quite smart, they really splashed out. Hang on, they only asked us on Mum and Dad's invitation—didn't they ask you as well?"

"They did," Tim said. "I don't think we could have gone."

"Well, you missed—" Daniel said. "Hey, I remember." He gave a big smile, and now it was a deliberately malicious one. "Yeah, you wrote a big letter to Bernie saying he was a fascist, or something, and it was in contravention of your political position, or whatever. Yeah, he showed it to me, we were really concerned about that, Mr. Sellers never knew he'd been in such danger of being put up against the wall when the revolution comes."

"Oh, for fuck's sake," Tim said. "Not everyone agrees with your political position, you know."

"I don't have a political position," Daniel said. "I've never voted in my life. They're all the same."

"That's exactly what all completely right-wing people always say," Tim said, attacking his quiche.

"Yeah, I bet," Daniel said, not ruffled. "I bet you're really proud of yourself, though, now Mrs. Sellers is in hospital and probably going to die."

"She's what?"

Tim was flushed still; it wasn't out of rage, just out of shame that Bernie might have come over the road to show the carefully argued letter he'd written explaining the facts of the case to Daniel. Probably to his mum and dad too—no, probably not. Tim remembered Bernie, his brusque, assessing manner, and it seemed most likely that he'd have waited to show it to Daniel, the one who would find it funny. He hadn't heard anything was wrong with Sandra's mum.

"It was at the weekend," Daniel said. He was, it seemed, not surprised that nobody would have thought to tell Tim something like this and, in fact, he hadn't spoken to any of his family for weeks. It wouldn't have occurred to them to pass this on. "Mum asked me to send over a few ready-made dishes from the kitchen that Bernie could heat up when he came in from the hospital, so I'm involved in the whole thing. Of course, we were pleased to," he said grandly. "It's no more work for us."

"That's generous of you," Tim said.

"She's had a brain haemorrhage," Daniel said. "It was lucky Bernie was in—he'd just got back from taking their son off to the station. What's his name?"

"Francis," Tim said.

"Francis, he was up from London, he was just going back. If it had happened when he was out, she'd have died, they reckon. She's probably still going to die. She's in a coma. They're over there at the Northern General day and night. Mum's been going every other day. I went with her, the day before yesterday, and Helen's been once, too."

"Helen's been?" Tim hardly knew Helen.

"She's quite upset about it. She felt she was just getting to know Alice. She liked her. I mean, she still likes her, she's not dead."

"What caused it?"

"I don't think anything much, not in particular," Daniel said. "Helen was there when the doctor came round. She went out, of course, she let him talk to Mr. Sellers and—Francis. Are you sure it's Francis? But they told her afterwards—it could have happened at any point in her life, there's some kind of weakness there anyway, and it just burst now. They showed us the scans. They're horrific."

Tim controlled himself. It seemed to him that this was the moment he'd been waiting for over the course of years. Every patient stroke of his conduct, every irregular and unconventional turn in his professional and personal path had, it seemed, been directed with keen rationality towards this exact end, and directed, despite himself, by his own mind, full of planning. He had read a book called *Love in the Time of Cholera* and had thrilled to the idea that you might wait fifty, sixty years and your love would return to you. It had happened to him at twenty-nine. Everything from the previous years—his taking up with Trudy, which had always appeared a decision and not a gut feeling, the chain of progress along the same line in the same building, which represented his career, even the house in Nether Edge, which, ugly as it was, offered a spare room on the narrow top floor, which, of course, of course, was there to be hers—everything seemed now in retrospect to have been arranged for this exact moment. He had been led through high-hedged path after high-hedged path, unable to see over the top, not to be told whether this was a maze or a road to a destination, and now he had been rewarded. It all made sense, as if he had been handed a map when he no longer had any need of it. All that—everything since, twenty years before, she had taken his head and pressed it in a need that was hers alone, since he had not known the need until it was being fulfilled—had led him to this point. That long-remembered face was taking on flesh again, moving. He was in Sheffield when she would return; he was there to offer her everything she now needed. He had had dreams in which she returned from Australia in a wheelchair, blind, and he was on the Tarmac to push her. A dead mother was nearly the next best thing.

"Has Sandra come back?" Tim said casually.

Daniel shifted in his chair, uncomfortably. "I wondered that," he said. "She hasn't. I don't think she's planning to."

"She's not coming back?" Tim said.

"I don't think so," Daniel said. "I know. I'm surprised. I mentioned her to Bernie—he's in a terrible state, Bernie. At the moment he's got other things to worry about, of course he has. I've never seen anyone cry so much. I don't think Francis is much use to him, either. Sooner or later, though, he's going to start thinking about Sandra. I'm really surprised at her. Bernie said he'd phoned her and she said that she would come over, but she couldn't at the moment. He wouldn't say but I think she said it was too expensive to get a ticket at that short notice."

"She wouldn't have said that."

"Maybe she didn't. It was just that when he was telling me, he said, 'I know everyone thinks she's making a lot of money over there.' But then he stopped himself. She must have said something of that sort."

"She must have been in Australia for ten years."

"More than that," Daniel said. "She was only out of university a year when she went. She's only been back once, and they've never gone at all. I know they keep in touch, though."

"What an old gossip you are," Tim said.

"Of course," Daniel said, stung. "It's nice of you to wonder immediately what you can do to help when someone's in trouble. I know you're so concerned about social problems."

Tim didn't think that a single rich woman in hospital was "social problems," but he also thought that if he said that, Daniel would immediately say that the Sellerses weren't rich in any obvious sense. A few moments ago, however, a bold and extraordinary idea had been unfolding in Tim's mind. If he had been disappointed to discover that, after all, the initial scenario of his helping, supporting Sandra at a time of need, would unfold another scenario, a more dramatic one, had immediately presented itself. He didn't know how he was going to achieve it; it seemed, however, exactly the thing he ought to be doing, even if he had to walk out on Trudy to do it, even if he had to cancel all his classes, supplying Hester Carver with the flimsiest of excuses for the purpose. He saw exactly what he was going to do. There was no reason not to.

"Where does she live?" Tim said.

"In Sydney," Daniel said, puzzled, because surely Tim would know this. "She calls herself Alex, these days. She lives in a place called Manly—I remember noticing, because I thought it was funny. She sends me a Christmas card most years . . . You know I was friends with her." Daniel, not always the brightest person, looked assessingly now at Tim. "Listen to me—you're not thinking of writing to her, are you?"

"Of course not," Tim said. "I don't know her. I'm not going to write to her. The older I get," he said, settling back—he'd finished his lunch, though the waitress took his empty plate and Daniel's near-full one away quite indifferently, "the older I get, the less I think I understand women. Take my students . . ."

And he had prepared this bit, explaining his menstruating fan club in non-carrying tones quite coherently. In fact, it was so coherent— he'd made so much sense out of it—that he couldn't quite recall why he'd wanted to ask Daniel's opinion. As he carried on, it seemed to Tim that he was talking in exactly the exuberant and amusing way that he'd heard other men talk at parties and at the ends of public bars about women, about the curious things their co-workers did, and were greeted with laughter; but Daniel's face was hardening with distaste, pulling back into a sort of disgusted sneer, as if it were trying to escape from Tim as fast as it possibly could.

"You're completely sick," Daniel said eventually. "You really want to see a psychiatrist."

None of that seemed to matter any more; he'd been handed a task, a big, shiny, beautiful task, and all he had to do was to carry it to the other side of the world. In fairy tales, that was the hardest thing of all, to go to the ends of the earth. These days, Tim thought, as he trudged into Bigg and Cleaver (there was an old Pelican he was looking for) to the welcoming fanfare of a drunk saxophonist falling out of a third-storey window and landing on a skip full of drums, that was a doddle. Anyone could go to the ends of the earth; after this, he was going to go to Thomas Cook and buy a ticket. Only then would he go home and tell Trudy where he was going, on his own.

Twelve years before, in 1982, a white Mercedes taxi was driving in thin, drizzly rain along an Australian highway. The driver was dark and hairy; Lebanese, he'd told his passenger, and gone on to guess, without asking her, that she was English. "Pale, you see," he'd said. He kept on talking, and was talking still; but Sandra's—Alexandra's—attention was fixed on the outside. It was extraordinary to get off and find rain here, too. It might have been the same rain that had been falling at Heathrow, twenty-four hours before, and it was certainly almost the same temperature. It seemed bizarre to have made so much effort; to have paid hundreds of pounds for the ticket; to have lugged two enormous suitcases across the country (a hundred and twenty pounds in excess baggage), to have sat, cramped, nearly at the back row of a plane for a whole cycle of a day, though the sun was swerving crazily around the plane's progress, making a sort of figure-of-eight; to have done all that to find exactly what she had left, a faint drizzle and only the accent on the car radio at all different. They had paused at Singapore, and she had gone out on to the airport terrace, and that had seemed worth travelling for: a huge slap of hot, wet air. Now it seemed as if they might as well have turned round and gone straight back to England.

But of course they had not done so. Alexandra was desperately tired; her watch said six, but she couldn't work out whether this grey drizzle was that of dawn or dusk. She focused on the world outside, and then, of course, it was different, gorgeously so, the gorgeousness residing only in the strange billboards, the boasting about what things cost in weird and unworkable currency, and behind them, some suggestion that this was a new country, an unfamiliar country; the trees were quite different. Could they be eucalyptus? She had no idea. She reminded herself that the stars, even, were different from the ones in England.

"Out here on holiday?" the taxi driver said, having run through his monologue.

"No," Alexandra said. "I don't know. I haven't thought about it. I don't know how long I'm staying."

She didn't know, it was true. The story was that she was here after a man; she'd told everyone that. There'd been an Australian in a bar in Zakynthos the August before last. He'd been travelling round Europe, and had ended up there. She'd ditched Michelle, her friend she'd gone on holiday with, and after one night, then a day on a boat trip to the nearest island with him, a second night, she'd gone back to her hotel in the morning and had moved her stuff into the flat Chris was renting. She'd left a note for Michelle with an apology; Michelle saw her and she saw Michelle, on her own, on the beach two days later, and she'd raised her book and ignored them both. They hadn't been such friends after that, and Michelle made a point of telling her, when they were back in England, that she'd had a really boring time on her own. It had been fun. Part of it was that she'd made up a whole load of stuff about herself. People often thought she was posher than she was, what with the drawl and the Alice band and the Alexandra, and she generally played up a bit to it, saying she'd been born in London but brought up in Yorkshire. That was what you needed to do, these days; people liked posh, and though Alexandra herself had never fooled anyone genuinely posher than herself, she managed all right with the sort of people who had gone to Warwick, and with most people since then. She'd never gone the whole hog so much, though, as she'd gone with Australian

Chris, and she suspected that part of her appeal for him was that he thought she was a dirty posh English girl, or however he put it to himself and, when they were alone, to his two pathetic "mates."

She'd put off her departure back from Zakynthos an extra week— it was at the end of the summer, she'd finished her summer job and wasn't supposed to start her new, her proper job in the insurance firm until 15 September anyway. It was probably a mistake. She left it until after her flight back had gone to try to change it, and learnt that it was an unchangeable ticket, and she'd have to buy a new one, and at that time of year it wasn't going to be easy to find anything. Chris, who'd been quite keen on her staying when she'd first suggested it, seemed to lose a little bit of interest when she really did stay. There was one day, too, when he just said in the morning that he was going off with Morgan and Ted, he hadn't spent any time with them for a week, and she could do what she liked, go and tan her skinny white English arse on the beach. But at the end of the holiday, they'd said goodbye in the right sort of way: on the terrace of the rented apartment he'd hugged her and hugged her, and then he'd fucked her, right there on the tiled balcony, and then he'd hugged her some more and said they'd be seeing each other pretty soon, he reckoned. He was going back to Australia, once they'd gone to Germany, to Munich for the Oktoberfest to get royally pissed, and then he was going to have to start the hard graft to learn the ropes in his father's garage. She did her best, and actually managed to cry a little bit; she treasured the memory of his face, looking, of all things, aghast, reaching round for anything and having to settle for his salt-encrusted T-shirt to wipe her face. She could remember that better than anything; better than the way his face looked. She only had three or four photographs of him to tell her that.

Back in England, it had been all too easy to work up what, after all, had been only a holiday romance. She loved the word "romance" for it; there'd been no sort of red roses and tables for two, only her bent double over the bed frame, the headboard banging furiously against the wall and the noise of the pair of them hammering and yelping away into the cicada-still Greek night, only a quick and inspirational blowjob behind the rocks in the heat of the day. As for tables for two, there were usually the rat-like Morgan and Ted tucked in there too, whining about the cost, saying it was more expensive than they'd heard. That was her holiday romance, it seemed, but showing the three or four photographs of suddenly very handsome Chris around, his good white teeth glowing out of the underexposed darkness of his suntan, like an apparition's, nobody thought it at all unlikely.

Even to her family, she'd kept up the story. She knew it sounded like a holiday romance, she said, but he was a nice guy, and you could meet somebody nice just as easily on holiday as anywhere else, she supposed.

"Did he and Michelle get on all right?" her mother had asked, and Alexandra had had to say—since Michelle was in England and could easily contradict that part of the story—that she hadn't seen a lot of Michelle after she met Chris.

"That's awful," her mother had said. "I hope you didn't just dump her. Poor Michelle, I'd be furious if I were her."

But the important thing was that Alexandra had met a man—there'd been men before, but she could see that it was starting to become important that there should be a steady man, even if he was on the other side of the world and in no sense going out with her. It made all sorts of things much easier.

Alexandra hadn't bothered to find anywhere to live, that summer after she'd finished at Warwick and come home to start her job in a Sheffield insurance company, a good job, a management trainee. She had been planning to find a flat in the week between coming back from Greece and starting work, but as things ended up, there was only a weekend between coming back from Greece and starting work, so she stayed where she was, upstairs in her parents' house. It was pretty dull. Francis was doing his A levels—he was going to go to Leeds University—and she didn't have a lot to say to him anyway. The downside of having a half-existent boyfriend in Australia was that you couldn't bring anyone else home, and if she was going to stay out, she'd have to arrange it in advance with some friend or other, give her a cover story. Which presupposed that there was anyone she wanted to mess about with; anyone she'd know about in advance, that was. In Alexandra's eyes, to go on beyond a second or a third time was to turn sex into an affair; to push a one-night stand in the direction of marriage. "You're not from Sheffield, are you?" more than one wide-eyed naïf had said to her, the morning after. For some people, a holiday romance might be an abbreviated thing; for Alexandra, that one was as long as she cared to let any relationship go on, and she counted the length of the relationship not in days or weeks, but in occasions of coupling. She had no real intention of discovering all the bored routine of marriage in what had originally been a chance encounter; and repetition carried the threat of exactly that.

Still, a one-night stand could be done, and after a cautious month or two, she suggested to one of the other girls who had started at the big insurance firm at the same time that they go out on the town on a Friday night.

"I don't know where to go," the girl, Sam, said, evidently a little surprised.

"Oh, I know a few places," Alexandra said. "I grew up here, actually."

Sam was even more surprised; Alexandra was aloof, hadn't given much away, only occasionally gave the impression of joining in, as it were. She knew that Sam was living in a flat on her own, bought for her by her home-counties father, and told her parents, though she didn't say anything to Sam, that she would be spending the night there, it being easier. If it came to nothing, she could always go home and say she had felt tired, had been offered a lift.

It didn't come to nothing; she went home with a student. It made her laugh, going back to a student hall of residence. She caught a glimpse of herself in the glass door of the hall of residence as he fumbled with the key and she fumbled with his crotch. In her little black dress, her slicked-back geometric bob and her slash of red lipstick, she looked like a fabulous beast in these striplit corridors, echoing with inconsiderate rock music at two a.m. She forgot his name; a month later, she went again to Casanova's with Sam—they'd had a good time. And again she told her parents that was where she'd be staying.

She should, perhaps, have been looking for somewhere to live, which would have made everything much easier. But she hated her job—hated it with a deliberate and instant hostility, and it hated her back, asking her if she was really committed to her profession through a succession of serious mouthpieces within a matter of months. In her head was always the memory of that dry little island in the Greek sea, a line of palm trees planted deliberately behind the beach for shade in place of the native pines, and a lithe hairy Australian banging her head against the headboard for whole quarter-hours. It seemed incredible, insulting to her, that she should have to live in the place she grew up, and incredible that she had been so stupid as to move back there after her chance to get away. Her mind filled with possibilities; she formed an idea of Australia.

Living at home made things easier. By the time she landed in Australia, she had twelve thousand pounds to be going on with. For the first two nights, she had booked a hotel room down by the quay, an expensive hotel, an international chain. She intended after that to find a cheaper one, and then, if things seemed to be working out, some sort of flat, and then—what? A job. She denied it even to herself, but when she was to look back, she had no doubt that as soon as she bought the one-way ticket for Sydney, she'd always known she would get here and stop here. (The voice in her head, how much of her unused, under-practised Sheffield voice it was!)

That first morning, she knew she would never forget a moment of it. She never knew whether, in fact, she had arrived at six in the morning, or six in the evening; she had either gone to bed and slept for thirteen hours or for twenty-five straight. There seemed no way of ever knowing. But she woke at eight in the morning, and when she opened the curtains what met her dazzled eyes from the nineteenth-floor window was, rushing up to greet her gaze, the great dazzling sweep of the harbour, what was, she knew, the Opera House, so different from almost above, the great bridge and a clean blaze of sun and sea and shining glass like nothing else she could ever have imagined. She had had only the vaguest idea that her room was so high up, she'd been so exhausted when she arrived. But her long sleep had wiped all that quite clean, and she felt like going out and seeing what the city held for her.

She had seen it all so many times in photographs, of course, but it still surprised; the ice-cream scoops of the Opera House so edibly the palest brown and from this position, on foot, not quite the shape you thought it would be. She went on walking, with the shine of the city already deep within her, and smiling quite stupidly at everyone she met, and found herself in a park that ran over a substantial hill. It was a botanical garden, apparently; she looked up into the heavy gloom of the trees, and there were vast fruit hanging there. She wondered if they were breadfruit—jackfruit—but then one moved somewhat, stretching out a membraned wing, and they were—what? Flying foxes, enormous bats? She had no idea. Amazing. And there, most marvellous of all, was a yellowing Greek-pillared building exactly like the old Graves Art Gallery, placed on top of a perfect green hill underneath a perfect blue sky. And it was an art gallery. That was absolutely hilarious. She didn't go in; she had a lifetime to go in. Over and over again, that beautiful first day, she felt as if she were in a Sheffield which had died and gone to heaven. So many times in Sheffield, toiling up a gloomy Victorian street, she had had the illusion that just over the brow of the hill it would give up its teasing seriousness and show some glorious expanse of sea. She had never known why she had always felt this; it never made the slightest ounce of sense. And here she was, and it looked so much the same, with its soft yellow and blackened buildings, its ambitious stabs at skyscrapers; but the people made it beautiful, getting around their lives in ways themselves beautiful—transporting themselves with wheeled heels, irresistible tugboats hooting as they set off from one wharf after another. And look—there—like the irruption of festive pleasures into an urban life, like the boys pounding up the hills with their rollerskates on, there was a supercilious white ibis stalking along the waterfront, like a bird that had lived its life among sand, in ancient Egypt, and had now earned its reward; and then—suddenly she was in a different place, and looking all the way across the harbour at the Opera House—quite at once there was, of all things, a parrot, just sitting there, eyeing her, like someone's escaped pet, a vivid green and red and, as it stretched and shook its wings, a beautiful sunset pink underneath. She stood there, entranced; it took off, and as she followed it with her eye, she saw something perhaps even more marvellous, a scrubbed-clean white hanging railway making its futuristic way through the high sandstone buildings. She looked at it all, from the far glitter of the open sea, the little huddle of cottages on one side of the bay, buried among dense greenery, the whole city, and could not believe that people walked through here looking nothing but happy; could not believe that they did not give way to their daily astonishment. She felt like buying presents, here, for   oh, she didn't know, but for everyone.

She sat on a wall and watched the people go by. Behind her was the sea; in front of her, a sort of promenade. After a few moments, a boy stopped—he was wearing a vest, a pair of vivid red shorts and, round his ankles, legwarmers. He had glided up on a skateboard, flicked it up with his toes, and now held it to his chest. He smiled as if he couldn't help it, could do nothing else, and his teeth and eyes shone like the day. "You wanna go?" he said.

"No, that's fine," Alexandra said, but smiling in helpless response. She didn't care whether he stayed or went: he'd contributed enough in three words.

"Suit yourself," the boy said, but in a perfectly friendly way. "Catch you later," and he was off.

Her first days in Sydney were just like that, spent wandering around, striking up conversations with any number of people, mostly as short but amiable as that first one—people of any age, they all talked to her, and they talked to her as if she were their oldest friend. She simply followed her instincts, and one day, down at the harbour front, saw on the board a destination: "Manly," it said, and it seemed like the continuation of a huge joke that everyone was in on. She bought a ticket, and took a seat at the front of the boat, on a green-painted seat like a park bench. It wasn't busy; it was the middle of the day in the week, and there were only a dozen or so other people on the boat. It set off, and Alexandra watched the landward sights, the glass palaces downtown, the Opera House, the bridge fall effortlessly into new vistas. A tiny island in the middle of the bay; a pair of scarlet speedboats, apparently racing each other round the harbour in effortless leisure; a yacht with sails of perfect whiteness. She tried to remember that there were sharks here, there were spiders that could kill you, crocodiles in the sea, even, but it all seemed impossible to imagine. There was nothing in this country that could hurt you.

Manly was a thin strip of land, carved up into tiny blocks of brilliant white and glass, and the joke seemed to be continued by its inhabitants; the Manly Grocers, the Manly Fishing Club, the Manly Supermarket. There were few people about, and their smiles seemed to suggest that this was a joke that had never palled. It must, in reality, be ordinary to them; their pleasure must come from a more deeply rooted place. The Manly Fishmongers, even; she enjoyed that. And in a few blocks more, there she was at the real ocean, roaring away. It was winter, she knew that, but the air was as fresh and full of promise as a lovely English May, and there were even surfers in the sea. She couldn't believe how perfectly all this was living up to her expectations; if she'd known how to draw a picture of an Australian surfer, they would have looked exactly like that. It was nearly one o'clock. Resolutely, she retraced her steps to the Manly Fishmongers, and there she bought a bag of cooked prawns, asked them to open a dozen oysters, and took them, slopping about in their juice in the bottom of a plastic bag, back to the beach, and ate them in sheer pleasure, feeding one every now and again to the shrieking demands of the seagulls. It was all too perfect, and when it was done, and she had wiped her hands by rubbing them in the coarse clean sand, she rewarded herself with a beer.

The perfection of the day surely heralded some big positive alteration in her circumstances, and on the way back, Alexandra paused outside the Manly Dress Shop. It wasn't really called that; it was called, just like Mrs. Grunbaum's shop in Broomhill, Belinda's. It was a proper dress shop, though, with a beige summer suit and a pink-and-black striped cocktail dress in raw silk in the window, the mannequins canted backwards as if recoiling from an explosion of light. She looked down at herself: although she had sat on a beach for an hour, her dress was elegant, and she could feel her hair might have been styled by the wind. She went in; she talked to the manageress; she asked for a job; and they gave it to her, just to see how it would work out. She told them her name was Alex, and they agreed to pay her, for the moment, cash in hand.

Any kind of ambition had, it seemed, been drained entirely away from her, and, within weeks, she was more happy than she had ever known, just advising rich girls from Sydney on the perfect look for them. It made her laugh; she couldn't believe that, even now, the way she had learnt how to talk gave her some kind of edge in this place full of beauty. They actually thought, some of them—and Marion, whose shop it was, was one—that Alex had some kind of innate sense of elegant European style because of where she came from and how she talked. Marion made suggestions to her customers nervously, looking over at Alex for frequent confirmation. "That's simply gorgeous," Alex would say, or, every so often, "It's a nice dress, but I don't think it's exactly—let me suggest—" And they were grateful. It was preposterous to Alex; she would have sacrificed a good deal to have been one of those people, dress sense and all. And yet she was utterly happy in her ill paid job, with no responsibilities, and her sunny little flat, on the second floor of a building three streets from the ocean. It was utterly enough.

Though she had made her way by being English—"terribly terribly" was the phrase they used of her, she couldn't understand it—she was damned if she was going to spend any time with the other English in Australia. Every single one she met seemed to drink like a fish, and to be regarded by the surrounding Australians with a kind of jocular terror, which tended to come out in tentative forays into insults. She was taken to an event at the modern art museum—she still hadn't made it to that transported Graves on the hill. She went with a group of those friends who, here, seemed to accumulate from nowhere; they'd suggested it, thought she'd enjoy it because it was an exhibition of new British painting, shipped all the way over here, classy. They'd lasted fifteen minutes of gazing into their glasses of free wine before Alex let them off the hook by saying, in her most pukka tones, "This is bloody awful, let's go to King's Cross and get awfully pissed." They liked that. She wouldn't care if she never saw another English person again.

Before long, she had to remind herself that she had any kind of family, and what had been a commitment to write every single week without fail was sometimes put aside. It wasn't that there was nothing to tell them; it was more that she didn't really want them to be tempted to come over here. She could feel herself shedding her ties like a dog shaking itself after a bathe. Even the question of getting in touch with Chris, who was supposedly the reason she had come, seemed repulsive, as if he were part of her English life; her letters home always contained a short paragraph, steadily growing shorter as the months went by, of plausible lies about the dickhead. She couldn't even remember what he had looked like. After six months, her voice, which was such a benefit to her in her pleasantly crummy job, started to grate on her.

She had a love affair; she enjoyed even its eventual unhappiness. He was older than her, and tanned into a leathery sort of state beyond his thirty-five years; the dry skin at his neck tasted like heavily salted crisps, and you expected him to dissolve under the tongue. He'd been married once; she'd moved back to Perth, his wife, with the nine-year-old twins, and he was putting too much weight on the relationship from day one. She didn't care; she gave it five months, and it took five months.

One weekend, he took her to a friend's house in the Blue Mountains. She hadn't been outside Sydney since she'd got there, and amused him by asking if they were in the outback yet as soon as they were clear of the suburbs. It was a glass and wood ranch house, way up a back road, bone-shatteringly bumpy by night, and when she woke in the morning, a vivid slash of red clay through the eucalyptus groves and, incredibly, full of kangaroos. She'd never thought of seeing such a thing, but he laughed at her when she woke him up to come and look at the kangaroos in the mist of the morning. "There's plenty to spare," he said.

She wandered out on to the veranda; there was a mother and a baby, grazing a couple of feet apart. They stopped when she came out, and beadily observed her. She took a step closer, and another, and another, stopping only when they thumped off in their laborious way. "It's all right," she said. "I'm not going to hurt you," but with one more step, the baby took a single leap and—she couldn't see how it was done—was feet first back into the mother's pouch, just the end of a foot and the black snub nose and a lumpiness under the fur to show that anything was there. The mother lumbered off. Alex had never seen anything so wonderful in her life.

But the weekend was a matter of grey tinned food and dried preparations and endless boring beer, and the television was up the creek,
and by the end of it she was pretty sick of Dirk. It wasn't his fault. They
were perfectly polite in the car going back—he talked, as he often did,
about the ways his first marriage had failed—and a couple of weeks
later she ended the relationship, badly. She couldn't mind anything;
it was all just fantastic. And immediately afterwards she regularized
her position with the authorities, left the dress shop and went to do
exactly the job she'd been doing in England for one of the biggest
insurance companies in Australia. Their billboards were everywhere—
you couldn't miss them; and after three more years she spoke like any
Australian, and she lived in a flat with a terrace in Manly.

Alex had heard once of a way of life that had tempted her: a girl she
had met at a party at university, somebody's elder sister, who said that
for four years, she'd worked each year for six months at an office job,
and then with what she'd earned and saved, she took off to some really
low-rent part of the world—Greece, India—and sat there for the next
six months. She'd been a confident, drawling sort of girl, and her existence seemed better organized and better planned in its concentrated
pleasures than any other Alex had ever heard of. "Like cocks and box,"
the girl had said, to an admiring but uncomprehending audience at the
party. It seemed to Alex that, though she couldn't plan a life like that,
here had quite naturally, in some respects, fallen into similar rhythms.
When she looked back over the five years since she had arrived in Sydney, it turned out that her life divided into two, and she alternated
between two positions. For five months each year she would be with a
man; it would come to an end, and she would be single again for seven
months before she started thinking it might be nice to have a boyfriend
again. Both had their pleasures; the pleasure of discovering somebody,
of the sex, of giving yourself over to somebody, of settling into domesticity, of anticipating the end, of looking forward to being single again;
or on the other hand the pleasure of being able to do exactly what you
wanted, of being able to go out on a Friday night with whoever you felt
like asking, of undertaking small domestic improvements, of staying in
and trying out face-packs, and, finally, of anticipating the pleasure of
meeting someone new again, to have someone dopy to go to bed with
and to take you out for dinner. The rhythm had reached a kind of
steady level, and it was surprising that the qualities of the man himself
weren't reflected in the length of the relationship. It always ended up
being around five or six months, for some reason.

She went on writing a letter every few weeks, but with less and less to say; she got herself a camera, and in the week before she was going to write, she generally took it out with her and photographed a beach party, a night out, lunch with some group of friends or another, just to have something to send and something to explain. She photographed, too, those small domestic improvements, once even sending a photograph to her parents of a new iron she had bought. Most of her letters were just accounts of one or other outing, giving not much away. After three years, she sent a letter saying that she and Chris had decided to call it a day; she thought it might grow awkward, never sending her parents a photograph that included the long-forgotten figure.

To her surprise, a week or ten days later, the telephone rang, and it was her mother, full of concern; it took her a moment to remember what she had to be concerned about, and she took three minutes to work out, from her mother's delicate questioning, that she might be under the impression that, without Chris, there was no point in Alex staying in Australia. That she might, incredible as it seemed, be thinking of going back to England. But England was dead to her or, as she put it, "I've really got my whole life here now." And once a year, towards the end of November, she always cleared an entire day, and sat down with an old list, and sent a pile of Christmas cards to anyone she could think of in England. In the first three or four years, she included a photocopied letter with the cards, saying what she'd been up to and how she was getting on, with a photocopied image of herself looking tanned and happy in a swimsuit on a beach. It would arrive in an England sooty and harsh, stripped of any colour. After a few years, she stopped including this, and her cards just said Love from Alex, and if she was sure there was no possibility of the invitation being taken up, she might add, to Daniel Glover, for instance, "You must try and come out some time—it'd be a blast . . ."

In reality she never thought of England. When she first arrived, she had thought immediately that this city was like a Sheffield that had died and gone to heaven. If, on the other side of the world, there was a city that was rooted deep in its geology, hauling up blackened shapeless treasure from the depths of the earth and turning it into money, here was a city that seemed to float on the surface of the water. She had no idea, really, how Sydney made any money; it just seemed a matter of unrooted confidence, exchanging sums, one for another. She learnt, too, a notion of family that suited her, however new and strange it at first appeared.

"I haven't seen them for years," Toni said—she was a journalist on the *Sydney Morning Herald*, decisive and punctual in her judgements. "It's stupid to keep it up when you've nothing in common with your parents."

"Do they live in Sydney?" Alex said. It was a late-night conversation; they were lying on a pile of beanbags on a veranda, overlooking the blue-black warm summer of the sea, a trail of silver leading across the surface to the huge moon and the silver Southern Cross Alex always looked for, as once she had looked for Orion and his belt. It was a party of some guy Alex had never met before; Toni had told her to come along, and she had.

"Mum and Dad?" Toni said. "No, I don't think so. I grew up in Canberra, you know—the last I heard, Dad had retired from the Civil Service and they went to live on the Gold Coast. I guess they play canasta with a lot of other retired civil servants all day long. I've got nothing in common with them. There wasn't a row, we just lost touch."

It seemed wonderful to Alex that you could do such a thing, cut yourself off from the guilt and burden of family, and live entirely in the surface-skimming world of this city, reflected in the water. She knew she couldn't do such a thing, and the letters and the Christmas cards continued without a break. What seemed strange to her at first was that Toni, for instance, was very hot on the idea of Australia's ancient history, on Aboriginal heritage, on the Australian earth's unbroken history over the millennia; she introduced Alex to people who told her, unblinkingly, that they were Aboriginal. She'd never say such a thing, but she couldn't help observing that some were hardly darker than she was, and some actually had blue eyes. She rethought her ideas of the culture; she did her best and bought two Aboriginal paintings from a gallery on the harbour front. But Toni laughed at her when she saw them.

"That's stuff for tourists," she said, when she saw them hanging, one on each side of Alex's big picture window. "They're done by Aborigines, sure, but it's not their culture. They just sit in a big shed near Alice Springs with a cut-out potato and four jars of poster paints, and they get on with it, all day long. You want to see proper Aboriginal painting, you need to go to the museum, but they go for a fortune now, a really good Clifford Possum Tjapaljarra."

"A what?" Alex said.

"Clifford Possum Tjapaljarra," Toni said, without hesitation. "That stuff's serious, but these, it's just interior decoration, right? It's not something you should have in your house if it's not your culture."

"Well, I just liked them," Alex said. "I don't care if they're worth anything or not."

"That's not the point," Toni said. It was as near as Alex had ever come to having an argument with anyone in Australia; even the men tended to come to an end with a brisk agreement, a chilly nod and a swift departure. And she did like the paintings and, most of all, she liked the feeling that she could get rid of them when they started to bore her. In any case, what was her culture? She couldn't say more than "England" when people asked her where she came from; she didn't belong where she was born, which was London; she didn't belong where her parents lived, which was Sheffield. She just didn't.

Alex had been away for a long weekend in the mountains—she had been in Australia for twelve years—when she got home to find two messages on her answer-phone, one from her father, another from her brother. It was about her mother, and she had to sit down for ten minutes. They didn't have her mobile-phone number—it had never occurred to her to give it to them. In a while the clarity of principle, of the shape of her life, made itself felt.

"Are you all right, babe?" Stewart said.

She felt sorry for him; they'd only been seeing each other for a few weeks, though they'd sort of known each other for longer. It had been his brother's veranda on which she'd had that conversation with Toni, and it had all been pretty relaxed until now, neither of them making much movement towards taking anything very seriously.

"Yeah," she said. "I suppose it had to happen sooner or later. They're getting on, my parents." But was that true—her mother, she would be, what, only fifty-nine.

"What are you going to do?" he said.

"There's nothing I can do," she said. "I could dash over there, but I'd just be in the way."

"No, you wouldn't," Stewart said at once. "She's your mother, they'd be glad to have you around."

"You don't know what it's like," Alex said. "I'm going to see what happens first. They wouldn't want me doing a mercy dash just because of this."

"You mean, you're going to wait and see, and you'll go back if your mother dies, eh?"

"No," Alex said. "I didn't mean that at all. I'm going to see what happens. I'll ask them if they want me to come, and if they say yes, course I'll get on a plane. They'll give me time off."

"Oh, well, that's the important consideration," Stewart said. She eyed him; she hadn't thought that he—that anyone—was likely to take that point of view. "I'd better be off. You don't want me around."

It was true, she didn't, and especially she didn't want him to listen to the conversation she then had with her father. Afterwards she worked out that it must have been seven in the morning over there. He sounded as if he hadn't been to bed; he sounded broken.

"They just don't know," he said. "In two or three weeks they're going to be able to carry out some surgery, but it's all too fragile now. She can't be moved, even into a side ward—she's in a main ward with a lot of geriatrics."

His voice, echoing under oceans, came at her twice, once feebly and then with its feebler underwater echo.

"Why can't they move her?" Alex said. "She needs peace and quiet, doesn't she?"

There was a pause; she couldn't tell whether he was digesting what she'd said, or whether the transmission took a second or two, and he was speaking at an ordinary rate of response. Their conversation was filled with silences, like a too-meaningful play.

"She's in a dangerous state," he said. "They're just waiting. She might have another bleed from the same place, and it increases the risk of that if they move her at all."

"And that would be bad," Alex said; she could hear herself, how Australian her voice had grown.

"The doctor's said—he said it quite plainly—that if she does have another haemorrhage at all, she'd definitely die. We're just waiting."

"Do you want me to come over?" Alex said. "I don't mind, if you think it would be helpful."

"I don't know about helpful," her father said—and there, surely, was a pause beyond the mechanics of telephone transmission. "It's up to you."

It was clear to Alex what she would do. She told nobody, not feeling responsible for anything Stewart might say, and carried on. If you asked somebody directly, and particularly an English person, whether they needed your support—if you could put it in a way that reflected on their own selfish needs—then of course they would decline. If you let them think for a moment that they were being supportive of you, let them start offering options that would be good for your welfare, then before you knew it you would be doing their bidding, and all in the name of your own needs. She would go over for Christmas, she reassured herself, and that was months away; and if anything happened, she would certainly make the effort and go over for that. Alex reckoned she could probably get the time off for something like that.

Quickly, Francis and Bernie settled into a regular routine. You could cope with almost anything like that. His father left home early in the morning, perhaps soon after seven, and sat with Alice until twelve or one. Francis went over at one, and Bernie went home. He returned at seven, and Francis either stayed or went home. Bernie came home at ten, and they had supper together before going to bed. The routine, over the first two weeks of Alice's coma, seemed to sustain them, and each other's presence kept them in a state of rationally expressed concern. Only sometimes, when either of them was alone, did they find themselves out of control and having to walk outside to nurse their tears.

For the first three days, Alice was in a common ward, with five other women, on the ground floor of the hospital. Three of the other women were old, and senile. Two of these were silent and still, allowing themselves glumly to be fed or to stare into space, but the third, her toothless face a nutcracker, chin and long nose coming together in incomprehensible resolve, resented being asked to stay in bed, and could not understand that she was in a hospital. "What they all doing here in my room?" Vera—her name—would call, clambering out of bed; and the nurses would explain, sometimes for the fourth time in an hour, that she was not in her own bedroom but in a hospital ward. Worse, her resentment often seemed to focus on Alice and, getting out of her own bed, she would come over to Alice's and start accusing her of having stolen her bed. She was a frail old lady, with bird-like wristbones and tendons, and could be led away before she attempted to upheave the mattress, to throw Alice on to the floor. The more sentient women in the ward noted that the nurses were bringing Bernie and Francis cups of tea, unrequested, and realized the seriousness of Alice's case; they limited themselves to remarking, as if to nobody in particular, that it was a terrible shame. After a day of this, the nurses drew a curtain about Alice's bed, and though Vera could be seen blundering about outside, her arms stretched out in front of her, like a terrible avenging sleepwalker, it seemed to take her a good deal longer to discover that her bed was within; they sat within a gauzy floral tent, and waited.

The doctor had explained that the situation was grave, and that all that could be hoped for was no alteration; any alteration at the moment would signal Alice's death. When the brain scans were returned, a different doctor showed them to Bernie and Francis, and explained the same thing. They looked extraordinarily like Rorschach tests and, like the mad, Bernie and Francis tried to find any kind of meaning or resemblance in these terrible black spills on the film. They were in a small yellow-brown room, overfilled with furniture, the approved images of bereavement cards—of flowers in mauve and pink, executed in pastels—on the wall. The doctor's manner was clipped and practical; Francis was grateful for the lack of emotional concern. His face in that too-small room—the Relatives' Room, it was called—was too close and unblinking to them. When the ward was being planned, this room had been designed for the purposes of breaking news to relations, and there was no need for it to be any particular size. The air was thick and warm; the clean smell of the doctor was apparent.

"How will you know that any change has taken place?" Francis said.

"That will become apparent from the equipment monitoring Alice," the doctor said.

"And if that happens, how soon—" Francis couldn't continue.

"Death would take place within a few hours," the doctor said. "I'm sorry not to be able to put it in any more comforting way."

"That's quite all right, Doctor," Bernie said. His language had undergone a change of formality; it had always had this tendency when speaking to doctors and other professional people, but the respect he evinced was by now almost painful.

"We can, however, move her now into a room of her own," the doctor said. "I understand there's been a problem with some of the other patients. I'm very sorry for that."

"We don't blame the patients," Bernie said. "I know you don't have dedicated geriatric wards any more."

They moved her; it was an intricate, massive undertaking involving four nurses. It reminded Francis of those films of whole houses being lifted from their foundations and transported on giant wheels to somewhere entirely new, nothing within, not even a plate in the kitchen cupboard, shaken loose. The new room was bare and clean; like the rest of the hospital, it had the rounded brick sanitary feel of an Edwardian object painted cream and hosed down ten thousand times; the odour of philanthropy was deep-imbued in the walls. There was more privacy here, though the door was only shut when the nurses gave Alice a bed bath, or changed her mysterious tubes and attachments, Bernie or Francis waiting outside.

"She's not conscious of anything that's going on," the doctor had said. "I must warn you, too, that if she does survive this, it's quite possible that her personality will be completely altered."

Francis did not believe any of that. He felt very strongly that she could be kept where she was—and that was the aim of the medical staff—by being made to listen to the familiar voices of her husband and son. He asked a nurse about it. "Well, I don't think it can do the slightest bit of harm," she said. It was clear that she might have added, but for long practice in consoling relations in this way, that anything which made Francis feel he was doing something would make him feel better. Francis overcame his embarrassment—he had never said anything so fiercely personal to his father before—and told Bernie that he was going to sit and talk to Alice for as long as it took. Bernie seemed incapable of taking anything in; all that was keeping him going was the possibility of thanking the doctors, of saying, "I understand," to them in the most formal and well-behaved manner. But he seemed to understand, and didn't say, "If you find it a comfort," as he might have done. Whether it was for his own comfort or not, he took to doing the same thing, and often when Francis arrived to take over the afternoon shift, as it were, he found Bernie murmuring in quite his old humorous style at Alice's side.

At first Francis's talk took the form of assurances of love, of telling Alice what sort of admirable person she was, with the sense that nobody had ever got round to boosting her self-worth by explaining this to her. It was all true, but he got to the end of it very quickly, and it was exhausting, embarrassing and unnatural to go on telling his mother how excellent a person she was, even if she hadn't known it. He went over the same ground four or five times in succession, but it sounded absurd to put something into words she would never listen to in—in real life, he found himself thinking. Alice's flushed and unkempt surfaces, her hair greying and spread over the pillow, her hands reaching up constantly to scratch her reddened neck—there was some side-effect, perhaps of some of the blood-pressure drugs, that made her itch and itch—or to try, out of consciousness, to pull out the cannula in the back of her hand. These movements seemed to emerge from some profound irritation of Alice's, which might have been caused by the shameful sincerity of Francis's expressions of love and worth, things nobody had ever thought themselves capable of saying out loud.

"That's right," the nurse said, interrupting one of Francis's murmured paragraphs. "She seems better today." It was difficult to know how they could tell. She paused at the door, having taken down the readings, and surprisingly added her own comment: "You're a good lad," she said, as if she had known him for ever. Though Francis and Bernie both became quickly expert in the significance of the blood-pressure figures, constantly maintained, and of the pace of the pulse monitor, Alice only seemed at all better when, after a bed bath and a clean-up, the nurses let them back to see a more smoothed and groomed Alice, her hair brushed in an approximation of how she usually wore it, the dirt under her fingernails, which accumulated so quickly from her scratching, cleaned gently away. And all, really, that was better then was her hair, which had never been ill in the first place. For the rest of it, she looked and sounded, in the periodic small noises she made, very ill; ill in quite an ordinary way, ill with the blush of flu, her lips dry and flaking with lack of liquid. She looked as if she had a temperature, and had managed to fall asleep, that was all.

Francis went on talking, and now he talked his way through any kind of memory he could dredge up, anything in which Alice took a part. He went through their last meeting, when he had brought the cat; and then he tried to do last Christmas, but that was more difficult, every Christmas that had ever been melting into the same one. He worked backwards; he reminded her of the time when they had gone with Sandra to the airport with her bags of luggage, and her saying goodbye, she'd be back soon, she had no doubt about it. Then, as if explaining how they had reached that point, he talked about the long period when Sandra had been living at home, and them driving him to Leeds, boxes of books, a stereo, two cheese plants obscuring the view from the back window. He talked, too, about the long series of driving lessons he'd taken, and them leading to nothing; he tried to make that a funny story. And then he remembered he'd forgotten something, and he talked about Bernie's retirement party, all the people who'd come, listing as many as he could think of, just saying the names. To fill up the long beeping hours with familiar knowledge, he went back over them, saying everything he could remember about Mrs. Arbuthnot, the Warners, the Glovers, everyone he could remember.

"You're all right," Bernie said. He was standing in the door of Alice's room, with two cups of tea, one in each hand. They were in china cups, so the nurses must have made them. It was the measure of their concern, and Francis looked forward to the day when they were thrown back on getting them out of the vending machine, like ordinary visitors.

"I was just talking to Mum," Francis said, feeling as if he had been caught out.

"It's a good idea," Bernie said. "I talk to her too. You don't know what's getting through to her."

"A familiar voice," Francis said.

"That's it," Bernie said. For the first time since his retirement, Bernie had taken to wearing a jacket and tie, and his shirts were ironed, his chin was shaven. He was keeping up appearances, just as he did when, at home, he took one of Daniel Glover's prepared dishes from the oven and put it on a table as scrupulously laid as any Alice had ever set out. "I don't mind taking over now."

"I'll call for a taxi," Francis said.

He liked to be in bed by the time Bernie was home. It was best not to face each other. He knew that for his father, the night, the end of the day's visiting when all possibility of being practical had gone and there was nothing to do but sleep as best he could, was the worst time, and he had trained himself not to listen to the noises that came from his parents' bedroom. If he listened, Francis could not sleep, and the noises of his father's terror and grief went on into the small hours.

The next day he resumed his narrative, and he went back, talking and thinking about every holiday they had ever taken; going back to when they had first come to Sheffield. There was a half-hour on Grandma Sellers, and another on Uncle Henry, everything he could think of and remember about them. He returned again to the recent past, and, interspersing memories now with frank statements of love, he went over the same ground. His mother shifted; her surfaces still flushed and tense, as if under some unknowable pain. From time to time the nurses came in, sometimes to take readings from the machine, sometimes to usher Francis out so that they could perform some rite of ablution. He returned, and, not knowing what else to start talking about, started telling her what he had never told her, about how he felt and what he was. He knew that he should have told her this long before, knew that she wanted to know what puzzled her, and now he explained that he was quite all right, that he was a failure in the eyes of the world but he didn't mind, that it wasn't important. Told her what he had long ago come to understand, that for whatever reason something in him was missing, that he had never felt any sexual desire for anyone, that some part, which to the world was indispensable, was not there. He told her how, always, he had led up to the fringe of desire, of expressed desire, whether he was on his own and in his own thoughts, or even when he was with another person and the possibility seemed, as best he could tell, to be in the air. He had been led away from it, and if he had desires of any sort, he did not know what form they would ultimately take. He explained what it was like to look at someone and know them beautiful, yet not respond; whether to a man or a woman; he explained about the sense of exclusion that knowledge had imposed from any society he had ever lived in. He explained all this, quite clearly, and as if to reassure her told her that he had never been so happy as when he had been hers, a child, not knowing and not missing what would never be his.

The knowledge that he was, at any rate, something—not someone who wanted his own sex, nor someone who wanted to change his own, a something that was nothing, a neutral—would console her, and he expanded, telling her over and over again that she was not to blame, that nobody was. In his own mind, knowing what Sandra had been, he felt that there was some fount of desire to be shared between his parents' children, which she had prematurely drained, leaving nothing for him; at her worst, she had surely said as much, taunting him, and he had had no reply. But now he had talked enough about himself; he went off, tired, and ate an awful sandwich in the hospital canteen, and came back, ready to talk.

He told her more things he had never told her, never told anyone else who hadn't laughed at the information; told her about the three novels he had written, exuberantly detailed epics on distant planets, whole imagined many-branching biologies and evolutions among three- and five-legged purple camel-like beings, the detailed invented languages and geologies, trade systems and entire millennia-long imaginary wars between planetary empires he had worked out and worked over for the purpose, in the end, of writing a trite love story that nobody could believe and nobody—he had tried each of his three novels on four different people—could read. They all said it was interesting, and evidently hadn't got more than fifty pages into any of them. Francis told her everything about the Gurganian Empire, ruled by the three- and five-legged camel-like beings with their purple fur, and its three typewritten narratives; no one had ever stayed so long and listened to its intricacies. It went on all afternoon, until Bernie returned.

"I don't know what you find to talk about," he admitted. "I go over old things. I've brought in—" he shamefacedly brought out a photograph album, an old family album "—I've brought in something to remind me of stuff I could talk to her about, things that might mean something even if she isn't—"

The euphemism eluded Bernie.

"Isn't clear in her head," Francis supplied, but Bernie shook his head irritably.

When Francis came back the next day, he had thought about these things, and brought with him a book. Five years before, as a Christmas present, he had given his parents a complete set of Sherlock Holmes, in nine handsome volumes, the complete lot. He didn't know whether they had read them; he himself had loved them crazily at sixteen or seventeen, read them over and over until the one-volume Penguin paperback had broken and shattered under its enormous weight. He brought one in—it was pocket-sized—and when Bernie had handed over, Francis shyly brought the volume out from his pocket, and explained to his mother, her eyes shut, what he was going to do. He started to read.

He had always loved to be read to. Though he had himself learnt to read so young that he couldn't remember any bedtime story, it was an accepted thing that if he was ill and tired as a child, his mother would come and read to him, anything he wanted her to. It was as part of an illness as tomato soup and Marmite on toast. There had been flu, a proper three-week flu when he was fourteen or so, and all the lights in the house had gone a sour yellow with his temperature. His eyes had been too tired and sore to rest on a page—"Fancy you not wanting to read," his mother had said teasingly. But he had asked her to read to him, and she had gone on from where he had got to with *Vanity Fair.* He rested, his eyes closed, feeling dizzy with illness, but he could follow the story. It was not a book she had ever read, she said, and he could hear the slight puzzlement in her voice as Becky Sharp went through the ballroom on the night before Waterloo. He knew what it was; she could tell, somehow, that all of this had nothing to do with him. He knew all about passion in literature; he knew the words and the tune it went along to. They had read five whole chapters, and George Osborne was lying dead on the battlefield by the time he was well enough to take it up again. "I've enjoyed it," she said. "I'll read it when you're finished with it." But he didn't think she had, and when he opened *The Casebook of Sherlock Holmes*, the boards were still as stiff as those of a volume in a bookshop.

He started to read, not putting any expression into his voice, but reading all the characters as if they were him. He felt that he did not know what her wounded brain would make of a gamut of pretended voices, and thought of *The Ordeal of Gilbert Pinfold*. As he read on, he grew absorbed in the story, and had to resist the temptation to fall silent, and read on rapidly in his own enchantment, his eye flying more swiftly over the page than his tongue could. Some were better than others, but he loved the rhythm of it; he loved the way the world, so baffling and meaningless at the beginning of each story, fell into place before Sherlock Holmes, so wonderful a reader of facts that everything made sense to him, everything under the most disparate and unnarrated surfaces.

The nurses came in, and the doctors from time to time, examining Alice's own surface. There seemed to be an obvious connection between the tasks of Sherlock Holmes and these medical investigations. It seemed to him that, like geologists wandering over a lawn buckled by seams of coal, the doctors were trying to work out the reality and the substance of profound events by means of the most external and conspicuous signs. What Alice's face and body now offered—what those machines, even, offered that were hooked up to her and reading, measuring her—were only the most exiguous clues, in the Conan Doyle sense; facts, curiosities that, though interesting perhaps in themselves or peculiar, made no connected sense to the Watson-like observer. These items of information formed to a Watson only a remote pattern of sense, reduced in the clipboard at the end of her bed to lines between points that nobody could really interpret. Only the Holmeses who came and went could look at these facts, and sagely nod, as the great Sherlock could look at a footprint in a Brixton garden and deduce the age and weight and race of the man who, days before, had placed it there.

The case before him, and Bernie, too, as the light failed and Francis's father took his place at the nightly vigil, seemed one that the great detective had never got round to, and Francis read the exchanges of Holmes's unreported, speculative cases with care and something like sorrow, as if their full details would supply him with the reason he was waiting for, as if the reason he waited for was tantamount to what he really wanted: a cure and an awakening. Most of all, he waited for and dwelt on the names of those cases Watson had never got round to telling, as if in these last ones might lie the secret causes that lay below Alice's hot surface.

> *have therefore recommended Mr. Ferguson to call upon you and lay the matter before you. We have not forgotten your successful action in the case of Matilda Briggs.*
> *We are, sir,*
> *Faithfully yours,*
> *Morrison, Morrison, and Dodd.*
> *per E. J. C.*

> *"Matilda Briggs was not the name of a young woman, Watson," said Holmes in a reminiscent voice. "It was a ship which is associated with the giant rat of Sumatra, a story for which the world is not yet prepared. But what do we know about vampires? Does it come within*

"Have you been reading all afternoon?" Bernie said, coming in, although it was really his voice that sounded so tired and broken.

"Most of it," Francis said.

"What is it? Sherlock Holmes? You used to like that a lot," Bernie said. "I remember you were always pestering us to know what we thought of it, the way kids do. There wasn't any point, I'd only seen it on the telly, I don't know anything about the books. It's yours, is it, the book?"

"Yes, I think so," Francis said, lying.

"I ought to read it some time," Bernie said. "Did she enjoy it?"

Francis smiled. "Oh, I think so," he said, welcoming this sign of his father, as much as anything, getting better. "Her blood pressure's down, too."

"She looks cooler, don't you think?" Bernie said. "Long way to go, though."

"I'll call a taxi," Francis said.

It was one of Daniel's ideas, and one of the things that made Get High on Your Own Supply so popular, that it should have some kind of home-like aspect. One of these aspects was that, from seven thirty to eight thirty every night, the bar should be made as much like a drinks party as it possibly could. It was a success; people often booked a table for eight thirty or even nine, but turned up at seven thirty on the dot to swan about the bar. Two of the waiters, Jerry and Mark, were deputed to walk about with silver platters on their shoulders laden with canapés. Scott, Jane's husband, had offered advice, but as Daniel said to Helen — neither of them quite knowing what degree of mockery or irony was involved in the statement—folk in Sheffield didn't want that kind of rubbish; they wouldn't stand for it even if it were free. So what went out on the silver platters was exactly the sort of thing Daniel remembered from parties ten or twenty years ago: mushroom and Coronation-chicken vol-au-vents, mini quiches, sausages on sticks, even. It had started at Daniel's quite successful monthly seventies nights in the restaurant; then Helen had pointed out how much quicker the ironic canapés went on seventies nights than the seriously meant stuff on every other night of the month. Folk in Sheffield—at any rate the folk in Sheffield who came to Get High on Your Own Supply—laughed when this sort of thing started turning up straight-facedly on every other night of the month, but they ate it and enjoyed it.

Tonight, Daniel was wandering through the crowd, meeting and greeting. He liked to keep up the appearance of a favoured guest at the party, perhaps some kind of famous client, rather than the *patron*, as Mark put it to Jerry, in a bogus French accent. He did it very well, laughing and joining in, giving the impression of getting just a little bit drunk on the company rather than the unattended Campari in his hand, never less than two-thirds down, never refilled. Jerry and Mark walked through the crowd gracefully, like synchronized swimmers carving arcs and swerves towards each other; it was a matter of walking constantly in a series of S shapes. Helen wasn't such a good party person, and liked to stand behind the frosted-glass bar with the reservations book, lending a hand with the drinks when it got a bit hectic. On the other hand, her mum and dad, Phil and Shirley, they loved it. They worked hard all day, Jerry's sister Emma, who doubled as a receptionist for the dance school, said, but always by seven thirty they were down here, pink and shining and delighted, with a drink in his right hand and a drink in her left hand, quite symmetrical, smiling at the newcomers but not approaching anyone, just standing there and taking the occasional canapé as if perfectly amazed and astonished that anyone could offer them any such thing for free, simply full of pleasure. "I can tell you something, Jerry," Phil had said one night after a third sherry, amazement high in his brown eyes. "I never expected it—but I'm getting to be a rich man. I can't believe it." Because of course it was mostly his money that had gone into Get High on Your Own Supply. He didn't look like the sort who had ever had much money to throw around, though now he'd settled into a uniform of smart brown shoes and quite dapper, brightly coloured woollen jackets, which didn't make him look too much like a Butlins funmonger. Jerry had wondered, and had wormed out of him, that the money had been his retirement or redundancy fund; he'd been a miner. He smiled as he said this, shyly embarrassed, looking at the floor, though it was impossible to imagine why. "Don't tell m'wife I said anything," Phil said, artificially maintaining the normal level of his voice. Jerry liked him a lot. "This is what I've always dreamed of doing, to tell you the truth, young man," Phil said, and refused, regretfully, the last vol-au-vent left on the tray.

Sometimes there were other people there, *amis de maison*, as Mark put it to Jerry in another of his irritating French phrases. One of the least popular with Jerry and Mark and the other staff was in tonight. He was supposed to be a great friend of Mr. Daniel's, though nobody had ever seen any concrete sign of it. He sat in the corner, nursing a drink that he clearly thought he shouldn't have been asked to pay for, his eyes following Daniel about the room as he mingled and greeted and laughed. Daniel carried on as usual; they could see, however, that he was quite aware of being watched and followed, and would deal with it in due course. He was wearing a sort of imitation of what Daniel was wearing, but his black shirt had been worn a good deal, and its colour had in the first place not been very good quality; it was greying round the cuffs and collar, its points curling inwards slightly. He must be getting on for forty. They'd seen him before: he came down, when he came down, for the party-like atmosphere between seven thirty and eight thirty, but he didn't stay for dinner.

"What's John Warner doing here?" Helen said to Daniel, as soon as she could, her tight little bob shaking crossly.

"He's allowed to come," Daniel said. "I didn't invite him. If he wants to come and have dinner, he's as welcome as anyone else. Has he come for dinner?"

Helen barely glanced at the reservations book. "No," she said.

"Well, he's welcome to come for a drink before dinner, then," Daniel said.

"Am I indeed?" Phil said, coming up. "That's nice to hear."

"We weren't talking about you, Phil," Daniel said. "It's already on the tray. Good afternoon?"

"Fair," Phil said, taking a handful of nuts and throwing them back in his throat before picking up his usual dry sherry. "That lad David's coming on. He's got a gift for it."

This David was the twelve-year-old son of one of the water-workers in one of the cottages at the reservoir, who had come in shyly one day with his saved-up pocket money and asked to learn to dance the Latin. His mum and his sisters had come from the start to cheer him on, and in a few weeks they'd all been learning, and their friends. But David, according to Phil, was the one with the gift.

"I'll be thinking of putting him in for competitions before the year's out," Phil said. "We've not got a girl of the same standard, though. Who were you talking about, anyway?"

"That chap over there," Helen said. "In the black shirt with the fringe falling in his eyes."

"Oh, that chap," Phil said. "I've seen him before. He's an old friend of yours, though, isn't he, Daniel?"

"His dad lives on my mum and dad's road," Daniel said. "Him and me, we used to go down town on a Friday night together."

"Knocking them dead," Helen said.

"That was before I met you, though," Daniel said. "Can't stand here nattering—"

And he was off in aid of the party-like atmosphere. "Party Like Atmosphere" was one of the names they'd considered for the restaurant, ruling it out because, as Helen said, what happened if it didn't have one?

Daniel more or less avoided John Warner until the bar started to empty, people moving through to the restaurant, a drink in one hand, a brown-paper handwritten menu in the other and the ladies with their handbags swinging from the crook of their arms. At that point in the evening, Daniel always liked to withdraw a little bit. They'd seen enough of him for the moment, and it was his firm belief that the one thing that got on people's nerves was intrusion at the dinner-table. No waiter of his would ever ask whether the food was all right; a waiter of his would be perfectly confident that it was. At this point Daniel disappeared; he'd go back into the restaurant to circulate when they'd moved on to coffee and maybe even liqueurs. Jerry and Mark and the others were good at their jobs, and everyone in Get High on Your

Own Supply ended up eating a pudding, and having a cup of coffee. He just stayed in the bar, and let them go through.

Before the bar was quite empty, he did go over to John Warner. "Sorry, mate," he said. "It's been mad."

"You're doing well," John said, now taking his vodka-tonic, in which all the ice had long since melted, and finishing it in a long swig, like a pint of beer. "I came down to see how well it was going."

"Yeah, it's been mad," Daniel said again. "The secret is, I reckon, don't try to do what you don't know how to do. There's always some-one else you can hire for that. We've got someone who can cook, and the front-of-house know what they're doing."

"Fascinating," John Warner said.

Daniel wasn't having that from someone like John Warner who'd never achieved anything in his life. "You need someone experienced in a new place," he said. "I wouldn't do it again, I think it's a fluke. If I started again, I'd work in a professional restaurant, an established one, for two years first. But everyone else knows what they're doing, they've all done it before. The other day, right, the suppliers turn up with sir-loins, Andy doesn't like the look of them, refuses to sign the docket, sends the whole lot back, crosses it off the menu, calm as anything. I'd have let myself be talked into taking them—well, not now, but I bet they'd have talked me into it a year ago. You need experience."

"Helen's enjoying herself?" John Warner said, twirling his glass pointedly.

"I reckon so," Daniel said. "How's your dad?"

"He's all right," John said. "Always the same."

"And you," Daniel said. "Are you still going down Casanova's like we used to? I haven't been for, I don't know, five years. We used to go every week, you remember?"

"Course," John said. "Yeah, I go down there. You ought to come—you don't want to get too middle-aged too soon. It's changed a bit, though. There's not those lads in suits hanging round the edge of the dance-floor any more, and there's not the girls dancing round their handbags in circles."

"You all right, John?" Helen said, coming up with his vodka-and-tonic in her hand. She handed it over in a somehow satirical way. "Seen any good new films recently, or, I should say, any good old films? I always enjoy hearing about Barbara Stanwyck's best films, you know."

"We were just talking about Casanova's," Daniel said. "John says it's changed," and John repeated what he'd just said.

"Well, I don't know how you fit in," Helen said to John, "since you were always one of the ones in suits hanging round the edges."

"As it happens, I dance," John said. "You ought to come down some time."

"I wouldn't have thought that's likely to happen again," Helen said. "I don't mind letting Daniel off the leash, though. You two should go for old times' sake. Just so long as you don't get off with a nurse—I mean you, Daniel."

"Yeah, why not?" John said. "I was going down there tonight—you want to come?"

"Some other night," Daniel said, but to his surprise, Helen joined in with the ridiculous request and, within ten minutes, he'd strangely agreed to go to Casanova's with John Warner that evening.

"Go on," Helen said, when they'd excused themselves and were in the office. "Go and have some fun. You've been working too hard, and on top of everything, taking meals up to, you know, Bernie three times a week."

Daniel hadn't known she knew about that.

"It's a nice gesture, Daniel, but it can't go on, and it's made everything just a little bit more hectic. Go on, have a night off. We'll manage."

It wasn't until she said that that he thought that, actually, he hadn't spent an evening apart from Helen for months and months. Driving from the restaurant to Walkley to change before going out, John Warner in the passenger seat—and how had he got down to Get High on Your Own Supply in the first place, had his dad brought him?—he tried out a more brutal way of putting it. "I haven't had a night off from Helen in six months," he said.

John Warner laughed unkindly, as he was supposed to. "How are the mighty fallen," he said. "Not let you out of her sight, does she?"

"Something like that," Daniel said. In fact, it wasn't until he had a night off from Helen, as he had coarsely put it for Warner's benefit, that it seemed clear to him that he didn't really want one. He wouldn't mind going down to Casanova's, but he'd much rather go with Helen than with John Warner, who was probably going to spend half his time telling Daniel what was wrong with him and the other half trying to get drinks out of him. Now that it was Daniel's money, he'd earned it, he resented glad-handing people with drinks much more. He hadn't cared so much about it when it was just his salary at the end of the month.

John Warner spent most of the journey talking jeeringly about the girl he'd picked up the week before, the things she'd said, the enthusiasm she'd expressed for seeing him again. Daniel listened, thinking that "the week before" probably meant six months ago, if not a year, and wondering why someone who seemed to dislike women as much as John Warner did devoted so much time to hunting them down. Perhaps that was the right phrase: hunting them down.

"Mind you," John said, "it's changed a bit, down at Casanova's. It's a riot. They all come, the ravers and that, and they dance till they chuck them out, and then they dance outside till the police come. They'll dance to the noise of police sirens if there's nothing else. Mind, they're on drugs, most of them. They all take that Ecstasy."

"At Casanova's?" Daniel said; it was only a couple of years since he'd been there in a suit and a tie, grooving round the dance floor to George Michael. Five years, tops.

"Oh, yeah, they all do it. The management, they don't like it, but it's full every night, now, and it stays open till four, five in the morning. They don't drink, though, that's the only thing, they just drink water. Casanova's, they put up the price of a bottle of water—it's two pounds now, a right small bottle, too."

"I wish I could get away with that," Daniel said, wondering if he was making a mistake in coming out with Warner.

"It's good for our sort of trade, too," John Warner said. "You know what I mean? Is this where you live?" as they drew up in the Walkley street outside Daniel's house. "It's quite nice, I wouldn't have thought of living in Walkley myself, but it's all right."

"Thanks," Daniel said, as John Warner followed him in.

"The thing is," John Warner said, hardly casting an eye round the hallway as he took off his jacket and hung it on a hook, "it's all good for our ancestral trade, if you know what I mean. The girls, the little ravers, they come down, they take their drugs, and then they get—do you know what they say? They call it getting 'loved up.' They love everyone. I tell you, I wouldn't normally stand a chance with some of those girls, but they're quite happy to ask you to come home with them, or even, you know, if they can't wait, they'll say, 'Come on, let's do it now, in the toilets,' and that."

"OK," Daniel said. "What happens, though, the next morning, when they wake up and they're in bed with someone old enough to be their dad?"

"I'm not as old as that," John Warner said. "I don't mind. It's not like they didn't want to do it."

"Sounds like fun," Daniel said, his heart sinking. "Get yourself a drink. I'll go and change."

"Thanks," John Warner said, going over to the walnut table where the bottles stood, and starting to go through them as if conducting an inventory. "Don't dress up, just put an old T-shirt on and some jeans or something. There's no point in wearing anything flash—they probably wouldn't let you in."

Daniel, halfway up the stairs, stopped and turned, came down again slowly. He watched John pour himself a good half a glass of Irish whiskey, and flop down on the long low black leather sofa. "Do you do all that, then?" Daniel said.

"What?" John Warner said. "I told you I did, didn't I?"

"I meant the drugs, you know," Daniel said. "Ecstasy and all that."

"I've done it sometimes," John Warner said. "It's all right, it makes you dance."

"I'm not going to," Daniel said. "I'm too old to be starting on something like that, I reckon."

"I wasn't going to offer you any," John Warner said, affronted, but Daniel thought it was probably more likely that he was going to end up paying for whatever pleasures Warner had developed.

"That's all right then," Daniel said, going back upstairs. "I won't be a minute."

The street in Walkley where they lived was steep and tree-lined; the houses, solid and Edwardian, attached to each other on one side but set solidly apart on the other. The road didn't lead anywhere in particular, and it was quiet all day long, and in the night there was absolute silence outside. That was one of the reasons they'd liked it so much. Helen was woken by the noise of a taxi drawing up outside, the door slamming, and then the creaking of the front gate as the taxi drove off. She looked at the bedside clock; it was half past three. She'd only been asleep an hour and a half. She listened, her body tensing back into consciousness, to Daniel scrabbling with his key in the lock, then a jangle outside, and him trying another key. "Oh, for heaven's sake," she said to herself. She had no idea why Daniel kept all his keys, for the restaurant as well as home, on the same key-ring: it always took him about five minutes to find the right one. The door opened and shut again; she could hear him breathing heavily in the hallway in the dark, then toppling upstairs. He opened the bedroom door with exaggerated care and came in; she lay there, not saying anything, quite enjoying the performance. With a thud and then another, he got his shoes off; and when she thought he'd managed to get his trousers off, she reached over and turned on the bedside light with a click.

"Christ, look at you," she said, and meant it: Daniel's hair was all over the place, mad and flaring, and the black T-shirt he was wearing was stained with a white tidemark of salt where he'd sweated. "Jesus, you stink."

"I know," Daniel said, placing his words carefully, judiciously, like swirls of cream on top of a tart. "I got into the taxi and said where I was going, and then the driver just opened all the windows. I can't smell it myself."

"He's such a twat, that friend of yours," Helen said.

"You don't know the half of it," Daniel said. "You know something?"

"What's that, Daniel?"

"I think I'm probably too old for that malarkey," he said.

"Didn't you have a good time, then?"

"It was all right," Daniel said. "I've never seen it so full. And everyone having a much better time than I was."

"That's the saddest thing I ever heard," Helen said.

"Fuck off," Daniel said. "Do you want to know something funny, though?"

"Go on," Helen said.

"Well," Daniel said, drawing a breath, and trying to get the buttons on his shirt undone. "You know. I've got this old friend called John Warner, I used to go down Casanova's with him. Only I stopped going, because I met this great woman, but he kept on going. And he's tried to keep up, and I haven't. And all his friends down there, they're about fifteen, twenty years younger than him, and they all like this music. You want to hear this music, love, it's like a washing-machine going round. No. It's like being inside, going round inside a washing-machine. Only there's one thing, one really quite sad thing, you might say, about being John Warner's age or, you know, being my age, and being in a club like that with about a thousand kids jumping up and down. You know what the really sad thing is?"

"No, Daniel, tell me."

"There was this girl, right," Daniel said, "and she's a right pretty girl, she's blonde, and it's not her fault she's got a green fur bikini top on and not much else. I wouldn't have said no, only . . ." He sat down on the bed, and started amateurishly to fumble away in the general area of Helen's chest, under the continental quilt.

"Oh, get off, Daniel, you stink," Helen said. "So this girl, you're trying to get off with her, and —"

"No," Daniel said. "No. No. It wasn't like that, Helen, it wasn't. She was trying to get off with me and I was saying, 'No, I don't, I really don't think so.' Apart from anything else, she was definitely on drugs."

"She'd have to be," Helen said. "The drugs haven't been invented that would persuade me to let you near me in your state right now. Seriously, get off me."

"She was, she was on drugs," Daniel said. "And do you know what she said to me?"

Daniel looked at Helen. It seemed, in whatever was left of Daniel's mind, to be a genuine question, and after a moment, she said, "No, love, I don't know what she said to you."

"She said to me," Daniel said, "she said, 'You're a friend of Granddad's.' That's what they call John Warner down there, Granddad."

"That's funny."

"That's not the worst of it," Daniel said. "She goes, 'You can do it to me if you like, I don't mind.' And I say, 'What do you mean, you don't mind?' And she says, 'I don't mind, you know what I mean.' "

"Poor old Daniel," Helen said.

" 'I don't mind,' " Daniel quoted again.

"Now get off the bed," Helen said. "And go and have a shower before you get in. It's not the end of the world. I'll still put up with you."

"I know you do," Daniel said. "The point is—"

But then he seemed to lose whatever point it was, and shortly got up, a puzzled and pained expression on his face, and went off to the bathroom in his damp and sagging underpants. Helen watched him go, and in a moment, she turned the light off again. She lay back and, as she often did before sleep, started totting up what they had made in the last few days. She found it soothing, and safe, and in only a few moments had sunk back into the confused thoughts of unconsciousness. She had no sense of Daniel coming into bed.

The library was exactly as it had always been, behind the grey block of its front. Inside, the smell was reassuringly unchanged; the yellowish varnish of the bookcases, and the black plastic labels at the end of each with the Dewey numbers and the categories. Now there were computers on tables containing the library's catalogue, too; there were people at each terminal, and readers waiting for one to come free. The tall-legged chests of drawers containing the card catalogue were still there, but no one was consulting them, and they had the air of obsolescence. That was rather sad; there was, surely, a pleasure in rifling through the ragged-edged cards with their neatly typed details, a sensuous pleasure, and also the pleasure of coming across the most unlikely-sounding book, a place or two before the book you were looking for. In a gesture of cussedness, Francis went to the card catalogue and opened a drawer, more or less at random, just to remember what it felt like, before it was too late.

It was a Saturday morning. Bernie had gone to the hospital, taking Katherine Glover with him in the car, and, rather than sit around the house, Francis had decided to go and do something positive. He'd taken compassionate leave, and felt he ought to be doing more to justify it. He'd asked his father if he could borrow his library card— "Well, I know I've got one," his father said doubtfully, though it was in his wallet—and had gone to town on the bus. For twenty minutes, he'd just walked around; he couldn't think of anything he wanted to do, or buy, or look at, so he'd done what he'd said he'd do and gone into the library.

For old times' sake, he gathered together five books, just as he used to; they were books he'd always meant to read and, actually, if he looked at the date stamps, some of them, ten years back, had probably been on his ticket. There was no doubt; he'd been a great one for taking books out hopefully, then returning them, three weeks later, still unstarted. He had them stamped—it seemed quite possible to him that the woman who stamped them out, blonde and snub-nosed, was the same person as an Alice-band girl he quite clearly remembered, give or take about forty pounds in weight. He put the books into his rucksack, and left. Nothing much had changed, apart from the computers; even the people selling their revolutionary newspapers at the bottom of the steps outside.

"I heard about your mum," one said, as he was about to walk past. Francis stopped and looked; it was, unmistakably, Timothy Glover.

"Oh," Francis said. "Thanks. I didn't recognize you, I'm sorry. Thanks. She's stable now."

"I know," Tim said. "My mother told me. I phoned her yesterday to find out how she was doing."

"Thanks, it's kind of you to be concerned," Francis said.

"We're all concerned," Tim said, and Francis looked at him in surprise. "I expect your sister's coming over, isn't she? She lives in Australia, I heard."

"I don't know," Francis said. "I don't think she can, not just at the moment."

The woman with Tim, selling their newspaper, now gave him a resolute and contemptuous look, and walked five paces away. He hardly gave her a glance.

"That's not on," Tim said. "Surely she can come over?"

"Well, I don't think she can," Francis said. "And my mum's stable now. I'm sure she'll come over when she can."

"I'm sure she won't," Tim said, with real venom. "Somebody ought to make her come. I can't believe she just can't be bothered."

Francis said nothing. What he remembered now was, long ago, in the playground of the junior school, and the history of that playground game, for so long now obscure in its rules and details. It came back to him, how Timothy, then, had forced his way in, had imposed, uninvited, his own convictions of right and of punishment. He had joined in, not for pleasure, but because he had seen possibilities of damage and destruction. It had been a good game, and Timothy had broken into the circle, and destroyed it for the pleasure of destruction. When Francis thought of the game and its history, he could not remember the details of how it was played, only, in general terms, its energy and allure. But he remembered how it had ended, with Andrew, who had really been one of the only friends he had ever had, his leg broken, and him being taken away to the hospital. He'd never rid himself of the conviction that Timothy Glover, in the end, had got his way, imposing his notions of punishment and right. Perhaps it was just the fact of the hospital that made Francis think of that terrible time again now; but he knew with certainty that they were talking, at bottom, about his mother, someone about whom a Timothy Glover certainly didn't care in the slightest.

"You know something?" Francis said, and his voice was trembling. "I don't think I really believe in 'Someone ought to do something.' "

"Pardon me?" Timothy said, shaking his head and laughing in an affected way.

"When people say, 'Someone ought to do something,' " Francis said. "I don't really believe in it. Particularly if it means 'you ought to do something.' It just seems quite an easy sort of thing to say, to tell other people what their duty is when it's none of your business."

"I'm sorry about your mother," Timothy said mildly, turning away. "I didn't express myself well. I didn't mean to start telling you what you ought to be doing."

Francis turned his back and was off. He'd never liked Timothy Glover; he would have preferred not to have had that conversation. That was the trouble with being so tall: people tended to recognize you, even when you wouldn't recognize them. It was time to go to the hospital.

As the weeks went on, Alice started becoming stable. That was the expression that was used, odd though it was; to start to become anything was surely to be in a condition of change and not stability. But she started to become stable. Her colour improved, and she lost the terrible rasping edge to her breath, through which she had appeared to be trying to swallow a lump of air as if it were a choking cube of meat. She had looked as if she were in the throes of a traumatic sleep and struggling against nightmares, her brow furrowed in pain. But now her brow had smoothed, and she looked not peacefully asleep—that was what was customarily said about the dead—but even as if she were awake and resting her eyes. There was a tranquillity about her now, which everyone commented on; she had lost that deep-sleep frown of suffering, and as Francis read to her, he occasionally had the illusion that she was listening to him and following the story, that at some point she might open her eyes at the end of a Sherlock Holmes and say how much she'd enjoyed that.

"I know it sounds strange," Katherine Glover said, "but your mother, she looks much better than she did two weeks ago."

"I think it's just the drugs," Francis said. "They've lowered her temperature and her blood pressure. I think that makes things easier for her."

The drugs had been changed slightly, and she no longer suffered under those storms of itching, the clouds of rash across her neck dissolving into her familiar milky skin tones. If she looked better, the machines by her bed confirmed the impression: the figures registering her blood pressure were lower, her temperature normal, her body starting to repair the damage that had taken place. The doctors came round less frequently, and had less to say to Francis and Bernie. They interpreted these abstruse clues in their best Sherlock Holmes style and, unlike Holmes, started to give not the veiled past but the uncertain future a cautious shape.

"If there are no setbacks," one said to Bernie and Francis, in the same small Relatives' Room, "we might start to think about moving Alice to the Hallamshire Hospital. They can look after her more thoroughly there, they have a dedicated neurology unit."

There was, too, a surgical procedure that needed to be carried out on Alice to secure her brain against further insults—it was a beautiful word Francis had learnt for the first time in the last weeks, and it seemed extraordinarily apt to him. Insult: it really was the right word for what had happened to his mother and to all of them, only wrong in the inadequacy of its scale. It struck him that, even though Alice was in a coma and presumably not listening, any more than, in reality, she was listening to or following the Sherlock Holmes recitations, the doctors showed a delicacy of feeling in not discussing her case in front of her, but in asking them to come to the Relatives' Room. Such delicacy of feeling was naturally at the opposite pole of behaviour to the insult Alice had suffered, and would naturally deplore it and work to undo that insult's worst effects.

"Oh, that's a good idea," Helen said, when appealed to; she had come one afternoon with Katherine, for company, when Malcolm was at work. "They'll want to move her to the Hallamshire if they can. There's a dedicated neurology unit there."

It had surprised Francis, and also, evidently, Bernie, with what dedication unexpected people had visited Alice, not once but repeatedly. She had liked Helen, on the few times they had met, but Helen's devotion, and her and Daniel's practical help, couldn't have been predicted. Their restaurant, about which Francis heard a good deal, and was grateful for the supply of a topic of conversation, was left largely to run itself. Over the weeks it seemed to Francis that his mother, without knowing it, had made a pair of new friends, and they had become intimate with Alice as she slept. He wondered what she would feel about that if she knew about it.

"Of course," Katherine said. "Helen used to work at the Hallamshire. She used to be a nurse, you ought to take her advice."

"I don't think there's any decisions to be made," Bernie said, and then, as if fearing he might have been rude, he added, "I mean, of course Alice will go wherever the doctors think is best." He took Alice's hand in both of his, and stroked the back of it.

Alice changed, and became stable, the two things in this unfamiliar world not contradicting each other, and around her things changed too. Francis and Bernie were less conscious of the other patients in the ward than they had been, now that Alice was in a room on her own. The freely offered cups of tea came to an end, marking the nurses' assessment of a less dangerous situation, and Francis went out more often to the hot-drinks machine in the octagonal foyer between the four sub-wards. There, struggling to find the right change, he came across other sets of visitors, and they became first familiar faces and then people he could talk to, and finally, after a few polite but anonymous conversations, names and a family member in a ward. "Is she a fighter, your mam?" one said to him one day, when he was outside on the steps, and Francis agreed that she was, hardly knowing whether his mother was or not. "She'll make it through," the other patient's relative said, and Francis nodded, pretending to be consoled, though he thought of asking her what the hell she knew about it. It would be a very easy thing to say, whatever the circumstances.

The patients sometimes arrived, and sometimes left; it was a shock one day to see a whole family in tears about the bedside of a middle-aged unconscious woman, to see himself and his father, as it were, down the vista of weeks enacting the terror and grief that had now subsided into worry and routine. Some of the patients changed out of their nightgowns into day clothes and left on the arm of a proud beaming son or husband, smiling to right and left like a new bride walking down the aisle on the arm of a husband, graciously acknowledging the nurses who had come out to say goodbye.

Others left in different ways. Vera, the frightened old woman who had so objected to Alice being in her bed, contracted flu that turned into a chest infection, into pneumonia, and was moved into the private room directly opposite Alice's. Alice now had regular and varied visitors—Francis, Bernie, Katherine, Malcolm, Helen, Daniel, Davina and David even, Anthea, Caroline and half a dozen others. The numbers had to be limited and a timetable drawn up. But Vera had no visitors: she had no family, the nurses said, as if inviting Francis to pop in and have a kind word if he had nothing better to do; and Francis would see her tiny body lying on its side on top of the sheets, her knees drawn up and her little claw-like hands waving as if to grasp something. One day he arrived after lunch, and through the door of Vera's room he could see she was not there, only a heavy green zipped-up sack like the bags suits came in, like a chrysalis. He went into his mother's room, and she was breathing peacefully, his father by her side, the machines beeping in their tranquil regular manner. A nurse popped her head round the door and said, "I'm just shutting this door for a moment," and did so; the noise of Vera's bed being wheeled past followed, and in a couple of minutes the nurse reopened the door. The proximity of death had been too recent for Bernie and Francis; the kind nurse had thought to spare them any sort of trauma, even what was not a trauma, the quite consoling sight of death having fallen on Vera, and for the moment missing Francis's mother.

Outside, the landscape changed, and the seasons began to give way to each other. The savage rains and grey days that had accompanied Alice's first awful days in the hospital grew less frequent; the land-scaped grounds of the hospital began to put out bulbs, and quite at once, one day, Francis noticed a drift of sun-yellow daffodils and white snowdrops, at forty degrees in the fierce and cheek-reddening wind. Outside Alice's window, through the Venetian blinds, had been a grim sort of little courtyard. One day he looked up from "The League of Red-Headed Men" and, to his astonishment, he saw that the tree out-side was spuming with blossom. The skies cleared and were blue again; small nursery-tale animals appeared in the grounds, shooting rat-like up trees with their furry little tails behind them. He could not make his mind up whether these things were altering under his observation, or whether the biggest change was in him, that the grief and inwardness that had cloaked him for weeks, if not months, if not years, was lifting and allowing him to see what he had never truly observed before. He felt as if he was starting to watch the movements of the spring in a way he had never been capable of, and sometimes now he set down his book and talked to his mother about it instead, describing, in minute detail, the blossoming tree out of the window, the sights of planted woodland in the landscaped gardens running down to the gate of the hospital. Alice listened attentively, her eyes closed but her face tranquil and relaxed. And then one day, without any warning, the clocks went back and the spring evening was light until well after seven.

"I don't know what you find to talk about," Bernie said, but he smiled forgivingly; they had taken now to sharing their evening meal, and giving Alice, as Bernie said, a bit of a rest from company for an hour or so. "You were never so chatty before."

Francis returned to work, but arranged to take Fridays and Monday mornings off, and went up to Sheffield every Thursday evening, returning on Monday mornings. The Department were being very good about it; he gave them the impression that he was an only child. Not much had changed in London. One of the lodgers had decided to move out, and the landlord asked Francis if he wanted to take over that room too. He hesitated, and then, to his surprise, said no. He had been paying some kind of attention without really knowing it, and house prices were now a lot lower than they had been for a long time. There was no reason why he should not himself buy a flat rather than go on renting three haphazard rooms on the top floor of someone else's.

Samson stayed in Sheffield. Bernie said he didn't mind him being around, he quite liked the company, and the butter trick seemed to have worked. Samson was almost too much at home, appropriating and curling up in Bernie's armchair, allowing himself to be thrown off but immediately returning to curl up and purr in Bernie's lap. There was no point at all, Francis's father said, in objecting; cats knew their own mind and this one was more determined than most. He seemed to have taken a definite liking to Bernie, Bernie said. "I don't know what your mother will think," he said. Two or three weeks ago he might have said "would."

And then one day Alice opened her eyes. Francis heard about it from his father, during the week, over the phone, and felt guilt and regret that he had not been there. The phone had rung in his room in London only five minutes after he had got home. Afterwards he wondered why his father had not called him at work; perhaps he thought, and perhaps rightly, that Francis would want to make sure of his own response. He wondered, too, how often he had called and left no message, waiting anxiously for Francis to pick up the phone and not wanting to leave a message that might, even for two minutes, be frightening, asking him to telephone as soon as possible. Francis picked up the phone, and immediately, his voice full of delight, his father said, "She opened her eyes today." She hadn't spoken, and probably couldn't, but she had eagerly drunk one glass of water, then another, and had even hungrily eaten some food before closing her eyes and sinking back into what, now, seemed very much like sleep. "She's lost a lot of weight," Bernie said. "At least from her face it looks as if she has. She must have been hungry, not eating all that time." Then he laughed, incredulous: the fact that Alice had not been eating was not something that had occurred to him at all.

It was a Wednesday night, and Francis went up on the Thursday night as usual, going straight from the office with his packed bag and determined that, if he could, he would stay an extra day after the weekend. On the train, he went to the buffet car, and with an experienced and tired eye ran through the seven choices of sandwich in the little fridge.

"Can I help you at all?" the steward said; he was snappy, camp, with one silver earring and an unsmiling lined face under his spiked black hair.

"Just a cup of tea," Francis said. He had had every single sandwich on this service over the last few weeks; he was sick of them all, and decided he was going to bring his own if he had to eat on the train.

He arrived at the hospital that evening full of apologies, but it wasn't quite clear to his father what he might be apologizing for. It didn't seem to him as though Francis, through a misplaced trust in personal duties and professional obligations, had excused himself from an important stage in his mother's recovery as a too-burdened young parent might miss, through his labours in a City office, his infant's first words, his infant's first steps. And in any case, tingeing their relief and delight was the remembered advice from the doctor that Alice, should she come through this—and surely, now, she had come through this—might well find herself in possession of a character not her own.

It was too early to say, Bernie said, and just as he did so, Alice in her bed opened her eyes again, like a child delighted to repeat a party trick to gather praise from a new guest. For a moment her eyes were the heartrendingly groggy-blank blue he had seen over and over when the nurses had lifted her eyelids against her will and called her name in her ear, to test for responses. But then something within her, something undeterminable by the clues being gathered by the machines by her bed, visibly gathered and tensed and focused on Francis; and, without any doubt, she knew him as he knew her. There was no change of personality in those blue eyes. Her mouth moved a little.

"She might want some water," Bernie said. Francis got up to fetch a cup from the side table, now bearing a familiar object, a small china angel that Francis recognized as always having been on her bedside table at home. When he returned, she had closed her eyes, but he gently raised the purple plastic cup with its infantile beaker-top to her mouth, and she opened them again, feasting them on him. She drank a little, but he sensed she hadn't particularly wanted that, and lowered it again. "What is it, Mum?" he said, and her mouth moved again. "It's all right now," he said. She had been trying to say something.

"I've told Sandra," Bernie said, when they were in the car going home. "Alex. About your mother coming round. She was delighted, and relieved, she said. She's hoping to come over to see us very soon."

"I don't know why she hasn't come already," Francis said crossly.

Bernie looked at him in surprise. "That's not like you," he said, pausing at some traffic-lights. "And it's not fair. You can't just pop over from Australia at the drop of a hat."

Francis thought, on the whole, that you could, but he didn't say anything more. It proved to him what he had never consciously thought but had, clearly enough, concluded within himself, that his father had given up on Sandra, and whatever regrets and pain that decision had caused him, he would be determinedly grateful for being allowed to telephone her if it did not occur to her to telephone them, for a telephone call from her when he might have hoped for a letter, for anything at all, any evidence of concern at the most extreme and painful episodes of family existence in place of what might be hoped for, her presence and her once-familiar face and love. In television dramas, in books, this kind of severance took place with abruptness and with some cause, after some splendid and memorable exchange of views. In England, though such a severance could and did take place, it required, it seemed, no such difference of views, no theft or violence, no long-hidden secret—or if there should be such a hidden secret, it was hidden from Francis and, he believed, from his father too. All that was required was a plane fare to Australia and a slowly dwindling evidence of effort and commitment, until it had dwindled away altogether to the level, perhaps, that it had always occupied, concealed only by the requirement and effort that were asked of you when you were actually around. Probably that was unfair. But Francis knew that if his father's memory was as good as his own, or had preserved the same moments, it would be with some pain that it returned to the back of a car driving up to Sheffield, to move house, twenty or more years before, and him saying to Francis in the back, "I wouldn't give you two hundred quid for Sandra. Maybe if you gave her a wash first." Francis hoped his father didn't remember that; he hoped that, in some way you read about in the newspapers these days, he'd made it up himself. He knew his father had never meant it.

. . .

One of the things to like about Stewart was how full of crazy ideas he was, suggested and implemented on the spur of the moment. He was perfectly capable of saying to Alex, "Let's go to Cairns for the weekend," or turning up with tickets to a rock concert that same evening, or putting Alex into his jeep and taking her off somewhere she'd never thought of going before, or simply saying as they woke up, "We're not going to get out of bed today." Alex liked it; she didn't always go along with it, but she liked it, and she much preferred it to the sort of man who planned outings weeks or months in advance, then seemed to blame her sourly when a weekend in the Blue Mountains lacked spontaneity. Of course, it helped that Stewart owned his own business, a historic-postcard emporium mostly run for him by his borderline-autistic assistant Gwilym. Gwilym, who had the fragile and blotchy pink skin, pale ginger hair and eyelashes and rained-out blue eyes of someone whose ancestors should never have left rainy North Wales, never minded being left alone in the shop, and Stewart never saw why he shouldn't take off now and again. Some people thought those washed-out blue eyes of Gwilym's gave him a misleadingly sly look that scared off customers, and that Stewart was a bit too relaxed about his priorities.

It was harder, though, for Alex, and she tried to channel Stewart's spontaneity into weekends, and otherwise only very occasionally go along with it. She liked her job, though most people wouldn't have thought there was much interesting in it. She liked the people she worked with, and she honestly didn't enjoy coming back the day after one of these excursions and telling a pack of lies about how ill she'd felt, one of those twenty-four-hour things.

Stewart lived over his shop; it was better than that made it sound. It was an old Victorian provisions merchant's, and the three storeys over the shop were solid, well-lit and spacious. He'd done it all himself, stripping it down and putting in industrial-style kitchen and bathroom. A woman from *Australian Interiors* had come to see if it would do for a photo-feature. Alex was standing at the raw-steel breakfast counter, with a wide bowl of milky coffee, chopping up a plate of papaya and mango and pineapple, one of Stewart's old football shirts barely covering her arse, when she heard Stewart coming downstairs behind her. It was half past seven in the morning; the sunlight was already bright through the thin muslin drapes drawn across the window. She could hear from the way he was placing his big feet on the creaking treads that he didn't want her to hear him, and she carried on slicing, artificially slowly, until she actually felt his restrained breath behind, on the back of her neck, felt his big roughened calloused foot-baller's hands sliding up her smooth thighs, up underneath the hem of the football shirt she was wearing, running up her sides. He was like Tigger, the way he bounced straight back; she sometimes wondered if he ever thought about anything else.

"You're up early," he said, after a time.

"Got to get moving," Alex said. "Time to get to work."

"Ah, I'm not doing that," Stewart said. "Gwil can enjoy himself today, have a day in charge."

"You give him too much to do," Alex said. "He takes more interest in the shop than you do."

"Yeah, I reckon he does," Stewart said, in his big, placid way. "Let's have a day off. It's a real beautiful day."

"Forget it," Alex said. "It'll be a beautiful day at the weekend, too."

"You want to take a chill pill," Stewart said. "I always forget what an uptight Pom you are. Take the girl out of England, but you can't take England out of the girl."

"Yeah, yeah," Alex said, who had heard that one before, and not just from Stewart.

"But I tell you what I had in mind," Stewart said. "I bet you've never been to the zoo, have you?"

"The zoo?"

"Yeah, you know, the zoo, collection of animals in their own habi-tats, you can go and stare at them. Australian animals mostly. Have you ever seen a koala bear?"

"You know what?" Alex said. "I never have. Apart from at the zoo in Manchester, actually. I've never ever seen one living in the wild here."

"You won't in Sydney, apart from at the zoo," Stewart said. "Come on, it's a gorgeous day, perfect for looking at koalas and kangaroos and Tasmanian Devils and duck-billed platypuses and black mambos. I bet you don't know what a black mambo is, do you?"

"I've absolutely no idea what a black mambo is, unless it's a dance, which I don't think it probably is from the context."

"No, it's the world's most venomous snake, and it lives right here in Australia."

"Waltzing fucking Matilda," Alex said, laughing at the peculiar forms Stewart's national pride took, but she was quite enjoying the attentions of his hands up her sides, and in another ten minutes she had agreed to call in sick and go off with Stewart to the zoo. It was safer than it sounded: Stewart's shop and the zoo weren't anywhere near Alex's office, and so long as they waited until after ten, they weren't likely to be seen by anyone.

Stewart was terrible, and she had to banish him out of her eyeline while she made the phone call, soon after nine. She made it as soon as there was going to be anyone in the office. Her boss, Kevin, was English like her, had come over only three years ago, and had a habit of not arriving until half past nine or ten. She had the feeling that insincerity or implausibility in her voice was much more obvious to him than it was to the others in the office, and she wanted to get in before she had to speak to him. She phoned at five past nine, and got Shannon, who sounded completely sympathetic. "It's some kind of—eurgh, eurgh—bug I picked up, I reckon, it feels like—eurgh, eurgh—a twenty-four-hour thing, but I'll get in—eurgh—the doctor if it's not better by tomorrow and—eurgh—I'm going back to bed now. I won't be answering the phone."

She put down the phone and turned to see Stewart, as she knew, still in his loose blue jockey pants, which hung like a washing-line from hipbone to gaunt hipbone, hugging a cushion to his mouth in silent hilarity. "You're absolutely shit at that," he said. "That was the most unconvincing thing I ever heard. 'Eurgh, eurgh,' " he quoted.

"It's not my fault," Alex said. "I asked you to break the news for me. You would have been much more convincing."

"Everyone knows," Stewart said cheerfully, "there's nothing more obviously fake than asking someone to call up on your behalf because you're too ill to come to the phone. You're never too ill to come to the phone unless you're in a coma."

"OK," Alex said.

"Jeeze, I'm sorry," Stewart said, aghast, "I didn't mean anything, anything about your mum, I wasn't thinking."

"That's fine," Alex said, smiling tightly. "I wasn't thinking about my mum either. Are you going to get dressed and we can go to the fucking zoo?"

"Sounds like a top plan," Stewart said.

She enjoyed her day, their day, though pretty soon they gave up on the zoo—after the few weird highlights, the showstoppers, most animals were the same as in any zoo anywhere, and you started to feel like somebody going through the archives. They were tickled by the koalas—they were just pissed old men, working up their trees step by step and looking seriously in danger of falling off at any moment from sheer drunkenness. Stewart and Alex watched, entranced, for twenty minutes at their slow, blunt-nosed race up and down the tree; a whole noisy class of schoolchildren came and went round them. But in front of most of the other enclosures, perched in an elevated arrangement up the side of a steep hill overlooking the harbour, a ribbon-like path wending downwards from the peak, they just talked; Stewart liked to hear stories about Alex's childhood, and today she told him about flashing her tits at Mr. Griffiths next door from the upstairs window, the day they'd moved house from London. He laughed at that, but she didn't tell him about the other thing she'd done, left a turd unflushed in the upstairs toilet to greet the new owners. She told him, in place of that, about the people in Sheffield, the ones who had removed every single lightbulb, and he laughed again. He wasn't so good at telling stories about his childhood, and the same ones tended to come up repeatedly, today the one about his auntie Pearl, who, one Christmas, had batted away a funnel web, flying right at her face, with a table-tennis paddle. She didn't mind hearing them; she quite liked them; but it was a bit of an inequality in their relationship. When they were out together with friends, it often fell to her to turn Gwilym's absurdities into a funny story, though Stewart had been there too. It was as if he didn't quite see things that happened in front of him as stories; in a way she liked that innocence in him.

Afterwards, trusting to their luck a little, they made a day of it by driving down to the harbour front and having a seafood lunch in the sun. Shelled things were what had kept her in Australia in the first place; she always felt that it had been the eating of the magical oysters and prawns on the beach at Manly that day that had anchored her there, as if the products of the seas of Australia carried a spell within them, like the island of the lotus-eaters. She always liked to be given a broad platter of high-piled shells and carapaces and a neat little line of surgeon's tools to pick away at them for forty minutes and leave, at the end, a pile of carapaces and detritus higher than the one she had been given, to let her fingers grow sticky and only at the end to rinse them in the bowl of warm water with a lemon in it, wipe them on the napkin, sit back behind her sunglasses and smile, replete. Stewart had a steak.

"I'd better get back," she said. "I've not been home for three days and I'd better check my messages. They might start to wonder if they've left a message from work and I don't call them back before five."

"What time is it now?"

"Three o'clock," Alex said.

"You don't want to do anything this afternoon?"

"Let's not push our luck," Alex said. "Drive me home, and I'll see you tomorrow."

Stewart looked downcast and red-nosed, but he'd been granted his day, more or less; it was always better to leave him while he'd not yet had enough of her. He dropped her off at the door to her apartment block in Manly. Over the road, a black limo was purring, the driver sitting behind tinted windows in his sunglasses, reading a tabloid, and as they kissed goodbye, the newsreader from the television came out from the back entrance of one of the seafront blocks. She left about this time every day, and today she was wearing a beige linen suit with her usual Ray-Bans on.

"That's Carol Walmer," Stewart observed. "Off the telly."

"Yeah, she lives there," Alex said. "She spends all Sunday walking up and down the esplanade looking for fans who want her autograph. It's a bit pathetic."

"I'll see you tomorrow," Stewart said. "Will you come over after work?"

As Alex was fumbling for her key, the door to flat six opened and Terry put his head out. He was a ludicrously fit and wizened old man, a pillar of the Manly running club, who even at sixty thought nothing of running ten miles up hill and down again, every day, and who, as he told Alex and anyone else he ever met, pretty well every time they saw each other, had never been outside Australia in his life because there was everything in this country a man could want. His wife, Vi, led a sad life, visible in her face as, for the third time that day, she started watering the hydrangeas on their balcony, which abutted on to Alex's.

"Someone looking for you," he said. "Someone come looking for you this morning."

"Who was it?" Alex said.

"*I* don't know," Terry said, as if affronted. "How should I know? I could hear your buzzer going, buzz, buzz, buzz, then it stops, like he's thinking, like, and then he only goes and buzzes on our bell."

"I'm sorry if you were disturbed," Alex said.

"Oh, *we* weren't disturbed, no worries," Terry said, now apparently aggrieved at the suggestion that they weren't good neighbours. "I tell you, I couldn't understand a blinking word he was saying, so I goes downstairs, to the main door, you know, the main door—"

"Yes," Alex said, still frozen with her key halfway to the door.

"—and it's this bloke, and he says he's looking for you, and can he come in and wait. It'd be about one, this was, we were just sitting down to a bite to eat."

"And you said no, I hope."

"Vi says to me, afterwards, like, 'You should have asked him in, be neighbourly,' but I dunno. Because I didn't let him in, I said to him, 'She's not here if you've been ringing on her buzzer and she's not answering, stands to reason.' I can tell you, he didn't like that, not one little bit. So I tells him to come back later and he goes away. He's a, he's from England, I reckon, like you."

"Oh, God," Alex said. "It must have been my boss, looking for me."

"He said he'll come back, later today. Who do you reckon it was, then?"

"I think it must have been my boss," Alex said patiently.

"Funny thing, though," Terry said. "He said he was looking for Sandra, I didn't know who he meant, but he'd got your surname right. He said he'd be back later today."

She'd drawn the blinds, three evenings ago, and had gone back to Stewart's without opening them. The flat had the dusty, unobserved look of an ancient tomb, and an ugly smell, which turned out to come from their dinner dishes, left soaking in the sink, and an open carton of milk for their after-dinner coffee, which she'd forgotten to put back in the fridge. Alex opened the blinds and pulled open the glass doors to the balcony, did the washing-up quickly, rinsing out the carton of its clotted curds before throwing it in the kitchen bin. She put a couple of bottles of beer and some water in the fridge for later. She played the red-blinking phone messages; there were five, including one from Stewart's sister wanting to talk to her about her wedding next month— she'd turned down an offer to be a bridesmaid, knowing that it meant letting herself in for a dress like a peach-coloured meringue—two silent ones and a concerned message from Kevin, telling her to get some rest and come in when she was better. On the message, he called her Alex; she couldn't remember that he'd ever called her anything else. Then she went downstairs, got into her car and drove out to the supermarket to get some tuna and salad leaves for her dinner; it was nice to have an evening off from Stewart, once in a while. All the way there and all the way back she was practising what she was going to tell Kevin the next day about why she hadn't been in when he'd popped round to see how ill she was. In the end, she'd decided that the best explanation was that Stewart had come round and taken her back to his house for a bit of TLC and hot-lemon drinks. Actually, she wasn't sure she'd said to Kevin that she was home in the first place.

Alex was careless about shutting the front door to the building, and when she got out of her car, it was ajar. If Terry had seen that, he'd have another go at her. She'd overdone it in the supermarket as usual, and toiled up the three flights of stairs with two heavy bags in each hand. It was because of that that she didn't see the man until she was nearly at her landing, her face down. He was standing in an awkward, uncertain posture, not calmly waiting but edgily, as if his bones were somehow uncomfortable in his own skin. She had seen that stance before. It was like those moments when, in a place long become deeply familiar in all its aspects, a school, a workplace, a lover's apartment, an unexpected flash of memory, erupting perhaps from a single object, an irregular angle of vision, the first experience of that place is rendered again with complete freshness, the lost flavour of newness imbuing a long-known interior. To look at this figure, or at other figures like it, glimpsed or observed in a steely way on the streets of Sydney, was to make that mental journey in reverse. For years Alex had lived now in a nation of people who did not hang their heads over their bodies and look at the pavement; who did not move their limbs or smile in tentative and experimental ways, not quite sure whether their hard internal struc-tures and their softer surfaces would agree to move together to the same purpose. She had lived for years in a nation that moved without thinking about it, and stretched without considering the matter first in the beautiful sun; and she herself now moved in the same way. She did not feel it in herself; rather, she knew that she walked like a person who had once learnt to dance from the fact that she, her body, now never considered anything about the way she held herself, and her body moved with unconscious grace. What now seemed bizarre and out of its place in Australia—in Sydney, in Australia—on the third floor of an apartment block in Manly outside the door of her own apartment had once seemed like the normal state of existence. Englishness, with all its self-consciousness and its occasional brash, lapel-holding exuberance assumed for an occasion, was no longer as normal as it had been for years, and she looked at the man in his odd posture and his pale awk-ward skin with an immediate impression not just of Englishness but of estrangement. She didn't know him, but he, it seemed, knew her.

"Sandra?" he said.

"Who are you?" she said, setting down her bags on the tiled floor.

"It's Tim," he said. "Timothy. Timothy Glover."

"Remind me," she said, but with a faint stirring of memory. "And how did you get in?"

"I used to live opposite you, in Rayfield Avenue," the man said, disappointed. "I was only a little boy, though, when you left. I've changed a lot. I'm Daniel's brother."

"Oh, right," Alex said, and then, more graciously, "Sheffield. So— welcome to Australia. You should have phoned, though. Are you here on holiday?" He didn't, after all, have his bags with him. This was a call and not an in-person request to be put up for two weeks.

"I tried to phone," the man said, "but I never got anything but the answer-phone message. I thought it would be best," he said, picking up her shopping and waiting as she put the key in the lock, following her into the flat, "to turn up and surprise you."

"Always the best thing," Alex said. "Are you here on holiday?" she asked again.

"Where shall I put these?" Tim said. "I'm here for ten days. I flew in yesterday."

"It's nice to see you," Alex said. "But you should have phoned. I might easily not have been around, and it's not all that convenient now—I'm going to have to rush out in an hour or two." Her initial relief that the Englishman who had been turning up was not, after all, her boss Kevin, and she was not in trouble for bunking off work, was giving way to a suspicion that someone turning up in this way was on an unwelcome mission. For some weeks now she had been living with the uncomfortable sense of what people in Sheffield thought, clearly enough, she ought to do with her mother sick in hospital and, at first, likely to die. There hadn't been a reprimand, or a suggestion of how she ought to behave in the circumstances. But Alex had the impression that the only reason for that was that she was speaking to them over the phone. Things might be different if she was talking to anyone about it face to face. In her darker thoughts she had wondered whether somebody might turn up in just this way, on her doorstep in Australia, and bring her back forcibly.

"Well," she said, at a loss, and Tim was in no hurry to take a hint. "Why don't you sit down for the moment, anyway?" He was a very unlikely emissary. She could hardly remember him.

The last thing Trudy had said to him as he left the house was a hateful thing. "Well, have a good time," she had said. "Whatever you're supposed to be doing. I'm sure you've got some good reason."

"It's good to do our own thing from time to time," he had said, his suitcase at his feet. It didn't even sound convincing to himself.

"That's right," she said. "You know, I'll get in touch with Stig while you're away. I haven't seen him for years. We'll go down the Leadmill or something. Bye, then."

She had turned and gone upstairs, her crumpled grey espadrilles trodden down at the back and slapping against her yellowing heels. At the sixth step, she paused. He didn't know why he had thought that she might turn round and say something more sympathetic, something regretful and imbued with the love which ought to lie beneath their life together.

Trudy had known her duty, however. She had said the offensive, the really hurtful thing. Neither of them had seen Stig for years. When he and Trudy had first started seeing each other, Stig had taken the opportunity to insult them, one after the other, and then drop them. The insults had been on the grounds of ideology, but the intention beneath it was clear. And when they'd got married at the registry office, the invitation to the piss-up at the Frog and Parrot had come back, broadly scrawled upon with a passion which was quite unreadable. Tim couldn't understand it, but he understood the way that, on those occasional meetings in the street, Tim looked straight in his face with a thousand-yard stare before walking past in a chilly way. He wondered what would happen if Trudy really did phone him.

He'd forgotten about it by the time he reached Heathrow. The coach to London had been cheaper than the train, but the front door was wedged open by some hydraulic failure, its piercing alarm ringing for the whole six hours. He hadn't known how to get to Heathrow, and the underground was a nightmare of stairs and corridors with his heavy oblong suitcase. He seemed to be the only person in the world who, nowadays, didn't have a set of little wheels on his suitcase. And then Heathrow, the security, the awful piles of businessmen setting off with their little briefcases, the awful piles of holidaymakers drinking in the bars. He looked about for somewhere to sit; the gate of his flight had not been announced yet. But there was no-where; there was only shopping.

It was only the thought of Sandra, bobbing up insistently and joyously now at regular intervals, as often as a Bedouin thinking of water, that drew him on; that, and the irreversibility of the security screening. It was a long way to go, and this was a lot to subject your-self to.

Tim would not shop; he would only buy a sandwich. And if he had thought about it in advance, he would have made himself a sandwich. He went to the shiny sandwich shop, and bought one bacon sandwich. He ate it. Then, thinking about the journey, he went and bought another, and placed it in its cellophane wrapping in his old canvas shoulder bag. Airlines did not feed you enough, and it might be a good idea to buy some more food, to fill the gaps between one meal and another.

But between London and Singapore; at Singapore, where the emaciated chill of the air in the terminal indicated the thick hot wet blanket of air in the outside; and in the long sleep which overtook him between Singapore and Sydney, so that he woke only when over the vast red continent with only three hours to go; all that time he was not hungry. When they landed and were out of the plane, they were asked, all the passengers, to place their bags on the floor. A sniffer dog was let loose, and ran with unerring insistence up to Tim's bag. The three hundred passengers craned and stared. Tim blushed, and, as the security staff insisted, opened his bag. It was only a bacon sandwich; he'd quite forgotten. He thought that would be the end of the matter, but it was not. Did he not realize that it was a serious offence to bring food into Australia? What had he thought he was doing?

There was a relief, however, in the bacon sandwich as they took it away. There was no sniffer dog who could detect the thing which Tim was bringing into the country; the thing which he was bringing to Sandra. He didn't know what it was. But he could feel it inside him.

The patient was moved, in an ambulance with flashing lights driving at ten miles an hour, avoiding every road with speed bumps in it, and, though Bernie went with Alice, holding her hand and gritting his teeth in terror throughout that long hour, she was in the end moved from the ground-floor room at the Northern General to the fifteenth floor of the Hallamshire Hospital. She seemed perfectly calm throughout the transfer, as if there was nothing much to it, and her lack of concern insulated her from the close observation of everyone else involved. In the end she was installed in another private room, with large windows giving out over the great sweep of the valley, and the constant and steady alteration in her state continued in its unpredictable way.

Bernie did not admit any change in his own response; he went on visiting at exactly the same times, and in exactly the same way. His routine, and Francis's when he came up on a Thursday night, remained exactly as it had been for the previous weeks. It was Alice who was following a narrative of her own, an old-fashioned melodrama full of twists and turns, of unsuspected developments in the plot, of dangers threatened and averted, in which actions undertaken long ago came back to the surface and had unpredicted effects. They were the dullest members of an audience at, perhaps, an underattended Saturday matinée; the brilliant actress giving her all and taking them through the immense convolutions of a frankly implausible plot was in the bed at the Hallamshire.

Alice had started to try to speak again, though her mouth, for the moment, would not make the right noises. The noises she made sounded like her; they had her sweetness of tone and gentle enunciation, and even the rhythms of proper sentences, observations, questions, which to Alice were obviously perfectly sensible, and probably were. Her visitors could not understand what she was saying, and after a few attempts, Alice would assume a look of enraged irritation and sink back into her pillow, before starting again on another subject. She had always had lovely manners, and the need to entertain her guests with some conversation had survived, whatever else was lost from her personality. It was just that they couldn't understand what she was saying. That would improve, and there was talk of speech therapists in due course.

Bernie was more concerned with something he could not talk to the doctors about. Alice's conversational sallies were not directed at him; they were directed at everyone other than him. She had a new expression of great, child-like sweetness; she had never had a knowing look, exactly, but had acquired adult guarded expressions just as anyone might in the course of fifty-eight years. All that veiled social range of measured pleasure, measured interest, controlled boredom had gone. Alice now had the immediate expressions of a child, and when someone entered whom she was pleased to see, her face lit up with delight; it sometimes took her a moment to get there, but she greeted Katherine, Francis, even Anthea, even Daniel, even Helen with a beautiful smile and a look in her eyes of glowing enjoyment, which was that of a girl. Her boredom, too, could be open, though perhaps it was only tiredness, and they had to be careful not to talk across her, or—everyone noticed—to talk too fast or simultaneously. That called up an expression of pained distress, Alice's eyes flickering backwards and forwards and finally collapsing in exhaustion. The simplicity of her response was not indiscriminate: no nurse or doctor entering could create any delighted welcome in her eyes and mouth, and she tended to look at them in rather a snooty way, as if they were servants. That response was obvious to everyone, and the nurses and doctors tended to divert from their general cosy Christian-name assumed intimacy and call her "Mrs. Sellers" without hesitation, as if she were someone accustomed to a high degree of respect. Bernie wondered, sometimes, if he gave the impression, with his old London voice and unmistakably ordinary background, of being the devoted chauffeur of their patient, looking down her nose in a blunt and undisguisedly haughty way, like a child, or the Red Queen.

Because, in fact, though Alice greeted all her other visitors with unalloyed frank pleasure, her eyes grew cold and snubbing when Bernie came into the little room. If anyone else was visiting at the same time, she would try to talk to them, would listen to what they had to say with her eyes fixed in open pleasure on their face as long as her energy lasted. She would turn her eyes away from Bernie, and if she looked at him, there was always cold anger in her expression. Mostly, if he was there on his own, he would talk away, telling her about his day, about anything that crossed his mind, maintaining cheerfulness and telling her how well she was doing. "Keeping her spirits up," he called it to himself. He didn't want to admit that her spirits seemed high when anyone but him was around.

The nurses and doctors started to try to divine her state with Alice's own help, and took to asking her searching questions to find out what had happened to her, or perhaps what knowledge now remained to her. Bernie liked this twice-daily oral exam, and particularly the one question: "Alice, could you tell us who the prime minister is?"

He thought that was funny; and Alice answered promptly. It was difficult to understand the long sentence she brought out. Perhaps it was "There was an election last year," or "Still the same one as it was this morning," or something similarly dismissive, but she made an effort and you could hear, through the muffled noises her tongue could make, the rhythm, at least, of "John Major." The nurse made a satisfied tick, and went away.

"We've just reinstated that one in the last couple of years," a nurse explained, when Bernie asked. "We found that however badly damaged a patient's mind was—even patients with quite advanced Alzheimer's—they always seemed to know that it was Mrs. Thatcher. And until quite recently you couldn't base much on them not remembering immediately that it was John Major. People with nothing wrong with them went on saying Mrs. Thatcher before remembering and correcting themselves, for a year, eighteen months. There was a doctor even who said once, 'I'm going to write to the prime minister—she'll do something,' without thinking about it."

"I know what you mean," Bernie said. Alice, who was listening to this, lay with her eyes angrily up to the ceiling, seemingly determined not to make any contribution, even by listening. If she could have stuck her fingers in her ears, she would.

In the course of a couple of weeks, Alice's speech cleared a good deal, like thick dark stormclouds after rain, and you could understand what she was saying. It turned out that her response to the prime-minister question was "It's still the same one, unless there's been an election since this morning." The curt and manorial style towards the nursing staff turned out not to be a wrong impression, and Alice's instructions to them, her comments on the food had a highly irascible quality. The staff, one confided in Bernie, thought Alice a perfect hoot and a love, and the more *grande dame* she grew, the more it seemed to amuse them and make them fond of her. Bernie didn't feel the same way. It broke his heart to see her turn away from him so pointedly, to reject him with every gesture and look at her disposal. He had always thought that a pretentious and meaningless thing to say, "to break your heart." Hearts did not break; no one died of a broken heart. People died of falling off ladders, of inadequately insulated plugs, of hair-dryers, but they did not die of a broken heart, and when they suffered, it was from some other cause.

But, all the same, Bernie's heart was breaking. When, at the end of a long day of looks and tight-drawn lips, he got into the car to drive home, alone, he felt as if something had broken inside his chest and would never be mended. Something seemed to have shattered and splintered within his ribcage, and splinters had caught at the base of his throat. Sometimes, when nobody was by, he found himself bending over in pain and crying, useless meaningless self-pitying phrases coming to his lips and emerging, unheard by anyone. He would not do it in the hospital, or in front of anyone else, but sometimes, when he was alone at home at night, or once or twice actually in the car—he'd had to draw over to the side of the road and wait until the storm of weeping had passed over him—it took hold of him. There was no such thing as a broken heart, he told himself, not perhaps knowing what a doctor could have told him, that there was such a thing as a stress-induced cardiomyopathy when, through weeping, a patient's ventricles could rebel against their casing, could imitate anything up to a myocardial infarction; he did not know that, in fact, there was such a thing as a broken heart, though his heart was doing its best to tell him so.

Nothing like this had ever happened between him and Alice, all the years of their marriage, and this was the longest period they had ever spent apart. Apart, to Bernie, meant "apart at night." Night terrified him, now that the depth and breadth of his love and dependence was revealed to him, and he thought, over and over, of the first months of their lives together. He recalled in exact detail their first outings, to the pictures, for a coffee in an espresso bar, to the youth-club dance. He remembered how lovely she had looked in her boned dress, full-skirted with a fitted bodice, swirling out when they danced, the feel of the heavy ruched white cotton under his hand, white cotton with a print of electric blue Himalayan poppies all over it. He remembered that dress much better than her wedding dress; the wedding itself had been a blur, and now was reduced to nothing more than what the photographs had recorded. He remembered the different stages of their relation-ship, going from single outings to courting, and then her coming home to meet his mother and Uncle Henry, her sitting down willingly and helping unpack the boxes of stockings, was it?, that his mother had acquired somehow and was going to make a profit out of through Mrs. Harris's market stall. How she'd done that cheerfully, only after-wards telling him she couldn't believe his mother made her way like that, but she'd liked his uncle Henry. And then the engagement; they hadn't had a party, as people tended to these days, and they'd known each other for what now seemed an incredibly short time, only six months before they'd got engaged, and in another six months they were married. That was thirty-five years ago. Ever since then he'd half taken her for granted, half existed in a state of astonished gratitude that had become utterly familiar, and only now was it being taken away from him. He'd thought he would lose it through the Insult, as the doctors called it, and now, quite unexpectedly, Alice was turning away from him, and he did not know why. In all those years she had never turned away from him. Most of all what broke his heart was, resur-rected in the purest clarity, the false memory of her in a red kilt with a big safety-pin and a grey jersey under a duffel coat, her breasts held separately and apart as the bras of the period did, coming through the door of his friend's party with two friends of her own and already laughing, and him looking at her and saying—and that must be a false memory—to himself, "I'm going to marry that girl." The first time he ever saw her.

The canteen at the Hallamshire was quite different in style from the one at the Northern General, and less brutally functional. There were trellises between tables, wound through with fake plastic ivy, and real potted plants on waist-high brass stands. Bernie had gone down there one Friday morning, and was sitting with a mug of coffee and a cheese scone. He had left Francis upstairs with Alice; she liked to have him to herself, Bernie thought, when he arrived after a few days, and he liked to see what progress she'd made in the few days since he'd seen her. It felt to Bernie that, in the weeks since the Insult, he and Francis had grown closer together than they had ever been before, but it was an intimacy of a peculiar kind. They had gone from not speaking openly to each other through reserve and restraint, the usual conditions of an English life, to a state in which nothing needed to be said because they both understood what the other was thinking, and what the other was dealing with. Bernie had said nothing to anyone, even Francis, about the way Alice was turning away from him. It seemed to him that it was paining Francis as much as it was him.

He had been in the canteen for an hour and a half, drawing out his cheese scone with a second mug of coffee—he had had breakfast, and in general he wasn't hungry these days—when Francis came in, looking around to find him. "I'm just going to get a coffee," he said. "Do you want anything?" Bernie waited, and in a moment Francis came back and sat down. He said immediately, "It's Mum. She's been thinking something, she hasn't told anyone. She just told me, though."

He had come in with Bernie that morning, and the difference in the way Alice greeted each of them had been marked. Bernie had disconsolately kissed her, Alice turning her cheek away as much as she could, and then said bravely that he'd leave the two of them to chat for a while and would be up in an hour or so. He'd left, and Francis, he said, just had to ask his mother what was wrong; the behaviour was so strange, and anything that suggested what the doctors had warned of, a change of personality, ought to be addressed rather than tactfully left alone. At first she had denied anything was on her mind; she conveyed to Francis that it seemed to her to be quite reasonable to be taking this attitude. She gave the impression that a "situation" had caused a rupture between her and Bernie, and nothing in this was her own fault.

Francis looked into his coffee, and then, haltingly, and with embarrassment, it came out. "It's some kind of delusion," he said. In the moment of the Insult, a fantasy had been planted in Alice's brain, and, with some kind of evil ingenuity, it had manufactured a grotesque explanation for the sequence of events that had ended with her lying in hospital.

"She doesn't believe, or she doesn't think she had a brain haemorrhage," Francis said. "I don't know whether she hasn't taken it in, or that she doesn't believe it."

"What does she think happened?" Bernie said, aghast.

Francis shuffled with his hands. "She thinks—sorry, this is a bit difficult," he said. "She thinks what happened was that you were both worried about me, that I didn't have enough money, or something, and agreed that you would both—that you would enter into a suicide pact. And she thinks she tried to do it but you decided that you wouldn't do it."

"That's—" Bernie said, but "ridiculous" didn't seem to cover it.

"Look, I've been explaining to her it wasn't like that," Francis said. "She can't remember—not just since the haemorrhage, but what was happening just before, with the cat and everything. Me bringing the cat up, I mean. I've been explaining to her what really happened."

"Is she all right now?"

"I don't know," Francis said. "She was quite angry at first, she thought you'd told me to tell her another story, but I told her that wasn't true. I talked to a doctor. They're going to explain to her again what's happened to her, that she couldn't possibly have done it to herself."

"I wish she'd said something," Bernie said.

"It's not easy," Francis said, and Bernie had to agree with that; he had seen how hard it was to talk even to your son about what you were feeling and what you believed, and there had been as little of that in his own marriage. The trust that had existed between them had been most beautifully unspoken, and there had never been any misunderstanding before. He had relied on silence and love, as Alice had.

Francis had arranged for a doctor to come and explain the facts to Alice, but it seemed as if he had broken Alice's belief with the conversation. He and Bernie came in together, Bernie feeling, of all things, shamefaced, and there was an immediate difference in the way Alice looked at him. She looked at him with quickness, alertness, surmise, and when he kissed her, she did not turn away from him. There was an expression of abashed silliness in her face, like a small child caught out and preparing an apology, and once they had talked it over in careful steps, and the doctor had come in to explain the events of the last few weeks, they felt that the worst of it had been dispersed.

It was difficult for Francis to tell his father this; as he went through the explanation, he felt like a headmaster laying out a child's wrongs. And Bernie felt this too, because he seemed to flush as if at something brought out into the open. There was nothing Francis could do: it was his plain duty to tell his father, and the doctor, what he had extracted from his mother. And the next day, as if to take the place of this delusion, another delusion arose. He arrived, and within ten minutes, his newly talkative mother was telling him that John Major had been pay ing a visit to the hospital the day before, that he had greeted her and asked her how she was. She was quite serious about it, making perfect sense, and by now Alice had returned so much to the state of reason that Francis found himself excusing himself, as if to go to the lavatory, and asking a nurse whether, by any chance . . .

For some reason, the delusion about the prime minister proved much harder to shift from Alice's mind than the one about her husband. She had let her belief about Bernie go swiftly, and gratefully, after a couple of anguished assurances; and there must always have been some deep-buried anchor of love in her which had known that he could not have done such a thing, that, indeed, whatever her brain was telling her, he had not. But Alice knew that the prime minister visited hospitals, and his name had been planted firmly in her mind by the twice-daily question; she grew insistent, then impatient, then finally angry with Francis when he maintained that her mind was playing tricks on her. These delusions continued; Bernie was better than Francis at securing agreement when Alice needed to be assured that she had had a brain haemorrhage and had not attempted suicide unsuccessfully, that the prime minister, but, oddly, never the Queen, had been speaking to her, that Sandra had visited the night before, after they had left. If it had been up to Francis, he would have humoured her, have allowed her to go on believing whatever she wanted to believe in that now borderless no man's land between memory and dream. It could do no harm. It was his father who firmly refused to stop correcting her. He had seen the nurses, who happily humoured her, saying, "That's nice," when she wondered out loud whether the prime minister had enjoyed his visit, and what prevented him saying the same sort of thing was the fact that, as they said, "That's nice," even though they were by Alice's bed, they raised their voices and enunciated. There was nothing wrong with Alice's hearing. It was just their habit when talking to anyone old or demented, and it was the raise of the voice that convinced Bernie and made him insist to Francis that to give way to Alice was to give up on her. So they went on correcting, and gently insisting, and Alice, finally, would allow her delusion to be erased. Once it had gone, she never went back to it; but there was no shortage of others to replace it.

To Francis, his mother was running through the literary genres, one after another, and after a long period in which she was a baffling complex of clues, laid out like a room for the forensic reconstructive narrative of a Sherlock Holmes, after a period when, in her reawakened state, she spoke the murmurs and cryptic nonsense of an Imagist poem, after the nineteenth-century limelit melodrama, the collapses and the unexpected revivals, of her attack and its consequences and the *bildungsroman* of her slow improvement, there seemed here to be a science-fiction epic of the most abstruse, tawdry and terrifying variety. It seemed to Francis that his mother was in some H. P. Lovecraft fantasy of body-snatching and remote control, in which thoughts, beliefs, a whole new external world were being inflicted on her by some malevolent outside power. The world had been erased, or partly erased; what was familiar to her had been extracted and placed within a new, unreal world of delusions and phantoms. It was not, however, from outside that this parallel narrative was being imposed: it was coming from within Alice, as her passively receiving and interpreting brain burst all its bounds, as love or blood or rivers did, and finally created a world for her. They would recede in time, the doctors said, and took not much specific readerly interest in even the most elaborate of Alice's constructions.

The alternative narrative taking place for Alice, in which an attempt at suicide, foiled, was rewarded by visits from the prime minister and, perhaps most upsettingly, from Sandra, tormented Francis in his three-day weekends, and in the end he thought, were he to write any of this down, he did not know whether he would choose to describe what had happened to him, or whether he would go on being the creator of the Gurganian Empire, and follow his mother's sad and consoling delusions. Her beliefs, it seemed to him, made more narrative sense, had more narrative power, than what had actually happened; and, more than that, they contained within them some promise of redemption and defeat. The doctors were talking about the insertion of a tiny silver coil, to seal the source of the bleed. That seemed a fiddly result, a solution dramatic only to one who was actually present, compared to the bounding heroes so clearly implied and required by the account his mother's brain was giving of the thing which had happened to it, to her.

"But what about love?" the man who had called himself Timothy said. He was glittering as if with fever. The end of his nose, the corners of his glistening eyes, his mouth plumped with a rush of blood—pink as a white rabbit's. "Have you thought, ever in your life, about that? What about love?"

"Oh, for Christ's sake," Sandra said, bravely in the circumstances. "Go fuck yourself."

They glared at each other.

The sun had long since set. For a while, she had been switching on one small lamp after another as the hours had gone by and the room sank into gloom. Each time she had done so with a feeling of being permitted to do so, as if he were her jailer in her own home, his eyes following her as she got up and turned on a light. From the restaurant terrace in the street below the calls of waiters had been succeeded by its usual music starting up—the old rumba you got so familiar with, night after night—and now the ebb and flow of conversation from its arriving crowd of customers. From the front, a block or two away, could be heard the hooting of car horns leisurely crawling up and down, promenading like humans. The phone had rung twice in the previous hour and a half, and it had been Stewart. The first time he'd left a message, the second time he'd put the phone down without speaking, though she'd known it had been him. She hadn't made a move to answer the phone, and now, as it started ringing again, she decided not to answer the phone, not to make any kind of sudden move.

"We'd get on a lot better," she said, after a long, conciliatory silence, "if you'd just sit down."

"I don't think so," he said in the end. He was, quite firmly, between her and the front door.

An hour and a half before, she had let him into her flat, had said, "Remind me," with a faint stirring of memory. "And how did you get in?"

"I used to live opposite you, in Rayfield Avenue."

"Oh, right," Sandra said. "Sheffield. So—welcome to Australia. You should have phoned, though. Are you here on holiday?"

"I tried to phone," the man said, "but I never got anything but the answer-phone message. I thought it would be best to turn up and surprise you."

"You've certainly done that," Sandra said. "Are you here on holiday?" she asked again.

"Where shall I put these?" Tim said, holding her bags of shopping. "I'm here for ten days. I flew in yesterday."

"It's nice to see you," Sandra said. "But you should have phoned. I might easily not have been around, and it's not all that convenient now—I'm going to have to rush out in an hour or two." She paused and looked at him. "Yes," she said slowly. "Yes, I remember you."

He stared at her. "I never thought you wouldn't."

"Well, I do."

"You sound—" He stopped, looked away from her, as if thinking of the right word.

"I've got to sound pretty Australian," Sandra said. "I know, if that's what you were about to say."

"Australian?" Timothy said, turning with a wild expression in his eyes.

"Is it the jet lag?" Sandra said, and tried what she used to call, jokingly, a light sociable Manly laugh. This was an old acquaintance, dropping in from England. "You seem pretty confused. It can really mess with your head. You're in Australia."

"That wasn't what I was going to say," Timothy said. "When you said—what you said—and I said—I said you sound—you sound like it's surprising, like it's some feat of memory that you remember me at all. I wasn't going to say you'd got an Australian accent."

She wandered over to the kitchen, kicking off her shoes against the breakfast bar, poking them back upright with her toes as she went. She opened the fridge door and began to put away the groceries, which Timothy had left on the kitchen counter. "Do you want a beer?" she said. "They're cold."

"No thanks," he said.

"Well, I'm going to have one, if you don't mind," Sandra said. She wondered what she was supposed to do with this guest; how she could get rid of him. In his behaviour it seemed as if she had invited him round, and instead of him explaining what the hell he was doing there, he was waiting for her to unveil the surprise outing she'd planned. She could hardly remember him; there was an obvious explanation for why he was here, but she couldn't imagine he was a likely ambassador from any source. She'd half expected someone to appear like this, but she'd expected, really, her brother. "What are you doing in Australia?" she said, pouring the beer with a judicious eye down the inner slope of a glass.

"It's hard to say," he said.

"I know what you mean," she said. "I don't know why I came to Australia. I just came and I stayed. I thought there'd be kangaroos everywhere. That's the only idea I had of Australia. But I stayed anyway. Have you just got here?"

"Yes, only this morning."

"You *must* be jet-lagged," Sandra said, sitting down on the edge of an armchair. "And you came straight over to see me?" She had a bit of a sinking feeling. "I'm really flattered."

"I thought I wouldn't waste time."

"And are you going to travel?" Sandra said, seeing in this a way to turn this obviously pointless visit into a purposeful one, and to get rid of what might be a clinging self-invited guest to Perth, Darwin, the outback, Ayers Rock, or Uluru, as it was called these days.

"I hadn't thought," Timothy said, and tried a smile in response to hers. Like those trick two-dimensional portraits, his eyes followed her as she moved about the room, tidying up. "I've got two weeks. Where would you go, if you were me?"

She hadn't been a great traveller herself since she arrived here. "Well," she said. There'd been trips with boyfriends to the Blue Mountains, now and again. There'd been the odd week on the Gold Coast. A few times she'd had to go to Darwin or Hobart to sort out the regional offices there—she'd always meant to stay on in Tasmania especially. There'd been that bloke from Melbourne she'd met at Irene's—he'd been Greek, her cousin, not a dentist—who'd seemed quite interested. For his sake, she'd spent half a dozen weekends in that unexpectedly Manchester-like city of industrial magnates and over-endowed palaces of art and insurance; in the end, she'd concluded that she'd always have to spend evenings with him chewing over where he'd gone wrong with his ex-wife, and called an end to it. There'd been, too, a girls' week in Fiji—they'd all taken half a dozen different bikinis, one for each day and the white one for towards the end when they'd got really brown, where they'd seen nothing of Fiji except a vast piss-cloudy swimming-pool of inlets and artificial waterfalls and flumes and lagoons, densely fringed with skirted waiters bringing cocktails to a hell of a lot of other Australians. It had been a blast. "I'm not much of a traveller myself," Sandra said, "but you ought to see as much as you can. Ayers Rock. The Great Barrier Reef. The Blue Mountains."

Timothy's eyes went beseechingly over her face, not looking at her, but as if searching for imperfections. "I hadn't really made any plans," he said.

"I must have changed a lot," Sandra said. "Would you have recognized me?"

"Oh, yes," Timothy said, with fervour. "I'd have recognized you."

That look, as of a spaniel being promised a held-up biscuit, had not left the man's face since he'd arrived. It seemed to be exaggerated by the fact that he had nothing in his hands, not even a drink. Sandra got up hastily and, without asking, went to the kitchen cupboard. She got one of the heavy blue Czech tumblers for whisky and, without asking, filled it with ice and a mixture of lemonade and orange juice from a carton. "Try this," she said, handing it over as if the drink was some secret recipe, handed down through her family.

He took it with surprise, but he took it, and sipped it cautiously. His eyes never left her; she realized that she'd handed it over and stood there watching him, like a strict-but-kind nurse. It occurred to her that, after all, she only had his word for who he said he was: the grown-up version of a little boy she barely remembered. He could—she supposed—be anyone. Looking at his sallow awkward English freckled skin hanging off his cheekbones, his awkwardnesses at elbow and knees, she could discern no clue to a lost memory of anyone. She just could not call the face to mind; only a single memory.

"I remember," Sandra said slowly, "the first time I saw you, you were screaming and shouting."

"I don't know about that," Timothy said.

"I remember," Sandra said. "It was the day we were moving in. Your mother came out of the house with a snake in both hands, and you were behind her, trying to get the snake off her, and screaming your head off. And she sort of threw it down and stamped on it, and you went into hysterics."

"Yes," Timothy said. He looked disinclined to think of this as a funny episode. "I remember."

"It was the strangest thing to see when you're moving in somewhere new," Sandra said. "At first I thought—I didn't know anything about the North—at first I thought, just for a moment, that there must be snakes in the north, like in that story you read at school, with the mongoose, and your mother had just found one and thrown it out."

"That wasn't it," Timothy muttered.

"No," Sandra said. "I guess it wasn't."

"Are there snakes here?" Timothy said, and suddenly she saw him as he had been, grinding out questions like a rusty machine, hardly caring what the answer was, whether there was any answer.

"Not that you'd notice," Sandra said.

"Eight out of the ten most venomous snakes in the world," Timothy said, "live in Australia. And the most venomous of all is the inland Taipan."

"Is that a fact?" Sandra said.

"It is," Timothy said, coming out of what might have been a small trance of memory. "I'd forgotten I knew that. I used to be mad keen on snakes when I was a kid. That's what all that was about."

"The —" Sandra mimed Katherine, a snake above her head in both hands, flinging it down, stomping on the head, grinding her heel round "—whole performance? I never really heard the story."

"There wasn't much to it," Tim said briskly. "I got crazy about snakes. You know how some kids always have some passionate interest on the go."

"I guess so," Sandra said.

"Well, with me, it was snakes. I don't know why!"

"I wasn't accusing you of anything."

Tim shrugged, finished his lemonade and orange juice in a single gulp.

"I got interested," he said, in a more reasonable tone. "I read a lot about snakes. I used to dream of finding one of those English snakes, an adder or a grass snake, down on the lower crags, you know?"

The lower crags: something very like a memory started up in Sandra. It was as if, on an old automatic gramophone, the needle had come to the end of an LP, had lifted, returned, lowered and once more begun to play unsuspected, familiar strains. The lower crags: this man was who he said he was.

"But you never see snakes in England, or hardly ever," he went on. "You have to get exactly the right terrain, and not often even there. So when I say I was interested in snakes, I mean I read about them in books. I borrowed books from the library—there was one I didn't take back for a year and a half, and then I didn't take it back, my mum found it and took it back, and I didn't get any pocket money for a whole year, really, not just a threat, I really didn't. I used to sit up and learn all their names, their Latin names, the inland Taipan is *Oxyripidus* something. I found out all about their habitats and what they ate, and how endangered they were, because most snakes are endangered to some degree. But mostly I wanted to have one of my own. Not a venomous one, I wanted a yellow python, and you could get them in this shop in Sheffield I knew about. I knew my mum and dad would never let me have one—well, my dad, maybe, he's got his hobbies and interests, he'd have understood, but my mum never would have. I saved up for about two years, I reckon."

"That was before you had your pocket money confiscated, I suppose," Sandra said, not greatly interested.

"Yes, of course," Timothy said. "That all happened long afterwards. I'd forgotten about the library book by then."

"Oh dear," Sandra said.

Timothy looked at her; she buried her expression in a glass of beer. "It wasn't enough, though, I had to make up in other ways. I took a couple of pounds from my dad's wallet every now and again. And then once, this never happened to me before and never since, I just found a five-pound note on the Manchester Road. You know how children are, how superstitious, and I thought that meant I was supposed to buy the snake. But of course my mum, she'd never have let me have one, so at first I just asked the man in the shop if I could have a snake of my own, there, to visit, which he wouldn't sell. And he did, and I went down there, but after a bit, you have to have the snake with you all the time, don't you? So I had to sneak a vivarium into the house, and put it under my bed, and then finally, when I knew no one was going to be at home, I went and collected Geoffrey, he was called Geoffrey, he was a yellow carpet python. I thought I'd be able to keep him there without anyone noticing, feed him on frozen mice, you get frozen mice from pet shops quite easily."

"Are they still frozen when the snakes eat them?"

"No, you defrost them first," Timothy said. "And some snakes won't eat dead mice at all, you have to feed them live ones. So I had this snake underneath my bed, and I suppose it was starting to smell a bit in there, quite quickly—my brother, Daniel, he went on about it. And then one day I thought I'd take Geoffrey out to show him the new people moving in opposite—"

"Oh dear," Sandra said. "I knew this was all going to be my fault somehow."

"It's not your fault," Tim said. "It was your mum, she saw Geoffrey and she told my mum, without knowing he was a secret, and then, well, you saw the rest." ·

"Right," Sandra said. They were silent for a moment. Sandra remembered not so much that, but that Katherine's husband had run off, that that was the first thing she'd announced, and a week later he was back again. It had taken ages for them to speak to each other, the two families, without embarrassment. For Timothy it was all about his stupid snake. "How is everyone in Sheffield, anyway?"

"Well," Timothy said. "You know, I think I will have a drink. A proper one." Sandra got up, and without asking further, fetched him a beer from the fridge, handed it to him with a fresh glass. "Your mum—well, you know about your mum . . ."

"Yes," Sandra said. This was what she had been expecting, and she sat down heavily, with a set look on her face. "She's making a good recovery. It was quite serious."

"It was quite serious," Timothy said. "They thought she was going to die, my mum says."

"She's recovering well," Sandra insisted. "My dad's been keeping me up to date. I would have come over, but I don't know what I could have done and, thank God, it worked out for the best."

"You know," Timothy said, "I don't think anyone understands why you didn't make more of an effort. It looked to most people as if you didn't care."

"Or it's working out," Sandra said. "She's getting better all the time. She'll be leaving hospital before too long. I'll come over soon. So people like you can just—"

"It didn't look very good," Timothy said. "People were surprised."

"Oh, for heaven's sake," Sandra said. "Who was surprised?"

"Well, most people," Timothy said. "Most people were surprised that you didn't come over. That's what I meant."

"I can tell you, my dad completely understood," Sandra said, who knew exactly what Timothy had meant, having expected it for some time. "He said straight away, he's gone on saying, he didn't expect me to come over."

"That's exactly what you would say in the circumstances," Timothy said. "I don't know whether he would have meant it."

"It's my dad," Sandra said. "I know whether he'd have meant it or not. I tell you something else. I know very well he wouldn't in a million years have asked you to come over and try to make me feel guilty. He wouldn't have asked you, and he wouldn't want to make me feel guilty. I don't know why you're here."

"I'm on holiday," Timothy said. "I happen to be here on holiday. I thought I'd drop in and keep you up to date."

"I don't believe it," Sandra said. "It's really none of your business, the whole thing. I'd rather not talk about it."

At this point, the telephone rang. "Excuse me," Sandra said, getting up, but Tim got up too. For a moment she thought he was, in some mistaken gesture of kindness, going to answer the telephone on her behalf, but before she could reach it, he grabbed her shoulder.

"Don't get that," he said.

"Don't you tell me—" she said, and twisted in abrupt rage—it was there so quickly, she must have been building up to it—and he gripped more firmly. Her blouse tore.

"Jesus, what the fuck do you think you're doing?" she said. "You've torn my fucking blouse."

The phone message came to an end—. . . *if you want to leave a message, speak after the beep* . . . and Stewart's voice started up, in the echoey acoustic of his shop. He just wanted to know what she was up to; she stood, furious, and held herself back from slapping Timothy.

"I think you'd better go," she said, as the phone message came to an end. "I don't know what you're doing here, or what you want, but I think you've said it all. That was my boyfriend."

"You've got a boyfriend," Timothy said, smiling.

"Yes, why shouldn't I?" she said. "I might even have a husband for all you know."

"No," Timothy said. "I would have known that."

"Look, you've made your point," she said. "I sincerely hope you really were coming to Australia on holiday. You've come a hell of a long way otherwise to be told something you're blaming me for is none of your business. It's none of anyone's business. All right?"

But Timothy made no move to go. He picked up a corner of the rent cloth, quite delicately, but as if he knew he could make a more decisive gesture, and let it drop again. He sat down, quite heavily. She remained standing, waiting for him to take the hint. Outside, in the street, it was growing dark; she switched on a light, returned to her cross posture. He smiled again, not looking at her.

"I expect you're probably wondering what I've been up to for the last few years," Timothy said. "I was only a little boy when I saw you last. I got interested in radical politics when I was still at school.

It's injustice that makes you burn, the injustice, it's in schools and you can see it, but it's everywhere, more hidden. I got eight O levels and four A levels, I did A levels in economics and history and German. And general studies. I thought I'd take German to read Marx in the original, but I never got to that point. I didn't do so well in German as I did in the others, I got a C for that, I got As for the others. I *could* have gone to university."

"Nobody's suggesting you couldn't," Sandra murmured, fingering her torn blouse, trying to see if it could be fixed, but it was no good: he'd bring out this triumph, he was going to introduce himself by summing up his life, give her the sense of the right he had to talk to her in this way. He talked over her as if she'd said nothing. She wondered whether he was like this with everyone he met; she thought, frighteningly, that this was probably a special occasion.

"I *could* have gone to university but I decided not to, not at first. I thought the radical moment had come, this was in 1984, there was no point in entering an institution to destroy it from within, it was going to be destroyed from outside within months, that's what we all thought in 1984. But the timing was wrong—that was all, it was the timing—we'd misread the signs. The popular movement fizzled out. So I went to university a couple of years late, and I—I went to the polytechnic in Sheffield, I wanted to stay, I had ties there. I *did all right*." This came out belligerently, and, like weather figures in a box on a wall, Sandra now sat down as Timothy stood up, paced around hectoring. "I got a first, I did social sciences. And then I got a master's and a PhD, and I got that in three years, writing about Goffman, Erving Goffman. You probably don't even know who that is, do you? Even though I started late I was still only twenty-seven when I finished and got the doctorate. I'm Doctor Timothy Glover, it says it on my passport. And they gave me a job teaching at the polytechnic—it's a university now, it's called Sheffield Hallam University. I've been doing that for two years, teaching there. I'm still involved with radical politics, only not so much with direct action. I'm getting so I can't run from the pigs like I used to. It's your blinking knees what go first, isn't it, it's always the knees first. Ooh, me knees—"

"You've still got some passionate interest on the go, then," Sandra said, pale with anger. But he ignored her, and she fell silent, not laughing as he faked a moment of hopping round her living room. She watched the performance; watched, too, the little china figurine on the glass occasional table. She hoped the idiot wasn't going to kick it over.

He subsided at length, straightened up, and gave her a look that went through all the stages; embarrassment, assessment, contempt. "That's what I've been doing," he said. "It's been quite a long time, you see."

"What happened in 1984?" Sandra said.

"Pardon?"

"You said something important happened in 1984," Sandra said. She could, with concentration, have worked out the events of that year, so famous, so anticipated, in advance, and so unlike its previous billing. For her, it could only have been one in a succession of years during which she relaxed, inch by inch, her body, her way of speaking, the tension of her former smile, all giving way under the blazing sun on a beach, on white and gleaming city streets full of well-dressed healthy people, under many nights of fresh and unrecognized stars. No: 1984, surely, was the year she gave up working at Belinda's and started work at the place she now worked at. It had been ten years ago. "What happened to you in 1984?"

Timothy wheeled round, as if at a dumb student request for something that had been covered earlier in the degree module. "It wasn't to me it happened," he said. "I'm talking about the miners' strike. The miners. You know. They went on strike."

"I heard about that," Sandra said. "I think I did. I was living such a long way away, though."

"Let me explain it to you," Timothy said heavily—he might have been talking with laborious irony, she just couldn't detect it any more. But this was certainly a step too far, and she interrupted him.

"Look," she said. "I really have no idea why you've come to see me. I really don't have any idea why you're still here. I don't remember you, not really. If you're on holiday here, it's nice of you to look me up. It's nice to see people from England, if they come. But that's all. My mother's got nothing to do with you. I've managed for ten years without knowing the ins and outs of some strike or other, so I guess I'll go on managing. You've burst in, you've assaulted me and torn my clothes. That seems like quite a lot in order to tell me about the miners' strike. Just tell me now what the result was, and I'll be happy enough with that."

The phone rang again. She made no move to answer it; he held her steady gaze. The message started up, then abruptly stopped; Stewart again.

"The result?" Timothy said, into the silence in the flat. "The result of what?"

"The miners' strike," Sandra said. "Who won?"

"It's not really a matter of—"

"Did the miners get what they wanted? What they were striking over?"

"No."

"So I guess the managers won, the coal company."

"It wasn't a company. It was the Government."

"I told you, I'm not interested."

"The thing is, it was really your father—do you know what he did? He was in charge of what they called strategy. He piled up coal—he made sure the miners wouldn't be needed, that they could be laid off for a year and save all that money there without any effects, and afterwards—"

There was a violence now in Timothy's accelerating certainties, his hands clenching into fists, unclenching, fist hitting palm as he made his point to a seated audience of one. As he strode and hit his fist into palm, his fist into palm, she concentrated hard on not blinking at each blow. She brought her knees together, and her ankles, tilted her legs to one side in self-protective lady-like posture. She placed her hands together in a praying position, or like a child about to applaud. She held her eyes wide open, and as he smacked his fist into his palm, she did not flinch, she did not blink.

"And afterwards—"

"Afterwards, what?"

"The thing is," Timothy said, lowering his voice a little, "the ironic and awful thing is that your father, he worked so hard to dismantle and sell off what belonged to everyone, because, you know, everything's so much better if they can make money out of it. Everybody buying and selling and boasting about what Sid told them and ending up with two hundred and sixty pounds worth of what used to be a public utility, you see, and then in the end, your father, his wife's brain turns on her and he doesn't think twice, he goes to the National Health Service, of course he does. Because most important things, they're run by the state for the people. You know something? What's the safest airline in the world?"

"I know the answer to this one," Sandra said. "I just don't have a buzzer in front of me, I'm afraid."

"It's Qantas," Timothy said. "It's the only major airline which has never had a crash. And who owns that? It's the state, isn't it?"

"No, it's not," Sandra said. "Even I know that. It got privatized last year. I bought some shares in it."

"Bully for you," Timothy said. "Let's see if it goes on being so safe now it's been denationalized. I hope you're on the first fucking plane that goes down because they've forgotten to tighten the bolts, and I hope you're on the way to visit your mother, finally, when it goes down."

"I've no idea what you're talking about," Sandra said. "And you can leave my mother out of it."

"Don't you see, though?" Timothy said, working himself up again. "It's all the same thing. Your mother, and you not caring and sitting here buying your little shares to enrich yourself by a few extra Australian dollars and not thinking about anyone else, and everything that was once for the common good, all that being thrown away to make a quick buck, it's all the same thing. My God, though, I might have known about you. You just don't care about anyone else. Let me tell you about me. I fell in love with someone, and I've been with her for nearly ten years, she's called Trudy, and we're together because we can care about each other, and we've got that ability, we care about each other and we care about people we know and we care about people we don't even know. It's all about love, in the end."

Timothy continued hitting his fist into his palm, almost in Sandra's face. She shrank back in her chair; he was standing halfway between the chair and the telephone, which now started ringing again.

"Better get that," he said, but she shook her head. He waited, as if politely, at this interruption, until the message started again and the caller hung up.

"Let's talk about you, on the other hand," he said. "Who do you care about? Not your parents or your family. You don't care about Daniel, who's supposed to be such a good friend of yours. I don't believe you care about anyone except yourself and the *dividends* you're going to get from some airline sell-off."

"That was my boyfriend on the phone," Sandra said. "You know nothing about me, nothing at all."

"You don't care about him, either," Timothy said. "I bet you don't. If you cared about him, you'd have answered the phone by now."

"I'm not answering the phone because you're here," Sandra said.

"I tell you, there's something missing in your life," Timothy said, "and it's love. Do you ever think about love? In the whole of your life, have you ever thought about love?"

"Oh, for Christ's sake," Sandra said. "Go and fuck yourself."

There was a long silence; they glared at each other.

"We'd get on a hell of a lot better," Sandra said, "if you'd sit down."

Timothy looked at his hands, clenched into fists and then, quite at once, without seeming to know what he was doing, he dropped on his knees, and started to cry in an entirely helpless way. She watched, uncaring, knowing that her disinterest in the spectacle would inevitably look like proof of what he had said. She waited for the storm to subside. Outside, the world, incredibly, was going about its business: teenagers with borrowed cars were driving up and down the dark front, hooting in greeting; dinners were being eaten by families and couples to a rumba soundtrack in the street below; Stewart was wondering, not very hard, where his girlfriend could have got to; perhaps her boss, now, was talking in his English voice to his Korean wife, Cindy, perhaps even saying that there was some kind of flu going round the office and that Alex had gone down with it. All that was happening outside, and inside her flat she was looking at a man crying and crumpling.

"Do you know what you've done?" he said in the end, wiping his reddened face with an angry wrist. "You've ruined my life. You really have."

"I don't know how you work that out," Sandra said. "I've done nothing wrong. Even now, you're not going to be in any trouble if you go and I never see you again. Not serious trouble. You just get up, and go back to your hotel and change your flight, fly back to England tomorrow and just accept that you never achieved whatever it was you thought you'd achieve by turning up here like this. I don't understand but, let me tell you, you're on a bit of a winning streak at the moment. If you just turn round and go now, I'm not going to tell anyone that you were ever here. I haven't ruined your life. That's a stupid thing to say."

"Not today," Timothy said, his face and eyes reddened, sore and gleaming. "It wasn't today you ruined it. You ruined it a long time ago. You don't know what it's been like, the last fifteen years, almost twenty years. You don't know what it's been like, living in my head. Every day, to wake up knowing that at some point there you are in my head, there you're going to be, fucking. Fucking Daniel, and then fucking someone else, fucking men, one after another, just bodies, I couldn't invent the faces, fucking the whole of Australia, fucking everyone, only not me, it's never going to be me."

"You're out of your fucking head," Sandra said. "This is some kind of joke, yeah? I never knew you, Timothy. I spoke to you about two times in my life. There's no way you could have been wanting to fuck me for the last fifteen years." She fingered, once more, the blouse torn at her shoulder, showing her bra strap and four square inches of shoulder flesh; she thought about going into the bedroom and changing into something, anything—a cape, a poncho, if she had one, a nun's wimple. But she wouldn't take off any of her clothes now with Timothy in the flat.

"It's all about fucking," Timothy said. "My brother fucking anyone he wants because he can, and Stig, the same, and my sister having a baby with her husband, they're at it all the time, and my mum, even, she fucked that man she worked in a flower shop with, I know she did. And me, what about me? I've only ever had sex with Trudy, the whole of my life. It's you I've been thinking about the whole time and now you say you don't even remember me, you think you only ever spoke to me twice, it's not true, it's not true."

"Who the hell's Stig?" Sandra said.

Timothy looked at her, startled. "It doesn't matter," he said in the end. There was a long silence between them, broken by a burst of raucous girls' laughter from the street. It came as a shock to her, the Australian sound of it. She might have been in Sheffield again for a moment, and the conditioned air a clean breeze off the moors. "Can I sit down?"

"No," she said. "You're going."

"You really don't remember," he said.

"I have no idea what you're talking about."

"And now you say you can't remember me, that you only ever talked to me twice," Timothy said. "You really don't remember."

"No, I don't remember anything in particular," Sandra said, although this was growing less and less true by the moment. "You were just at the end of the table when I came round for dinner—I only came round about twice—and that was it. You just sat and talked about what you'd been doing at school."

"You *can* remember," Timothy said. "You can remember one day—I don't know why you were there, but you were upstairs in the spare bedroom on your own. You don't remember? And you were lying on the bed and asked me in. You must have been fifteen, I'd be—what— ten? And your blouse was undone, and you lay back and undid it some more. Do you remember now? Do you?"

"You're making it up," Sandra said, but she felt less sure now. "This is just your sick fantasy. No one would be like that with a ten-year-old."

"Oh, but you were," Timothy said. "You undid your top and you let me undo your bra. Do you want corroborative evidence? I remember your bra, it undid at the front, I'd never heard of such a thing, I'd only ever seen my mum's bras in the washing basket, and they fastened at the back. I thought all bras did. I reckon it was a new thing, around then. If you don't remember me, do you remember buying a front-fastening bra? I bet you do. Do you want more corroboration? Your back was really spotty. I hadn't expected that, either."

"You should just go now, fuck off, go," Sandra said, with a sense of her own bravery. If she herself didn't say it, didn't remember it, none of it was true. Just now the spare bedroom upstairs in the Rayfield Avenue house, Sheffield, England, seemed not just remote and long ago, but nothing more than a fantasy of Timothy Glover's. He had dreamt the whole vanished country up, had invented her motivations and reasons from twenty years ago, had derived from his fantasies further fantasies, believed it had all happened. None of it ever had. He had dreamt up reasons why she had done it, and made it all real in his own head. All the same, she remembered the front-fastening bra: she'd bought it in Chelsea Girl.

"I'll fuck off when I'm finished," Timothy said. "I've waited long enough for this. You don't even know what I've been through. You haven't given a moment's thought to what you did. Don't you remember? You let me take off your bra, and you took off your shirt, and you pushed my face down between your tits."

"Listen to yourself," Sandra said. "You'd never have thought people might actually enjoy doing it."

"You'd have let me fuck you," Timothy said insistently.

"You were ten years old," Sandra shouted. "You weren't physically capable of it."

"Yes," Timothy shouted. "I was ten years old. Do you honestly think it's right to behave like that to a ten-year-old boy?"

"Ah, fuck off," Sandra said. "Like you give a shit. Like you regret that happened to you. Like you wouldn't have got round to hating women anyway, you little shit. Like I wasn't a child myself. You really are a stupid fucking twat. What harm did it do you that you wouldn't have done yourself?"

"You want to know what harm it did me? Let me tell you—"

"No, fuck off, shut the fuck up, I know exactly. Or I know in what ways you're fucked up that you're going to blame on me. You never got to fuck me because you were ten when the opportunity arose and the opportunity never arose again. And you've thought about it quite a lot. Don't tell me that all this—the plane ticket, the denunciation about not dashing back to be with my dear old mum in her hour of need, the miners' strike crap—don't tell me it's all because you never got a chance to fuck me? You're off your fucking head."

"It's more than that—"

"No, it's not," Sandra said. "OK, then. Let's put it right. You can fuck me now. I don't give a shit. I'm a grown-up, even if you're not. I've fucked a few men, one more won't make any difference. And then you get on the plane back to England and both of us get on with our lives. I promise you, you're not going to go on like this, once you've actually had sex with me. Whatever's in your head, I can't possibly live up to it. So, what about it, then? Hey? Hey?"

She went over to him, prodding him even as she unbuttoned her shirt.

"No," he said, backing away. "I don't think that's what I want."

"And ain't that a surprise?" Sandra said. With a grotesque wink, she hoicked one breast out of the tear in her blouse like an old stripper. "You're just like every other Communist in the world."

"I'm not a Communist," Timothy said. "I'm a Marxist. There's a difference."

"Forgive me for not giving a shit," Sandra said. "So you sit around going, oh, yeah, I really want to fuck Sandra, or I really want to live in a place run by the workers for the workers, but you only say that, you know it ain't gonna happen. That's a kind of luxury, don'tcha think, big boy? And let's say one day Sandra, she says to you, 'Go on, let's fuck, then,' because that's what you really want, or say one day, the workers' paradise suddenly turns up, it's really gonna happen. You know what a little shit like you's gonna say? You'd go, 'No thanks, love, you're all right.' You don't want that crap. You just say you do, like you tell your-self it's me who's ruined your life. It's just a bit easier to live your life like that."

"You don't know I don't want it all, not really," Timothy said bravely.

"Oh yes I do," Sandra said, "because nobody could. Now fuck off out of it, and think yourself fucking lucky you're not leaving here attached to a big black Sydney police officer."

She had manoeuvred both him and herself about the room, inching about and letting him give way to her. And there she was, by the breakfast bar, there he was at the door to the flat. She gracefully bobbed a curtsy and came back smiling with the business end of a kitchen knife pointing at his stomach.

"And one more thing before you go," Sandra said. "When you get back to England, tell your brother Daniel I want to come and eat in his restaurant some time. I hear it's a top night out."

Somehow, she had reached behind him as she spoke, and unhitched the front door, passing the carving knife from one hand to another. It was almost an embrace, this complicated move, juggling knife, door handle and Timothy. He found himself walking backwards through an open door, his face sore and his throat rawly snatching at itself in the aftermath of weeping convulsions. There was something in his way; his elbow caught something rough and sinewy and boned, which proved to be the mahogany-hued big-nosed face of an elderly Australian in singlet and skirt-wide shiny blue shorts, with an outraged expression and, behind him, a wife (unmistakably) peering out from the door opposite. He had been about to ring the doorbell of Sandra's flat.

Timothy extracted himself sideways, and Sandra readjusted her stance, evidently seeing that she was pointing a carving knife at her next-door-neighbour's chest. "You all right, Terry?" she said.

"What the hell is going on?" Terry said. "All this racket, Alex, it's not like you, and—"

That was what he had prepared, and he had brought it out regardless. He hadn't expected to be greeted by a bellicose Sandra with a carving knife in her hand, and his comments died away as an—

"And I'm not sure we appreciate overhearing all this effing and blinding and—"

"That's right," the wife put in from behind, her arms folded. It seemed to Timothy that the situation of ultimatum, horrified prissiness and being-proved-right-all-along, in terms of the three different people about him, had frozen permanently, and, for themselves, they could remain in those postures, however extreme, indefinitely. It was up to him to bring the situation to an end, and it was only he who could do it.

"I'll be off," he said bathetically, not knowing how else to put it, and slid, head down, between Sandra and her neighbour, not looking at the neighbour's wife, and down the communal marble stairs, the segs on his shoes clattering on the marble as he went. He had brought no bag, and he went lightly. The door to the apartment complex was shut. He tugged at it uselessly, startling and then amusing a couple on the street side walking past, who stared at him on the other side of the glass door. He tugged again, before seeing to one side the green rubber plunger that unlocked it.

Outside, the warm floating air was a shock after the Northern brisk-ness of the building's air-conditioning—he could not say how long he had been inside. He looked about in astonishment. It seemed like the world was coming to an end. It looked to Timothy like the world as it was before Christ came to it, or Marx. Above him only the blazing angry sky of stars, the jumble of familiar and unfamiliar and shaken-up and distorted and the completely new, all in a blaze of stage-effect. And then around him, a crowd of pleasure, going about their unblamable business, festive, clean, laughing—they looked, all of them, so stupid. They were so stupid. A crowd out for fun, and none of them, not one, was drunk. Timothy, though, he felt drunk, and soiled, and stared-at, as a filthy tramp might be in an ordinary Sheffield street. He looked down at his hand; it was red with gripping. Across the road, there was a restaurant, and a terrace, and a thought, a sensible thought occurred to him. He could get something to eat. He stumbled over and stood for a moment between two miniature trimmed bay-tree bushes. He could see the waiters inspecting him, talking to each other, and finally one came over—obviously delegated. He approached so upright, in his blinding white shirt and ballgown-like apron, right down to his ankles over his black trousers, that Timothy almost cringed.

"Can I help you?" the waiter said; he was dark and good-looking, and his accent, now, was not Australian but French.

Timothy uttered his request.

"I'm afraid not," the waiter said. "Tonight—" He gestured at the full restaurant, the full terrace, the people enjoying themselves, all with their friends, their lovers, their lives on show.

Timothy turned away. It was a stupid idea, anyway. He could go back to the hotel and order something from the café in the foyer. Any-way, he wasn't hungry. But at the end of the road, he turned, not right back towards the ferry stop, but left towards the beachfront, where he had sat and waited for hours that afternoon, gazing out to sea, waiting for Sandra to come back. He felt so alone now that the thought of Trudy came like an irrelevance. If he were ever to be admitted to that enclave behind the bay trees, if he were ever to be less than alone, who would mitigate that loneliness? The thought of Trudy, standing with him just then, at the bay tree, both of them smiling and well-dressed and ungrievanced, struck him as an incredible fable. That would never happen. He went on walking. He seemed to see himself from outside, as these stupid, stupid handsome people saw him. He walked out into the road, between moving cars; but here on the seafront they were moving so slowly, cruising almost to the point of stasis, that they just slowed a little bit more, not hooting, just letting him pass as they were letting other people pass between them. He reached the other side, still seeing himself, grubby, shabby, hunched, through the eyes of the fit and stupid and rich and share-owning young of this seaside Arcadia, and there was an opening in the barrier.

He dropped through it, and on to the beach; the soft sand made an unexpected hard thud against the soles of his shoes. For a moment he thought of taking his shoes off, but realized he would need them on. That would help. The light cast by the seafront buildings, the flats, the shops, the offices, fell on to the near half of the beach. There was a group of surfers to one side, in the form of some mystic circle, a round of cross-legged devotees now the sea had subsided into dark, summoning up all the demons of the South with a glowing brand, passed from cupped hand to cupped hand. He would not go to them. He swerved away to the left, and as he walked further towards the sea, he walked, as it were, into darkness. "Hey, look at that guy," he heard one of the surfers say, unconcerned, but then someone else seemed to say something at the same time, either over there or nearer, perhaps within his own head. And then the texture underfoot changed, became softer and harder, more packed and more yielding simultaneously, then changed again as a shock of water washed over his shoes, ran inside, soaking his feet. It was only with that sensation that every other sensation clarified: the noise, which had been of traffic, clarified itself as the noise of the surf, and the smell, which had been the salt of barbecue and the smell of fish laid out in restaurant windows, gave way to the great wash of the sea. He did not know which was the sea here, the Pacific or what. The great Southern sea. It was nauseatingly warm. He went on walking, and he might have heard a voice behind him, calling from the surfers' group, but it sounded uninvolved, if it had spoken at all, and soon it stopped calling altogether. The sea was about his knees, his thighs, as he waded onwards into the dark. It pulled at his clothes with a dense suction. For a second he thought of his wallet, thick with advanced Australian dollars. He had had a use for them, and now they were in his pocket, being soaked by sea water. He made sense of his thoughts, and strode onwards, dragging the sea behind him like a cloak. The weight of sea water against his chest; he felt overpowered, and this was no longer a wade into the fringes of the ocean he had waited for, but a medium in which who knew what might live, things bigger and hungrier and more widely jawing than even an inland Taipan. And then the first wave—it must have been a wave that in day-light surfers would watch and wait for—struck him direct in the face. At the same time, something seized his ankles, pulling them out from under him, and he fell, his arms struggling against the sheer weight all around him, the roar like an audience's laughter in his ears. He began to change his mind; he thrashed out, but there was nothing to thrash against; and something now seized his legs like a rope, and it pulled him, down, into those whole unpurchased burdens of warm salt water. Hatloads of it, he said to himself, his mouth and his eyes open and fill-ing. Buckets.

One weekend Francis looked out of the window of his parents' house and thought the grass needed cutting. Bernie had never been much of a gardener, and many of the shrubs, which had now grown shapelessly leggy, or squat and shapeless, were actually the plants that had been left so many years before by the Watsons. They were the ones who had taken all the lightbulbs, a story told every high season and holiday by Bernie, with additions; for some years, in the retelling, he had been hurling himself to his knees as the last and youngest Watson exited the house, begging tearfully for at least one lightbulb in the downstairs toilet to shit by. It hadn't happened quite like that, and the Watsons'd left, at any rate, a few shrubs in the garden. There'd been an occasional addition, a camellia and some sticks, which you always forgot about until they put leaves out and flowered. But Bernie's gardening was on a different sort of scale to, say, Malcolm Glover's: he was forever ripping out trees and installing six-inch saplings that would only look like any-thing in thirty years' time. Bernie, on the other hand, had bought the camellia (for instance) already in bloom. He didn't get a great deal done beyond mowing the lawn.

When Francis noticed that the lawn was growing thick and shaggy, like a mane, he couldn't leave it for a moment longer. His situation, his and his father's, was in danger of turning into that horrible warning up the road: the house where the mother had died. It hadn't been painted for decades; there were weeds and unkempt growths in the front garden; the rubbish piled up in the front porch and was thrown into the long grass. It looked, actually, quite a lot like the house Francis lived in in London. It had happened here, in this neat street, because the mother had died and the father and son hadn't known how to keep it up. With the childish habit of naming things that had never left him, Francis called it the Sad House in his mind, just as Anthea Arbuthnot, whose name he knew perfectly well, had always been Nosy Woman.

Living as he did in a bedsit or three, Francis was conscious of the neatness of his parents' house. An ornament, once chipped, would never be allowed to stay on the shelf on the grounds that most of it was whole; a mug with a crack like a hair in it was promptly thrown out. Things here were looked after, and replaced. Unlike the Sad House, up the road, it wasn't his mother's sole attention that kept things like this: Bernie, too, was neat in his ways, couldn't bear disorder. "If you'd been in the army . . ." he used to say reproachfully, whenever he'd come across anything Francis or Sandra had dropped on the floor, a plate left dirty and unattended on a table. Perhaps it had been his two years' national service, decades ago, that had made him neat. Though he'd kept the house shipshape, the garden had passed him by, and the lawn had grown.

The fly-mower was kept in the garage, and Francis fetched it out one afternoon. When he took the cover off, the blades had been carefully wiped after its last outing. He set it on the long grass, and went inside to the utility room to plug the machine in. He must have knocked the on/off switch when taking it out; as he put the plug in, the machine started up outside, with a buzz and then a kind of stubby, choking series of grunts. The window upstairs opened.

"I don't think that's going to work," Bernie said. "I was looking the other day, I think the grass has got too long. Something more radical's called for."

"I could give it a go," Francis said. "Improve the look of it a bit anyway, if I gave it a once-over."

"It'll make things worse," Bernie said. "When the grass is as long as that, the fly-mower just tears it out by the root and it ruins the blades. I'm going to have to get a man in with a scythe."

Francis unplugged the mower, wiped the blades, wound up the coil, replaced the cover and put the mower back where it had come from.

But then he crossed the road to Mr. Glover, who, after all, knew about gardening.

"Hello, Francis," Mrs. Glover said, opening the door with a Saturday magazine in her hand and her reading-glasses on. "Have you been down to see your mum today? She seemed very cheerful yesterday."

"She'll be home in a week or two," Francis said.

"That seems quick," Mr. Glover said, coming to the door too. He had got, quite suddenly, a good deal older, his slightness and thinness developing deep ridges, and, when he smiled, the weatherbeaten quality of a retired jockey. He had never looked much like a jockey before; but now he looked like a retired one. He and Katherine, unexpectedly, had grown to look like each other: they could have been brother and sister. It was since she had had her hair cut short; it was practical, but quite flattering to her thin white hair. "They never let you hang around in hospitals, these days, do they?"

"They wouldn't be talking of sending her home unless they were completely sure," Mrs. Glover said. "They must be happy about the way the operation went."

Francis explained his errand.

"A scythe?" Mr. Glover said. "I'm not sure. I don't think you mean a scythe, that's an enormous two-handed job—one of those could take your legs off if you weren't careful. You want what we used to call a bagging hook—it's, what, a sort of sickle. The sort of thing you see medieval peasants walking around with in the films, you know, over their shoulders."

Francis thought it was the sort of thing Death always had, as well, but only said, "I don't suppose you've got one of those, then?"

"A bagging hook?" Mr. Glover said. "I used to have one, I know."

"One more piece of supposedly historic rubbish cluttering up the garage," Mrs. Glover said, much less surprised at this than might have been expected, "I'll be bound."

"Some of that stuff's very valuable," Mr. Glover said warmly.

"If you ever wonder why it is we have to keep the car outside in all weathers," Mrs. Glover said, gesturing to their new car with the rolled-up magazine, a surprisingly saucy four-door sports car in bright red, "that'll be because of all the very valuable stuff in the garage." She spoke casually; it was obviously a favourite topic of dissension around here.

"But the sickle," Mr. Glover said. "It's not something you use all that often. There's a difference between a sickle and a bagging hook, but I don't know what it is exactly. Let me have a rummage—I don't think *I* threw it away, at all events."

"Don't look at me," Katherine said, turning round and going back inside the house. "I don't throw anything away, my life wouldn't be worth living."

"I daresay that's true," Malcolm said. "Let's have a bit of a rummage."

When the garage door was raised, it wasn't quite the Oriental bazaar Katherine had suggested, but there wasn't any chance that a car could have fitted in there. There was a bench with metal-working tools and a half-finished breastplate in a clamp, and above it, three dozen neatly labelled plastic drawers, like a well-stocked ironmonger's; there was a potting bench, with green egg-trays in stacks and two large, comfortable pillows, potting compost in plastic sacks, as well as the small tools of the potter's trade. On the other side of the garage, the hardier tools of the garden, the rake, spade, electric mower, trowels in different sizes, and some odder things that could only have been there, as Mrs. Glover had said, for the historical importance, including—

"I knew I had one," Mr. Glover said. "It's been there so long, and I've never used it, so you sort of stop seeing it. Do you know how to use it?"

They went back together over the road, and, for half an hour, gingerly, they tried the thing out. It was very tricky: Francis, a foot taller than Malcolm, had to stoop to get near the grass at all. They found that you only got into the rhythm with quite small swings; if you were too ambitious, took too wide a sweep, you were apt to lose your balance and fall over. Bernie came out with a cup of tea, and watched, making unhelpful suggestions, but in half an hour, Francis had somehow developed the right kind of action, and was making three or four swings in succession, stepping sideways at the right moment. He'd manage it for a little while, and then he'd somehow become aware of what he was doing—it must look odd, this antique task in a back garden on a Saturday morning in Sheffield—and lose it again, have to stop, take a practice swing, begin again. Malcolm was much more the height for it, but somehow couldn't do it, and after a while he and Bernie sat down and watched Francis get on with it. The regularity of it, the difficulty, hypnotized Francis; he was almost finished before he realized how tired he was, his shirt dripping with sweat. He felt as if he'd done a good job, but the lawn seemed to have had the haircut of a blind madman, patches of near-baldness and spikes of untouched grass alternating.

"I'd leave round the pond," Bernie called. "You'll break the blade on the bricks."

Francis saw the sense of this, and sat down for a rest on the low brick wall around the pond at the end of the garden. There'd once been fish in this pond, he remembered; something else the Watsons had left. They must have been pretty strange people.

"Didn't there used to be—" he called, but at that exact moment, a fat red fish, exactly what he remembered, surfaced lazily as if, one more time, taking a look at a surprised Francis.

"What's that?" Bernie said, ambling up the garden.

"There are fish in this pond," Francis said, astonished. "I mean, there still are."

"Of course there are," Bernie said comfortably. "Fancy you not knowing that."

"How old are they?" Francis said. "They must be—"

"No idea," Bernie said. "Decades, probably."

"How have they survived all this time, with no one looking after them?" Francis said in amazement.

"They don't take much looking after," Bernie said, slightly reproachfully. It hadn't occurred to Francis that anyone might look after the fish. It seemed to him that, had they been his responsibility, he'd have neglected them, left them to die. The easy assumption of responsibility, of achievement on the part of others was always the cause of self-reproach in Francis. He found it so difficult to do what anyone else did as a matter of routine, and he had never had that knack of application. He looked about him now at the garden; he had enjoyed the task when he was in the middle of it, had taken pleasure in the swinging of the blade through the long grass, but now that it was done, he could see that he'd made a careless, untidy job without much concentration. He could never be much good at anything. He'd made the garden look a much worse mess than it had looked to start with; he'd not managed, these last weeks, to be much in the way of help or support to his parents, even. His mother was coming home in a week or two; he knew that his dad, once he'd gone back to London, would do what he'd been planning to do in any case, get in a professional gardener to sort out the lawn.

When he said goodbye to his mother the next day, in hospital, she said what she'd taken to saying on his farewells: "You're a good boy." It was, roughly, what a nurse had said once; he wondered whether she and her nurses had discussed it, and come to this point together, or whether he carried it in front of him like a consolation prize. He gave her a kiss, and said goodbye to his father, then took a taxi to the station. He'd got to know the Sunday-afternoon trains, and there was only ten minutes to wait. Usually he bought a magazine of some sort; today he thought he wouldn't.

The trains on Sunday were unpredictable. It must have been about an hour after it left Sheffield that Francis raised himself from his thoughts and noticed that the train had come to a stop, and hadn't moved for a good stretch of time. Outside, a patch of unremarkable countryside; a green hill, crested with a copse, a slope scattered with sheep, a pool of standing water. The train was silent; there were only two or three other people in the carriage, and no announcement—Francis was fairly sure of it—had been made. Nobody went and nobody came. Brought back from his thoughts, he opened his fat brief-case, and took out the manuscript of his half-finished novel and, rattling round the bottom, one of a long series of green Pentel pens. He looked at the scale of the book; nobody would ever read it; and then, yielding to something he couldn't have explained, he turned the first page of the manuscript over and began to write, very quickly.

He didn't notice when the train started again, and it must have been an hour or more later when he looked up. Outside the train, the yellow lights of the outskirts of London; and, to his surprise, inside the train at the table facing him was someone who must have joined the train at where, Bedford, Leicester? He hadn't noticed the train stopping, or anyone getting on, or anyone sitting down at the table. The man was inspecting him with sparkling pleasure, and when Francis caught his eye, he broke out into an enormous and brilliantly white smile. He was a handsome man, Indian or at any rate Asian, his eyes and teeth and hair all shining in their different ways, and giving off a sense of life and enjoyment; and Francis, for once, didn't look away in shyness, but smiled back. It felt as if every smile he had ever smiled in his life until then had been an attempt at a smile, and not a very good one; Francis had often seen himself trying to smile in photographs, and had had to accept that his smiles looked as unconvincing and unpractised from the outside as they always felt from within. But now he smiled, and it was a smile you could have put on the cover of a magazine.

"You were completely lost in your writing," the man said. "I was going to ask you if you wanted a cup of tea, but I couldn't disturb you."

"I'm sorry if I ignored you," Francis said.

"That's quite all right," the man said. "But hello, anyway."

"Hello," Francis said, and for the second time that afternoon, he seemed to feel something long neglected, something he had not even known was there inside him, begin to stir and move. Everything in this afternoon seemed quite unlike him; nothing now seemed like an effort; and he set down his pen, stretched his long arms, and started to talk to his new friend.

There was no doubt about it. Daniel was driving everybody mad. Bethany, the new chef, was the only one to do anything about it. He had wandered into the kitchen at eleven o'clock, and had inspected the deliveries, one after the other, lifting the cloth and peering at the contents. It was all fine: Bethany had signed for everything. He clearly wasn't really looking at it, in any case. He went out of the kitchen, into the dining room, and walked around in his stately plump way, moving pepper pots an inch or two on the tables, running a finger along the top of the four or five paintings around the walls. He went behind the bar, and tapped a finger against the line of optics. Gareth, the sous-chef, was watching all this. Then he came back into the kitchen and, all over again, lifted up the covers on the boxes of vegetables. Bethany put down her knife, and went to the kitchen telephone, speaking briefly and sharply, and in a minute Helen came down from the office. "For heaven's sake," she said, coming in, "find something to do and stop bothering Bethany and Gareth."

"I'm not bothering them," Daniel said.

"You're loitering and being generally annoying," Helen said. "Haven't you got anything to do?"

"I was thinking," Daniel said.

"I dread it when you start thinking," Helen said. "I never know what's going to come out next when a thought starts rattling round the empty great box you've got on your shoulders and between your ears."

"I was thinking," Daniel said, "we've not changed the look of the restaurant in ten years, have we?"

"I knew it," Bethany said, and then called, "Gareth, hey, I win my bet. It was redecorating."

"We repainted," Helen said. "We repainted two years ago, that wall. It used to be mauve before it was that mustard colour."

"Apart from that," Daniel said.

"No, that's all we've needed to do."

"It just needs," Daniel said, then huffed and shrugged. "It just needs a bit more in the way of clutter, somehow."

"Clutter?" Helen said.

"Don't you think it looks a bit too much like a restaurant?" Daniel said.

"Well, there's a reason for that," Bethany murmured, sniffing through her twelfth onion in a row, wiping her nose on her shoulder.

"Oh, for heaven's sake, Daniel," Helen said. "If you've got something to say that isn't actually extremely stupid, then now might be the moment to say it."

"No," Daniel said. "You know what I mean. The menu's the food you would cook at home, if you could cook and if you could take the trouble, but the look of the room, it's just like any other restaurant. We need more clutter."

"I can do quite well without any clutter, personally speaking," Helen said. "You're not pregnant by any chance, are you, Daniel?"

Bethany laughed, enjoying this.

"I was wondering that myself," Gareth said, looking up with red eyes from an eight-inch mountain of chopped onions.

"I'd go to the gym more if I had any time," Daniel said, hurt.

"For once, Daniel," Helen said, "I wasn't making a point about the size of your gut. I only meant that if you were pregnant, that would explain any sudden nest-building tendencies. As far as I'm concerned, the restaurant looks absolutely fine as it is."

Daniel hardly knew, in fact, what he meant, and soon after that, the desultory speculation subsided in a more practical suggestion that one thing he might do some time soon might be to buy a few new white shirts. It was that suggestion which sent him into town a couple of mornings later. For some reason, Cole's car park was full, a placard placed in front of the entrance. Daniel turned the Saab round, wending through the one-way system, trying to think of another car park—he always used Cole's. In the end, he found himself going back up from Division Street, and in the nick of time before the turning, remembered there was one just by Bigg and Cleaver.

It was the second-hand bookshop that Tim had got most of his books from. It was with a mixture of motives that Daniel, having paid and displayed and locked the Saab, found himself going into the shop. There had been so little respect shown to Tim after his death. It had been Daniel who had paid for the repatriation of his body and its cremation, when, two weeks after Tim had been reported missing, the body had been washed up, gnawed, to be identified only by professional means. The funeral had been formal, well attended, small in its emotions. You could not say that the death of your brother was experienced as, in any sense, the lifting of a burden, but Daniel could not tell anyone that the writing of the enormous cheque felt like a paying of respects, a paying-off of obligations. The funeral and its aftermath were occasions only of regret, and hardly at all of grief. Only Jane, gripping Scott's hand tightly, had cried—had cried buckets—and that was probably postpartum weeping. The baby they had left behind. Trudy had come, had shaken their hands, had not come back to the house. Perhaps contributing to the peculiar atmosphere of the funeral had been Alice's presence; she had been out of hospital only a week or two, and, though changed in appearance, looking frail and much older than before, she was able to smile. Many people found it easier to say the right thing to Bernie about Alice's recovery than to Katherine and Malcolm about Tim's death, and that was understandable.

That sense of the deferring of respect might have led Daniel through the doors of Ruby Tuesday, four doors along, where he had once had lunch with Tim. But lingering propriety brought him into Bigg and Cleaver instead. It couldn't be said that the shop had a hushed atmosphere, though: as Daniel came in, the record-player was just building up to a full-scale assault on a political prisoner with hurled drums and cymbals, oboes and saxophones at full shrieking pitch. Daniel stood there, a little unsure of what he was really there for, and then another motive asserted itself, a more immediate one: the feeling that what the restaurant needed was clutter. He could see it quite clearly: instead of that blue and green abstract on the short wall in the bar of Get High on Your Own Supply, a shelf of handsome brown old books. He'd never much liked that blue and green abstract; they'd bought two paintings, and then thought they might as well have a third rather than leave one wall blank.

The man behind the counter, the record-player to his left hand, the till to the right, was no more contemptuously amused than Daniel had thought he'd be at the request. "We can do that," he said. "People like you come in from time to time, asking for books for their pub, for their bar, for 'the snug,' whatever. They furnish a room." His colleague, sorting through a box of LPs behind him gave out a honking laugh for some reason. "So, what's it going to be? Do you want a big lovely set with matching gold bindings?"

"Nothing too expensive," Daniel said.

"It won't be expensive if it's something no one wants any more," the man said. "You'd be surprised how many twelve-volume sets of collected sermons got printed in the nineteenth century. They look wonderful."

"They used to hollow them out, didn't they?" Daniel said, trying out a piece of bibliographical knowledge. "Put bottles of whisky inside."

"That's a myth," the man said. "It only happens in Benny Hill sketches. But, right, we've got a by-the-yard interior-decoration service. What's the effect you're aiming at?"

"I sort of thought—well, not grand, not like a library in a stately home. More a bit homey, but not, you know, tatty old paperbacks, and—I don't know. I know those bookshelves you see in pubs, they always look as if they're full of books from a junk shop. They never really look like bookshelves in someone's house, I don't know why. I want it to look like a case of books from someone's house. Does that make any sense?"

"Well," the man said, "we can do our best. I suppose what you want is a shelf of books that people might have heard of, and some runs of authors, maybe? Something that looks as if—let's say—something that looks as if the person who put it together might have had some interests in life."

"Can you do that?"

The man looked Daniel up and down, and there was now a definite amusement in his voice. "Can we do sincerity, you mean?" he said.

"Yes, I suppose I do."

"Well, we can fake it," he said.

They agreed a price—Daniel might have tried to haggle upwards, it seemed pretty low—and he told Daniel to come back in three hours' time, there'd be a decent couple of boxes for him. He knew a carpenter, too, to put up shelves; actually, his workshop was a few doors down on Division Street. Daniel went round there first, and the carpenter agreed to come round in two weeks' time to put up two or three shelves. He apologized for it not being sooner: "You're lucky it can be as soon as that," he said. "We've got more work than we know what to do with, just these last few months."

He sounded disgusted, but pretending to complain about everything was just how Sheffield was, and Daniel limited himself to remarking, in the same sick-to-the-back-teeth tone, that it never rained but it poured. It was quite a cosy chat they had. Afterwards, knowing that he'd been given licence to fritter away three hours or so, Daniel wandered down towards Cole's. There were all sorts of new shops and bars opening up down here; strange little fashion-student shops for the kids in the clubs, silversmiths not long out of college, a sweaty little cave painted black inside and selling techno records. There was a new bar next to the fire station, too; an enormous one. They must know what they were doing. He didn't go into any of them; he went off to Cole's, and extravagantly bought six white cotton shirts, all exactly the same. It was lunchtime, and Daniel, in accordance with his mood, went into a restaurant he'd never been in before, a new one, and, just for the hell of it, had one of the stalwarts off the Get High on Your Own Supply menu, the fish pie. He quite enjoyed it not being as good as theirs, too.

"What in the name of Christ is that you've got there?" Helen said, as Daniel and Jerry lugged a box—the first of three—into the office. She didn't turn round: she carried on looking at the spreadsheet on the computer screen.

"I bought some books," Daniel said, and explained. Helen spun the office chair round and looked at him in astonishment.

"Clutter," Helen said. Daniel and Jerry, who had been hovering and puffing, made some mysterious communication without looking at each other, and exited. They could see an argument coming.

"Erm," Daniel said. "Well, yes, clutter. I thought, what would be quite nice, just a bookcase, over there—a sort of, you know, cosy, homey, er—"

"I despair," Helen said. "It could be worse, I suppose. I thought you were thinking about knick-knacks and cushions. Personally, I think it's going to look just a little bit stupid, one bookcase on its own, but I won't stand in your way."

"Anything else you want to get off your chest?" Daniel said. "Do you want to start going on at me to lose some weight, like everyone else around here? What about that?"

"Oh, for heaven's sake, Daniel, get off your high horse, no one's having a go at you," Helen said.

"You could have fooled me," Daniel said.

"All I meant was I thought we were supposed to be partners in this business," Helen said.

"Well, we are," Daniel said. He had had practice in the last months in not saying the observations that came into his head, and now he thought: That'll be all we are if things don't improve around here from your side. He managed not to say it.

"In my opinion," Helen said, "the look of the restaurant is something we should discuss and agree on. You don't just go out and spend a thousand pounds on something because you think it might be nice without talking about it."

"We talked about it," Daniel said.

"No, Daniel," Helen said. "What happened was that you mentioned something in very general terms, I said I didn't think so, and then you went out. There's a difference."

Helen turned back to the computer as if she were right. There was plenty more to say from Daniel's side, but the trouble was, most of it was wrong, and Helen was actually right. It probably was stupid to put up a bookshelf of randomly chosen books in a restaurant. There was no doubt Helen and everyone else was right when they said what they said, that he needed to lose some weight. He didn't know how that had happened—it hadn't happened to his dad or to his mum, both of them still perfectly trim in their sixties. Daniel, in what was really more of a performance of petulance than anything else, bent down and opened one of the boxes. On top was quite a new book; it looked as if it hadn't been read, and he took it out, standing up with a bit of the heavy-breathing routine. He hadn't known the shop was going to put new books in; he'd thought it would be entirely what lay underneath this book, a line of quite untempting-looking worn readers' copies of classic-looking type thingies. It wouldn't go along with those, this new hardback with a shiny dustjacket; he wondered why they'd put it in. He straightened up and, with a shake of the head, went off with this single book to the restaurant bar. There was never anyone there at this time of day; he pulled round a big armchair, facing the corner of the room, kicked off his shoes, put his book in his lap and began to read.

It was three hours later when Helen came out of the office, yawning and stretching her arms in an arch above her head, then gripping them, hand in elbow, behind her back. As she often did when there was no one about, she took off her rings, two on her left hand, one on the right, laid them carefully on the bar and cracked her fingers, one after the other, pulling them, starting with the little finger and ending up with the thumb. They went off like firecrackers—"You'll get arthritis," she said silently to herself, a piece of playground wisdom. She put her rings back on, and went behind the bar. From the shelf underneath the till, she picked up the remote control from the CD player, and, not caring what was on, just pressed the play button. It was probably going to begin whatever had happened to be on the machine the last time anyone had used it. Often, in these circumstances, Helen had been startled by the irruption into a calm afternoon of the night before's music. What the kids in the kitchen had put on to entertain themselves while they were finishing off when all the customers had gone. None of them could cook to music. She'd discovered that when a radio she'd bought as a kind thought had languished untouched in the corner of the kitchen for weeks. The music only came on when they were cleaning up and tidying away.

Now she pressed the button and a woman's scornful voice asked what she was looking at before a dance beat started up. It had been left at top volume, so that it would be heard in the kitchen through the doors, and from a chair in the corner of the bar—she hadn't thought anyone was in it—a head, Daniel's, leapt up.

"Christ, you made me jump," he said cheerfully. "Can you turn that racket down a bit?"

"I was just about to," Helen said, and did so.

"What time is it?" Daniel said, then looked at his watch. "My God, I've been sitting here three hours."

"Did you drop off?" Helen said.

"No, I've been reading," Daniel said. "Don't tell me off, I've got nothing much to do today anyway."

"What are you reading?" Helen said, coming over. "One of your books from this morning?"

"I think it got in by mistake," Daniel said, showing her the cover. He had his thumb in the book, a hundred or so pages in. "I only asked for tasteful-looking old books. This is a new one."

"What's it about?" Helen said.

"Oh, I don't know," Daniel said. "It's sort of about people like us, I think."

And he showed her the first page. " 'So the garden—' " she read.

"I can't be sitting around all day, love," Helen said. "I'll read it when you're done. Is my dad finished upstairs?"

"Must be nearly," Daniel said, and yawned and stretched, watching her go, the movement of her rump, a dancer's movements, with still that old pleasure. "I'll not be putting up the bookcase," he called after her. "I thought about it. It was a stupid idea, really." She kept on going, and it was only by a sort of satisfied, approving movement of her head that he saw she'd heard him. He picked up the book, and weighed it in his hand. Soon the first customers would be arriving. His mum and dad had said they were coming down this evening with Jane and Scott and baby Archie, up for the weekend. He'd recommend the fish pie, and get Helen to sit down and eat with them. All those books: all made from what people remember. Memory, in a block, six inches by four by two. Maybe Helen was right when she said she knew why the second-hand bookshop was so glad to be shot of them. Or perhaps that was just in her fit of rage with him for spending the money so ineffectually and thoughtlessly. He watched her coming back from the bar, with a shining glass for him in her hand, a slice of lemon on top, and he smiled. And she smiled back. What he'd wasted today; it was only money, after all. And time, of course. There had never been any real doubt in his mind that she would forgive him.

London—Khartoum—Topsham
March 2007

A Note About the Author

Philip Hensher's novels include *Kitchen Venom*, which won the Somerset Maugham Award, and *The Mulberry Empire*, which was long-listed for the Man Booker Prize. Chosen by *Granta* as one of its best young British novelists, he is professor of creative writing at Exeter University and a columnist for the *Independent*. He lives in London.

A Note on the Type

This book was set in Janson, a typeface long thought to have been made by the Dutchman Anton Janson, a practicing type-founder in Leipzig during the years 1668–1687. However, it has been conclusively demonstrated that these types are actually the work of Nicholas Kis (1650–1702), a Hungarian, who most probably learned his trade from the master Dutch typefounder Dirk Voskens. The type is an excellent example of the influential and sturdy Dutch types that prevailed in England up to the time William Caslon (1692–1766) developed his own incomparable designs from them.

Composed by Creative Graphics,
Allentown, Pennsylvania
Printed and bound by Berryville Graphics,
Berryville, Virginia